TRUTH | BEAUTY | GOODNESS | COMMITMENT

Philosophy & Literature

Cameron Thompson

PINE MANOR JUNIOR COLLEGE, WELLESLEY, MASSACHUSETTS

Authors Choice Press

San Jose New York Lincoln Shanghai

ABOUT THE AUTHOR

Cameron Thompson has taught English on both the secondary and college levels. At Pine Manor Junior College, where he was chairman of the English department for many years, he teaches an Introduction to Philosophy course and several courses in English. Mr. Thompson received his B.A. and M.A. degrees from Princeton University and also did graduate work in philosophy at Harvard University.

Philosophy & Literature
Truth, Beauty, Goodness, Commitment

Authors Choice Press
an imprint of iUniverse.com, Inc.

For information address:
iUniverse.com, Inc.
5220 S 16th, Ste. 200
Lincoln, NE 68512
www.iuniverse.com

Originally published by Harcourt Brace

ISBN: 0-595-18756-0

Printed in the United States of America

ACKNOWLEDGMENTS

ACKNOWLEDGMENTS: For permission to reprint copyrighted material, grateful acknowledgment is made to the following publishers, authors, and agents:

CYRILLY ABELS: "Mac's Masterpiece" by Frank O'Connor from *The London Mercury.*

BRANDT & BRANDT: "By the Waters of Babylon" from *Selected Works of Stephen Vincent Benét*, Holt, Rinehart and Winston, Inc., copyright 1937 by Stephen Vincent Benét, copyright renewed © 1964 by Thomas C. Benét, Stephanie B. Mahin and Rachel Benét Lewis.

COLLINS-KNOWLTON-WING, INC.: "A Pinch of Salt" from *Fairies and Fusiliers* by Robert Graves, copyright © 1918 by Robert Graves.

DODD, MEAD & COMPANY, INC.: "Sagacity" from *Golden Fleece* by William Rose Benét, copyright 1933, 1935 by Dodd, Mead & Company, Inc., copyright renewed.

KENNETH DURANT and SATURDAY REVIEW: "Try Tropic (For a sick generation)" from *Collected Poems* by Genevieve Taggard, Harper & Row, Publishers. Originally published in *Saturday Review*, October 13, 1928.

NORMA MILLAY ELLIS: "Euclid Alone Has Looked on Beauty Bare" from *Collected Poems* by Edna St. Vincent Millay, Harper & Row, Publishers, copyright 1923, 1951 by Edna St. Vincent Millay and Norma Millay Ellis.

ERNST, CANE, BERNER & GITLIN: "Young Man Axelbrod" by Sinclair Lewis, copyright 1917 by Sinclair Lewis, copyright renewed 1945 by Sinclair Lewis.

GROVE PRESS, INC.: "Orchard" from *H. D. Selected Poems,* copyright © 1957 by Norman Holmes Pearson.

Contents

BEAUTY

GOODNESS

COMMITMENT

Foreword

This volume has been built around values: the values of Truth, Beauty, Goodness, and Commitment. The first three of these have had continued recognition as superior values in western civilization since Plato first singled them out centuries ago. Commitment, the fourth value, is also of ancient origin. It is included in this book because it has sufficient contemporary relevance to deserve a treatment more respectful than one which would reduce it to some combination of Truth, Beauty, and Goodness.

Values are usually distinguished as being either quantitative or qualitative. Quantitative values are primarily symbols of measurement: Is this bottle of milk, this automobile, or this house worth the price? Qualitative values refer to our less tangible concerns. Why are you fond of a friend? Is your family a happy one? Do you find religion meaningful? These two types of values—quantitative and qualitative—often overlap, of course. For example, one's home can have a "market price" value quite different from its "meaning" value to oneself, so that in considering the sale of a home one can undergo major difficulties in attempting to balance the quantitative and the qualitative values involved.

Although there is this everyday overlap of values, the present book is solely concerned with the qualitative aspects of the four values mentioned: Truth, Beauty, Goodness, Commitment. Both philosophers and writers have been—must be—interested in such qualitative values. The difference between the two groups is basically a difference of approach to their common interest. The philosopher normally (but not always) approaches the particular value in terms of the abstract; the writer normally (but not always) approaches it in terms of the concrete. To illustrate this distinction, I should like you to read the following sonnet by George Santayana, who was an eminent philosopher and an able poet as well:

O World, Thou Choosest Not the Better Part!

> O world, thou choosest not the better part!
> It is not wisdom to be only wise,
> And on the inward vision close the eyes,
> But it is wisdom to believe the heart.
> Columbus found a world, and had no chart
> Save one that faith deciphered in the skies;
> To trust the soul's invincible surmise
> Was all his science and his only art.
> Our knowledge is a torch of smoky pine
> That lights the pathway but one step ahead
> Across a void of mystery and dread.

> Bid, then, the tender light of faith to shine
> By which alone the mortal heart is led
> Unto the thinking of the thought divine.

In his poem Santayana is implying a value judgment about Truth, a judgment which is capsulated in the second line, "It is not wisdom to be only wise, . . ." This line, lifted from the poem and placed on a chalkboard for class discussion, would represent an abstract statement regarding Truth with which you might, or might not, agree. But is it not equally evident that the poem as a whole is a "dramatic" illumination of the insight expressed in this second line: that this line and the other lines, taken together, make concrete (through expansion, imagery, and rhythmic effects) the abstract value judgment which you are free to infer from the poem?[1]

Each section of this volume begins with philosophical selections and is followed by selections from literature. I emphasize this distinction between the abstract and the concrete approaches to the field of values because I do not want you to search for interrelationships between the two types of selections when, in fact, no such interrelationships usually exist. Specifically, I do not want you to consider the literary selections as "illustrations" of any philosophical points of view which have preceded them. Should you recognize that Millay's poem, "Euclid Alone Has Looked on Beauty Bare" (p. 215), is clearly Platonic in its "philosophy," this recognition may well enrich the poem for you. I did not, however, include the poem in this book as an example of Platonism-in-literature but rather as an effective poetic expression of one writer's approach to the value under consideration. In short, keep in mind that philosophers and creative writers share (with all of us) a concern for values, but that each group has its own characteristic perspective and manner of expression.

---

[1] That the process I have suggested with respect to Santayana's sonnet can be reversed is evident from a reading of Plato's "Allegory of the Den" (p. 5), where the concrete element (that is, Plato's "story") can be extracted from the total context—but only at the risk of missing the abstract meaning for which Plato invented his story.

TRUTH

Introduction

The complexions—and complexities—of Truth are greater than one might first suspect. It is easy enough to say that everybody knows the "truths" that 2 plus 2 always equals 4 and that Christmas always comes on December 25th. But what is true love? true Americanism? true art? How is a person true to himself?

Here is a poem I once wrote:

Wisdom

There was a scholar
Who sat in his study, brooding.
There came a knock at his door
And an old man dressed in motley entered.
"Good morning, sir. I am 'Wisdom,' " he announced.
"No, old man, you are a buffoon," the scholar replied,
And he thrust the visitor so violently from his study
That the old man died of a broken neck.

The scholar returned to his study—
And was never seen again.

In this poem I am attempting, poetically, to distinguish between two kinds of "truth": in this case, the dry-as-dust kind of truth represented by the conventional scholar, and the far broader (and deeper) kind of truth represented by the old man. Is not the Santayana poem in the Foreword making much the same point?

Many mathematical and scientific "truths" have been overthrown or modified in the light of fresh advances—and this healthful process continues. In religion and in the arts, disagreement has been so prevalent as to lead many thoughtful people to the conclusion that the word truth is not applicable to these areas at all.

If we accept this conclusion, we will agree with the point made in one of Carl Sandburg's poems:

Elephants Are Different to Different People

Wilson and Pilcer and Snack stood before the zoo elephant.

Wilson said, "What is its name? Is it from Asia or Africa? Who feeds it? Is it a he or a she? How old is it? Do they have twins? How much does it cost to feed? How much does it weigh? If it dies, how much will another one cost? If it dies, what will they use the bones, the fat, and the hide for? What use is it besides to look at?"

Pilcer didn't have any questions; he was murmuring to himself, "It's a house by itself, walls and windows, the ears came from tall cornfields, by God; the architect of those legs was a workman, by God; he stands like a bridge out across deep water; the face is sad and the eyes are kind; I know elephants are good to babies."

Snack looked up and down and at last said to himself, "He's a tough son-of-a-gun outside and I'll bet he's got a strong heart, I'll bet he's strong as a copper-riveted boiler inside."

They didn't put up any arguments.

They didn't throw anything in each other's faces.

Three men saw the elephant three ways

And let it go at that.

They didn't spoil a sunny Sunday afternoon;

"Sunday comes only once a week," they told each other.

There is, however, another approach possible and one which you should at least consider. This is to recognize the value of approaching "truth" both horizontally and vertically. Historically, this is not an entirely new attempt to solve the "truth problems" I have suggested, but it has present appeal because it is associated with one of our most distinguished contemporary thinkers—Reinhold Niebuhr.

Niebuhr's horizontal–vertical distinction may be illustrated in this way. A routine photograph of a landscape will give one an extremely accurate reproduction of that landscape in the ' horizontal" sense; a painter, however, may disregard or distort the details of the same landscape and yet "catch its feel," its significant "truth," in a revelation not possible to the documentary camera. The painter's approach may be said to be "vertical."

Niebuhr's distinction is not one I impose on you. I offer it merely as one example, an introductory example, of the attempts by philosophers and by creative writers to answer the ever-nagging question: What is Truth?

Plato

[427–347 B.C.]

Plato makes a good beginning for this section, for he was passionately concerned about the nature of Truth. The selection I have chosen is a famous one: partly because it expresses a basic Platonic conviction, and partly because the writing itself is so superior in its clarity and sharpness of imagery.

A word about the term allegory. It represents what I think of as a two-level situation; that is to say, in an allegory one has a "story" level and one also has a "meaning" level. Allegory, therefore, fuses the specific and the general. In effect, it dramatizes the thematic concern of the author. In doing so, it constitutes a blending of the "concrete" and the "abstract" of which I have spoken in the Foreword.

In form, the selection is a dialogue between Socrates, the inspiring teacher of Plato in whose name Plato commonly presented his own views, and Glaucon, a representative citizen of Athens. Plato believed that most people can only comprehend profound philosophical insights by the use of easily understood "stories," just as Jesus later used parables to convey religious insights.

In content, Plato is asserting that most of us are the victims of illusion so far as recognizing Truth. If one has always been a prisoner in a den, condemned to see only reflections of the Truth, he will assume that these reflections are really true. He will believe this so firmly that he will not believe a fellow prisoner who has escaped his bondage, has seen Truth, and has returned to inform the prisoners of their mistaken confidence in the "truth" of their shadow world.

Read the selection fairly quickly on the story level. Then return to it, more thoughtfully, on the meaning level until you are confident that you have grasped the "truth" which Socrates—that is, Plato—is attempting to convey to Glaucon—who is yourself.

The Allegory of the Den

[Socrates speaks.] And now, I said, let me show in a parable how far our nature is enlightened or unenlightened: Behold! human beings living in an underground den, which has a mouth open toward the light and reaching all along the den. Here they have been from their childhood, and have their legs and necks chained so that they cannot move, and can only see before them, being prevented by the chains from turning round their heads. Above and behind them a fire is blazing at a distance, and

Excerpt from Book VII of *The Republic,* translated by Benjamin Jowett.

between the fire and the prisoners there is a raised way,[1] and you will
see, if you look, a low wall built along the way, like the screen which
10 marionette players have in front of them, over which they show the
puppets.

I see, [Glaucon replied].

Objects/making the Shadows

And do you see, I said, men passing along the wall carrying all sorts
of vessels, and statues and figures of animals made of wood and stone
and various materials, which appear over the wall? Some of them are
talking, others silent.

You have shown me a strange image, and they are strange prisoners.

Like ourselves, I replied; and they see only their own shadows, or the
shadows of one another, which the fire throws on the opposite wall of
20 the cave?

True, he said; how could they see anything but the shadows if they
were never allowed to move their heads?

And of the objects which are being carried in like manner, they would
only see the shadows?

Yes, he said.

And if they were able to converse with one another, would they not
suppose that they were naming what was actually before them?

Very true.

And suppose further that the prison had an echo which came from the
30 other side. Would they not be sure to fancy when one of the passers-by
spoke that the voice which they heard came from the passing shadow?

No question, he replied.

To them, I said, the truth would be literally nothing but the shadows
of the images.

That is certain.

And now look again, and see what will naturally follow if the prisoners are released and disabused of their error. At first, when any of
them is liberated and compelled suddenly to stand up and turn his neck
round and walk and look toward the light, he will suffer sharp pains; the
40 glare will distress him, and he will be unable to see the realities of which
in his former state he had seen the shadows; and then conceive some
one saying to him, that what he saw before was an illusion, but that
now, when he is approaching nearer to being and his eye is turned
toward more real existence, he has a clearer vision—what will be his
reply? And you may further imagine that his instructor is pointing to the
objects as they pass and requiring him to name them, will he not be
perplexed? Will he not fancy that the shadows which he formerly saw
are truer than the objects which are now shown to him?

Far truer.

50 And if he is compelled to look straight at the light, will he not have a

[1] *way:* walk.

pain in his eyes which will make him turn away to take refuge in the objects of vision which he can see, and which he will conceive to be in reality clearer than the things which are now being shown to him?

True, he said.

And suppose once more, that he is reluctantly dragged up a steep and rugged ascent and held fast until he is forced into the presence of the sun himself. Is he not likely to be pained and irritated? When he approaches the light, his eyes will be dazzled, and he will not be able to see anything at all of what are now called realities.

60   Not all in a moment, he said.

He will have to grow accustomed to the sight of the upper world. And first he will see the shadows best, next the reflections of men and other objects in the water, and then the objects themselves; then he will gaze upon the light of the moon and the stars and the spangled heaven; and he will see the sky and the stars by night better than the sun or the light of the sun by day?

Certainly.

Last of all he will be able to see the sun, and not mere reflections of it in the water, but he will see it in his own proper place, and not in 70 another; and he will contemplate it as it is.

Certainly.

He will then proceed to argue that this is what gives the season and the years, and is the guardian of all that is in the visible world, and in a certain way the cause of all things which he and his fellows have been accustomed to behold?

Clearly, he said, he would first see the sun and then reason about it.

And when he remembered his old habitation, and the wisdom of the den and his fellow-prisoners, do you not suppose that he would felicitate 80 himself on the change, and pity them?

Certainly, he would.

And if they were in the habit of conferring honors among themselves on those who were quickest to observe the passing shadows and to remark which of them went before, and which followed after, and which were together; and who were therefore best able to draw conclusions as to the future, do you think that he would care for such honors and glories, or envy the possessors of them? Would he not say with Homer,

> Better to be the poor servant of a poor master

and to endure anything, rather than think as they do and live after their 90 manner?

Yes, he said, I think that he would rather suffer anything than entertain these false notions and live in this miserable manner.

Imagine once more, I said, such a one coming suddenly out of the sun to be replaced in his old situation; would he not be certain to have his eyes full of darkness?

To be sure, he said.

And if there were a contest, and he had to compete in measuring the shadows with the prisoners who had never moved out of the den, while his sight was still weak, and before his eyes had become steady (and the time which would be needed to acquire this new habit of sight might be very considerable), would he not be ridiculous? Men would say of him that up he went and down he came without his eyes; and that it was better not even to think of ascending; and if any one tried to loose another and lead him up to the light, let them only catch the offender, and they would put him to death.

No question, he said.

This entire allegory, I said, you may now append, dear Glaucon, to the previous argument; the prison-house is the world of sight, the light of the fire is the sun, and you will not misapprehend me if you interpret the journey upward to be the ascent of the soul into the intellectual world according to my poor belief, which, at your desire, I have expressed—whether rightly or wrongly God knows. But, whether true or false, my opinion is that in the world of knowledge the idea of good appears last of all, and is seen only with an effort; and, when seen, is also inferred to be the universal author of all things beautiful and right, parent of light and of the lord of light in this visible world, and the immediate source of reason and truth in the intellectual; and that this is the power upon which he who would act rationally either in public or private life must have his eye fixed.

I agree, he said, as far as I am able to understand you.

Moreover, I said, you must not wonder that those who attain to this beatific vision are unwilling to descend to human affairs; for their souls are ever hastening into the upper world where they desire to dwell; which desire of theirs is very natural, if our allegory may be trusted.

Yes, very natural.

And is there anything surprising in one who passes from divine contemplations to the evil state of man, misbehaving himself in a ridiculous manner; if, while his eyes are blinking and before he has become accustomed to the surrounding darkness, he is compelled to fight in courts of law, or in other places, about the images or the shadows of images of justice, and is endeavoring to meet the conceptions of those who have never yet seen absolute justice?

Anything but surprising, he replied.

Anyone who has common sense will remember that the bewilderments of the eyes are of two kinds, and arise from two causes, either from coming out of the light or from going into the light, which is true of the mind's eye, quite as much as of the bodily eye; and he who remembers this when he sees anyone whose vision is perplexed and weak, will not be too ready to laugh; he will first ask whether that soul of man has 140 come out of the brighter life, and is unable to see because unaccustomed to the dark, or having turned from darkness to the day is dazzled by excess of light. And he will count the one happy in his condition and state of being, and he will pity the other; or, if he have a mind to laugh at the soul which comes from below into the light, there will be more reason in this than in the laugh which greets him who returns from above out of the light into the den.

FOR STUDY AND DISCUSSION

1. Restate in your own words the physical situation in which the prisoners exist. Remembering that this selection is an allegory, can you suggest other "caves" in modern life in which people might be "imprisoned"— or feel imprisoned?

2. If a prisoner is released from the cave and compelled to look toward the light, he will at first suffer pain. Why? He will also be perplexed and "fancy that the shadows which he formerly saw are truer than the objects which are now shown to him." Why would he be perplexed and make this mistake?

3. What are the stages of the liberated prisoner's experience outside of the cave?

4. Socrates says that if such a liberated prisoner returned to the cave, his former companions would find him "ridiculous." Why would they find him ridiculous? Who is basically ridiculous?

5. By line 107, Socrates has completed the "story" level of his allegory. He proceeds to "translate" it; that is, to indicate its significant "meaning" level and to suggest some of its implications. In your own words, what is this meaning level, and what are some of its implications? To what extent do you find Socrates's point about our human tendency to confuse "shadows" with "reality" relevant today?

René Descartes

[1596–1650]

Descartes is sometimes called the "father of modern philosophy." During the medieval period, which separates Descartes and Plato, significant philosophical contributions were made, notably in the monumental work of St. Thomas Aquinas.[1] But these contributions could not reflect the coming scientific and cultural reorientations spurred by the Renaissance. Although primarily a mathematician, Descartes was alert to the philosophical implications of the "new thinking." In applying the open and tentative approach of the scientist to philosophical problems, he set the course for the history of post-Renaissance philosophy.

When I use the phrase "open and tentative approach," you may properly conclude that I mean "skeptical," but you must be cautious in the use of this word, for philosophers commonly make a significant distinction between methodological and absolute skepticism. The difference between Descartes' method and his final position affords an excellent example of this distinction. He employs the skeptical method and yet he reaches a positive or non-skeptical conclusion.

As you will discover in the following excerpt from his work, Descartes begins by deliberately doubting everything: God, the outside world, even his own existence. He soon reaches the conclusion that he cannot doubt his own existence because the very phrase "I doubt" implies the presence of an "I" who does the "doubting." The skeptical method has, therefore, given him a firm foundation on which to build. But this "I," which seems to be firmly established, may still be deceived by its impressions of the external world, for all of us are deceived by dreams, illusions, and hallucinations. Suppose, argues Descartes, that God is a malevolent, not a benign, Being, who has set out to deceive us in our supposed knowledge of the external world.

At this point, Descartes' argument becomes subtle—and, perhaps, more questionable. You will see that he asserts that the idea of God exists in himself, and that since he could not have generated such an idea by himself, it must have been God-induced. Further, since the "idea" of God includes the concept of His perfection, and since perfection includes truthfulness, it follows that God cannot be a deceiver. Thus the material world, which was once held up to systematic doubt is now established as a "clear and distinct" reality—to use a favorite phrase of Descartes.

The selection which follows is not too difficult to read for Descartes is one of the most stylistically clear of all philosophical writers. My primary

---

[1] St. Thomas Aquinas [1225–1274]: great medieval theologian and philosopher who made the first—and still very influential—survey of the Catholic position on matters of religion and philosophy. Present followers of Aquinas are commonly called Thomists

concern is that you follow his argumentation and that you remain alert to question whatever flaws in his logic you feel you have detected.

From Skepticism to Conviction

I had been nourished on letters since my childhood, and since I was given to believe that by their means a clear and certain knowledge could be obtained of all that is useful in life, I had an extreme desire to acquire instruction.

But as soon as I had achieved the entire course of study at the close of which one is usually received into the ranks of the learned, I entirely changed my opinion. . . .

As regards all the opinions which, up to that time, I had embraced, I thought I could not do better than try once and for all to sweep them
10 completely away. Later on they might be replaced, either by others which were better, or by the same when I had made them conform to the uniformity of a rational scheme. I firmly believe that by this means I should succeed much better than if I had built on foundations and principles of which I had allowed myself to be persuaded in youth without having inquired into their truth. My design has never extended beyond trying to reform my own opinions and to build on a foundation which is entirely my own.

I was not seeking to imitate the skeptics, who only doubt for the sake of doubting and pretend always to be uncertain. On the contrary, my
20 design was only to provide myself with good ground for assurance, to reject the quicksand and mud in order to find the rock or clay. . . .

I suppose, then, that all the things that I see are false. I persuade myself that nothing has ever existed of all that my fallacious memory represents to me. I consider that I possess no senses. I imagine that body, figure, extension, motion, and place are but the fictions of my mind. What, then, can be esteemed as true? Perhaps nothing at all, unless that there is nothing in the world that is certain.

But immediately I notice that while I wish to think all things false, it is nonetheless absolutely essential that I, who wish to think this, should
30 truly exist. There is a powerful and cunning deceiver who employs his ingenuity in misleading me. Let it be granted. It follows the more that I exist, if he deceives me. If I did not exist, he could not deceive me. This truth, "I think, therefore I am; *cogito, ergo sum,*" is so certain, so assured, that all the most extravagant skepticism is incapable of shaking it. This truth, "I am, I exist," I can receive without scruple as the first principle of the philosophy for which I am seeking. . . .

Excerpts from *Discourse on Method* and *Meditations on First Philosophy*, as adapted in *An Introduction to Modern Philosophy* by Alburey Castell, © 1963, The Macmillan Company.

I am certain that I am a thing which thinks. But if I am indeed certain of this, I must know what is requisite to render me certain of anything. I must possess a standard of certainty. In this first knowledge which I
40 have gained, what is there that assures me of its truth? Nothing except the clear and distinct perception of what I state. . . .

All things which I perceive very clearly and very distinctly are true. If I have heretofore judged that such matters could be doubted, it was because it came into my mind that perhaps a God might have endowed me with such a nature that I might have been deceived even concerning things which seemed to me most manifest. I see no reason to believe that there is a God who is a deceiver; however, as yet I have not satisfied myself that there is a God at all.

I must inquire whether there is a God. And, if I find that there is a
50 God, I must also inquire whether He may be a deceiver. For, without a knowledge of these two truths, I do not see that I can ever be certain of anything. . . .

There is the idea of God. Is this idea something that could have originated in, been caused by, me? By the name *God* I understand a being that is infinite, eternal, immutable, independent, all-knowing, all-powerful, by which I myself and everything else (if anything else does exist) have been created.

Now, all these qualities are such that the more diligently I attend to them, the less do they appear capable of originating in me alone. Hence,
60 from what was premised above, we must conclude that God necessarily exists as the origin of this idea I have of Him. . . .

The whole strength of the argument which I have here used to prove the existence of God consists in this: It is not possible that my nature should be what it is, and that I should have in myself the idea of a God, if God did not exist. God, whose idea is in me, possesses all those supreme perfections of which our mind may have some idea but without understanding them all, is liable to no errors or defects, and has none of those marks which denote imperfection. From this it is manifest that He cannot be a deceiver, since fraud and deception proceed from some
70 defect.

[Lastly] He has given me a very great inclination to believe that my ideas of sensible objects are sent or conveyed to me by external material objects. I do not see how He could be defended from the accusation of deceit if these ideas were produced in me by any cause other than material objects. Hence we must allow that material objects exist.

Summary of Argument [margin annotation]

FOR STUDY AND DISCUSSION

1. In order to reach fundamental convictions he can regard as his own, Descartes determines to sweep aside all the opinions he had learned "at school." However, he is careful to distinguish his position from that of the skeptics. What is the distinction he makes?
2. As a first step, Descartes assumes that everything he observes is false. How, then, does he reach his basic certainty: his own existence?
3. On what grounds does he say, "All things which I perceive very clearly and very distinctly are true"?
4. What is his argument for the existence of God? his argument that God cannot be a deceiver? Restate both of these arguments in your own words.
5. Having answered these questions to his own satisfaction, why is it now easy for Descartes confidently to assert the existence of an external world which he had at first deliberately doubted?

William James

[1842–1910]

Plato and Descartes are, in philosophical terminology, rationalists. They believe that it is primarily by reasoning, by making logical connections, that we arrive at truth. This confidence in reason was questioned even in their own times and has been increasingly questioned since the rise of modern science with its emphasis on observation and experimentation. No one has dramatized the earlier attacks on rationalism more than William James, a distinguished psychologist and one of America's greatest philosophers.

James is associated with a philosophical position called pragmatism, which holds that the truth of an idea is determined by how well it works in practice. Pragmatism, in turn, is part of the broader anti-rationalist movement in philosophy called empiricism which holds that truth is based on experience and can only be reached by controlled observation. John Dewey [1859–1952], another great modern empiricist, once likened rationalists to spiders, who spin webs out of themselves. In contrast, he maintained, the empiricists are more like bees, who collect their material from the outside world and then transform it creatively into something valuable. James is even harsher toward the rationalists: he calls them "tender-minded," whereas the empiricists are "tough-minded."

These comments are background for this selection from James, for you can readily guess that a "tough-minded" empiricist has a disturbing problem in dealing with areas such as religion and morality (art might well be added), where the scientific method does not seem to apply. James's "solution" to this problem is that these areas present a different kind of "truth situation." In the tradition of the French philosopher Blaise Pascal [1623–1662], who asserted that "The heart hath its reasons, which the reason knows not of," James affirms the validity of man's non-scientific experiences. In the following selection, he proposes that in the areas of religion and morality we can never hope for "final" evidence (in the empirical-scientific sense). Yet he also asserts that such convictions ("forced options," as he calls them) are the only trustworthy guides to types of truth vital to our most fundamental concerns.

Belief

Let us give the name of *hypothesis* to anything that may be proposed to our belief. And, just as electricians speak of live and dead wires, let us speak of a hypothesis as either *live* or *dead*. A live hypothesis is one which appeals as real possibility to him to whom it is proposed. . . .

A living option is one in which both hypotheses are live ones. If I say

Excerpt from *The Will to Believe.*

to you: "Be a theosophist or be a Mohammedan," it is probably a dead option, because for you neither hypothesis is likely to be alive. But if I say: "Be an agnostic or be a Christian," it is otherwise. Trained as you are, each hypothesis makes some appeal, however small, to your belief.

A forced option is one which arises when there is no standing outside of the alternative hypothesis. If I say to you: "Choose between going out with your umbrella or without it," I do not offer you a forced option. You can easily avoid it by not going out at all. But if I say: "Either accept this truth or go without it," I put on you a forced option, for there is no third alternative and no standing outside of these two alternatives.

A momentous option is one that is presented when the opportunity is unique, when the stake is significant, or when the decision is irreversible if it later prove unwise. If I were Dr. Nansen and proposed to you to join my North Pole expedition, your option would be momentous; for this would probably be your only opportunity, and your choice now would either exclude you from the North Pole sort of immortality altogether, or put at least the chance of it into your hands. *Per contra*, the option is trivial when the opportunity is not unique, when the stake is insignificant, or when the decision is reversible if it later prove unwise.

An option is genuine when it is of the living, forced, momentous kind. . . .

The thesis I defend is this: *Our passional nature* [1] *not only lawfully may, but must, decide an option between propositions, whenever it is a genuine option that cannot by its nature be decided on intellectual grounds.* . . .

The next question arises: Are there any such forced options in our speculative opinions? Are there some options between opinions in which this passional influence must be regarded both as an inevitable and as a lawful determinant of our choice?

Moral questions immediately present themselves. A moral question is a question not of what exists, but of what is good, or would be good if it did exist.

Science can tell us what exists; but to compare the worths, both of what exists and what does not exist, we must consult not science, but what Pascal calls our "heart," i.e., our passional nature. Science, herself, consults her heart when she lays it down that the infinite ascertainment of fact and correction of false belief are the supreme goods for man. Challenge the statement, and science can only repeat it oracularly, or else prove it by showing that such ascertainment and correction bring man all sorts of other goods which man's heart in turn declares desirable.

Let us pass to the question of religious faith. What do we mean by the

[1] *passional nature:* emotional nature, as opposed to intellectual nature.

religious hypothesis? Broadly it is this: Science says things are; morality
50 says some things are better than other things; religion says that the best
things are the more eternal things, the things in the universe that throw
the last stone, so to speak, and say the final word, and that we are better
off, even now, if we believe her first affirmation to be true. . . .

Now, let us consider what the logical elements of this situation are *in
case the religious hypothesis in both its branches be really true.* We must
admit that possibility at the outset.

We see, first, that religion offers itself as a momentous option. We are
supposed to gain, even now, by our belief, and to lose by our nonbelief,
a certain vital good.

60 We see, second, that religion is a forced option so far as that vital
good is concerned. We cannot escape the issue by remaining skeptical,
because although we do avoid error in that way *if religion be untrue,* we
lose the good, *if it be true.* Skepticism, then, is not an avoidance of the
option. . . .

If we had an infallible intellect with its objective certitudes, we might
feel ourselves disloyal to such a perfect organ of knowledge in not
trusting to it exclusively, in not waiting for its releasing word. But if we
are empiricists, if we believe that no bell in us tolls to let us know for
certain when truth is in our grasp, then it seems a piece of idle fantasti-
70 cality to preach so solemnly our duty of waiting for the bell. Indeed we
may wait if we will—I hope you do not think that I am denying that—
but if we do so, we do so at our peril as much as if we believed.

I, therefore, for one, cannot see my way to accepting the agnostic
rules for truth-seeking, or to willfully agree to keep my willing nature
out of the game. I cannot do so for this plain reason, that *a rule of
thinking which would absolutely prevent me from acknowledging certain
kinds of truth, if those kinds of truth were really there, would be an
irrational rule.*

FOR STUDY AND DISCUSSION

1. What does James mean by the word *option?* He asserts that there are
   three different kinds of options. What are they?
2. I would like you to reflect on James's paragraph beginning on line 28,
   "The thesis I defend is this: . . ." Can you bring arguments to support
   this position? Can you argue against it?
3. Why does he maintain that "forced options" are inescapable in the field
   of morality?
4. Why does he maintain that religious options are not only "forced" but
   are "momentous"?
5. How, in the instances of both morality and religion, does he distinguish
   these kinds of "truth" from scientific "truth"?

FICTION

Introduction to Fiction and Poetry

I follow the philosophical excerpts with readings from fiction and poetry. Since the same procedure will be repeated in the remaining sections of the book, I want to make two points very clear in order to avoid needless repetition.

In the first place, I want you to keep in mind that a successful story or poem is rarely written to demonstrate a "truth." I remind you that creative writing, with special exceptions (such as allegory), is concrete, not abstract. Thus, Truth, as illuminated in the stories and poems that follow, is not a logical argumentation but is a "truth of insight" about life which has found natural expression in the writer's chosen form. Incidentally, I trust you will agree with me that this comment about our immediate concern, literature, is equally applicable to all other arts. Each, in its own manner, is a way of seeing—then creatively interpreting—some provocative aspect of human life.

My second reminder is a related one. I have attempted to choose literary selections interestingly relevant to the four philosophical values I am concerned with in this anthology—Truth, Beauty, Goodness, Commitment— but it must always be remembered that there is often an overlapping of these values in any given piece of literature. Let me give you two examples which should illustrate my point. The examples are two poems by Emily Dickinson [1830–1886]. I have condensed the first one, omitting the three middle stanzas.

To Hear an Oriole Sing

To hear an oriole sing
May be a common thing,
Or only [1] a divine.

. . .

The "tune is in the tree,"
The skeptic showeth me;
"No, sir! In thee!"

This poem is obviously about a type of Truth, but it clearly has overtones about the nature of Beauty. Here is a more difficult poem by Emily Dickinson:

[1] only: truly.

17

What Soft, Cherubic Creatures

What soft, cherubic creatures
  These gentlewomen are!
One would as soon assault a plush
  Or violate a star.

Such dimity convictions,
  A horror so refined
Of freckled human nature,
  Of Deity ashamed,—

It's such a common glory,
  A fisherman's degree!
Redemption, brittle lady,
  Be so ashamed of thee.

The vocabulary and the subtlety of allusions in this second poem may be obstacles to your enjoyment, so let me give you an informal prose summary. Some modern women have become so shallowly "refined" (today we might call them "status-conscious") that they have lost significant contact with "lesser" human beings, forgetting that Christianity was founded by "ordinary" people and that the Christian ideal of redemption from sin must always imply divine contempt for the false values which these women exhibit.

Here, too, one is aware that the author is reflecting a kind of Truth, but in this latter poem one also senses that what I have called an "overlap" is more consistent with Goodness than with Beauty. In short, in neither case is the author marshaling thoughts in the type of straight-line development associated with the philosopher. It is therefore necessary that, as you read the short stories, poems, and plays in this book, you be alert to a characteristic mingling of values in many of them—a mingling which can be highly suggestive of the complex responses all of us have to our most rich experiences.

The Bet

A N T O N   P.   C H E K H O V
[1860–1904]

"The Bet" illustrates the two major points made in the introduction to this section: it dramatizes certain "truths"; also it is a reminder that in most effective short stories there is the kind of overlapping of values which I have mentioned. Here the overlapping is between Truth and Goodness; the story could clearly have been chosen to illustrate how a creative writer has dealt with the latter value.

I have chosen to include "The Bet" under the Truth section of this book because I think it an excellent starting point for questions and ideas which might well intrigue you while reading each of the remaining five stories. For example, I would like you to decide whether the theme of the story—and its overtones—is "true" to life. Whatever your decision, I would like you to be able to defend it convincingly.

I

It was a dark autumn night. The old banker was pacing from corner to corner of his study, recalling to his mind the party he gave in the autumn fifteen years before. There were many clever people at the party and much interesting conversation. They talked among other things of capital punishment. The guests, among them not a few scholars and journalists, for the most part disapproved of capital punishment. They found it obsolete as a means of punishment, unfitted to a Christian State, and immoral. Some of them thought that capital punishment should be replaced universally by life-imprisonment.

"I don't agree with you," said the host. "I myself have experienced neither capital punishment nor life-imprisonment, but if one may judge *a priori,* then in my opinion capital punishment is more moral and more humane than imprisonment. Execution kills instantly, life-imprisonment kills by degrees. Who is the more humane executioner, one who kills you in a few seconds or one who draws the life out of you incessantly, for years?"

"They're both equally immoral," remarked one of the guests, "because their purpose is the same, to take away life. The State is not God. It has no right to take away that which it cannot give back, if it should so desire."

Among the company was a lawyer, a young man of about twenty-five. On being asked his opinion, he said:

"Capital punishment and life-imprisonment are equally immoral; but if I were offered the choice between them, I would certainly choose the second. It's better to live somehow than not to live at all."

There ensued a lively discussion. The banker, who was then younger and more nervous, suddenly lost his temper, banged his fist on the table, and turning to the young lawyer, cried out:

"It's a lie. I bet you two millions you wouldn't stick in a cell even for five years."

"If you mean it seriously," replied the lawyer, "then I bet I'll stay not five but fifteen."

"Fifteen! Done!" cried the banker. "Gentlemen, I stake two millions."

"Agreed. You stake two millions, I my freedom," said the lawyer.

So this wild, ridiculous bet came to pass. The banker, who at that time had too many millions to count, spoiled and capricious, was beside himself with rapture. During supper he said to the lawyer jokingly:

"Come to your senses, young man, before it's too late. Two millions are nothing to me, but you stand to lose three or four of the best years of your life. I say three or four, because you'll never stick it out any longer. Don't forget either, you unhappy man, that voluntary is much heavier than enforced imprisonment. The idea that you have the right to free yourself at any moment will poison the whole of your life in the cell. I pity you."

And now the banker, pacing from corner to corner, recalled all this and asked himself:

"Why did I make this bet? What's the good? The lawyer loses fifteen years of his life and I throw away two millions. Will it convince people that capital punishment is worse or better than imprisonment for life? No, no! all stuff and rubbish. On my part, it was the caprice of a well-fed man; on the lawyer's, pure greed of gold."

He recollected further what happened after the evening party. It was decided that the lawyer must undergo his imprisonment under the strictest observation, in a garden wing of the banker's house. It was agreed that during the period he would be deprived of the right to cross the threshold, to see living people, to hear human voices, and to receive letters and newspapers. He was permitted to have a musical instrument, to read books, to write letters, to drink wine and smoke tobacco. By the agreement he could communicate, but only in silence, with the outside world through a little window specially constructed for this purpose. Everything necessary, books, music, wine, he could receive in any quantity by sending a note through the window. The agreement provided for all the minutest details, which made the confinement strictly solitary, and it obliged the lawyer to remain exactly fifteen years from twelve o'clock of November 14th, 1870 to twelve o'clock of November 14th, 1885. The least attempt on his part to violate the conditions, to escape if only for two minutes before the time, freed the banker from the obligation to pay him the two millions.

During the first year of imprisonment, the lawyer, as far as it was possible to judge from his short notes, suffered terribly from loneliness and boredom. From his wing day and night came the sound of the piano. He rejected wine and tobacco. "Wine," he wrote, "excites desires, and desires are the chief foes of a prisoner; besides, nothing is more boring than to drink good wine alone, and tobacco spoils the air in his room." During the first year the lawyer was sent books of a light character: novels with a complicated love interest, stories of crime and fantasy, comedies, and so on.

In the second year the piano was heard no longer and the lawyer asked only for classics. In the fifth year, music was heard again, and the prisoner asked for wine. Those who watched him said that during the whole of that year he was only eating, drinking, and lying on his bed. He yawned often and talked angrily to himself. Books he did not read. Sometimes at nights he would sit down to write. He would write for a long time and tear it all up in the morning. More than once he was heard to weep.

In the second half of the sixth year, the prisoner began zealously to study languages, philosophy, and history. He fell on these subjects so hungrily that the banker hardly had time to get books enough for him. In the space of four years about six hundred volumes were bought at his request. It was while that passion lasted that the banker received the following letter from the prisoner: "My dear gaoler, I am writing these lines in six languages. Show them to experts. Let them read them. If they do not find one single mistake, I beg you to give orders to have a gun fired off in the garden. By the noise I shall know that my efforts have not been in vain. The geniuses of all ages and countries speak in different languages; but in them all burns the same flame. Oh, if you knew my heavenly happiness now that I can understand them!" The prisoner's desire was fulfilled. Two shots were fired in the garden by the banker's order.

Later on, after the tenth year, the lawyer sat immovable before his table and read only the New Testament. The banker found it strange that a man who in four years had mastered six hundred erudite volumes should have spent nearly a year in reading one book, easy to understand and by no means thick. The New Testament was then replaced by the history of religions and theology.

During the last two years of his confinement the prisoner read an extraordinary amount, quite haphazard. Now he would apply himself to the natural sciences, then he would read Byron or Shakespeare. Notes used to come from him in which he asked to be sent at the same time a book on chemistry, a textbook of medicine, a novel, and some treatise on philosophy or theology. He read as though he were swimming in the sea among broken pieces of wreckage, and in his desire to save his life was eagerly grasping one piece after another.

II

The banker recalled all this, and thought:

"Tomorrow at twelve o'clock he receives his freedom. Under the agreement, I shall have to pay him two millions. If I pay, it's all over with me. I am ruined forever . . ."

Fifteen years before he had too many millions to count, but now he was afraid to ask himself which he had more of, money or debts. Gambling on the Stock Exchange, risky speculation, and the recklessness of which he could not rid himself even in old age, had gradually brought his business to decay; and the fearless, self-confident, proud man of business had become an ordinary banker, trembling at every rise and fall in the market.

"That cursed bet," murmured the old man clutching his head in despair. "Why didn't the man die? He's only forty years old. He will take away my last farthing, marry, enjoy life, gamble on the Exchange, and I will look on like an envious beggar and hear the same words from him every day: 'I'm obliged to you for the happiness of my life. Let me help you.' No, it's too much! The only escape from bankruptcy and disgrace is that the man should die."

The clock had just struck three. The banker was listening. In the house every one was asleep, and one could hear only the frozen trees whining outside the windows. Trying to make no sound, he took out of his safe the key of the door which had not been opened for fifteen years, put on his overcoat, and went out of the house. The garden was dark and cold. It was raining. A damp, penetrating wind howled in the garden and gave the trees no rest. Though he strained his eyes, the banker could see neither the ground, nor the white statues, nor the garden wing, nor the trees. Approaching the garden wing, he called the watchman twice. There was no answer. Evidently the watchman had taken shelter from the bad weather and was now asleep somewhere in the kitchen or the greenhouse.

"If I have the courage to fulfill my intention," thought the old man, "the suspicion will fall on the watchman first of all."

In the darkness he groped for the steps and the door and entered the hall of the garden-wing, then poked his way into a narrow passage and struck a match. Not a soul was there. Someone's bed, with no bedclothes on it, stood there, and an iron stove loomed dark in the corner. The seals on the door that led into the prisoner's room were unbroken.

When the match went out, the old man, trembling from agitation, peeped into the little window.

In the prisoner's room a candle was burning dimly. The prisoner himself sat by the table. Only his back, the hair on his head and his hands were visible. Open books were strewn about on the table, the two chairs, and on the carpet near the table.

Five minutes passed and the prisoner never once stirred. Fifteen years' confinement had taught him to sit motionless. The banker tapped on the window with his finger, but the prisoner made no movement in reply. Then the banker cautiously tore the seals from the door and put the key into the lock. The rusty lock gave a hoarse groan and the door creaked. The banker expected instantly to hear a cry of surprise and the sound of steps. Three minutes passed and it was as quiet inside as it had been before. He made up his mind to enter.

Before the table sat a man, unlike an ordinary human being. It was a skeleton, with tight-drawn skin, with long curly hair like a woman's, and a shaggy beard. The color of his face was yellow, of an earthy shade; the cheeks were sunken, the back long and narrow, and the hand upon which he leaned his hairy beard was so lean and skinny that it was painful to look upon. His hair was already silvering with grey, and no one who glanced at the senile emaciation of the face would have believed that he was only forty years old. On the table, before his bended head, lay a sheet of paper on which something was written in a tiny hand.

"Poor devil," thought the banker, "he's asleep and probably seeing millions in his dreams. I have only to take and throw this half-dead thing on the bed, smother him a moment with the pillow, and the most careful examination will find no trace of unnatural death. But, first, let us read what he has written here."

The banker took the sheet from the table and read:

"Tomorrow at twelve o'clock midnight, I shall obtain my freedom and the right to mix with people. But before I leave this room and see the sun I think it necessary to say a few words to you. On my own clear conscience and before God who sees me, I declare to you that I despise freedom, life, health, and all that your books call the blessings of the world.

"For fifteen years I have diligently studied earthly life. True, I saw neither the earth nor the people, but in your books I drank fragrant wine, sang songs, hunted deer and wild boar in the forests, loved women. . . . And beautiful women, like clouds ethereal, created by the magic of your poets' genius, visited me by night and whispered to me wonderful tales, which made my head drunken. In your books I climbed the summits of Elburz and Mont Blanc and saw from there how the sun rose in the morning, and in the evening suffused the sky, the ocean, and the mountain ridges with a purple gold. I saw from there how above me lightnings glimmered cleaving the clouds; I saw green forests, fields, rivers, lakes, cities; I heard sirens singing, and the playing of the pipes of Pan; I touched the wings of beautiful devils who came flying to me to speak of God. . . . In your books I cast myself into bottomless abysses, worked miracles, burned cities to the ground, preached new religions, conquered whole countries. . . .

"Your books gave me wisdom. All that unwearying human thought created in the centuries is compressed to a little lump in my skull. I know that I am cleverer than you all.

"And I despise your books, despise all worldly blessings and wisdom. Everything is void, frail, visionary and delusive as a mirage. Though you be proud and wise and beautiful, yet will death wipe you from the face of the earth like the mice underground; and your posterity, your history, and the immortality of your men of genius will be as frozen slag, burnt down together with the terrestrial globe.

"You are mad, and gone the wrong way. You take falsehood for truth and ugliness for beauty. You would marvel if suddenly apple and orange trees should bear frogs and lizards instead of fruit, and if roses should begin to breathe the odor of a sweating horse. So do I marvel at you, who have bartered heaven for earth. I do not want to understand you.

"That I may show you in deed my contempt for that by which you live, I waive the two millions of which I once dreamed as of paradise, and which I now despise. That I may deprive myself of my right to them, I shall come out from here five minutes before the stipulated term, and thus shall violate the agreement."

When he had read, the banker put the sheet on the table, kissed the head of the strange man, and began to weep. He went out of the wing. Never at any other time, not even after his terrible losses on the Exchange, had he felt such contempt for himself as now. Coming home, he lay down on his bed, but agitation and tears kept him a long time from sleeping. . . .

The next morning the poor watchman came running to him and told him that they had seen the man who lived in the wing climb through the window into the garden. He had gone to the gate and disappeared. The banker instantly went with his servants to the wing and established the escape of his prisoner. To avoid unnecessary rumors he took the paper with the renunciation from the table and, on his return, locked it in his safe.

FOR STUDY AND DISCUSSION

1. Does the argument at the beginning of the story convincingly lay the ground for the bet?
2. Why are the banker and the lawyer not specified by name?
3. Do you find a relationship between the kinds of books the lawyer read and his final decision?
4. What is the lawyer saying about truth in his final document?
5. What do the mixed reactions of the banker at the end suggest about certain "truths" of human life?

By the Waters of Babylon

STEPHEN VINCENT BENÉT

[1898–1943]

The north and the west and the south are good hunting ground, but it is forbidden to go east. It is forbidden to go to any of the Dead Places except to search for metal, and then he who touches the metal must be a priest or the son of a priest. Afterward, both the man and the metal must be purified. These are the rules and the laws; they are well-made. It is forbidden to cross the great river and look upon the place that was the Place of the Gods—this is most strictly forbidden. We do not even say its name though we know its name. It is there that spirits live, and demons—it is there that there are the ashes of the Great Burning. These things are forbidden—they have been forbidden since the beginning of time.

My father is a priest; I am the son of a priest. I have been in the Dead Places near us, with my father—at first, I was afraid. When my father went into the house to search for the metal, I stood by the door and my heart felt small and weak. It was a dead man's house, a spirit house. It did not have the smell of man, though there were old bones in a corner. But it is not fitting that a priest's son should show fear. I looked at the bones in the shadow and kept my voice still.

Then my father came out with the metal—a good, strong piece. He looked at me with both eyes but I had not run away. He gave me the metal to hold—I took it and did not die. So he knew that I was truly his son and would be a priest in my time. That was when I was very young—nevertheless my brothers would not have done it, though they are good hunters. After that, they gave me the good piece of meat and the warm corner by the fire. My father watched over me—he was glad that I should be a priest. But when I boasted or wept without a reason, he punished me more strictly than my brothers. That was right.

After a time, I myself was allowed to go into the dead houses and search for metal. So I learned the ways of those houses—and if I saw bones, I was no longer afraid. The bones are light and old—sometimes they will fall into dust if you touch them. But that is a great sin.

I was taught the chants and the spells—I was taught how to stop the running of blood from a wound and many secrets. A priest must know many secrets—that was what my father said. If the hunters think we do all things by chants and spells, they may believe so—it does not hurt them. I was taught how to read in the old books and how to make the old writings—that was hard and took a long time. My knowledge made me happy—it was like a fire in my heart. Most of all, I liked to hear of the Old Days and the stories of the gods. I asked myself many questions that I could not answer, but it was good to ask them. At night, I would lie awake and listen to the wind—it seemed to me that it was the voice of the gods as they flew through the air.

We are not ignorant like the Forest People—our women spin wool on the wheel, our priests wear a white robe. We do not eat grubs from the tree, we have not forgotten the old writings, although they are hard to understand. Nevertheless, my knowledge and my lack of knowledge burned in me—I wished to know more. When I was a man at last, I came to my father and said, "It is time for me to go on my journey. Give me your leave."

He looked at me for a long time, stroking his beard; then he said at last, "Yes. It is time." That night, in the house of the priesthood, I asked for and received purification. My body hurt but my spirit was a cool stone. It was my father himself who questioned me about my dreams.

He bade me look into the smoke of the fire and see—I saw and told what I saw. It was what I have always seen—a river, and, beyond it, a great Dead Place and in it the gods walking. I have always thought about that. His eyes were stern when I told him—he was no longer my father but a priest. He said, "This is a strong dream."

"It is mine," I said, while the smoke waved and my head felt light. They were singing the Star song in the outer chamber, and it was like the buzzing of bees in my head.

He asked me how the gods were dressed, and I told him how they were dressed. We know how they were dressed from the book, but I saw them as if they were before me. When I had finished, he threw the sticks three times and studied them as they fell.

"This is a very strong dream," he said. "It may eat you up."

"I am not afraid," I said and looked at him with both eyes. My voice sounded thin in my ears, but that was because of the smoke.

He touched me on the breast and the forehead. He gave me the bow and the three arrows.

"Take them," he said. "It is forbidden to travel east. It is forbidden to cross the river. It is forbidden to go to the Place of the Gods. All these things are forbidden."

"All these things are forbidden," I said, but it was my voice that spoke and not my spirit. He looked at me again.

"My son," he said. "Once I had young dreams. If your dreams do not eat you up, you may be a great priest. If they eat you, you are still my son. Now go on your journey."

I went fasting, as is the law. My body hurt but not my heart. When the dawn came, I was out of sight of the village. I prayed and purified myself, waiting for a sign. The sign was an eagle. It flew east.

Sometimes signs are sent by bad spirits. I waited again on the flat rock, fasting, taking no food. I was very still—I could feel the sky above me and the earth beneath. I waited till the sun was beginning to sink. Then three deer passed in the valley going east—they did not mind me or see me. There was a white fawn with them—a very great sign.

I followed them, at a distance, waiting for what would happen. My heart was troubled about going east, yet I knew that I must go. My head hummed with my fasting—I did not even see the panther spring upon the white fawn. But, before I knew it, the bow was in my hand. I shouted and the panther lifted his head from the fawn. It is not easy to kill a panther with one arrow but the arrow went through his eye and into his brain. He died as he tried to spring—he rolled over, tearing at the ground. Then I knew I was meant to go east—I knew that was my journey. When the night came, I made my fire and roasted meat.

It is eight suns' journey to the east and a man passes by many Dead Places. The Forest People are afraid of them but I am not. Once I made my fire on the edge of a Dead Place at night and, next morning, in the dead house, I found a good knife, little rusted. That was small to what came afterward but it made my heart feel big. Always when I looked for game, it was in front of my arrow, and twice I passed hunting parties of the Forest People without their knowing. So I knew my magic was strong and my journey clean, in spite of the law.

Toward the setting of the eighth sun, I came to the banks of the great river. It was half-a-day's journey after I had left the god-road—we do not use the god-roads now for they are falling apart into great blocks of stone, and the forest is safer going. A long way off, I had seen the water through trees but the trees were thick. At last, I came out upon an open place at the top of a cliff. There was the great river below, like a giant in the sun. It is very long, very wide. It could eat all the streams we know and still be thirsty. Its name is Ou-dis-sun, the Sacred, the Long. No man of my tribe had seen it, not even my father, the priest. It was magic and I prayed.

Then I raised my eyes and looked south. It was there, the Place of the Gods.

How can I tell what it was like—you do not know. It was there, in the red light, and they were too big to be houses. It was there with the red light upon it, mighty and ruined. I knew that in another moment the gods would see me. I covered my eyes with my hands and crept back into the forest.

Surely, that was enough to do, and live. Surely it was enough to spend the night upon the cliff. The Forest People themselves do not come near. Yet, all through the night, I knew that I should have to cross the river and walk in the places of the gods, although the gods ate me up. My magic did not help me at all, and yet there was a fire in my bowels, a fire in my mind. When the sun rose, I thought, "My journey has been clean. Now I will go home from my journey." But, even as I thought so, I knew I could not. If I went to the Place of the Gods, I would surely die, but if I did not go, I could never be at peace with my spirit again. It is better to lose one's life than one's spirit, if one is a priest and the son of a priest.

Nevertheless, as I made the raft, the tears ran out of my eyes. The Forest People could have killed me without fight, if they had come upon me then, but they did not come. When the raft was made, I said the sayings for the dead and painted myself for death. My heart was cold as a frog and my knees like water, but the burning in my mind would not let me have peace. As I pushed the raft from the shore, I began my death song—I had the right. It was a fine song.

> "I am John, son of John," I sang. "My people are the Hill People. They are the men.
> I go into the Dead Places but I am not slain.
> I take the metal from the Dead Places but I am not blasted.
> I travel upon the god-roads and am not afraid. E-yah! I have killed the panther, I have killed the fawn!
> E-yah! I have come to the great river. No man has come there before.
> It is forbidden to go east, but I have gone, forbidden to go on the great river, but I am there.
> Open your hearts, you spirits, and hear my song.
> Now I go to the Place of the Gods, I shall not return.
> My body is painted for death and my limbs weak, but my heart is big as I go to the Place of the Gods!"

All the same, when I came to the Place of the Gods, I was afraid, afraid. The current of the great river is very strong—it gripped my raft with its hands. That was magic, for the river itself is wide and calm. I could feel evil spirits about me, in the bright morning; I could feel their breath on my neck as I was swept down the stream. Never have I been so much alone—I tried to think of my knowledge, but it was a squirrel's heap of winter nuts. There was no strength in my knowledge any more and I felt small and naked as a new-hatched bird—alone upon the great river, the servant of the gods.

Yet, after a while, my eyes were opened and I saw. I saw both banks of the river—I saw that once there had been god-roads across it, though now they were broken and fallen like broken vines. Very great they were, and wonderful and broken—broken in the time of the Great Burning when the fire fell out of the sky. And always the current took me nearer to the Place of the Gods, and the huge ruins rose before my eyes.

I do not know the customs of rivers—we are the People of the Hills. I tried to guide my raft with the pole but it spun around. I thought the river meant to take me past the Place of the Gods and out into the Bitter Water of the legends. I grew angry then—my heart felt strong. I said aloud, "I am a priest and the son of a priest!" The gods heard me—they showed me how to paddle with the pole on one side of the raft. The current changed itself—I drew near to the Place of the Gods.

When I was very near, my raft struck and turned over. I can swim in our lakes—I swam to the shore. There was a great spike of rusted metal sticking out into the river—I hauled myself up upon it and sat there, panting. I had saved my bow and two arrows and the knife I found in the Dead Place but that was all. My raft went whirling downstream toward the Bitter Water. I looked after it, and thought if it had trod me under, at least I would be safely dead. Nevertheless, when I had dried my bowstring and re-strung it, I walked forward to the Place of the Gods.

It felt like ground underfoot; it did not burn me. It is not true what some of the tales say, that the ground there burns forever, for I have been there. Here and there were the marks and stains of the Great Burning, on the ruins, that is true. But they were old marks and old stains. It is not true either, what some of our priests say, that it is an island covered with fogs and enchantments. It is not. It is a great Dead Place—greater than any Dead Place we know. Everywhere in it there are god-roads, though most are cracked and broken. Everywhere there are the ruins of the high towers of the gods.

How shall I tell what I saw? I went carefully, my strung bow in my hand, my skin ready for danger. There should have been the wailings of spirits and the shrieks of demons, but there were not. It was very silent and sunny where I had landed—the wind and the rain and the birds that drop seeds had done their work—the grass grew in the cracks of the broken stone. It is a fair island—no wonder the gods built there. If I had come there, a god, I also would have built.

How shall I tell what I saw? The towers are not all broken—here and there one still stands, like a great tree in a forest, and the birds nest high. But the towers themselves look blind, for the gods are gone. I saw a fish-hawk, catching fish in the river. I saw a little dance of white butterflies over a great heap of broken stones and columns. I went there and looked about me—there was a carved stone with cut-letters, broken in half. I can read letters but I could not understand these. They said UBTREAS. There was also the shattered image of a man or a god. It had been made of white stone and he wore his hair tied back like a woman's. His name was ASHING, as I read on the cracked half of a stone. I thought it wise to pray to ASHING, though I do not know that god.

How shall I tell what I saw? There was no smell of man left, on stone or metal. Nor were there many trees in that wilderness of stone. There are many pigeons, nesting and dropping in the towers—the gods must have loved them, or, perhaps, they used them for sacrifices. There are wild cats that roam the god-roads, green-eyed, unafraid of man. At night they wail like demons, but they are not demons. The wild dogs are more dangerous, for they hunt in a pack, but them I did not meet till later. Everywhere there are the carved stones, carved with magical numbers or words.

I went north—I did not try to hide myself. When a god or a demon saw me, then I would die, but meanwhile I was no longer afraid. My hunger for knowledge burned in me—there was so much that I could not understand. After a while, I knew that my belly was hungry. I could have hunted for my meat, but I did not hunt. It is known that the gods did not hunt as we do—they got their food from enchanted boxes and jars. Sometimes these are still found in the Dead Places—once, when I was a child and foolish, I opened such a jar and tasted it and found the food sweet. But my father found out and punished me for it strictly, for, often, that food is death. Now, though, I had long gone past what was forbidden, and I entered the likeliest towers, looking for the food of the gods.

I found it at last in the ruins of a great temple in the mid-city. A mighty temple it must have been, for the roof was painted like the sky at night with its stars—that much I could see, though the colors were faint and dim. It went down into great caves and tunnels—perhaps they kept their slaves there. But when I started to climb down, I heard the squeaking of rats, so I did not go—rats are unclean, and there must have been many tribes of them, from the squeaking. But near there, I found food, in the heart of a ruin, behind a door that still opened. I ate only the fruits from the jars—they had a very sweet taste. There was drink, too, in bottles of glass—the drink of the gods was strong and made my head swim. After I had eaten and drunk, I slept on the top of a stone, my bow at my side.

When I woke, the sun was low. Looking down from where I lay, I saw a dog sitting on his haunches. His tongue was hanging out of his mouth; he looked as if he were laughing. He was a big dog, with a gray-brown coat, as big as a wolf. I sprang up and shouted at him but he did not move—he just sat there as if he were laughing. I did not like that. When I reached for a stone to throw, he moved swiftly out of the way of the stone. He was not afraid of me; he looked at me as if I were meat. No doubt I could have killed him with an arrow, but I did not know if there were others. Moreover, night was falling.

I looked about me—not far away there was a great, broken god-road, leading north. The towers were high enough, but not so high, and while many of the dead-houses were wrecked, there were some that stood. I went toward this god-road, keeping to the heights of the ruins, while the dog followed. When I had reached the god-road, I saw that there were others behind him. If I had slept later, they would have come upon me asleep and torn out my throat. As it was, they were sure enough of me; they did not hurry. When I went into the dead-house, they kept watch at the entrance—doubtless they thought they would have a fine hunt. But a dog cannot open a door and I knew, from the books, that the gods did not like to live on the ground but on high.

I had just found a door I could open when the dogs decided to rush. Ha! They were surprised when I shut the door in their faces—it was a good door, of strong metal. I could hear their foolish baying beyond it, but I did not stop to answer them. I was in darkness—I found stairs and climbed. There were many stairs, turning around till my head was dizzy. At the top was another door—I found the knob and opened it. I was in a long small chamber—on one side of it was a bronze door that could not be opened, for it had no handle. Perhaps there was a magic word to open it but I did not have the word. I turned to the door in the opposite side of the wall. The lock of it was broken and I opened it and went in.

Within, there was a place of great riches. The god who lived there must have been a powerful god. The first room was a small anteroom—I waited there for some time, telling the spirits of the place that I came in peace and not as a robber. When it seemed to me that they had had time to hear me, I went on. Ah, what riches! Few, even, of the windows had been broken—it was all as it had been. The great windows that looked over the city had not been broken at all though they were dusty and streaked with many years. There were coverings on the floors, the colors not greatly faded, and the chairs were soft and deep. There were pictures upon the walls, very strange, very wonderful—I remember one of a bunch of flowers in a jar—if you came close to it, you could see nothing but bits of color, but if you stood away from it, the flowers might have been picked yesterday. It made my heart feel strange to look at this picture—and to look at the figure of a bird, in some hard clay, on a table and see it so like our birds. Everywhere there were books and writings, many in tongues that I could not read. The god who lived there must have been a wise god and full of knowledge. I felt I had a right there, as I sought knowledge also.

Nevertheless, it was strange. There was a washing place but no water— perhaps the gods washed in air. There was a cooking place but no wood, and though there was a machine to cook food, there was no place to put fire in it. Nor were there candles or lamps—there were things that looked like lamps but they had neither oil nor wick. All these things were magic, but I touched them and lived—the magic had gone out of them. Let me tell one thing to show. In the washing place, a thing said "Hot" but it was not hot to the touch—another thing said "Cold" but it was not cold. This must have been a strong magic but the magic was gone. I do not understand—they had ways—I wish that I knew.

It was close and dry and dusty in their house of the gods. I have said the magic was gone but that is not true—it had gone from the magic things but it had not gone from the place. I felt the spirits about me, weighing upon me. Nor had I ever slept in a Dead Place before—and yet, tonight, I must sleep there. When I thought of it, my tongue felt dry in my throat, in spite of my wish for knowledge. Almost I would have gone down again and faced the dogs, but I did not.

I had not gone through all the rooms when the darkness fell. When it fell, I went back to the big room looking over the city and made fire. There was a place to make fire and a box with wood in it, though I do not think they cooked there. I wrapped myself in a floor-covering and slept in front of the fire—I was very tired.

Now I tell what is very strong magic. I woke in the midst of the night.

When I woke, the fire had gone out and I was cold. It seemed to me that all around me there were whisperings and voices. I closed my eyes to shut them out. Some will say that I slept again, but I do not think that I slept. I could feel the spirits drawing my spirit out of my body as a fish is drawn on a line.

Why should I lie about it? I am a priest and the son of a priest. If there are spirits, as they say, in the small Dead Places near us, what spirits must there not be in that great Place of the Gods? And would not they wish to speak? After such long years? I know that I felt myself drawn as a fish is drawn on a line. I had stepped out of my body—I could see my body asleep in front of the cold fire, but it was not I. I was drawn to look out upon the city of the gods.

It should have been dark, for it was night, but it was not dark. Everywhere there were lights—lines of lights—circles and blurs of light—ten thousand torches would not have been the same. The sky itself was alight—you could barely see the stars for the glow in the sky. I thought to myself "This is strong magic" and trembled. There was a roaring in my ears like the rushing of rivers. Then my eyes grew used to the light and my ears to the sound. I knew that I was seeing the city as it had been when the gods were alive.

That was a sight indeed—yes, that was a sight: I could not have seen it in the body—my body would have died. Everywhere went the gods, on foot and in chariots—there were gods beyond number and counting, and their chariots blocked the streets. They had turned night to day for their pleasure—they did not sleep with the sun. The noise of their coming and going was the noise of many waters. It was magic what they could do—it was magic what they did.

I looked out of another window—the great vines of their bridges were mended and the god-roads went east and west. Restless, restless, were the gods and always in motion! They burrowed tunnels under rivers—they flew in the air. With unbelievable tools, they did giant works—no part of the earth was safe from them, for if they wished for a thing, they summoned it from the other side of the world. And always, as they labored and rested, as they feasted and made love, there was a drum in their ears—the pulse of the giant city, beating and beating like a man's heart.

Were they happy? What is happiness to the gods? They were great, they were mighty, they were wonderful and terrible. As I looked upon them and their magic, I felt like a child—but a little more, it seemed to me, and they would pull down the moon from the sky. I saw them with wisdom beyond wisdom and knowledge beyond knowledge. And yet not all they did was well done—even I could see that—and yet their wisdom could not but grow until all was peace.

Then I saw their fate come upon them, and that was terrible past speech. It came upon them as they walked the streets of their city. I have been in the fights with the Forest People—I have seen men die. But this was not like that. When gods war with gods, they use weapons we do not know. It was fire falling out of the sky and a mist that poisoned. It was the time of the Great Burning and the Destruction. They ran about like ants in the streets of their city— poor gods, poor gods! Then the towers began to fall. A few escaped—yes, a few. The legends tell it. But, even after the city had become a Dead Place, for many years the poison was still in the ground. I saw it happen, I saw the last of them die. It was darkness over the broken city and I wept.

All this, I saw. I saw it as I have told it, though not in the body. When I woke in the morning, I was hungry, but I did not think first of my hunger for my heart was perplexed and confused. I knew the reason for the Dead Places, but I did not see why it had happened. It seemed to me it should not have happened, with all the magic they had. I went through the house looking for an answer. There was so much in the house I could not understand—and yet I am a priest and the son of a priest. It was like being on one side of the great river, at night, with no light to show the way.

Then I saw the dead god. He was sitting in his chair, by the window, in a room I had not entered before and, for the first moment, I thought that he was alive. Then I saw the skin on the back of his hand—it was like dry leather. The room was shut, hot and dry—no doubt that had kept him as he was. At first I was afraid to approach him—then the fear left me. He was sitting looking out over the city—he was dressed in the clothes of the gods. His age was neither young nor old—I could not tell his age. But there was wisdom in his face and great sadness. You could see that he would have not run away. He had sat at his window, watching his city die—then he himself had died. But it is better to lose one's life than one's spirit—and you could see from the face that his spirit had not been lost. I knew that if I touched him, he would fall into dust—and yet, there was something unconquered in the face.

That is all of my story, for then I knew he was a man—I knew then that they had been men, neither gods nor demons. It is a great knowledge, hard to tell and believe. They were men—they went a dark road, but they were men. I had no fear after that—I had no fear going home, though twice I fought off the dogs and once I was hunted for two days by the Forest People. When I saw my father again, I prayed and was purified. He touched my lips and my breast, he said, "You went away a boy. You come back a man and a priest." I said, "Father, they were men! I have been in the Place of the Gods and seen it! Now slay me, if it is the law—but still I know they were men."

He looked at me out of both eyes. He said, "The law is not always the same shape—you have done what you have done. I could not have done it in my time, but you come after me. Tell!"

I told and he listened. After that, I wished to tell all the people but he showed me otherwise. He said, "Truth is a hard deer to hunt. If you eat too much truth at once, you may die of the truth. It was not idly that our fathers forbade the Dead Places." He was right—it is better the truth should come little by little. I have learned that, being a priest. Perhaps, in the old days, they ate knowledge too fast.

Nevertheless, we make a beginning. It is not for the metal alone we go to the Dead Places now—there are the books and the writings. They are hard to learn. And the magic tools are broken—but we can look at them and wonder. At least, we make a beginning. And, when I am chief priest we shall go beyond the great river. We shall go to the Place of the Gods—the place newyork—not one man but a company. We shall look for the images of the gods and find the god ASHING and the others—the gods LINCOLN and BILTMORE and MOSES. But they were men who built the city, not gods or demons. They were men. I remember the dead man's face. They were men who were here before us. We must build again.

In Another Country

ERNEST HEMINGWAY

[1899–1961]

In the fall the war [1] was always there, but we did not go to it any more. It was cold in the fall in Milan and the dark came very early. Then the electric lights came on, and it was pleasant along the streets looking in the windows. There was much game hanging outside the shops, and the snow powdered in the fur of the foxes and the wind blew their tails. The deer hung stiff and heavy and empty, and small birds blew in the wind and the wind turned their feathers. It was a cold fall and the wind came down from the mountains.

We were all at the hospital every afternoon, and there were different ways of walking across the town through the dusk to the hospital. Two of the ways were alongside canals, but they were long. Always, though, you crossed a bridge across a canal to enter the hospital. There was a choice of three bridges. On one of them a woman sold roasted chestnuts. It was warm, standing in front of her charcoal fire, and the chestnuts were warm afterward in your pocket. The hospital was very old and very beautiful, and you entered through a gate and walked across a courtyard and out a gate on the other side. There were usually funerals starting from the courtyard. Beyond the old hospital were the new brick pavilions, and there we met every afternoon and were all very polite and interested in what was the matter, and sat in the machines that were to make so much difference.

The doctor came up to the machine where I was sitting and said: "What did you like best to do before the war? Did you practice a sport?"

I said: "Yes, football."

"Good," he said. "You will be able to play football again better than ever."

My knee did not bend, and the leg dropped straight from the knee to the ankle without a calf, and the machine was to bend the knee and make it move as in riding a tricycle. But it did not bend yet, and instead the machine lurched when it came to the bending part. The doctor said: "That will all pass. You are a fortunate young man. You will play football again like a champion."

In the next machine was a major who had a little hand like a baby's. He winked at me when the doctor examined his hand, which was between two leather straps that bounced up and down and flapped the stiff fingers, and said: "And will I too play football, captain-doctor?" He had been a very great fencer, and before the war the greatest fencer in Italy.

[1] *the war:* World War I, in Italy.

The doctor went to his office in a back room and brought a photograph which showed a hand that had been withered almost as small as the major's, before it had taken a machine course, and after was a little larger. The major held the photograph with his good hand and looked at it very carefully. "A wound?" he asked.

"An industrial accident," the doctor said.

"Very interesting, very interesting," the major said, and handed it back to the doctor.

"You have confidence?"

"No," said the major.

There were three boys who came each day who were about the same age I was. They were all three from Milan, and one of them was to be a lawyer, and one was to be a painter, and one had intended to be a soldier, and after we were finished with the machines, sometimes we walked back together to the Café Cova, which was next door to the Scala. We walked the short way through the Communist quarter because we were four together. The people hated us because we were officers, and from a wineshop someone called out, "*A basso gli ufficiali!*" [1] As we passed. Another boy who walked with us sometimes and made us five wore a black silk handkerchief across his face because he had no nose then and his face was to be rebuilt. He had gone out to the front from the military academy and been wounded within an hour after he had gone into the front line for the first time. They rebuilt his face, but he came from a very old family and they could never get the nose exactly right. He went to South America and worked in a bank. But this was a long time ago, and then we did not any of us know how it was going to be afterward. We only knew then that there was always the war, but that we were not going to it any more.

We all had the same medals, except the boy with the black silk bandage across his face, and he had not been at the front long enough to get any medals. The tall boy with a very pale face who was to be a lawyer had been a lieutenant of Arditi and had three medals of the sort we each had only one of. He had lived a very long time with death and was a little detached. We were all a little detached, and there was nothing that held us together except that we met every afternoon at the hospital. Although, as we walked to the Cova through the tough part of town, walking in the dark, with light and singing coming out of the wine shops, and sometimes having to walk into the street when the men and women would crowd together on the sidewalk so that we would have had to jostle them to get by, we felt held together by there being something that had happened that they, the people who disliked us, did not understand.

We ourselves all understood the Cova, where it was rich and warm and not

[1] *A basso gli ufficiali!:* Down with the officers!

too brightly lighted, and noisy and smoky at certain hours, and there were always girls at the tables and the illustrated papers on a rack on the wall. The girls at the Cova were very patriotic, and I found that the most patriotic people in Italy were the café girls—and I believe they are still patriotic.

The boys at first were very polite about my medals and asked me what I had done to get them. I showed them the papers, which were written in very beautiful language and full of *fratellanza* and *abnegazione* [1] but which really said, with the adjectives removed, that I had been given the medals because I was an American. After that their manner changed a little toward me, although I was their friend against outsiders. I was a friend, but I was never really one of them after they had read the citations, because it had been different with them and they had done very different things to get their medals. I had been wounded, it was true; but we all knew that being wounded, after all, was really an accident. I was never ashamed of the ribbons, though, and sometimes, after the cocktail hour, I would imagine myself having done all the things they had done to get their medals; but walking home at night through the empty streets with the cold wind and all the shops closed, trying to keep near the street lights, I knew that I would never have done such things, and I was very much afraid to die, and often lay in bed at night by myself, afraid to die and wondering how I would be when I went back to the front again.

The three with the medals were like hunting-hawks; and I was not a hawk, although I might seem a hawk to those who had never hunted; they, the three, knew better and so we drifted apart. But I stayed good friends with the boy who had been wounded his first day at the front, because he would never know how he would have turned out; so he could never be accepted either, and I liked him because I thought perhaps he would not have turned out to be a hawk either.

The major, who had been the great fencer, did not believe in bravery, and spent much time while we sat in the machines correcting my grammar. He had complimented me on how I spoke Italian, and we talked together very easily. One day I had said that Italian seemed such an easy language to me that I could not take a great interest in it; everything was so easy to say. "Ah, yes," the major said. "Why, then, do you not take up the use of grammar?" So we took up the use of grammar, and soon Italian was such a difficult language that I was afraid to talk to him until I had the grammar straight in my mind.

The major came very regularly to the hospital. I do not think he ever missed a day, although I am sure he did not believe in the machines. There was a time when none of us believed in the machines, and one day the major said it was all nonsense. The machines were new then and it was we who were to prove them. It was an idiotic idea, he said, "a theory, like another." I had

---

[1] *fratellanza* and *abnegazione:* brotherhood and self-sacrifice.

not learned my grammar, and he said I was a stupid impossible disgrace, and he was a fool to have bothered with me. He was a small man and he sat straight up in his chair with his right hand thrust into the machine and looked straight ahead at the wall while the straps thumped up and down with his fingers in them.

"What will you do when the war is over if it is over?" he asked me. "Speak grammatically!"

"I will go to the States."

"Are you married?"

"No, but I hope to be."

"The more of a fool you are," he said. He seemed very angry. "A man must not marry."

"Why, Signor Maggiore?"

"Don't call me 'Signor Maggiore.' "

"Why must not a man marry?"

"He cannot marry. He cannot marry," he said angrily. "If he is to lose everything, he should not place himself in a position to lose that. He should not place himself in a position to lose. He should find things he cannot lose."

He spoke very angrily and bitterly, and looked straight ahead while he talked.

"But why should he necessarily lose it?"

"He'll lose it," the major said. He was looking at the wall. Then he looked down at the machine and jerked his little hand out from between the straps and slapped it hard against his thigh. "He'll lose it," he almost shouted. "Don't argue with me!" Then he called to the attendant who ran the machines. "Come and turn this damned thing off."

He went back into the other room for the light treatment and the massage. Then I heard him ask the doctor if he might use his telephone and he shut the door. When he came back into the room, I was sitting in another machine. He was wearing his cape and had his cap on, and he came directly toward my machine and put his arm on my shoulder.

"I am so sorry," he said, and patted me on the shoulder with his good hand. "I would not be rude. My wife has just died. You must forgive me."

"Oh——" I said, feeling sick for him. "I am *so* sorry."

He stood there biting his lower lip. "It is very difficult," he said. "I cannot resign myself."

He looked straight past me and out through the window. Then he began to cry. "I am utterly unable to resign myself," he said and choked. And then crying, his head up looking at nothing, carrying himself straight and soldierly, with tears on both his cheeks and biting his lips, he walked past the machines and out the door.

The doctor told me that the major's wife, who was very young and whom he had not married until he was definitely invalided out of the war, had died of pneumonia. She had been sick only a few days. No one expected her to die. The major did not come to the hospital for three days. Then he came at the usual hour, wearing a black band on the sleeve of his uniform. When he came back, there were large framed photographs around the wall, of all sorts of wounds before and after they had been cured by the machines. In front of the machine the major used were three photographs of hands like his that were completely restored. I do not know where the doctor got them. I always understood we were the first to use the machines. The photographs did not make much difference to the major because he only looked out of the window.

Young Archimedes

ALDOUS HUXLEY

[1894–1963]

It was the view which finally made us take the place. True, the house had its disadvantages. It was a long way out of town and had no telephone. The rent was unduly high, the drainage system poor. On windy nights, when the ill-fitting panes were rattling so furiously in the window frames that you could fancy yourself in a hotel omnibus, the electric light, for some mysterious reason, used invariably to go out and leave you in the noisy dark. There was a splendid bathroom; but the electric pump, which was supposed to send up water from the rainwater tanks in the terrace, did not work. Punctually every autumn the drinking well ran dry. And our landlady was a liar and a cheat.

But these are the little disadvantages of every hired house, all over the world. For Italy they were not really at all serious. I have seen plenty of houses which had them all and a hundred others, without possessing the compensating advantages of ours—the southward-facing garden and terrace for the winter and spring, the large cool rooms against the midsummer heat, the hilltop air and freedom from mosquitoes, and finally the view.

And what a view it was! Or rather, what a succession of views. For it was different every day; and without stirring from the house one had the impression of an incessant change of scene: all the delights of travel without its fatigues. There were autumn days when all the valleys were filled with mist and the crests of Apennines rose darkly out of a flat white lake. There were days when the mist invaded even our hilltop and we were enveloped in a soft vapor in which the mist-colored olive trees, that sloped away below our windows toward the valley, disappeared as though into their own spiritual essence; and the only firm and definite things in the small, dim world within which we found ourselves confined were the two tall black cypresses growing on a little projecting terrace a hundred feet down the hill. Black, sharp, and solid, they stood there, twin pillars of Hercules at the extremity of the known universe; and beyond them there was only pale cloud and round them only the cloudy olive trees.

These were the wintry days; but there were days of spring and autumn, days unchangingly cloudless, or—more lovely still—made various by the huge floating shapes of vapor that, snowy above the far-away snow-capped mountains, gradually unfolded, against the pale bright blue, enormous heroic gestures. And in the height of the sky the bellying draperies, the swans, the aerial marbles, hewed and left unfinished by gods grown tired of creation almost before they had begun, drifted sleeping along the wind, changing form as they moved. And the sun would come and go behind them; and now the town in the valley would fade and almost vanish in the shadow, and now, like an immense fretted jewel between the hills, it would glow as though by its own light. And looking across the nearer tributary valley that wound from below our crest down toward the Arno, looking over the low dark shoulder of hill on whose extreme promontory stood the towered church of San Miniato, one saw the huge dome airily hanging on its ribs of masonry, the square campanile, the sharp spire of Santa Croce, and the canopied tower of the Signoria, rising above the intricate maze of houses, distinct and brilliant, like small treasures carved out of precious stones. For a moment only, and then their light would fade away once more, and the traveling beam would pick out, among the indigo hills beyond, a single golden crest.

There were days when the air was wet with passed or with approaching rain, and all the distances seemed miraculously near and clear. The olive trees detached themselves one from another on the distant slopes; the far-away villages were lovely and pathetic like the most exquisite small toys. There were days in summertime, days of impending thunder when, bright and sunlit against huge bellying masses of black and purple, the hills and the white houses shone as it were precariously, in a dying splendor, on the brink of some fearful calamity.

How the hills changed and varied! Every day and every hour of the day, almost, they were different. There would be moments when, looking across the plain of Florence, one would see only a dark blue silhouette against the sky. The scene had no depth; there was only a hanging curtain painted flatly with the symbols of mountains. And then, suddenly almost, with the passing of a cloud, or when the sun had declined to a certain level in the sky, the flat scene transformed itself; and where there had been only a painted curtain, now there were ranges behind ranges of hills, graduated tone after tone from brown, or gray, or a green-gold to far-away blue. Shapes that a moment before had been fused together indiscriminately into a single mass, now came apart into their constituents. Fiesole, which had seemed only a spur of Monte Morello, now revealed itself as the jutting headland of another system of hills, divided from the nearest bastions of its greater neighbor by a deep and shadowy valley.

At noon, during the heats of summer, the landscape became dim, powdery, vague, and almost colorless under the midday sun; the hills disappeared into the trembling fringes of the sky. But as the afternoon wore on, the landscape emerged again, it dropped its anonymity, it climbed back out of nothingness into form and life. And its life, as the sun sank and slowly sank through the long afternoon, grew richer, grew more intense with every moment. The level light, with its attendant long, dark shadows, laid bare, so to speak, the anatomy of the land; the hills—each western escarpment shining, and each slope averted from the sunlight profoundly shadowed—became massive, jutty, and solid. Little folds and dimples in the seemingly even ground revealed themselves. Eastward from our hilltop, across the plain of the Ema, a great bluff cast its ever-increasing shadow; in the surrounding brightness of the valley a whole town lay eclipsed within it. And as the sun expired on the horizon, the further hills flushed in its warm light, till their illumined flanks were the color of tawny roses; but the valleys were already filled with the blue mist of evening. And it mounted, mounted; the fire went out of the western windows of the populous slopes; only the crests were still alight, and at last they too were all extinct. The mountains faded and fused together again into a flat painting of mountains against the pale evening sky. In a little while it was night; and if the moon were full, a ghost of the dead scene still haunted the horizons.

Changeful in its beauty, this wide landscape always preserved a quality of humanness and domestication which made it, to my mind at any rate, the best of all landscapes to live with. Day by day one traveled through its different beauties; but the journey, like our ancestors' Grand Tour, was always a journey through civilization. For all its mountains, its steep slopes and deep valleys, the Tuscan scene is dominated by its inhabitants. They have cultivated every rood of ground that can be cultivated; their houses are thickly scattered even over the hills, and the valleys are populous. Solitary on the hilltop, one is not alone in a wilderness. Man's traces are across the country, and already—one feels it with satisfaction as one looks out across it—for centuries, for thousands of years, it has been his, submissive, tamed, and humanized. The wide, blank moorlands, the sands, the forests of innumerable trees—these are places for occasional visitation, healthful to the spirit which submits itself to them for not too long. But fiendish influences as well as divine haunt these total solitudes. The vegetative life of plants and things is alien and hostile to the human. Men cannot live at ease except where they have mastered their surroundings and where their accumulated lives outnumber and outweigh the vegetative lives about them. Stripped of its dark woods, planted, terraced, and tilled almost to the mountains' tops, the Tuscan landscape is humanized and safe. Sometimes upon those who live in the midst of it there comes a longing for some place that is solitary, inhuman, lifeless, or peopled only with alien life. But the longing is soon satisfied, and one is glad to return to the civilized and submissive scene.

I found that house on the hilltop the ideal dwelling-place. For there, safe in the midst of a humanized landscape, one was yet alone; one could be as solitary as one liked. Neighbors whom one never sees at close quarters are the ideal and perfect neighbors.

Our nearest neighbors, in terms of physical proximity, lived very near. We had two sets of them, as a matter of fact, almost in the same house with us. One was the peasant family, who lived in a long, low building, part dwelling-house, part stables, storerooms and cowsheds, adjoining the villa. Our other neighbors—intermittent neighbors, however, for they only ventured out of town every now and then, during the most flawless weather—were the owners of the villa, who had reserved for themselves the smaller wing of the huge L-shaped house—a mere dozen rooms or so—leaving the remaining eighteen or twenty to us.

They were a curious couple, our proprietors. An old husband, gray, listless, tottering, seventy at least; and a signora of about forty, short, very plump, with tiny fat hands and feet and a pair of very large, very dark black eyes, which she used with all the skill of a born comedian. Her vitality, if you could have harnessed it and made it do some useful work, would have supplied a whole town with electric light. The physicists talk of deriving energy from the atom; they would be more profitably employed nearer home—in discovering some way of tapping those enormous stores of vital energy which accumulate in unemployed women of sanguine temperament and which, in the present imperfect state of social and scientific organization, vent themselves in ways that are generally so deplorable: in interfering with other people's affairs, in working up emotional scenes, in thinking about love and making it, and in bothering men till they cannot get on with their work.

Signora Bondi got rid of her superfluous energy, among other ways, by "doing in" her tenants. The old gentleman, who was a retired merchant with a reputation for the most perfect rectitude, was allowed to have no dealings with us. When we came to see the house, it was the wife who showed us round. It was she who, with a lavish display of charm, with irresistible rolling of the eyes, expatiated on the merits of the place, sang the praises of the electric pump, glorified the bathroom (considering which, she insisted, the rent was remarkably moderate), and when we suggested calling in a surveyor to look over the house, earnestly begged us, as though our well-being were her only consideration, not to waste our money unnecessarily in doing anything so superfluous. "After all," she said, "we are honest people. I wouldn't dream of letting you the house except in perfect condition. Have confidence." And she looked at me with an appealing, pained expression in her magnificent eyes, as though begging me not to insult her by my coarse suspiciousness. And leaving us no time to pursue the subject of surveyors any further, she began assuring us that our little boy was the most beautiful angel she had ever seen. By the time our interview with Signora Bondi was at an end, we had definitely decided to take the house.

"Charming woman," I said, as we left the house. But I think that Elizabeth was not quite so certain of it as I.

Then the pump episode began.

On the evening of our arrival in the house we switched on the electricity. The pump made a very professional whirring noise; but no water came out of the taps in the bathroom. We looked at one another doubtfully.

"Charming woman?" Elizabeth raised her eyebrows.

We asked for interviews; but somehow the old gentleman could never see us, and the Signora was invariably out or indisposed. We left notes; they were never answered. In the end, we found that the only method of communicating with our landlords, who were living in the same house with us, was to go down into Florence and send a registered express letter to them. For this they had to sign two separate receipts and even, if we chose to pay forty centimes more, a third incriminating document, which was then returned to us. There could be no pretending, as there always was with ordinary letters or notes, that the communication had never been received. We began at last to get answers to our complaints. The Signora, who wrote all the letters, started by telling us that, naturally, the pump didn't work, as the cisterns were empty, owing to the long drought. I had to walk three miles to the post office in order to register my letter reminding her that there had been a violent thunderstorm only last Wednesday, and that the tanks were consequently more than half full. The answer came back: bath water had not been guaranteed in the contract; and if I wanted it, why hadn't I had the pump looked at before I took the house? Another walk into town to ask the Signora next door whether she remembered her adjurations to us to have confidence in her, and to inform her that the existence in a house of a bathroom was in itself an implicit guarantee of bath water. The reply to that was that the Signora couldn't continue to have communications with people who wrote so rudely to her. After that I put the matter into the hands of a lawyer. Two months later the pump was actually replaced. But we had to serve a writ on the lady before she gave in. And the costs were considerable.

One day, toward the end of the episode, I met the old gentleman in the road, taking his big maremman dog for a walk—or being taken, rather, for a walk by the dog. For where the dog pulled, the old gentleman had perforce to follow. And when it stopped to smell, or scratch the ground, or leave against a gatepost its visiting card or an offensive challenge, patiently, at his end of the leash, the old man had to wait. I passed him standing at the side of the road, a few hundred yards below our house. The dog was sniffing at the roots of one of the twin cypresses which grew one on either side of the entry to a farm; I heard the beast growling indignantly to itself, as though it scented an intolerable insult. Old Signor Bondi, leashed to his dog, was waiting. The knees inside the tubular gray trousers were slightly bent. Leaning on his cane, he stood gazing mournfully and vacantly at the view. The whites of his old eyes were discolored, like ancient billiard balls. In the gray, deeply wrinkled face, his nose was dyspeptically red. His white moustache, ragged and yellowing at the fringes, drooped in a melancholy curve. In his black tie he wore a very large diamond; perhaps that was what Signora Bondi had found so attractive about him.

I took off my hat as I approached. The old man stared at me absently, and it was only when I was already almost past him that he recollected who I was.

"Wait," he called after me, "wait!" And he hastened down the road in pursuit. Taken utterly by surprise and at a disadvantage—for it was engaged in retorting to the affront imprinted on the cypress roots—the dog permitted itself to be jerked after him. Too much astonished to be anything but obedient, it followed its master. "Wait!"

I waited.

"My dear sir," said the old gentleman, catching me by the lapel of my coat and blowing most disagreeably in my face, "I want to apologize." He looked around him, as though afraid that even here he might be overheard. "I want to apologize," he went on, "about that wretched pump business. I assure you that, if it had been only my affair, I'd have put the thing right as soon as you asked. You were quite right: a bathroom is an implicit guarantee of bath water. I saw from the first that we should have no chance if it came to court. And besides, I think one ought to treat one's tenants as handsomely as one can afford to. But my wife"—he lowered his voice—"the fact is that she likes this sort of thing, even when she knows that she's in the wrong and must lose. And besides, she hoped, I dare say, that you'd get tired of asking and have the job done yourself. I told her from the first that we ought to give in; but she wouldn't listen. You see, she enjoys it. Still, now she sees that it must be done. In the course of the next two or three days you'll be having your bath water. But I thought I'd just like to tell you how . . ." But the Maremmano, which had recovered by this time from its surprise of a moment since, suddenly bounded, growling, up the road. The old gentleman tried to hold the beast, strained at the leash, tottered unsteadily, then gave way and allowed himself to be dragged off. ". . . how sorry I am," he went on, as he receded from me, "that this little misunderstanding . . ." But it was no use. "Good-bye." He smiled politely, made a little deprecating gesture, as though he had suddenly remembered a pressing engagement, and had no time to explain what it was. "Good-bye." He took off his hat and abandoned himself completely to the dog.

A week later the water really did begin to flow, and the day after our first bath Signora Bondi, dressed in dove-gray satin and wearing all her pearls, came to call.

"Is it peace now?" she asked, with a charming frankness, as she shook hands.

We assured her that, so far as we were concerned, it certainly was.

"But why *did* you write me such dreadfully rude letters?" she said, turning on me a reproachful glance that ought to have moved the most ruthless malefactor to contrition. "And then that writ. How *could* you? To a lady . . ."

I mumbled something about the pump and our wanting baths.

"But how could you expect me to listen to you while you were in that mood? Why didn't you set about it differently—politely, charmingly?" She smiled at me and dropped her fluttering eyelids.

I thought it best to change the conversation. It is disagreeable, when one is in the right, to be made to appear in the wrong.

A few weeks later we had a letter—duly registered and by express messenger—in which the Signora asked us whether we proposed to renew our lease (which was only for six months), and notifying us that, if we did, the rent would be raised 25 percent, in consideration of the improvements which had been carried out. We thought ourselves lucky, at the end of much bargaining, to get the lease renewed for a whole year with an increase in the rent of only 15 percent.

It was chiefly for the sake of the view that we put up with these intolerable extortions. But we had found other reasons, after a few days' residence, for liking the house. Of these the most cogent was that, in the peasant's youngest child, we had discovered what seemed the perfect playfellow for our own small boy. Between little Guido—for that was his name—and the youngest of his brothers and sisters there was a gap of six or seven years. His two elder brothers worked with their father in the fields; since the time of the mother's death, two or three years before we knew them, the eldest sister had ruled the house, and the younger, who had just left school, helped her and in betweenwhiles kept an eye on Guido, who by this time, however, needed very little looking after; for he was between six and seven years old and as precocious, self-assured, and responsible as the children of the poor, left as they are to themselves almost from the time they can walk, generally are.

Though fully two and a half years older than little Robin—and at that age thirty months are crammed with half a lifetime's experience—Guido took no undue advantage of his superior intelligence and strength. I have never seen a child more patient, tolerant, and untyrannical. He never laughed at Robin for his clumsy efforts to imitate his own prodigious feats; he did not tease or bully, but helped his small companion when he was in difficulties and explained when he could not understand. In return, Robin adored him, regarded him as the model and perfect Big Boy, and slavishly imitated him in every way he could.

These attempts of Robin's to imitate his companion were often exceedingly ludicrous. For by an obscure psychological law, words and actions in themselves quite serious become comic as soon as they are copied; and the more accurately, if the imitation is a deliberate parody, the funnier—for an overloaded imitation of someone we know does not make us laugh so much as one that is almost indistinguishably like the original. The bad imitation is only ludicrous when it is a piece of sincere and earnest flattery which does not quite come off. Robin's imitations were mostly of this kind. His heroic and unsuccessful attempts to perform the feats of strength and skill, which Guido could do with ease, were exquisitely comic. And his careful, long-drawn imitations of Guido's habits and mannerisms were no less amusing. Most ludicrous of all, because most earnestly undertaken and most incongruous in the imitator, were Robin's impersonations of Guido in the pensive mood. Guido was a thoughtful child, given to brooding and sudden abstractions. One would find him sitting in a corner by himself, chin in hand, elbow on knee, plunged, to all appearances, in the profoundest meditation. And sometimes, even in the midst of his play, he would suddenly break off, to stand, his hands behind his back, frowning and staring at the ground. When this happened, Robin became overawed and a little disquieted. In a puzzled silence he looked at his companion. "Guido," he would say softly, "Guido." But Guido was generally too much preoccupied to answer; and Robin, not venturing to insist, would creep near him, and throwing himself as nearly as possible into Guido's attitude—standing Napoleonically, his hands clasped behind him, or sitting in the posture of Michelangelo's Lorenzo the Magnificent—would try to meditate too. Every few seconds he would turn his bright blue eyes toward the elder child to see whether he was doing it quite right. But at the end of a minute he began to grow impatient; meditation wasn't his strong point. "Guido," he called again and, louder, "Guido!" And he would take him by the hand and try to pull him away. Sometimes Guido roused himself from his reverie and went back to the interrupted game. Sometimes he paid no attention. Melancholy, perplexed, Robin had to take himself off to play by himself. And Guido would go on sitting or standing there, quite still; and his eyes, if one looked into them, were beautiful in their grave and pensive calm.

They were large eyes, set far apart and, what was strange in a dark-haired Italian child, of a luminous pale blue-gray color. They were not always grave and calm, as in these pensive moments. When he was playing, when he talked or laughed, they lit up; and the surface of those clear, pale lakes of thought seemed, as it were, to be shaken into brilliant sun-flashing ripples. Above those eyes was a beautiful forehead, high and steep and domed in a curve that was like the subtle curve of a rose petal. The nose was straight, the chin small and rather pointed, the mouth drooped a little sadly at the corners.

I have a snapshot of the two children sitting together on the parapet of the terrace. Guido sits almost facing the camera, but looking a little to one side and downward; his hands are crossed in his lap and his expression, his attitude are thoughtful, grave, and meditative. It is Guido in one of those moods of abstraction into which he would pass even at the height of laughter and play—quite suddenly and completely, as though he had all at once taken it into his head to go away and had left the silent and beautiful body behind, like an empty house, to wait for his return. And by his side sits little Robin, turning to look up at him, his face half averted from the camera, but the curve of his cheek showing that he is laughing; one little raised hand is caught at the top of a gesture, the other clutches at Guido's sleeve, as though he were urging him to come away and play. And the legs dangling from the parapet have been seen by the blinking instrument in the midst of an impatient wriggle; he is on the point of slipping down and running off to play hide-and-seek in the garden. All the essential characteristics of both the children are in that little snapshot.

"If Robin were not Robin," Elizabeth used to say, "I could almost wish he were Guido."

And even at that time, when I took no particular interest in the child, I agreed with her. Guido seemed to me one of the most charming little boys I had ever seen.

We were not alone in admiring him. Signora Bondi when, in those cordial intervals between our quarrels, she came to call, was constantly speaking of him. "Such a beautiful, beautiful child!" she would exclaim with enthusiasm. "It's really a waste that he should belong to peasants who can't afford to dress him properly. If he were mine, I should put him into black velvet; or little white knickers and a white knitted silk jersey with a red line at the collar and cuffs; or perhaps a white sailor suit would be pretty. And in winter a little fur coat, with a squirrel skin cap, and possibly Russian boots . . ." Her imagination was running away with her. "And I'd let his hair grow, like a page's, and have it just curled up a little at the tips. And a straight fringe across his forehead. Every one would turn round and stare after us if I took him out with me in Via Tornabuoni."

What you want, I should have liked to tell her, is not a child; it's a clockwork doll or a performing monkey. But I did not say so—partly because I could not think of the Italian for a clock-work doll and partly because I did not want to risk having the rent raised another 15 percent.

"Ah, if only I had a little boy like that!" She sighed and modestly dropped her eyelids. "I adore children. I sometimes think of adopting one—that is, if my husband would allow it."

I thought of the poor old gentleman being dragged along at the heels of his big white dog and inwardly smiled.

"But I don't know if he would," the Signora was continuing, "I don't know if he would." She was silent for a moment, as though considering a new idea.

A few days later, when we were sitting in the garden after luncheon, drinking our coffee, Guido's father, instead of passing with a nod and the usual cheerful good-day, halted in front of us and began to talk. He was a fine handsome man, not very tall, but well proportioned, quick and elastic in his movements, and full of life. He had a thin brown face, featured like a Roman's and lit by a pair of the most intelligent-looking gray eyes I ever saw. They exhibited almost too much intelligence when, as not infrequently happened, he was trying, with an assumption of perfect frankness and a childlike innocence, to take one in or get something out of one. Delighting in itself, the intelligence shone there mischievously. The face might be ingenuous, impassive, almost imbecile in its expression; but the eyes on these occasions gave him completely away. One knew, when they glittered like that, that one would have to be careful.

Today, however, there was no dangerous light in them. He wanted nothing out of us, nothing of any value—only advice, which is a commodity, he knew, that most people are only too happy to part with. But he wanted advice on what was, for us, rather a delicate subject: on Signora Bondi. Carlo had often complained to us about her. The old man is good, he told us, very good and kind indeed. Which meant, I dare say, among other things, that he could easily be swindled. But his wife . . . Well, the woman was a beast. And he would tell us stories of her insatiable rapacity: she was always claiming more than the half of the produce which, by the laws of the métayage system,[1] was the proprietor's due. He complained of her suspiciousness: she was forever accusing him of sharp practices, of downright stealing—him, he struck his breast the soul of honesty. He complained of her shortsighted avarice: she wouldn't spend enough on manure, wouldn't buy him another cow, wouldn't have electric light installed in the stables. And we had sympathized, but cautiously, without expressing too strong an opinion on the subject. The Italians are wonderfully noncommittal in their speech; they will give nothing away to an interested person until they are quite certain that it is right and necessary and, above all, safe to do so. We had lived long enough among them to imitate their caution. What we said to Carlo would be sure, sooner or later, to get back to Signora Bondi. There was nothing to be gained by unnecessarily embittering our relations with the lady—only another 15 percent, very likely, to be lost.

Today he wasn't so much complaining as feeling perplexed. The Signora had sent for him, it seemed, and asked him how he would like it if she were to make an offer—it was all very hypothetical in the cautious Italian style—to adopt little Guido. Carlo's first instinct had been to say that he wouldn't like it at all. But an answer like that would have been too coarsely committal. He had preferred to say that he would think about it. And now he was asking for our advice.

Do what you think best was what in effect we replied. But we gave it distantly but distinctly to be understood that we didn't think that Signora Bondi would make a very good foster mother for the child. And Carlo was inclined to agree. Besides, he was very fond of the boy.

"But the thing is," he concluded rather gloomily, "that if she has really set her heart on getting hold of the child, there's nothing she won't do to get him—nothing."

He too, I could see, would have liked the physicists to start on unemployed childless women of sanguine temperament before they tried to tackle the atom. Still, I reflected, as I watched him striding away along the terrace, singing powerfully from a brazen gullet as he went, there was force there, there was life enough in those elastic limbs, behind those bright gray eyes, to put up a good fight even against the accumulated vital energies of Signora Bondi.

It was a few days after this that my gramophone and two or three boxes of

---

[1] *métayage system:* in continental Europe, the equivalent of the American system of sharecropping; that is, the practice of a landlord in rural areas of providing his tenant farmers with seed, tools, and the like, with the understanding that a designated amount of their harvests be given to him.

records arrived from England. They were a great comfort to us on the hilltop, providing as they did the only thing in which that spiritually fertile solitude— otherwise a perfect Swiss Family Robinson's island—was lacking: music. There is not much music to be heard nowadays in Florence. The times when Dr. Burney could tour through Italy, listening to an unending succession of new operas, symphonies, quartets, cantatas, are gone. Gone are the days when a learned musician, inferior only to the Reverend Father Martini of Bologna, could admire what the peasants sang and the strolling players thrummed and scraped on their instruments. I have traveled for weeks through the peninsula and hardly heard a note that was not "Salome" or the Fascists' song. Rich in nothing else that makes life agreeable or even supportable, the northern metropolises are rich in music. That is perhaps the only inducement that a reasonable man can find for living there. The other attractions—organized gaiety, people, miscellaneous conversation, the social pleasures—what are those, after all, but an expense of spirit that buys nothing in return? And then the cold, the darkness, the moldering dirt, the damp and squalor. . . . No, where there is no necessity that retains, music can be the only inducement. And that, thanks to the ingenious Edison, can now be taken about in a box and unpacked in whatever solitude one chooses to visit. One can live at Benin, or Nuneaton, or Tozeur in the Sahara, and still hear Mozart quartets, and selections from the Well-Tempered Clavichord, and the Fifth Symphony, and the Brahms clarinet quintet, and motets by Palestrina.

Carlo, who had gone down to the station with his mule and cart to fetch the packing-case, was vastly interested in the machine.

"One will hear some music again," he said, as he watched me unpacking the gramophone and the discs. "It is difficult to do much oneself."

Still, I reflected, he managed to do a good deal. On warm nights we used to hear him, where he sat at the door of his house, playing his guitar and softly singing; the eldest boy shrilled out the melody on the mandolin, and sometimes the whole family would join in, and the darkness would be filled with their passionate, throaty singing. Piedigrotta songs they mostly sang; and the voices drooped slurringly from note to note, lazily climbed or jerked themselves with sudden sobbing emphases from one tone to another. At a distance and under the stars the effect was not unpleasing.

"Before the war," he went on, "in normal times" (and Carlo had a hope, even a belief, that the normal times were coming back and that life would soon be as cheap and easy as it had been in the days before the flood), "I used to go and listen to the operas at the Politeama. Ah, they were magnificent. But it costs five lire now to get in."

"Too much," I agreed.

"Have you got *Trovatore?*" he asked.

I shook my head.

"*Rigoletto?*"

"I'm afraid not."

"*Boheme? Fanciulla del West? Pagliacci?*"

I had to go on disappointing him.

"Not even *Norma?* Or the *Barbiere?*"

I put on Battistini in "La ci darem" out of *Don Giovanni.* He agreed that the singing was good; but I could see that he didn't much like the music. Why not? He found it difficult to explain.

"It's not like *Pagliacci,*" he said at last.

"Not palpitating?" I suggested, using a word with which I was sure he would be familiar; for it occurs in every Italian political speech and patriotic leading article.

"Not palpitating," he agreed.

And I reflected that it is precisely by the difference between *Pagliacci* and *Don Giovanni,* between the palpitating and the nonpalpitating, that modern musical taste is separated from the old. The corruption of the best, I thought, is the worst. Beethoven taught music to palpitate with his intellectual and spiritual passion. It has gone on palpitating ever since, but with the passion of inferior men. Indirectly, I thought, Beethoven is responsible for *Parsifal, Pagliacci,* and the *Poem of Fire;* still more indirectly for *Samson and Delilah* and "Ivy, cling to me." Mozart's melodies may be brilliant, memorable, infectious; but they don't palpitate, don't catch you between wind and water, don't send the listener off into erotic ecstasies.

Carlo and his elder children found my gramophone, I am afraid, rather a disappointment. They were too polite, however, to say so openly; they merely ceased, after the first day or two, to take any interest in the machine and the music it played. They preferred the guitar and their own singing.

Guido, on the other hand, was immensely interested. And he liked, not the cheerful dance tunes, to whose sharp rhythms our little Robin loved to go stamping round and round the room, pretending that he was a whole regiment of soldiers, but the genuine stuff. The first record he heard, I remember, was that of the slow movement of Bach's Concerto in D Minor for two violins. That was the disc I put on the turntable as soon as Carlo had left me. It seemed to me, so to speak, the most musical piece of music with which I could refresh my long-parched mind—the coolest and clearest of all draughts. The movement had just got under way and was beginning to unfold its pure and melancholy beauties in accordance with the laws of the most exacting intellectual logic, when the two children, Guido in front and little Robin breathlessly following, came clattering into the room from the loggia.

Guido came to a halt in front of the gramophone and stood there, motionless, listening. His pale blue-gray eyes opened themselves wide; making a little nervous gesture that I had often noticed in him before, he plucked at his lower lip with his thumb and forefinger. He must have taken a deep breath; for I noticed that, after listening for a few seconds, he sharply expired and drew in a fresh gulp of air. For an instant he looked at me—a questioning, astonished, rapturous look—gave a little laugh that ended in a kind of nervous shudder, and turned back toward the source of the incredible sounds. Slavishly imitating his elder comrade, Robin had also taken up his stand in front of the gramophone, and in exactly the same position, glancing at Guido from time to time to make sure that he was doing everything, down to plucking at his lip, in the correct way. But after a minute or so he became bored.

"Soldiers," he said, turning to me; "I want soldiers. Like in London." He remembered the ragtime and the jolly marches round and round the room.

I put my fingers to my lips. "Afterward," I whispered.

Robin managed to remain silent and still for perhaps another twenty seconds. Then he seized Guido by the arm, shouting, *"Vieni, Guido!* Soldiers. *Soldati. Vieni giuocare soldati."*

It was then, for the first time, that I saw Guido impatient. *"Vai!"* he whispered angrily, slapped at Robin's clutching hand and pushed him roughly away. And he leaned a little closer to the instrument, as though to make up by yet intenser listening for what the interruption had caused him to miss.

Robin looked at him, astonished. Such a thing had never happened before. Then he burst out crying and came to me for consolation.

When the quarrel was made up—and Guido was sincerely repentant, was as nice as he knew how to be when the music had stopped and his mind was free to think of Robin once more—I asked him how he liked the music. He said he thought it was beautiful. But *bello* in Italian is too vague a word, too easily and frequently uttered, to mean very much.

"What did you like best?" I insisted. For he had seemed to enjoy it so much that I was curious to find out what had really impressed him.

He was silent for a moment, pensively frowning. "Well," he said at last, "I liked the bit that went like this." And he hummed a long phrase. "And then there's the other thing singing at the same time—but what are those things," he interrupted himself, "that sing like that?"

"They're called violins," I said.

"Violins." He nodded. "Well, the other violin goes like this." He hummed again. "Why can't one sing both at once? And what is in that box? What makes it make that noise?" The child poured out his questions.

I answered him as best I could, showing him the little spirals on the disc, the needle, the diaphragm. I told him to remember how the string of the guitar trembled when one plucked it; sound is a shaking in the air, I told him, and I tried to explain how those shakings get printed on the black disc. Guido listened to me very gravely, nodding from time to time. I had the impression that he understood perfectly well everything I was saying.

By this time, however, poor Robin was so dreadfully bored that in pity for him I had to send the two children out into the garden to play. Guido went obediently; but I could see that he would have preferred to stay indoors and listen to more music. A little while later, when I looked out, he was hiding in the dark recesses of the big bay tree, roaring like a lion, and Robin, laughing, but a little nervously, as though he were afraid that the horrible noise might possibly turn out, after all, to be the roaring of a real lion, was beating the bush with a stick, and shouting, "Come out, come out! I want to shoot you."

After lunch, when Robin had gone upstairs for his afternoon sleep, he reappeared. "May I listen to the music now?" he asked. And for an hour he sat there in front of the instrument, his head cocked slightly on one side, listening while I put on one disc after another.

Thenceforward he came every afternoon. Very soon he knew all my library of records, had his preferences and dislikes, and could ask for what he wanted by humming the principal theme.

"I don't like that one," he said of Strauss's "Till Eulenspiegel." "It's like what we sing in our house. Not really like, you know. But somehow rather like, all the same. You understand?" He looked at us perplexedly and appealingly, as though begging us to understand what he meant and so save him from going on explaining. We nodded. Guido went on. "And then," he said, "the end doesn't seem to come properly out of the beginning. It's not like the one you played the first time." He hummed a bar or two from the slow movement of Bach's D Minor Concerto.

"It isn't," I suggested, "like saying: All little boys like playing. Guido is a little boy. Therefore Guido likes playing."

He frowned. "Yes, perhaps that's it," he said at last. "The one you played first is more like that. But, you know," he added, with an excessive regard for truth, "I don't like playing as much as Robin does."

Wagner was among his dislikes; so was Debussy. When I played the record of one of Debussy's Arabesques, he said, "Why does he say the same thing over and over again? He ought to say something new, or go on, or make the thing grow. Can't he think of anything different?" But he was less censorious about the *Après-midi d'un Faune*. "The things have beautiful voices," he said.

Mozart overwhelmed him with delight. The duet fom *Don Giovanni,* which his father had found insufficiently palpitating, enchanted Guido. But he preferred the quartets and the orchestral pieces.

"I like music," he said, "better than singing."

Most people, I reflected, like singing better than music; are more interested in the executant than in what he executes, and find the impersonal orchestra less moving than the soloist. The touch of the pianist is the human touch, and the soprano's high C is the personal note. It is for the sake of his touch, that note, that audiences fill the concert hall.

Guido, however, preferred music. True, he liked *"La ci darem"*; he liked *"Deh vizni alla finestra"*; he thought *"Che soave zefiretto"* so lovely that almost all our concerts had to begin with it. But he preferred the other things. The *Figaro* overture was one of his favorites. There is a passage not far from the beginning of the piece, where the first violins suddenly go rocketing up into the heights of loveliness; as the music approached that point, I used always to see a smile developing and gradually brighten on Guido's face, and when, punctually, the thing happened, he clapped his hands and laughed aloud with pleasure.

On the other side of the same disc, it happened, was recorded Beethoven's *Egmont* overture. He liked that almost better than *Figaro*.

"It has more voices," he explained. And I was delighted by the acuteness of the criticism; for it is precisely in the richness of its orchestration that *Egmont* goes beyond *Figaro*.

But what stirred him almost more than anything was the *Coriolan* overture. The third movement of the Fifth Symphony, the second movement of the Seventh, the slow movement of the Emperor Concerto—all these things ran it pretty close. But none excited him so much as *Coriolan*. One day he made me play it three or four times in succession; then he put it away.

"I don't think I want to hear that any more," he said.

"Why not?"

"It's too . . . too . . ." he hesitated, "too big," he said at last. "I don't really understand it. Play me the one that goes like this." He hummed the phrase from the D Minor Concerto.

"Do you like that one better?" I asked.

He shook his head. "No, it's not that exactly. But it's easier."

"Easier?" It seemed to me rather a queer word to apply to Bach.

"I understand it better."

One afternoon, while we were in the middle of our concert, Signora Bondi was ushered in. She began at once to be overwhelmingly affectionate toward the child; kissed him, patted his head, paid him the most outrageous compliments on his appearance. Guido edged away from her.

"And do you like music?" she asked.

The child nodded.

"I think he has a gift," I said. "At any rate, he has a wonderful ear and a power of listening and criticizing such as I've never met with in a child of that age. We're thinking of hiring a piano for him to learn on."

A moment later I was cursing myself for my undue frankness in praising the boy. For Signora Bondi began immediately to protest that, if she could have the upbringing of the child, she would give him the best masters, bring out his talent, make an accomplished maestro of him—and, on the way, an infant prodigy. And at that moment, I am sure, she saw herself sitting maternally, in pearls and black satin, in the lea of the huge Steinway, while an angelic Guido, dressed like little Lord Fauntleroy, rattled out Liszt and Chopin, to the loud delight of a thronged auditorium. She saw the bouquets and all the elaborate floral tributes, heard the clapping and the few well-chosen words with which the veteran maestri, touched almost to tears, would hail the coming of the little genius. It became more than ever important for her to acquire the child.

"You've sent her away fairly ravening," said Elizabeth, when Signora

Bondi had gone. "Better tell her next time that you made a mistake and that the boy's got no musical talent whatever."

In due course, the piano arrived. After giving him the minimum of preliminary instruction, I let Guido loose on it. He began by picking out for himself the melodies he had heard, reconstructing the harmonies in which they were embedded. After a few lessons, he understood the rudiments of musical notation and could read a simple passage at sight, albeit very slowly. The whole process of reading was still strange to him; he had picked up his letters somehow, but nobody had yet taught him to read whole words and sentences.

I took occasion, next time I saw Signora Bondi, to assure her that Guido had disappointed me. There was nothing in his musical talent, really. She professed to be very sorry to hear it; but I could see that she didn't for a moment believe me. Probably she thought that we were after the child too, and wanted to bag the infant prodigy for ourselves, before she could get in her claim, thus depriving her of what she regarded almost as her feudal right. For, after all, weren't they her peasants? If anyone was to profit by adopting the child it ought to be herself.

Tactfully, diplomatically, she renewed her negotiations with Carlo. The boy, she put it to him, had genius. It was the foreign gentleman who had told her so, and he was the sort of man, clearly, who knew about such things. If Carlo would let her adopt the child, she'd have him trained. He'd become a great maestro and get engagements in the Argentine and the United States, in Paris and London. He'd earn millions and millions. Think of Caruso, for example. Part of the millions, she explained, would of course come to Carlo. But before they began to roll in, those millions, the boy would have to be trained. But training was very expensive. In his own interest, as well as in that of his son, he ought to let her take charge of the child. Carlo said he would think it over, and again applied to us for advice. We suggested that it would be best in any case to wait a little and see what progress the boy made.

He made, in spite of my assertions to Signora Bondi, excellent progress. Every afternoon, while Robin was asleep, he came for his concert and his lesson. He was getting along famously with his reading; his small fingers were acquiring strength and agility. But what to me was more interesting was that he had begun to make up little pieces on his own account. A few of them I took down as he played them and I have them still. Most of them, strangely enough, as I thought then, are canons. He had a passion for canons. When I explained to him the principles of the form he was enchanted.

"It is beautiful," he said, with admiration. "Beautiful, beautiful. And so easy!"

Again the word surprised me. The canon is not, after all, so conspicuously simple. Thenceforward he spent most of his time at the piano in working out little canons for his own amusement. They were often remarkably ingenious. But in the invention of other kinds of music he did not show himself so fertile as I had hoped. He composed and harmonized one or two solemn little airs like hymn tunes, with a few sprightlier pieces in the spirit of the military march. They were extraordinary, of course, as being the inventions of a child. But a great many children can do extraordinary things; we are all geniuses up to the age of ten. But I had hoped that Guido was a child who was going to be a genius at forty; in which case what was extraordinary for an ordinary child was not extraordinary enough for him. "He's hardly a Mozart," we agreed, as we played his little pieces over. I felt, it must be confessed, almost aggrieved. Anything less than a Mozart, it seemed to me, was hardly worth thinking about.

He was not a Mozart. No. But he was somebody, as I was to find out, quite as extraordinary. It was one morning in the early summer that I made the discovery. I was sitting in the warm shade of our westward-facing balcony, working. Guido and Robin were playing in the little enclosed garden below. Absorbed in my work it was only, I suppose, after the silence had prolonged itself a considerable time that I became aware that the children were making remarkably little noise. There was no shouting, no running about; only a quiet talking. Knowing by experience that when children are quiet it generally means that they are absorbed in some delicious mischief, I got up from my chair and looked over the balustrade to see what they were doing. I expected to catch them dabbling in water, making a bonfire, covering themselves with tar. But what I actually saw was Guido, with a burnt stick in his hand, demonstrating on the smooth paving-stones of the path that the square on the hypotenuse of a right-angled triangle is equal to the sum of the squares on the other two sides.

Kneeling on the floor, he was drawing with the point of his blackened stick on the flagstones. And Robin, kneeling imitatively beside him, was growing, I could see, rather impatient with this very slow game.

"Guido," he said. But Guido paid no attention. Pensively frowning, he went on with his diagram. "Guido!" The younger child bent down and then craned round his neck so as to look up into Guido's face. "Why don't you draw a train?"

"Afterward," said Guido. "But I just want to show you this first. It's *so* beautiful," he added cajolingly.

"But I want a train," Robin persisted.

"In a moment. Do just wait a moment." The tone was almost imploring. Robin armed himself with renewed patience. A minute later Guido had finished both his diagrams.

"There!" he said triumphantly, and straightened himself up to look at them. "Now I'll explain."

And he proceeded to prove the theorem of Pythagoras—not in Euclid's way, but by the simpler and more satisfying method which was, in all probability, employed by Pythagoras himself. He had drawn a square and dissected it, by a pair of crossed perpendiculars, into two squares and two equal rectangles. The equal rectangles he divided up by their diagonals into four equal right-angled triangles. The two squares are then seen to be the squares on the two sides of any one of these triangles other than the hypotenuse. So much for the first diagram. In the next he took the four right-angled triangles into which the rectangles had been divided and rearranged them round the original square so that their right angles filled the corners of the square, the hypotenuses looked inward, and the greater and less sides of the triangles were in continuation along the sides of the square (which are each equal to the sum of these sides). In this way the original square is redissected into four right-angled triangles and the square on the hypotenuse. The four triangles are equal to the two rectangles of the original dissection. Therefore the square on the hypotenuse is equal to the sum of the two squares—the squares on the other two sides—into which, with the rectangles, the original square was first dissected.

In very untechnical language, but clearly and with a relentless logic, Guido expounded his proof. Robin listened, with an expression on his bright, freckled face of perfect incomprehension.

"*Treno*," he repeated from time to time. "*Treno*. Make a train."

"In a moment," Guido implored. "Wait a moment. But do just look at this. *Do*." He coaxed and cajoled. "It's so beautiful. It's so easy."

So easy. . . . The theorem of Pythagoras seemed to explain for me Guido's musical predilections. It was not an infant Mozart we had been cherishing; it was a little Archimedes with, like most of his kind, an incidental musical twist.

"*Treno, treno!*" shouted Robin, growing more and more restless as the exposition went on. And when Guido insisted on going on with his proof, he lost his temper. "*Cattivo Guido*," he shouted, and began to hit out at him with his fists.

"All right," said Guido resignedly. "I'll make a train." And with his stick of charcoal he began to scribble on the stones.

I looked on for a moment in silence. It was not a very good train. Guido might be able to invent for himself and prove the theorem of Pythagoras; but he was not much of a draftsman.

"Guido!" I called. The two children turned and looked up. "Who taught you to draw those squares?" It was conceivable, of course, that somebody might have taught him.

"Nobody." He shook his head. Then, rather anxiously, as though he were afraid there might be something wrong about drawing squares, he went on to apologize and explain. "You see," he said, "it seemed to me so beautiful. Because those squares"—he pointed at the two small squares in the first figure—"are just as big as this one." And, indicating the square on the hypotenuse in the second diagram, he looked up at me with a deprecating smile.

I nodded. "Yes, it's very beautiful," I said—"it's very beautiful indeed."

An expression of delighted relief appeared on his face; he laughed with pleasure. "You see, it's like this," he went on, eager to initiate me into the glorious secret he had discovered. "You cut these two long squares"—he meant the rectangles—"into two slices. And then there are four slices, all just the same, because, because—oh, I ought to have said that before—because these long squares are the same, because those lines, you see . . ."

"But I want a train," protested Robin.

Leaning on the rail of the balcony, I watched the children below. I thought of the extraordinary thing I had just seen and of what it meant.

I thought of the vast differences between human beings. We classify men by the color of their eyes and hair, the shape of their skulls. Would it not be more sensible to divide them up into intellectual species? There would be even wider gulfs between the extreme mental types than between a Bushman and a Scandinavian. This child, I thought, when he grows up, will be to me, intellectually, what a man is to a dog. And there are other men and women who are, perhaps, almost as dogs to me.

Perhaps the men of genius are the only true men. In all the history of the race there have been only a few thousand real men. And the rest of us—what are we? Teachable animals. Without the help of the real men, we should have found out almost nothing at all. Almost all the ideas with which we are familiar could never have occurred to minds like ours. Plant the seeds there and they will grow; but our minds could never spontaneously have generated them.

There have been whole nations of dogs, I thought; whole epochs in which no Man was born. From the dull Egyptians the Greeks took crude experience and rules of thumb and made sciences. More than a thousand years passed before Archimedes had a comparable successor. There has been only one Buddha, one Jesus, only one Bach that we know of, one Michelangelo.

Is it by a mere chance, I wondered, that a Man is born from time to time? What causes a whole constellation of them to come contemporaneously into being and from out of a single people? Taine thought that Leonardo, Michelangelo, and Raphael were born when they were because the time was ripe for great painters and the Italian scene congenial. In the mouth of a rationalizing nineteenth-century Frenchman the doctrine is strangely mystical; it may be none the less true for that. But what of those born out of time? Blake, for example. What of those?

This child, I thought, has had the fortune to be born at a time when he will be able to make good use of his capacities. He will find the most elaborate analytical methods lying ready to his hand; he will have a prodigious experience behind him. Suppose him born while Stonehenge was building; he might have spent a lifetime discovering the rudiments, guessing darkly where now he might have had a chance of proving. Born at the time of the Norman Conquest, he would have had to wrestle with all the preliminary difficulties created by an inadequate symbolism; it would have taken him long years, for example, to learn the art of dividing MMMCCCCLXXXVIII by MCMXIX. In five years, nowadays, he will learn what it took generations of Men to discover.

And I thought of the fate of all the Men born so hopelessly out of time that they could achieve little or nothing of value. Beethoven born in Greece, I thought, would have had to be content to play thin melodies on the flute or lyre; in those intellectual surroundings it would hardly have been possible for him to imagine the nature of harmony.

From drawing trains, the children in the garden below had gone on to playing trains. They were trotting round and round; with blown round cheeks and pouting mouth, like the cherubic symbol of a wind, Robin puff-puffed, and Guido, holding the skirt of his smock, shuffled behind him, tooting. They ran forward, backed, stopped at imaginary stations, shunted, roared over bridges, crashed through tunnels, met with occasional collisions and derailments. The young Archimedes seemed to be just as happy as the little tow-headed barbarian. A few minutes ago he had been busy with the theorem of Pythagoras. Now, tooting indefatigably along imaginary rails, he was perfectly content to shuffle backward and forward among the flower beds, between the pillars of the loggia, in and out of the dark tunnels of the laurel tree. The fact that one is going to be Archimedes does not prevent one from being an ordinary cheerful child meanwhile. I thought of this strange talent distinct and separate from the rest of the mind, independent, almost, of experience. The typical child prodigies are musical and mathematical; the other talents ripen slowly under the influence of emotional experience and growth. Till he was thirty Balzac gave proof of nothing but ineptitude; but at four the young Mozart was already a musician, and some of Pascal's most brilliant work was done before he was out of his teens.

In the weeks that followed, I alternated the daily piano lessons with lessons in mathematics. Hints rather than lessons they were; for I only made suggestions, indicated methods, and left the child himself to work out the ideas in detail. Thus I introducd him to algebra by showing him another proof of the theorem of Pythagoras. In this proof one drops a perpendicular from the right angle onto the hypotenuse, and arguing from the fact that the two triangles thus created are similar to one another and to the original triangle, and that the proportions which their corresponding sides bear to one another are therefore equal, one can show in algebraical form that $c^2 + d^2$ (the squares on the other two sides) are equal to $a^2 + b^2$ (the squares on the two segments of the hypotenuse) $+2ab$; which last, it is easy to show geometrically, is equal to $(a + b)^2$, or the square on the hypotenuse. Guido was as much enchanted by the rudiments of algebra as he would have been if I had given him an engine worked by steam, with a methylated spirit lamp to heat the boiler; more enchanted, perhaps—for the engine would have got broken, and, remaining always itself, would in any case have lost its charm, while the rudiments of algebra continued to grow and blossom in his mind with an unfailing luxuriance. Every day he made the discovery of something which seemed to him exquisitely beautiful; the new toy was inexhaustible in its potentialities.

In the intervals of applying algebra to the second book of Euclid, we experimented with circles; we stuck bamboos into the parched earth, measured their shadows at different hours of the day, and drew exciting conclusions from our observations. Sometimes, for fun, we cut and folded sheets of paper so as to make cubes and pyramids. One afternoon Guido arrived carrying carefully between his small and rather grubby hands a flimsy dodecahedron.[1]

"E tanto bello!" he said, as he showed us his paper crystal; and when I asked him how he had managed to make it, he merely smiled and said it had been so easy. I looked at Elizabeth and laughed. But it would have been more symbolically to the point, I felt, if I had gone down on all fours, wagged the spiritual outgrowth of my os coccyx, and barked my astonished admiration.

It was an uncommonly hot summer. By the beginning of July our little Robin, unaccustomed to these high temperatures, began to look pale and tired; he was listless, had lost his appetite and energy. The doctor advised mountain air. We decided to spend the next ten or twelve weeks in Switzerland. My parting gift to Guido was the first six books of Euclid in Italian. He turned over the pages, looking ecstatically at the figures.

"If only I knew how to read properly," he said "I'm so stupid. But now I shall really try to learn."

From our hotel near Grindelwald we sent the child, in Robin's name, various post cards of cows, Alp-horns, Swiss chalets, edelweiss, and the like. We received no answers to these cards; but then we did not expect answers. Guido could not write, and there was no reason why his father or his sisters should take the trouble to write for him. No news, we took it, was good news. And then one day, early in September, there arrived at the hotel a strange letter. The manager had it stuck up on the glass-fronted noticeboard in the hall, so that all the guests might see it, and whoever conscientiously thought that it belonged to him might claim it. Passing the board on the way into lunch, Elizabeth stopped to look at it.

"But it must be from Guido," she said.

I came and looked at the envelope over her shoulder. It was unstamped and black with postmarks. Traced out in pencil, the big uncertain capital letters sprawled across its face. In the first line was written: *AL BABBO DI ROBIN,* and there followed a travestied version of the name of the hotel and the place. Round the address bewildered postal officials had scrawled suggested emendations. The letter had wandered for a fortnight at least, back and forth across the face of Europe.

"Al Babbo di Robin. To Robin's father." I laughed. "Pretty smart of the postmen to have got it here at all." I went to the manager's office, set forth the justice of my claim to the letter and, having paid the fifty-centime surcharge

[1] *dodecahedron:* in mathematics, a solid having twelve plane faces.

for the missing stamp, had the case unlocked and the letter given me. We went in to lunch.

"The writing's magnificent," we agreed, laughing as we examined the address at close quarters. "Thanks to Euclid," I added. "That's what comes of pandering to the ruling passion."

But when I opened the envelope and looked at its contents I no longer laughed. The letter was brief and almost telegraphical in style. *"Sono dalla padrona,"* it ran, *"Non mi place ha Rubato il mio Libro non Voglio Suonare piu Voglio Tornare a Casa Venga Subito Guido."*

"What is it?"

I handed Elizabeth the letter. "That blasted woman's got hold of him," I said.

Busts of men in Homburg hats, angels bathed in marble tears extinguishing torches, statues of little girls, cherubs, veiled figures, allegories and ruthless realisms—the strangest and most diverse idols beckoned and gesticulated as we passed. Printed indelibly on tin and embedded in the living rock, the brown photographs looked out, under glass, from the humbler crosses, headstones, and broken pillars. Dead ladies in the cubistic geometrical fashions of thirty years ago—two cones of black satin meeting point to point at the waist, and the arms; a sphere to the elbow, a polished cylinder below—smiled mournfully out of their marble frames; the smiling faces, the white hands, were the only recognizably human things that emerged from the solid geometry of their clothes. Men with black moustaches, men with white beards, young clean-shaven men, stared or averted their gaze to show a Roman profile. Children in their stiff best opened wide their eyes, smiled hopefully in anticipation of the little bird that was to issue from the camera's muzzle, smiled skeptically in the knowledge that it wouldn't, smiled laboriously and obediently because they had been told to. In spiky Gothic cottages of marble the richer dead privately reposed; through grilled doors one caught a glimpse of pale Inconsolables weeping, of distraught Geniuses guarding the secret of the tomb. The less prosperous sections of the majority slept in communities, close-crowded but elegantly housed under smooth continuous marble floors, whose every flagstone was the mouth of a separate grave.

These continental cemeteries, I thought, as Carlo and I made our way among the dead, are more frightful than ours, because these people pay more attention to their dead than we do. That primordial cult of corpses, that tender solicitude for their material well-being, which led the ancients to house their dead in stone, while they themselves lived between wattles and under thatch, still lingers here; persists, I thought, more vigorously than with us. There are a hundred gesticulating statues here for every one in an English graveyard. There are more family vaults, more "luxuriously appointed" (as they say of liners and hotels) than one would find at home. And embedded in every tombstone there are photographs to remind the powdered bones within what form they will have to resume on the Day of Judgment; beside each are little hanging lamps to burn optimistically on All Soul's Day. To the Man who built the Pyramids they are neater, I thought, than we.

"If I had known," Carlo kept repeating, "if only I had known." His voice came to me through my reflections as though from a distance. "At the time he didn't mind at all. How should I have known that he would take it so much to heart afterward? And she deceived me, she lied to me."

I assured him yet once more that it wasn't his fault. Though, of course, it was, in part. It was mine too, in part; I ought to have thought of the possibility and somehow guarded against it. And he shouldn't have let the child go, even temporarily and on trial, even though the woman was bringing pressure to bear on him. And the pressure had been considerable. They had worked on the same holding for more than a hundred years, the men of Carlo's family; and now she had made the old man threaten to turn him out. It would be a dreadful thing to leave the place; and besides, another place wasn't so easy to find. It was made quite plain, however, that he could stay if he let her have the child. Only for a little to begin with; just to see how he got on. There would be no compulsion whatever on him to stay if he didn't like it. And it would be all to Guido's advantage; and to his father's, too, in the end. All that the Englishman had said about his not being such a good musician as he had thought at first was obviously untrue—mere jealousy and little-mindedness: the man wanted to take credit for Guido himself, that was all. And the boy, it was obvious, would learn nothing from him. What he needed was a real good professional master.

All the energy that, if the physicists had known their business, would have been driving dynamos, went into this campaign. It began the moment we were out of the house, intensively. She would have more chance of success, the Signora doubtless thought, if we weren't there. And besides, it was essential to take the opportunity when it offered itself and get hold of the child before we could make our bid—for it was obvious to her that we wanted Guido just as much as she did.

Day after day she renewed the assault. At the end of a week she sent her husband to complain about the state of the vines: they were in a shocking condition; he had decided, or very nearly decided, to give Carlo notice. Meekly, shamefacedly, in obedience to higher orders, the old gentleman uttered his threats. Next day Signora Bondi returned to the attack. The pa-drone, she declared, had been in a towering passion; but she'd do her best, her very best, to mollify him. And after a significant pause she went on to talk about Guido.

In the end Carlo gave in. The woman was too persistent and she held too many trump cards. The child could go and stay with her for a month or two on trial. After that, if he really expressed a desire to remain with her, she could formally adopt him.

At the idea of going for a holiday to the seaside—and it was to the seaside, Signora Bondi told him, that they were going—Guido was pleased and excited. He had heard a lot about the sea from Robin. *Tanta acqua!* It had sounded almost too good to be true. And now he was actually to go and see this marvel. It was very cheerfully that he parted from his family.

But after the holiday by the sea was over, and Signora Bondi had brought him back to her town house in Florence, he began to be homesick. The Signora, it was true, treated him exceedingly kindly, bought him new clothes, took him out to tea in the Via Tornabuoni and filled him up with cakes, iced strawberryade, whipped cream, and chocolates. But she made him practice the piano more than he liked, and what was worse, she took away his Euclid, on the score that he wasted too much time with it. And when he said that he wanted to go home, she put him off with promises and excuses and downright lies. She told him that she couldn't take him at once, but that next week, if he was good and worked hard at his piano meanwhile, next week . . . And when the time came, she told him that his father didn't want him back. And she redoubled her petting, gave him expensive presents, and stuffed him with yet unhealthier foods. To no purpose. Guido didn't like his new life, didn't want to practice scales, pined for his book, and longed to be back with his brothers and sisters. Signora Bondi, meanwhile, continued to hope that time and chocolates would eventually make the child hers; and to keep his family at a distance, she wrote to Carlo every few days letters which still purported to come from the seaside (she took the trouble to send them to a friend, who posted them back again to Florence), and in which she painted the most charming picture of Guido's happiness.

It was then that Guido wrote his letter to me. Abandoned, as he supposed, by his family—for that they shouldn't take the trouble to come to see him when they were so near was only to be explained on the hypothesis that they really had given him up—he must have looked to me as his last and only hope. And the letter, with its fantastic address, had been nearly a fortnight on its way. A fortnight—it must have seemed hundreds of years; and as the centuries succeeded one another, gradually, no doubt, the poor child became convinced that I too had abandoned him. There was no hope left.

"Here we are," said Carlo.

I looked up and found myself confronted by an enormous monument. In a kind of grotto hollowed in the flanks of a monolith of gray sandstone, Sacred Love, in bronze, was embracing a funerary urn. And in bronze letters riveted into the stone was a long legend to the effect that the inconsolable Ernesto Bondi had raised this monument to the memory of his beloved wife, Annunziata, as a token of his undying love for one whom, snatched from him by a premature death, he hoped very soon to join beneath this stone. The first Signora Bondi had died in 1912. I thought of the old man leashed to his white dog; he must always, I reflected, have been a most uxorious husband.

"They buried him here."

We stood there for a long time in silence. I felt the tears coming into my eyes as I thought of the poor child lying there underground. I thought of those luminous grave eyes, and the curve of that beautiful forehead, the droop of the melancholy mouth, of the expression of delight which illumined his face when he learned of some new idea that pleased him, when he heard a piece of music that he liked. And this beautiful small being was dead; and the spirit that inhabited this form, the amazing spirit, that too had been destroyed almost before it had begun to exist.

And the unhappiness that must have preceded the final act, the child's despair, the conviction of his utter abandonment—those were terrible to think of, terrible.

"I think we had better come away now," I said at last, and touched Carlo on the arm. He was standing there like a blind man, his eyes shut, his face slightly lifted toward the light; from between his closed eyelids the tears welled out, hung for a moment, and trickled down his cheeks. His lips trembled and I could see that he was making an effort to keep them still. "Come away," I repeated.

The face which had been still in its sorrow was suddenly convulsed; he opened his eyes, and through the tears they were bright with a violent anger. "I shall kill her," he said, "I shall kill her. When I think of him throwing himself out, falling through the air . . ." With his two hands he made a violent gesture, bringing them down from over his head and arresting them with a sudden jerk when they were on a level with his breast. "And then crash." He shuddered. "She's as much responsible as though she had pushed him down herself. I shall kill her." He clenched his teeth.

To be angry is easier than to be sad, less painful. It is comforting to think of revenge. "Don't talk like that," I said. "It's no good. It's stupid. And what would be the point?" He had had those fits before, when grief became too painful and he had tried to escape from it. Anger had been the easiest way of escape. I had had, before this, to persuade him back into the harder path of grief. "It's stupid to talk like that," I repeated, and I led him away through the ghastly labyrinth of tombs, where death seemed more terrible even than it is.

By the time we had left the cemetery and were walking down from San Miniato toward the Piazzale Michelangelo below, he had become calmer. His anger had subsided again into the sorrow from which it had derived all its strength and its bitterness. In the Piazzale we halted for a moment to look down at the city in the valley below us. It was a day of floating clouds—great shapes, white, golden, and gray; and between them patches of a thin, transparent blue. Its lantern level, almost, with our eyes, the dome of the cathedral revealed itself in all its grandiose lightness, its vastness and aerial strength. On the innumerable brown and rosy roofs of the city the afternoon sunlight lay softly, sumptuously, and the towers were as though varnished and enameled with an old gold. I thought of all the Men who had lived here and left the visible traces of their spirit and conceived extraordinary things. I thought of the dead child.

The Bear

W I L L I A M   F A U L K N E R

[1897–1962]

He was ten. But it had already begun, long before that day when at last he wrote his age in two figures and he saw for the first time the camp where his father and Major de Spain and old General Compson and the others spent two weeks each November and two weeks again each June. He had already inherited then, without ever having seen it, the tremendous bear with one trap-ruined foot which, in an area almost a hundred miles deep, had earned itself a name, a definite designation like a living man.

He had listened to it for years: the long legend of corncribs rifled, of shotes and grown pigs and even calves carried bodily into the woods and devoured, of traps and deadfalls overthrown and dogs mangled and slain, and shotgun and even rifle charges delivered at point-blank range and with no more effect than so many peas blown through a tube by a boy—a corridor of wreckage and destruction beginning back before he was born, through which sped, not fast but rather with the ruthless and irresistible deliberation of a locomotive, the shaggy tremendous shape.

It ran in his knowledge before he ever saw it. It looked and towered in his dreams before he even saw the unaxed woods where it left its crooked print, shaggy, huge, red-eyed, not malevolent but just big—too big for the dogs which tried to bay it, for the horses which tried to ride it down, for the men and the bullets they fired into it, too big for the very country which was its constricting scope. He seemed to see it entire with a child's complete divination before he ever laid eyes on either—the doomed wilderness whose edges were being constantly and punily gnawed at by men with axes and plows who feared it because it was wilderness, men myriad and nameless even to one another in the land where the old bear had earned a name, through which ran not even a mortal animal but an anachronism, indomitable and invincible, out of an old dead time, a phantom, epitome and apotheosis of the old wild life at which the puny humans swarmed and hacked in a fury of abhorrence and fear, like pygmies about the ankles of a drowsing elephant: the old bear solitary, indomitable and alone, widowered, childless, and absolved of mortality—old Priam reft of his old wife and having outlived all his sons.

Until he was ten, each November he would watch the wagon containing the dogs and the bedding and food and guns and his father and Tennie's Jim, the Negro, and Sam Fathers, the Indian, son of a slave woman and a Chickasaw chief, depart on the road to town, to Jefferson, where Major de Spain and the others would join them. To the boy, at seven, eight, and nine, they were not going into the Big Bottom to hunt bear and deer, but to keep yearly rendezvous with the bear which they did not even intend to kill. Two weeks later they would return, with no trophy, no head and skin. He had not expected it. He had not even been afraid it would be in the wagon. He believed that even after he was ten and his father would let him go too, for those two weeks in November, he would merely make another one, along with his father and Major de Spain and General Compson and the others, the dogs which feared to bay at it and the rifles and shotguns which failed even to bleed it, in the yearly pageant of the old bear's furious immortality.

Then he heard the dogs. It was in the second week of his first time in the camp. He stood with Sam Fathers against a big oak beside the faint crossing where they had stood each dawn for nine days now, hearing the dogs. He had heard them once before, one morning last week—a murmur, sourceless, echoing through the wet woods, swelling presently into separate voices which he could recognize and call by name. He had raised and cocked the gun as Sam told him and stood motionless again while the uproar, the invisible course, swept up and past and faded; it seemed to him that he could actually see the deer, the buck, blond, smoke-colored, elongated with speed, fleeing, vanishing, the woods, the gray solitude, still ringing even when the cries of the dogs had died away.

"Now let the hammers down," Sam said.

"You knew they were not coming here too," he said.

"Yes," Sam said. "I want you to learn how to do when you didn't shoot. It's after the chance for the bear or the deer has done already come and gone that men and dogs get killed."

"Anyway," he said, "it was just a deer."

Then on the tenth morning he heard the dogs again. And he readied the too-long, too-heavy gun as Sam had taught him, before Sam even spoke. But this time it was no deer, no ringing chorus of dogs running strong on a free scent, but a moiling yapping an octave too high, with something more than indecision and even abjectness in it, not even moving very fast, taking a long time to pass completely out of hearing, leaving then somewhere in the air that echo, thin, slightly hysterical, abject, almost grieving, with no sense of a fleeing, unseen, smoke-colored, grass-eating shape ahead of it, and Sam, who had taught him first of all to cock the gun and take position where he could see everywhere and then never move again, had himself moved up beside him; he could hear Sam breathing at his shoulder, and he could see the arched curve of the old man's inhaling nostrils.

"Hah," Sam said. "Not even running. Walking."

"Old Ben!" the boy said. "But up here!" he cried. "Way up here!"

"He do it every year," Sam said. "Once. Maybe to see who in camp this time, if he can shoot or not. Whether we got the dog yet that can bay and hold him. He'll take them to the river, then he'll send them back home. We may as well go back too; see how they look when they come back to camp."

When they reached the camp the hounds were already there, ten of them crouching back under the kitchen, the boy and Sam squatting to peer back into the obscurity where they had huddled, quiet, the eyes luminous, glowing at them and vanishing, and no sound, only that effluvium of something more than dog, stronger than dog and not just animal, just beast, because still there had been nothing in front of that abject and almost painful yapping save the solitude, the wilderness, so that when the eleventh hound came in at noon and with all the others watching—even old Uncle Ash, who called himself first a cook—Sam daubed the tattered ear and the raked shoulder with turpentine and axle grease, to the boy it was still no living creature, but the wilderness which, leaning for the moment down, had patted lightly once the hound's temerity.

"Just like a man," Sam said. "Just like folks. Put off as long as she could having to be brave, knowing all the time that sooner or later she would have to be brave to keep on living with herself, and knowing all the time beforehand what was going to happen to her when she done it."

That afternoon, himself on the one-eyed wagon mule which did not mind the smell of blood nor, as they told him, of bear, and with Sam on the other one, they rode for more than three hours through the rapid, shortening winter day. They followed no path, no trail even that he could see; almost at once they were in a country which he had never seen before. Then he knew why Sam had made him ride the mule which would not spook. The sound one stopped short and tried to whirl and bolt even as Sam got down, blowing its breath, jerking and wrenching at the rein, while Sam held it, coaxing it forward with his voice, since he could not risk tying it, drawing it forward while the boy got down from the marred one.

Then, standing beside Sam in the gloom of the dying afternoon, he looked down at the rotted overturned log, gutted and scored with claw marks and, in the wet earth beside it, the print of the enormous warped two-toed foot. He knew now what he had smelled when he peered under the kitchen where the dog huddled. He realized for the first time that the bear which had run in his listening and loomed in his dreams since before he could remember to the contrary, and which, therefore, must have existed in the listening and dreams of his father and Major de Spain and even old General Compson, too, before they began to remember in their turn, was a mortal animal, and that if they had departed for the camp each November without any actual hope of bringing its trophy back, it was not because it could not be slain, but because so far they had had no actual hope to.

"Tomorrow," he said.

"We'll try tomorrow," Sam said. "We ain't got the dog yet."

"We've got eleven. They ran him this morning."

"It won't need but one," Sam said. "He ain't here. Maybe he ain't nowhere. The only other way will be for him to run by accident over somebody that has a gun."

"That wouldn't be me," the boy said. "It would be Walter or Major or—"

"It might," Sam said. "You watch close in the morning. Because he's smart. That's how come he has lived this long. If he gets hemmed up and has to pick out somebody to run over, he will pick out you."

"How?" the boy said. "How will he know—" He ceased. "You mean he already knows me, that I ain't never been here before, ain't had time to find out yet whether I—" He ceased again, looking at Sam, the old man whose face revealed nothing until it smiled. He said humbly, not even amazed, "It was me he was watching. I don't reckon he did need to come but once."

The next morning they left the camp three hours before daylight. They rode this time because it was too far to walk, even the dogs in the wagon; again the first gray light found him in a place which he had never seen before, where Sam had placed him and told him to stay and then departed. With the gun which was too big for him, which did not even belong to him, but to Major de Spain, and which he had fired only once—at a stump on the first day, to learn the recoil and how to reload it—he stood against a gum tree beside a little bayou whose black still water crept without movement out of a canebrake and crossed a small clearing and into cane again, where, invisible, a bird—the big woodpecker called Lord-to-God by Negroes—clattered at a dead limb.

It was a stand like any other, dissimilar only in incidentals to the one where he had stood each morning for ten days; a territory new to him, yet no less familiar than that other one which, after almost two weeks, he had come to believe he knew a little—the same solitude, the same loneliness through which human beings had merely passed without altering it, leaving no mark, no scar, which looked exactly as it must have looked when the first ancestor of Sam Fathers' Chickasaw predecessors crept into it and looked about, club or stone ax or bone arrow drawn and poised; different only because, squatting at the edge of the kitchen, he smelled the hounds huddled and cringing beneath it and saw the raked ear and shoulder of the one who, Sam said, had had to be brave once in order to live with herself, and saw yesterday in the earth beside the gutted log the print of the living foot.

He heard no dogs at all. He never did hear them. He only heard the drumming of the woodpecker stop short off and knew that the bear was looking at him. He never saw it. He did not know whether it was in front of him or behind him. He did not move, holding the useless gun, which he had not even had warning to cock and which even now he did not cock, tasting in his saliva that taint as of brass which he knew now because he had smelled it when he peered under the kitchen at the huddled dogs.

Then it was gone. As abruptly as it had ceased, the woodpecker's dry, monotonous clatter set up again, and after a while he even believed he could hear the dogs—a murmur, scarce a sound even, which he had probably been hearing for some time before he even remarked it, drifting into hearing and then out again, dying away. They came nowhere near him. If it was a bear they ran, it was another bear. It was Sam himself who came out of the cane and crossed the bayou, followed by the injured bitch of yesterday. She was almost at heel, like a bird dog, making no sound. She came and crouched against his leg, trembling, staring off into the cane.

"I didn't see him," he said. "I didn't, Sam!"

"I know it," Sam said. "He done the looking. You didn't hear him neither, did you?"

"No," the boy said. "I—"

"He's smart," Sam said. "Too smart." He looked down at the hound, trembling faintly and steadily against the boy's knee. From the raked shoulder a few drops of fresh blood oozed and clung. "Too big. We ain't got the dog yet. But maybe someday. Maybe not next time. But someday."

So I must see him, he thought. *I must look at him.* Otherwise, it seemed to him that it would go on like this forever, as it had gone on with his father and Major de Spain, who was older than his father, and even with old General Compson, who had been old enough to be a brigade commander in 1865. Otherwise, it would go on so forever, next time and next time, after and after and after. It seemed to him that he could never see the two of them, himself and the bear, shadowy in the limbo from which time emerged, becoming time; the old bear absolved of mortality and himself partaking, sharing a little of it, enough of it. And he knew now what he had smelled in the huddled dogs and tasted in his saliva. He recognized fear. *So I will have to see him,* he thought, without dread or even hope. *I will have to look at him.*

It was in June of the next year. He was eleven. They were in camp again, celebrating Major de Spain's and General Compson's birthdays. Although the one had been born in September and the other in the depth of winter and in another decade, they had met for two weeks to fish and shoot squirrels and turkey and run coons and wildcats with the dogs at night. That is, he and Boon Hoggenbeck and the Negroes fished and shot squirrels and ran the coons and cats, because the proved hunter, not only Major de Spain and old General Compson, who spent those two weeks sitting in a rocking chair before a tremendous iron pot of Brunswick stew, stirring and tasting, with old Ash to quarrel with about how he was making it and Tennie's Jim to pour whiskey from the demijohn into the tin dipper from which he drank it, but even the boy's father and Walter Ewell, who were still young enough, scorned such, other than shooting the wild gobblers with pistols for wagers on their marksmanship.

Or, that is, his father and the others believed he was hunting squirrels. Until the third day, he thought that Sam Fathers believed that too. Each morning he would leave the camp right after breakfast. He had his own gun now, a Christmas present. He went back to the tree beside the bayou where he had stood that morning. Using the compass which old General Compson had given him, he ranged from that point; he was teaching himself to be a better-than-fair woodsman without knowing he was doing it. On the second day he even found the gutted log where he had first seen the crooked print. It was almost completely crumbled now, healing with unbelievable speed, a passionate and almost visible relinquishment, back into the earth from which the tree had grown.

He ranged the summer woods now, green with gloom; if anything, actually dimmer than in November's gray dissolution, where, even at noon, the sun fell only in intermittent dappling upon the earth, which never completely dried out and which crawled with snakes—moccasins and water snakes and rattlers, themselves the color of the dappling gloom, so that he would not always see them until they moved, returning later and later, first day, second day, passing in the twilight of the third evening the little log pen enclosing the log stable where Sam was putting up the horses for the night.

"You ain't looked right yet," Sam said.

He stopped. For a moment he didn't answer. Then he said peacefully, in a peaceful rushing burst as when a boy's miniature dam in a little brook gives way, "All right. But how? I went to the bayou. I even found that log again. I—"

"I reckon that was all right. Likely he's been watching you. You never saw his foot?"

"I," the boy said—"I didn't—I never thought—"

"It's the gun," Sam said. He stood beside the fence motionless—the old man, the Indian, in the battered faded overall and the five-cent straw hat which in the Negro's race had been the badge of his enslavement and was now the regalia of his freedom. The camp—the clearing, the house, the barn and its tiny lot with which Major de Spain in his turn had scratched punily and evanescently at the wilderness—faded in the dusk, back into the immemorial darkness of the woods. *The gun,* the boy thought. *The gun.*

"Be scared," Sam said. "You can't help that. But don't be afraid. Ain't nothing in the woods going to hurt you unless you corner it, or it smells that you are afraid. A bear or a deer, too, has got to be scared of a coward the same as a brave man has got to be."

The gun, the boy thought.

"You will have to choose," Sam said.

He left the camp before daylight, long before Uncle Ash would wake in his quilts on the kitchen floor and start the fire for breakfast. He had only the compass and a stick for snakes. He could go almost a mile before he would begin to need the compass. He sat on a log, the invisible compass in his invisible hand, while the secret night sounds, fallen still at his movements, scurried again and then ceased for good, and the owls ceased and gave over to the waking of day birds, and he could see the compass. Then he went fast yet still quietly; he was becoming better and better as a woodsman, still without having yet realized it.

He jumped a doe and a fawn at sunrise, walked them out of the bed, close enough to see them—the crash of undergrowth, the white scut, the fawn scudding behind her faster than he had believed it could run. He was hunting right, upwind, as Sam had taught him; not that it mattered now. He had left the gun; of his own will and relinquishment he had accepted not a gambit, not a choice, but a condition in which not only the bear's heretofore inviolable anonymity but all the old rules and balances of hunter and hunted had been abrogated. He would not even be afraid, not even in the moment when the fear would take him completely—blood, skin, bowels, bones, memory from the long time before it became his memory—all save that thin, clear, immortal lucidity which alone differed him from this bear and from all the other bear and deer he would ever kill in the humility and pride of his skill and endurance, to which Sam had spoken when he leaned in the twilight on the lot fence yesterday.

By noon he was far beyond the little bayou, farther into the new and alien country than he had ever been. He was traveling now not only by the old, heavy, biscuit-thick silver watch which had belonged to his grandfather. When he stopped at last, it was for the first time since he had risen from the log at dawn when he could see the compass. It was far enough. He had left the camp nine hours ago; nine hours from now, dark would have already been an hour old. But he didn't think that. He thought, *All right. Yes. But what?* and stood for a moment, alien and small in the green and topless solitude, answering his own question before it had formed and ceased. It was the watch, the compass, the stick—the three lifeless mechanicals with which for nine hours he had fended the wilderness off; he hung the watch and compass carefully on a bush and leaned the stick beside them and relinquished completely to it.

He had not been going very fast for the last two or three hours. He went no faster now, since distance would not matter even if he could have gone fast. And he was trying to keep a bearing on the tree where he had left the compass, trying to complete a circle which would bring him back to it or at least intersect itself, since direction would not matter now either. But the tree was not there, and he did as Sam had schooled him—made the next circle in the opposite direction, so that the two patterns would bisect somewhere, but crossing no print of his own feet, finding the tree at last, but in the wrong place—no bush, no compass, no watch—and the tree not even the tree, because there was a down log beside it and he did what Sam Fathers had told him was the next thing and the last.

As he sat down on the log he saw the crooked print—the warped, tremendous, two-toed indentation which, even as he watched it, filled with water. As he looked up, the wilderness coalesced, solidified—the glade, the tree he sought, the bush, the watch and the compass glinting where a ray of sunshine touched them. Then he saw the bear. It did not emerge, appear; it was just there, immobile, solid, fixed in the hot dappling of the green and windless noon, not as big as he had dreamed it, but as big as he had expected it, bigger, dimensionless, against the dappled obscurity, looking at him where he sat quietly on the log and looked back at it.

Then it moved. It made no sound. It did not hurry. It crossed the glade,

walking for an instant into the full glare of the sun; when it reached the other
side it stopped again and looked back at him across one shoulder while his
quiet breathing inhaled and exhaled three times.

Then it was gone. It didn't walk into the woods, the undergrowth. It faded,
sank back into the wilderness as he had watched a fish, a huge old bass, sink
and vanish into the dark depths of its pool without even any movement of its
fins.

He thought, *It will be next fall.* But it was not next fall, nor the next nor the
next. He was fourteen then. He had killed his buck, and Sam Fathers had
marked his face with the hot blood, and in the next year he killed a bear. But
even before that accolade he had become as competent in the woods as many
grown men with the same experience; by his fourteenth year he was a better
woodsman than most grown men with more. There was no territory within
thirty miles of the camp that he did not know—bayou, ridge, brake, land-
mark, tree and path. He could have led anyone to any point in it without
deviation, and brought them out again. He knew the game trails that even
Sam Fathers did not know; in his thirteenth year he found a buck's bedding
place, and unbeknown to his father he borrowed Walter Ewell's rifle and lay
in wait at dawn and killed the buck when it walked back to the bed, as Sam
had told him how the old Chickasaw fathers did.

But not the old bear, although by now he knew its footprints better than he
did his own, and not only the crooked one. He could see any one of the three
sound ones and distinguish it from any other, and not only by its size. There
were other bears within these thirty miles which left tracks almost as large,
but this was more than that. If Sam Fathers had been his mentor and the
back-yard rabbits and squirrels at home his kindergarten, then the wilderness
the old bear ran was his college, the old male bear itself, so long unwifed and
childless as to have become its own ungendered progenitor, was his alma
mater. But he never saw it.

He could find the crooked print now almost whenever he liked, fifteen or
ten or five miles, or sometimes nearer the camp than that. Twice while on
stand during the three years he heard the dogs strike its trail by accident; on
the second time they jumped it seemingly, the voices high, abject, almost
human in hysteria, as on that first morning two years ago. But not the bear
itself. He would remember that noon three years ago, the glade, himself and
the bear fixed during that moment in the windless and dappled blaze, and it
would seem to him that it had never happened, that he had dreamed that too.
But it had happened. They had looked at each other, they had emerged from
the wilderness old as earth, synchronized to the instant by something more
than the blood that moved the flesh and bones which bore them, and touched,
pledged something, affirmed, something more lasting than the frail web of
bones and flesh which any accident could obliterate.

Then he saw it again. Because of the very fact that he thought of nothing else, he had forgotten to look for it. He was still hunting with Walter Ewell's rifle. He saw it cross the end of a long blow-down, a corridor where a tornado had swept, rushing through rather than over the tangle of trunks and branches as a locomotive would have, faster than he had ever believed it could move, almost as fast as a deer even, because a deer would have spent most of that time in the air, faster than he could bring the rifle sights up with it. And now he knew what had been wrong during all the three years. He sat on a log, shaking and trembling as if he had never seen the woods before nor anything that ran them, wondering with incredulous amazement how he could have forgotten the very thing which Sam Fathers had told him and which the bear itself had proved the next day and had now returned after three years to reaffirm.

And now he knew what Sam Fathers had meant about the right dog, a dog in which size would mean less than nothing. So when he returned alone in April—school was out then, so that the sons of farmers could help with the land's planting, and at last his father had granted him permission, on his promise to be back in four days—he had the dog. It was his own, a mongrel of the sort called by Negroes a fyce, a ratter, itself not much bigger than a rat and possessing that bravery which had long since stopped being courage and had become foolhardiness.

It did not take four days. Alone again, he found the trail on the first morning. It was not a stalk; it was an ambush. He timed the meeting almost as if it were an appointment with a human being. Himself holding the fyce muffled in a feed sack and Sam Fathers with two of the hounds on a piece of a plowline rope, they lay down wind of the trail at dawn of the second morning. They were so close that the bear turned without even running, as if in surprised amazement at the shrill and frantic uproar of the released fyce, turning at bay against the trunk of a tree, on its hind feet; it seemed to the boy that it would never stop rising, taller and taller, and even the two hounds seemed to take a desperate and despairing courage from the fyce, following it as it went in.

Then he realized that the fyce was actually not going to stop. He flung, threw the gun away, and ran; when he overtook and grasped the frantically pin-wheeling little dog, it seemed to him that he was directly under the bear.

He could smell it, strong and hot and rank. Sprawling, he looked up to where it loomed and towered over him like a cloudburst and colored like a thunderclap, quite familiar, peacefully and even lucidly familiar, until he remembered: This was the way he had used to dream about it. Then it was gone. He didn't see it go. He knelt, holding the frantic fyce with both hands, hearing the abashed wailing of the hounds drawing farther and farther away, until Sam came up. He carried the gun. He laid it down quietly beside the boy and stood looking down at him.

"You've done seed him twice now with a gun in your hands," he said. "This time you couldn't have missed him."

The boy rose. He still held the fyce. Even in his arms and clear of the ground, it yapped frantically, straining and surging after the fading uproar of the two hounds like a tangle of wire springs. He was panting a little, but he was neither shaking nor trembling now.

"Neither could you!" he said. "You had the gun! Neither did you!"

"And you didn't shoot," his father said. "How close were you?"

"I don't know, sir," he said. "There was a big wood tick inside his right hind leg. I saw that. But I didn't have the gun then."

"But you didn't shoot when you had the gun," his father said. "Why?"

But he didn't answer, and his father didn't wait for him to, rising and crossing the room, across the pelt of the bear which the boy had killed two years ago and the larger one which his father had killed before he was born, to the bookcase beneath the mounted head of the boy's first buck. It was the room which his father called the office, from which all the plantation business was transacted; in it for the fourteen years of his life he had heard the best of all talking. Major de Spain would be there and sometimes old General Compson, and Walter Ewell and Boon Hoggenback and Sam Fathers and Tennie's Jim, too, were hunters, knew the woods and what ran them.

He would hear it, not talking himself but listening—the wilderness, the big woods, bigger and older than any recorded document of white man fatuous enough to believe he had bought any fragment of it or Indian ruthless enough to pretend that any fragment of it had been his to convey. It was of the men, not white nor black nor red, but men, hunters with the will and hardihood to endure and the humility and skill to survive, and the dogs and the bear and deer juxtaposed and reliefed against it, ordered and compelled by and within the wilderness in the ancient and unremitting contest by the ancient and immitigable rules which voided all regrets and brooked no quarter, the voices quiet and weighty and deliberate for retrospection and recollection and exact remembering, while he squatted in the blazing firelight as Tennie's Jim squatted, who stirred only to put more wood on the fire and to pass the bottle from one glass to another. Because the bottle was always present, so that after a while it seemed to him that those fierce instants of heart and brain and courage and wiliness and speed were concentrated and distilled into that brown liquor which not women, not boys and children, but only hunters drank, drinking not of the blood they had spilled but some condensation of the wild immortal spirit, drinking it moderately, humbly even, not with the pagan's base hope of acquiring the virtues of cunning and strength and speed, but in salute to them.

His father returned with the book and sat down again and opened it. "Listen," he said. He read the five stanzas aloud, his voice quiet and deliberate in the room where there was no fire now because it was already spring. Then he looked up. The boy watched him. "All right," his father said. "Listen." He read again, but only the second stanza this time, to the end of it, the last two lines, and closed the book and put it on the table beside him. "She cannot fade, though thou hast not thy bliss, forever wilt thou love, and she be fair," he said.[1]

"He's talking about a girl," the boy said.

"He had to talk about something," his father said. Then he said, "He was talking about truth. Truth doesn't change. Truth is one thing. It covers all things which touch the heart—honor and pride and pity and justice and courage and love. Do you see now?"

He didn't know. Somehow it was simpler than that. There was an old bear, fierce and ruthless, not merely just to stay alive, but with the fierce pride of liberty and freedom, proud enough of the liberty and freedom to see it threatened without fear or even alarm; nay, who at times even seemed deliberately to put that freedom and liberty in jeopardy in order to savor them, to remind his old strong bones and flesh to keep supple and quick to defend and preserve them. There was an old man, son of a Negro slave and an Indian king, inheritor on the one side of the long chronicle of a people who had learned humility through suffering, and pride through the endurance which survived the suffering and injustice, and on the other side, the chronicle of a people even longer in the land than the first, yet who no longer existed in the land at all save in the solitary brotherhood of an old Negro's alien blood and the wild and invincible spirit of an old bear. There was a boy who wished to learn humility and pride in order to become skillful and worthy in the woods, who suddenly found himself becoming so skillful so rapidly that he feared he would never become worthy because he had not learned humility and pride, although he had tried to, until one day and as suddenly he discovered that an old man who could not have defined either had led him, as though by the hand, to that point where an old bear and a little mongrel of a dog showed him that, by possessing one thing other, he would possess them both.

And a little dog, nameless and mongrel and many-fathered, grown, yet weighing less than six pounds, saying as if to itself, "I can't be dangerous, because there's nothing much smaller than I am; I can't be fierce, because they would call it just a noise; I can't be humble, because I'm already too close to the ground to genuflect; I can't be proud, because I wouldn't be near enough to it for anyone to know who was casting the shadow, and I don't even know that I'm not going to heaven, because they have already decided that I don't possess an immortal soul. So all I can be is brave. But it's all right. I can be that, even if they still call it just noise."

That was all. It was simple, much simpler than somebody talking in a book about youth and a girl he would never need to grieve over, because he could never approach any nearer her and would never have to get any farther away. He had heard about a bear, and finally got big enough to trail it, and he trailed it four years and at last met it with a gun in his hands and he didn't shoot. Because a little dog— But he could have shot long before the little dog covered the twenty yards to where the bear waited, and Sam Fathers could have shot at any time during that interminable minute while Old Ben stood on

[1] These lines come from Keats's "Ode on a Grecian Urn." See page 220.

his hind feet over them. He stopped. His father was watching him gravely across the spring-rife twilight of the room; when he spoke, his words were as quiet as the twilight, too, not loud, because they did not need to be because they would last. "Courage, and honor, and pride," his father said, "and pity, and love of justice and of liberty. They all touch the heart, and what the heart holds to becomes truth, as far as we know the truth. Do you see now?"

Sam, and Old Ben, and Nip, he thought. And himself too. He had been all right too. His father had said so. "Yes, sir," he said.

The Author Discusses "The Bear"

FROM CLASS CONFERENCES AT THE UNIVERSITY OF VIRGINIA, 1957–58

Q. In "The Bear," Mr. Faulkner, was there a dog, a real Lion? [1]

A. Yes, there was. I can remember that dog—I was about the age of that little boy—and he belonged to our pack of bear and deer dogs, and he was a complete individualist. He didn't love anybody. The other dogs were all afraid of him, he was a savage, but he did love to run the bear. Yes, I remember him quite well. He was mostly airedale, he had some hound and Lord only knows what else might have been in him. He was a tremendous big brute—stood about that high, must have weighed seventy-five or eighty pounds.

Q. In any bear hunt that Lion participated in, did he ever perform a heroic action like the one in the story?

A. No, not really. There's a case of the sorry, shabby world that don't quite please you, so you create one of your own, so you make Lion a little braver than he was, and you make the bear a little more of a bear than he actually was. I am sure that Lion could have done that and would have done it, and it may be at times when I wasn't there to record the action, he did do things like that.

Q. Mr. Faulkner, you seem to put so much meaning in the hunt. Could you tell us just why you hunted when you were a little boy, or what meaning the hunt has to you?

A. The hunt was simply a symbol of pursuit. Most of anyone's life is a pursuit of something. That is, the only alternative to life is immobility, which is death. This was a symbolization of the pursuit which is a normal part of

---

[1] In a different version of "The Bear," Faulkner gives the name of Lion to the "right dog" the boy finally gets. Notice that in this interview Faulkner describes Lion as "a tremendous big brute," whereas in the version of the story reprinted in the text he refers to the fyce as ". . . not much bigger than a rat. . . ." If you prefer one designation to the other, defend your choice in terms of the story's theme.

anyone's life, while he stays alive, told in terms which were familiar to me and dramatic to me. The protagonist could have been anything else besides that bear. I simply told a story which was a natural, normal part of anyone's life in familiar and to me interesting terms without any deliberate intent to put symbolism in it. I was simply telling something which was in this case the child—the need, the compulsion of the child to adjust to the adult world. It's how he does it, how he survives it, whether he is destroyed by trying to adjust to the adult world or whether despite his small size he does adjust within his capacity. And always to learn something, to learn something of—not only to pursue but to overtake and then to have the compassion not to destroy, to catch, to touch, and then let go because then tomorrow you can pursue again. If you destroy it, what you caught, then it's gone, it's finished. And that to me is sometimes the greater part of valor but always it's the greater part of pleasure, not to destroy what you have pursued. The pursuit is the thing, not the reward, not the gain.

Q. Sir, one of the most interesting aspects of "The Bear" to me is the conflict between man and the wilderness. I would like to ask you if you intend for the reader to sympathize more with Old Ben in his conflict with the hunters or toward the hunters in their conflict with Old Ben.

A. Well, not "sympathize." I doubt if the writer's asking anyone to sympathize, to choose sides. That is the reader's right. What the writer's asking is compassion, understanding, that change must alter, must happen, and change is going to alter what was. That no matter how fine anything seems, it can't endure, because once it stops, abandons motion, it is dead. It's to have compassion for the anguish that the wilderness itself may have felt by being ruthlessly destroyed by axes, by men who simply wanted to make that earth grow something they could sell for a profit, which brought into it a condition based on an evil like human bondage. It's not to choose sides at all—just to compassionate the good splendid things which change must destroy, the splendid fine things which are a part of man's past too, part of man's heritage too, but they were obsolete and had to go. But that's no need to not feel compassion for them simply because they were obsolete.

Q. I'd like to ask you . . . if you saw a symbol in the bear in the short story "The Bear."

A. Since I've been up here and discussed it, I've seen lots of symbols that I was too busy at the time—

Q. [I wish you'd please] tell me one so that I could tell my class.

A. Well, one symbol was the bear represented the vanishing wilderness. The little dog that wasn't scared of the bear represented the indomitable spirit of man. I'll have to dig back and get up some more of those symbols, because I have learned around an even dozen that I put into that story without knowing it. But there are two pretty good ones that you can hold to.

In the Penal Colony

FRANZ KAFKA

[1883–1924]

"It's a curious machine," said the officer to the explorer, and despite the fact that he was well acquainted with the apparatus, he nevertheless looked at it with a certain admiration, as it were. It was apparently merely out of courtesy that the explorer had accepted the invitation of the commanding officer to attend the execution of a private soldier condemned for disobedience and insulting a superior officer. Nor did there appear to be great interest in this execution in the penal colony. At any rate, here in the deep, sandy little valley shut in on every side by naked slopes, there were present, beside the officer and the explorer, only the condemned man—an obtuse, wide-mouthed fellow, with neglected face and hair—and a soldier acting as guard. The latter held the heavy chain to which were attached the little chains that fettered the offender's ankles and wrists as well as his neck, and which were themselves linked together by connecting chains. As a matter of fact, however, the condemned man looked so doglike and submissive, one had the impression that he might be allowed to run freely about the slopes, and that, when the execution was about to begin, one would have only to whistle for him to come right back.

The explorer had little thought for the apparatus and started walking up and down behind the condemned man with almost visible indifference. Meanwhile, the officer began the final preparations, now crawling beneath the machine, which was built deep in the ground, now climbing a ladder in order to inspect the upper parts. These were tasks which could easily have been left to a mechanic, but the officer performed them with great zeal, either because he was a special advocate of this apparatus, or because for other reasons the work could not be entrusted to anyone else. "Now everything's ready," he finally called out and climbed down the ladder. He was exceedingly fatigued, breathing with his mouth wide open, and had stuck two dainty lady's handkerchiefs under the collar of his uniform. "These uniforms are much too heavy for the tropics," commented the explorer instead of making inquiries about the machine, as the officer had expected him to do. "Certainly," said the officer, washing his hands, stained with oil and grease, in a pail of water that stood ready nearby, "but they are the symbols of home, and we don't want to lose our homeland. But take a look at this machine," he added immediately, as he dried his hands with a towel, pointing at the same time to the apparatus. "Up till now, it still had to be worked by hand; now it works entirely alone." The explorer nodded and followed the officer. The latter, wanting to safeguard himself against all eventualities, said: "Of course disturbances do occur; I hope there will be none today, yet we must always reckon with one. For the apparatus has to run for twelve consecutive hours. But if there should be any disturbances, they will only be insignificant ones, and they will be repaired at once."

"Don't you want to sit down?" he finally asked, and choosing a wicker chair from a heap of others, he offered it to the explorer, who could not refuse. He was now sitting on the edge of a pit, into which he cast a fugitive glance. It was not very deep. On one side of the pit the turned-up earth had been heaped into a wall: on the other side stood the machine. "I don't know," said the officer, "if the commanding officer has already explained the apparatus to you." The explorer made a vague gesture of the hand; the officer asked nothing better, for now he could explain the apparatus himself. "This machine," he said, grasping the crankshaft, on which he was leaning, "is an invention of our former commanding officer. I collaborated with him in the early experiments and took part in all the stages of the work up till the end. But credit for the invention belongs to him alone. Have you ever heard of our former commander? No? Well, I'm not exaggerating when I say that the organizing of the entire penal colony is his work. We who were his friends knew already, at the time of his death, that the organization of the colony was so complete in itself, that his successor, even though he were to have a thousand new ideas in his head, would not be able to change anything for many years to come, at least. What we foresaw has come about: the new commander has had to recognize this. It's too bad you did not know the former commander. But"—here the officer interrupted himself, "here I am gabbling away, and his apparatus is standing right here before us. It consists, as you see, of three parts. In the course of time, each of these parts has come to be designated by certain folk names, as it were. The lower one is called the 'bed,' the upper one the 'draughtsman,' and the middle one hanging up there is called the 'harrow.' " "The harrow?" asked the explorer. He had not been listening with undivided attention; the sun was much too tightly ensnared in the shadowless valley; it was hard to concentrate one's thoughts. The officer seemed to him all the more admirable, therefore, as he explained his cause so zealously, in his tight dress uniform, heavy with epaulets and hung with gold braid. Moreover, as he spoke he was busying himself with a screwdriver, tightening a screw here and there. The soldier seemed to be in a state of mind similar to that of the explorer. He had tied the condemned man's chain around both his wrists and was now leaning with one hand on his gun, his head drooping from the nape of his neck, indifferent to everything. The explorer was not surprised by this, for the officer was speaking French and certainly neither the soldier nor the condemned man understood French. It was, therefore, all the more striking that the condemned man should nevertheless have made an effort to follow the explanations of the officer. With a kind of sleepy perseverance he continued to direct his glance where the officer happened to be pointing. When the latter was now interrupted by a question from the explorer, he, too, looked, as did the officer, at the explorer.

"Yes, harrow," said the officer. "It's a suitable name. The needles are arranged as in a harrow and the whole thing is worked like a harrow, although always on the same spot, and much more artistically. You'll understand it right away, anyhow. The condemned man is laid here on the bed.—But I shall first of all describe the apparatus, and after that, I'll get the operation itself under way. You will then be able to follow it more easily. Also, there is a cog-wheel in the draughtsman which has gotten too worn down; it makes a creaking noise when it runs so that a person can hardly understand what is being said. Spare parts are hard to get here, too, unfortunately.—Well, then, as I said, here's the bed. It is entirely covered with a layer of cotton, the purpose of which you will learn later on. The condemned man is laid on this cotton, belly down and naked, of course; these straps for the hands, these for the feet, these for the throat, so as to fasten him tight. Here, at the head of the bed where, as I said, the man first lies on his face, there is this little ball of felt, which can be easily adjusted so that it goes right into the man's mouth. Its purpose is to prevent his screaming and biting his tongue. Of course, the man must take hold of the ball of felt since, otherwise, his neck would be broken by the throat-straps." "Is this cotton?" asked the explorer, bending forward. "Why certainly," said the officer smiling, "just feel it yourself." He seized the explorer's hand and guided it across the bed. "It's a specially prepared cotton, that's why it looks so unfamiliar; I'll have something to say about its purpose later on." The explorer was already won over a little in favor of the apparatus; he put his hands over his eyes as a protection against the sun and looked up at it. It was a large structure. The bed and the draughtsman were of equal dimensions and looked like two dark chests. The draughtsman was placed about two meters above the bed; both were connected at the corners by four brass poles which almost gave forth rays in the sunlight. The harrow was hanging between the chests, on a steel band.

The officer had hardly noticed the explorer's earlier indifference; he became aware, however, that his interest was now awakening; he therefore interrupted his explanations to give the explorer time for undisturbed contemplation. The condemned man imitated the explorer; since he could not place his hand over his eyes, he blinked directly upward.

"So the man lies down," said the explorer, and he leaned back in his armchair, crossing his legs.

"Yes," said the officer, pushing his cap back a little and passing his hand over his hot face, "now listen! Both the bed and the draughtsman have their own electric batteries; the bed needs one for itself, the draughtsman one for the harrow. As soon as the man has been strapped down, the bed is put in motion. It quivers simultaneously from side to side, as well as up and down, in tiny, very rapid vibrations. You will probably have seen similar machines in hospitals; only, in the case of our bed, all the motions are very precisely calculated; for they have to be painstakingly accorded to the motions of the harrow. But the execution proper of the sentence is left to this harrow."

"What is the sentence, anyway?" asked the explorer. "So you don't know that, either?" said the officer with astonishment, biting his lips. "Please excuse me; if my explanations are perhaps a bit disjointed, I sincerely beg your pardon. For these explanations were formerly given by the commanding officer; the new commander, however, has shunned this duty of rank; but that he should have failed to enlighten such an important visitor"—the explorer sought to wave away the mark of honor with both hands, but the officer insisted on the expression—"such an important visitor, about the form of our sentence, is another innovation which—" he had a curse on his lips, but restrained himself and said: "I was not informed, it is not my fault. As a matter of fact, I am the best qualified to explain our ways of judging, for I carry here"—he tapped his breast pocket—"the original drawings on the subject, made by the former commander."

"Drawings made by the commander himself?" asked the explorer. "Did he combine everything in his own person? Was he a soldier, a judge, a builder, a chemist, a draughtsman, all in one?"

"Surely," said the officer, nodding his head with a fixed, meditative expression. Then he examined his hands: they did not seem to him to be clean enough to touch the drawings; so he went to the pail and washed them once more. Then he took out a small leather brief case. "Our sentence does not sound severe," he said. "The law which the condemned man broke is written on his body with the harrow. For instance, this offender"—the officer pointed to the condemned man—"will have inscribed on his body: 'HONOR YOUR SUPERIOR.'"

The explorer gave a fleeting glance at the man; when the officer pointed toward him, he hung his head and seemed to be concentrating all his powers of hearing, on finding out something. But the motions of his tightly pressed, puffy lips showed clearly that he could understand nothing. The explorer had wanted to ask various questions but at the sight of the man he only asked: "Does he know his sentence?" "No," the officer said, and wanted to go right ahead with his explanations. But the explorer interrupted him: "So he does not know his sentence?" "No," said the officer again, and he hesitated a moment, as if demanding further justification of his question from the explorer. "It would be useless to announce it to him," he said, "he'll learn it anyway, on his own body." The explorer was inclined to remain silent, when he felt the condemned man's gaze upon him; it seemed to be asking if he could approve of the procedure described. So the explorer, who had already leaned back, bent forward once more and asked: "But he certainly must know that he has been condemned, doesn't he?" "He doesn't know that either," said the officer, smiling at the explorer, as if expecting further strange disclosures. "Well, then," said the explorer, passing his hand over his forehead, "so this man still does not know how his defense was undertaken?" "He had no opportunity of defending himself," said the officer, and looked to one side, as if he were talking to himself and did not want to embarrass the explorer by telling these things which seemed to him self-evident. "But he must surely have had a chance to defend himself?" said the explorer, rising from the armchair.

The officer realized that he was in danger of being held up for some time in his explanation of the apparatus. So he walked over to the explorer, took his arm, pointed toward the condemned man who, seeing that interest was so obviously directed his way, now stood at attention, while the guard drew the chain tighter. "The situation is as follows," said the officer. "I was appointed judge in the penal colony, despite my youth. For I was assistant to the former commander in all punitive matters and I am the one who knows the machine best. The principle on which I base my decisions is this: There is never any doubt about the guilt! Other courts cannot follow this principle, for they consist of many heads and also have still higher courts over them. Such is not the case here, or at least it was not the case with our former commander. To be sure, the new commander has already shown an inclination to meddle with my decisions, but I have always succeeded so far in warding him off, and I shall continue to do so. You wanted an explanation of this case: it is as simple as all of them. The captain notified us this morning that this man, who had been assigned to his personal service and who slept in front of his door, had fallen asleep while on duty. For it is his duty to get up each time the hour strikes and salute before the captain's door. This is certainly not a difficult duty, but it is a necessary one, for he must be alert while on guard as well as while serving his superior. Last night the captain wanted to see if the servant was doing his duty. He opened the door at two o'clock sharp and found him asleep in a crouching position. He took his riding whip and lashed the man across the face. Now, instead of getting up and asking forgiveness, the man seized his superior by the legs, shook him, and shouted: 'Throw that whip away, or I'll eat you up.' These are the facts. The captain came to me an hour ago. I wrote down his statement and added the sentence immediately. Then I ordered the man to be put in chains. That was all very simple. If I had called the man first and questioned him, it would have only resulted in confusion. He would have lied; then, if I had succeeded in contradicting the first lies, he would have replaced these with new ones, and so forth. But now I've got hold of him, and I'll not let him go. Is everything clear now? But time passes, the execution should have begun, and I am not yet through with the explanation of the apparatus." He forced the explorer back into his armchair, went back over to the machine and began: "As you see, this harrow corresponds to the form of a human being; here is the harrow for the upper part of the body, here are the harrows for the legs. For the head, this little burin [1] alone is designated. Have I made myself clear?" He bent amiably toward the explorer, prepared to give the most exhaustive explanations.

The explorer looked at the harrow with wrinkled forehead. The information about the court proceedings had not satisfied him. After all, he was

---

[1] *burin:* a sharply pointed engraver's tool.

forced to tell himself, this was a penal colony; special measures were necessary here, and they were obliged to proceed according to military regulations
up to the very last detail. Besides, he placed some hope in the new commander, who obviously intended to introduce—slowly, to be sure—a new
procedure which could not penetrate the limited mind of this officer. This
train of thought led the explorer to ask: "Is the commander going to attend
the execution?" "That's not certain," said the officer, painfully affected by the
unmotivated question, and his friendly expression became distorted. "That's
exactly why we have to hurry," he continued. "I shall even have to cut my
explanations short, as much as I regret to do so. But then I might add further
explanations tomorrow, when the apparatus will have been cleaned again—
the fact that it gets so dirty is its only defect. So now I'll give you only the
most essential facts. When the man lies on the bed and it has been made to
vibrate, the harrow is lowered onto the body. Of itself it assumes a position
that permits the sharp points just barely to touch the body; once it is in place,
this steel cord tautens at once into a rod. And then the play begins. The
uninitiated notice no external difference in the penalties. The harrow appears
to be working uniformly. Tremblingly it sticks its points into the body, which
has begun to tremble too, because of the bed. To make it possible for everyone to verify the execution of the sentence, the harrow was made of glass. A
few technical difficulties had to be surmounted in order to fasten the needles
into it, but we finally succeeded after many attempts. We simply spared no
pains. And now everyone can watch the progress of the writing on the body
through the glass. Would you mind coming nearer to look at the needles?"

Slowly the explorer arose, walked over, and bent over the harrow. "You can
see," said the officer, "two kinds of needles in different arrangements. Each
long one has a short one next to it. For the long one writes and the short one
sprays water in order to wash off the blood, and so keep the writing always
clear. The bloody water is then conducted into little drains and finally flows
into this principal drain which has an overflow pipe leading into the ditch."
The officer pointed out the exact direction which the blood-water had to take.
As he held both hands to the mouth of the overflow pipe in order to best
illustrate his point, the explorer lifted his head and, groping behind him, was
about to return to his seat. At that moment he saw to his horror that the
condemned man, like himself, had acted on the invitation of the officer to
inspect closely the construction of the harrow. He had dragged the drowsy
guard a little way forward with his chain, and was also bending over the glass.
He could be seen looking with uncertain eyes for the thing the two gentlemen
had just been examining but, because he lacked the explanation, he was not
successful. He bent first to one side, then to the other. Again and again his eye
roved over the glass. The explorer wanted to push him back, for what he was
doing was probably punishable. But the officer held the explorer back with
one hand, took a clod of earth from the ditch with the other, and threw it at
the guard. The latter lifted his eyes suddenly, saw what the condemned man

had dared do, let his gun drop and, digging his heels into the ground, he wrenched the condemned man back so that he fell right over. The guard looked down at the man as he writhed and clanked his chains. "Stand him up straight!" the officer shouted, for he noticed that the explorer's attention was far too diverted by the offender. What's more, the explorer was bending across the harrow, without bothering about it, intent only on finding out what was going to happen to the condemned man. "Handle him carefully," the officer shouted again. He ran around the apparatus, seized the condemned man, whose feet kept slipping from under him, by the shoulders and stood him upright, with the help of the guard.

"Now I know everything," said the explorer when the officer came back to him again. "Except the most important part," said the latter and grasping the explorer by the arm, he pointed upward; "There, in the draughtsman is the clockwork that determines the motions of the harrow, and this clockwork is regulated according to the drawing called for by the sentence. I still use the sketches made by the former commanding officer. Here they are,"—he pulled a few sheets out of his leather briefcase—"but unfortunately I cannot let you take them in your hand, for they are my most precious possession. Please sit down, I'll show them to you from this distance, so that you may see everything well." He showed him the first page. The explorer would have liked to say a word of approval, but he only saw labyrinthine lines that frequently crossed and recrossed each other and covered the paper so densely that one could recognize only with difficulty the white spaces in between. "Please read this," said the officer. "I can't," said the explorer. "Why, it's perfectly clear," said the officer. "It's undoubtedly very artistic," said the explorer evasively, "but I cannot decipher it." "Of course," said the officer laughing, as he put the briefcase away, "it's not fine penmanship for schoolchildren. You have to pore over it for a long while. In the end, you too would certainly make it out. Naturally it can't be ordinary handwriting, for it is not supposed to kill at once, but within an average space of twelve hours; the turning point being calculated for the sixth hour. The writing proper has to be surrounded by many, many embellishments; the real writing only encircles the body in a narrow girdle; the rest of the body is intended for decorative effects. Can you now understand the value of the work of the harrow, and of the entire machine? Just look at this!" He jumped onto the ladder, turned a wheel and called down: Look out! step aside!" Everything began to move. If the wheel had not creaked, it would have been wonderful. As if surprised by this disturbing wheel, the officer threatened it with his fist; then, excusing himself, stretched his arms out toward the explorer and hurriedly climbed down in order to observe the action of the apparatus from below. Something was still out of order which he alone noticed. He climbed up again, grasped the inner part of the draughtsman with both hands and then, in order to get down quickly, instead of using the ladder, slid down one of the rods. To make himself understood above the noise, he shouted as loudly as possible into the ear of the explorer: "Do you understand what's happening now? The harrow is beginning to write: when it has finished the first inscription on the man's back, the layer of cotton begins to furl up and rolls the body slowly over on its side so as to present a fresh surface to the harrow. In the meantime, the wound-written parts take their place on the cotton, which stops the bleeding at once, by means of a special preparation, and makes further deepening of the writing possible. Just here, the spikes on the edge of the harrow tear the cotton from the wounds, as the body is turned over again, hurl it into the ditch, and the harrow starts working again. Thus it writes more and more deeply during the whole twelve hours. The first six hours the condemned man lives about as before, he only suffers pain. After two hours the piece of felt is removed, for the man hasn't the strength to scream any more. Here, at the head end, we put warm rice porridge into this electrically heated tray, from which the man, if he cares to, can eat whatever he can lap up with his tongue. None of them ever misses this opportunity. I know really of none, and my experience is great. Only around the sixth hour does he lose his pleasure in eating. Then I usually kneel down here and observe the following phenomenon. Rarely does the man swallow the last morsel. All he does is to turn it about in his mouth and spit it out into the ditch. I have to stoop over then; otherwise I would catch it in the face. But around the sixth hour how quiet the man becomes! Even the dullest begins to understand. It starts around the eyes. From here it spreads out. It's a sight which could tempt you to lie down under the harrow with him. But nothing further happens, the man is just beginning to decipher the writing, and he purses his lips as if listening. You have seen that it is not easy to decipher the writing with the eye; but our man deciphers it with his wounds. Of course, that means a lot of work; he needs six hours to accomplish it. Then the harrow spears him clean through and hurls him into the ditch, where he plumps down into the bloody water and cotton. The tribunal is ended and we, the soldier and I, shovel him under."

The explorer had bent his ear to the officer and, with his hands in his coat pockets, observed the work of the machine. The condemned man was also observing it but without comprehension. He leaned over a little to follow the oscillating needles, when the guard, at a sign from the officer, slashed his shirt and trousers from behind with a knife so that they fell down off him. The man tried to seize the falling garments in order to cover his nakedness, but the soldier lifted him into the air and shook the last shreds from him. The officer brought the machine to a standstill and in the silence that now reigned the condemned man was placed under the harrow. The chains were undone and straps fastened in their place. Just at first it seemed almost to spell relief for the condemned man. Then the harrow settled down a bit lower, for he was a thin man. When the points touched him, a shudder ran over his skin; while the guard was busy with his right hand, he reached out blindly with his left; but it was toward where the explorer was standing. Uninterruptedly the officer kept looking at the explorer from the side, as if trying to read on his face the impression that the execution, which he had explained to him at least superficially, was making on him.

The strap intended for the wrist broke; the guard had probably pulled on it too hard. The guard showed him the broken bit of strap and the officer was obliged to help. Turning his face toward the explorer, he walked over to the guard and said: "This machine is quite complicated; here and there something is bound to tear or break; but one should not for this reason allow oneself to be misled as to one's general judgment. As a matter of fact, a substitute for the strap may be had promptly; I am going to use a chain, only the delicacy of the vibration of the right arm will in that case of course be reduced." And as he attached the chain, he added: "The means at my disposal for the upkeep of the machine are very limited now. Under the former commander there existed a fund intended only for this purpose, to which I had free access. There was also a warehouse here in which all kinds of spare parts were kept. I confess I was almost wasteful with them, I mean formerly, not now, as the new commander—to whom everything is only a pretext for combating old institutions—asserts. Now he administers the Machine Fund himself, and whenever I send for a new strap, the broken one is required as proof, the new one takes ten days to arrive, then it's of poor quality and not worth much. But in the meantime how am I to make the machine go without straps? Nobody bothers about that!"

The explorer reflected: It is always a delicate matter to intervene effectively in other people's affairs. He was neither a citizen of the penal colony nor a citizen of the state to which it belonged. If he wanted to condemn the execution, or even to prevent it, they could say to him: You are a foreigner, be silent. To this he would not be able to reply other than to add that as far as this matter was concerned, he didn't understand it himself, for he was traveling with the sole intention of observing and certainly not with that of changing foreign court procedures. But here, however, the situation appeared to be very tempting. There was no doubt about the injustice of the proceedings and the inhumanity of the execution. Nobody would assume that the explorer had any personal interest in the matter, for the condemned man was a stranger to him. They were not compatriots, nor was he at all a man who invited pity. The explorer himself had recommendations from high officials, he had been received with great courtesy, and the fact that he had been asked to the execution seemed even to indicate that they might desire his opinion concerning this procedure. This was all the more likely in fact since the commanding officer, as he had just heard distinctly, was not a partisan of this procedure and maintained an almost hostile attitude toward the officer.

At that moment, the explorer heard a cry of rage from the officer. Not without difficulty, he had just succeeded in shoving the felt gag into the mouth of the offender, when the latter closed his eyes in an irresistible nausea and vomited. Hurriedly the officer wrenched him away from the gag and tried to turn his head towards the ditch; but it was too late, the slop was already running all over the machine. "All this is the commander's fault!" the officer cried and shook the brass rods in front without rhyme or reason. "They're getting my machine as filthy as a stable." His hands shaking, he showed the explorer what had happened. "Haven't I tried for hours to make the commander understand that no meals should be given for a day before the execution? But the new, lenient tendency disagrees. The ladies of the commander's family stuff the man's mouth with sweets before he is led away. All his life he has fed on stinking fish, and now he has to eat candy! But it certainly would be possible, I wouldn't object—why on earth don't they get a new felt gag, as I have urged for the last three months? How can anyone take into his mouth, without loathing, a gag on which more than a hundred dying men have sucked and bitten?"

The condemned man had laid his head back and looked very peaceful, the guard was busy cleaning the machine with the condemned man's shirt. The officer walked toward the explorer, who took a step backward in some sort of premonition, but the officer took his hand and drew him to one side. "I want to say a few words to you in confidence," he said. "May I?" "Certainly," said the explorer, and listened, his eyes lowered.

"This procedure and this execution, which you now have the opportunity to admire, no longer have any open adherents in our colony at present. I am their only advocate, as well as the only advocate of the old commander's legacy. I am no longer able to consider further improvements of the procedure; I exhaust all my strength trying to preserve what already exists. During the old commander's lifetime, the colony was filled with his adherents; I possess some of his strength of conviction, but I entirely lack his power; in consequence, the adherents have slipped away. There are still a good many, but nobody admits it. If you go to the teahouse today, that is, on an execution day, and listen around a bit, you will perhaps hear only ambiguous utterances. These people are all adherents, but they are quite useless to me under the present commander with his present views. And now I ask you: Shall such a lifework as this"—here he pointed to the machine—"be allowed to perish just because of this commander and the women in his family who influence him? Can we allow this? Even though one is only on our island for a few days, as a stranger? But there is no time to lose, there is something afoot to undermine my jurisdiction; discussions are already taking place in the commander's office to which I am not summoned. Even your visit today seems to me to be characteristic of the entire situation; they are cowards, so they send you, a stranger, ahead of them. How different the executions were in the old days! Already, a day before the execution, the entire valley was overcrowded with people; they all came just to watch; early in the morning the commander appeared with his ladies; a flourish of trumpets awakened the entire encampment; I made the announcement that everything was ready; the society people—no high official was allowed to be absent—took their places around the machine; this heap of wicker chairs is a miserable relic of those times. The machine was freshly painted and shone brightly, I used new spare parts for almost every execution. Before hundreds of eyes—all the spectators stood on tiptoe as far back as those slopes over there—the condemned man was laid under the harrow by the commander himself. What a common soldier is allowed to do today, was then my task, as presiding judge, and I felt honored by it. And now the execution began! Not a single discord disturbed the work of the machine. Many stopped looking, even, and just lay there in the sand with their eyes closed. Everybody realized: Justice is now being done. In the stillness only the sighing of the condemned man, muffled by the felt, could be heard. Today the machine no longer succeeds in wringing from the condemned man a sigh that is sufficiently loud for the felt not to stifle it. In those days, however, the writing needles dripped a corrosive liquid which we are not allowed to use today. Well, then came the sixth hour! It was impossible to grant all the petitions to be allowed to witness the spectacle from close by. The commander in his wisdom gave orders that the children should be considered first; of course I was always allowed to stand close by on account of my position; many's the time I used to crouch there with a small child in each arm. How we all absorbed the expression of transfiguration from the man's tortured face, how we lifted our cheeks into the glow of this justice, finally achieved and already fading! What times those were, comrade!" The officer had evidently forgotten who it was standing before him; he had embraced the explorer and laid his head on his shoulder. The latter was greatly embarrassed and looked impatiently beyond the officer. The guard had finished the cleaning job and was now pouring rice porridge from a can into the tray. The condemned man, who seemed to have almost completely recovered, no sooner noticed this than he began to clack with his tongue for the porridge. The guard kept shoving him away, for the porridge was undoubtedly intended for a later moment, but it was nevertheless unseemly for him to put his dirty hands in the tray and eat out of it in front of the ravenous offender.

The officer quickly pulled himself together. "I was not really trying to touch your emotions," he said. "I know it is impossible to make those times comprehensible today. Besides, the machine still works and can speak for itself. It speaks for itself, even when it is standing all alone in this valley. And in the end, the corpse still falls with an unbelievably gentle flying motion into the ditch, even though there are no longer hundreds to gather around the ditch like flies, as there used to be. At that time we had to put up a strong railing around the ditch, but that has been torn down long ago."

The explorer looked aimlessly about him, wanting to keep his face from the officer. The latter, thinking he was looking at the barrenness of the valley, seized his hands and walked around him in order to catch his glance: "Do you see the shame of it?" he said.

But the explorer remained silent. For a little while the officer left him alone; with outspread legs and his hands on his hips, he stood still, looking at the ground. Then he smiled encouragingly at the explorer and said: "I was standing nearby yesterday, when the commander gave you the invitation. I heard it. I know the commander. I understood at once what he had in mind with that invitation. Although his power would be sufficient to take measures against me, he does not yet dare do so; but he wants to expose me to your judgment, as being that of a distinguished foreigner. He has made a careful calculation; this is your second day on the island, you did not know the old commander and his thought processes, you are prejudiced by the European point of view, you are perhaps, on principle, an opponent of capital punishment in general, and of such a machinelike type of execution in particular; furthermore you see how the execution takes place, without public sympathy, sadly, on a machine that is already somewhat damaged; now would it not be easily possible—this is what the commander thinks—that you should not approve of my procedure? And if you did not approve of it, would you not keep silent about it—I am still speaking from the commander's point of view—for you certainly have complete confidence in your own much tried convictions? You have surely seen and learned to appreciate the different peculiarities of many peoples; therefore you will in all probability not speak out with all your might against the procedure as you would, perhaps, do in your own country. But that isn't at all necessary for the commander. A haphazard, merely an incautious, word suffices. It need not in any way correspond to your convictions, if only it appears to meet with his wishes. I am sure he will question you with all the cunning he possesses. And the ladies will sit around in a circle, all ears. You'll probably say: 'In our country the court proceedings are different,' or, 'In our country the accused is examined before judgment is pronounced,' or, 'In our country there are other penalties than the death penalty,' or, 'In our country there have been no tortures since the Middle Ages.' These are all observations that are as right as they appear self-evident to you; innocent observations that do not touch my procedure. But how will the commander take them? I can see him now, our friend the commander, as he pushes his chair aside and hurries to the balcony, I can see his ladies flocking after him, I can hear his voice—the ladies call it a thunder voice—as he says: 'A great occidental researcher designated to examine court proceedings in many countries, has just announced that our procedure in accordance with old customs is an inhuman one. After this judgment, pronounced by such a distinguished man, it is of course no longer possible for me to tolerate this method. Beginning today, I therefore issue the following order —and so forth.' You want to protest, you did not really say what he announces you did, you did not call my method inhuman; on the contrary, in your innermost thoughts you regard it as the most human and most worthy of humanity; you also admire this mechanism—but it is too late; you can't even reach the balcony, which is already crowded with ladies; you try to attract attention, you try to shout, but a lady's hand holds your mouth shut—and I, and the old commander's work, are lost."

The explorer had to suppress a smile; so the task he had regarded as being so difficult was really as easy as that. He said evasively, "You overestimate my influence; the commander has read my letter of introduction; he knows that I am no connoisseur of court proceedings. If I were to express an opinion, it would be the opinion of a private individual, of no more importance than that of anyone else, and certainly much less important than that of the commander who, unless I am mistaken, has very extensive powers in this penal colony. If his opinion concerning this procedure is such a positive one as you believe, then, I am afraid that its end is indeed here, without there being any need of my modest cooperation."

Did the officer understand this? No, he did not yet understand. He shook his head vigorously and threw a brief glance back at the condemned man and the soldier, who was startled and let go of the rice. The officer came quite near the explorer, and without looking at him directly but at something or other on his coat, said more softly than before: "You don't know the commander; you are, as it were, under no obligations—if you'll pardon my expression—to him, or to us all. Believe me, your influence cannot be too highly estimated. I was indeed delighted when I heard that you were to attend the execution alone. This order of the commander was aimed at me, but now I am going to turn it to my own advantage. Uninfluenced by false insinuations and contemptuous looks—which would have been inevitable with a larger attendance at the execution—you have listened to my explanations, you have seen the machine and are now about to witness the execution. Surely your judgment is already formed; should there still be a few uncertainties in your mind, the sight of the execution will do away with them. And now I make this plea to you: Help me with the commander!"

The explorer did not allow him to continue. "But how could l do that?" he cried. "That's quite impossible. I am as powerless to help you as to hinder you."

"You certainly can," said the officer. The explorer noticed somewhat anxiously that the officer's fists were clenched. "You certainly can," he repeated, still more insistently. "I have a plan that must succeed. You believe your influence is insufficient. I know it is sufficient. But allowing that you're right, isn't it necessary then to try everything, even what may possibly fail, in order to maintain this procedure? So listen to my plan. In order to carry it out, it is above all necessary for you to be as reticent as possible concerning your judgment of this procedure in the colony today. Unless someone questions you directly, you must by no means say anything; your utterances should be brief and vague; people should notice that it becomes increasingly difficult for you to talk about it, that you are acrimonious, that you practically have to burst into invective, were you to talk openly. I don't ask you to lie, in any sense; you should give only the briefest answers, such as: 'Yes, I've seen the execution,' or, 'Yes, I've heard all the explanations.' Of that, no more. Of course there is sufficient cause for the acrimony people should notice in you, even though it does not correspond to the commander's viewpoint. Of course he will misunderstand completely and give it his own interpretation. That is the basis of my plan. Tomorrow an important meeting of all the higher administrative officers will take place under the chairmanship of the commander at headquarters. The commander naturally knows how to make a spectacle out of these sessions. A gallery has been built which is always occupied by spectators. I am obliged to attend these consultations, but I am loath to do so. In any case, you will certainly be invited to this meeting; if you will follow my plan today, the invitation will become an urgent request. Should you not be invited, however, for some undiscoverable reason, you must ask for an invitation; you will get it then without any doubt. So tomorrow you're seated with the ladies in the commander's box. He reassures himself frequently, by looking upward, that you are there. After disposing of diverse indifferent and ludicrous subjects, calculated solely to interest the spectators—mostly about port constructions, eternally about port constructions—the court procedure also comes up for discussion. If this point should not occur to the commander, or rather not early enough, I'll see to it that it does. I'll stand up and make a report of today's execution. Quite brief, only a report. Such a report is not customary, but I make it nevertheless. The commander thanks me, as always, with a friendly smile; and then he cannot restrain himself; he sees his chance: 'A report of today's execution has just been made,' he will say, or something similar to this. 'I'd only like to add to this report that this particular execution was attended by the great scholar, whose visit—an exceptional honor for our colony—you all know about. Our session today also takes on an added significance as a result of his presence. Let us now question this great scholar as to his opinion of this execution, carried out in accordance with early customs, as well as of the procedure that led up to it.' Naturally, applause throughout the house, and general approval; I am the loudest. The commander makes a bow before you and says: 'Then I put the question in the name of everyone present.' And now you step up to the balustrade. Lay your hands on it, so that they are visible to everybody; otherwise the ladies will take hold of them and dally with your fingers. And now, finally, comes a word from you. I don't know how I shall stand the tension of the hours until that moment. You must place no limit on your speech, blare forth the truth; lean over the balustrade, bellow your opinion, yes, bellow it, at the commander, your unshakable opinion! But maybe you don't want to do this, maybe it does not correspond to your character; in your country people act differently in such situations; this too is all right; this too is quite sufficient; don't get up at all, say only a few words, whisper them so that they may be heard by the officials below you; that'll do. You needn't even mention the small attendance at the execution, the creaking wheel, the broken strap, the repulsive felt gag; no, I'll take care of everything else. And believe me, if my speech doesn't chase him from the hall, it'll force him to his knees, so that he will have to acknowledge: I bow down before you, old commander!—That's my plan; won't you help me to carry it out? But of course you will; what's more, you must." And the officer seized the explorer by both arms and looked into his face, breathing heavily. He had shouted the last sentences so loudly that even the guard and the condemned man became attentive; although they understood nothing, they stopped eating and looked toward the explorer, chewing the while.

The explorer had no doubt from the very beginning as to the answer he would have to give. He had experienced too much in his life to vacillate now; at bottom he was an honest man, and he was not afraid. Nevertheless, he hesitated, just the time of a breath, at the sight of the soldier and the condemned man. But finally he said what he had to say: "No." The officer blinked several times and did not take his eyes off him. "Do you want an explanation?" asked the explorer. The officer nodded silently. "I am opposed to this procedure," the explorer then said. "Before you even took me into your confidence—I'll not abuse this confidence, of course, under any circumstances—I had already considered whether I would be justified in taking steps against this procedure, and whether there would be the slightest prospect of success in case I did so. It was clear to me to whom I should have to turn first: to the commander, of course. You have made it still clearer, but without having strengthened my resolution; on the contrary, your honest conviction moves me, even though it could never influence me."

The officer remained silent, turned to the machine and, seizing one of the brass rods, leaned slightly backward to look up at the draughtsman, as if to check whether or not everything was in order. The guard and the condemned man seemed to have become friends; the condemned man was making signs to the guard, despite the fact that the tight straps which bound him made this difficult: the soldier bent over toward him; the condemned man whispered something to him and the soldier nodded.

The explorer followed the officer: "You don't know yet what I am going to do," he said. "Of course, I shall give my opinion about the procedure to the commander, not at the meeting, however, but *tête-à-tête;* nor shall I stay here long enough to be drawn into any meeting: I am going away early tomorrow morning, or at least I'll board ship then."

It seemed as though the officer had been listening. "So the procedure did not convince you," he said to himself, and smiled as an old man smiles at a child's nonsense, withholding his own real musings behind the smile.

"Then the time has come," he said finally, and looked suddenly at the explorer, his eyes shining with a certain challenge, a certain appeal for cooperation. "Time for what?" the explorer asked anxiously, but received no answer.

"You're free," said the officer to the condemned man in the latter's own language. At first the condemned man did not believe it. "You're free now," the officer said. The face of the condemned man showed signs of life for the first time. Was this the truth? Or was it only a passing whim on the part of the officer? Had the foreign explorer obtained pardon for him? Which was it? His face seemed to ask these questions. But not for long. Whatever it might be, if he could, he really wanted to be free, and he began to shake himself as much as the harrow permitted.

"You're breaking my straps," the officer shouted. "Keep quiet, we'll unfasten them for you." And with the help of the guard, to whom he had made a sign, he got to work. The condemned man chuckled gently to himself, saying nothing; he turned his face first to the left toward the officer, then to the right toward the guard; not forgetting the explorer.

"Pull him out," the officer ordered the guard. To do this, they were obliged to move with a certain caution, on account of the harrow. The condemned man, due to his impatience, already had a few slight lacerations on his back.

From this moment on, however, the officer hardly bothered about him any more. He walked over to the explorer, took out again his small leather briefcase, rummaged through it, finally found the paper he was looking for and showed it to the explorer. "Read this," he said. "I can't," said the explorer. "I told you before I can't read those pages." "But take a good look at the page anyway," said the officer, stepping to the explorer's side to read with him. When this did not help, either, in order to facilitate the explorer's reading, he ran his little finger across the page, well above it, as if the paper must not be touched under any condition. The explorer made an effort, in order to be agreeable to the officer at least in this, but it was impossible. Now the officer began to spell out the writing, then he read it once more connectedly. "It says: 'BE JUST!'—Now you can read it," he said. The explorer bent so low over the paper that the officer drew it back, fearing he might touch it; actually the explorer said nothing more, but it was clear that he still had not been able to read it. "It says: 'BE JUST!'" the officer repeated. "That may be so," said the explorer, "I believe that's what it says." "All right then," said the officer, at least partially satisfied, and he climbed the ladder still holding the page; with great caution he laid it on the draughtsman, and then began apparently to rearrange the entire mechanism; it was a very tedious job, for the wheels in question must have been very tiny; sometimes his head disappeared completely in the draughtsman, he was obliged to examine the wheelwork so closely.

The explorer continued to follow the work from below, his neck grew stiff, his eyes began to smart from the sunlight-flooded sky. The guard and the condemned man were now occupied only with each other. With the point of his bayonet, the guard lifted up the condemned man's shirt and trousers which were lying in the ditch. The shirt was frightfully dirty, and the condemned man washed it in the water-pail. Both had to laugh aloud when the condemned man put the shirt and trousers on, for both garments had been slashed in two behind. Perhaps the offender thought it his duty to entertain the guard; in his slit clothes he made circles around the guard, who was crouching on the ground, laughing and beating his knees. Nevertheless they restrained themselves somewhat, out of respect for the presence of the two gentlemen.

When the officer had finally finished up above, he smilingly surveyed the whole in all its parts once more, banged shut the cover of the draughtsman, which until now had been open, climbed down and looked first into the ditch, then at the condemned man; noticed with satisfaction that the latter had recovered his garments, walked toward the pail to wash his hands, recognized too late the repulsive filth in it, became saddened at the fact that now he could not wash his hands, at last dipped his fingers in the sand—this substitute did not suffice but he had to accommodate himself—then rose and began to unbutton the coat of his uniform. At this, the two lady's handkerchiefs which he had stuck in his collar fell into his hands. "Here, take your handkerchiefs," he said, and threw them toward the condemned man. In explanation he said to the explorer: "Gifts from the ladies."

In spite of the evident hurry with which he took off his coat and then undressed completely, he nevertheless handled each garment very carefully. He even let his fingers run over the silver cord on his tunic and shook one of the tassels straight. Yet it was little in keeping with this carefulness that, as soon as he had finished handling a garment, he immediately threw it into the ditch, with an angry gesture. The last thing that remained was his smallsword and belt. He drew the sword from its scabbard, broke it, then gathered everything together—the pieces of the sword, the scabbard and the belt—and threw them away so violently that they clinked together in the ditch.

Now he stood there naked. The explorer bit his lips and said nothing. To be sure, he knew what was going to happen, yet he had no right to prevent the officer from doing anything. If the court procedure to which the officer was so attached really was about to be abolished—possibly as a consequence of the action which the explorer had felt obliged to take—then the officer was acting entirely rightly; the explorer would not have acted differently in his place.

The guard and the condemned man understood nothing at first; in the beginning, they did not even look on. The condemned man was overjoyed at having got back his pocket handkerchiefs, but he was not allowed to enjoy them very long, for the soldier snatched them away from him with a quick, unpredictable gesture. The condemned man now tried once more to pull the handkerchiefs from the soldier's belt, into which the latter had carefully put them, but the soldier was on his guard. So they struggled, half in jest. Only when the officer was completely naked did they pay any attention to him. The condemned man especially seemed to be seized with a foreboding of some great change. What had happened to him was now happening to the officer. It might even go on to the very end. Most likely, the foreign explorer had given the order for it. So this was revenge. Without himself having suffered to the end, he was nevertheless avenged to the end. A broad, noiseless laughter appeared now in his face, and remained there.

The officer turned toward the machine. If it had already been clear before that he understood the machine well, it was now almost horrifying to see the way he took charge of it, and the way it obeyed him. He had hardly brought his hand near the harrow when it rose and sank several times until it had reached the right position to receive him; he took hold of the bed by the edge only, and it started to vibrate right away; the ball of felt came toward his mouth. One saw that the officer did not really want to take it, but his hesitancy lasted just a moment, he submitted at once and took it in his mouth. Everything was ready, only the straps were still hanging down at the sides, but they were obviously unnecessary, as the officer did not need to be strapped in. Then the condemned man noticed the hanging straps; in his opinion the execution would not be complete unless the straps were tightly fastened; he waved excitedly to the guard and both of them ran to buckle the officer in. The latter had already stretched out one foot in order to push the crank that was to start the draughtsman going; then he saw that the two men had come near him. He drew his foot back and let himself be strapped in. Now, however, he was no longer able to reach the crank; neither the guard nor the condemned man would be able to find it, and the explorer was determined not to make a move. This was not necessary; hardly had the straps been fastened, when the machine began to work; the bed trembled, the needles danced on the skin, the harrow swung up and down. The explorer had been staring at it quite a while before he remembered that a wheel in the draughtsman should have made a creaking noise; yet all was silent, not the slightest hum was to be heard.

Because of this silent action the machine ceased to be the focus of attention. The explorer looked over toward the soldier and the condemned man. The latter was the more lively of the two; everything about the machine interested him; first he would bend down; then he would stretch himself, holding his index finger constantly extended to point out something to the guard. The explorer felt uncomfortable. He was determined to remain there till the end, but he could not have borne the sight of the two men very long. "Go home," he said. The soldier would, perhaps, have been ready to go, but the condemned man considered the order as a sort of punishment. He begged and implored with clasped hands to be allowed to stay, and when the explorer, shaking his head, refused to give in, he even went on his knees. The explorer saw that orders were of no avail here and he was about to go over and drive the two of them away. At that moment he heard a noise up in the draughtsman. He looked up. Could that one cogwheel be giving trouble? But it was something else. Slowly the cover of the draughtsman rose and then fell wide open. The teeth of a cogwheel began to show, then rose up; soon the whole wheel appeared; it was as if some great force were pressing the draughtsman together so that there was no room left for this wheel; it kept rotating till it reached the edge of the draughtsman, fell down, reeled upright a bit in the sand, then lay there. But already another one rose up above, followed by many more, big ones, little ones, and others that could hardly be told apart; the same thing happened to them all, one kept thinking that the draughtsman must surely be emptied by now, when a new, particularly numerous lot appeared, rose up, fell down, reeled in the sand, and lay there. At the sight of this occurrence the condemned man forgot all about the explorer's orders; the cogwheels completely fascinated him; he kept trying to seize one of them, at the same time urging the soldier to help him; but he withdrew his hand in fright, for another cogwheel always followed at once, and this, at least at first when it would come rolling toward him, frightened him.

The explorer, however, was very disturbed; the machine was evidently going to pieces; its quiet action was a delusion; he had the feeling that he would have to care for the officer now, since the latter was no longer able to care for himself. But while the dropping of the cogwheels had claimed his entire attention, he had neglected to watch the rest of the machine; now, however, when the last cogwheel had left the draughtsman, he bent over the harrow, only to have a fresh, more annoying surprise. The harrow was not writing, it was just sticking the body, nor was the bed rolling it but just lifting it, trembling, up to the needles. The explorer wanted to interfere and, if possible, bring the whole thing to a stop, for this was not the torture the officer had wanted to arrive at, this was outright murder. He stretched out his hands. But at that moment the harrow was already beginning to rise sideways with the impaled body, the way it usually did only at the twelfth hour. Blood was flowing in a hundred streams, unmixed with water, for the little water pipes had also failed this time. And now the last thing failed too, the body did not release itself from the long needles, but, bleeding profusely, hung over the ditch without falling into it. The harrow was ready to fall back into its usual position, but, as if it had noticed itself that it was not yet freed of its burden, it remained suspended above the ditch. "Why don't you help?" the explorer shouted over to the guard and the condemned man, as he, himself, seized the officer's feet. He tried to hold the feet down on his side and the other two were to take hold of the officer's head from the other side, so that he might be slowly lifted off the needles. But the two could not make up their minds to join him; the condemned man practically turned away; the explorer had to go over to them and force them to come over near the officer's head. Just here he saw the face of the corpse, almost against his will. It was as it had been in life; no sign of the promised redemption was to be detected; that which all the others had found in the machine, the officer had not found; his lips were tightly pressed together, his eyes were open, and had an expression of life; their look was calm and convinced; the point of the big iron prong pierced his forehead.

When the explorer reached the first houses of the colony, with the soldier and the condemned man behind him, the soldier pointed at one house and said, "That's the teahouse."

On the ground floor of one house there was a deep, low, cavernous room with smoke-stained walls and ceiling. On the street side it was wide open. Although the tea house differed little from the other houses in the colony, which were all very run-down, with the exception of the palatial structures that housed headquarters, it nevertheless gave the impression to the explorer of a historic memory, and he felt the power of other days. He walked nearer and, followed by his companions, he passed between the unoccupied tables standing on the street before the teahouse, and inhaled the cool, musty air which came from the inside. "The old man's buried here," said the soldier. "The priest refused him a place in the cemetery. At first they were undecided as to where to bury him, but they finally buried him here. I'm sure the officer did not tell you anything about it, for that was the thing he was most ashamed of. He even tried a few times to disinter the old man at night, but he was always chased away." "Where is the grave?" asked the explorer, who found it hard to believe the guard. Both the guard and the condemned man immediately dashed ahead of him and with outstretched hands pointed to the spot where the grave was to be found. They led the explorer straight to the back wall where customers were sitting at a few of the tables. They were probably longshoremen, sturdy-looking men with short, glossy, full black beards. All of them were coatless, their shirts torn; they were poor humble folk. As the explorer approached, several of them rose, flattened themselves up against the wall and looked in his direction. "He's a foreigner," was the whisper that went about the explorer; "he wants to see the grave." They shoved one of the tables aside, underneath which there really was a tombstone. It was a simple slab, low enough to be hidden under the table. On it was an inscription in quite small letters, to read which the explorer was obliged to kneel down. It read: "HERE LIES THE OLD COMMANDER. HIS ADHERENTS, WHO MAY NO LONGER BEAR A NAME, HAVE DUG THIS GRAVE FOR HIM AND ERECTED THIS STONE. THERE EXISTS A PROPHECY TO THE EFFECT THAT, AFTER A CERTAIN NUMBER OF YEARS, THE COMMANDER WILL RISE FROM THE DEAD AND LEAD THEM OUT OF THIS HOUSE TO THE RECONQUEST OF THE COLONY. BELIEVE AND WAIT!" When he had finished reading, the explorer rose and saw the men standing about him and smiling as if they had read the inscription with him, had found it ridiculous, and were calling upon him to join in their viewpoint. The explorer acted as though he had noticed nothing, distributed a few coins among them, waited until the table had been shoved back over the grave, then left the teahouse and walked toward the port.

The guard and the condemned man had come across acquaintances in the teahouse who detained them. But they must have torn themselves away soon after, for the explorer was no further than the middle of the long stairway leading to the boats, when they came running after him. They probably wanted to force the explorer at the last moment to take them along. While the explorer was negotiating with a sailor down below for his crossing to the liner, the two men rushed down the steps, silently, for they did not dare cry out. But when they arrived below, the explorer was already in the boat and the sailor was just about to shove off. They might still have been able to jump into the boat, but the explorer picked up a heavy, knotted towrope from the floor, threatened them with it, and thus prevented them from jumping.

FICTION: FOR STUDY AND DISCUSSION

Because these stories have been collected under the Truth section of this book, perhaps your first task should be to determine the particular "truth" about life that each story dramatizes. In effect, this is the same as stating the theme of each story.

The above point leads me to comment on the word *realism* in fiction. I suppose that *realism* means "true to real life," but a story which faithfully reproduces traffic noises may be realistic without ever telling the reader any significant truth about life. Such a story might well be more of a "documentary" than a literary achievement. On the other hand, such stories as "By the Waters of Babylon" and "In the Penal Colony," which are very unlike "real life," are profoundly "true" in their allegorical representations of the human condition.

The word *allegorical* is closely associated with the word *symbolical*. However, a symbol is normally restricted to a single thing (or, sometimes, a person) standing for an abstract idea, whereas an allegory is a story told through a series of connected symbols. Thus, to the young American in "In Another Country," the hawk becomes a symbol of courage. The bear in Faulkner's story has a comparable symbolic significance (although the other related symbols in this story lead the story somewhat closer to an allegorical classification). Now consider "In the Penal Colony." One starts with the basic symbol of the prison: the world is a prison. As one continues, one realizes that there is almost a point-to-point correspondence between events (and persons) on the *story* level and ideas on the *meaning* level. So completely formal and intellectually demanding an allegory infuriates many readers, yet distinguished writers (and distinguished philosophers, such as Plato) have been convinced that the most profound insights can only be expressed in allegorical form. I encourage you to argue the point.

It is sometimes (I emphasize *sometimes*) useful after reading a story to go back to its title. The title of "The Bet" reveals little about the meanings of the story; in contrast, your understanding of "In Another Country" will be enhanced if you sense that this title has two levels of meaning. What about the title "Young Archimedes"?

I do not know whether you are familiar with the term "initiation story." An initiation story typically deals with the initiation of a relatively young person into some aspect of the adult world. I would call three of the stories in this section initiation stories. Try to pick the three and attempt to explain the type of initiation in each case.

POETRY

Truth Is as Old as God

EMILY DICKINSON

[1830–1886]

Students sometimes think of poems as "wordy," even "flowery." In point of fact, good poems—whether long or short—are notable for their preciseness. When F. Scott Fitzgerald's daughter was a freshman at Vassar, he wrote her this fatherly advice based on his very considerable and very successful experience in creative writing:

> *The chief fault in your style is its lack of distinction . . . [And] the only thing that will help you is poetry, which is the most concentrated form of style. . . .*

Emily Dickinson's style is an almost blinding reminder of a great poet's capacity to "concentrate" style. In "Truth Is as Old as God," she has, in eight lines, expressed her own insight into a problem which has perplexed students of philosophy and religion for many centuries. Your job in reading her poem is primarily to understand the philosophical–religious question involved, then to sense (and explain) the impact with which the poem can "hit" one in a manner that is less possible in formal prose.

Truth is as old as God,—
His twin identity—
And will endure as long as He,
A co-eternity,
And perish on the day
That He is borne away
From mansion of the universe,
A lifeless Deity.

FOR STUDY AND DISCUSSION

1. In the first two lines, the poet says:

> Truth is as old as God,—
> His twin identity—

It is clear, philosophically speaking, that these lines are open to question. For example, what *kinds* of truth? One might (but not necessarily) assert that

the "truths" of pure science and of the arts have this identity with God, but what about the "true" evils of the world as we know them?
2. Now setting aside the philosophical complexities of Miss Dickinson's position, consider the selection in terms of its poetic effectiveness alone. For example, the two lines quoted above are a striking affirmation of Miss Dickinson's devotion to Truth. What makes them so effective?
3. What is the advantage of endowing both Truth and God with life?
4. In this connection, what is the force of the phrase "A lifeless Deity" in the last line?

The Brain Is Wider than the Sky

EMILY DICKINSON

The brain is wider than the sky,
   For, put them side by side,
The one the other will include
   With ease, and you beside.

The brain is deeper than the sea,   5
   For, hold them, blue to blue,
The one the other will absorb,
   As sponges, buckets do.

The brain is just the weight of God,
   For, lift them, pound for pound,   10
And they will differ, if they do,
   As syllable from sound.

The Wayfarer

STEPHEN CRANE

[1871–1900]

The wayfarer,
Perceiving the pathway to truth,
Was struck with astonishment.
It was thickly grown with weeds.
"Ha," he said,   5
"I see that no one has passed here
In a long time."
Later he saw that each weed
Was a singular knife.
"Well," he mumbled at last,   10
"Doubtless there are other roads."

The Bear

ROBERT FROST

[1875–1963]

The bear puts both arms around the tree above her
And draws it down as if it were a lover
And its choke cherries lips to kiss good-by,
Then lets it snap back upright in the sky.
Her next step rocks a boulder on the wall   5
(She's making her cross-country in the fall).
Her great weight creaks the barbed-wire in its staples
As she flings over and off down through the maples,
Leaving on one wire tooth a lock of hair.
Such is the uncaged progress of the bear.   10
The world has room to make a bear feel free;
The universe seems cramped to you and me.   *Discussing mankind*
Man acts more like the poor bear in a cage –
That all day fights a nervous inward rage,
His mood rejecting all his mind suggests.   15

He paces back and forth and never rests
The toe-nail click and shuffle of his feet,
The telescope at one end of his beat,
And at the other end the microscope,
Two instruments of nearly equal hope,   20
And in conjunction giving quite a spread.
Or if he rests from scientific tread,
'Tis only to sit back and sway his head
Through ninety odd degrees of arc, it seems,
Between two metaphysical extremes.   25
He sits back on his fundamental butt
With lifted snout and eyes (if any) shut,
(He almost looks religious but he's not),
And back and forth he sways from cheek to cheek,
At one extreme agreeing with one Greek,   30
At the other agreeing with another Greek
Which may be thought, but only so to speak.
A baggy figure, equally pathetic
When sedentary and when peripatetic.[1]

---

[1] "The Bear" is built around a *paradox*. In the formal dictionary meaning a paradox is any self-contradictory statement, but in literature (as well as in much general conversation) the contradiction on the literal level implies a meaning which in fact is true. Thus, in "To the Evening Star" William Blake uses the phrase "speak silence." This phrase is strictly speaking impossible, but it is true within the context of the poem in much the same manner as our colloquial comment that "actions speak louder than words." It is helpful to remember that there are paradoxes of *situation* as well as of *statement* since it is the former type that Frost primarily employs in "The Bear."

The Egg and the Machine

ROBERT FROST

He gave the solid rail a hateful kick.
From far away there came an answering tick
And then another tick. He knew the code:
His hate had roused an engine up the road.
He wished when he had had the track alone 5
He had attacked it with a club or stone
And bent some rail wide open like a switch
So as to wreck the engine in the ditch.
Too late though, now he had himself to thank.
Its click was rising to a nearer clank. 10
Here it came breasting like a horse in skirts.
(He stood well back for fear of scalding squirts.)
Then for a moment all there was was size
Confusion and a roar that drowned the cries
He raised against the gods in the machine. 15
Then once again the sandbank lay serene.
The traveler's eye picked up a turtle trail,
Between the dotted feet a streak of tail,
And followed it to where he made out vague
But certain signs of buried turtle's egg; 20
And probing with one finger not too rough,
He found suspicious sand, and sure enough,
The pocket of a little turtle mine.
If there was one egg in it there were nine,
Torpedo-like, with shell of gritty leather 25
All packed in sand to wait the trump together.
"You'd better not disturb me any more,"
He told the distance, "I am armed for war.
The next machine that has the power to pass
Will get this plasm in its goggle glass." 30

When I Heard the Learned Astronomer

WALT WHITMAN
[1819–1892]

When I heard the learned astronomer,
When the proofs, the figures, were ranged in columns before me,
When I was shown the charts and diagrams, to add, divide, and measure them,
When I sitting heard the astronomer where he lectured with much applause in
    the lecture room,
How soon unaccountable I became tired and sick,
Till rising and gliding out I wandered off by myself,
In the mystical moist night air, and from time to time,   *weird part of*
Looked up in perfect silence at the stars.   *Story*

To a Steam Roller

MARIANNE MOOPE
[BORN 1887]

The illustration
is nothing to you without the application.
    You lack half wit. You crush all the particles down
        into close conformity, and then walk back and forth on them.

Sparkling chips of rock
are crushed down to the level of the parent block.
    Were not "impersonal judgment in aesthetic
        matters, a metaphysical impossibility," you

might fairly achieve
it. As for butterflies, I can hardly conceive
    of one's attending upon you, but to question
        the congruence of the complement is vain, if it exists.[1]

---

[1] In this poem Miss Moore looks with a jaundiced eye on a symbol of man's technological advance: a steam roller. You will notice that she personifies the steam roller; ask
yourselves how this personification emphasizes her point of view. For example, what do
the two lines beginning with "You crush all the particles down . . ." suggest about modern man's worship of the machine? What is the irony in the phrase she "quotes" which
begins "impersonal judgment . . ."? What single word in this possibly made-up quota-
tion comes closest to identifying Miss Moore's fundamental criticism of the steam roller?
What is the function of the "butterflies" in emphasizing her theme?

Pegasus Lost

ELINOR WYLIE
[1885–1928]

And there I found a gray and ancient ass,
With dull glazed stare, and stubborn wrinkled smile,
Sardonic, mocking my wide-eyed amaze.
A clumsy hulking form in that white place
At odds with the small stable, cleanly, Greek,   5
The marble manger and the golden oats.
With loathing hands I felt the ass's side,
Solidly real and hairy to the touch.
Then knew I that I dreamed not, but saw truth;
And knowing, wished I still might hope I dreamed.   10
The door stood wide, I went into the air.
The day was blue and filled with rushing wind,
A day to ride high in the heavens and taste
The glory of the gods who tread the stars.
Up in the mighty purity I saw   15
A flashing shape that gladly sprang aloft—
My little Pegasus, like a far white bird
Seeking sun-regions, never to return.
Silently then I turned my steps about,
Entered the stable, saddled the slow ass;   20
Then on its back I journeyed dustily
Between sun-wilted hedgerows into town.

Sagacity

WILLIAM ROSE BENÉT
[1886–1950]

We knew so much; when her beautiful eyes could lighten,
   Her beautiful laughter follow our phrase;
Or the gaze go hard with pain, the lips tighten,
   On the bitterer days.

Oh, ours was all knowing then, all generous displaying.
   Such wisdom we had to show!
And now there is merely silence, silence, silence saying
   All we did not know.

Morning Song from *Senlin*

CONRAD AIKEN
[BORN 1889]

It is morning, Senlin says, and in the morning
When the light drips through the shutters like the dew,
I arise, I face the sunrise,
And do the things my fathers learned to do.
Stars in the purple dusk above the rooftops   5
Pale in a saffron mist and seem to die,
And I myself on a swiftly tilting planet
Stand before a glass and tie my tie.

Vine leaves tap my window,
Dew-drops sing to the garden stones,   10
The robin chirps in the chinaberry tree
Repeating three clear tones.

It is morning. I stand by the mirror
And tie my tie once more.
While waves far off in a pale rose twilight   15
Crash on a coral shore.
I stand by a mirror and comb my hair:
How small and white my face!—
The green earth tilts through a sphere of air
And bathes in a flame of space.   20

There are houses hanging above the stars
And stars hung under a sea.
And a sun far off in a shell of silence
Dapples my walls for me.

It is morning, Senlin says, and in the morning   25
Should I not pause in the light to remember god?
Upright and firm I stand on a star unstable,
He is immense and lonely as a cloud.
I will dedicate this moment before my mirror
To him alone, for him I will comb my hair.   30
Accept these humble offerings, clouds of silence!
I will think of you as I descend the stair.

Vine leaves tap my window,
The snail-track shines on the stones,

Dew-drops flash from the chinaberry tree 35
Repeating two clear tones.

It is morning, I awake from a bed of silence,
Shining I rise from the starless waters of sleep.
The walls are about me still as in the evening,
I am the same, and the same name still I keep. 40
The earth revolves with me, yet makes no motion,
The stars pale silently in a coral sky.
In a whistling void I stand before my mirror,
Unconcerned, and tie my tie.

There are horses neighing on far-off hills 45
Tossing their long white manes,
And mountains flash in the rose-white dusk,
Their shoulders black with rains.
It is morning. I stand by the mirror
And surprise my soul once more; 50
The blue air rushes above my ceiling,
There are suns beneath my floor.

. . . It is morning, Senlin says, I ascend from darkness
And depart on the winds of space for I know not where,
My watch is wound, a key is in my pocket, 55
And the sky is darkened as I descend the stair.
There are shadows across the windows, clouds in heaven,
And a god among the stars; and I will go
Thinking of him as I might think of daybreak
And humming a tune I know. 60

Vine leaves tap at the window,
Dew-drops sing to the garden stones,
The robin chirps in the chinaberry tree
Repeating three clear tones.[1]

---

[1] I direct your attention to two points about this poem. The first is its **highly musical** quality. Its rhythms are complex but superbly controlled. Observe the sustained pattern of variation in the length of lines and the manner in which groups of lines consistently play against one another. Notice, for example, the shift in tone given by the three stanzas beginning "Vine-leaves . . ." Notice, too, that these three stanzas within themselves show variations on a pattern. Throughout the poem there is a subtle use of alliteration, internal rhymes, and half-rhymes. The identification of these will help you to explain the poem's lyrical effectiveness.

My second point is worded as a question: How do these lyric qualities reinforce the comment on life which Aiken is making in his poem?

The Last Days of Alice

ALLEN TATE

[BORN 1899]

Alice grown lazy, mammoth but not fat,
Declines upon her lost and twilight age,
Above in the dozing leaves the grinning cat
Quivers forever with his abstract rage;

Whatever light swayed on the perilous gate   5
Forever sways, nor will the arching grass
Caught when the world clattered undulate
In the deep suspension of the looking-glass.

Bright Alice! always pondering to gloze
The spoiled cruelty she had meant to say   10
Gazes learnedly down her airy nose
At nothing, nothing thinking all the day:

Turned absent-minded by infinity
She cannot move unless her double move,
The All-Alice of the world's entity   15
Smashed in the anger of her hopeless love,

Love for herself who, as an earthly twain,
Pouted to join her two in a sweet one:
No more the second lips to kiss in vain
The first she broke, plunged through the glass alone—   20

Alone to the weight of impassivity
Incest of spirit, theorem of desire
Without will as chalky cliffs by the sea
Empty as the bodiless flesh of fire;

All space that heaven is a dayless night,   25
A nightless day driven by perfect lust
For vacancy, in which her bored eyesight
Stares at the drowsy cubes of human dust.

We, too, back to the world shall never pass
Through the shattered door, a dumb shade-harried crowd,   30
Being all infinite, function depth and mass
Without figure; a mathematical shroud

Hurled at the air—blessèd without sin!
O God of our flesh, return us to Your wrath,
Let us be evil could we enter in   35
Your grace, and falter on the stony path!

$E = mc^2$

MORRIS BISHOP

[BORN 1893]

What was our trust, we trust not;
    What was our faith, we doubt;
Whether we must or must not,
    We may debate about.
The soul, perhaps, is a gust of gas   5
    And wrong is a form of right—
But we know that Energy equals Mass
    By the Square of the Speed of Light.

What we have known, we know not;
    What we have proved, abjure;   10
Life is a tangled bowknot,
    But one thing still is sure.
Come, little lad; come, little lass—
    Your docile creed recite:
"We know that Energy equals Mass   15
    By the Square of the Speed of Light."

Statistics

STEPHEN SPENDER

[BORN 1909]

Lady, you think too much of speeds,
    Pulleys and cranes swing in your mind;
    The Woolworth Tower has made you blind
To Egypt and the pyramids.

Too much impressed by motor-cars   5
    You have a false historic sense.
    But I, perplexed at God's expense
Of electricity on stars,

From Brighton pier shall weigh the seas,
    And count the sands along the shore: 10
    Despite all moderns, thinking more
Of Shakespeare and Praxiteles.

Golly, How Truth Will Out!

OGDEN NASH

[BORN 1902]

How does a person get to be a capable liar?
That is something that I respectfully inquiar,
Because I don't believe a person will ever set the world on fire
Unless they are a capable lire.
Some wise man said that words were given to us to conceal our thoughts   5
But if a person has nothing but truthful words why their thoughts haven't
    even the protection of a pair of panties or shoughts,
And a naked thought is ineffectual as well as improper,
And hasn't a chance in the presence of a glib chinchilla-clad whopper.
One of the greatest abilities a person can have, I guess,   10
Is the ability to say Yes when they mean No and No when they mean
    Yes.
Oh to be Machiavellian, oh to be unscrupulous, oh, to be glib!
Or to be ever prepared with a plausible fib!
Because then a dinner engagement or a contract or treaty is no   15
    longer a fetter,
Because liars can just logically lie their way out of it if they don't like
    it or if one comes along that they like better;
And do you think their conscience prickles?
No, it tickles.   20
And please believe that I mean every one of these lines as I am writing
    them
Because once there was a small boy who was sent to the drugstore to
    buy some bitter stuff to put on his nails to keep him from biting
    them,   25

And in his humiliation he tried to lie to the clerk
And it didn't work,
Because he said My mother sent me to buy some bitter stuff for a
    friend of mine's nails that bites them, and the clerk smiled wisely and
    said I wonder who that friend could be,   30
And the small boy broke down and said Me,
And it was me, or at least I was him,
And all my subsequent attempts at subterfuge have been equally grim,
And that is why I admire a suave prevarication because I prevaricate
    so awkwardly and gauchely,   35
And that is why I can never amount to anything politically or socially.

The Indian upon God

WILLIAM BUTLER YEATS

[1865–1939]

I passed along the water's edge below the humid trees,
My spirit rocked in evening light, the rushes round my knees,
My spirit rocked in sleep and sighs; and saw the moorfowl pace
All dripping on a grassy slope, and saw them cease to chase
Each other round in circles, and heard the eldest speak: 5
Who holds the world between His bill and made us strong or weak
Is an undying moorfowl, and He lives beyond the sky.
The rains are from His dripping wing, the moonbeams from His eye.
I passed a little further on and heard a lotus talk:
Who made the world and ruleth it, He hangeth on a stalk,   10
For I am in His image made, and all this tinkling tide
Is but a sliding drop of rain between His petals wide.
A little way within the gloom a roebuck raised his eyes
Brimful of starlight, and he said: *The Stamper of the Skies,*
He is a gentle roebuck; for how else, I pray, could He   15
Conceive a thing so sad and soft, a gentle thing like me?
I passed a little further on and heard a peacock say:
Who made the grass and made the worms and made my feathers gay,
He is a monstrous peacock, and He waveth all the night
His languid tail above us, lit with myriad spots of light.   20

Hap

THOMAS HARDY
[1840–1928]

If but some vengeful god would call to me
From up the sky, and laugh: "Thou suffering thing,
Know that thy sorrow is my ecstasy,
That thy love's loss is my hate's profiting!"

Then would I bear it, clench myself, and die,   5
Steeled by the sense of ire unmerited;
Half-eased in that a Powerfuller than I
Had willed and meted me the tears I shed.

But not so. How arrives it joy lies slain,
And why unblooms the best hope ever sown?   10
—Crass Casualty obstructs the sun and rain,
And dicing Time for gladness casts a moan. . . .
These purblind Doomsters had as readily strown
Blisses about my pilgrimage as pain.[1]

---

[1] "Hap" is essentially a sonnet although its appearance might obscure that fact. The significant "turn" comes in the ninth line. Having identified this turn, you should concentrate on understanding its function toward emphasizing the final statement about truth in the remaining lines. A point which you might wish to investigate and discuss is whether the last six lines are expressing the "fatalism" commonly associated with Hardy or an interesting modification of that philosophy. You might start by looking up the word *hap,* preferably in the *Oxford English Dictionary.*

Preludes

T. S. E L I O T
[1888–1965]

I

The winter evening settles down
With smell of steaks in passageways.
Six o'clock.
The burnt-out ends of smoky days.
And now a gusty shower wraps   5
The grimy scraps
Of withered leaves about your feet
And newspapers from vacant lots;
The showers beat
On broken blinds and chimney-pots,   10
And at the corner of the street
A lonely cab-horse steams and stamps.
And then the lighting of the lamps.

II

The morning comes to consciousness
Of faint stale smells of beer   15
From the sawdust-trampled street
With all its muddy feet that press
To early coffee-stands.
With the other masquerades
That time resumes,   20
One thinks of all the hands
That are raising dingy shades
In a thousand furnished rooms.

III

You tossed a blanket from the bed,
You lay upon your back, and waited;   25
You dozed, and watched the night revealing
The thousand sordid images
Of which your soul was constituted;

They flickered against the ceiling.
And when all the world came back   30
And the light crept up between the shutters
And you heard the sparrows in the gutters,
You had such a vision of the street
As the street hardly understands;
Sitting along the bed's edge, where   35
You curled the papers from your hair,
Or clasped the yellow soles of feet
In the palms of both soiled hands.

IV

His soul stretched tight across the skies
That fade behind a city block,   40
Or trampled by insistent feet
At four and five and six o'clock;
And short square fingers stuffing pipes,
And evening newspapers, and eyes
Assured of certain certainties,   45
The conscience of a blackened street
Impatient to assume the world.

I am moved by fancies that are curled
Around these images, and cling:
The notion of some infinitely gentle   50
Infinitely suffering thing.

Wipe your hand across your mouth, and laugh;
The worlds revolve like ancient women
Gathering fuel in vacant lots.[1]

---

[1] "Preludes" was written relatively early in Eliot's distinguished career. It foreshadows his more famous "negative" poems such as "The Waste Land" and "The Hollow Men." Throughout the poem the impossibility of individuality in an industrialized world is stressed, an emphasis especially evident in the first three stanzas. In the fourth stanza a sensitive person is introduced, but it is made clear that he, too, is powerless against an environment vulgarly "assured of certain certainties." In the last seven lines the poet makes his last sad protest against the human predicament of so many individuals caught in a meaningless existence of "vacant lots."

The Kingdom of God

"In No Strange Land"

FRANCIS THOMPSON

[1859–1907]

O world invisible, we view thee,
O world intangible, we touch thee,
O world unknowable, we know thee,
Inapprehensible, we clutch thee!

Does the fish soar to find the ocean,   5
The eagle plunge to find the air—
That we ask of the stars in motion
If they have rumor of thee there?

Not where the wheeling systems darken,
And our benumbed conceiving soars!—   10
The drift of pinions, would we hearken,
Beats at our own clay-shuttered doors.

The angels keep their ancient places;—
Turn but a stone, and start a wing!
'Tis ye, 'tis your estrangèd faces,   15
That miss the many-splendored thing.

But (when so sad thou canst not sadder)
Cry;—and upon thy so sore loss
Shall shine the traffic of Jacob's ladder
Pitched betwixt Heaven and Charing Cross.   20

Yea, in the night, my Soul, my daughter,
Cry,—clinging Heaven by the hems;
And lo, Christ walking on the water
Not of Gennesareth, but Thames! [1]

---

[1] Francis Thompson, a devout English Catholic poet, is most often associated with a single poem, "The Hound of Heaven." I have always found "The Kingdom of God" more striking in its imagery and more contemporary in its thematic appeal. It might be interesting to compare this poem with Whitman's "When I Heard the Learned Astronomer" (p. 104). As a start you might discuss how each poet, in his own manner, is expressing doubt about the conventional avenues toward truth.

Calmly We Walk Through This April's Day

DELMORE SCHWARTZ

[1913–1966]

Calmly we walk through this April's day,
Metropolitan poetry here and there,
In the park sit pauper and *rentier*,[1]
The screaming children, the motor car
Fugitive about us, running away,   5
Between the worker and the millionaire.
Number provides all distances,
It is Nineteen Thirty-Seven now,
Many great dears are taken away,
What will become of you and me   10
(This is the school in which we learn . . .)
Besides the photo and the memory?
(. . . that time is the fire in which we burn.)

(This is the school in which we learn . . .)
What is the self amid this blaze?   15
What am I now that I was then
Which I shall suffer and act again,
The theodicy [2] I wrote in my high school days
Restored all life from infancy,
The children shouting are bright as they run   20
(This is the school in which they learn . . .)
Ravished entirely in their passing play!
(. . . that time is the fire in which they burn.)

Avid its rush, that reeling blaze!
Where is my father and Eleanor?   25
Not where are they now, dead seven years,
But what they were then?
                   No more? No more?
From Nineteen-Fourteen to the present day,
Bert Spira and Rhoda consume, consume   30
Not where they are now (where are they now?)
But what they were then, both beautiful;

[1] *rentier:* one who receives his income from stocks, bonds, real estate—commonly called "unearned" income.
[2] *theodicy:* an attempt to reconcile God's benevolence with the evils of the world.

Each minute bursts in the burning room,
The great globe reels in the solar fire,
Spinning the trivial and unique away.   35
(How all things flash! How all things flare!)
What am I now that I was then?
May memory restore again and again
The smallest color of the smallest day:
Time is the school in which we learn,   40
Time is the fire in which we burn.

Light Breaks Where No Sun Shines

DYLAN THOMAS
[1914–1953]

Light breaks where no sun shines;
Where no sea runs, the waters of the heart
Push in their tides;
And, broken ghosts with glowworms in their heads,
The things of light   5
File through the flesh where no flesh decks the bones.

A candle in the thighs
Warms youth and seed and burns the seeds of age;
Where no seed stirs,
The fruit of man unwrinkles in the stars,   10
Bright as a fig;
Where no wax is, the candle shows its hairs.

Dawn breaks behind the eyes;
From poles of skull and toe the windy blood
Slides like a sea;   15
Nor fenced, nor staked, the gushers of the sky
Spout to the rod
Divining in a smile the oil of tears.

Night in the sockets rounds,
Like some pitch moon, the limit of the globes;   20
Day lights the bone;

Where no cold is, the skinning gales unpin
The winter's robes;
The film of spring is hanging from the lids.

Light breaks on secret lots,   25
On tips of thought where thoughts smell in the rain;
When logics die,
The secret of the soil grows through the eye,
And blood jumps in the sun;
Above the waste allotments the dawn halts.   30

POETRY: FOR STUDY AND DISCUSSION

Roughly since the Renaissance, and increasingly since the Industrial Revolution
(now so greatly accelerated), the mind and responses of modern man have been
largely science-oriented. For most people this orientation has been a material blessing. The applications of "pure science" have led to higher wages, lesser work
loads, and many conveniences which we have now come to take for granted.

However, reflection suggests the other side of the coin: what is the price we
have paid for our immense technological advances? William Wordsworth [1770–
1850] wrote:

> The world is too much with us; late and soon,
> Getting and spending, we lay waste our powers;
> Little we see in Nature that is ours;
> We have given our hearts away, a sordid boon!
> This sea that bares her bosom to the moon;
> The winds that will be howling at all hours,
> And are up-gathered now like sleeping flowers;
> For this, for everything, we are out of tune;
> It moves us not. . . .

Whitman ("When I Heard the Learned Astronomer") page 104, raises the same
question. Bishop ("E = mc²"), page 109, goes further, for he is clearly suggesting that in a topsy-turvy way we are now making a *religion* of science.

Such reactions raise the question of *how* a poem speaks to us and for us in our
human search for the nonquantitative values in life. Emerson once remarked that
"the poet is the man without impediment." I take Emerson's comment to mean
that just as a few of us have an actual physical impediment of speech, so most of
us are linguistically impeded from depicting effectively the many delights and sorrows of our shared existence. Thus the poet (as, to be sure, all other artists) ar-
ticulates experiences which more handicapped human beings feel but cannot successfully express.

Basically, I suppose, the poet's superior capacity for articulation rests on his natural (and developed) sense of imagery and of rhythm. This book is not directed toward the techniques of literary composition, but I believe it most important to emphasize that it is the mastery of such techniques that permits the poet to communicate to a responsive reader—assuming, of course, that the poet has superior talent to begin with. Always remember, I would suggest, that the poet is "building a bridge" (to use an obvious *image*) between himself and his reader. To make this connection, he will make vivid his perspective by images that relate the reader and himself. Rhythms perform the same function: they, too, are resources of communication which reinforce other aspects of the poem in assuring its success.[1]

Understood in this manner, a satisfactory poem provides a dimension to truth not possible in even the most careful prose account. I can best illustrate my point by asking you to read again "The Last Days of Alice" by Allen Tate on page 108. Then read the following explanatory note on the poem by Mr. Tate. I think you will agree that the poem, *as a poem,* says something which is more subtle and sinks deeper than Mr. Tate's own prose statement.

Here is Mr. Tate's comment on "The Last Days of Alice":

> I suppose that what the poem "says" is that man has dehumanized himself, not that science has dehumanized him. He is allowing himself to see the sciences as an *end* in itself, instead of as an instrument for the control of nature for human ends. The simple conceit that the poem is based upon is that Carroll's Alice, having got through to the other side of the looking glass, can't get back again; the other side is the dead world of abstraction which our intellectual pride has created. At the end of the poem the "I," the speaker of the poem, cries out that he would rather be in the imperfect human world, where sin and the wrath of God prevail, than in the perfect but dead world of mathematical forms.[2]

I would like you to review the poems of this section in the light of what I have been saying. You might then take a poem you have particularly liked and compose a clear statement of its essential meaning. (You would do well to use Mr. Tate's letter as a model.) This accomplished, return to the poem and prepare yourself to specify those elements which distinguish it from even your best prose "translation."

---

[1] There are many handbooks to help you on the technical aspects of poetry. My own favorite is Babette Deutsch's *Poetry Handbook* (revised edition), Funk and Wagnalls, New York, 1962.

[2] Reprinted by permission of Mr. Tate.

BEAUTY

Introduction

Beauty, like truth, cannot be adequately defined. When I was young, I recall that older people remarked of a girl I was dating that she had beauty but was not beautiful. At the same time, I was puzzled—perhaps offended—by this distinction. Now I know better, for I have come to realize that the "completely beautiful" is a Platonic ideal.

It is reassuring for Keats to sing in "Endymion,"

> A thing of beauty is a joy forever.

Poetically, the line expresses with great impact a profound truth about the human experience: A thing of beauty is, indeed, a joy forever, whether it be a girl, a garden, a landscape, or a religious symbol.

Such a sentiment is all very well, and if one is willing to remain half-educated, one can rest content in this type of half-truth. In point of fact, however, girls grow old, gardens are often neglected, landscapes are commonly obliterated—and religious symbols are declared "dead."

A repeated assertion is that only Nature is truly beautiful, and that man's attempts to create beauty represent his imperfect efforts to "imitate" Nature's dazzling display. Ralph Waldo Emerson [1803–1882] supports this view in a poem called "The Snow-Storm":

> Announced by all the trumpets of the sky,
> Arrives the snow, and driving o'er the fields,
> Seems nowhere to alight: the whited air
> Hides hills and woods, the river, and the heaven,
> And veils the farmhouse at the garden's end.   5
> The sled and traveller stopped, the courier's feet
> Delayed, all friends shut out, the housemates sit
> Around the radiant fireplace, enclosed
> In a tumultuous privacy of storm.
>
>   Come see the north wind's masonry.   10
> Out of an unseen quarry evermore
> Furnished with tile, the fierce artificer
> Curves his white bastions with projected reef
> Round every windward stake, or tree, or deer.
> Speeding, the myriad-handed, his wild work   15
> So fanciful, so savage, nought cares he
> For number or proportion. Mockingly,
> A swanlike form invests the hidden thorn;
> Fills up the farmer's lane from wall to wall,
> Maugre [1] the farmer's sighs and at the gate   20

[1] Maugre: in spite of.

A tapering turret overtops the work.
And when his hours are numbered, and the world
Is all his own, retiring, as he were not,
Leaves, when the sun appears, astonished Art
To mimic in slow structures, stone by stone,   25
Built in an age, the mad wind's night-work,
The frolic architecture of the snow.

The view of art expressed in lines 24–27 has a respectful—even reverential
—attitude toward Nature. However, it is a view which has been strongly con-
tested. Take, for example, these lines of Matthew Arnold [1822–1888]:

To an Independent Preacher

Who Preached That We Should Be "in Harmony with Nature"

"In harmony with Nature?" Restless fool,
Who with such heat dost preach what were to thee,
When true, the last impossibility;
To be like Nature strong, like Nature cool:—
Know, man hath all which Nature hath, but more,   5
And in that *more* lie all his hopes of good.
Nature is cruel; man is sick of blood:
Nature is stubborn; man would fain adore:
Nature is fickle; man hath need of rest:
Nature forgives no debt, and fears no grave;   10
Man would be mild, and with safe conscience blest.
Man must begin, know this, where Nature ends;
Nature and man can never be fast friends.
Fool, if thou canst not pass her, rest her slave!

This difference of opinion can have profound philosophical implications.
At this point, however, it is perhaps sufficient to remind you that there are
kinds of beauty as there are kinds of truth. In short, if Man cannot make a
snowstorm, Nature cannot compose a poem about a snowstorm.

Leo Tolstoy

[1828–1910]

That branch of philosophy which deals with the nature of beauty is called aesthetics. In this field it is usually considered a waste of time to compare natural beauty with the beauties of artistic production. That is to say, one admits that a tranquil pond, a towering mountain, a delightful waterfall, a charming flower, a first snowfall of winter are beautiful, but such instances of beauty are not of our own making: we can, at best, only conserve and enhance them. Art, on the other hand, finds in "given" beauties (and even in outward ugliness) a stimulus for the creation of man-made beauty in such forms as literature, music, painting, and sculpture. The fundamental question of aesthetics thus becomes (as indicated in Tolstoy's title): What is art?[1]

As usual, the Greeks were the first to become curious about this question, and Aristotle's Poetics is a classic in the literature on aesthetics. In subsequent centuries, an enormous variety of answers to the basic problem has been suggested. Art has been said to be intuition; it has been called the concrete universal; it has been designated harmony (or proportion); it has been called significant form. Art has been given many other such final definitions. Tolstoy's position is especially interesting because it is the judgment of a great artist rather than of a professional philosopher. Of course you should remember that because Tolstoy was a literary genius, it does not follow that he has the answer to his own question: What is art. I offer this selection to you merely as a historically important (and as a somewhat influential) view of the fundamental nature and standards of art.

Tolstoy's position can be summarized by saying that for him art is the communication of emotion. As he proposes it: "Art begins when one person with the object of joining another or others to himself in one and the same feeling, expresses that feeling by certain external indications." He points out that the feelings with which the artist "infects" others may be of all sorts, but "If only the spectators or auditors are infected by the feelings which the author has felt, it is art." Tolstoy concludes by listing the three conditions upon which the degree of this infectiousness depends: the individuality of the artist's emotion, the clarity with which it is communicated, the sincerity with which it is felt by him.

---

[1] I am here reiterating some observations made in the introduction to this section, especially my concluding remarks. I am also aware of the argument that natural beauties can be considered works of art produced by a Divine Artist. This argument may have religious persuasiveness, but it is too purely speculative to permit aesthetic investigation of a helpful sort.

What Is Art?

The activity of art is based on the fact that a man receiving through his sense of hearing or sight another man's expression of feeling is capable of experiencing the emotion which moved the man who expressed it. To take the simplest example: one man laughs and another who hears becomes merry, or a man weeps and another who hears feels sorrow. A man is excited or irritated, and another man seeing him is brought to a similar state of mind. By his movements or by the sounds of his voice a man expresses courage and determination or sadness and calmness, and this state of mind passes on to others. A man suffers, manifesting his sufferings by groans and spasms, and this suffering transmits itself to other people; a man expresses his feelings of admiration, devotion, fear, respect, or love, to certain objects, persons, or phenomena, and others are infected by the same feelings of admiration, devotion, fear, respect, or love, to the same objects, persons, or phenomena.

Art begins when one person with the object of joining another or others to himself in one and the same feeling expresses that feeling by certain external indications. To take the simplest example: a boy having experienced, let us say, fear on encountering a wolf, relates that encounter; and in order to evoke in others the feeling he has experienced, describes himself, his condition before the encounter, the surroundings, the wood, his own lightheartedness, and then the wolf's appearance, its movements, the distance between himself and the wolf, and so forth. All this—if only the boy when telling the story again experiences the feelings he had lived through, and infects the hearers and compels them to feel what he had experienced—is art. Even if the boy had not seen a wolf but had frequently been afraid of one, and if wishing to evoke in others the fear he had felt, he invented an encounter with a wolf and recounted it so as to make his hearers share the feelings he experienced when he feared the wolf, that also would be art. And just in the same way it is art if a man, having experienced either the fear of suffering or the attraction of enjoyment (whether in reality or in imagination), expresses these feelings on canvas or in marble so that others are infected by them. And it is also art if a man feels, or imagines to himself, feelings of delight, gladness, sorrow, despair, courage, or despondency, and the transition from one to another of these feelings, and expresses them by sounds so that the hearers are infected by them and experience them as they were experienced by the composer.

The feelings with which the artist infects others may be most various —very strong or very weak, very important or very insignificant, very bad or very good: feelings of love of one's country, self-devotion and submission to fate or to God expressed in a drama, raptures of lovers

Excerpt from *What Is Art?* translated by A. Maude.

described in a novel, feelings of voluptuousness expressed in a picture, courage expressed in a triumphal march, merriment evoked by a dance, humor evoked by a funny story, the feeling of quietness transmitted by an evening landscape or by a lullaby, or the feeling of admiration evoked by a beautiful arabesque—it is all art.

If only the spectators or auditors are infected by the feelings which the author has felt, it is art.

To evoke in oneself a feeling one has once experienced and having
50 *evoked it in oneself then by means of movements, lines, colors, sounds, or forms expressed in words, so to transmit that feeling that others experience the same feeling—this is the activity of art.*

Art is a human activity consisting in this, that one man consciously by means of certain external signs, hands on to others feelings he has lived through, and that others are infected by these feelings and also experience them.

Art is not, as the metaphysicians say, the manifestation of some mysterious Idea of beauty or God; it is not, as the aesthetic physiologists say, a game in which man lets off his excess of stored-up energy; it
60 is not the expression of man's emotions by external signs; it is not the production of pleasing objects; and, above all, it is not pleasure; but it is a means of union among men joining them together in the same feelings, and indispensable for the life and progress toward well-being of individuals and of humanity.

There is one indubitable sign distinguishing real art from its counterfeit—namely, the infectiousness of art. If a man without exercising effort and without altering his standpoint, on reading, hearing, or seeing another man's work experiences a mental condition which unites him with that man and with others who are also affected by that work, then
70 the object evoking that condition is a work of art.

And not only is infection a sure sign of art, but the degree of infectiousness is also the sole measure of excellence in art.

The stronger the infection, the better is the art, as art, speaking of it now apart from its subject-matter—that is, not considering the value of the feelings it transmits.

And the degree of the infectiousness of art depends on three conditions:

(1) On the greater or lesser individuality of the feeling transmitted;
(2) on the greater or lesser clearness with which the feeling is trans-
80 mitted; (3) on the sincerity of the artist, that is, on the greater or lesser force with which the artist himself feels the emotion he transmits.

FOR STUDY AND DISCUSSION

1. Before he defines what art *is,* Tolstoy is concerned to determine what art is *based on.* What is it based on for him?

2. How does his use of the boy and the wolf example conform to the basis of art which he has asserted? How does it imply that this basis is a very broad one?

3. In lines 49–56 Tolstoy proceeds to give his definition of art. Examine this definition with care. What aspects of art does it emphasize? Do you agree with this definition? Can you think of any aspects of art that are not accounted for in Tolstoy's view of art?

4. Shortly after giving his definition of art, Tolstoy makes this statement: ". . . [art] is a means of union among men, joining them together in the same feelings, and indispensable for the life and progress toward well-being of individuals and of humanity." Do you see a potential danger in this view of the function of art?

5. He concludes with renewed insistence on "infectiousness" as the criterion of evaluating art, and lists three conditions that determine the degree of infectiousness in given cases. Can you think of instances where one or more of these conditions would hardly apply in judging the quality of works of art?

George Santayana

[1863–1952]

George Santayana is one of the most enticing writers of this century. By background, he is both Spanish and American. He is also both Catholic and anti-Catholic (a paradox suggested by a typical phrase of his that Catholicism is "that splendid error"). He is, in philosophy, an avowed materialist,[1] yet no philosopher has paid greater tribute to the symbolic insights which both religion and the arts contribute to our human situation.

In general, Santayana is distrustful of the presumptions of the human intellect to soar beyond given experience. This distrust permeates the following sonnet he once wrote:

On the Death of a Metaphysician [2]

Unhappy dreamer, who outwinged in flight
The pleasant region of the things I love,
And soared beyond the sunshine, and above
The golden cornfields and the dear and bright
Warmth of the hearth,—blasphemer of delight,   5
Was your proud bosom not at peace with Jove,
That you sought, thankless for his guarded grove,
The empty horror of abysmal night?
Ah, the thin air is cold above the moon!
I stood and saw you fall, befooled in death,   10
As, in your numbèd spirit's fatal swoon,
You cried you were a god, or were to be;
I heard with feeble moan your boastful breath
Bubble from the depths of the Icarian sea.[3]

For Santayana, then, the world of values (of which beauty is one) is the world as we experience it, not the world as we intellectualize it. This ap-

---

[1] *materialist:* a philosopher who believes that the fundamental nature of the universe is material (or physical) rather than spiritual (or mental).

[2] metaphysician: In philosophy, a metaphysician is one who attempts to identify ultimate reality: thus Plato, as a metaphysician, "found" ultimate reality in the trinity of Truth, Beauty, and Goodness—of which Goodness was the godhead.

[3] The allusion in the last line to Icarus is from Greek mythology. On wings of wax, fashioned by his father (Daedalus), Icarus flew too close to the sun. His wings melted and he dropped to his death in the sea below. In literature Icarus has become a symbol of one who, bravely but foolishly, endeavors to fly upward beyond his natural limitations.

proach is emphasized in the following selection. He expresses the point at
the beginning of the second paragraph: "Values spring from the immediate
and inexplicable reaction of vital impulse, and from the irrational part of
our nature." He goes on to distinguish between aesthetic and moral judgments. Largely on the basis of the distinction, Santayana concludes that
the appreciation of beauty is part of our "holiday life," that aesthetics is
solely concerned with enjoyment, and that beauty is thereby best understood as pleasure objectified (as, for example, in the arts).

Art as Pleasure

It would be easy to find a definition of *beauty* that should give in a
few words a telling paraphrase of the word. We know on excellent
authority that beauty is truth, that it is the expression of the ideal, the
symbol of divine perfection, and the sensible manifestation of the good.
A litany of these titles of honor might easily be compiled and repeated
in praise of our divinity. Such phrases stimulate thought and give us a
momentary pleasure, but they hardly bring any permanent enlighten-
ment. A definition that should really define must be nothing less than the
exposition of the origin, place, and elements of beauty as an object of
10 human experience. We must learn from it, as far as possible, why, when,
and how beauty appears, what conditions an object must fulfill to be
beautiful, what elements of our nature make us sensible of beauty, and
what the relation is between the constitution of the object and the excitement of our susceptibility. Nothing less will really define beauty or
make us understand what aesthetic appreciation is. . . .

Values spring from the immediate and inexplicable reaction of vital
impulse, and from the irrational part of our nature. The rational part is
by its essence relative; it leads us from data to conclusions, or from
parts to wholes; it never furnishes the data with which it works. If any
20 preference or precept were declared to be ultimate and primitive, it
would thereby be declared to be irrational, since mediation, inference,
and synthesis are the essence of rationality. The ideal of rationality is
itself as arbitrary, as much dependent on the needs of a finite organisa-
tion, as any other ideal. Only as ultimately securing tranquillity of mind,
which the philosopher instinctively pursues, has it for him any necessity.
In spite of the verbal propriety of saying that reason demands rationality, what really demands rationality, what makes it a good and indispensable thing and gives it all its authority, is not its own nature, but our
need of it both in safe and economical action and in the pleasures of
30 comprehension.

It is evident that beauty is a species of value, and what we have said
of value in general applies to this particular kind. . . .

Excerpt from *The Sense of Beauty*.

The relation between aesthetic and moral judgments, between the spheres of the beautiful and the good, is close, but the distinction between them is important. One factor of this distinction is that while aesthetic judgments are mainly positive, that is, perceptions of good, moral judgments are mainly and fundamentally negative, or perceptions of evil. Another factor of the distinction is that whereas, in the perception of beauty, our judgment is necessarily intrinsic and based on the

40 character of the immediate experience, and never consciously on the idea of an eventual utility in the object, judgments about moral worth, on the contrary, are always based, when they are positive, upon the consciousness of benefits probably involved. . . .

weird part of story

The appreciation of beauty and its embodiment in the arts are activities which belong to our holiday life, when we are redeemed for the moment from the shadow of evil and the slavery to fear, and are following the bent of our nature where it chooses to lead us. The values, then, with which we here deal are positive; they were negative in the sphere of morality. The ugly is hardly an exception, because it is not the

50 cause of any real pain. In itself it is rather a source of amusement. If its suggestions are vitally repulsive, its presence becomes a real evil toward which we assume a practical and moral attitude. And, correspondingly, the pleasant is never, as we have seen, the object of a truly moral injunction. . . .

Definition of Beauty

We have now reached our definition of beauty, which, in the terms of our successive analysis and narrowing of the conception, is value positive, intrinsic, and objectified. Or, in less technical language, Beauty is pleasure regarded as the quality of a thing.

This definition is intended to sum up a variety of distinctions and

60 identifications which should perhaps be here more explicitly set down. Beauty is a value; that is, it is not a perception of a matter of fact or of a relation: it is an emotion, an affection of our volitional and appreciative nature. An object cannot be beautiful if it can give pleasure to nobody: a beauty to which all men were forever indifferent is a contradiction in terms.

In the second place, this value is positive, it is the sense of the presence of something good, or (in the case of ugliness) of its absence. It is never the perception of a positive evil, it is never a negative value. That we are endowed with the sense of beauty is a pure gain which

70 brings no evil with it. When the ugly ceases to be amusing or merely uninteresting and becomes disgusting, it becomes indeed a positive evil: but a moral and practical, not an aesthetic one. In aesthetics that saying is true—often so disingenuous in ethics—that evil is nothing but the absence of good: for even the tedium and vulgarity of an existence without beauty is not itself ugly so much as lamentable and degrading. The absence of aesthetic goods is a moral evil: the aesthetic evil is

merely relative, and means less of aesthetic good than was expected at the place and time. No form in itself gives pain, although some forms give pain by causing a shock of surprise even when they are really beautiful: as if a mother found a fine bull pup in her child's cradle, when her pain would not be aesthetic in its nature.

80

Further, this pleasure must not be in the consequence of the utility of the object or event, but in its immediate perception; in other words, beauty is an ultimate good, something that gives satisfaction to a natural function, to some fundamental need or capacity of our minds. Beauty is therefore a positive value that is intrinsic; it is a pleasure. These two circumstances sufficiently separate the sphere of aesthetics from that of ethics. Moral values are generally negative, and always remote. Morality has to do with the avoidance of evil and the pursuit of good: aesthetics only with enjoyment. . . .

90

2ⁿᵈ Definition

Thus beauty is constituted by the objectification of pleasure. It is pleasure objectified. *-Pleasure comes with experience*

- Beauty isn't the Painting but the pleasure we get from the painting.

FOR STUDY AND DISCUSSION

1. In lines 16–17, Santayana says: "Values spring from the immediate and inexplicable reaction of vital impulse, and from the irrational part of our nature." It is important, here, that you not misunderstand the word *irrational*. Santayana means with the word to designate an area—the area of values—which is *nonrational* in its nature. How does the remainder of the paragraph support this interpretation?

2. Moral and aesthetic responses are both "value-experiences" in the sense just discussed, but Santayana is at pains to distinguish between the two. What are the two points of distinction he makes?

3. Santayana elaborates upon his asserted distinction between morality and aesthetics. Can you offer further arguments, coupled with examples, from your own experiences and observations which either support or oppose his position?

4. Tolstoy, I believe, would not agree with Santayana's definition of beauty or his supporting arguments. Why not?

5. Reread the last two sentences carefully. The word *objectification* refers to our tendency to ascribe the quality of a sensation (which, by definition, is subjective) to the object which produces the sensation: in short, to objectify the quality. Thus, when eating a piece of candy, we may experience the sensation of sweetness. If we do, we will then objectify our sensation and call the candy "sweet" even though the candy, in itself, is only a mixture of ingredients capable of evoking the quality (sweetness) of this particular sensation. In the light of this explanation what does Santayana mean when he asserts that beauty is pleasure objectified?

John Dewey

[1859–1952]

John Dewey has been the most influential American philosopher of modern times. The impact of his thoughts on the nature of democracy, society, and education (as well as his professional philosophical studies) is so great that many who have never heard of Dewey—much less read his works—reflect in their opinions and behavior the impress of his conclusions.

In the tradition of William James (page 14), Dewey is essentially a pragmatist. He is interested in ideas not so much "for their own sake" but in ideas as stimuli and guides to action in the various fields of human endeavor. In an early volume, How We Think, Dewey insists that constructive thinking is essentially the solving of specific problems in any given area of concern and that this area is in no sense limited to the "academic" or "intellectual." To him, our minds are seen as instruments which can further the growth and satisfaction of life. We are engaged in a ceaseless (but rewarding) struggle to conquer the manifold obstacles of human experience —whether these be to learn to drive a car, to cook, to garden, to promote a business, to prepare a classroom paper, to create a work of art.

In aesthetics Dewey's emphasis is again on activity. He distrusts the word beauty (especially when it is capitalized) because, he believes, it suggests a static finality which too often draws attention away from the dynamic interplay between the artist, his formative material, and a potentially responsive audience. For Dewey the artist's problem is to control his medium with a success that fulfills the vision which prompted his undertaking. The complementary problem for an audience is the challenge to re-create imaginatively the artist's experience—to share that experience vicariously with the artist.

The title of Dewey's major work on aesthetics (Art As Experience) is suggestive of much of this background information, and the following excerpt from that volume deals with related concerns. Thus, he begins by asserting that no subject matter is inappropriate to art: "Impulsion beyond all limits that are externally set inheres in the very nature of the artist's work," and that "the interest of an artist is the only limitation placed upon use of material, and this limitation is not restrictive." So, too, "Interest becomes one-sided and morbid only when it ceases to be frank, and becomes sly and furtive—as it doubtless does in much contemporary exploitation of sex." He agrees, in part, with Tolstoy's emphasis on the importance of the sincerity of the artist, but he rejects the merit of art that is solely used for propagandistic purposes. For Dewey, "the undefined pervasive quality of an experience is that which binds together all the defined elements, the objects of which we are focally aware, making them a whole," and "a work of art elicits and accentuates this quality of being a whole and of belonging to the large, all-inclusive whole which is the universe in which we live." He goes on to suggest that the aesthetic experience provides a deeper dimension to reality than our ordinary preoccupations permit, and he concludes, "where egoism is not made the measure of reality and value, we are citizens of this vast world beyond ourselves, and any intense realization of its presence with and in us brings a peculiarly satisfying sense of unity in itself and with ourselves."

The Totality of Art

What subject-matter is appropriate for art? Are there materials inherently fit and others unfit? Or are there none which are common and unclean with respect to artistic treatment? The answer of the arts themselves has been steadily and progressively in the direction of an affirmative answer to the last question.

Impulsion beyond all limits that are externally set inheres in the very nature of the artist's work. It belongs to the very character of the creative mind to reach out and seize any material that stirs it so that the value of that material may be pressed out and become the matter of a
10 new experience. Refusal to acknowledge the boundaries set by convention is the source of frequent denunciations of objects of art as immoral. But one of the functions of art is precisely to sap the moralistic timidity that causes the mind to shy away from some materials and refuse to admit them into the clear and purifying light of perceptive consciousness.

The interest of an artist is the only limitation placed upon use of material, and this limitation is not restrictive. It but states a trait inherent in the work of the artist, the necessity of sincerity; the necessity that he shall not fake and compromise. The universality of art is so far away from denial of the principle of selection by means of vital interest that it
20 depends upon interest. Other artists have other interests, and by their collective work, unembarrassed by fixed and antecedent rule, all aspects and phases of experience are covered. Interest becomes one-sided and morbid only when it ceases to be frank, and becomes sly and furtive—as it doubtless does in much contemporary exploitation of sex. . . .

In his desire to restrict the material of art to themes drawn from the life of the common man, factory worker and especially peasant, Tolstoy paints a picture of the conventional restrictions that is out of perspective. But there is truth enough in it to serve as illustration of one all-important characteristic of art: Whatever narrows the boundaries of the
30 material fit to be used in art hems in also the artistic sincerity of the individual artist. It does not give fair play and outlet to his vital interest. It forces his perceptions into channels previously worn into ruts and

Excerpt from *Art as Experience.*

clips the wings of his imagination. I think the idea that there is a moral obligation on an artist to deal with "proletarian" material, or with any material on the basis of its bearing on proletarian fortune and destiny is an effort to return to a position that art has historically outgrown. But as far as proletarian interest marks a new direction of attention and involves observation of materials previously passed over, it will certainly call into activity persons who were not moved to expression by former
40 materials, and will disclose and thus help break down boundaries of which they were not previously aware. I am somewhat skeptical about Shakespeare's alleged personal aristocratic bias. I fancy that his limitation was conventional, familiar, and therefore congenial to pit as well as to stalls. But whatever its source, it limited his "universality." . . .

About every explicit and focal object there is a recession into the implicit which is not intellectually grasped. In reflection we call it dim and vague. But in the original experience it is not identified as the vague. It is a function of the whole situation, and not an element in it, as it would have to be in order to be apprehended as vague. At twilight, dusk
50 is a delightful quality of the whole world. It is its appropriate manifestation. It becomes a specialized and obnoxious trait only when it prevents distinct perception of some particular thing we desire to discern.

The undefined pervasive quality of an experience is that which binds together all the defined elements, the objects of which we are focally aware, making them a whole. The best evidence that such is the case is our constant sense of things as belonging or not belonging, of relevancy, a sense of which is immediate. It cannot be a product of reflection, even though it requires reflection to find out whether some particular consideration is pertinent to what we are doing or thinking. For unless the
60 sense were immediate, we should have no guide to our reflection. The sense of an extensive and underlying whole is the context of every experience, and it is the essence of sanity. For the mad, the insane, thing to us is that which is torn from the common context and which stands alone and isolated, as anything must which occurs in a world totally different from ours. Without an indeterminate and undetermined setting, the material of any experience is incoherent.

A work of art elicits and accentuates this quality of being a whole and of belonging to the large, all-inclusive whole which is the universe in which we live. This fact, I think, is the explanation of that feeling of
70 exquisite intelligibility and clarity we have in the presence of an object that is experienced with aesthetic intensity. It explains also the religious feeling that accompanies intense aesthetic perception. We are, as it were, introduced into a world beyond this world which is nevertheless the deeper reality of the world in which we live in our ordinary experiences. We are carried out beyond ourselves to find ourselves. I can see no psychological ground for such properties of an experience save that,

somehow, the work of art operates to deepen and to raise to great clarity that sense of an enveloping undefined whole that accompanies every normal experience. This whole is then felt as an expansion of ourselves.

80 For only one frustrated in a particular object of desire upon which he had staked himself, like Macbeth, finds that life is a tale told by an idiot, full of sound and fury, signifying nothing. Where egotism is not made the measure of reality and value, we are citizens of this vast world beyond ourselves, and any intense realization of its presence with and in us brings a peculiarly satisfying sense of unity in itself and with ourselves.

FOR STUDY AND DISCUSSION

1. "What subject-matter is appropriate for art"? Dewey begins with this provocative question. As he points out, it is the very nature of the artist to go beyond all limits "externally set." What does he mean by limits "externally set"?

2. He then states that "The interest of an artist is the only limitation placed upon use of material, and this limitation is not restrictive." Yet he qualifies this statement somewhat. What qualification does he make?

3. To what extent does he both agree and disagree with Tolstoy's emphasis on "sincerity" and the "moral obligation" of art?

4. In the concluding paragraphs of this selection, Dewey is examining the more complex contributions of art. Notice, for example, his illustration of "dusk." Is it not true that the same dusk which is an annoyance and a hazard to the motorist hurrying home from his job can also be "a delightful quality of the whole world" when seen from a different perspective? Can you suggest other comparable examples?

5. Wordsworth wrote, "The world is too much with us . . ." (page 118). Whether you recall the poem or not, in what sense do you think he was using the word *world?* How is this sentence of Dewey's about the aesthetic experience in harmony with Wordsworth's suggestion and with the example of "dusk": "We are . . . introduced into a world which is nevertheless the deeper reality of the world in which we live in our ordinary experiences"?

FICTION

The Birthmark

NATHANIEL HAWTHORNE
[1804–1864]

*I remind you that Chekhov's "The Bet," the first story in the section on
Truth, showed an intermingling of values: in that instance, an intermingling
of comments on both truth and goodness. In Hawthorne's "The Birthmark"
all three values—truth, goodness, and beauty—are intimately related.*

*Hawthorne chooses to orient his story around a specific instance of beauty
in the person of Georgiana and the reactions to her beauty of such people
as other women, former suitors, her husband, her husband's assistant, and
herself. Yet, as the story proceeds, it becomes increasingly evident that the
"defect" in Georgiana's beauty, her birthmark, is symbolic of the intrinsic
defects in all human nature: whether they be defects of beauty or of truth
or of goodness.*

*"The Birthmark" is both a tale to be read for entertainment and an
allegory to be interpreted in terms of the comment it is making about the
human condition. Hawthorne, himself, encourages this approach when he
speaks of the "impressive moral" which the tale illuminates.*

In the latter part of the last century there lived a man of science, an
eminent proficient in every branch of natural philosophy, who not long before
our story opens had made experience of a spiritual affinity more attractive
than any chemical one. He had left his laboratory to the care of an assistant,
cleared his fine countenance from the furnace smoke, washed the stain of
acids from his fingers, and persuaded a beautiful woman to become his wife.
In those days when the comparatively recent discovery of electricity and other
kindred mysteries of Nature seemed to open paths into the region of miracle,
it was not unusual for the love of science to rival the love of woman in its
depth and absorbing energy. The higher intellect, the imagination, the spirit,
and even the heart might all find their congenial ailment in pursuits which, as
some of their ardent votaries believed, would ascend from one step of powerful intelligence to another, until the philosopher should lay his hand on the
secret of creative force and perhaps make new worlds for himself. We know
not whether Aylmer possessed this degree of faith in man's ultimate control
over Nature. He had devoted himself, however, too unreservedly to scientific
studies ever to be weaned from them by any second passion. His love for his
young wife might prove the stronger of the two; but it could only be by
intertwining itself with his love of science, and uniting the strength of the
latter to his own.

Such a union accordingly took place, and was attended with truly remarkable consequences and a deeply impressive moral. One day, very soon after

their marriage, Aylmer sat gazing at his wife with a trouble in his countenance that grew stronger as he spoke.

"Georgiana," said he, "has it never occurred to you that the mark upon your cheek might be removed?"

"No, indeed," said she, smiling; but perceiving the seriousness of his manner, she blushed deeply. "To tell you the truth, it has been so often called a charm that I was simple enough to imagine it might be so."

"Ah, upon another face perhaps it might," replied her husband; "but never on yours. No, dearest Georgiana, you came so nearly perfect from the hand of Nature that this slightest possible defect, which we hesitate whether to term a defect or a beauty, shocks me, as being the visible mark of earthly imperfection."

"Shocks you, my husband!" cried Georgiana, deeply hurt; at first reddening with momentary anger, but then bursting into tears. "Then why did you take me from my mother's side? You cannot love what shocks you!"

To explain this conversation it must be mentioned that in the center of Georgiana's left cheek there was a singular mark, deeply interwoven, as it were, with the texture and substance of her face. In the usual state of her complexion—a healthy though delicate bloom—the mark wore a tint of deeper crimson, which imperfectly defined its shape amid the surrounding rosiness. When she blushed it gradually became more indistinct, and finally vanished amid the triumphant rush of blood that bathed the whole cheek with its brilliant glow. But if any shifting motion caused her to turn pale there was the mark again, a crimson stain upon the snow, in what Aylmer sometimes deemed an almost fearful distinctness. Its shape bore not a little similarity to the human hand, though of the smallest pygmy size. Georgiana's lovers were wont to say that some fairy at her birth hour had laid her tiny hand upon the infant's cheek, and left this impress there in token of the magic endowments that were to give her such sway over all hearts. Many a desperate swain would have risked life for the privilege of pressing his lips to the mysterious hand. It must not be concealed, however, that the impression wrought by this fairy sign manual varied exceedingly, according to the difference of temperament in the beholders. Some fastidious persons—but they were exclusively of her own sex—affirmed that the bloody hand, as they chose to call it, quite destroyed the effect of Georgiana's beauty and rendered her countenance even hideous. But it would be as reasonable to say that one of those small blue stains which sometimes occur in the purest statuary marble would convert the Eve of Powers to a monster. Masculine observers, if the birthmark did not heighten their admiration, contented themselves with wishing it away, that the world might possess one living specimen of ideal loveliness without the semblance of a flaw. After his marriage—for he thought little or nothing of the matter before—Aylmer discovered that this was the case with himself.

Had she been less beautiful—if Envy's self could have found aught else to sneer at—he might have felt his affection heightened by the prettiness of this mimic hand, now vaguely portrayed, now lost, now stealing forth again and glimmering to and fro with every pulse of emotion that throbbed within her heart; but seeing her otherwise so perfect, he found this one defect grow more and more intolerable with every moment of their united lives. It was the fatal flaw of humanity which Nature, in one shape or another, stamps ineffaceably on all her productions, either to imply that they are temporary and finite, or that their perfection must be wrought by toil and pain. The crimson hand expressed the ineludible gripe in which mortality clutches the highest and purest of earthly mold, degrading them into kindred with the lowest, and even with the very brutes, like whom their visible frames return to dust. In this manner, selecting it as the symbol of his wife's liability to sin, sorrow, decay, and death Aylmer's somber imagination was not long in rendering the birthmark a frightful object, causing him more trouble and horror than ever Georgiana's beauty, whether of soul or sense, had given him delight.

At all the seasons which should have been their happiest, he invariably and without intending it, nay, in spite of a purpose to the contrary, reverted to this one disastrous topic. Trifling as it at first appeared, it so connected itself with innumerable trains of thought and modes of feeling that it became the central point of all. With the morning twilight Aylmer opened his eyes upon his wife's face and recognized the symbol of imperfection; and when they sat together at the evening hearth his eyes wandered stealthily to her cheek, and beheld, flickering with the blaze of the wood fire, the spectral hand that wrote mortality where he would fain have worshiped. Georgiana soon learned to shudder at his gaze. It needed but a glance with the peculiar expression that his face often wore to change the roses of her cheek into a deathlike paleness, amid which the crimson hand was brought strongly out, like a bas-relief of ruby on the whitest marble.

Late one night when the lights were growing dim, so as hardly to betray the stain on the poor wife's cheek, she herself, for the first time, voluntarily took up the subject.

"Do you remember, my dear Aylmer," said she, with a feeble attempt at a smile, "have you any recollection of a dream last night about this odious hand?"

"None! none whatever!" replied Aylmer, starting; but then he added, in a dry, cold tone, affected for the sake of concealing the real depth of his emotion, "I might well dream of it; for before I fell asleep it had taken a pretty firm hold of my fancy."

"And you did dream of it!" continued Georgiana, hastily; for she dreaded lest a gush of tears should interrupt what she had to say. "A terrible dream! I wonder that you can forget it. Is it possible to forget this one expression?—'It is in her heart now; we must have it out!' Reflect, my husband; for by all means I would have you recall that dream."

The mind is in a sad state when Sleep, the all-involving, cannot confine her specters within the dim region of her sway, but suffers them to break forth, affrighting this actual life with secrets that perchance belong to a deeper one. Aylmer now remembered his dream. He had fancied himself with his servant Aminadab, attempting an operation for the removal of the birthmark; but the deeper went the knife, the deeper sank the hand, until at length its tiny grasp appeared to have caught hold of Georgiana's heart; whence, however, her husband was inexorably resolved to cut or wrench it away.

When the dream had shaped itself perfectly in his memory, Aylmer sat in his wife's presence with a guilty feeling. Truth often finds its way to the mind close muffled in robes of sleep, and then speaks with uncompromising directness of matters in regard to which we practice an unconscious self-deception during our waking moments. Until now he had not been aware of the tyrannizing influence acquired by one idea over his mind, and of the lengths which he might find in his heart to go for the sake of giving himself peace.

"Aylmer," resumed Georgiana, solemnly, "I know not what may be the cost to both of us to rid me of this fatal birthmark. Perhaps its removal may cause cureless deformity; or it may be the stain goes as deep as life itself. Again: do we know that there is a possibility, on any terms, of unclasping the firm gripe of this little hand which was laid upon me before I came into the world?"

"Dearest Georgiana, I have spent much thought upon the subject," hastily interrupted Aylmer. "I am convinced of the perfect practicability of its removal."

"If there be the remotest possibility of it," continued Georgiana, "let the attempt be made at whatever risk. Danger is nothing to me; for life, while this hateful mark makes me the object of your horror and disgust—life is a burden which I would fling down with joy. Either remove this dreadful hand, or take my wretched life! You have deep science. All the world bears witness of it. You have achieved great wonders. Cannot you remove this little, little mark, which I cover with the tips of two small fingers? Is this beyond your power, for the sake of your own peace, and to save your poor wife from madness?"

"Noblest, dearest, tenderest wife," cried Aylmer, rapturously, "doubt not my power. I have already given this matter the deepest thought—thought which might almost have enlightened me to create a being less perfect than yourself. Georgiana, you have led me deeper than ever into the heart of science. I feel myself fully competent to render this dear cheek as faultless as its fellow; and then, most beloved, what will be my triumph when I shall have corrected what Nature left imperfect in her fairest work! Even Pygmalion, when his sculptured woman assumed life, felt not greater ecstasy than mine will be."

"It is resolved, then," said Georgiana, faintly smiling. "And, Aylmer, spare me not, though you should find the birthmark take refuge in my heart at last."

Her husband tenderly kissed her cheek—her right cheek—not that which bore the impress of the crimson hand.

The next day Aylmer apprised his wife of a plan that he had formed whereby he might have opportunity for the intense thought and constant watchfulness which the proposed operation would require; while Georgiana, likewise, would enjoy the perfect repose essential to its success. They were to seclude themselves in the extensive apartments occupied by Aylmer as a laboratory, and where, during his toilsome youth, he had made discoveries in the elemental powers of Nature that had roused the admiration of all the learned societies in Europe. Seated calmly in this laboratory, the pale philosopher had investigated the secrets of the highest cloud region and of the profoundest mines; he had satisfied himself of the causes that kindled and kept alive the fires of the volcano; and had explained the mysteries of fountains, and how it is that they gush forth, some so bright and pure, and others with such rich medicinal virtues, from the dark bosom of the earth. Here, too, at an earlier period, he had studied the wonders of the human frame, and attempted to fathom the very process by which Nature assimilates all her precious influences from earth and air, and from the spiritual world, to create and foster man, her masterpiece. The latter pursuit, however, Aylmer had long laid aside in unwilling recognition of the truth—against which all seekers sooner or later stumble—that our great creative Mother, while she amuses us with apparently working in the broadest sunshine, is yet severely careful to keep her own secrets, and, in spite of her pretended openness, shows us nothing but results. She permits us, indeed, to mar, but seldom to mend, and, like a jealous patentee, on no account to make. Now, however, Aylmer resumed these half-forgotten investigations; not, of course, with such hopes or wishes as first suggested them; but because they involved much physiological truth and lay in the path of his proposed scheme for the treatment of Georgiana.

As he led her over the threshold of the laboratory, Georgiana was cold and tremulous. Aylmer looked cheerfully into her face, with intent to reassure her, but was so startled with the intense glow of the birthmark upon the whiteness of her cheek that he could not restrain a strong convulsive shudder. His wife fainted.

"Aminadab! Aminadab!" shouted Aylmer, stamping violently on the floor.

Forthwith there issued from an inner apartment a man of low stature, but bulky frame, with shaggy hair hanging about his visage, which was grimed with the vapors of the furnace. This personage had been Aylmer's underworker during his whole scientific career, and was admirably fitted for that office by his great mechanical readiness and the skill with which, while incapable of comprehending a single principle, he executed all the details of his master's experiments. With his vast strength, his shaggy hair, his smoky aspect, and the indescribable earthiness that incrusted him, he seemed to represent man's physical nature; while Aylmer's slender figure and pale, intellectual face, were no less apt a type of the spiritual element.

"Throw open the door of the boudoir, Aminadab," said Aylmer, "and burn a pastille."

"Yes, master," answered Aminadab, looking intently at the lifeless form of

Georgiana; and then he muttered to himself, "If she were my wife, I'd never part with that birthmark."

When Georgiana recovered consciousness she found herself breathing an atmosphere of penetrating fragrance, the gentle potency of which had recalled her from her deathlike faintness. The scene around her looked like enchantment. Aylmer had converted those smoky, dingy, somber rooms, where he had spent his brightest years in recondite pursuits, into a series of beautiful apartments not unfit to be the secluded abode of a lovely woman. The walls were hung with gorgeous curtains, which imparted the combination of grandeur and grace that no other species of adornment can achieve; and as they fell from the ceiling to the floor, their rich and ponderous folds, concealing all angles and straight lines, appeared to shut in the scene from infinite space. For aught Georgiana knew, it might be a pavilion among the clouds. And Aylmer, excluding the sunshine, which would have interfered with his chemical processes, had supplied its place with perfumed lamps, emitting flames of various hue, but all uniting in a soft, empurpled radiance. He now knelt by his wife's side, watching her earnestly, but without alarm; for he was confident in his science, and felt that he could draw a magic circle round her within which no evil might intrude.

"Where am I? Ah, I remember," said Georgiana, faintly; and she placed her hand over her cheek to hide the terrible mark from her husband's eyes.

"Fear not, dearest!" exclaimed he. "Do not shrink from me! Believe me, Georgiana, I even rejoice in this single imperfection, since it will be such a rapture to remove it."

"Oh, spare me!" sadly replied his wife. "Pray do not look at it again. I never can forget that convulsive shudder."

In order to soothe Georgiana, and, as it were, to release her mind from the burden of actual things, Aylmer now put in practice some of the light and playful secrets which science had taught him among its profounder lore. Airy figures, absolutely bodiless ideas, and forms of unsubstantial beauty came and danced before her, imprinting their momentary footsteps on beams of light. Though she had some indistinct idea of the method of these optical phenomena, still the illusion was almost perfect enough to warrant the belief that her husband possessed sway over the spiritual world. Then again, when she felt a wish to look forth from her seclusion, immediately, as if her thoughts were answered, the procession of external existence flitted across a screen. The scenery and the figures of actual life were perfectly represented, but with that bewitching, yet indescribable difference which always makes a picture, an image, or a shadow so much more attractive than the original. When wearied of this, Aylmer bade her cast her eyes upon a vessel containing a quantity of earth. She did so, with little interest at first; but was soon startled to perceive the germ of a plant shooting upward from the soil. Then came the slender stalk; the leaves gradually unfolded themselves; and amid them was a perfect and lovely flower.

"It is magical!" cried Georgiana. "I dare not touch it."

"Nay, pluck it," answered Aylmer—"pluck it, and inhale its brief perfume while you may. The flower will wither in a few moments and leave nothing save its brown seed vessels; but thence may be perpetuated a race as ephemeral as itself."

But Georgiana had no sooner touched the flower than the whole plant suffered a blight, its leaves turning coal-black as if by the agency of fire.

"There was too powerful a stimulus," said Aylmer, thoughtfully.

To make up for this abortive experiment, he proposed to take her portrait by a scientific process of his own invention. It was to be effected by rays of light striking upon a polished plate of metal. Georgiana assented; but, on looking at the result, was affrighted to find the features of the portrait blurred and indefinable; while the minute figure of a hand appeared where the cheek should have been. Aylmer snatched the metallic plate and threw it into a jar of corrosive acid.

Soon, however, he forgot these mortifying failures. In the intervals of study and chemical experiment he came to her flushed and exhausted, but seemed invigorated by her presence, and spoke in glowing language of the resources of his art. He gave a history of the long dynasty of the alchemists, who spent so many ages in quest of the universal solvent by which the golden principle might be elicited from all things vile and base. Aylmer appeared to believe that, by the plainest scientific logic, it was altogether within the limits of possibility to discover this long-sought medium; "but," he added, "a philosopher who should go deep enough to acquire the power would attain too lofty a wisdom to stoop to the exercise of it." Not less singular were his opinions in regard to the *elixir vitae*. He more than intimated that it was at his option to concoct a liquor that should prolong life for years, perhaps interminably; but that it would produce a discord in Nature which all the world, and chiefly the quaffer of the immortal nostrum, would find cause to curse.

"Aylmer, are you in earnest?" asked Georgiana, looking at him with amazement and fear. "It is terrible to possess such power, or even to dream of possessing it."

"Oh, do not tremble, my love," said her husband. "I would not wrong either you or myself by working such inharmonious effects upon our lives; but I would have you consider how trifling, in comparison, is the skill requisite to remove this little hand."

At the mention of the birthmark, Georgiana, as usual, shrank as if a red-hot iron had touched her cheek.

Again Aylmer applied himself to his labors. She could hear his voice in the distant furnace room giving directions to Aminadab, whose harsh, uncouth, misshapen tones were audible in response, more like the grunt or growl of a brute than human speech. After hours of absence, Aylmer reappeared and proposed that she should now examine his cabinet of chemical products and natural treasures of the earth. Among the former he showed her a small vial, in which, he remarked, was contained a gentle yet most powerful fragrance, capable of impregnating all the breezes that blow across a kingdom. They were of inestimable value, the contents of that little vial; and, as he said so, he threw some of the perfume into the air and filled the room with piercing and invigorating delight.

"And what is this?" asked Georgiana, pointing to a small crystal globe containing a gold-colored liquid. "It is so beautiful to the eyes that I could imagine it the elixir of life."

"In one sense it is," replied Aylmer; "or, rather, the elixir of immortality. It is the most precious poison that ever was concocted in this world. By its aid I could apportion the lifetime of any mortal at whom you might point your finger. The strength of the dose would determine whether he were to linger out years, or drop dead in the midst of a breath. No king on his guarded throne could keep his life if I, in my private station, should deem that the welfare of millions justified me in depriving him of it."

"Why do you keep such a terrific drug?" inquired Georgiana in horror.

"Do not mistrust me, dearest," said her husband, smiling; "its virtuous potency is yet greater than its harmful one. But see! here is a powerful cosmetic. With a few drops of this in a vase of water, freckles may be washed away as easily as the hands are cleansed. A stronger infusion would take the blood out of the cheek, and leave the rosiest beauty a pale ghost."

"Is it with this lotion that you intend to bathe my cheek?" asked Georgiana, anxiously.

"Oh, no," hastily replied her husband; "this is merely superficial. Your case demands a remedy that shall go deeper."

In his interviews with Georgiana, Aylmer generally made minute inquiries as to her sensations and whether the confinement of the rooms and the temperature of the atmosphere agreed with her. These questions had such a particular drift that Georgiana began to conjecture that she was already subjected to certain physical influences, either breathed in with the fragrant air or taken with her food. She fancied likewise, but it might be altogether fancy, that there was a stirring up of her system—a strange, indefinite sensation creeping through her veins, and tingling, half painfully, half pleasurably, at her heart. Still, whenever she dared to look into the mirror, there she beheld herself pale as a white rose and with the crimson birthmark stamped upon her cheek. Not even Aylmer now hated it so much as she.

To dispel the tedium of the hours which her husband found it necessary to devote to the processes of combination and analysis, Georgiana turned over the volumes of his scientific library. In many dark old tomes she met with chapters full of romance and poetry. They were works of philosophers of the middle ages, such as Albertus Magnus, Cornelius Agrippa, Paracelsus, and the famous friar who created the prophetic Brazen Head. All these antique naturalists stood in advance of their centuries, yet were imbued with some of their credulity, and therefore were believed, and perhaps imagined themselves to have acquired from the investigation of Nature a power above Nature, and from physics a sway over the spiritual world. Hardly less curious and imaginative were the early volumes of the *Transactions of the Royal Society* in which the members, knowing little of the limits of natural possibility, were continually recording wonders or proposing methods whereby wonders might be wrought.

But to Georgiana the most engrossing volume was a large folio from her husband's own hand, in which he recorded every experiment of his scientific career, its original aim, the methods adopted for its development, and its final success or failure, with the circumstances to which either event was attributable. The book, in truth, was both the history and emblem of his ardent, ambitious, imaginative, yet practical and laborious life. He handled physical details as if there were nothing beyond them; yet spiritualized them all, and redeemed himself from materialism by his strong and eager aspiration toward the infinite. In his grasp the veriest clod of earth assumed a soul. Georgiana, as she read, reverenced Aylmer and loved him more profoundly than ever, but with a less entire dependence on his judgment than heretofore. Much as he had accomplished, she could not but observe that his most splendid successes were almost invariably failures, if compared with the ideal at which he aimed. His brightest diamonds were the merest pebbles, and felt to be so by himself, in comparison with the inestimable gems which lay hidden beyond his reach. The volume, rich with achievements that had won renown for its author, was yet as melancholy a record as ever mortal hand had penned. It was the sad confession and continual exemplification of the shortcomings of the composite man, the spirit burdened with clay and working in matter, and of the despair that assails the higher nature at finding itself so miserably thwarted by the earthly part. Perhaps every man of genius in whatever sphere might recognize the image of his own experience in Aylmer's journal.

So deeply did these reflections affect Georgiana that she laid her face upon the open volume and burst into tears. In this situation she was found by her husband.

"It is dangerous to read in a sorcerer's books," said he with a smile, though his countenance was uneasy and displeased. "Georgiana, there are pages in that volume which I can scarcely glance over and keep my senses. Take heed lest it prove as detrimental to you."

"It has made me worship you more than ever," said she.

"Ah, wait for this one success," rejoined he, "then worship me if you will. I shall deem myself hardly unworthy of it. But come, I have sought you for the luxury of your voice. Sing to me, dearest."

So she poured out the liquid music of her voice to quench the thirst of his spirit. He then took his leave with a boyish exuberance of gayety, assuring her that her seclusion would endure but a little longer, and that the result was already certain. Scarcely had he departed when Georgiana felt irresistibly impelled to follow him. She had forgotten to inform Aylmer of a symptom which for two or three hours past had begun to excite her attention. It was a sensation in the fatal birthmark, not painful, but which induced a restlessness throughout her system. Hastening after her husband, she intruded for the first time into the laboratory.

The first thing that struck her eye was the furnace, that hot and feverish worker, with the intense glow of its fire, which by the quantities of soot clustered above it seemed to have been burning for ages. There was a distilling apparatus in full operation. Around the room were retorts, tubes, cylinders, crucibles, and other apparatus of chemical research. An electrical machine stood ready for immediate use. The atmosphere felt oppressively close, and was tainted with gaseous odors which had been tormented forth by the processes of science. The severe and homely simplicity of the apartment, with its naked walls and brick pavement, looked strange, accustomed as Georgiana had become to the fantastic elegance of her boudoir. But what chiefly, indeed almost solely, drew her attention, was the aspect of Aylmer himself.

He was pale as death, anxious and absorbed, and hung over the furnace as if it depended upon his utmost watchfulness whether the liquid which it was distilling should be the draught of immortal happiness or misery. How different from the sanguine and joyous mien that he had assumed for Georgiana's encouragement!

"Carefully now, Aminadab; carefully, thou human machine; carefully, thou man of clay!" muttered Aylmer, more to himself than his assistant. "Now, if there be a thought too much or too little, it is all over."

"Ho! ho!" mumbled Aminadab. "Look, master! look!"

Aylmer raised his eyes hastily, and at first reddened, then grew paler than ever, on beholding Georgiana. He rushed toward her and seized her arm with a gripe that left the print of his fingers.

"Why do you come hither? Have you no trust in your husband?" cried he, impetuously. "Would you throw the blight of that fatal birthmark over my labors? It is not well done. Go, prying woman, go!"

"Nay, Aylmer," said Georgiana with the firmness of which she possessed no stinted endowment, "it is not you that have a right to complain. You mistrust your wife; you have concealed the anxiety with which you watch the development of this experiment. Think not so unworthily of me, my husband. Tell me all the risk we run, and fear not that I shall shrink; for my share in it is far less than your own."

"No, no, Georgiana!" said Aylmer, impatiently; "it must not be."

"I submit," replied she calmly. "And, Aylmer, I shall quaff whatever draught you bring me; but it will be on the same principle that would induce me to take a dose of poison if offered by your hand."

"My noble wife," said Aylmer, deeply moved, "I knew not the height and depth of your nature until now. Nothing shall be concealed. Know, then, that this crimson hand, superficial as it seems, has clutched its grasp into your being with a strength of which I had no previous conception. I have already administered agents powerful enough to do aught except to change your entire physical system. Only one thing remains to be tried. If that fail us we are ruined."

"Why did you hesitate to tell me this?" asked she.

"Because, Georgiana," said Aylmer in a low voice, "there is danger."

"Danger? There is but one danger—that this horrible stigma shall be left upon my cheek!" cried Georgiana. "Remove it, remove it, whatever be the cost, or we shall both go mad!"

"Heaven knows your words are too true," said Aylmer, sadly. "And now, dearest, return to your boudoir. In a little while all will be tested."

He conducted her back and took leave of her with a solemn tenderness which spoke far more than his words how much was now at stake. After his departure Georgiana became rapt in musings. She considered the character of Aylmer, and did it completer justice than at any previous moment. Her heart exulted, while it trembled, at his honorable love—so pure and lofty that it would accept nothing less than perfection nor miserably make itself contented with an earthlier nature than he had dreamed of. She felt how much more precious was such a sentiment than that meaner kind which would have borne with the imperfection for her sake and have been guilty of treason to holy love by degrading its perfect ideal to the level of the actual; and with her whole spirit she prayed that, for a single moment, she might satisfy his highest and deepest conception. Longer than one moment she well knew it could not be; for his spirit was ever on the march, ever ascending, and each instant required something that was beyond the scope of the instant before.

The sound of her husband's footsteps aroused her. He bore a crystal goblet containing a liquor colorless as water, but bright enough to be the draught of immortality. Aylmer was pale; but it seemed rather the consequence of a highly wrought state of mind and tension of spirit than of fear or doubt.

"The concoction of the draught has been perfect," said he, in answer to Georgiana's look. "Unless all my science have deceived me, it cannot fail."

"Save on your account, my dearest Aylmer," observed his wife, "I might wish to put off this birthmark of mortality by relinquishing mortality itself in preference to any other mode. Life is but a sad possession to those who have attained precisely the degree of moral advancement at which I stand. Were I weaker and blinder it might be happiness. Were I stronger, it might be endured hopefully. But, being what I find myself, methinks I am of all mortals the most fit to die."

"You are fit for heaven without tasting death!" replied her husband. "But why do you speak of dying? The draught cannot fail. Behold its effect upon this plant."

On the window seat there stood a geranium diseased with yellow blotches, which had overspread all its leaves. Aylmer poured a small quantity of the liquid upon the soil in which it grew. In a little time, when the roots of the plant had taken up the moisture, the unsightly blotches began to be extinguished in a living verdure.

"There needed no proof," said Georgiana, quietly. "Give me the goblet. I joyfully stake all upon your word."

"Drink, then, thou lofty creature!" exclaimed Aylmer with fervid admiration. "There is no taint of imperfection on thy spirit. Thy sensible frame, too, shall soon be all perfect."

She quaffed the liquid and returned the goblet to his hand.

"It is grateful," said she with a placid smile. "Methinks it is like water from a heavenly fountain; for it contains I know not what of unobtrusive fragrance and deliciousness. It allays a feverish thirst that had parched me for many days. Now, dearest, let me sleep. My earthly senses are closing over my spirit like the leaves around the heart of a rose at sunset."

She spoke the last words with a gentle reluctance, as if it required almost more energy than she could command to pronounce the faint and lingering syllables. Scarcely had they loitered through her lips ere she was lost in slumber. Aylmer sat by her side, watching her aspect with the emotions proper to a man the whole value of whose existence was involved in the process now to be tested. Mingled with this mood, however, was the philosophic investigation characteristic of the man of science. Not the minutest symptom escaped him. A heightened flush of the cheek, a slight irregularity of breath, a quiver of the eyelid, a hardly perceptible tremor through the frame —such were the details which, as the moments passed, he wrote down in his folio volume. Intense thought had set its stamp upon every previous page of that volume, but the thoughts of years were all concentrated upon the last.

While thus employed, he failed not to gaze often at the fatal hand, and not without a shudder. Yet once, by a strange and unaccountable impulse, he pressed it with his lips. His spirit recoiled, however, in the very act; and Georgiana, out of the midst of her deep sleep, moved uneasily and murmured as if in remonstrance. Again Aylmer resumed his watch. Nor was it without avail. The crimson hand, which at first had been strongly visible upon the marble paleness of Georgiana's cheek, now grew more faintly outlined. She remained not less pale than ever; but the birthmark, with every breath that came and went, lost somewhat of its former distinctness. Its presence had been awful; its departure was more awful still. Watch the stain of the rainbow fading out the sky, and you will know how the mysterious symbol passed away.

"By Heaven! it is well-nigh gone!" said Aylmer to himself, in almost irrepressible ecstasy. "I can scarcely trace it now. Success! success! And now it is like the faintest rose color. The lightest flush of blood across her cheek would overcome it. But she is so pale!"

He drew aside the window curtain and suffered the light of natural day to fall into the room and rest upon her cheek. At the same time he heard a gross, hoarse chuckle, which he had long known as his servant Aminadab's expression of delight.

"Ah, clod! ah, earthly mass!" cried Aylmer, laughing in a sort of frenzy, "you have served me well! Matter and spirit—earth and heaven—have both done their part in this! Laugh, thing of the senses! You have earned the right to laugh."

These exclamations broke Georgiana's sleep. She slowly unclosed her eyes and gazed into the mirror which her husband had arranged for that purpose. A faint smile flitted over her lips when she recognized how barely perceptible was now that crimson hand which had once blazed forth with such disastrous brilliancy as to scare away all their happiness. But then her eyes sought Aylmer's face with a trouble and anxiety that he could by no means account for.

"My poor Aylmer!" murmured she.

"Poor? Nay, richest, happiest, most favored!" exclaimed he. "My peerless bride, it is successful! You are perfect!"

"My poor Aylmer," she repeated with a more than human tenderness, "you have aimed loftily; you have done nobly. Do not repent that with so high and pure a feeling, you have rejected the best the earth could offer. Aylmer, dearest Aylmer, I am dying!"

Alas! it was too true! The fatal hand had grappled with the mystery of life, and was the bond by which an angelic spirit kept itself in union with a mortal frame. As the last crimson tint of the birthmark—that sole token of human imperfection—faded from her cheek, the parting breath of the now perfect woman passed into the atmosphere, and her soul, lingering a moment near her husband, took its heavenward flight. Then a hoarse, chuckling laugh was heard again! Thus ever does the gross fatality of earth exult in its invariable triumph over the immortal essence which, in this dim sphere of half-development, demands the completeness of a higher state. Yet, had Aylmer reached a profounder wisdom, he need not thus have flung away the happiness which would have woven his mortal life of the selfsame texture with the celestial. The momentary circumstance was too strong for him; he failed to look beyond the shadowy scope of time, and, living once for all in eternity, to find the perfect future in the present.

FOR STUDY AND DISCUSSION

1. To Aylmer, Georgiana's birthmark becomes agonizing. Why?
2. Because of her love for Aylmer, Georgiana genuinely wants the birthmark removed. However, as time passes, she becomes increasingly less confident of full success. Why?
3. Symbolically, whom does Aylmer's assistant Aminadab represent? To help you with a hint, what is Hawthorne conveying when he has Aminadab say, "If she were my wife, I'd never part with that birthmark"?
4. Although some of Aylmer's experiments are preposterous, Hawthorne does not dismiss him merely as a "mad scientist." What does the author's attitude toward Aylmer seem to be? What is his attitude toward Aminadab?
5. Finally, the inevitable question: What is the "impressive moral" (last line on page 137) which Hawthorne believes his story dramatizes?

Young Man Axelbrod

S I N C L A I R   L E W I S

[1885–1951]

The cottonwood is a tree of a slovenly and plebeian habit. Its woolly wisps turn gray the lawns and engender neighborhood hostilities about our town. Yet it is a mighty tree, a refuge and an inspiration; the sun flickers in its towering foliage, whence the tattoo of locusts enlivens our dusty summer afternoons. From the wheat country out to the sagebrush plains between the buttes and the Yellowstone it is the cottonwood that keeps a little grateful shade for sweating homesteaders.

In Joralemon we call Knute Axelbrod "Old Cottonwood." As a matter of fact, the name was derived not so much from the quality of the man as from the wide grove about his gaunt white house and red barn. He made a comely row of trees on each side of the country road, so that a humble, daily sort of a man, driving beneath them in his lumber wagon, might fancy himself lord of a private avenue.

And at sixty-five Knute was like one of his own cottonwoods, his roots deep in the soil, his trunk weathered by rain and blizzard and baking August noons, his crown spread to the wide horizon of day and the enormous sky of a prairie night.

This immigrant was an American even in speech. Save for a weakness about his j's and w's, he spoke the twangy Yankee English of the land. He was the more American because in his native Scandinavia he had dreamed of America as a land of light. Always through disillusion and weariness he beheld America as the world's nursery for justice, for broad, fair towns, and eager talk; and always he kept a young soul that dared to desire beauty.

As a lad Knute Axelbrod had wished to be a famous scholar, to learn the ease of foreign tongues, the romance of history, to unfold in the graciousness of wise books. When he first came to America, he worked in a sawmill all day and studied all evening. He mastered enough book-learning to teach district school for two terms; then, when he was only eighteen, a great-hearted pity for faded little Lena Wesselius moved him to marry her. Gay enough, doubtless, was their hike by prairie schooner to new farmlands, but Knute was promptly caught in a net of poverty and family. From eighteen to fifty-eight he was always snatching children away from death or the farm away from mortgages.

He had to be content—and generously content he was—with the second-hand glory of his children's success and, for himself, with pilfered hours of reading—that reading of big, thick, dismal volumes of history and economics which the lone mature learner chooses. Without ever losing his desire for strange cities and the dignity of towers, he stuck to his farm. He acquired a half-section, free from debt, fertile, well-stocked, adorned with a cement silo, a chicken-run, a new windmill. He became comfortable, secure, and then he was ready, it seemed, to die; for at sixty-three his work was done, and he was unneeded and alone.

His wife was dead. His sons had scattered afar, one a dentist in Fargo, another a farmer in the Golden Valley. He had turned over his farm to his daughter and son-in-law. They had begged him to live with them, but Knute refused.

"No," he said, "you must learn to stand on your own feet. I vill not give you the farm. You pay me four hundred dollars a year rent, and I live on that and vatch you from my hill."

On a rise beside the lone cottonwood which he loved best of all his trees Knute built a tar-paper shack, and here he "bached it"; cooked his meals, made his bed, sometimes sat in the sun, read many books from the Joralemon library, and began to feel that he was free of the yoke of citizenship which he had borne all his life.

For hours at a time he sat on a backless kitchen chair before the shack, a wide-shouldered man, white-bearded, motionless; a seer despite his grotesquely baggy trousers, his collarless shirt. He looked across the miles of stubble to the steeple of the Jackrabbit Forks church and meditated upon the uses of life. At first he could not break the rigidity of habit. He rose at five, found work in cleaning his cabin and cultivating his garden, had dinner exactly at twelve, and went to bed by afterglow. But little by little he discovered that he could be irregular without being arrested. He stayed abed till seven or even eight. He got a large, deliberate, tortoise-shell cat, and played games with it; let it lap milk upon the table, called it the Princess, and confided to it that he had a "sneaking idee" that men were fools to work so hard. Around this coatless old man, his stained waistcoat flapping about a huge torso, in a shanty of rumpled bed and pine table covered with sheets of food-daubed newspaper, hovered all the passionate aspiration of youth and the dreams of ancient beauty.

He began to take long walks by night. In his necessitous life night had ever been a period of heavy slumber in close rooms. Now he discovered the mystery of the dark; saw the prairies wide-flung and misty beneath the moon, heard the voices of grass and cottonwoods and drowsy birds. He tramped for miles. His boots were dew-soaked, but he did not heed. He stopped upon hillocks, shyly threw wide his arms, and stood worshiping the naked, slumbering land.

These excursions he tried to keep secret, but they were bruited abroad. Neighbors, good, decent fellows with no sense about walking in the dew at night, when they were returning late from town, drunk, lashing their horses and flinging whisky bottles from racing democrat wagons, saw him, and they spread the tidings that Old Cottonwood was "getting nutty since he give up his farm to that son-in-law of his and retired. Seen the old codger wandering around at midnight. Wish I had his chance to sleep. Wouldn't catch me out in the night air."

Any rural community from Todd Center to Seringapatam is resentful of any person who varies from its standard, and is morbidly fascinated by any hint of madness. The countryside began to spy on Knute Axelbrod, to ask him questions, and to stare from the road at his shack. He was sensitively aware of it and inclined to be surly to inquisitive acquaintances. Doubtless that was the beginning of his great pilgrimage.

As a part of the general wild license of his new life—really, he once roared at that startled cat, the Princess: "By gollies! I ain't going to brush my teeth tonight. All my life I've brushed 'em, and alvays wanted to skip a time vunce"—Knute took considerable pleasure in degenerating in his taste in scholarship. He wilfully declined to finish *The Conquest of Mexico,* and began to read light novels borrowed from the Joralemon library. So he rediscovered the lands of dancing and light wines, which all his life he had desired. Some economics and history he did read, but every evening he would stretch out in his buffalo-horn chair, his feet on the cot and the Princess in his lap, and invade Zenda or fall in love with Trilby.

Among the novels he chanced upon a highly optimistic story of Yale in which a worthy young man "earned his way through" college, stroked the crew, won Phi Beta Kappa, and had the most entertaining, yet moral, conversations on or adjacent to "the dear old fence."

As a result of this chronicle, at about three o'clock one morning, when Knute Axelbrod was sixty-four years of age, he decided that he would go to college. All his life he had wanted to. Why not do it?

When he awoke he was not so sure about it as when he had gone to sleep. He saw himself as ridiculous, a ponderous, oldish man among clean-limbed youths, like a dusty cottonwood among silver birches. But for months he wrestled and played with that idea of a great pilgrimage to the Mount of Muses; for he really supposed college to be that sort of place. He believed that all college students, except for the wealthy idlers, burned to acquire learning. He pictured Harvard and Yale and Princeton as ancient groves set with marble temples, before which large groups of Grecian youths talked gently about astronomy and good government. In his picture they never cut classes or ate.

With a longing for music and books and graciousness such as the most ambitious boy could never comprehend, this thick-faced farmer dedicated himself to beauty, and defied the unconquerable power of approaching old age. He sent for college catalogues and school books, and diligently began to prepare himself for college.

He found Latin irregular verbs and the whimsicalities of algebra fiendish. They had nothing to do with actual life as he had lived it. But he mastered them; he studied twelve hours a day, as once he had plodded through eighteen hours a day in the hayfield. With history and English literature he had comparatively little trouble; already he knew much of them from his recreative reading. From German neighbors he had picked up enough Plattdeutsch to make German easy. The trick of study began to come back to him from his small school teaching of forty-five years before. He began to believe that he could really put it through. He kept assuring himself that in college, with rare and sympathetic instructors to help him, there would not be this baffling search, this nervous strain.

But the unreality of the things he studied did disillusion him, and he tired of his new game. He kept it up chiefly because all his life he had kept up onerous labor without any taste for it. Toward the autumn of the second year of his eccentric life he no longer believed that he would ever go to college.

Then a busy little grocer stopped him on the street in Joralemon and quizzed him about his studies, to the delight of the informal club which always loafs at the corner of the hotel.

Knute was silent, but dangerously angry. He remembered just in time how he had once laid wrathful hands upon a hired man, and somehow the man's collar bone had been broken. He turned away and walked home, seven miles, still boiling. He picked up the Princess, and, with her mewing on his shoulder, tramped out again to enjoy the sunset.

He stopped at a reedy slough. He gazed at a hopping plover without seeing it. Suddenly he cried:

"I am going to college. It opens next veek. I t'ink that I can pass the examinations."

Two days later he had moved the Princess and his sticks of furniture to his son-in-law's house, had bought a new slouch hat, a celluloid collar, and a solemn suit of black, had wrestled with God in prayer through all of a star-clad night, and had taken the train for Minneapolis, on the way to New Haven.

While he stared out of the car window Knute was warning himself that the millionaires' sons would make fun of him. Perhaps they would haze him. He bade himself avoid all these sons of Belial and cleave to his own people, those who "earned their way through."

At Chicago he was afraid with a great fear of the lightning flashes that the swift crowds made on his retina, the batteries of ranked motor cars that charged at him. He prayed, and ran for his train to New York. He came at last to New Haven.

Not with gibing rudeness, but with politely quizzical eyebrows, Yale received him, led him through entrance examinations, which, after sweaty plowing with the pen, he barely passed, and found for him a roommate. The roommate was a large-browed soft white grub named Ray Gribble, who had been teaching school in New England and seemed chiefly to desire college training so that he might make more money as a teacher. Ray Gribble was a hustler; he instantly got work tutoring the awkward son of a steel man, and for board he waited on table.

He was Knute's chief acquaintance. Knute tried to fool himself into thinking he liked the grub, but Ray couldn't keep his damp hands off the old man's soul. He had the skill of a professional exhorter of young men in finding out Knute's motives, and when he discovered that Knute had a hidden desire to sip at gay, polite literature, Ray said in a shocked way:

"Strikes me a man like you, that's getting old, ought to be thinking more about saving your soul than about all these frills. You leave this poetry and stuff to these foreigners and artists, and you stick to Latin and math, and the Bible. I tell you, I've taught school, and I've learned by experience."

With Ray Gribble, Knute lived grubbily, an existence of torn comforters and smelly lamp, of lexicons and logarithm tables. No leisurely loafing by fireplaces was theirs. They roomed in West Divinity, where gather the theologues, the lesser sort of law students, a whimsical genius or two, and a horde of unplaced freshmen and "scrub seniors."

Knute was shockingly disappointed, but he stuck to his room because outside of it he was afraid. He was a grotesque figure, and he knew it, a white-polled giant squeezed into a small seat in a classroom, listening to instructors younger than his own sons. Once he tried to sit on the fence. No one but "ringers" sat on the fence any more, and at the sight of him trying to look athletic and young, two upper-class men snickered, and he sneaked away.

He came to hate Ray Gribble and his voluble companions of the submerged tenth of the class, the hewers of tutorial wood. It is doubtless safer to mock the flag than to question that best-established tradition of our democracy— that those who "earn their way through" college are necessarily stronger, braver, and more assured of success than the weaklings who talk by the fire. Every college story presents such a moral. But tremblingly the historian submits that Knute discovered that waiting on table did not make lads more heroic than did football or happy loafing. Fine fellows, cheerful and fearless, were many of the boys who "earned their way," and able to talk to richer classmates without fawning; but just as many of them assumed an abject respectability as the most convenient pose. They were pickers up of unconsidered trifles; they toadied to the classmates whom they tutored; they wriggled before the faculty committee on scholarships; they looked pious at Dwight Hall prayer meetings to make an impression on the serious minded; and they drank one glass of beer at Jake's to show the light minded that they meant nothing offensive by their piety. In revenge for cringing to the insolent athletes whom they tutored, they would, when safe among their own kind, yammer about the "lack of democracy of college today." Not that they were so indiscreet as to do anything about it. They lacked the stuff of really rebellious souls. Knute listened to them and marveled. They sounded like young hired men talking behind his barn at harvest time.

This submerged tenth hated the dilettantes of the class even more than they hated the bloods. Against one Gilbert Washburn, a rich aesthete with more manner than any freshman ought to have, they raged righteously. They spoke of seriousness and industry till Knute, who might once have desired to know lads like Washburn, felt ashamed of himself as a wicked, wasteful old man.

Humbly though he sought, he found no inspiration and no comradeship. He was the freak of the class, and aside from the submerged tenth, his classmates were afraid of being "queered" by being seen with him.

As he was still powerful, one who could take up a barrel of pork on his knees, he tried to find friendship among the athletes. He sat at Yale Field, watching the football tryouts, and tried to get acquainted with the candidates. They stared at him and answered his questions grudgingly—beefy youths who in their simple-hearted way showed that they considered him plain crazy.

The place itself began to lose the haze of magic through which he had first seen it. Earth is earth, whether one sees it in Camelot or Joralemon or on the Yale campus—or possibly even in the Harvard yard! The buildings ceased to be temples to Knute; they became structures of brick or stone, filled with young men who lounged at windows and watched him amusedly as he tried to slip by.

The Gargantuan hall of Commons became a tri-daily horror because at the table where he dined were two youths who, having uncommonly penetrating minds, discerned that Knute had a beard, and courageously told the world about it. One of them, named Atchison, was a superior person, very industrious and scholarly, glib in mathematics and manners. He despised Knute's lack of definite purpose in coming to college. The other was a playboy, a wit and a stealer of street signs, who had a wonderful sense for a subtle jest; and his references to Knute's beard shook the table with jocund mirth three times a day. So these youths of gentle birth drove the shambling, wistful old man away from Commons, and thereafter he ate at the lunch counter at the Black Cat.

Lacking the stimulus of friendship, it was the harder for Knute to keep up the strain of studying the long assignments. What had been a week's pleasant reading in his shack was now thrown at him as a day's task. But he would not have minded the toil if he could have found one as young as himself. They were all so dreadfully old, the money-earners, the serious laborers at athletics, the instructors who worried over their life work of putting marks in class-record books.

Then, on a sore, bruised day, Knute did meet one who was young.

Knute had heard that the professor who was the idol of the college had berated the too-earnest lads in his Browning class and insisted that they read *Alice in Wonderland*. Knute floundered dustily about in a second-hand book-shop till he found an "Alice," and he brought it home to read over his lunch of a hot-dog sandwich. Something in the grave absurdity of the book appealed to him, and he was chuckling over it when Ray Gribble came into the room and glanced at the reader.

"Huh!" said Mr. Gribble.

"That's a fine, funny book," said Knute.

"Huh! *Alice in Wonderland!* I've heard of it. Silly nonsense. Why don't you read something really fine, like Shakespeare or *Paradise Lost?*"

"Vell——" said Knute, all he could find to say.

With Ray Gribble's glassy eye on him, he could no longer roll and roar with the book. He wondered if indeed he ought not to be reading Milton's pompous anthropological misconceptions. He went unhappily out to an early history class, ably conducted by Blevins, Ph.D.

Knute admired Blevins, Ph.D. He was so tubbed and eyeglassed and terribly right. But most of Blevins's lambs did not like Blevins. They said he was a "crank." They read newspapers in his class and covertly kicked one another.

In the smug, plastered classroom, his arm leaning heavily on the broad tablet-arm of his chair, Knute tried not to miss one of Blevins's sardonic proofs that the correct date of the second marriage of Themistocles was two years and seven days later than the date assigned by that illiterate ass, Frutari of Padua. Knute admired young Blevins's performance, and he felt virtuous in application to these hard, unnonsensical facts.

He became aware that certain lewd fellows of the lesser sort were playing poker just behind him. His prairie-trained ear caught whispers of "Two to dole," and "Raise you two beans." Knute revolved and frowned upon these mockers of sound learning. As he turned back he was aware that the offenders were chuckling and continuing their game. He saw that Blevins, Ph.D., perceived that something was wrong; he frowned, but he said nothing. Knute sat in meditation. He saw Blevins as merely a boy. He was sorry for him. He would do the boy a good turn.

When class was over he hung about Blevins's desk till the other students had clattered out. He rumbled:

"Say, Professor, you're a fine fellow. I do something for you. If any of the boys make themselves a nuisance, you yust call on me, and I spank the son of a guns."

Blevins, Ph.D., spake in a manner of culture and nastiness:

"Thanks so much, Axelbrod, but I don't fancy that will ever be necessary. I am supposed to be a reasonably good disciplinarian. Good day. Oh, one moment. There's something I've been wishing to speak to you about. I do wish you wouldn't try quite so hard to show off whenever I call on you during quizzes. You answer at such needless length, and you smile as though there were something highly amusing about me. I'm quite willing to have you regard me as a humorous figure, privately, but there are certain classroom conventions, you know, certain little conventions."

"Why, Professor!" wailed Knute, "I never make fun of you! I didn't know I smile. If I do, I guess it's yust because I am so glad when my stupid old head gets the lesson good."

"Well, well, that's very gratifying, I'm sure. And if you will be a little more careful——"

Blevins, Ph.D., smiled a toothy, frozen smile, and trotted off to the Graduates' Club, to be witty about old Knute and his way of saying "yust," while in the deserted classroom Knute sat chill, an old man and doomed. Through the windows came the light of Indian summer; clean, boyish cries rose from the campus. But the lover of autumn smoothed his baggy sleeve, stared at the blackboard, and there saw only the gray of October stubble about his distant shack. As he pictured the college watching him, secretly making fun of him and his smile, he was now faint and ashamed, now bull-angry. He was lonely for his cat, his fine chair of buffalo horns, the sunny doorstep of his shack, and the understanding land. He had been in college for about one month.

Before he left the classroom he stepped behind the instructor's desk and looked at an imaginary class.

"I might have stood there as a prof if I could have come earlier," he said softly to himself.

Calmed by the liquid autumn gold that flowed through the streets, he walked out Whitney Avenue toward the butte-like hill of East Rock. He observed the caress of the light upon the scarped rock, heard the delicate music of leaves, breathed in air pregnant with tales of old New England. He exulted: " 'Could write poetry now if I yust—if I yust could write poetry!"

He climbed to the top of East Rock, whence he could see the Yale buildings like the towers of Oxford, and see Long Island Sound, and the white glare of Long Island beyond the water. He marveled that Axelbrod of the cottonwood country was looking across an arm of the Atlantic to New York state. He noticed a freshman on a bench at the edge of the rock, and he became irritated. The freshman was Gilbert Washburn, the snob, the dilettante, of whom Ray Gribble had once said: "That guy is the disgrace of the class. He doesn't go out for anything, high stand or Dwight Hall or anything else. Thinks he's so doggone much better than the rest of the fellows that he doesn't associate with anybody. Thinks he's literary, they say, and yet he doesn't even heel the 'Lit,' like the regular literary fellows! Got no time for a loafing, mooning snob like that."

As Knute stared at the unaware Gil, whose profile was fine in outline against the sky, he was terrifically public-spirited and disapproving and that sort of moral thing. Though Gil was much too well dressed, he seemed moodily discontented.

"What he needs is to vork in a threshing crew and sleep in the hay," grumbled Knute almost in the virtuous manner of Gribble. "Then he vould know when he vas vell off, and not look like he had the earache. Pff!" Gil Washburn rose, trailed toward Knute, glanced at him, sat down on Knute's bench.

"Great view!" he said. His smile was eager.

That smile symbolized to Knute all the art of life he had come to college to find. He tumbled out of his moral attitude with ludicrous haste, and every wrinkle of his weathered face creased deep as he answered:

"Yes. I t'ink the Acropolis must be like this here."

"Say, look here, Axelbrod; I've been thinking about you."

"Yas?"

"We ought to know each other. We two are the class scandal. We came here to dream, and these busy little goats like Atchison and Giblets, or whatever your roommate's name is, think we're fools not to go out for marks. You may not agree with me, but I've decided that you and I are precisely alike."

"What makes you t'ink I come here to dream?" bristled Knute.

"Oh, I used to sit near you at Commons and hear you try to quell old Atchison whenever he got busy discussing the reasons for coming to college. That old, moth-eaten topic! I wonder if Cain and Abel didn't discuss it at the Eden Agricultural College. You know, Abel the mark-grabber, very pious and high stand, and Cain wanting to read poetry."

"Yes," said Knute, "and I guess Prof. Adam say, 'Cain, don't you read this poetry; it von't help you in algebry.' "

"Of course. Say, wonder if you'd like to look at this volume of Musset I was sentimental enough to lug up here today. Picked it up when I was abroad last year."

From his pocket Gil drew such a book as Knute had never seen before, a slender volume, in a strange language, bound in hand-tooled crushed levant, an effeminate bibelot over which the prairie farmer gasped with luxurious pleasure. The book almost vanished in his big hands. With a timid forefinger he stroked the levant, ran through the leaves.

"I can't read it, but that's the kind of book I alvays t'ought there must be some like it," he sighed.

"Listen!" cried Gil. "Ysaye is playing up at Hartford tonight. Let's go hear him. We'll trolley up. Tried to get some of the fellows to come, but they thought I was a nut."

What an Ysaye was, Knute Axelbrod had no notion; but "Sure!" he boomed.

When they got to Hartford they found that between them they had just enough money to get dinner, hear Ysaye from gallery seats, and return only as far as Meriden. At Meriden Gil suggested:

"Let's walk back to New Haven, then. Can you make it?"

Knute had no knowledge as to whether it was four miles or forty back to the campus, but "Sure!" he said. For the last few months he had been noticing that, despite his bulk, he had to be careful, but tonight he could have flown.

In the music of Ysaye, the first real musician he had ever heard, Knute had found all the incredible things of which he had slowly been reading in William Morris and "Idylls of the King." Tall knights he had beheld, and slim princesses in white samite, the misty gates of forlorn towns, and the glory of the chivalry that never was.

They did walk, roaring down the road beneath the October moon, stopping to steal apples and to exclaim over silvered hills, taking a puerile and very natural joy in chasing a profane dog. It was Gil who talked, and Knute who listened, for the most part; but Knute was lured into tales of the pioneer days, of blizzards, of harvesting, and of the first flame of the green wheat. Regarding the Atchisons and Gribbles of the class both of them were youthfully bitter and supercilious. But they were not bitter long, for they were atavisms tonight. They were wandering minstrels, Gilbert the troubadour with his man-at-arms.

They reached the campus at about five in the morning. Fumbling for words that would express his feeling, Knute stammered:

"Vell, it vas fine. I go to bed now and I dream about———"

"Bed? Rats! Never believe in winding up a party when it's going strong. Too few good parties. Besides, it's only the shank of the evening. Besides, we're hungry. Besides—oh, besides! Wait here a second. I'm going up to my room to get some money, and we'll have some eats. Wait! Please do!"

Knute would have waited all night. He had lived almost seventy years and traveled fifteen hundred miles and endured Ray Gribble to find Gil Washburn.

Policemen wondered to see the celluloid-collared old man and the expensive-looking boy rolling arm in arm down Chapel Street in search of a restaurant suitable to poets. They were all closed.

"The Ghetto will be awake by now," said Gil. "We'll go buy some eats and take 'em up to my room. I've got some tea there."

Knute shouldered through dark streets beside him as naturally as though he had always been a nighthawk, with an aversion to anything as rustic as beds. Down on Oak Street, a place of low shops, smoky lights, and alley mouths, they found the slum already astir. Gil contrived to purchase boxed biscuits, cream cheese, chicken-loaf, a bottle of cream. While Gil was chaffering, Knute stared out into the street milkily lighted by wavering gas and the first feebleness of coming day; he gazed upon Kosher signs and advertisements in Russian letters, shawled women and bearded rabbis; and as he looked he gathered contentment which he could never lose. He had traveled abroad tonight.

The room of Gil Washburn was all the useless, pleasant things Knute wanted it to be. There was more of Gil's Paris days in it than of his freshman-hood: Persian rugs, a silver tea service, etchings, and books. Knute Axelbrod of the tar-paper shack and piggy farmyards gazed in satisfaction. Vast bearded, sunk in an easy chair, he clucked amiably while Gil lighted a fire.

Over supper they spoke of great men and heroic ideals. It was good talk, and not unspiced with lively references to Gribble and Atchison and Blevins, all asleep now in their correct beds. Gil read snatches of Stevenson and Anatole France; then at last he read his own poetry.

It does not matter whether that poetry was good or bad. To Knute it was a miracle to find one who actually wrote it.

The talk grew slow, and they began to yawn. Knute was sensitive to the lowered key of their Indian-summer madness, and he hastily rose. As he said good-bye he felt as though he had but to sleep a little while and return to this unending night of romance.

But he came out of the dormitory upon day. It was six-thirty of the morning, with a still, hard light upon red-brick walls.

"I can go to his room plenty times now; I find my friend," Knute said. He held tight the volume of Musset, which Gil had begged him to take.

As he started to walk the few steps to West Divinity Knute felt very tired. By daylight the adventure seemed more and more incredible.

As he entered the dormitory he sighed heavily:

"Age and youth, I guess they can't team together long." As he mounted the stairs he said: "If I saw the boy again, he vould get tired of me. I tell him all I got to say." And as he opened his door, he added: "This is what I come to college for—this one night. I go avay before I spoil it."

He wrote a note to Gil and began to pack his telescope. He did not even wake Ray Gribble, sonorously sleeping in the stale air.

At five that afternoon, on the day coach of a westbound train, an old man sat smiling. A lasting content was in his eyes, and in his hands a small book in French.

How Beautiful with Shoes

WILBUR DANIEL STEELE
[BORN 1886]

By the time the milking was finished, the sow, which had farrowed [1] the past week, was making such a row that the girl spilled a pint of the warm milk down the trough lead to quiet the animal before taking the pail to the well house. Then in the quiet she heard a sound of hoofs on the bridge, where the road crossed the creek a hundred yards below the house, and she set the pail down on the ground beside her bare, barn-soiled feet. She picked it up again. She set it down. It was as if she calculated its weight.

That was what she was doing, as a matter of fact, setting off against its pull toward the well house the pull of that wagon team in the road, with little more of personal will or wish in the matter than has a wooden weather vane between two currents in the wind. And as with the vane, so with the wooden girl—the added behest of a whiplash cracking in the distance was enough; leaving the pail at the barn door she set off in a deliberate, docile beeline through the cow yard, over the fence, and down in a diagonal across the farm's one tilled field toward the willow brake that walled the road at the dip. And once under way, though her mother came to the kitchen door and called in her high, flat voice, "Amarantha, where you goin', Amarantha?" the girl went on, apparently unmoved, as though she had been as deaf as the woman in the doorway; indeed, if there was emotion in her it was the purely sensuous one of feeling the clods of the furrows breaking softly between her toes. It was springtime in the mountains.

"Amarantha, why don't you answer me, Amarantha?"

For moments after the girl had disappeared beyond the willows the widow continued to call, unaware through long habit of how absurd it sounded, the name which that strange man her husband had put upon their daughter in one of his moods. Mrs. Doggett had been deaf so long she did not realize that nobody else ever thought of it for the broad-fleshed, slow-minded girl, but called her Mary, or, even more simply, Mare.

Ruby Herter had stopped his team this side of the bridge, the mules' heads turned into the lane to his father's farm beyond the road. A big-barreled, heavy-limbed fellow with a square, sallow, not unhandsome face, he took out youth in ponderous gestures of masterfulness; it was like him to have cracked his whip above his animal's ears the moment before he pulled them to a halt. When he saw the girl getting over the fence under the willows he tongued the wad of tobacco out of his mouth into his palm, threw it away beyond the road, and drew a sleeve of his jumper across his lips.

"Don't run yourself out o' breath, Mare; I got all night."

[1] *farrowed:* given birth.

"I was comin'." It sounded sullen only because it was matter-of-fact.

"Well, keep a-comin' and give us a smack." Hunched on the wagon seat, he remained motionless for some time after she had arrived at the hub, and when he stirred it was but to cut a fresh bit of tobacco, as if already he had forgotten why he threw the old one away. Having satisfied his humor, he unbent, climbed down, kissed her passive mouth, and hugged her up to him, roughly and loosely, his hands careless of contours. It was not out of the way; they were used to handling animals both of them; and it was spring. A slow warmth pervaded the girl, formless, nameless, almost impersonal.

Her betrothed pulled her head back by the braid of her yellow hair. He studied her face, his brows gathered and his chin out.

"Listen, Mare, you wouldn't leave nobody else hug and kiss you, dang you!"

She shook her head, without vehemence or anxiety.

"Who's that?" She hearkened up the road. "Pull your team out," she added, as a Ford came in sight around the bend above the house, driven at speed. "Geddap!" she said to the mules herself.

But the car came to a halt near them, and one of the five men crowded in it called, "Come on, Ruby, climb in. They's a loony loose out o' Dayville Asylum, and they got him trailed over somewheres on Split Ridge, and Judge North phoned up to Slosson's store for ever'body come help circle him—come on, hop the runnin' board!"

Ruby hesitated, an eye on his team.

"Scared, Ruby?" The driver raced his engine. "They say this boy's a killer."

"Marc, take the team in and tell Pa." The car was already moving when Ruby jumped it. A moment after it had sounded on the bridge it was out of sight.

"Amarantha, Amarantha, why don't you come, Amarantha?"

Returning from her errand fifteen minutes later, Mare heard the plaint lifted in the twilight. The sun had dipped behind the back ridge, and though the sky was still bright with day, the dusk began to smoke up out of the plowed field like a ground fog. The girl had returned through it, got the milk, and started toward the well house before the widow saw her.

"Daughter, seems to me you might!" she expostulated without change of key. "Here's some young man friend o' yourn stopped to say howdy, and I been rackin' my lungs out after you. . . . Put that milk in the cool and come!"

Some young man friend? But there was no good to be got from puzzling. Mare poured the milk in the pan in the dark of the low house over the well, and as she came out, stooping, she saw a figure waiting for her, black in silhouette against the yellowing sky.

"Who are you?" she asked, a native timidity making her sound sulky.

" 'Amarantha!' " the fellow mused. "That's poetry." And she knew then that she did not know him.

She walked past, her arms straight down and her eyes front. Strangers always affected her with a kind of muscular terror simply by being strangers. So she gained the kitchen steps, aware by his tread that he followed. There, taking courage, she turned on him, her eyes down at the level of his knees.

"Who are you and what d' y' want?"

He still mused. "Amarantha! Amarantha in Carolina! That makes me happy!"

Mare hazarded one upward look. She saw that he had red hair, brown eyes, and hollows under his cheekbones, and though the green sweater he wore on top of a gray overall was plainly not meant for him, sizes too large as far as girth went, yet he was built so long of limb that his wrists came inches out of the sleeves and made his big hands look even bigger.

Mrs. Doggett complained. "Why don't you introduce us, daughter?"

The girl opened her mouth and closed it again. Her mother, unaware that no sound had come out of it, smiled and nodded, evidently taking to the tall, homely fellow and tickled by the way he could not seem to get his eyes off her daughter. But the daughter saw none of it, all her attention centered upon the stranger's hands.

Restless, hard-fleshed, and chap-bitten, they were like a countryman's hands; but the fingers were longer than the ordinary, and slightly spatulate at their ends, and these ends were slowly and continuously at play among themselves.

The girl could not have explained how it came to her to be frightened and at the same time to be calm, for she was inept with words. It was simply that in an animal way she knew animals, knew them in health and ailing, and when they were ailing she knew by instinct, as her father had known, how to move so as not to fret them.

Her mother had gone in to light up; from beside the lamp shelf she called back, "If he's aimin' to stay to supper you should've told me, Amarantha, though I guess there's plenty of the side meat to go round, if you'll bring me in a few more turnips and potatoes, though it is late."

At the words the man's cheeks moved in and out. "I'm very hungry," he said.

Mare nodded deliberately. Deliberately, as if her mother could hear her, she said over her shoulder, "I'll go get the potatoes and turnips, Ma." While she spoke she was moving, slowly, softly, at first, toward the right of the yard, where the fence gave over into the field. Unluckily her mother spied her through the window.

"Amarantha, where *are* you goin'?"

"I'm goin' to get the potatoes and turnips." She neither raised her voice nor glanced back, but lengthened her stride. "He won't hurt her," she said to herself. "He won't hurt her; it's me, not her," she kept repeating, while she got over the fence and down into the shadow that lay more than ever like a fog on the field.

The desire to believe that it actually did hide her, the temptation to break from her rapid but orderly walk, grew till she could no longer fight it. She saw the road willows only a dash ahead of her. She ran, her feet floundering among the furrows.

She neither heard nor saw him, but when she realized he was with her she knew he had been with her all the while. She stopped, and he stopped, and so they stood, with the dark open of the field all around. Glancing sidewise presently, she saw he was no longer looking at her with those strangely importunate brown eyes of his, but had raised them to the crest of the wooded ridge behind her.

By and by, "What does it make you think of?" he asked. And when she made no move to see, "Turn around and look!" he said, and though it was low and almost tender in its tone, she knew enough to turn.

A ray of the sunset hidden in the west struck through the tops of the topmost trees, far and small up there, a thin, bright hem.

"What does it make you think of, Amarantha? . . . Answer!"

"Fire," she made herself say.

"Or blood."

"Or blood, yeh. That's right, or blood." She had heard a Ford going up the road beyond the willows, and her attention was not on what she said.

The man soliloquized. "Fire and blood, both; spare one or the other, and where is beauty, the way the world is? It's an awful thing to have to carry, but Christ had it. Christ came with a sword. I love beauty, Amarantha. . . . I say, I love beauty!"

"Yeh, that's right, I hear." What she heard was the car stopping at the house.

"Not prettiness. Prettiness'll have to go with ugliness, because it's only ugliness trigged up. But beauty!" Now again he was looking at her. "Do you know how beautiful you are, Amarantha, *Amarantha sweet and fair?*" Of a sudden, reaching behind her, he began to unravel the meshes of her hair braid, the long, flat-tipped fingers at once impatient and infinitely gentle. *"Braid no more that shining hair!"*

Flat-faced Mare Doggett tried to see around those glowing eyes so near to hers, but, wise in her instinct, did not try too hard. "Yeh," she temporized. "I mean, no, I mean."

"Amarantha, I've come a long, long way for you. Will you come away with me now?"

"Yeh—that is—in a minute I will, mister—yeh. . . ."

"Because you want to, Amarantha? Because you love me as I love you? Answer!"

"Yeh—sure—uh . . . *Ruby!*"

The man tried to run, but there were six against him, coming up out of the dark that lay in the plowed ground. Mare stood where she was while they knocked him down and got a rope around him; after that she walked back toward the house with Ruby and Older Haskins, her father's cousin.

Ruby wiped his brow and felt of his muscles. "Gees, you're lucky we come, Mare. We're no more'n past the town, when they come hollerin' he'd broke over this way."

When they came to the fence the girl sat on the rail for a moment and rebraided her hair before she went into the house, where they were making her mother smell ammonia.

Lots of cars were coming. Judge North was coming, somebody said. When Mare heard this she went into her bedroom off the kitchen and got her shoes and put them on. They were brand-new two-dollar shoes with cloth tops, and she had only begun to break them in last Sunday; she wished afterwards she had put her stockings on, too, for they would have eased the seams. Or else that she had put on the old button pair, even though the soles were worn through.

Judge North arrived. He thought first of taking the loony straight through to Dayville that night, but then decided to keep him in the lockup at the courthouse till morning and make the drive by day. Older Haskins stayed in, gentling Mrs. Doggett, while Ruby went out to help get the man into the judge's sedan. Now that she had them on, Mare didn't like to take the shoes off till Older went; it might make him feel small, she thought.

Older Haskins had a lot of facts about the loony.

"His name's Humble Jewett," he told them. "They belong back in Breed County, all them Jewetts, and I don't reckon there's none of 'em that's not a mite unbalanced. He went to college though, worked his way, and he taught somethin' 'rother in some academy school a spell, till he went off his head all of a sudden and took after folks with an ax. I remember it in the paper at the time. They give out one while how the principal wasn't goin' to live, and there was others—there was a girl he tried to strangle. That was four-five years back."

Ruby came in guffawing. "Know the only thing they can get 'im to say, Mare? Only God thing he'll say is 'Amarantha, she's goin' with me.' . . . Mare!"

"Yeh, I know."

The cover of the kettle the girl was handling slid off on the stove with a clatter. A sudden sick wave passed over her. She went out to the back, out into the air. It was not till now she knew how frightened she had been.

Ruby went home, but Older Haskins stayed to supper with them and helped Mare do the dishes afterward; it was nearly nine when he left. The mother was already in bed, and Mare was about to sit down to get those shoes off her wretched feet at last, when she heard the cow carrying on up at the barn, lowing and kicking, and next minute the sow was in it with a horning note. It might be a fox passing by to get at the henhouse, or a weasel. Mare forgot her feet, took a broom handle they used in boiling clothes, opened the back door, and stepped out. Blinking the lamplight from her eyes, she peered up toward the outbuildings and saw the gable end of the barn standing like a red arrow in the dark, and the top of a butternut tree beyond it drawn in skeleton traceries, and just then a cock crowed.

She went to the right corner of the house and saw where the light came from, ruddy above the woods down the valley. Returning into the house, she bent close to her mother's ear and shouted, "Somethin's afire down to the town, looks like," then went out again and up to the barn. "Soh! Soh!" she called in to the animals. She climbed up and stood on the top of the rail of the cowpen fence, only to find she could not locate the flame even there.

Ten rods behind the buildings a mass of rock mounted higher than their ridgepoles, a chopped-off buttress of the back ridge, covered with oak scrub and wild grapes and blackberries, whose thorny ropes the girl beat away from her as she scrambled up in the wine-colored dark. Once at the top, and the brush held aside, she could see the tongue tip of the conflagration half a mile away at the town. And she knew by the bearing of the two church steeples that it was the building where the lockup was that was burning.

There is a horror in knowing animals trapped in a fire, no matter what the animals.

"O my God!" Mare said.

A car went down the road. Then there was a horse galloping. That would be Older Haskins probably. People were out at Ruby's father's farm; she could hear their voices raised. There must have been another car up from the other way, for lights wheeled and shouts were exchanged in the neighborhood of the bridge. Next thing she knew, Ruby was at the house below, looking for her probably.

He was telling her mother. Mrs. Doggett was not used to him, so he had to shout even louder than Mare had to.

"What y' reckon he done, the hellion! He broke the door and killed Lew Fyke and set the courthouse afire! . . . Where's Mare?"

Her mother would not know. Mare called. "Here, up the rock here."

She had better go down. Ruby would likely break his bones if he tried to climb the rock in the dark, not knowing the way. But the sight of the fire fascinated her simple spirit, the fearful element, more fearful than ever now, with the news. "Yes, I'm comin'," she called sulkily, hearing feet in the brush. "You wait; I'm comin'."

When she turned and saw it was Humble Jewett, right behind her among the branches, she opened her mouth to screech. She was not quick enough. Before a sound came out he got one hand over her face and the other arm around her body.

Mare had always thought she was strong, and the loony looked gangling, yet she was so easy for him that he need not hurt her. He made no haste and little noise as he carried her deeper into the undergrowth. Where the hill began to mount it was harder though. Presently he set her on her feet. He let the hand that had been over her mouth slip down to her throat, where the broad-tipped fingers wound, tender as yearning, weightless as caress.

"I was afraid you'd scream before you knew who 'twas, Amarantha. But I didn't want to hurt your lips, dear heart, your lovely, quiet lips."

It was so dark under the trees she could hardly see him, but she felt his breath on her mouth, near to. But then, instead of kissing her, he said, "No! No!" took from her throat for an instant the hand that had held her mouth, kissed its palm, and put it back softly against her skin.

"Now, my love, let's go before they come."

She stood stock-still. Her mother's voice was to be heard in the distance, strident and meaningless. More cars were on the road. Nearer, around the rock, there were sounds of tramping and thrashing. Ruby fussed and cursed. He shouted, "Mare, dang you, where are you, Mare?" his voice harsh with uneasy anger. Now, if she aimed to do anything, was the time to do it. But there was neither breath nor power in her windpipe. It was as if those yearning fingers had paralyzed the muscles.

"Come!" The arm he put around her shivered against her shoulder blades. It was anger. "I hate killing. It's a dirty, ugly thing. It makes me sick." He gagged, judging by the sound. But then he ground his teeth. "Come away, my love!"

She found herself moving. Once when she broke a branch underfoot with an instinctive awkwardness he chided her. "Quiet, my heart, else they'll hear!" She made herself heavy. He thought she grew tired and bore more of her weight till he was breathing hard.

Men came up the hill. There must have been a dozen spread out, by the angle of their voices as they kept touch. Always Humble Jewett kept caressing Mare's throat with one hand; all she could do was hang back.

"You're tired and you're frightened," he said at last. "Get down here."

There were twigs in the dark, the overhang of a thicket of some sort. He thrust her in under this, and lay beside her on the bed of ground pine. The hand that was not in love with her throat reached across her; she felt the weight of its forearm on her shoulder and its fingers among the strands of her hair, eagerly, but tenderly, busy. Not once did he stop speaking, no louder than breathing, his lips to her ear.

"*Amarantha sweet and fair—Ah, braid no more that shining hair . . .*"

Mare had never heard of Lovelace, the poet; she thought the loony was just going on, hardly listened, got little sense. But the cadence of it added to the lethargy of all her flesh.

"*Like a clew of golden thread—Most excellently ravellèd . . .*"

Voices loudened; feet came tramping; a pair went past not two rods away.

"*. . . Do not then wind up the light—In ribbands, and o'ercloud in night . . .*"

The search went on up the woods, men shouting to one another and beating the brush.

". . . *But shake your head and scatter day!* I've never loved, Amarantha. They've tried me with prettiness, but prettiness is too cheap, yes, it's too cheap."

Mare was cold, and the coldness made her lazy. All she knew was that he talked on.

"But dogwood blowing in the spring isn't cheap. The earth of a field isn't cheap. Lots of times I've lain down and kissed the earth of a field, Amarantha. That's beauty, and a kiss for beauty." His breath moved up her cheek. He trembled violently. "No, no, not yet!" He got to his knees and pulled her by an arm. "We can go now."

They went back down the slope, but at an angle, so that when they came to the level they passed two hundred yards to the north of the house and crossed the road there. More and more her walking was like sleepwalking, the feet numb in their shoes. Even where he had to let go of her, crossing the creek on stones, she stepped where he stepped with an obtuse docility. The voices of the searchers on the back ridge were small in distance when they began to climb the face of Coward Hill, on the opposite side of the valley.

There is an old farm on top of Coward Hill, big hayfields as flat as tables. It had been half-past nine when Mare stood on the rock above the barn; it was toward midnight when Humble Jewett put aside the last branches of the woods and led her out on the height, and half a moon had risen. And a wind blew there, tossing the withered tops of last year's grasses, and mists ran with the wind, and ragged shadows with the mists, and mares'-tails of clear moonlight among the shadows, so that now the boles of birches on the forest's edge beyond the fences were but opal blurs and now cut alabaster. It struck so cold against the girl's cold flesh, this wind, that another wind of shivers blew through her, and she put her hands over her face and eyes. But the madman stood with his eyes wide open and his mouth open, drinking the moonlight and the wet wind.

His voice, when he spoke at last, was thick in his throat.

"Get down on your knees." He got down on his and pulled her after. "And pray!"

Once in England a poet sang four lines. Four hundred years have forgotten his name, but they have remembered his lines. The daft man knelt upright, his face raised to the wild scud, his long wrists hanging to the dead grass. He began simply:

> *O western wind, when wilt thou blow*
> *That the small rain down can rain?*

The Adam's apple was big in his bent throat. As simply he finished:

> *Christ, that my love were in my arms*
> *And I in my bed again!*

Mare got up and ran. She ran without aim or feeling in the power of the wind. She told herself again that the mists would hide her from him, as she had done at dusk. And again, seeing that he ran at her shoulder, she knew he had been there all the while, making a race for it, flailing the air with his long arms for joy of play in the cloud of spring, throwing his knees high, leaping the moon-blue waves of the brown grass, shaking his bright hair; and her own hair was a weight behind her, lying level on the wind. Once a shape went bounding ahead of them for instants; she did not realize it was a fox till it was gone.

She never thought of stopping; she never thought anything, except once, "O my God, I wish I had my shoes off!" And what would have been the good in stopping or in turning another way, when it was only play? The man's ecstasy magnified his strength. When a snake fence came at them he took the top rail in flight, like a college hurdler and, seeing the girl hesitate and half turn as if to flee, he would have releaped it without touching a hand. But then she got a loom of buildings, climbed over quickly, before he should jump, and ran along the lane that ran with the fence.

Mare had never been up there, but she knew that the farm and the house belonged to a man named Wyker, a kind of cousin of Ruby Herter's, a violent, bearded old fellow who lived by himself. She could not believe her luck. When she had run half the distance and Jewett had not grabbed her, doubt grabbed her instead. "O my God, go careful!" she told herself. "Go slow!" she implored herself, and stopped running, to walk.

Here was a misgiving the deeper in that it touched her special knowledge. She had never known an animal so far gone that its instincts failed it; a starving rat will scent the trap sooner than a fed one. Yet, after one glance at the house they approached, Jewett paid it no further attention, but walked with his eyes to the right, where the cloud had blown away, and wooded ridges, like black waves rimed with silver, ran down away toward the Valley of Virginia.

"I've never lived!" In his single cry there were two things, beatitude and pain.

Between the bigness of the falling world and his eyes the flag of her hair blew. He reached out and let it whip between his fingers. Mare was afraid it would break the spell then, and he would stop looking away and look at the house again. So she did something almost incredible; she spoke.

"It's a pretty—I mean—a beautiful view down that-a-way."

"God Almighty beautiful, to take your breath away. I knew I'd never loved, Belovèd——" He caught a foot under the long end of one of the boards that covered the well and went down heavily on his hands and knees. It seemed to make no difference. "But I never knew I'd never lived," he finished in the same tone of strong rapture, quadruped in the grass, while Mare ran for the door and grabbed the latch.

When the latch would not give, she lost what little sense she had. She pounded with her fists. She cried with all her might: "Oh—hey—in—there—hey—in there!" Then Jewett came and took her gently between his hands and drew her away, and then, though she was free, she stood in something like an awful embarrassment while he tried shouting.

"Hey! Friend! Whoever you are, wake up and let my love and me come in!"

"No!" wailed the girl.

He grew peremptory. "Hey, wake up!" He tried the latch. He passed to full fury in a wink's time; he cursed, he kicked, he beat the door till Mare thought he would break his hands. Withdrawing, he ran at it with his shoulder; it burst at the latch, went slamming in, and left a black emptiness. His anger dissolved in a big laugh. Turning in time to catch her by a wrist, he cried joyously, "Come, my Sweet One!"

"No! No! Please—aw—listen. There ain't nobody there. He ain't to home. It wouldn't be right to go in anybody's house if they wasn't to home, you know that."

His laugh was blither than ever. He caught her high in his arms.

"I'd do the same by his love and him if 'twas my house, I would." At the threshold he paused and thought, "That is, if she was the true love of his heart forever."

The room was the parlor. Moonlight slanted in at the door, and another shaft came through a window and fell across a sofa, its covering dilapidated, showing its wadding in places. The air was sour, but both of them were farm-bred.

"Don't, Amarantha!" His words were pleading in her ear. "Don't be so frightened."

He set her down on the sofa. As his hands let go of her they were shaking.

"But look, I'm frightened too." He knelt on the floor before her, reached out his hands, withdrew them. "See, I'm afraid to touch you." He mused, his eyes rounded. "Of all the ugly things there are, fear is the ugliest. And yet, see, it can be the very beautifulest. That's a strange, queer thing."

The wind blew in and out of the room, bringing the thin, little bitter sweetness of new April at night. The moonlight that came across Mare's shoulders fell full upon his face, but hers it left dark, ringed by the aureole of her disordered hair.

"Why do you wear a halo, Love?" He thought about it. "Because you're an angel, is that why?" The swift, untempered logic of the mad led him to dismay. His hands came flying to hers, to make sure they were of earth; and he touched her breast, her shoulders, and her hair. Peace returned to his eyes as his fingers twined among the strands.

"Thy hair is as a flock of goats that appear from Gilead . . ." He spoke like a man dreaming. *"Thy temples are like a piece of pomegranate within thy locks."*

Mare never knew that he could not see her for the moonlight.

"Do you remember, Love?"

She dared not shake her head under his hand. "Yeh, I reckon," she temporized.

"You remember how I sat at your feet, long ago, like this, and made up a song? And all the poets in all the world have never made one to touch it, have they, Love?"

"Ugh-ugh—never."

"How beautiful are thy feet with shoes . . . Remember?"

"O my God, what's he sayin' now?" she wailed to herself.

> *How beautiful are thy feet with shoes, O prince's daughter! the*
> *joints of thy thighs are like jewels, the work of the hands*
> *of a cunning workman.*
> *Thy navel is like a round goblet, which wanteth not liquor; thy*
> *belly is like an heap of wheat set about with lilies.*
> *Thy two breasts are like two young roes that are twins.*

Mare had not been to church since she was a little girl, when her mother's black dress wore out. "No, no!" she wailed under her breath. "You're awful to say such awful things." She might have shouted it; nothing could have shaken the man now, rapt in the immortal, passionate periods of Solomon's song:

> . . . *now also thy breasts shall be as clusters of the vine, and*
> *the smell of thy nose like apples.*

Hotness touched Mare's face for the first time. "Aw, no, don't talk so!"

> *And the roof of thy mouth like the best wine for my belovèd*
> . . . *causing the lips of them that are asleep to speak.*

He had ended. His expression changed. Ecstasy gave place to anger, love to hate. And Mare felt the change in the weight of the fingers in her hair.

"What do you mean, I mustn't say it like that?" But it was not to her his fury spoke, for he answered himself straightway. "Like poetry, Mr. Jewett; I won't have blasphemy around my school."

"Poetry! My God! If that isn't poetry—if that isn't music——" . . . "It's Bible, Jewett. What you're paid to teach here is *literature*."

"Dr. Ryeworth, you're the blasphemer and you're an ignorant man." . . .

"And your principal. And I won't have you going around reading sacred allegory like earthly love."

"Ryeworth, you're an old man, a dull man, a dirty man, and you'd be better dead."

Jewett's hands had slid down from Mare's head. "Then I went to put my fingers around his throat, so. But my stomach turned, and I didn't do it. I went to my room. I laughed all the way to my room. I sat in my room at my table and I laughed. I laughed all afternoon and long after dark came. And then, about ten, somebody came and stood beside me in my room.

" 'Wherefore dost thou laugh, son?'

"I didn't laugh any more. He didn't say any more. I kneeled down, bowed my head.

" 'Thy will be done! Where is he, Lord?'

" 'Over at the girls' dormitory, waiting for Blossom Sinckley.'

"Brassy Blossom, dirty Blossom . . ."

It had come so suddenly it was nearly too late. Mare tore at his hands with hers, tried with all her strength to pull her neck away.

"Filthy Blossom! And him an old filthy man, Blossom! And you'll find him in hell when you reach there, Blossom . . ."

It was more the nearness of his face than the hurt of his hands that gave her power of fright to choke out three words.

"I—ain't—Blossom!"

Light ran in crooked veins. Through the veins she saw his face bewildered. His hands loosened. One fell down and hung; the other he lifted and put over his eyes, took it away again and looked at her.

"Amarantha!" His remorse was fearful to see. "What have I done!" His hands returned to hover over the hurts, ravening with pity, grief, and tenderness. Tears fell down his cheeks. And with that, dammed desire broke its dam.

"Amarantha, my love, my dove, my beautiful love——"

"And I ain't Amarantha neither, I'm Mary! Mary, that's my name!"

She had no notion what she had done. He was like a crystal crucible that a chemist watches, changing hue in a wink with one adeptly added drop; but hers was not the chemist's eye. All she knew was that she felt light and free of him; all she could see of his face as he stood away above the moonlight were the whites of his eyes.

"Mary!" he muttered. A slight paroxysm shook his frame. So in the transparent crucible desire changed its hue. He retreated farther, stood in the dark by some tall piece of furniture. And still she could see the whites of his eyes.

"Mary! Mary Adorable!" A wonder was in him. "Mother of God!"

Mare held her breath. She eyed the door, but it was too far. And already he came back to go on his knees before her, his shoulders so bowed and his face so lifted that it must have cracked his neck, she thought; all she could see on the face was pain.

"Mary Mother, I'm sick to my death. I'm so tired."

She had seen a dog like that, one she had loosed from a trap after it had been there three days, its caught leg half gnawed free. Something about the eyes.

"Mary Mother, take me in your arms . . ."

Once again her muscles tightened. But he made no move.

". . . and give me sleep."

No, they were worse than the dog's eyes.

"Sleep, sleep! Why won't they let me sleep? Haven't I done it all yet, Mother? Haven't I washed them yet of all their sins? I've drunk the cup that was given me; is there another? They've mocked me and reviled me, broken my brow with thorns and my hands with nails, and I've forgiven them, for they knew not what they did. Can't I go to sleep now, Mother?"

Mare could not have said why, but now she was more frightened than she had ever been. Her hands lay heavy on her knees, side by side, and she could not take them away when he bowed his head and rested his face upon them.

After a moment he said one thing more. "Take me down gently when you take me from the Tree."

Gradually the weight of his body came against her shins, and he slept.

The moon streak that entered by the eastern window crept north across the floor, thinner and thinner; the one that fell through the southern doorway traveled east and grew fat. For a while Mare's feet pained her terribly and her legs, too. She dared not move them, though, and by and by they did not hurt so much.

A dozen times, moving her head slowly on her neck, she canvassed the shadows of the room for a weapon. Each time her eyes came back to a heavy earthenware pitcher on a stand some feet to the left of the sofa. It would have had flowers in it when Wyker's wife was alive; probably it had not been moved from its dust ring since she died. It would be a long grab, perhaps too long; still, it might be done if she had her hands.

To get her hands from under the sleeper's head was the task she set herself. She pulled first one, then the other, infinitesimally. She waited. Again she tugged a very, very little. The order of his breathing was not disturbed. But at the third trial he stirred.

"Gently! Gently!" His own muttering waked him more. With some drowsy instinct of possession he threw one hand across her wrists, pinning them together between thumb and fingers. She kept dead quiet, shut her eyes, lengthened her breathing, as if she too slept.

There came a time when what was pretense grew a peril; strange as it was, she had to fight to keep her eyes open. She never knew whether or not she really napped. But something changed in the air, and she was wide awake again. The moonlight was fading on the doorsill, and the light that runs before dawn waxed in the window behind her head.

And then she heard a voice in the distance, lifted in maundering song. It was old man Wyker coming home after a night, and it was plain he had had some whisky.

Now a new terror laid hold of Mare.

"Shut up, you fool you!" she wanted to shout. "Come quiet, quiet!" She might have chanced it now to throw the sleeper away from her and scramble and run, had his powers of strength and quickness not taken her simple imagination utterly in thrall.

Happily the singing stopped. What had occurred was that the farmer had espied the open door and, even befuddled as he was, wanted to know more about it quietly. He was so quiet that Mare began to fear he had gone away. He had the squirrel hunter's foot, and the first she knew of him was when she looked and saw his head in the doorway, his hard, soiled whiskery face half upside down with craning.

He had been to the town. Between drinks he had wandered in and out of the night's excitement; had even gone a short distance with one search party himself. Now he took in the situation in the room. He used his forefinger. First he held it to his lips. Next he pointed it with a jabbing motion at the sleeper. Then he tapped his own forehead and described wheels. Lastly, with his whole hand, he made pushing gestures, for Mare to wait. Then he vanished as silently as he had appeared.

The minutes dragged. The light in the east strengthened and turned rosy. Once she thought she heard a board creaking in another part of the house, and looked down sharply to see if the loony stirred. All she could see of his face was a temple with freckles on it and the sharp ridge of a cheekbone, but even from so little she knew how deeply and peacefully he slept. The door darkened. Wyker was there again. In one hand he carried something heavy; with the other he beckoned.

"Come jumpin'!" he said out loud.

Mare went jumping, but her cramped legs threw her down halfway to the sill; the rest of the distance she rolled and crawled. Just as she tumbled through the door it seemed as if the world had come to an end above her; two barrels of a shotgun discharged into a room make a noise. Afterwards all she could hear in there was something twisting and bumping on the floor boards. She got up and ran.

Mare's mother had gone to pieces; neighbor women put her to bed when Mare came home. They wanted to put Mare to bed, but she would not let them. She sat on the edge of her bed in her lean-to bedroom off the kitchen, just as she was, her hair down all over her shoulders and her shoes on, and stared away from them, at a place in the wallpaper.

"Yeh, I'll go myself. Lea' me be!"

The women exchanged quick glances, thinned their lips, and left her be. "God knows," was all they would answer to the questionings of those that had not gone in, "but she's gettin' herself to bed."

When the doctor came through he found her sitting just as she had been, still dressed, her hair down on her shoulders and her shoes on.

"What d' y' want?" she muttered and stared at the place in the wallpaper.

How could Doc Paradise say, when he did not know himself?

"I didn't know if you might be—might be feeling very smart, Mary."

"I'm all right. Lea' me be."

It was a heavy responsibility. Doc shouldered it. "No, it's all right," he said to the men in the road. Ruby Herter stood a little apart, chewing sullenly and looking another way. Doc raised his voice to make certain it carried. "Nope, nothing."

Ruby's ears got red, and he clamped his jaws. He knew he ought to go in and see Mare, but he was not going to do it while everybody hung around waiting to see if he would. A mule tied near him reached out and mouthed his sleeve in idle innocence; he wheeled and banged a fist against the side of the animal's head.

"Well, what d' y' aim to do 'bout it?" he challenged its owner.

He looked at the sun then. It was ten in the morning. "Hell, I got work!" he flared and set off down the road for home. Doc looked at Judge North, and the judge started after Ruby. But Ruby shook his head angrily. "Lea' me be!" He went on, and the judge came back.

It got to be eleven and then noon. People began to say, "Like enough she'd be as thankful if the whole neighborhood wasn't camped here." But none went away.

As a matter of fact they were no bother to the girl. She never saw them. The only move she made was to bend her ankles over and rest her feet on edge; her shoes hurt terribly and her feet knew it, though she did not. She sat all the while staring at that one figure in the wallpaper, and she never saw the figure.

Strange as the night had been, this day was stranger. Fright and physical pain are perishable things once they are gone. But while pain merely dulls and telescopes in memory and remains diluted pain, terror looked back upon has nothing of terror left. A gambling chance taken, at no matter what odds, and won was a sure thing since the world's beginning; perils come through safely were never perilous. But what fright does do in retrospect is this—it heightens each sensuous recollection, like a hard, clear lacquer laid on wood, bringing out the color and grain of it vividly.

Last night Mare had lain stupid with fear on ground pine beneath a bush, loud footfalls and light whispers confused in her ear. Only now, in her room, did she smell the ground pine.

Only now did the conscious part of her brain begin to make words of the whispering.

"*Amarantha,*" she remembered, "*Amarantha sweet and fair.*" That was as far as she could go for the moment, except that the rhyme with "fair" was "hair." But then a puzzle, held in abeyance, brought other words. She wondered what "ravel Ed" could mean. "*Most excellently ravellèd.*" It was left to her mother to bring the end.

They gave up trying to keep her mother out at last. The poor woman's prostration took the form of fussiness.

"Good gracious, daughter, you look a sight. Them new shoes, half ruined;

ain't your feet *dead?* And look at your hair, all tangled like a wild one!"
She got a comb.

"Be quiet, daughter; what's ailin' you? Don't shake your head!"

"But shake your head and scatter day."

"What you say, Amarantha?" Mrs. Doggett held an ear down.

"Go 'way! Lea' me be!"

Her mother was hurt and left. And Mare ran, as she stared at the wall-paper.

"Christ, that my love were in my arms . . ."

Mare ran. She ran through a wind white with moonlight and wet with "the small rain." And the wind she ran through, it ran through her, and made her shiver as she ran. And the man beside her leaped high over the waves of the dead grasses and gathered the wind in his arms, and her hair was heavy and his was tossing, and a little fox ran before them in waves of black and silver, more immense than she had ever known the world could be, and more beautiful.

"God Almighty beautiful, to take your breath away!"

Mare wondered, and she was not used to wondering. "Is it only crazy folks ever run like that and talk that way?"

She no longer ran; she walked; for her breath was gone. And there was some other reason, some other reason. Oh yes, it was because her feet were hurting her. So, at last, and roundabout, her shoes had made contact with her brain.

Bending over the side of the bed, she loosened one of them mechanically. She pulled it half off. But then she looked down at it sharply, and she pulled it on again.

"How beautiful . . ."

Color overspread her face in a slow wave.

"How beautiful are thy feet with shoes . . ."

"Is it only crazy folks ever say such things?"

"O prince's daughter!"

"Call you that?"

By and by there was a knock at the door. It opened, and Ruby Herter came in.

"Hello, Mare old girl!" His face was red. He scowled and kicked at the floor. "I'd-a been over sooner, except we got a mule down sick." He looked at his dumb betrothed. "Come on, cheer up, forget it! He won't scare you no more, not that boy, not what's left o' him. What you lookin' at, sourface? Ain't you glad to see me?"

Mare quit looking at the wallpaper and looked at the floor.

"Yeh," she said.

"That's more like it, babe." He came and sat beside her; reached down behind her and gave her a spank. "Come on, give us a kiss, babe!" He wiped his mouth on his jumper sleeve, a good farmer's sleeve, spotted with milking.

He put his hands on her; he was used to handling animals. "Hey, you, warm up a little; reckon I'm goin' to do all the lovin'?"

"Ruby, lea' me be!"

"What!"

She was up, twisting. He was up, purple.

"What's ailin' of you, Mare? What you bawlin' about?"

"Nothin'—only go 'way!"

She pushed him to the door and through it with all her strength, and closed it in his face, and stood with her weight against it, crying, "Go 'way! Go 'way! Lea' me be!"

The Chrysanthemums

JOHN STEINBECK

[1902–1968]

The high gray-flannel fog of winter closed the Salinas Valley from the sky and from the rest of the world. On every side it sat like a lid on the mountains and made of the great valley a closed pot. On the broad, level land floor the gang plows bit deep and left the black earth shining like metal where the shares had cut. On the foot-hill ranches across the Salinas River the yellow stubble fields seemed to be bathed in pale cold sunshine; but there was no sunshine in the valley now in December. The thick willow scrub along the river flamed with sharp and positive yellow leaves.

It was a time of quiet and of waiting. The air was cold and tender. A light wind blew up from the southwest so that the farmers were mildly hopeful of a good rain before long; but fog and rain do not go together.

Across the river, on Henry Allen's foot-hill ranch there was little work to be done, for the hay was cut and stored and the orchards were plowed up to receive the rain deeply when it should come. The cattle on the higher slopes were becoming shaggy and rough-coated.

Elisa Allen, working in her flower garden, looked down across the yard and saw Henry, her husband, talking to two men in business suits. The three of them stood by the tractor shed, each man with one foot on the side of the Little Fordson. They smoked cigarettes and studied the machine as they talked.

Elisa watched them for a moment and then went back to her work. She was thirty-five. Her face was lean and strong and her eyes were as clear as water. Her figure looked blocked and heavy in her gardening costume, a man's black hat pulled low down over her eyes, clodhopper shoes, a figured print dress almost completely covered by a big corduroy apron with four big pockets to hold the snips, the trowel and scratcher, the seeds and the knife she worked with. She wore heavy leather gloves to protect her hands while she worked.

She was cutting down the old year's chrysanthemum stalks with a pair of short and powerful scissors. She looked down toward the men by the tractor shed now and then. Her face was eager and mature and handsome; even her work with the scissors was overeager, overpowerful. The chrysanthemum stems seemed too small and easy for her energy.

She brushed a cloud of hair out of her eyes with the back of her glove, and left a smudge of earth on her cheek in doing it. Behind her stood the neat white farmhouse with red geraniums close-banked round it as high as the windows. It was a hard-swept-looking little house, with hard-polished windows and a clean mat on the front steps.

Elisa cast another glance toward the tractor shed. The stranger men were getting into their Ford coupé. She took off a glove and put her strong fingers down into the forest of new green chrysanthemum sprouts that were growing round the old roots. She spread the leaves and looked down among the close-growing stems. No aphids were there, no sow bugs nor snails nor cut worms. Her terrier fingers destroyed such pests before they could get started.

Elisa started at the sound of her husband's voice. He had come near quietly and he leaned over the wire fence that protected her flower garden from cattle and dogs and chickens.

"At it again," he said. "You've got a strong new crop coming."

Elisa straightened her back and pulled on the gardening glove again. "Yes. They'll be strong this coming year." In her tone and on her face there was a little smugness.

"You've got a gift with things," Henry observed. "Some of those yellow chrysanthemums you had last year were ten inches across. I wish you'd work out in the orchard and raise some apples that big."

Her eyes sharpened. "Maybe I could do it too. I've a gift with things all right. My mother had it. She would stick anything in the ground and make it grow. She said it was having planter's hands that knew how to do it."

"Well, it sure works with flowers," he said.

"Henry, who were those men you were talking to?"

"Why, sure, that's what I came to tell you. They were from the Western Meat Company. I sold those thirty head of three-year-old steers. Got nearly my own price too."

"Good," she said. "Good for you."

"And I thought," he continued, "I thought how it's Saturday afternoon, and we might go into Salinas for dinner at a restaurant and then to a picture show—to celebrate, you see."

"Good," she repeated. "Oh, yes. That will be good."

Henry put on his joking tone. "There's fights tonight. How'd you like to go to the fights?"

"Oh, no," she said breathlessly. "No, I wouldn't like fights."

"Just fooling, Elisa. We'll go to a movie. Let's see. It's two now. I'm going to take Scotty and bring down those steers from the hill. It'll take us maybe two hours. We'll go in town about five and have dinner at the Cominos Hotel. Like that?"

"Of course I'll like it. It's good to eat away from home."

"All right then. I'll go get up a couple of horses."

She said, "I'll have plenty of time to transplant some of these sets, I guess."

She heard her husband calling Scotty down by the barn. And a little later she saw the two men ride up the pale-yellow hillside in search of the steers.

There was a little square sandy bed kept for rooting the chrysanthemums. With her trowel she turned the soil over and over and smoothed it and patted it firm. Then she dug ten parallel trenches to receive the sets. Back at the chrysanthemum bed she pulled out the little crisp shoots, trimmed off the leaves of each one with her scissors, and laid it on a small orderly pile.

A squeak of wheels and plod of hoofs came from the road. Elisa looked up. The country road ran along the dense bank of willows and cottonwoods that bordered the river, and up this road came a curious vehicle, curiously drawn. It was an old spring-wagon, with a round canvas top on it like the cover of a prairie schooner. It was drawn by an old bay horse and a little gray-and-white burro. A big stubble-bearded man sat between the cover flaps and drove the crawling team. Underneath the wagon, between the hind wheels, a lean and rangy mongrel dog walked sedately. Words were painted on the canvas in clumsy, crooked letters: "Pots, pans, knives, scissors, lawn mowers, Fixed." Two rows of articles, and the triumphantly definitive "Fixed" below. The black paint had run down in little sharp points beneath each letter.

Elisa, squatting on the ground, watched to see the crazy loose-jointed wagon pass by. But it didn't pass. It turned into the farm road in front of her house, crooked old wheels skirling and squeaking. The rangy dog darted from beneath the wheels and ran ahead. Instantly the two ranch shepherds flew out at him. Then all three stopped, and with stiff and quivering tails, with taut straight legs, with ambassadorial dignity, they slowly circled, sniffing daintily. The caravan pulled up to Elisa's wire fence and stopped. Now the newcomer dog, feeling outnumbered, lowered his tail and retired under the wagon with raised hackles and bared teeth.

The man on the wagon seat called out, "That's a bad dog in a fight when he gets started."

Elisa laughed. "I see he is. How soon does he generally get started?"

The man caught up her laughter and echoed it heartily. "Sometimes not for weeks and weeks," he said. He climbed stiffly down over the wheel. The horse and the donkey dropped like unwatered flowers.

Elisa saw that he was a very big man. Although his hair and beard were graying, he did not look old. His worn black suit was wrinkled and spotted with grease. The laughter had disappeared from his face and eyes the moment his laughing voice ceased. His eyes were dark and they were full of the brooding that gets in the eyes of teamsters and of sailors. The calloused hands he rested on the fence were cracked, and every crack was a black line. He took off his battered hat.

"I'm off my general road, ma'am," he said. "Does this dirt road cut over across the river to the Los Angeles highway?"

Elisa stood up and shoved the thick scissors in her apron pocket. "Well, yes, it does, but it winds around and then fords the river. I don't think your team could pull through the sand."

He replied with some asperity, "It might surprise you what them beasts can pull through."

"When they get started?" she asked.

He smiled for a second. "Yes. When they get started."

"Well," said Elisa, "I think you'll save time if you go back to the Salinas road and pick up the highway there."

He drew a big finger down the chicken wire and made it sing. "I ain't in any hurry, ma'am. I go from Seattle to San Diego and back every year. Takes all my time. About six months each way. I aim to follow nice weather."

Elisa took off her gloves and stuffed them in the apron pocket with the scissors. She touched the under edge of her man's hat, searching for fugitive hairs. "That sounds like a nice kind of a way to live," she said.

He leaned confidentially over the fence. "Maybe you noticed the writing on my wagon. I mend pots and sharpen knives and scissors. You got any of them things to do?"

"Oh, no," she said quickly. "Nothing like that." Her eyes hardened with resistance.

"Scissors is the worst thing," he explained. "Most people just ruin scissors trying to sharpen 'em, but I know how. I got a special tool. It's a little bobbit kind of thing and patented. But it sure does the trick."

"No. My scissors are all sharp."

"All right then. Take a pot," he continued earnestly, "a bent pot or a pot with a hole. I can make it like new so you don't have to buy no new ones. That's a saving for you."

"No," she said shortly. "I tell you I have nothing like that for you to do."

His face fell to an exaggerated sadness. His voice took on a whining undertone. "I ain't had a thing to do today. Maybe I won't have no supper tonight. You see I'm off my regular road. I know folks on the highway clear from Seattle to San Diego. They save their things for me to sharpen up because they know I do it so good and save them money."

"I'm sorry," Elisa said irritably. "I haven't anything for you to do."

His eyes left her face and fell to searching the ground. They roamed about until they came to the chrysanthemum bed where she had been working. "What's them plants, ma'am?"

The irritation and resistance melted from Elisa's face. "Oh, those are chrysanthemums, giant whites and yellows. I raise them every year, bigger than anybody around here."

"Kind of a long-stemmed flower? Looks like a quick puff of colored smoke?" he asked.

"That's it. What a nice way to describe them!"

"They smell kind of nasty till you get used to them," he said.

"It's a good bitter smell," she retorted, "not nasty at all."

He changed his tone quickly. "I like the smell myself."

"I had ten-inch blooms this year," she said.

The man leaned farther over the fence. "Look. I know a lady down the road a piece has got the nicest garden you ever seen. Got nearly every kind of flower but no chrysanthemums. Last time I was mending a copperbottom wash tub for her (that's a hard job but I do it good), she said to me, 'If you ever run acrost some nice chrysanthemums, I wish you'd try to get me a few seeds.' That's what she told me."

Elisa's eyes grew alert and eager. "She couldn't have known much about chrysanthemums. You *can* raise them from seed, but it's much easier to root the little sprouts you see there."

"Oh," he said. "I s'pose I can't take none to her then."

"Why yes, you can," Elisa cried. "I can put some in damp sand, and you can carry them right along with you. They'll take root in the pot if you keep them damp. And then she can transplant them."

"She'd sure like to have some, ma'am. You say they're nice ones?"

"Beautiful," she said. "Oh, beautiful!" Her eyes shone. She tore off the battered hat and shook out her dark pretty hair. "I'll put them in a flower pot, and you can take them right with you. Come into the yard."

While the man came through the picket gate Elisa ran excitedly along the geranium-bordered path to the back of the house. And she returned carrying a big red flower pot. The gloves were forgotten now. She kneeled on the ground by the starting bed and dug up the sandy soil with her fingers and scooped it into the bright new flower pot. Then she picked up the little pile of shoots she had prepared. With her strong fingers she pressed them into the sand and tamped round them with her knuckles. The man stood over her. "I'll tell you what to do," she said. "You remember so you can tell the lady."

"Yes, I'll try to remember."

"Well, look. These will take root in about a month. Then she must set them out, about a foot apart in good rich earth like this, see?" She lifted a handful of dark soil for him to look at. "They'll grow fast and tall. Now remember this. In July tell her to cut them down, about eight inches from the ground."

"Before they bloom?" he asked.

"Yes, before they bloom." Her face was tight with eagerness. "They'll grow right up again. About the last of September the buds will start."

She stopped and seemed perplexed. "It's the budding that takes the most care," she said hesitantly. "I don't know how to tell you." She looked deep into his eyes searchingly. Her mouth opened a little, and she seemed to be listening. "I'll try to tell you," she said. "Did you ever hear of planting hands?"

"Can't say I have, ma'am."

"Well, I can only tell you what it feels like. It's when you're picking off the buds you don't want. Everything goes right down into your fingertips. You watch your fingers work. They do it themselves. You can feel how it is. They pick and pick the buds. They never make a mistake. They're with the plant. Do you see? Your fingers and the plant. You can feel that, right up your arm. They know. They never make a mistake. You can feel it. When you're like that you can't do anything wrong. Do you see that? Can you understand that?"

She was kneeling on the ground looking up at him. Her breast swelled passionately.

The man's eyes narrowed. He looked away self-consciously. "Maybe I know," he said. "Sometimes in the night in the wagon there—"

Elisa's voice grew husky. She broke in on him. "I've never lived as you do, but I know what you mean. When the night is dark—the stars are sharp-pointed, and there's quiet. Why, you rise up and up!"

Kneeling there, her hand went out toward his legs in the greasy black trousers. Her hesitant fingers almost touched the cloth. Then her hand dropped to the ground.

He said, "It's nice, just like you say. Only when you don't have no dinner it ain't."

She stood up then, very straight, and her face was ashamed. She held the flower pot out to him and placed it gently in his arms. "Here. Put it in your wagon, on the seat, where you can watch it. Maybe I can find something for you to do."

At the back of the house she dug in the can pile and found two old and battered aluminum sauce pans. She carried them back and gave them to him. "Here, maybe you can fix these."

His manner changed. He became professional. "Good as new I can fix them." At the back of his wagon he set a little anvil, and out of an oily tool box dug a small machine hammer. Elisa came through the gate to watch him while he pounded out the dents in the kettles. His mouth grew sure and knowing. At a difficult part of the work he sucked his under-lip.

"You sleep right in the wagon?" Elisa asked.

"Right in the wagon, ma'am. Rain or shine I'm dry as a cow in there."

"It must be nice," she said. "It must be very nice. I wish women could do such things."

"It ain't the right kind of a life for a woman."

Her upper lip raised a little, showing her teeth. "How do you know? How can you tell?" she said.

"I don't know, ma'am," he protested. "Of course I don't know. Now here's your kettles, done. You don't have to buy no new ones."

"How much?"

"Oh, fifty cents'll do. I keep my prices down and my work good. That's why I have all them satisfied customers up and down the highway."

Elisa brought him a fifty-cent piece from the house and dropped it in his hand. "You might be surprised to have a rival sometime. I can sharpen scissors too. And I can beat the dents out of little pots. I could show you what a woman might do."

He put his hammer back in the oily box and shoved the little anvil out of sight. "It would be a lonely life for a woman, ma'am, and a scary life, too, with animals creeping under the wagon all night." He climbed over the single-tree, steadying himself with a hand on the burro's white rump. He settled himself in the seat, picked up the lines. "Thank you kindly, ma'am," he said. "I'll do like you told me; I'll go back and catch the Salinas road."

"Mind," she called, "if you're long in getting there, keep the sand damp."

"Sand, ma'am—Sand? Oh, sure. You mean around the chrysanthemums. Sure I will." He clucked his tongue. The beasts leaned luxuriously into their collars. The mongrel dog took his place between the back wheels. The wagon turned and crawled out the entrance road and back the way it had come, along the river.

Elisa stood in front of her wire fence watching the slow progress of the caravan. Her shoulders were straight, her head thrown back, her eyes half-closed, so that the scene came vaguely into them. Her lips moved silently, forming the words "Good-bye—good-bye." Then she whispered, "That's a bright direction. There's a glowing there." The sound of her whisper startled her. She shook herself free and looked about to see whether anyone had been listening. Only the dogs had heard. They lifted their heads toward her from their sleeping in the dust, and then stretched out their chins and settled asleep again. Elisa turned and ran hurriedly into the house.

In the kitchen she reached behind the stove and felt the water tank. It was full of hot water from the noonday cooking. In the bathroom she tore off her soiled clothes and flung them into the corner. And then she scrubbed herself with a little block of pumice, legs and thighs, loins and chest and arms, until her skin was scratched and red. When she had dried herself she stood in front of a mirror in the bedroom and looked at her body. She tightened her stomach and threw out her chest. She turned and looked over her shoulder at her back.

After a while she began to dress slowly. She put on her newest under-clothing and her nicest stockings and the dress which was the symbol of her prettiness. She worked carefully on her hair, penciled her eyebrows, and rouged her lips.

Before she was finished she heard the little thunder of hoofs and the shouts of Henry and his helper as they drove the red steers into the corral. She heard the gate bang shut and set herself for Henry's arrival.

His step sounded on the porch. He entered the house calling, "Elisa, where are you?"

"In my room, dressing. I'm not ready. There's hot water for your bath. Hurry up. It's getting late."

When she heard him splashing in the tub, Elisa laid his dark suit on the bed, and shirt and socks and tie beside it. She stood his polished shoes on the floor beside the bed. Then she went to the porch and sat primly and stiffly down. She looked toward the river road where the willow-line was still yellow with frosted leaves so that under the high gray fog they seemed a thin band of sunshine. This was the only color in the gray afternoon. She sat unmoving for a long time.

Henry came banging out of the door, shoving his tie inside his vest as he came. Elisa stiffened and her face grew tight. Henry stopped short and looked at her. "Why—why, Elisa. You look so nice!"

"Nice? You think I look nice? What do you mean by 'nice'?"

Henry blundered on. "I don't know. I mean you look different, strong and happy."

"I am strong? Yes, strong. What do you mean 'strong'?"

He looked bewildered. "You're playing some kind of a game," he said helplessly. "It's a kind of a play. You look strong enough to break a calf over your knee, happy enough to eat it like a watermelon."

For a second she lost her rigidity. "Henry! Don't talk like that. You didn't know what you said." She grew complete again. "I am strong," she boasted. "I never knew before how strong."

Henry looked down toward the tractor shed, and when he brought his eyes back to her, they were his own again. "I'll get out the car. You can put on your coat while I'm starting."

Elisa went into the house. She heard him drive to the gate and idle down his motor, and then she took a long time to put on her hat. She pulled it here and pressed it there. When Henry turned the motor off she slipped into her coat and went out.

The little roadster bounced along on the dirt road by the river, raising the birds and driving the rabbits into the brush. Two cranes flapped heavily over the willow-line and dropped into the river-bed.

Far ahead on the road Elisa saw a dark speck in the dust. She suddenly felt empty. She did not hear Henry's talk. She tried not to look; she did not want to see the little heap of sand and green shoots, but she could not help herself. The chrysanthemums lay in the road close to the wagon tracks. But not the pot; he had kept that. As the car passed them she remembered the good bitter smell, and a little shudder went through her. She felt ashamed of her strong planter's hands that were no use, lying palms up in her lap.

The roadster turned a bend and she saw the caravan ahead. She swung full round toward her husband so that she could not see the little covered wagon and the mismatched team as the car passed.

In a moment they had left behind them the man who had not known or needed to know what she said, the bargainer. She did not look back.

To Henry, she said loudly, to be heard above the motor, "It will be good, tonight, a good dinner."

"Now you're changed again," Henry complained. He took one hand from the wheel and patted her knee. "I ought to take you in to dinner oftener. It would be good for both of us. We get so heavy out on the ranch."

"Henry," she asked, "could we have wine at dinner?"

"Sure. Say! That will be fine."

She was silent for a while; then she said, "Henry, at those prize fights do the men hurt each other very much?"

"Sometimes a little, not often. Why?"

"Well, I've read how they break noses, and blood runs down their chests. I've read how the fighting gloves get heavy and soggy with blood."

He looked round at her. "What's the matter, Elisa? I didn't know you read things like that." He brought the car to a stop, then turned to the right over the Salinas River bridge.

"Do any women ever go to the fights?" she asked.

"Oh, sure, some. What's the matter, Elisa? Do you want to go? I don't think you'd like it, but I'll take you if you really want to go."

She relaxed limply in the seat. "Oh, no. I don't want to go. I'm sure I don't." Her face was turned away from him. "It will be enough if we can have wine. It will be plenty." She turned up her coat collar so he could not see that she was crying weakly—like an old woman.

Mac's Masterpiece

FRANK O'CONNOR

[1903–1966]

Two or three times a year Mac, a teacher in the monks' school, took to his bed for four or five days. That was understood. But when he gave up taking food his landlady thought it was getting serious. She told his friends she wanted to have him certified. Not another day would she keep him in the house after the abominable language he had used to her.

His friends, Boyd, Devane, and Corbett, came. Mac refused to open the bedroom door. He asked to be allowed to die in peace. It was only when Boyd took a hatchet to the lock that he appeared in his nightshirt, haggard and distraught, a big, melancholy mountain of a man, dribbling, his hair in tumult.

"Almighty God!" he cried. "Won't I even be allowed that one little comfort?"

They wrapped him in blankets and set him by the fire among his discarded toys, his dumbbells, chest developers, Indian clubs, sabers, shotgun, camera, cinema, gramophone, and piano, while Corbett, the bright young man from the local newspaper, heated the water for the punch. At this Mac came to himself a little and insulted Boyd. Boyd was his foil; a narrow-chested, consumptive-looking chemist with a loud voice and a yapping laugh like a fox's bark. He wore a bowler hat at various extraordinary angles and was very disputatious.

"Bad luck to you!" growled Boyd. "I don't believe there's anything up with you."

"Nothing up with me!" jeered Mac. "Devane, did you hear that? You know, Devane, that hog, unless you had a broken neck or a broken bottom, he'd say there was nothing up with you. He'd say there was nothing up with Othello or Hamlet. 'Nothing up with you!' Did anybody ever hear such a barbarous locution?"

"Come on away, Corbett," said Boyd angrily. "We might have known the old cod was only play-acting as usual."

"Don't rouse me now," said Mac with quiet scorn.

"Like an old actress when she's going off, pretending her jewelry is stolen."

"I won't be roused," said Mac earnestly. "What's that Lear says—'No, I'll not weep, this heart shall crack. . . .' You Philistine, you Christian Brothers' brat, you low, porter-drinking sot," he snarled with sudden violence, "I have a soul above disputing with you. . . . Devane," he added mournfully, "you understand me. You have a grand Byronian soul."

"I have nervous dyspepsia," groaned Devane, who was organist in the parish church. He felt himself in two or three places. "I get terrible pains here and here."

"I see you now as I saw you twenty years ago with the fire of genius in your eyes," Mac went on. "And now, God help you, you go about the streets as though you were making a living by collecting lost hairpins."

Devane refused punch. It made his stomach worse, he said.

"You're better off," said Mac, falling serious once more. "I say you're better off. You see your misery plain. You're only a little maggot yourself now, a measly little maggot of a man, hoping the Almight God won't crush you too soon, but you're a consistent maggot, a maggot by night and by day. But in my dreams I'm still a king, and then comes the awakening, the horror, the gray dawn."

He shuddered, wrapped in his blanket. Corbett rose and began to fiddle with the gramophone.

"Don't break that machine," said Mac irritably. "It cost a lot."

"What you want is a wife," said Corbett. "All those gadgets are only substitute wives. Did you ever get an hour's real pleasure out of any of them? I bet you never play that gramophone."

"You have a low mind, Corbett," snarled Mac. "You impute the basest motives to everyone."

At that very moment Corbett placed the needle on the record. There was a startling series of cracks, and then it began to give off "La Donna è Mobile." Mac jumped up as though he had been shot.

"O God, not that, not that! Turn it off! There, you've done it now."

"What?" asked Corbett innocently.

"Sunlight on the Mediterranean, moonlight on the Swiss lakes, the glow-worms in the grass, young love, hope, passion."

He began to stride up and down the room, swinging his blanket like a toga.

"The last time I heard that"—he stretched out his arm in a wild gesture— " 'twas in Galway on a rainy night. Galway in the rain and the statue of O Conaire in the Park and the long western faces like—like bullocks. There they were over the roulette tables, counting out their coppers; they had big cloth purses. Then suddenly, the what-you-may-call-it organ began. . . . Magic, by God, magic! It mounted and mounted and you knew by the shudder down your spine that 'twas all on fire; a sort of—a sort of pyramid—that's it!—a pyramid of light over your head. Turning and turning, faster and faster, the pyramid, I mean, and the lights crackling and changing; blue, red, orange. Man, I rushed back to the hotel, fearing something would spoil it on me. The last light was setting over the church tower, woodbine-colored light and a black knot of weeping cloud."

"Bravo, Mac!" said Boyd with his coarse laugh. He stuck his thumbs into the armholes of his waistcoat. "The old warrior is himself again. Haw?"

"Until the next time," said Corbett with a sneer.

"There'll be no next time," said Mac solemnly. "I'm after being down to hell and coming back. I see it all now. The Celtic mist is gone. I see it all clear before me in the Latin light."

And sure enough there was a change in Mac's behavior. He almost gave up drink and began to talk of the necessity for solitude. Solitude, he said, was the mind's true home. Solitude filled the cistern; company emptied it. He would stay at home and read or think. He began to talk of a vast novel on the subject of the clash between idealism and materialism in the Irish soul.

But the discipline was a hard one. Though he told the maid to say he was out, he hated to hear the voices of Boyd or Corbett as they went off together down the quay. One evening as they were moving away he knocked at the window and raised the blind, looking out at them and nodding. He tried to assume a superior, amused air, but there was wistfulness in his eyes. Finally he raised the window.

"Come on out, man!" said Boyd scornfully.

"No, no, I couldn't," replied Mac weakly.

" 'Tis a lovely night."

"What way did ye come?"

"Down High Street. All the shawlies [1] were out singing. Look, 'tis a gorgeous night. Stars! Millions of them!"

Softly in a wheezy tenor Boyd sang "Night of Stars and Night of Love" with declamatory gestures. Mac's resolution wavered.

"Come on in for a minute."

They climbed over the low sill, Boyd still singing and gesturing. As usual, he had an interesting item of news for Mac. The latest scandal; piping hot; another piece of jobbery perpetrated by a religious secret society. Mac groaned.

"My God, 'tis awful," he agreed. " 'Tis, do you know what it is, 'tis scandalous."

"Well, isn't that what we were always looking for?" exclaimed Boyd, shaking his fist truculently. "Government by our own? Now we have it. Government by the gunmen and the priests and the secret societies."

" 'Tis our own fault," said Mac gloomily.

"How so-a?"

" 'Tis our own fault. We're the intellect of the country and what good are we? None. Do we ever protest? No. All we do is live in burrows and growl at all the things we find wrong."

"And what else can we do? A handful of us?"

"Thousands of us."

"A handful! How long would I keep me business if I said or did what I thought was right? I make two hundred a year out of parish priests with indigestion. Man, dear, is there one man, one man in this whole town that can call his soul his own?"

---

[1] *shawlies:* fisherwomen.

"You're all wrong," said Mac crossly, his face going into a thousand wrinkles.

"Is there one man?" shouted Boyd with lifted finger.

"Bogy men!" said Mac, "that's all that frightens ye. Bogy men! If we were in earnest all that tangle of circumstance would melt away."

"Oh, melt away, melt away? Would it, indeed?"

"Of course it would. The human will can achieve anything. The will is the divine faculty in man."

"This is a new sort of theology."

" 'Tisn't theology at all; 'tis common sense. Let me alone now; I thought all this out long ago. The only obstacles we ever see are in ourselves."

"Ah, what nonsense are you talking? How are they in ourselves?"

"When the will is diseased, it creates obstacles where they never existed."

"Answer me," bawled Boyd, spitting into the fire. "Answer my question. Answer it now and let Corbett hear you. How are the obstacles in ourselves? Can a blind man paint a picture, can he? Can a cripple run the thousand yards? Haw?"

"Boyd," said Mac with a fastidious shudder, "you have a very coarse mind."

"I have a very realistic mind."

"You have a very coarse mind; you have the mind of a Christian Brothers' boy. But if you persist in that—that unpleasant strain, I'm more ready to believe that a blind man can paint a picture than that a normal, healthy man can be crippled from birth by a tangle of irrelevant circumstances."

"Circumstances are never irrelevant."

"Between the conception and the achievement all circumstances are irrelevant."

"You don't believe in matther? [1] Isn't that what it all comes to?"

"That has nothing to do with it."

"Do you or do you not believe in matther?" repeated Boyd throwing his bowler viciously on to the floor.

"I believe in the human will," snapped Mac.

"That means you don't believe in life."

"Not as you see it."

"Because I believe in life," said Boyd, his lantern jaw working sideways. "I believe that in all the life about me a divine purpose is working itself out."

"Oh, God," groaned Mac. "Animal stagnation! Chewing the cud! The City Council! Wolfe Tone Street! Divine purpose, my sweet God! Don't you see, you maggot, you clodhopper, you corner boy, that life can't be directed from outside? If there is a divine purpose—I don't know whether there is or not—it can only express itself through some human agency; and how the devil can you have a human agency if you haven't the individual soul, the man representing humanity? Do you think institutions, poetry, painting, the Roman

[1] *matther:* matter.

Empire, were created by maggots and clodhoppers? Do you? Do you? Do you?"

Just then there was a ring at the door and Devane came in, looking more than ever like a collector of lost hairpins.

"How are you, Devane?" asked Corbett.

"Rotten," said Devane.

"I never saw you any other way," growled Mac.

"I never am any other way," replied Devane.

"You're just in time," said Corbett.

"How so-a?"

"We're getting the will versus determinism; 'tis gorgeous. Go on, Mac. You were talking about the Roman Empire."

Mac suddenly threw himself into a chair, covering his face with his hands.

"My God, my God," he groaned softly between his fingers. "I'm at it again. I'm fifty-four years of age and I'm talking about the human will. A man whose life is over talking about the will. Go away and let me write me novel. For God's sake let me do one little thing before I die."

After that night Mac worked harder than ever. He talked a great deal about his novel. The secret of the Irish soul, he had discovered, was the conflict between the ideal and the reality.

Boyd, with whom he discussed it one night when they met accidentally, disputed this as he disputed everything.

"Idealism my eye!" he said scornfully. "The secret is bloody hypocrisy."

"No, Boyd," protested Mac. "You have a mind utterly without refinement. Hypocrisy is a noble and enlightened vice; 'tis far beyond the capacity of the people of this country. The English have been called hypocritical. Now, nobody could ever talk about the hypocritical Gael. The English had their walled cities, their castles, their artillery, as the price of their hypocrisy; all the unfortunate gulls of Irishmen ever got out of their self-deception was a raggy cloak and a bed in a wood."

"And is that what you're going to say in your novel?"

"I'm going to say lots of things in my novel."

"You'd better mind yourself."

"I'm going to tell the truth at last. I'm going to show that what's wrong with all of you people is your inability to reconcile the debauched sentimentalism of your ideals with the disorderly materialism of your lives."

"What?" Boyd stopped dead, hands in his pockets, head forward. "Are you calling me a sentimentalist?"

"I'm only speaking generally."

"Are you calling me a sentimentalist?"

"I'm not referring to you at all."

"Because I'm no sentimentalist. I'm a realist."

"You're a disappointed idealist like all the rest, that's what you are."

"A disappointed idealist? How do you make that out?"

"Boyd, I see ye all now quite clearly. I see ye as if I was looking at ye from eternity. I see what's wrong with ye. Ye aim too high. Ye hitch yeer wagon to too many bloody stars at the one time. Then comes the first snag and the first compromise. After that ye begin to sink, sink, sink till ye're tied hand and foot, till ye even deny the human soul."

"Are you back to that again? Are you denying the existence of matther again?"

"Materialist! Shabby little materialist, with your sentimental dreams. I see ye all there with yeer heads tied to yeer knees, pretending 'tis circumstance and 'tis nothing only the ropes ye spin out of yeer own guts."

Boyd was furious. It was bad enough to have Mac dodging him, telling the maid to say he was out, forcing him to spend long, lonely evenings; but then to call him a sentimentalist, a materialist, a disappointed idealist! In fact, all Mac's friends resented the new state of things. They jeered at the tidy way he now dressed himself. They jeered at the young woman with whom he was seen taking tea at the Ambassadors'.

Elsie Deignan was a pretty young woman of thirty-two or three. She was a teacher in the nuns' school in the South parish and had literary leanings. As a result of her experiences with the nuns, she was slightly tinged with anti-clericalism. For the first time in his life Mac felt he had met a woman whose conversation he might conceivably tolerate over an extended period. He fell badly in love.

The resentment of Mac's friends grew when he was seen walking out with her. And there were strange stories in circulation about the things he was saying in his novel. They were all going into it, and in a ridiculous fashion. They were pleased when Corbett told them that Mac's employers, the monks, were getting uneasy, too. Mac knew far too much about the Order. He had often referred scornfully to the disparity between their professions and their practice; was it possible that he was revealing all this? Corbett swore he was; he also said that one chapter described the initiation of a young man into the Knights of Columbanus, skulls, cowls, blindfolding, oaths and all.

"I suppose he thinks he'll be able to retire on the proceeds of it," said Boyd in disgust. "The English will lap that up. I hate a man that fouls his own nest."

"Well, don't we all?" groaned Devane, who alone of the gang was disposed to be merciful.

"That's different," said Boyd. "We can say things like that among ourselves, in the family, so to speak, but we don't want everyone to know about it."

"He showed me a couple of chapters," said Devane mournfully. "I didn't see anything at all in it. Sentimental stuff, that's how it looked to me."

"Ah, but you didn't see the big scenes," said Corbett. "And for a good reason."

"What reason?"

"There are several nasty things about you in it."

"He couldn't say anything about me," said Devane.

"That's all you know."

"By God," said Boyd, "he deserves all he gets. If there's anything worse than a man using his friends for copy, I don't know what it is."

Devane, perturbed, slipped away. After a good deal of thought he went along the quays to Mac's lodgings, his head down, his umbrella hanging over his joined hands, a picture of misery. Mac was busy and cheerful. Sheets of foolscap littered the table. He had been drinking tea.

"So you're still at it," said Devane.

"Still at it."

"You're a brave man."

"How so?"

"All the dove-cots you're after putting a-flutter."

"What the hell are you talking about?"

"I hear the monks are very uneasy."

"About my novel?" asked Mac with a start.

"Yes."

"How did they get to hear of it?"

"How do I know? Corbett says they were talking to the Canon about you."

Mac grew pale.

"Who's spreading stories about me?"

"I don't know, I tell you. What did you say about me?"

"I said nothing about you."

"You'd better not. You'll cause trouble enough."

"Sure, I'm not saying anything about anybody," said Mac, his face beginning to twitch.

"Well, they think you are."

"My God, there's a hole to work in." Mac suddenly sat back, haggard, his hands spread wide before him. "By God, I have a good mind to roast them all. And I didn't get to the serious part at all yet. That's only a description of his childhood."

"I didn't see anything wrong with it—what you showed me," said Devane, rubbing his nose.

"By God, I have," repeated Mac passionately, "a thorough good mind to roast them."

"You're too old," said Devane, and his metallic voice sounded like the spinning of a rattle. "Why don't you have sense? I used to want to be a musician one time. I don't want anything now only to live till I get me pension. You ought to have sense," he went on in a still crankier tone. "Don't you know they'll all round on you, like they did on me the time I got the organ?"

" 'Tis the curse of the tribe," declared Mac despairingly. "They hate to see anyone separating himself from the tribe."

"I don't know what it is," said Devane, "and I don't give a damn. I used to be trying to think out explanations, too, one time, but I gave it up. What's the use when you can read Jane Austen? Read Jane Austen, MacCarthy, she's grand and consoling, and there isn't a line in her that would remind you of anything at all. I like Jane Austen and Trollope, and I like Rameau and Lully and Scarlatti, and I'd like Bach too if he was satisfied with writing nice little dance tunes instead of bloody big elephants of Masses that put you in mind of your last end."

Devane left Mac very depressed. The news about the novel had spread. People discussed it everywhere; his enemies said they had never expected anything else from him; his friends were uneasy and went about asking if they shouldn't, as old friends of Mac's, advise him. They didn't, and as a result the scandal only spread farther.

With Elsie, Mac permitted himself to rage.

"By God, I will roast them now," he said. "I'm going to change the whole center part of the book. I see now where I went wrong. My idea was to show the struggle in a man's soul between idealism and materialism; you know, the Celtic streak, soaring dreams, 'the singing masons building roofs of gold'; the quest of the absolute, and then show how 'tis dragged down by the mean little everyday nature of the Celt; the mean, vain, money-grubbing, twisty little nature that kept him from ever doing anything in the world only suffer and twist and whine. But now I see a bigger theme emerging; the struggle with the primitive world—colossal!"

"You're marvelous," said Elsie. "How do you think of it all?"

"Because I'm it," said Mac vehemently. "I am the Celt. I feel it in my blood. The Celts are only emerging into civilization. I and people like me are the forerunners. We feel the whole conflict of the nation in ourselves; the individual soul and at the same time the sense of the tribe; the Latin pride and the primitive desire to merge ourselves in the crowd. I can see how 'twill go. My fellow will have to sink himself time and time again and then at last the trumpet call! His great moment has come. He must say farewell to the old world and stand up, erect and defiant."

Still, Mac found his novel heavy going. It wasn't that ideas didn't come to him; he had too many, but always there was the sense of a hundred malicious faces peering over his shoulder; the Canon and Corbett; Devane, Cronin, Boyd; the headmaster.

Then one evening the maid came to his room.

"Oh, by the way, Mr. MacCarthy, the Canon called looking for you."

"Oh, did he?" said Mac, but his heart missed a beat.

"He said he'd call back another time."

"Did he say what he wanted?"

"No, Mr. MacCarthy, but he seemed a bit worried."

The pages he had written formed a blur before Mac's eyes. He could not write. Instead he put on his hat and went up to Elsie's.

" 'Tis all up," he said.

"What?" she asked.

"Everything. Turned out on the roadside at my age to earn my living what way I can."

"Do you mean you're sacked?"

"No, but I will be. 'Tis only a matter of days. The Canon called to see me. He never called to see me before. But I don't care. Let them throw me out. I'll starve, but I'll show them up."

"You're exaggerating, Dan. Sure, you didn't do anything at all yet."

"No, but they know what I can do. They're afraid of me. They see the end of their world is coming."

"But did anything else happen? Are you guessing all this or did somebody tell you?"

"I only wish to God I did it thirty years ago," said Mac, striding moodily about the room. "That was the time when I was young and strong and passionate. But I'm not afraid of them. I may be a fallen giant, but I'm still a giant. They can destroy me, but I'll pull their damn temple about their ears, the way Samson did. It's you I'm sorry for, girl. I didn't know I was bringing you into this."

"I'm not afraid," she said.

"Ah, I'm a broken man, a broken man. Ten years ago I could have given you something to be proud of. I had genius then."

After leaving her, he called at Dolan's for a drink. Corbett and some of the others were there and Mac felt the necessity for further information. He resolved to get it by bluff. He'd show them just what he thought of all the pother.

"I hear the Church is going to strike," he said with a cynical laugh.

"Did you hear that, too?" exclaimed Corbett.

"So you know?"

"Only that old Brother Reilly was supposed to be up complaining of you to the Canon."

"Aha! So that's it, is it?"

"I hope to goodness it won't be anything serious," said Corbett despondently.

"Oh, I don't care. I won't starve."

"You're a bloody fool," said Cronin, the fat painter who had done the Stations of the Cross for the new parish church. "Don't you know damn well you won't get another job?"

"I won't. I know quite well I won't."

"And what are you going to do? I declare to God I thought you had more sense. At your age, too! You have a fine cushy job and you won't mind it."

"Not at that price."

"What price? What are you talking about? Haven't we all to stand it and put the best face we can on it?"

"And damn well you paid for it, Cronin!"

"How so?"

"You're—how long are you painting?—twenty-five years? And worse and worse you're getting till now you're doing Stations of the Cross in the best Bavarian style. Twenty-five years ago you looked as though you might have had the makings of a painter in you, but now what are you? A maggot like the rest of us, a measly little maggot! Oh, you can puff out your chest and eat your mustache as much as you like, but that's what you are. A maggot, a five-bob-an-hour drawing master."

"MacCarthy," said Boyd, "you want your backside kicked, and you're damn well going to get it kicked."

"And who's going to do it, pray?" asked Mac coolly.

"You wait till you get the Canon down on you; he won't be long about it."

"Aha," said Mac. "So the Canon is our new hero! The Deliverer! This, as I always guessed, is what all the old talk was worth. Ye gas and gas about liberty of conscience, but at the first whiff of powder ye run and hide under the Canon's soutane. Well, here's to the Canon! Anyway, he's a man."

"Are you accusing me of turning me coat?" bawled Boyd.

"Quiet now, Boyd, quiet!"

"Are you?"

"Boyd, I won't even take the trouble to quarrel with you," said Mac gravely. "You've lost even the memory of a man. I suppose when you were twenty-five or so you did hear the clock, but you don't hear it any longer." He sipped his pint and suddenly grew passionate. "Or do you? Do you? Do you hear the inexorable hour when all your wasted years spring out like little toy soldiers from the clock and present arms? And does it never occur to you that one of these days they'll step out and present arms and say: 'Be off now, you bloody old cod! We're going back to barracks!' "

It was late when he left the pub. He was very pleased with himself. He had squelched Cronin, made Boyd ridiculous, reinstated himself with the gang, proved he was still the master of them all. As he came through the side streets he began to feel lonely. When he came to the bridge he leaned over it and watched the river flowing by beneath.

"Christ, what a fool I am! What a fool!" he groaned.

For a long time he stood on the quay outside his own lodgings, afraid to go in. The shapes of human beings began to crowd round him, malevolent and fierce, the Canon, the head, Cronin, Boyd, Devane. They all hated him, all wished him ill, would stop at nothing to destroy him.

In the early morning he went downstairs, made a bonfire of his novel, and sobbed himself to sleep.

Début Recital

EDWARD NEWHOUSE

[BORN 1911]

Marie Berthelot's large studio was a working room. Its furnishings consisted of two concert grand pianos and their stools, two Morris chairs, three music cabinets, a gilded plaster death mask of Chopin, and some framed portraits inscribed to her with assurances of affection and high regard from Rachmaninoff, Fauré, Busoni, and Schnabel. Though she was older now than those men had been at the times they posed for the pictures, Mme. Berthelot was still in the habit of walking the mile from her studio to Carnegie Hall when there was anything worth hearing. Concertgoers who saw her making her way up the stairs to one of the boxes thought she was somebody's cook.

She had never been a handsome woman, and so time had played no unkind tricks on her. She was small and thick-waisted, and scarcely cared what clothes she put on her back. Her once black hair was now mouse-colored and frizzy. At the collar of her plain, tailored blouse, she wore a plain diamond bar pin that had belonged to her mother. She wore no other jewelry. An attentive person might have guessed from the way she crossed and uncrossed her ankles that they were her one point of vanity. Her eyes, set deep in wrinkled lids, were pale blue and businesslike.

At the sound of the doorbell, she got rather heavily out of the Morris chair, which must have been as old as she was. She looked at her watch. That would be Mr. Vaughn downstairs, she thought—Harley's father. On time.

She sighed. Ordinarily she did not look forward to sessions with parents of her students. The mothers were apt to be too anxious, the fathers too demanding. Too many of them asked too many questions that could not be answered. They pushed their children too hard. Or not hard enough. They worried about the boy practicing too much or too little. They ran out of money and proposed to pay less for an hour than they would have had to give a plumber for replacing a pair of washers. Or they brought a more expensive present than they could possibly afford.

Frederick Vaughn did not fit into any of these categories. An investment banker of some means, he paid, on the first of each month, Mme. Berthelot's regular fee, which was that of a fashionable analyst. He did better than stay in the background. He kept out of sight. During all the years that Mme. Berthelot had been teaching Harley Vaughn, she had met the boy's father only once; Mr. Vaughn had come to hear his son play the Schumann Concerto in A Minor with a student orchestra. Such conferring as seemed indicated had always been with Mrs. Vaughn, a lovely, mild woman of perhaps forty-five. She had taught her boy beautiful manners, rare in his generation, still rarer in a gifted young musician.

In many ways, the Vaughns were unique in Mme. Berthelot's long experience as a piano teacher. Serious young students in this country were usually the children of first- or second-generation immigrants, and the Vaughns were of old American stock. Somewhere in the childhood of every real instrumentalist will be found a period of saturation in music, nearly always the result of having a musician in the home, more often than not a professional. This is not likely to be the case in a conventional American family. Given such a background, even a boy with supreme native talents will always in time be talked or ignored out of developing them into a career.

There had, of course, been Albert Spalding. But Spalding's mother, unlike Mrs. Vaughn, had been an accomplished amateur pianist and singer. And all of Spalding's early training had taken place in Italy and France, while Harley Vaughn had never been abroad. Harley's period of saturation was begun simply by his discovery of Station WQXR on the radio; at the age of six, he announced that all he wanted for Christmas was more records. And now, at nineteen, Harley was probably a bigger talent than Spalding had ever been. Marie Berthelot, a careful woman, had high hopes for the boy's Town Hall début next month. She wondered what Mr. Vaughn had come to see her about.

She remembered Mr. Vaughn from that concert Harley had played with the student orchestra; a very tall man, strongly made, with a face and manner that Mme. Berthelot could easily imagine as dominating a mutinous Board of Directors. After the inevitable remark that he knew nothing of music, Mr. Vaughn had professed to be pleased with Harley's performance, really pleased. "Thanks to you and my wife," he had said. Mrs. Vaughn had stood at his side, trying valiantly not to look too proud of her boy and not succeeding altogether. What a lovely mother the boy has, Mme. Berthelot had thought, what an impressive father: good stock; good boy.

Nonetheless, at the sound of the doorbell the old woman sighed. Something extraordinary must be going on to bring Frederick Vaughn here in the middle of the afternoon, and she did not like too many extraordinary things to come up so shortly before a début recital. She thought she had sensed an urgency in his phone call earlier in the day.

Mrs. Tierney, the housekeeper, ushered Vaughn in. He cast a quick glance around. "Two pianos?" he said. "I've never seen a room with two pianos. I had imagined you sit looking over shoulders."

"Sometimes I do."

When they were seated in the Morris chairs, Mme. Berthelot said, "How's Mrs. Vaughn? It's been quite some time since I've seen her."

"Not at all well. In fact . . ." Vaughn paused. "In fact, that's partly what I've come to talk to you about. But before I do, there are . . . I should like to ask a few questions, and I hope you take nothing for granted in answering. I'm totally ignorant in your field, Mme. Berthelot. All I know is what I've picked up listening to Harley and his mother, and that isn't much. So I must beg your indulgence."

"I'm terribly sorry to hear about Mrs. Vaughn."

"Yes. Now, in my field—I'm a banker—sometimes I'm handed a report on a company, and it might run to a hundred pages or more. But I've learned to go through it and pick out what's important. I suppose you can do the same—with all your experience. I know it's not exactly the same. No figures, not much past performance. I'm asking you to tell me about Harley—truthfully, please. What has he got? What are his chances?"

"Harley has a great deal," said Mme. Berthelot. "He's technically sound. He has flair; temperament. He works. And he can hear what he plays—good critical sense. He responds to teaching. I think he'll give an outstanding recital next month."

"This is not the profession I would have chosen for him. But that's neither here nor there. He'll always have a little something to live on. So he might as well be doing what he wants. I agreed to his not going to college. A lot of boys in his position . . . Well, this is what he wants to do. All right. I'm glad he's found it. You think he's going to play an outstanding recital. Will he be able to follow it up?"

"That there is no way of knowing."

"Why not? You know he's going to have backing. So it must be something in him. You've told me what he has. Now tell me what he hasn't."

"There really is no way of telling, at this stage. Harley hasn't done enough concert work for me to tell. It still remains to be seen, for instance, if he has the performer's temperament."

"I understood you to say he did have temperament."

"Musical temperament was what I had in mind. A performer's temperament is something else; and just as hard to describe. Let me try. I've had students who were virtuosos in this room, but in front of an audience they messed up every time. Perhaps not every time. Some of them will put on enough of an act to get a good start on a career, even a brilliant start. But somewhere along the way there'll be trouble. Their wife will decide it's not good for the baby to be dragged around on a long European tour. And they'll give in. A performer doesn't care what his wife decides. He doesn't care what you think or I think. It's between him and his audience."

Marie Berthelot had much more to say, but she stopped. She did not know how far she ought to go with Harley's father in exploring the doubts she had about the boy. The last thing she wanted was that Harley should learn at this point that there were any doubts at all. She thought, I must remember to tell him not to discuss any of this with the boy. Vaughn was leaning forward too intently.

"What you're talking about is drive," he said. "The drive to succeed. That's not restricted to concert artists. I've seen enough of that in my own profession."

The old woman shook her head. "No. Not just drive. It's a special quality, Churchill has it. Would you like to know who else? Napoleon in Egypt saying, 'Soldiers, from the summit of yonder pyramids, forty centuries look down upon you.' Lincoln at Gettysburg. Sarah Bernhardt." Mme. Berthelot nodded toward one of the pictures on the wall. "My old teacher, Busoni, knew her. I'll tell you a story he told me, and you'll see what I mean. When Sarah was a very little girl, she lived with her mother and her aunt, both cocottes. She was sitting in a second-story window and saw her aunt going by with a gentleman. She asked to go along, but the aunt refused her. Apparently it wasn't one of those gentlemen who liked to have little girls along. So Sarah threw herself out of the window and broke I forget how many arms and legs. She was a performer making a point to a difficult audience. Not temper—temperament. Instinctive. The occasion called for a drastic gesture, and she produced. J. P. Morgan wouldn't have thought of it in a million years."

"I don't know about Sarah Bernhardt," Vaughn said. "I do know a little about Lincoln. He wasn't just a performer."

"None of the great ones are *just* performers. They have all the other stuff. But they won't be able to put it over unless they *are* performers, too. Do you remember Lincoln's stunts as a trial lawyer? Do you remember how he finished Douglas off in those debates? No one but a performer could have preserved a public face with that half-mad wife gnawing away at him year in, year out. There you had a sustained performance that makes the speech at Gettysburg look like nothing at all. The endless spinning of yarns, the periods of depression, it all adds up to the pattern of the performer."

"And it's a pattern that you're not sure Harley fits into. In other words, you don't think he's brat enough to throw himself out of the window."

Marie Berthelot saw that she had gone too far. She said, "This much is true: Harley is a joy to work with. He's a very nice boy. Most performing musicians are not nice at all. They are, if you like, brats. But there are always exceptions—Fritz Kreisler—and Harley may be one of them. I think he is. I do not think this is the time to plant any doubts in his mind. Or in yours, Mr. Vaughn. This is the sort of thing that will work itself out, one way or the other."

"Just how nice Harley is, I'm not at this moment prepared to say. You may know more about him than I. People in a family . . ." Vaughn clasped his hands. He seemed to be formulating his next remark. "Harley's mother is in the hospital, Mme. Berthelot. She's dying of cancer. The doctors give her only a few more weeks. She could go at any time, they say."

"How horrible," the old woman said. "How horrible. I had no idea. Harley didn't tell me."

"No. She's under sedation. Conscious only a few hours each day. But when she's conscious, she knows everything that's going on. She knows why she's there. She's in great pain."

"So young."

Marie Berthelot had already outlived too many of her contemporaries. After the death of her sister Léonie, who had kept house for her, she thought, Now there is no one left that I cannot bear to lose. The rest will be easier.

. . . But it never got easier. Why had Vaughn let her ramble on with those irrelevant theories?

"Forty-four," said Vaughn. "Harley and I have been going to the hospital each day. It seems to help her a little to have us there. But now Harley wants to stop going. He says it's interfering with his preparation for this concert. Up to a point, I can understand that. Of course. He wants to do his best."

Vaughn drew a deep breath. Marie Berthelot waited.

"What I can't understand is why it's necessary to have this concert next month. Why can't it be postponed till the fall? Harley talks about advertisements stuck up on bulletin boards all over town, tickets printed—what's that got to do with it? I've offered to buy him a better date in the fall, and he says the first-string critics will be tied up then with Rubinstein or the Philharmonic. How can those things even occur to him at a time like this? She's in there dying. Her whole life has revolved around him. How can I get it through to him that for the next few weeks, maybe days, his mother comes before everything else?"

There must be more to it, the old woman thought; there is always more to it. She waited again.

"I can't get through to him," Vaughn said. "It's as though we were talking separate languages. I suppose to some degree it's my own fault. Perhaps I haven't made enough of an attempt to understand Harley these past few years, and what communication we've had has been mostly through his mother. They've been very close. All the more reason why what he now proposes to do strikes me as so inhuman. Mme. Berthelot, he must continue coming to the hospital each day. Won't you talk to him?"

"I can talk to him about the possibility of postponing the recital," Marie Berthelot said slowly. "Awkward move, professionally, but I can find out how he feels. About the other thing, going to the hospital, I'm afraid that must be between you and Harley. That's a family thing, Mr. Vaughn. It wouldn't be my place to . . ." She trailed off. She had to keep Harley's confidence, she thought. Harley was her student. It was more important to keep Harley's full confidence than to gain Frederick Vaughn's.

"Is that a principle of yours?" Vaughn asked. "If it is, I shan't ask you to violate it for my wife's sake."

The old woman did not much like the word principle. People resorted to it when they did not feel like lifting a finger. To exonerate themselves.

"It's a family thing," she found herself reduced to saying again. "I must see how Harley feels. This is Thursday. Next Monday, he comes for his lesson."

"Next Monday, his mother may be dead." Vaughn stood up. "I'm very sorry to have troubled you with all this. I was really trying to put my job off on you. It's my job to see that he does what he must. I assure you he will."

The Chairman of the Board, Marie Berthelot thought; an overpowering man; Harley didn't stand a chance.

She said, "It's terrible about Mrs. Vaughn. Please tell her I . . . Tell her Harley is a wonderful boy. He is, you know."

She saw Vaughn to the door. Coming back, she met Mrs. Tierney, who said exactly what Mme. Berthelot thought she would say: "What a fine-looking gentleman."

After dinner, Harley phoned. He was calling from the drugstore on the corner, and wanted to know if he could come up. Then he must have started running and caught the elevator just right, because he was in the studio before his teacher had really settled back into the Morris chair.

Harley was almost as tall as his father: a handsome boy, with a crew cut and the face of a youngster training for a high-school track meet, not a Town Hall recital. He took his usual place on the piano stool.

"Your mother?"

"The same. We were up there till about an hour ago. No change. I haven't told you about her, because then I wouldn't have been able to talk about much else, and the work had to be done. I didn't want my father to come here."

"It's all right, Harley. It's just as well I know about it. Awful."

"I've been there every day. Sometimes with my father, sometimes by myself. She must be in agony. She doesn't talk about that."

The boy did not look at his teacher as he spoke. His eyes seemed to be fixed on one of the music cabinets.

"And I can't always think of things to say to her. So I just sit there. She can't always think of something, either. When she turns her head toward the wall, I know she's crying. It's a little better when my father is around. He can keep the talk pretty casual, mostly. Stuff about the house and the office, stuff like that. I can't do it so well. I run out of talk, and she turns her head to the wall."

Harley spoke in a tight monotone that his teacher had not heard him use before. He paused to swallow, and then the tight voice went on: "I get all churned up. I go home, I sit down to the piano, and I can't work. It's three and a half weeks before my concert, and I get worse every day. Last lesson, when I played the Franck for you, I felt it was just right, and you did, too. This morning I tried it, and it fell to pieces."

"We'll play it again next Monday. You'll get it back."

"Not if I keep going to that hospital, I won't. I love my mother, Mme. Berthelot. She's been—oh, everything to me. But what good am I doing by visiting her? All the good in the world, my father says. I don't believe it. She gets shaken up, too. Then she turns to the wall. How can I explain to my father what it means to prepare for a concert as important as this?"

"You have tried?"

"Every night. And he keeps saying it's still more important for her to see me while she can. He insists we put this concert off till the fall. He can't see the disgrace of it. The disgrace— It isn't that I care so much about that. What gets me is that I had the whole concert in my fingers, and now I'm losing it. I don't want to wait till the fall. I want to play this concert now."

Harley took his eyes off the music cabinet and looked at his teacher.

He said, "This crazy idea of my father's, about making her last days easier—it's crazy. How is it going to make it easier on her to know that I'm going to fall flat on my face at Town Hall?"

"You surely haven't told her that."

"No. But when she's conscious, she knows everything. She asks me how the work is going, and I say it's going fine. But she knows. I've never been able to kid her. I can't kid her now. It's insane to expect me to go on as though she were in there with a bad cold or a sprained ankle. I don't see how my father does it. I can't."

The boy stopped talking.

"What would you like me to do, Harley?"

"Talk to my father again, if you would. Tell him what it means to call off this kind of a concert. . . . No, I've told him all that. He won't listen to that. If you could explain in terms of what I . . . how a pianist works . . . the concentration that must not be broken—just the way you've explained it to me. He might listen to you."

Marie Berthelot shook her head gently. "I'm afraid I can't do that. It wouldn't be my place to. As I've told your father, this is a family thing, Harley. Between you and him."

"He won't listen to me. *She's* all he thinks about now. I'm nowhere in this, nowhere. When he leaves his work at the office to spend the afternoon at the hospital, someone else takes over. But me—who's going to play the Franck for me next month? I'm alone out there with the piano. If the Franck falls apart in my hands, who's going to put it together? How does ruining me help *her?*"

The boy still believes he is going to play next month, she thought; he still doesn't know he has no chance against that Chairman of the Board.

"You come in Monday, and we'll work on nothing but the Franck."

Harley's eyes filled with tears. "You won't talk to him?"

"I can't, dear boy. Not about this."

"Can I at least tell him what you've explained about concentration—how nothing must be permitted to break it? What you said?"

"I suppose so. I don't see why not."

"He looks at me. But he doesn't see me. All he sees is my mother on that bed. He doesn't care about me."

"Yes, he does. I can tell you he does."

"I don't want to wait till the fall. I've got to play this concert now. He's got to understand that."

"Have you been sleeping all right?"

"I don't know."

"Get all the sleep you can, Harley. Come in Monday, and we'll work on the Franck. Come Sunday, too, if you like. I'm teaching through tomorrow and Saturday, but you can always call up and come in the evening."

"Thank you. Thank you very much. I'll try not to disturb you. I'm sorry I had to disturb you today."

"For something like this, any time. It's terrible about your mother. Such a dear person. So young."

She saw the boy to the door, though she felt very tired. This was Marie Berthelot's forty-first year of teaching people to play the piano.

When Harley did not call during the weekend, the old woman began to fret. The boy's morale was bound to be disrupted by his mother's death and the postponing of the concert, but the damage, however bad, was also apt to be temporary. More permanent and more dangerous would be his loss of her as the one who stood between him and that Chairman of the Board. Marie Berthelot had been grateful for Vaughn's lack of interference in the boy's development; now she saw that lack as resulting from other lacks—of involvement and sympathy. She remembered what Vaughn had said: "This is not the profession I would have chosen for him." With his wife's influence gone, Vaughn was not a man to be reticent about making his choices clear. The old woman was afraid for the boy.

Monday morning, Harley came in for his regular lesson. In answer to Mme. Berthelot's inquiry, he said, "She's just the same. No change." He did not seem to want to go into details. Instead, he sat right down and played the Franck, played it beautifully.

The piece had lost none of the shapeliness and verve it had a week ago. And there were some things that had not been there before, subtle little changes of pace and dynamics. A week ago, Mme. Berthelot had been a trifle concerned about a long passage that had teetered on the brink of facile sentiment; now it was pure tenderness, profoundly felt.

"Good," the old woman said.

"I don't know. I'll work on it some more." Harley swung around on the stool and faced his teacher. "You told me to get some sleep, and I did. Beginning Friday night, I did. Thursday, my father and I stayed up all night, fighting. God, he's stubborn. He kept repeating the same thing over and over. As though I really could help her by going to the hospital day after day. It was awful. . . . This afternoon I'll go in, and then maybe not for a week. Friday night, I slept. Saturday, I started working and I got the Franck back, didn't I? And I'm going to play it next month just as I played it today."

"He's letting you go through with the concert?"

"He had to, Mme. Berthelot, he had to. Didn't I get the Franck back? Didn't I? Do you want to hear me play it again?"

"Yes. Sure. Play it again."

The boy played it again, securely, with enormous authority. Astonished, the old woman listened. This was, this must have been, the same authority that had prevailed against the Chairman of the Board. Harley would do well in Town Hall next month and in other halls in other years. Marie Berthelot wished Mrs. Vaughn could have lived to see and hear it. She wished there were something important she could do for Mrs. Vaughn. But she could not think of anything. She was not, after all, in the business of providing solace for dying women. She was in the business of teaching people to play the piano.

She said, "Now play something else."

FICTION: FOR STUDY AND DISCUSSION

You should first try to specify what beauty has meant in the lives of the main characters of the stories offered in this section: Is it a challenge? a worship? an escape from some personal problem?

Next, I would ask you to analyze what beauty means in your own life. Your analysis could be a good subject for a composition or the starting point for a class discussion. Let me suggest some guides. For example, do you respond more to natural beauty (trees, mountains, the sky, the sea, and the like), or do you prefer "man-made" beauty (opera, sculpture, poetry, dance, and the like)?

Perhaps you will say that you like both types of beauty. This may well be true, but then (philosophically speaking) you are now running straight into a plaguing problem: What is the relationship between these two *kinds* of beauty? And a related problem: Is, or is not, one kind of beauty superior to the other? Take, for instance, a painting of the color of autumn leaves. Is the painting superior to the reality in its impact? Is it inferior? Is its impact just as great but in a different way?

Now come back to my first paragraph: How does Aylmer ("The Birthmark") *see* Beauty? Axelrod ("Young Man Axelrod")? Amarantha ("How Beautiful with Shoes")? Elisa ("The Chrysanthemums")? Mac ("Mac's Masterpiece")? Harley ("Début Recital")? Do not these few stories suggest some of the complexities possible in our responses to the beautiful?

You are doubtless familiar with the terms *plot* (the pattern of a story's development), *character* (the people who populate a story), *setting* (the environment in which a story takes place), and *theme* (the comment on life which a story is making). Each of these elements of a story should be harmonious with the others. I should like you to examine the six stories in this section to see whether their authors have (or have not) been successful in effectively blending the four elements. As an example, you might start with two such apparently different stories as "The Chrysanthemums" and "Début Recital."

You are, also, doubtless aware of the term *conflict* as it is used in fiction. These six stories offer interesting illustrations of the use of fictional conflict. It is conflict which pushes the story forward to its natural conclusion. It may be an *external* conflict (one person against another or one person against his environment); it may be an *internal* conflict (a person torn between choices: Hamlet's anguished expression "To be or not to be" is a classic example of internal conflict); it may very well be (as it so often is in "real" life) a subtle combination of both types.

Since you have such conflicts in your own lives, it should not be difficult for you to make the "leap of imagination" necessary to identify the comparable conflicts present in these stories. The characters and their environments may often be very unfamiliar to you, but in each case a human predicament is presented with which you should be able to establish some sympathy of identification.

Pied Beauty

GERARD MANLEY HOPKINS

[1844–1889]

Most of Hopkins's poems reflect profound insights. They are also, usually, brilliantly executed. In the following poem, Hopkins expresses poetically his conviction on one of the oldest and most recurring problems of philosophical thought: namely, does there exist in our world of changes and varieties any single unifying principle which holds together these diverse elements?

In our Western culture, man's search for a One that holds together the Many preceded both Greek philosophical thinking and the early Christian theologians. That the pursuit continues into this day suggests that it represents a very basic drive in man to bring a satisfactory order out of the disorder which has always confronted him.

Hopkins was Catholic (a Jesuit) and a man of intense religious sensitivity and devotion. To him, the philosophical problem of "the One and the Many" could have only one answer. Regardless of your own beliefs, I trust you will share with me an admiration for Hopkins's evident fervor of conviction and for the dazzling techniques he uses to convey his conviction.

Glory be to God for dappled things—
    For skies of couple-color as a brinded cow;
      For rose-moles all in stipple upon trout that swim;
Fresh-firecoal chestnut-falls; finches' wings;
    Landscapes plotted and pieced—fold, fallow, and plow;   5
      And all trades, their gear and tackle and trim.

All things counter, original, spare, strange;
    Whatever is fickle, freckled (who knows how?)
      With swift, slow; sweet, sour; adazzle, dim;
He fathers-forth whose beauty is past change: 10
      Praise Him.

FOR STUDY AND DISCUSSION

1. If you do not know the meaning of the word *pied* in the title, look it up.
2. How does the opening line establish, with great effectiveness, the *first* point of Hopkins's attitude toward beauty?
3. What do the next eight lines contribute toward supporting this attitude? What effect do the examples that Hopkins uses have? the vocabulary? the rhythm?
4. Reread the last two lines very carefully, for they express the *second* (and basic) point of Hopkins's attitude toward Beauty. Notice how the pace of the poem changes markedly here. Show how this rhythmic change is poetically appropriate to the poet's final emphasis.

I Died for Beauty

EMILY DICKINSON

[1830–1886]

I died for beauty, but was scarce
Adjusted in the tomb,
When one who died for truth was lain
In an adjoining room.

He questioned softly why I failed?   5
"For beauty," I replied.
"And I for truth,—the two are one;
We brethren are," he said.

And so, as kinsmen met a night,
We talked between the rooms,   10
Until the moss had reached our lips
And covered up our names.

I Reckon, When I Count at All

EMILY DICKINSON

I reckon, when I count at all,
First Poets—then the Sun—
Then Summer—then the Heaven of God—
And then the list is done.
But looking back—the first so seems   5
To comprehend the whole—
The others look a needless show,
So I write Poets—All.
Their summer lasts a solid year,
They can afford a sun   10
The East would deem extravagant,
And if the final Heaven
Be beautiful as they disclose
To those who trust in them,
It is too difficult a grace   15
To justify the dream.

Ten Definitions of Poetry

CARL SANDBURG
[1878–1967]

1 Poetry is a projection across silence of cadences arranged to break that
silence with definite intentions of echoes, syllables, wave lengths.
2 Poetry is the journal of a sea animal living on land, wanting to fly the air.
3 Poetry is a series of explanations of life, fading off into horizons too swift
for explanations.
4 Poetry is a search for syllables to shoot at the barriers of the unknown
and the unknowable.
5 Poetry is a theorem of a yellow-silk handkerchief knotted with riddles,
sealed in a balloon tied to the tail of a kite flying in a white wind
against a blue sky in spring.
6 Poetry is the silence and speech between a wet struggling root of a flower
and a sunlit blossom of that flower.
7 Poetry is the harnessing of the paradox of earth cradling life and then
entombing it.
8 Poetry is a phantom script telling how rainbows are made and why they
go away.
9 Poetry is the achievement of the synthesis of hyacinths and biscuits.
10 Poetry is the opening and closing of a door, leaving those who look
through to guess about what is seen during a moment.

Petit, the Poet

EDGAR LEE MASTERS
[1869–1950]

Seeds in a dry pod, tick, tick, tick,
Tick, tick, tick, like mites in a quarrel—
Faint iambics that the full breeze wakens—
But the pine tree makes a symphony thereof.
Triolets, villanelles, rondels, rondeaus.   5
Ballades by the score with the same old thought:
The snows and the roses of yesterday are vanished;
And what is love but a rose that fades?
Life all around me here in the village:

*Ryming &
Not allowed
Anymore*

Tragedy, comedy, valor, and truth,   10
Courage, constancy, heroism, failure—
All in the loom, and, oh, what patterns!
Woodlands, meadows, streams, and rivers—
Blind to all of it all my life long.
Triolets, villanelles, rondels, rondeaus,   15
Seeds in a dry pod, tick, tick, tick,
Tick, tick, tick, what little iambics,
While Homer and Whitman roared in the pines! [1]

January

WILLIAM CARLOS WILLIAMS

[1883–1963]

Again I reply to the triple winds
running chromatic fifths of derision
outside my window:
                            Play louder.
You will not succeed. I am   5
bound more to my sentences
the more you batter at me
to follow you.
                            And the wind,
as before, fingers perfectly   10
its derisive music.

---

[1] Masters is here imagining the "self-written" epitaph of an unimportant poet who (suggestively) bore the name of Petit. Petit looks back on his poetic endeavors as wasted ones since he concerned himself only with the traditional forms and themes of poetry. How is this point brought out in specific lines of Masters' own poem?

In contrast to Petit's imagined poetry, Masters' poem is written in free verse. For the observation he is making about Petit's life, the choice of free verse is clearly a good one. Do you think, though, that Masters is implying that free verse, in itself, is superior to verse that follows one of the many metrical patterns available? Robert Frost is said to have commented that writing free verse is like playing tennis with the net down. This is a wittily expressed criticism, but you should be aware that Frost was given to tossing off barbed remarks which he did not expect anyone to accept as final authority.

Spring Night

SARA TEASDALE
[1884–1933]

The park is filled with night and fog,
   The veils are drawn about the world,
The drowsy lights along the paths
   Are dim and pearled.

Gold and gleaming the empty streets,   5
   Gold and gleaming the misty lake,
The mirrored lights like sunken swords,
   Glimmer and shake.

Oh, is it not enough to be
Here with this beauty over me?   10
My throat should ache with praise, and I
Should kneel in joy beneath the sky.
O, beauty, are you not enough?
Why am I crying after love,
With youth, a singing voice and eyes   15
To take earth's wonder with surprise?
Why have I put off my pride,
Why am I unsatisfied,—
I for whom the pensive night
Binds her cloudy hair with light,—   20
I, for whom all beauty burns
Like incense in a million urns?
O, beauty, are you not enough?
Why am I crying after love?

Orchard

H. D. (HILDA DOOLITTLE)
[1886–1961]

I saw the first pear
as it fell—
the honey-seeking, golden-banded,
the yellow swarm,
was not more fleet than I,   5
(spare us from loveliness!)
and I fell prostrate,
crying:
you have flayed us with your blossoms,
spare us the beauty   10
of the fruit-trees!

The honey-seeking
paused not;
and the air thundered their song,
and I alone was prostrate.   15

O rough-hewn
god of the orchard,
I bring you an offering—
do you, alone unbeautiful,
son of the god,   20
spare us from loveliness:

these fallen hazel-nuts,
stripped late of their green sheaths,
grapes, red-purple,
their berries   25
dripping with wine;
pomegranates already broken,
and shrunken figs,
and quinces untouched,
I bring you as offering.[1]   30

---

[1] H. D. belonged to a group of poets called Imagists, who believed that ". . . poetry should render particulars exactly and not deal in vague generalities. . . ." Notice that in "Orchard" H. D. does not use the general word *autumn* but evokes that season by reference to the ripened pear and the bees which it attracts. Observe that the bees themselves are not named but are particularized by images associated with them. In a like manner the "god" (Dionysius) is not so much designated as he is characterized ("rough-hewn"). The prayerful tone is delicately suggested by the repetition of "spare us . . ." and by the images of "prostrate" in line 7 and of "offering" in the last line.

Poetry

MARIANNE MOORE
[BORN 1887]

I, too, dislike it: there are things that are important beyond all this
    fiddle.
  Reading it, however, with a perfect contempt for it, one discovers
    in
  it, after all, a place for the genuine.
      Hands that can grasp, eyes
      that can dilate, hair that can rise
        if it must, these things are important not because a

high-sounding interpretation can be put upon them but because they
    are
  useful. When they become so derivative as to become unintelligible,
  the same thing may be said for all of us, that we
    do not admire what
    we cannot understand: the bat
      holding on upside down or in quest of something to

eat, elephants pushing, a wild horse taking a roll, a tireless wolf under
  a tree, the immovable critic twitching his skin like a horse that
    feels a flea, the base-
  ball fan, the statistician—
    nor is it valid
      to discriminate against "business documents and

schoolbooks"; all these phenomena are important. One must make a
    distinction
  however: when dragged into prominence by half poets, the result
    is not poetry,
  nor till the poets among us can be
    "literalists of
    the imagination"—above
      insolence and triviality and can present

5

10

15

20

25

for inspection, "imaginary gardens with real toads in them," shall   30
    we have
it. In the meantime, if you demand on the one hand,
the raw material of poetry in
    all its rawness and
    that which is on the other hand   35
        genuine, you are interested in poetry.[1]

Divinely Superfluous Beauty

ROBINSON JEFFERS
[1887–1962]

The storm-dances of gulls, the barking game of seals,
Over and under the ocean . . .
Divinely superfluous beauty
Rules the games, presides over destinies, makes trees grow
And hills tower, waves fall.   5
The incredible beauty of joy
Stars with fire the joining of lips, O let our loves too
Be joined, there is not a maiden
Burns and thirsts for love
More than my blood for you, by the shore of seals while the wings   10
Weave like a web in the air
Divinely superfluous beauty.

[1] Miss Moore begins her poem with the disarming statement, "I, too, dislike it . . ."
Since, as a poet, she must to some extent "like" poetry, how do you explain her comment? In answering this question, I direct your attention to the following phrases:

    ". . . a place for the genuine." (line 5)
    ". . . high-sounding interpretation . . ." (line 9)
    ". . . imaginary gardens with real toads in them . . ." (line 30)

Also observe that Miss Moore repeats the word *genuine* in the last sentence and couples it with the phrase ". . . the raw material of poetry. . . ." How does this concluding comment and what has preceded it resolve the puzzle of "I, too, dislike it . . ."?

Piazza Piece

J O H N   C R O W E   R A N S O M
[BORN 1888]

—I am a gentleman in a dustcoat trying
To make you hear. Your ears are soft and small
And listen to an old man not at all,
They want the young men's whispering and sighing.
But see the roses on your trellis dying   5
And hear the spectral singing of the moon;
For I must have my lovely lady soon.
I am a gentleman in a dustcoat trying.

—I am a lady young in beauty waiting
Until my truelove comes, and then we kiss.   10
But what gray man among the vines is this
Whose words are dry and faint as in a dream?
Back from my trellis, Sir, before I scream!
I am a lady young in beauty waiting.[1]

Euclid Alone Has Looked on Beauty Bare

E D N A   S T.   V I N C E N T   M I L L A Y
[1892–1950]

Euclid alone has looked on Beauty bare.
Let all who prate of Beauty hold their peace,
And lay them prone upon the earth and cease
To ponder on themselves, the while they stare
At nothing, intricately drawn nowhere   5
In shapes of shifting lineage; let geese
Gabble and hiss, but heroes seek release
From dusty bondage into luminous air.

[1] There is a type of poem called a *carpe diem* poem. The phrase, usually associated with the Latin poet Horace, means literally "seize the day." It implies that if we do not, we will have lost an opportunity not likely to be offered again. Inevitably, *carpe diem* poems tend to focus on young love. In English poetry you are no doubt familiar with Robert Herrick's line, "Gather ye rosebuds while ye may. . . ." Most readers consider Andrew Marvell's "To His Coy Mistress" the finest sustained expression of this philosophy in our literature. How does Ransom's "Piazza Piece" employ the *carpe diem* theme?

O blinding hour, O holy, terrible day,
When first the shaft into his vision shone   10
Of light anatomized! Euclid alone
Has looked on Beauty bare. Fortunate they
Who, though once only and then but far away,
Have heard her massive sandal set on stone.[1]

A Pinch of Salt

ROBERT GRAVES
[BORN 1895]

When a dream is born in you
    With a sudden clamorous pain,
When you know the dream is true
    And lovely, with no flaw nor stain,
O then, be careful, or with sudden clutch   5
You'll hurt the delicate thing you prize so much.

Dreams are like a bird that mocks,
    Flirting the feathers of his tail.
When you seize at the salt box,
    Over the hedge you'll see him sail.   10
Old birds are neither caught with salt nor chaff:
They watch you from the apple bough and laugh.

Poet, never chase the dream.
    Laugh yourself, and turn away.
Mask your hunger; let it seem   15
    Small matter if he come or stay;
But when he nestles in your hand at last,
Close up your fingers tight and hold him fast.

[1] Among philosophers, Plato alone can claim a large number of poems which closely reflect his essential position. Plato's position is that there are absolute values which escape sensory perception and are grasped only by the mind. Shelley's "Hymn to Intellectual Beauty" suggests by its very title a joyful acceptance of Platonic assumptions. Perhaps you are also familiar with Wordsworth's Platonic "Intimations of Immortality from Recollections of Early Childhood." Millay's sonnet is clearly in this tradition with its insistence that only the great mathematician can hope to see Beauty in its ideal form, stripped of all sensory embellishments: Beauty bare.

The Express

STEPHEN SPENDER

[BORN 1909]

After the first powerful, plain manifesto
The black statement of pistons, without more fuss
But gliding like a queen, she leaves the station.
Without bowing and with restrained unconcern
She passes the houses which humbly crowd outside,   5
The gasworks, and at last the heavy page
Of death, printed by gravestones in the cemetery.
Beyond the town, there lies the open country
Where, gathering speed, she acquires mystery,
The luminous self-possession of ships on ocean.   10
It is now she begins to sing—at first quite low
Then loud, and at last with a jazzy madness—
The song of her whistle screaming at curves,
Of deafening tunnels, brakes, innumerable bolts.
And always light, aerial, underneath,   15
Retreats the elate meter of her wheels.
Steaming through metal landscape on her lines,
She plunges new eras of white happiness,
Where speed throws up strange shapes, broad curves
And parallels clean like trajectories from guns.   20
At last, further than Edinburgh or Rome,
Beyond the crest of the world, she reaches night
Where only a low stream-line brightness
Of phosphorus on the tossing hills is light.
Ah, like a comet through flame, she moves entranced,   25
Wrapt in her music no bird song, no, nor bough
Breaking with honey buds, shall ever equal.[1]

---

[1] It should be interesting to discuss *why* Spender considers the express train an object of beauty and *how* he effectively conveys his appreciation. What is he emphasizing in the last three lines? Another poem about a train, quite close to Spender's in many ways, is Whitman's "To a Locomotive in Winter." Another (very different in perspective) is Emily Dickinson's "I Like to See It Lap the Miles."

Delight in Disorder

ROBERT HERRICK

[1591–1674]

A sweet disorder in the dress
Kindles in clothes a wantonness:
A lawn about the shoulders thrown
Into a fine distraction:
An erring lace, which here and there   5
Enthralls the crimson stomacher:
A cuff neglectful, and thereby
Ribbands to flow confusedly:
A winning wave (deserving note)
In the tempestuous petticoat: 10
A careless shoestring, in whose tie
I see a wild civility: [1]
Do more bewitch me, than when art
Is too precise in every part.

Sonnet 18

WILLIAM SHAKESPEARE

[1564–1616]

Shall I compare thee to a summer's day?
Thou art more lovely and more temperate:
Rough winds do shake the darling buds of May,
And summer's lease hath all too short a date;
Sometime too hot the eye of heaven shines,   5
And often is his gold complexion dimmed;
And every fair from fair sometime declines,
By chance, or nature's changing course untrimmed;
But thy eternal summer shall not fade
Nor lose possession of that fair thou owest,   10
Nor shall Death brag thou wanderest in his shade,
When in eternal lines to time thou growest—
    So long as men can breathe, or eyes can see,
    So long lives this, and this gives life to thee.

---

[1] *civility:* proper behavior, good breeding.

Sailing to Byzantium [1]

WILLIAM BUTLER YEATS
[1865–1939]

I

That is no country for old men. The young
In one another's arms, birds in the trees
—Those dying generations—at their song,
The salmon-falls, the mackerel-crowded seas,
Fish, flesh, or fowl, commend all summer long   5
Whatever is begotten, born, and dies.
Caught in that sensual music all neglect
Monuments of unaging intellect.

II

An aged man is but a paltry thing,
A tattered coat upon a stick, unless   10
Soul clap its hands and sing, and louder sing
For every tatter in its mortal dress,
Nor is there singing school but studying
Monuments of its own magnificence;
And therefore I have sailed the seas and come   15
To the holy city of Byzantium.

III

O sages standing in God's holy fire
As in the gold mosaic of a wall,
Come from the holy fire, perne in a gyre, [2]
And be the singing-masters of my soul.   20
Consume my heart away; sick with desire
And fastened to a dying animal
It knows not what it is; and gather me
Into the artifice of eternity.

---

[1] Byzantium is the ancient name for the city of Istanbul, in Turkey. It is used here as a symbol for the ageless quality of art in contrast to the emphasis a younger generation places on the physical (as indicated in the opening lines).

[2] *perne:* the spool on which thread is wound. *gyre:* a moving circle (as in *gyroscope*). Hence the total phrase is suggestive of the revolving motion characteristic of the continual rebirth of art within the pattern of history.

IV

Once out of nature I shall never take   25
My bodily form from any natural thing,
But such a form as Grecian goldsmiths make
Of hammered gold and gold enameling
To keep a drowsy Emperor awake;
Or set upon a golden bough to sing   30
To lords and ladies of Byzantium
Of what is past, or passing, or to come.

Ode on a Grecian Urn

JOHN KEATS
[1795–1821]

Thou still unravished bride of quietness,
    Thou foster child of silence and slow time,
Sylvan historian, who canst thus express
    A flowery tale more sweetly than our rhyme:
What leaf-fringed legend haunts about thy shape   5
    Of deities or mortals, or of both,
        In Tempe [1] or the dales of Arcady? [2]
What men or gods are these? What maidens loth?
    What mad pursuit? What struggle to escape?
        What pipes and timbrels? [3] What wild ecstasy? 10

Heard melodies are sweet, but those unheard
    Are sweeter; therefore, ye soft pipes, play on;
Not to the sensual ear, but, more endeared,
    Pipe to the spirit ditties of no tone.
Fair youth, beneath the trees, thou canst not leave   15
    Thy song, nor ever can those trees be bare;
        Bold Lover, never, never canst thou kiss,
Though winning near the goal—yet, do not grieve;
    She cannot fade, though thou hast not thy bliss,
        Forever wilt thou love, and she be fair!   20

[1] *Tempe:* a valley in Thessaly, Greece.
[2] *Arcady:* a picturesque region of Greece.
[3] *timbrels:* tambourines.

Ah, happy, happy boughs! that cannot shed
  Your leaves, nor ever bid the Spring adieu:
And, happy melodist, unwearièd,
  Forever piping songs forever new;
More happy love! more happy, happy love!   25
  Forever warm and still to be enjoyed,
    Forever panting, and forever young;
All breathing human passion far above,
  That leaves a heart high-sorrowful and cloyed,
    A burning forehead, and a parching tongue.   30

Who are these coming to the sacrifice?
  To what green altar, O mysterious priest,
Lead'st thou that heifer lowing at the skies,
  And all her silken flanks with garlands dressed?
What little town by river or sea shore,   35
  Or mountain-built with peaceful citadel,
    Is emptied of this folk, this pious morn?
And, little town, thy streets for evermore
  Will silent be; and not a soul to tell
    Why thou are desolate, can e'er return.   40

O Attic shape! Fair attitude! with brede [1]
  Of marble men and maidens overwrought,
With forest branches and the trodden weed;
  Thou, silent form, dost tease us out of thought
As doth eternity: Cold Pastoral!   45
  When old age shall this generation waste,
    Thou shalt remain, in midst of other woe
Than ours, a friend to man, to whom thou say'st,
  "Beauty is truth, truth beauty"—that is all
    Ye know on earth, and all ye need to know.[2]   50

---

[1] *brede:* embroidery.

[2] Both the theme of this poem and some of its individual lines have been the subject of analysis and controversy. For example, is Keats's view toward art basically similar to Yeats's ("Sailing to Byzantium") and therefore in marked contrast to the attitudes expressed by Emerson ("The Snow-Storm") and by Williams ("January")? What does Keats mean by the statement "Beauty is truth, truth beauty"? Clearly this phrase is in the Platonic tradition and may remind you of Millay's sonnet "Euclid Alone Has Looked on Beauty Bare," but its meaning within the context of the poem is more elusive. Incidentally, you are no doubt aware that it is to Keats's poem that the father is referring in the concluding paragraphs of Faulkner's "The Bear."

Composed upon Westminster Bridge

WILLIAM WORDSWORTH

[1770–1850]

Earth has not anything to show more fair:
Dull would he be of soul who could pass by
A sight so touching in its majesty:
This city now doth, like a garment, wear
The beauty of the morning; silent, bare,   5
Ships, towers, domes, theaters, and temples lie
Open unto the fields, and to the sky;
All bright and glittering in the smokeless air.
Never did sun more beautifully steep
In his first splendor, valley, rock, or hill;   10
Ne'er saw I, never felt, a calm so deep!
The river glideth at his own sweet will:
Dear God! the very houses seem asleep;
And all that mighty heart is lying still!

In a Station of the Metro [1]

EZRA POUND

[BORN 1885]

The apparition of these faces in the crowd;
Petals on a wet, black bough.[2]

---

[1] *Metro:* underground railway, subway.

[2] An awareness that the poet finds beauty in unexpected places and then transmits his discovery to the responsive reader is not a new one. Sandburg's "Nocturne in a Deserted Brickyard" suggests this point in its very title. Pound's poem, however, is an especially remarkable achievement because of its skillful compression. The poem was written over a year's period, the first version having thirty lines, the next one half that number, the final one just two lines. It is apparent that this drastic condensation crystallizes the core of Pound's response to what he once "saw" in the Metro station. What, in more ordinary terms, did he see? How does he evoke for us the immediacy of his experience and its individual quality?

Incidentally, for a very different perspective on subways, you might look up Oscar Williams's surrealistic poem "The Leg in the Subway."

POETRY: FOR STUDY AND DISCUSSION

The fundamental nature of Beauty is so elusive that many philosophers (and even more literary artists) have rejected efforts to define it. Still, one is nagged by a question Plato attacked so many centuries ago: What *is* beauty? Keats wrote,

> "Beauty is truth, truth beauty"—that is all
> Ye know on earth, and all ye need to know.

Keats's lines are very much in the Platonic tradition of an essential identity of Truth, Beauty, and Goodness. Incidentally, this is an opinion alluded to by Faulkner in the closing paragraphs of "The Bear" (page 101).

A contrary opinion is that Beauty is where one finds it: that one *brings* Beauty to a scene or to a person and thereby endows such particulars with significant Beauty. Samuel Taylor Coleridge [1772–1834] expressed this view in these lines from "Dejection: An Ode":

> . . . we receive but what we give,
> And in our life alone does Nature live:
> Ours is her wedding garment, ours her shroud!
> And would we aught behold, of higher worth,
> Than that inanimate cold world allowed   5
> To the poor loveless ever anxious crowd,
> Ah! from the soul itself must issue forth
> A light, a glory, a fair luminous cloud
> Enveloping the Earth—
> And from the soul itself must there be sent   10
> A sweet and potent voice, of its own birth,
> Of all sweet sounds the life and element!

Whatever you may decide about these contrasting philosophical positions about beauty, please do not make the error of thinking that because a selected poem is "beautifully written" it is *about* beauty. Three examples will suggest what I have in mind. The first is beautiful in expression, but is not *about* beauty:

Rose Aylmer

WALTER SAVAGE LANDOR
[1775–1864]

Ah, what avails the sceptred race,
  Ah, what the form divine!
What every virtue, every grace!
  Rose Aylmer, all were thine.

Rose Aylmer, whom these wakeful eyes
  May weep, but never see,
A night of memories and of sighs
  I consecrate to thee.

The second example, a lovely poem, suggests an attitude toward beauty:

Loveliest of Trees

A. E. HOUSMAN
[1859–1936]

Loveliest of trees, the cherry now
Is hung with bloom along the bough,
And stands about the woodland ride
Wearing white for Eastertide.

Now, of my threescore years and ten,   5
Twenty will not come again,
And take from seventy springs a score,
It leaves me only fifty more.

And since to look at things in bloom
Fifty springs are little room,   10
About the woodlands I will go
To see the cherry hung with snow.

The third example is Edna St. Vincent Millay's poem on page 215, which in its first line ("Euclid alone has looked on Beauty bare") initiates an explicit philosophical position regarding the nature of beauty, a position which aligns the writer with Plato and Keats.

Now, then, I would like you to return to the poems in this section (all of which are primarily *about* beauty) and be able to specify the particular type of beauty with which each is concerned, for some deal with natural beauty, others with artistic beauty. Next, you should attempt to make clear the attitude toward the chosen type of beauty which each poem expresses, for some are more optimistic than others and some adopt a more serious tone than others. Finally, you should examine the ways by which each poem effectively communicates to us its individual way of "seeing" an aspect of beauty.

GOODNESS

Introduction

Man has always wished to be good. Since he has so often, instead, achieved evil, this statement requires some explanation. I think this explanation consists of two parts: in the first place, man rationalizes his "evil" acts and calls them "good" (as, for example, Hitler and Stalin did on a national level); secondly, and more justifiably, he is confused by the distinction between good and evil.

This confusion can be a very honest and profound one. William Blake [1757–1827] gave it religious and philosophical significance in a poem with which many of you are familiar.

The Tiger

Tiger! Tiger! burning bright
In the forests of the night,
What immortal hand or eye
Could frame thy fearful symmetry?

In what distant deeps or skies   5
Burnt the fire of thine eyes?
On what wings dare he aspire?
What the hand dare seize the fire?

And what shoulder, and what art,
Could twist the sinews of thy heart?   10
And when thy heart began to beat,
What dread hand? and what dread feet?

What the hammer? what the chain?
In what furnace was thy brain?
What the anvil? what dread grasp   15
Dare its deadly terrors clasp?

When the stars threw down their spears,
And water'd heaven with their tears,
Did he smile his work to see?
Did he who made the Lamb make thee?   20

Tiger! Tiger! burning bright
In the forests of the night,
What immortal hand or eye,
Dare frame thy fearful symmetry?

Aside from this ultimate problem of how and why good and evil seem to coexist, inherently, in our world, for most of us there is the more immediate problem of living "the good life" in terms of our various personal needs and ideals.

Thus, the pursuit of pleasure has been a recurring standard since the days of the Greeks. Yet even that long ago, thoughtful men realized that there are significant distinctions between pleasures. For example, food and drink provide immediate and intense pleasure; but are not a lasting friendship, a happy family life, and a satisfying career sources of more enduring happiness?

The opposite extreme of the pursuit of pleasure also has both ancient and modern advocates. The Stoics, in particular, believed that serenity could best be attained by escaping the "human bondage" of the senses through strenuous self-discipline. Christianity, too, has traditionally stressed this position within its own ethical context.

An "in-between" view, which also has an honorable history, has in recent generations found favor because of more precise anthropological studies and, consequently, an increased sensitivity to the cultures of different nations and races. This position tends to be skeptical of an "absolute" Good or an "absolute" Evil. Rather, it emphasizes that an individual's conception of "the good life" is primarily determined by his environment—national, social, physical, familial, and the like.

Is this, then, the final answer? Of course not. Not only have philosophers and creative writers offered many differing versions of what constitutes "the good life," but their own views have commonly changed from time to time. Thus, I do not offer you any single platform; rather, I recommend to you the wisdom of a remark by William James: "To know the chief rival attitudes toward life . . . and to have heard some of the reasons they can give for themselves ought to be considered an essential part of liberal education."

Aristotle

[384–322 B.C.]

Aristotle was Plato's great student. Although he reflected much that he had absorbed from Plato, his own background and temperament led him to different emphases. It is said that everyone is, fundamentally, either a Platonist or an Aristotelian. This half-truth is suggestive of the distinction in interest and expression between the two men: Plato is "otherworldly" in his philosophic position and highly imaginative in his depiction of it; Aristotle is more "practical" and scientifically concerned and more specific in the analysis of his convictions.

The range of Aristotle's achievements is unparalleled in the history of our civilization. He is the father of biology (especially marine biology); he invented the science of logic; he was the first literary critic in the Western world; he was a distinguished political thinker; and his general philosophical conclusions have had an immeasurable impact on the history of our intellectual development. One of his greatest inquiries was in the field of morality and is presented in his Nicomachean Ethics (from which the following selection has been taken).

Aristotle had what today we might call a functional view of "the good life." Briefly, this means that the good for any organism lies in the full development of the capacities with which it has been endowed. In man these capacities are physical, rational, and spiritual. It is in the harmonious fulfillment of these three capacities that man achieves the good life and the happiness which accompanies it. You should attempt to relate the argument of the following selection to this broader idea of "the good life." Observe that Aristotle does not deny that pleasure is desired and is desirable as an essential component of the good life, but that he also insists that we must distinguish between different kinds of pleasure. As a related point, observe how he links pleasure to activity so that the greatest pleasures flow from the exercise of our superior capacities. Finally, observe how this line of argumentation leads Aristotle to the conclusion that since reason is man's highest faculty, it is through the full activity of reason that we are brought to the most satisfying happiness.

Pleasure and Happiness

Some people say that the [highest] good is pleasure; others, on the contrary, that pleasure is something utterly bad, whether, as is possible, they are convinced that it really is so, or they think it better in the interest of human life to represent pleasure as an evil, even if it is not so, feeling that men are generally inclined to pleasure and are the slaves of

Excerpt from *Nicomachean Ethics*, translated by J. E. C. Welldon.

their pleasures, and that it is a duty therefore to lead them in the contrary direction, as they will so arrive at the mean [1] *or proper* state.

But I venture to think that this is not a right statement of the case. For in matters of the emotions and actions, theories are not so trustworthy as facts; and thus, when theories disagree with the facts of perception, they fall into contempt and involve the truth itself in their destruction. For if a person censures pleasure and yet is seen at times to make pleasure his aim, he is thought to incline to pleasure as being entirely desirable; for it is beyond the power of ordinary people to make distinctions. It seems then the true [conventional] theories are exceedingly useful, not only as the means of knowledge but as guides of life; for as being in harmony with facts, they are believed, and being believed they encourage people who understand them to regulate their lives in accordance with them.

Perhaps the truth may be stated thus: Pleasures are desirable, but not if they are immoral in their origin, just as wealth is pleasant, but not if it be obtained at the cost of turning traitor to one's country, or health, but not at the cost of eating any food, however disagreeable. Or it may be said that pleasures are of different kinds, those which are noble in their origin are different from those which are dishonorable, and it is impossible to enjoy the pleasure of the just man without being just, or that of the musician without being musical, and so on. The distinction drawn between a friend and a flatterer seems to bring out clearly the truth that pleasure is not a good, or that there are pleasures of different kinds; for it seems that while the object of the friend in social intercourse is good, that of the flatterer is pleasure, and while the flatterer is censured, the friend for his disinterestedness is praised.

Again, nobody would choose to live all his life with the mind of a child, although he should enjoy the pleasures of childhood to the utmost, or to delight in doing what is utterly shameful, although he were never to suffer pain for doing it. There are many things too upon which we should set our hearts, even if they brought no pleasure with them, e.g., sight, memory, knowledge, and the possession of the virtues; and if it be true that these are necessarily attended by pleasures, it is immaterial, as we should desire them even if no pleasure resulted from them. It seems to be clear then that pleasure is not the good, nor is every pleasure desirable, and that there are some pleasures which are desirable in themselves, and they differ in kind or in origin from the others.

It may be asked then, How is it that nobody feels pleasure continuously? It is probably because we grow weary. Human beings are incapable of continuous activity, and as the activity comes to an end, so does the pleasure; for it is a concomitant of the activity. It is for the

---

[1] *mean:* Aristotle uses the word *mean* as the intelligent choice between two extremes: thus courage is a mean between recklessness and cowardice.

same reason that some things give pleasure when they are new, but give less pleasure afterward; for the intelligence is called into play at first, and applies itself to its object with intense activity, as when we look a person full in the face in order to recognize him, but afterward the activity ceases to be so intense and becomes remiss, and consequently the pleasure also fades away.

It may be supposed that everybody desires pleasure, for everybody clings to life. But life is a species of activity and a person's activity displays itself in the sphere and with the means which are after his own heart. Thus a musician exercises his ears in listening to music, a student his intellect in speculation, and so on.

But pleasure perfects the activities; it therefore perfects life, which is the aim of human desire. It is reasonable then to aim at pleasure, as it perfects life in each of us, and life is an object of desire.

Whether we desire life for the sake of pleasure or pleasure for the sake of life is a question which may be dismissed for the moment. For it appears that pleasure and life are yoked together and do not admit of separation, as pleasure is impossible without activity and every activity is perfected by pleasure.

As has been frequently said, . . . it is the things which are honorable and pleasant to the virtuous man that are really honorable and pleasant. But everybody feels that activity which accords with his own moral state to be most desirable, and accordingly the virtuous man regards the activity in accordance with virtue as most desirable.

Happiness then does not consist in amusement. It would be paradoxical to hold that the end of human life is amusement, and that we should toil and suffer all our life for the sake of amusing ourselves. For we may be said to desire all things as means to something else, except indeed happiness, as happiness is the end *or perfect state*.

If happiness consists in virtuous activity, it is only reasonable to suppose that it is the activity of the highest virtue, or in other words, of the best part of our nature. Whether it is the reason or something else which seems to exercise rule and authority by a natural right, and to have a conception of things noble and divine, either as being itself divine or as relatively the most divine part of our being, it is the activity of this part in accordance with its proper virtue which will be the perfect happiness.

If . . . reason is divine in comparison with the rest of Man's nature, the life which accords with reason will be divine in comparison with human life in general. Nor is it right to follow the advice of people who say that the thoughts of men should not be too high for humanity or the thoughts of mortals too high for mortality; for a man, as far as in him lies, should seek immortality and do all that is in his power to live in accordance with the highest part of his nature, as, although that part is insignificant in size, yet in power and honor it is far superior to all the rest.

It would seem too that this is the true self of everyone, if a man's true self is his supreme or better part. It would be absurd then that a man should desire not the life which is properly his own but the life which properly belongs to some other being. The remark already made will be appropriate here. It is what is proper to everyone that is in its nature best and pleasantest for him. It is the life which accords with reason then that will be best and pleasantest for Man, as a man's reason is in the highest sense himself. This will therefore be also the happiest life.

100

FOR STUDY AND DISCUSSION

1. In the first paragraph Aristotle states that some people think that pleasure is the highest good and others that it is utterly bad. He goes on to say, "But I venture to think that this is not a right statement of the case." Why not?
2. He goes on to distinguish between *kinds* of pleasure and to insist—on the basis of his comments—that pleasure cannot be "the good." What is his line of argument on this point? What are some of the examples he gives?
3. Although, for Aristotle, pleasure in itself cannot be "the good," pleasure is the reward of life-giving activities. Thus, if you are interested in a sport, the pleasure "goes with" successful activity in that sport. Can you suggest examples of your own where activity and pleasure are yoked together?
4. Aristotle relates this point to his earlier one about the different *kinds* of pleasure and concludes that the highest form of happiness will accompany the activities of "the best part of our nature." Can you apply this idea to your own pleasures in reading or music or art? Would you say you have greater or less pleasure from these activities now compared with when you were a small child? Do you expect your pleasure in these fields to increase or decrease as you mature? Why?
5. Aristotle's own conclusion is that since reason is man's unique and highest possession, the full activity of reason will carry with it, so to speak, the greatest happiness: the good life in its highest development. To what extent do you agree (or disagree) with this argument?

Immanuel Kant

[1724-1804]

Immanuel Kant is one of the monumental figures in the history of Western philosophy. His interests ranged, but his two greatest volumes are his Critique of Pure Reason (which deals with the nature and extent of human knowledge) and his Critique of Practical Reason (which deals with the nature and extent of our ethical possibilities). It is the substance of the latter volume which concerns us here.

It is important to realize that Kant attempted to reconcile the world of science and the world of morality. He accepted the "modern" science of his time and assumed that man, as a biological creation, is subject to the irreversible laws of nature: one must eventually eat; one cannot indefinitely stop breathing. However, he was equally impressed by contrasting moral laws which, in their own sphere, seemed to imply freedom of choice. This latter conviction is expressed in his assertion. "I ought; therefore, I can."

For Kant, in this moral realm the "good will" is primary; it is the only good for its own sake. All other "goods," such as money, social position, even health, are secondary. The "good will" is given concreteness in Kant's "categorical imperative of duty": to treat every person as an end in himself, never merely as a means to one's own end. In philosophical terms, this position is clearly close to the traditional religious insistence that we are all one in the eyes of God and should treat one another as brothers.

Kant's ethical demands are most exacting. For example, within this basic expectation of "duty," you will see that he makes a sharp demarcation between what he calls "in accord with duty" and "because of duty." He uses his own example of an honest dealer to clarify the distinction, but I will add one or two. If you write a letter once a week, by agreement, to a friend or a member of your family, you are, for Kant, performing an act merely "in accord with duty." Similarly, if a teacher (or student) meets his professional obligations from day-to-day, he is acting "in accord with duty." On the other hand, if you have forced yourself to write a letter which you owed but dreaded to compose, or if a teacher (or student) forced himself to meet a class—in spite of acceptable excuses—then that person would, for Kant, be acting "because of duty."

Kant's conception of "the good life" is austere and demanding. At the same time, it continues to provide philosophical encouragement to those who instinctively feel that an enduring sense of moral well-being must be grounded on an uncompromising code of stern ethical standards.

A Good Will and Duty

Nothing can possibly be conceived in the world, or even out of it, which can be called good without qualification, except a Good Will. Intelligence, wit, judgment, and the other *talents* of the mind, however they may be named, or courage, resolution, perseverance, as qualities of temperament, are undoubtedly good and desirable in many respects; but these gifts of nature may also become extremely bad and mischievous if the will which is to make use of them, and which, therefore, constitutes what is called *character,* is not good. It is the same with the *gifts of fortune.* Power, riches, honor, even health, and the general well-being and contentment with one's condition, which is called *happiness,* inspire pride, and often presumption, if there is not a good will to correct the influence of these on the mind, and with this also to rectify the whole principle of acting, and adapt it to its end. The sight of a being who is not adorned with a single feature of a pure and good will, enjoying unbroken prosperity, can never give pleasure to an impartial rational spectator. Thus a good will appears to constitute the indispensable condition even of being worthy of happiness. . . .

A good will is good not because of what it performs or effects, not by its aptness for the attainment of some proposed end, but simply by virtue of the volition; that is, it is good in itself, and considered by itself is to be esteemed much higher than all that can be brought about by it in favor of any inclination, nay even of the sum total of all inclinations. Even if it should happen that, owing to special disfavor of fortune, or the niggardly provision of a stepmotherly nature, this will should wholly lack power to accomplish its purpose, if with its greatest efforts it should yet achieve nothing, and there should remain only the good will (not, to be sure, a mere wish, but the summoning of all means in our power), then, like a jewel, it would still shine by its own light, as a thing which has its whole value in itself. Its usefulness or fruitlessness can neither add nor take away anything from this value. It would be, as it were, only the setting to enable us to handle it the more conveniently in common commerce, or to attract to it the attention of those who are not yet connoisseurs, but not to recommend it to true connoisseurs, or to determine its value. . . .

We have then to develop the notion of a will which deserves to be highly esteemed for itself, and is good without a view to anything further, a notion which exists already in the sound natural understanding, requiring rather to be cleared up than to be taught, and which in estimating the value of our actions always takes the first place, and consti-

Excerpt from *Fundamental Principles of the Metaphysics of Morals,* translated by Thomas Kingsmill Abbott.

40 tutes the condition of all the rest. In order to do this we will take the notion of duty, which includes that of a good will, although implying certain subjective restrictions and hindrances. These, however, far from concealing it, or rendering it unrecognizable, rather bring it out by contrast, and make it shine forth so much the brighter.

I omit here all actions which are already recognized as inconsistent with duty, although they may be useful for this or that purpose, for with these the question whether they are done *from duty* cannot arise at all, since they even conflict with it. I also set aside those actions which really conform to duty, but to which men have *no* direct *inclination,* perform-
50 ing them because they are impelled thereto by some other inclination. For in this case we can readily distinguish whether the action which agrees with duty is done *from duty,* or from a selfish view. It is much harder to make this distinction when the action accords with duty, and the subject has besides a *direct* inclination to it. For example, it is always a matter of duty that a dealer should not overcharge an inexperienced purchaser, and wherever there is much commerce the prudent tradesman does not overcharge, but keeps a fixed price for every one, so that a child buys of him as well as any other. Men are thus *honestly* served; but this is not enough to make us believe that the tradesman has
60 so acted from duty and from principles of honesty: his own advantage required it; it is out of the question in this case to suppose that he might besides have a direct inclination in favor of the buyers, so that, as it were, from love he should give no advantage to one another. Accordingly the action was done neither from duty nor from direct inclination, but merely with a selfish view. . . .

To be beneficent when we can is a duty; and besides this, there are many minds so sympathetically constituted that, without any other motive of vanity or self-interest, they find a pleasure in spreading joy around them, and can take delight in the satisfaction of others so far as
70 it is their own work. But I maintain that in such a case an action of this kind, however proper, however amiable it may be, has nevertheless no true moral worth, but is on a level with other inclinations, e.g., the inclination to honor, which, if it is happily directed to that which is in fact of public utility and accordant with duty, and consequently honorable, deserves praise and encouragement, but not esteem. For the maxim wants the moral import, namely, that such actions be done *from duty,* not from inclination. Put the case that the mind of that philanthropist were clouded by sorrow of his own, extinguishing all sympathy with the lot of others, and that while he still has the power to benefit others in
80 distress, he is not touched by their trouble because he is absorbed with his own; and now suppose that he tears himself out of this dead insensibility, and performs the action without any inclination to it, but simply from duty, then first has his action its genuine moral worth. Further

still; if nature has put little sympathy in the heart of this or that man; if he, supposed to be an upright man, is by temperament cold and indifferent to the sufferings of others, perhaps because in respect of his own he is provided with the special gift of patience and fortitude, and supposes, or even requires, that others should have the same—and such a man would certainly not be the meanest product of nature—but if nature had
₉₀ not specially framed him for a philanthropist, would he not still find in himself a source from whence to give himself a far higher worth than that of a good-natured temperament could be? Unquestionably. It is just in this that the moral worth of the character is brought out which is incomparably the highest of all, namely, that he is beneficent, not from inclination, but from duty.

To secure one's own happiness is a duty, at least indirectly; for discontent with one's condition, under a pressure of many anxieties and amidst unsatisfied wants, might easily become a great *temptation to transgression of duty*. But here again, without looking to duty, all men
₁₀₀ have already the strongest and most intimate inclination to happiness, because it is just in this idea that all inclinations are combined in one total. But the precept of happiness is often of such a sort that it greatly interferes with some inclinations, and yet a man cannot form any definite and certain conception of the sum of satisfaction of all of them which is called happiness. It is not then to be wondered at that a single inclination, definite both as to what it promises and as to the time within which it can be gratified, is often able to overcome such a fluctuating idea, and that a gouty patient, for instance, can choose to enjoy what he likes, and to suffer what he may, since, according to his calculation, on
₁₁₀ this occasion at least, he has (only) not sacrificed the enjoyment of the present moment to a possibly mistaken expectation of a happiness which is supposed to be found in health. But even in this case, if the general desire for happiness did not influence his will, and supposing that in his particular case health was not a necessary element in this calculation, there yet remains in this, as in all other cases, this law, namely, that he should promote his happiness not from inclination but from duty, and by this would his conduct acquire true moral worth.

It is in this manner, undoubtedly, that we are to understand those passages of Scripture also in which we are commanded to love our
₁₂₀ neighbor, even our enemy. For love, as an affection, cannot be commanded, but beneficence for duty's sake may; even though we are not impelled to it by any inclination—nay, are even repelled by a natural and unconquerable aversion. This is *practical* love, and not *pathological*—a love which is seated in the will, and not in the propensions of sense—in principles of action and not of tender sympathy; and it is this love alone which can be commanded.

FOR STUDY AND DISCUSSION

1. Kant speaks elsewhere of being especially impressed by two things: "The starry heavens above and the moral law within." What comment about Kant that I made in my introduction might this phrase remind you of?
2. Kant says that "nothing . . . can be called good without qualification, except a Good Will." In what ways might lesser "goods" require "qualification"?
3. He goes on to discuss his conception of "duty," emphasizing his distinction between the moral worth of actions done *in accord with* duty (or by "inclination") and those done *because of* duty. How would you express this distinction in your own words?
4. To support his distinction Kant offers four examples: (a) the dealer who does not overcharge his customers, (b) the philanthropist who is not touched by others' troubles, (c) the desire of every man to secure happiness, and (d) the Scriptural admonition "to love our neighbor, even our enemy." Which do you think are the most convincing of these examples? Which do you think are the least convincing?
5. Kant has been criticized for placing so much emphasis on the *motive* ("good will," "duty") of an act that he has neglected the importance of the *consequences* of an act in judging its moral worth. Thus, the English philosopher John Stuart Mill [1806–1873] has asserted that we must distinguish between the morality of an act and the morality of the person committing the act. For example, Mill insists that a man who saves a person from drowning commits a morally worthy *act* even though his *motive* may have been a hope for financial reward. Whether you agree with Mill or not, can you give additional examples which would seem to support his position?

Martin Buber

[1872–1966]

Martin Buber is a fascinating example of a profoundly religious existentialist.[1] Although Buber was one of the intellectual leaders of the new state of Israel and thoroughly steeped in the Hebraic religion, his philosophy of religion transcends any one faith. Buber's philosophy has seemed persuasive to many who are uncomfortable dealing with the technicalities of conventional theology.

This appraisal is not meant to suggest that Buber is easily understood, for he is not. Both his highly poetic style and the subtleties of his thought require considerable concentration. However, to many readers (including myself) the lyric form of Buber's writing increasingly becomes the "exactly right" vehicle for the type of semi-mystical philosophy it is expressing.

The selection I have chosen is taken from Buber's I and Thou, his most widely read and most influential volume. In this work he combines his broad (but deep) religious convictions with his existential sense that for one's religion to be relevant it must involve a sustained, meaningful relationship between the I (oneself) and the Thou (another person or, ultimately, God).

More than the title of his book indicates, Buber's customary use of a hyphen between I and Thou suggests the "oneness" of an I–Thou relationship. You will also see that he contrasts the more concrete relationship implied by I–Thou with the more abstract relationship implied by I–It. There is a vital distinction between these two phrases (these two "primary words," as Buber more precisely calls them), so let me give you a little help at this point before you move on to the selection itself.

It may first be said that an I–Thou relationship cannot be "explained": it simply is. Love is the ideal example, for the love of two people for one another is a felt relationship which does not call for—indeed, does not permit—rational explanation of its meaningfulness to the lovers involved. In contrast, an It is a "thing" (a person, an object in nature, a work of art) to which one has an objective relationship capable of being analyzed and classified—as when one says, "I am your parent," "I like mountains," "I am studying Shakespeare." In such cases, the concreteness, the unspoken immediacy of an existential I–Thou relationship has been replaced by an abstract, articulated I–It relationship.

The second point to be made is that the distinction between I–Thou and I–It is not absolute. One may begin—in marriage, for example—with an I–Thou relationship which increasingly becomes an I–It (husband–wife) relationship. In contrast, an I–It relationship can be transformed to an I–Thou one when full and spontaneous identity replaces a

---

[1] existentialist: There is no simple definition of this word. For a discussion of its meaning, see page 392.

merely "stated" relationship. As with most existentialists, Buber believes that the modern world, with its scientific and institutional orientations, is more inclined to encourage the changing of an I–Thou relationship into an I–It relationship than the opposite possibility.

It is important to keep in mind that, for Buber, both of his two relationships have significant relevance to modern living. In many of our capacities and operations we must treat the objects of our concerns as "things." However, he insists that the danger of this necessity is that by doing so we will increasingly abandon our profound human need of existential values for which there are no adequate substitutes. Buber has expressed this insight: "In all seriousness of Truth, hear this: without It man cannot live. But he who lives with It alone is not a man."

Fundamental Relations: I–Thou versus I–It

To man the world is twofold, in accordance with his twofold attitude.

The attitude of man is twofold, in accordance with the twofold nature of the primary words which he speaks.

The primary words are not isolated words, but combined words.

The one primary word is the combination I–Thou.

The other primary word is the combination I–It; wherein, without a change in the primary word, one of the words He and She can replace It.

Hence the I of man is also twofold.

10 For the I of the primary word I–Thou is a different I from that of the primary word I–It. . . .

There is no I taken in itself, but only the I of the primary word I–Thou and the I of the primary word I–It.

When a man says I, he refers to one or other of these. The I to which he refers is present when he says I. Further, when he says Thou or It, the I of one of the two primary words is present.

The existence of I and the speaking of I are one and the same thing.

When a primary word is spoken, the speaker enters the word and takes his stand in it. . . .

20 I perceive something. I am sensible of something. I imagine something. I will something. I feel something. I think something. The life of human beings does not consist of all this and the like alone.

This and the like together establish the realm of It.

But the realm of Thou has a different basis.

When Thou is spoken, the speaker has no thing for his object. For where there is a thing there is another thing. Every It is bounded by

Excerpts from I and Thou, translated by R. G. Smith.

others. *It* exists only through being bounded by others. But when *Thou* is spoken, there is no thing. *Thou* has no bounds.

When *Thou* is spoken, the speaker has no *thing;* he has indeed nothing. But he takes his stand in relation.

It is said that man experiences his world. What does that mean?

Man travels over the surface of things and experiences them. He extracts knowledge about their constitution from them: he wins an experience from them. He experiences what belongs to the things.

But the world is not presented to man by experiences alone. These present him only with a word composed of *It* and *He* and *She* and *It* again. . . .[1]

As experience, the world belongs to the primary word *I–It.*
The primary word *I–Thou* establishes the world of relation. . . .

I consider a tree.

I can look on it as a picture: stiff column in a shock of light, or splash of green shot with the delicate blue and silver of the background.

I can perceive it as movement: flowing veins on clinging, pressing pith, suck of the roots, breathing of the leaves, ceaseless commerce with earth and air—and the obscure growth itself.

I can classify it in a species and study it as a type in its structure and mode of life.

I can subdue its actual presence and form so sternly that I recognize it only as an expression of law—of the laws in accordance with which a constant opposition for forces is continually adjusted, or of those in accordance with which the component substances mingle and separate.

I can dissipate it and perpetuate it in number, in pure numerical relation.

In all this the tree remains my object, occupies space and time, and has its nature and constitution. . . .

If I face a human being as my *Thou,* and say the primary word *I–Thou* to him, he is not a thing among things, and does not consist of things.

Thus human being is not *He* or *She,* bounded from every other *He* and *She,* a specific point in space and time within the net of the world; nor is he a nature able to be experienced and described, a loose bundle of named qualities. But with no neighbor, and whole in himself, he is *Thou* and fills the heavens. This does not mean that nothing exists except himself. But all else lives in *his* light. . . .

I do not experience the man to whom I say *Thou.* But I take my stand

[1] This is in contrast to the primary word *I–Thou.*

in relation to him, in the sanctity of the primary word. Only when I step out of it do I experience him once more. In the act of experience *Thou* is far away.

Even if the man to whom I say *Thou* is not aware of it in the midst of his experience, yet relation may exist. For *Thou* is more than *It* realizes. No deception penetrates here; here is the cradle of the Real Life. . . .

. . . this is the exalted melancholy of our fate, that every *Thou* in our world must become an *It*. It does not matter how exclusively present the *Thou* was in the direct relation. As soon as the relation has been worked out or has been permeated with a means, the *Thou* becomes an object among objects—perhaps the chief, but still one of them, fixed in its size and its limits. In the work of art, realization in one sense means loss of reality in another. Genuine contemplation is over in a short time; now the life in nature, that first unlocked itself to me in the mystery of mutual action, can again be described, taken to pieces, and classified —the meeting point of manifold systems of laws. And love itself cannot persist in direct relation. It endures, but in interchange of actual and potential being. The human being who was even now single and uncon- ditioned, not something lying to hand, only present, not able to be experienced, only able to be fulfilled, has now become again a *He* or a *She,* a sum of qualities, a given quantity with a certain shape. Now I may take out from him again the color of his hair or of his speech or of his goodness. But so long as I can do this he is no more my *Thou* and cannot be my *Thou* again. . . .

The extended lines of relations meet in the eternal *Thou.*

Every particular *Thou* is a glimpse through to the eternal *Thou;* by means of every particular *Thou* the primary word addresses the eternal *Thou.* Through this mediation of the *Thou* of all beings fulfilment, and non-fulfilment, of relations comes to them: the inborn *Thou* is realized in each relation and consummated in none. It is consummated only in the direct relation with the *Thou* that by its nature cannot become *It.*

Men have addressed their eternal *Thou* with many names. In singing of Him who was thus named they always had the *Thou* in mind: the first myths were hymns of praise. Then the names took refuge in the lan- guage of *It;* men were more and more strongly moved to think of and to address their eternal *Thou* as an *It.* But all God's names are hallowed, for in them He is not merely spoken about, but also spoken to. . . .

God cannot be inferred in anything—in nature, say, as its author, or in history as its master, or in the subject as the self that is thought in it. Something else is not "given" and God then elicited from it; but God is the Being that is directly, most nearly, and lastingly, over against us, that may properly only be addressed, not expressed. . . .

I know nothing of a "world" and a "life in the world" that might separate man from God. What is thus described is actually life with an alienated world of *It,* which experiences and uses. He who truly goes out to meet the world goes out also to God. . . .

FOR STUDY AND DISCUSSION

1. What does Buber mean when he observes in line 4 that "the primary words are not isolated words, but combined words"? He goes on to state that there are two such primary words. What are the two primary words?
2. He says, "When a primary word is spoken, the speaker enters the word and takes his stand in it." Thus, the speaker determines whether he is expressing the *I–It* of our ordinary response to "things" (material or human) or is expressing the *I–Thou* of immediate and unquestioned relationship. How does Buber's illustration of the tree show various types of an *I–It* experience? For example, do you see that although the tree can be considered in different lights, it remains an "object," a "thing," thus an *It?*
3. Buber goes on to remark that, by way of contrast, "if I face a human being as my *Thou* . . . he is not a thing among things, and does not consist of things." Do you perceive that he is here insisting that the *I–Thou* relationship is the significant reality (although it is, incidentally, a most difficult one to write about or talk about because of the danger of automatically converting the *Thou* to an *It* in the process)?
4. Buber observes that "[it is] the exalted melancholy of our fate, that every *Thou* in our world must become an *It.*" An example might be marriage: two people very much in love (an *I–Thou* relationship) marry, but gradually the woman becomes "my wife" to the man, and the man becomes "my husband" to the woman, thus subtly moving toward an *I–It* context. Have you had comparable experiences in family life or with friendships?
5. For Buber, all *I–Thou* relationships find their consummation in our potential relationship with God: "by means of every particular *Thou* the primary word addresses the eternal *Thou.*" Yet here, too, Buber warns that God can become an *It.* What are some of the ways by which the eternal *Thou* might become an *It?*

FICTION

The Leader of the People

JOHN STEINBECK
[1902–1968]

Steinbeck's story places interesting emphasis on a problem of "goodness."
It is obviously more concentrated on that particular value than Chekhov's
"The Bet" or Hawthorne's "The Birthmark" are concentrated on their
respective themes of truth and beauty. I would suggest, then, that for this
selection you focus on these aspects of goodness which Steinbeck has chosen
to dramatize in fictional form.

The story is primarily dealing with the recurring difficulty of different
generations in communicating—and in sharing sympathetically with one an-
other—values deeply felt by each. The grandfather represents an older
generation which now takes proper pride in its great role of opening up the
American West. Yet, his son-in-law has an equally proper pride in what
his generation has done to consolidate these pioneering efforts by establishing
itself and its families on the productive, well-managed farms which are, in
effect, its pioneering contribution.

Thus, as you consider this story in relation to its interest in types and
degrees of "goodness," it is important to keep a very clear perspective. Do
not let your natural sympathy for the grandfather prevent you from seeing
that there is also good in Tiflin's dreams and achievements—even though
the time has long since passed when an individual can significantly be a
"leader of the people" in the manner once possible.

On Saturday afternoon Billy Buck, the ranch-hand, raked together the last
of the old year's haystack and pitched small forkfuls over the wire fence to a
few mildly interested cattle. High in the air small clouds like puffs of cannon
smoke were driven eastward by the March wind. The wind could be heard
whishing in the brush on the ridge crests, but no breath of it penetrated down
into the ranchcup.

The little boy, Jody, emerged from the house eating a thick piece of but-
tered bread. He saw Billy working on the last of the haystack. Jody tramped
down scuffing his shoes in a way he had been told was destructive to good
shoe-leather. A flock of white pigeons flew out of the black cypress tree as
Jody passed, and circled the tree and landed again. A half-grown tortoise-
shell cat leaped from the bunkhouse porch, galloped on stiff legs across the
road, whirled and galloped back again. Jody picked up a stone to help the
game along, but he was too late, for the cat was under the porch before the
stone could be discharged. He threw the stone into the cypress tree and
started the white pigeons on another whirling flight.

Arriving at the used-up haystack, the boy leaned against the barbed wire
fence. "Will that be all of it, do you think?" he asked.

The middle-aged ranch-hand stopped his careful raking and stuck his fork into the ground. He took off his black hat and smoothed down his hair. "Nothing left of it that isn't soggy from ground moisture," he said. He replaced his hat and rubbed his dry leathery hands together.

"Ought to be plenty mice," Jody suggested.

"Lousy with them," said Billy. "Just crawling with mice."

"Well, maybe, when you get all through, I could call the dogs and hunt the mice."

"Sure, I guess you could," said Billy Buck. He lifted a forkful of the damp ground-hay and threw it into the air. Instantly three mice leaped out and burrowed frantically under the hay again.

Jody sighed with satisfaction. Those plump, sleek, arrogant mice were doomed. For eight months they had lived and multiplied in the haystack. They had been immune from cats, from traps, from poison, and from Jody. They had grown smug in their security, overbearing and fat. Now the time of disaster had come; they would not survive another day.

Billy looked up at the top of the hills that surrounded the ranch. "Maybe you better ask your father before you do it," he suggested.

"Well, where is he? I'll ask him now."

"He rode up to the ridge ranch after dinner. He'll be back pretty soon."

Jody slumped against the fence post. "I don't think he'd care."

As Billy went back to his work, he said ominously, "You'd better ask him anyway. You know how he is."

Jody did know. His father, Carl Tiflin, insisted upon giving permission for anything that was done on the ranch, whether it was important or not. Jody sagged farther against the post until he was sitting on the ground. He looked up at the little puffs of wind-driven cloud. "Is it like to rain, Billy?"

"It might. The wind's good for it, but not strong enough."

"Well, I hope it don't rain until after I kill those damn mice." He looked over his shoulder to see whether Billy had noticed the mature profanity. Billy worked on without comment.

Jody turned back and looked at the side-hill where the road from the outside world came down. The hill was washed with lean March sunshine. Silver thistles, blue lupins, and a few poppies bloomed among the sage bushes. Halfway up the hill Jody could see Doubletree Mutt, the black dog, digging in a squirrel hole. He paddled for a while and then paused to kick bursts of dirt out between his hind legs, and he dug with an earnestness which belied the knowledge he must have had that no dog had ever caught a squirrel by digging in a hole.

Suddenly, while Jody watched, the black dog stiffened and backed out of the hole and looked up the hill toward the cleft in the ridge where the road came through. Jody looked up too. For a moment Carl Tiflin on horseback stood out against the pale sky, and then he moved down the road toward the house. He carried something white in his hand.

The boy started to his feet. "He's got a letter," Jody cried. He trotted away toward the ranch house, for the letter would probably be read aloud and he wanted to be there. He reached the house before his father did, and ran in. He heard Carl dismount from his creaking saddle and slap the horse on the side to send it to the barn where Billy would unsaddle it and turn it out.

Jody ran into the kitchen. "We got a letter!" he cried.

His mother looked up from a pan of beans. "Who has?"

"Father has. I saw it in his hand."

Carl strode into the kitchen then, and Jody's mother asked, "Who's the letter from, Carl?"

He frowned quickly. "How did you know there was a letter?"

She nodded her head in the boy's direction. "Big-Britches Jody told me."

Jody was embarrassed.

His father looked down at him contemptuously. "He *is* getting to be a Big-Britches," Carl said. "He's minding everybody's business but his own. Got his big nose into everything."

Mrs. Tiflin relented a little. "Well, he hasn't enough to keep him busy. Who's the letter from?"

Carl still frowned on Jody. "I'll keep him busy if he isn't careful." He held out a sealed letter. "I guess it's from your father."

Mrs. Tiflin took a hairpin from her head and slit open the flap. Her lips pursed judiciously. Jody saw her eyes snap back and forth over the lines. "He says," she translated, "he says he's going to drive out Saturday to stay for a little while. Why, this is Saturday. The letter must have been delayed." She looked at the postmark. "This was mailed day before yesterday. It should have been here yesterday." She looked up questioningly at her husband, and then her face darkened angrily. "Now what have you got that look on you for? He doesn't come often."

Carl turned his eyes away from her anger. He could be stern with her most of the time, but when occasionally her temper arose, he could not combat it.

"What's the matter with you?" she demanded again.

In his explanation there was a tone of apology Jody himself might have used. "It's just that he talks," Carl said lamely. "Just talks."

"Well, what of it? You talk yourself."

"Sure I do. But your father only talks about one thing."

"Indians!" Jody broke in excitedly. "Indians and crossing the plains!"

Carl turned fiercely on him. "You get out, Mr. Big-Britches! Go on, now! Get out!"

Jody went miserably out the back door and closed the screen with elaborate quietness. Under the kitchen window his shamed, downcast eyes fell upon a curiously shaped stone, a stone of such fascination that he squatted down and picked it up and turned it over in his hands.

The voices came clearly to him through the open kitchen window. "Jody's damn well right," he heard his father say. "Just Indians and crossing the plains. I've heard that story about how the horses got driven off about a thousand times. He just goes on and on, and he never changes a word in the things he tells."

When Mrs. Tiflin answered, her tone was so changed that Jody, outside the window, looked up from his study of the stone. Her voice had become soft and explanatory. Jody knew how her face would have changed to match the tone. She said quietly, "Look at it this way, Carl. That was the big thing in my father's life. He led a wagon train clear across the plains to the coast, and when it was finished, his life was done. It was a big thing to do, but it didn't last long enough. Look!" she continued, "it's as though he was born to do that, and after he finished it, there wasn't anything more for him to do but think about it and talk about it. If there'd been any farther west to go, he'd have gone. He's told me so himself. But at last there was the ocean. He lives right by the ocean where he had to stop."

She had caught Carl, caught him and entangled him in her soft tone.

"I've seen him," he agreed quietly. "He goes down and stares off west over the ocean." His voice sharpened a little. "And then he goes up to the Horseshoe Club in Pacific Grove, and he tells people how the Indians drove off the horses."

She tried to catch him again. "Well, it's everything to him. You might be patient with him and pretend to listen."

Carl turned impatiently away. "Well, if it gets too bad, I can always go down to the bunkhouse and sit with Billy," he said irritably. He walked through the house and slammed the front door after him.

Jody ran to his chores. He dumped the grain to the chickens without chasing any of them. He gathered the eggs from the nests. He trotted into the house with the wood and interlaced it so carefully in the woodbox that two armloads seemed to fill it to overflowing.

His mother had finished the beans by now. She stirred up the fire and brushed off the stove-top with a turkey wing. Jody peered cautiously at her to see whether any rancor toward him remained. "Is he coming today?" Jody asked.

"That's what his letter said."

"Maybe I better walk up the road to meet him."

Mrs. Tiflin clanged the stove-lid shut. "That would be nice," she said. "He'd probably like to be met."

"I guess I'll just do it then."

Outside, Jody whistled shrilly to the dogs. "Come on up the hill," he commanded. The two dogs waved their tails and ran ahead. Along the roadside the sage had tender new tips. Jody tore off some pieces and rubbed them on his hands until the air was filled with the sharp wild smell. With a rush the dogs leaped from the road and yapped into the brush after a rabbit. That was the last Jody saw of them, for when they failed to catch the rabbit, they went back home.

Jody plodded on up the hill toward the ridge top. When he reached the little cleft where the road came through, the afternoon wind struck him and blew up his hair and ruffled his shirt. He looked down on the little hills and ridges below and then out at the huge green Salinas Valley. He could see the white town of Salinas far out in the flat and the flash of its windows under the waning sun. Directly below him, in an oak tree, a crow congress had convened. The tree was black with crows all cawing at once.

Then Jody's eyes followed the wagon road down from the ridge where he stood, and lost it behind a hill, and picked it up again on the other side. On that distant stretch he saw a cart slowly pulled by a bay horse. It disappeared behind the hill. Jody sat down on the ground and watched the place where the cart would reappear again. The wind sang on the hilltops, and the puffball clouds hurried eastward.

Then the cart came into sight and stopped. A man dressed in black dismounted from the seat and walked to the horse's head. Although it was so far away, Jody knew he had unhooked the check-rein, for the horse's head dropped forward. The horse moved on, and the man walked slowly up the hill beside it. Jody gave a glad cry and ran down the road toward them. The squirrels bumped along off the road, and a roadrunner flirted its tail and raced over the edge of the hill and sailed out like a glider.

Jody tried to leap into the middle of his shadow at every step. A stone rolled under his foot and he went down. Around a little bend he raced, and there, a short distance ahead, were his grandfather and the cart. The boy dropped from his unseemly running and approached at a dignified walk.

The horse plodded stumble-footedly up the hill, and the old man walked beside it. In the lowering sun their giant shadows flickered darkly behind them. The grandfather was dressed in a black broadcloth suit, and he wore kid congress gaiters and a black tie on a short, hard collar. He carried his black slouch hat in his hand. His white beard was cropped close, and his white eyebrows overhung his eyes like mustaches. The blue eyes were sternly merry. About the whole face and figure there was a granite dignity, so that every motion seemed an impossible thing. Once at rest, it seemed the old man would be stone, would never move again. His steps were slow and certain. Once made, no step could ever be retraced; once headed in a direction, the path would never bend nor the pace increase nor slow.

When Jody appeared around the bend, Grandfather waved his hat slowly in welcome, and he called, "Why, Jody! Come down to meet me, have you?"

Jody sidled near and turned and matched his step to the old man's step and stiffened his body and dragged his heels a little. "Yes, sir," he said. "We got your letter only today."

"Should have been here yesterday," said Grandfather. "It certainly should. How are all the folks?"

"They're fine, sir." He hesitated and then suggested shyly, "Would you like to come on a mouse hunt tomorrow, sir?"

"Mouse hunt, Jody?" Grandfather chuckled. "Have the people of this generation come down to hunting mice? They aren't very strong, the new people, but I hardly thought mice would be game for them."

"No, sir. It's just play. The haystack's gone. I'm going to drive out the mice to the dogs. And you can watch, or even beat the hay a little."

The stern, merry eyes turned down on him. "I see. You don't eat them, then. You haven't come to that yet."

Jody explained, "The dogs eat them, sir. It wouldn't be much like hunting Indians, I guess."

"No, not much—but then later, when the troops were hunting Indians and shooting children and burning tepees, it wasn't much different from your mouse hunt."

They topped the rise and started down into the ranch cup, and they lost the sun from their shoulders. "You've grown," Grandfather said. "Nearly an inch, I should say."

"More," Jody boasted. "Where they mark me on the door, I'm up more than an inch since Thanksgiving even."

Grandfather's rich throaty voice said, "Maybe you're getting too much water and turning to pith and stalk. Wait until you head out, and then we'll see."

Jody looked quickly into the old man's face to see whether his feelings should be hurt, but there was no will to injure, no punishing nor putting-in-your-place light in the keen blue eyes. "We might kill a pig," Jody suggested.

"Oh, no! I couldn't let you do that. You're just humoring me. It isn't the time and you know it."

"You know Riley, the big boar, sir?"

"Yes. I remember Riley well."

"Well, Riley ate a hole into that same haystack, and it fell down on him and smothered him."

"Pigs do that when they can," said Grandfather.

"Riley was a nice pig, for a boar, sir. I rode him sometimes, and he didn't mind."

A door slammed at the house below them, and they saw Jody's mother standing on the porch waving her apron in welcome. And they saw Carl Tiflin walking up from the barn to be at the house for the arrival.

The sun had disappeared from the hills by now. The blue smoke from the house chimney hung in flat layers in the purpling ranchcup. The puffball clouds, dropped by the falling wind, hung listlessly in the sky.

Billy Buck came out of the bunkhouse and flung a wash basin of soapy water on the ground. He had been shaving in midweek, for Billy held Grandfather in reverence, and Grandfather said that Billy was one of the few men of the new generation who had not gone soft. Although Billy was in middle age, Grandfather considered him a boy. Now Billy was hurrying toward the house too.

When Jody and Grandfather arrived, the three were waiting for them in front of the yard gate.

Carl said, "Hello, sir. We've been looking for you."

Mrs. Tiflin kissed Grandfather on the side of his beard, and stood still while his big hand patted her shoulder. Billy shook hands solemnly, grinning under his straw mustache. "I'll put up your horse," said Billy, and he led the rig away.

Grandfather watched him go, and then, turning back to the group, he said as he had said a hundred times before, "There's a good boy. I knew his father, old Mule-tail Buck. I never knew why they called him Mule-tail except he packed mules."

Mrs. Tiflin turned and led the way into the house. "How long are you going to stay, Father? Your letter didn't say."

"Well, I don't know. I thought I'd stay about two weeks. But I never stay as long as I think I'm going to."

In a short while they were sitting at the white oilcloth table eating their supper. The lamp with the tin reflector hung over the table. Outside the dining-room windows the big moths battered softly against the glass.

Grandfather cut his steak into tiny pieces and chewed slowly. "I'm hungry," he said. "Driving out here got my appetite up. It's like when we were crossing. We all got so hungry every night we could hardly wait to let the meat get done. I could eat about five pounds of buffalo meat every night."

"It's moving around does it," said Billy. "My father was a government packer. I helped him when I was a kid. Just the two of us could about clean up a deer's ham."

"I knew your father, Billy," said Grandfather. "A fine man he was. They called him Mule-tail Buck. I don't know why except he packed mules."

"That was it," Billy agreed. "He packed mules."

Grandfather put down his knife and fork and looked around the table. "I remember one time we ran out of meat—" His voice dropped to a curious low singsong, dropped into a tonal groove the story had worn for itself. "There was no buffalo, no antelope, not even rabbits. The hunters couldn't even shoot a coyote. That was the time for the leader to be on the watch. I was the leader, and I kept my eyes open. Know why? Well, just the minute the people began to get hungry they'd start slaughtering the team oxen. Do you believe that? I've heard of parties that just ate up their draft cattle. Started from the middle and worked toward the ends. Finally they'd eat the lead pair, and then the wheelers. The leader of a party had to keep them from doing that."

In some manner a big moth got into the room and circled the hanging kerosene lamp. Billy got up and tried to clap it between his hands. Carl struck with a cupped palm and caught the moth and broke it. He walked to the window and dropped it out.

"As I was saying," Grandfather began again, but Carl interrupted him.

"You'd better eat some more meat. All the rest of us are ready for our pudding."

Jody saw a flash of anger in his mother's eyes. Grandfather picked up his knife and fork. "I'm pretty hungry, all right," he said. "I'll tell you about that later."

When supper was over, when the family and Billy Buck sat in front of the fireplace in the other room, Jody anxiously watched Grandfather. He saw the signs he knew. The bearded head leaned forward; the eyes lost their sternness and looked wonderingly into the fire; the big lean fingers laced themselves on the black knees. "I wonder," he began, "I just wonder whether I ever told you how those thieving Piutes drove off thirty-five of our horses."

"I think you did," Carl interrupted. "Wasn't it just before you went up into the Tahoe country?"

Grandfather turned quickly toward his son-in-law. "That's right. I guess I must have told you that story."

"Lots of times," Carl said cruelly, and he avoided his wife's eyes. But he felt the angry eyes on him, and he said, " 'Course I'd like to hear it again."

Grandfather looked back at the fire. His fingers unlaced and laced again. Jody knew how he felt, how his insides were collapsed and empty. Hadn't Jody been called a Big-Britches that very afternoon? He arose to heroism and opened himself to the term Big-Britches again. "Tell about Indians," he said softly.

Grandfather's eyes grew stern again. "Boys always want to hear about Indians. It was a job for men, but boys want to hear about it. Well, let's see. Did I ever tell you how I wanted each wagon to carry a long iron plate?"

Everyone but Jody remained silent. Jody said, "No. You didn't."

"Well, when the Indians attacked, we always put the wagons in a circle and fought from between the wheels. I thought that if every wagon carried a long plate with rifle holes, the men could stand the plates on the outside of the wheels when the wagons were in the circle and they would be protected. It would save lives, and that would make up for the extra weight of the iron. But of course the party wouldn't do it. No party had done it before and they couldn't see why they should go to the expense. They lived to regret it, too."

Jody looked at his mother, and knew from her expression that she was not listening at all. Carl picked at a callus on his thumb, and Billy Buck watched a spider crawling up the wall.

Grandfather's tone dropped into its narrative groove again. Jody knew in advance exactly what words would fall. The story droned on, speeded up for the attack, grew sad over the wounds, struck a dirge at the burials on the great plains. Jody sat quietly watching Grandfather. The stern blue eyes were detached. He looked as though he were not very interested in the story himself.

When it was finished, when the pause had been politely respected as the frontier of the story, Billy Buck stood up and stretched and hitched his trousers. "I guess I'll turn in," he said. Then he faced Grandfather. "I've got an old powder horn and a cap and ball pistol down to the bunkhouse. Did I ever show them to you?"

Grandfather nodded slowly. "Yes, I think you did, Billy. Reminds me of a pistol I had when I was leading the people across." Billy stood politely until the little story was done, and then he said, "Good night," and went out of the house.

Carl Tiflin tried to turn the conversation then. "How's the country between here and Monterey? I've heard it's pretty dry."

"It is dry," said Grandfather. "There's not a drop of water in the Laguna Seca. But it's a long pull from '87. The whole country was powder then, and in '61 I believe all the coyotes starved to death. We had fifteen inches of rain this year."

"Yes, but it all came too early. We could do with some now." Carl's eye fell on Jody. "Hadn't you better be getting to bed?"

Jody stood up obediently. "Can I kill the mice in the old haystack, sir?"

"Mice? Oh! Sure, kill them all off. Billy said there isn't any good hay left."

Jody exchanged a secret and satisfying look with Grandfather. "I'll kill every one tomorrow," he promised.

Jody lay in his bed and thought of the impossible world of Indians and buffaloes, a world that had ceased to be forever. He wished he could have been living in the heroic time, but he knew he was not of heroic timber. No one living now, save possibly Billy Buck, was worthy to do the things that had been done. A race of giants had lived then, fearless men, men of a staunchness unknown in this day. Jody thought of the wide plains and of the wagons moving across like centipedes. He thought of Grandfather on a huge white horse, marshaling the people. Across his mind marched the great phantoms, and they marched off the earth and they were gone.

He came back to the ranch for a moment, then. He heard the dull rushing sound that space and silence make. He heard one of the dogs, out in the doghouse, scratching a flea and bumping his elbow against the floor with every stroke. Then the wind arose again and the black cypress groaned and Jody went to sleep.

He was up half an hour before the triangle sounded for breakfast. His mother was rattling the stove to make the flames roar when Jody went through the kitchen. "You're up early," she said. "Where are you going?"

"Out to get a good stick. We're going to kill the mice today."

"Who is 'we'?"

"Why, Grandfather and I."

"So you've got him in it. You always like to have someone in with you in case there's blame to share."

"I'll be right back," said Jody. "I just want to have a good stick ready for after breakfast."

He closed the screen door after him and went out into the cool blue morning. The birds were noisy in the dawn, and the ranch cats came down from the hill like blunt snakes. They had been hunting gophers in the dark, and although the four cats were full of gopher meat, they sat in a semicircle at the back door and mewed piteously for milk. Doubletree Mutt and Smasher moved sniffing along the edge of the brush, performing the duty with rigid ceremony, but when Jody whistled, their heads jerked up and their tails waved. They plunged down to him, wriggling their skins and yawning. Jody patted their heads seriously and moved on to the weathered scrap pile. He selected an old broom handle and a short piece of inch-square scrap wood. From his pocket he took a shoelace and tied the ends of the sticks loosely together to make a flail. He whistled his new weapon through the air and struck the ground experimentally, while the dogs leaped aside and whined with apprehension.

Jody turned and started down past the house toward the old haystack ground to look over the field of slaughter, but Billy Buck, sitting patiently on the back steps, called to him, "You better come back. It's only a couple of minutes till breakfast."

Jody changed his course and moved toward the house. He leaned his flail against the steps. "That's to drive the mice out," he said. "I'll bet they're fat. I'll bet they don't know what's going to happen to them today."

"No, nor you either," Billy remarked philosophically, "nor me, nor anyone."

Jody was staggered by this thought. He knew it was true. His imagination twitched away from the mouse hunt. Then his mother came out on the back porch and struck the triangle, and all thoughts fell in a heap.

Grandfather hadn't appeared at the table when they sat down. Billy nodded at his empty chair. "He's all right? He isn't sick?"

"He takes a long time to dress," said Mrs. Tiflin. "He combs his whiskers and rubs up his shoes and brushes his clothes."

Carl scattered sugar on his mush. "A man that's led a wagon train across the plains has got to be pretty careful how he dresses."

Mrs. Tiflin turned on him. "Don't do that, Carl! Please don't!" There was more of threat than of request in her tone. And the threat irritated Carl.

"Well, how many times do I have to listen to the story of the iron plates, and the thirty-five horses? That time's done. Why can't he forget it, now it's done?" He grew angrier while he talked, and his voice rose. "Why does he have to tell them over and over? He came across the plains. All right! Now it's finished. Nobody wants to hear about it over and over."

The door into the kitchen closed softly. The four at the table sat frozen. Carl laid his mush spoon on the table and touched his chin with his fingers.

Then the kitchen door opened and Grandfather walked in. His mouth smiled tightly and his eyes were squinted. "Good morning," he said, and he sat down and looked at his mush dish.

Carl could not leave it there. "Did—did you hear what I said?"

Grandfather jerked a little nod.

"I don't know what got into me, sir. I didn't mean it. I was just being funny."

Jody glanced in shame at his mother, and he saw that she was looking at Carl, and that she wasn't breathing. It was an awful thing that he was doing. He was tearing himself to pieces to talk like that. It was a terrible thing to him to retract a word, but to retract it in shame was infinitely worse.

Grandfather looked sidewise. "I'm trying to get right side up," he said gently. "I'm not being mad. I don't mind what you said, but it might be true, and I would mind that."

"It isn't true," said Carl. "I'm not feeling well this morning. I'm sorry I said it."

"Don't be sorry, Carl. An old man doesn't see things sometimes. Maybe you're right. The crossing is finished. Maybe it should be forgotten, now it's done."

Carl got up from the table. "I've had enough to eat. I'm going to work. Take your time, Billy!" He walked quickly out of the dining room. Billy gulped the rest of his food and followed soon after. But Jody could not leave his chair.

"Won't you tell any more stories?" Jody asked.

"Why, sure I'll tell them, but only when—I'm sure people want to hear them."

"I like to hear them, sir."

"Oh! Of course you do, but you're a little boy. It was a job for men, but only little boys like to hear about it."

Jody got up from his place. "I'll wait outside for you, sir. I've got a good stick for those mice."

He waited by the gate until the old man came out on the porch. "Let's go down and kill the mice now," Jody called.

"I think I'll just sit in the sun, Jody. You go kill the mice."

"You can use my stick if you like."

"No, I'll just sit here a while."

Jody turned disconsolately away and walked down toward the old hay-stack. He tried to whip up his enthusiasm with thoughts of the fat juicy mice. He beat the ground with his flail. The dogs coaxed and whined about him, but he could not go. Back at the house he could see Grandfather sitting on the porch, looking small and thin and black.

Jody gave up and went to sit on the steps at the old man's feet.

"Back already? Did you kill the mice?"

"No, sir. I'll kill them some other day."

The morning flies buzzed close to the ground, and the ants dashed about in front of the steps. The heavy smell of sage slipped down the hill. The porch boards grew warm in the sunshine.

Jody hardly knew when Grandfather started to talk. "I shouldn't stay here, feeling the way I do." He examined his strong old hands. "I feel as though the crossing wasn't worth doing." His eyes moved up the side-hill and stopped on a motionless hawk perched on a dead limb. "I tell those old stories, but they're not what I want to tell. I only know how I want people to feel when I tell them.

"It wasn't Indians that were important, nor adventures, nor even getting out here. It was a whole bunch of people made into one big crawling beast. And I was the head. It was westering and westering. Every man wanted something for himself, but the big beast that was all of them wanted only westering. I was the leader, but if I hadn't been there, someone else would have been the head. The thing had to have a head.

"Under the little bushes the shadows were black at white noonday. When we saw the mountains at last, we cried—all of us. But it wasn't getting here that mattered, it was movement and westering.

"We carried life out here and set it down the way those ants carry eggs. And I was the leader. The westering was as big as God, and the slow steps that made the movement piled up and piled up until the continent was crossed.

"Then we came down to the sea, and it was done." He stopped and wiped his eyes until the rims were red. "That's what I should be telling instead of stories."

When Jody spoke, Grandfather started and looked down at him. "Maybe I could lead the people some day," Jody said.

The old man smiled. "There's no place to go. There's the ocean to stop you. There's a line of old men along the shore hating the ocean because it stopped them."

"In boats I might, sir."

"No place to go, Jody. Every place is taken. But that's not the worst—no, not the worst. Westering has died out of the people. Westering isn't a hunger any more. It's all done. Your father is right. It is finished." He laced his fingers on his knee and looked at them.

Jody felt very sad. "If you'd like a glass of lemonade, I could make it for you."

Grandfather was about to refuse, and then he saw Jody's face. "That would be nice," he said. "Yes, it would be nice to drink a lemonade."

Jody ran into the kitchen where his mother was wiping the last of the breakfast dishes. "Can I have a lemon to make a lemonade for Grandfather?"

His mother mimicked— "And another lemon to make a lemonade for you."

"No, ma'am. I don't want one."

"Jody! You're sick!" Then she stopped suddenly. "Take a lemon out of the cooler," she said softly. "Here, I'll reach the squeezer down to you."

FOR STUDY AND DISCUSSION

1. The conflict between Tiflin and his father-in-law reaches a climax at the breakfast scene. Analyze carefully the behavior (and the reasons for the behavior) of (a) the grandfather, (b) Mr. Tiflin, and (c) Mrs. Tiflin.
2. Why are Jody and his grandfather especially sympathetic to one another?
3. What role does Billy Buck play in bringing out the different types of "goodness" with which the story is dealing?

Gooseberries

ANTON P. CHEKHOV
[1860–1904]

The whole sky had been overcast with rain-clouds from early morning; it was a still day, not hot, but heavy, as it is in gray dull weather when the clouds have been hanging over the country for a long while, when one expects rain and it does not come. Ivan Ivanovich, the veterinary surgeon, and Burkin, the high school teacher, were already tired from walking, and the fields seemed to them endless. Far ahead of them they could just see the windmills of the village of Mironositskoe; on the right stretched a row of hillocks which disappeared in the distance behind the village, and they both knew that this was the bank of the river, that there were meadows, green willows, homesteads there, and that if one stood on one of the hillocks one could see from it the same vast plain, telegraph wires, and a train which in the distance looked like a crawling caterpillar, and that in clear weather one could even see the town. Now, in still weather, when all nature seemed mild and dreamy, Ivan Ivanovich and Burkin were filled with love of the countryside, and both thought how great, how beautiful a land it was.

"Last time we were in Prokofy's barn," said Burkin, "you were about to tell me a story."

"Yes; I meant to tell you about my brother."

Ivan Ivanovich heaved a deep sigh and lighted a pipe to begin to tell his story, but just at that moment the rain began. And five minutes later heavy rain came down, covering the sky, and it was hard to tell when it would be over. Ivan Ivanovich and Burkin stopped in hesitation; the dogs, already drenched, stood with their tails between their legs gazing at them feelingly.

"We must take shelter somewhere," said Burkin. "Let us go to Alehin's; it's close by."

"Come along."

They turned aside and walked through mown fields, sometimes going straight forward, sometimes turning to the right, till they came out on the road. Soon they saw poplars, a garden, then the red roofs of barns; there was a gleam of the river, and the view opened onto a broad expanse of water with a windmill and a white bathhouse: this was Sofino, where Alehin lived.

The watermill was at work, drowning the sound of the rain; the dam was shaking. Here wet horses with drooping heads were standing near their carts, and men were walking about covered with sacks. It was damp, muddy, and desolate; the water looked cold and malignant. Ivan Ivanovich and Burkin were already conscious of a feeling of wetness, messiness, and discomfort all over; their feet were heavy with mud, and when, crossing the dam, they went up to the barns, they were silent, as though they were angry with one another.

In one of the barns there was the sound of a winnowing machine, the door was open, and clouds of dust were coming from it. In the doorway was standing Alehin himself, a man of forty, tall and stout, with long hair, more like a professor or an artist than a landowner. He had on a white shirt that badly needed washing, a rope for a belt, drawers instead of trousers, and his boots, too, were plastered up with mud and straw. His eyes and nose were black with dust. He recognized Ivan Ivanovich and Burkin, and was apparently much delighted to see them.

"Go into the house, gentlemen," he said, smiling; "I'll come directly, this minute."

It was a big two-storied house. Alehin lived in the lower story, with arched ceilings and little windows, where the bailiffs had once lived; here everything was plain, and there was a smell of rye bread, cheap vodka, and harness. He went upstairs into the best rooms only on rare occasions, when visitors came. Ivan Ivanovich and Burkin were met in the house by a maidservant, a young woman so beautiful that they both stood still and looked at one another.

"You can't imagine how delighted I am to see you, my friends," said Alehin, going into the hall with them. "It is a surprise! Pelageya," he said, addressing the girl, "give our visitors something to change into. And, by the way, I will change too. Only I must first go and wash, for I almost think I have not washed since spring. Wouldn't you like to come into the bathhouse? And meanwhile they will get things ready here."

Beautiful Pelageya, looking so refined and soft, brought them towels and soap, and Alehin went to the bathhouse with his guests.

"It's a long time since I had a wash," he said, undressing. "I have got a nice bathhouse, as you see—my father built it—but I somehow never have time to wash."

He sat down on the steps and soaped his long hair and his neck, and the water round him turned brown.

"Yes, I must say," said Ivan Ivanovich meaningly, looking at his head.

"It's a long time since I washed . . ." said Alehin with embarrassment, giving himself a second soaping, and the water near him turned dark blue, like ink.

Ivan Ivanovich went outside, plunged into the water with a loud splash, and swam in the rain, flinging his arms out wide. He stirred the water into waves which set the white lilies bobbing up and down; he swam to the very middle of the millpond and dived, and came up a minute later in another place, and swam on, and kept on diving, trying to touch bottom.

"Oh, my goodness!" he repeated continually, enjoying himself thoroughly. "Oh, my goodness!" He swam to the mill, talked to the peasants there, then returned and lay on his back in the middle of the pond, turning his face to the rain. Burkin and Alehin were dressed and ready to go, but he still went on swimming and diving. "Oh, my goodness! . . ." he said. "Oh, Lord, have mercy on me! . . ."

"That's enough!" Burkin shouted to him.

They went back to the house. And only when the lamp was lighted in the big drawing room upstairs, and Burkin and Ivan Ivanovich, attired in silk dressing-gowns and warm slippers, were sitting in armchairs; and Alehin, washed and combed, in a new coat, was walking about the drawing room, evidently enjoying the feeling of warmth, cleanliness, dry clothes, and light shoes; and when lovely Pelageya, stepping noiselessly on the carpet and smiling softly, handed tea and jam on a tray—only then Ivan Ivanovich began on his story, and it seemed as though not only Burkin and Alehin were listening, but also the ladies, young and old, and the officers who looked down upon them sternly and calmly from their gold frames.

"There are two of us brothers," he began—"I, Ivan Ivanovich, and my brother, Nikolay Ivanovich, two years younger. I went in for a learned profession and became a veterinary surgeon, while Nikolay sat in a government office from the time he was nineteen. Our father, Chimsha-Himalaisky, was the son of a private, but he himself rose to be an officer and left us a little estate and the rank of nobility. After his death the little estate went in debts and legal expenses; but, anyway, we had spent our childhood running wild in the country. Like peasant children, we passed our days and nights in the fields and the woods, looked after horses, stripped the bark off the trees, fished and so on. . . . And, you know, whoever has once in his life caught perch or has seen the migrating of the thrushes in autumn, watched how they float in flocks over the village on bright, cool days, he will never be a real townsman, and will have a yearning for freedom to the day of his death. My brother was miserable in the government office. Years passed by, and he went on sitting in the same place, went on writing the same papers and thinking of one and the same thing—how to get into the country. And this yearning by degrees passed into a definite desire, into a dream of buying himself a little farm somewhere on the banks of a river or a lake.

"He was a gentle, good-natured fellow, and I was fond of him, but I never sympathized with this desire to shut himself up for the rest of his life in a little farm of his own. It's the correct thing to say that a man needs no more than six feet of earth. But six feet is what a corpse needs, not a man. And they say, too, now, that if our intellectual classes are attracted to the land and yearn for a farm, it's a good thing. But these farms are just the same as six feet of earth. To retreat from town, from the struggle, from the bustle of life, to retreat and bury oneself in one's farm—it's not life, it's egoism, laziness, it's monasticism of a sort, but monasticism without good works. A man does not need six feet of earth or a farm, but the whole globe, all nature, where he can have room to display all the qualities and peculiarities of his free spirit.

"My brother Nikolay, sitting in his government office, dreamed of how he would eat his own cabbages, which would fill the whole yard with such a savory smell, take his meals on the green grass, sleep in the sun, sit for whole hours on the seat by the gate gazing at the fields and the forest. Gardening books and the agricultural hints in calendars were his delight, his favorite spiritual sustenance; he enjoyed reading newspapers, too, but the only things he read in them were the advertisements of so many acres of arable land and a grass meadow with farmhouses and buildings, a river, a garden, a mill and millponds, for sale. And his imagination pictured the garden paths, flowers and fruit, starling cotes, the carp in the pond, and all that sort of thing, you know. These imaginary pictures were of different kinds according to the advertisements which he came across, but for some reason in every one of them he always had to have gooseberries. He could not imagine a homestead, he could not picture an idyllic nook, without gooseberries.

" 'Country life has its conveniences,' he would sometimes say. 'You sit on the veranda and you drink tea, while your ducks swim on the pond, there is a delicious smell everywhere, and . . . and the gooseberries are growing.'

"He used to draw a map of his property, and in every map there were the same things—(a) house for the family, (b) servants' quarters, (c) kitchen garden, (d) gooseberry bushes. He lived parsimoniously, was frugal in food and drink, his clothes were beyond description; he looked like a beggar, but kept on saving and putting money in the bank. He grew fearfully avaricious. I did not like to look at him, and I used to give him something and send him presents for Christmas and Easter, but he used to save that too. Once a man is absorbed by an idea there is no doing anything with him.

"Years passed: he was transferred to another province. He was over forty, and he was still reading the advertisements in the papers and saving up. Then I heard he was married. Still with the same object of buying a farm and having gooseberries, he married an elderly and ugly widow without a trace of feeling for her, simply because she had filthy lucre. He went on living frugally after marrying her, and kept her short of food, while he put her money in the bank in his name.

"Her first husband had been a postmaster, and with him she was accustomed to pies and homemade wines, while with her second husband she did not get enough black bread; she began to pine away with this sort of life, and three years later she gave up her soul to God. And I need hardly say that my brother never for one moment imagined that he was responsible for her death. Money, like vodka, makes a man queer. In our town there was a merchant who, before he died, ordered a plateful of honey and ate up all his money and lottery tickets with the honey, so that no one might get the benefit of it. While I was inspecting cattle at a railway station a cattle-dealer fell under an engine and had his leg cut off. We carried him into the waiting room, the blood was flowing—it was a horrible thing—and he kept asking them to look for his leg and was very much worried about it; there were twenty roubles in the boot on the leg that had been cut off, and he was afraid they would be lost."

"That's a story from a different opera," said Burkin.

"After his wife's death," Ivan Ivanovich went on, after thinking for half a minute, "my brother began looking out for an estate for himself. Of course, you may look about for five years and yet end by making a mistake, and buying something quite different from what you have dreamed of. My brother Nikolay bought through an agent a mortgaged estate of three hundred and thirty acres, with a house for the family, with servants' quarters, with a park, but with no orchard, no gooseberry bushes, and no duck pond; there was a river, but the water in it was the color of coffee, because on one side of the estate there was a brickyard and on the other a factory for burning bones. But Nikolay Ivanovich did not grieve much; he ordered twenty gooseberry bushes, planted them, and began living as a country gentleman.

"Last year I went to pay him a visit. I thought I would go and see what it was like. In his letters my brother called his estate 'Chumbaroklov Waste, alias Himalaiskoe.' I reached 'alias Himalaiskoe' in the afternoon. It was hot. Everywhere there were ditches, fences, hedges, fir trees planted in rows, and there was no knowing how to get to the yard, where to put one's horse. I went up to the house, and was met by a fat red dog that looked like a pig. It wanted to bark, but was too lazy. The cook, a fat, barefooted woman, came out of the kitchen, and she, too, looked like a pig, and said that her master was resting. I went in to see my brother. He was sitting up in bed with a quilt over his legs; he had grown older, fatter, wrinkled; his cheeks, his nose, and his mouth all stuck out—he looked as though he might begin grunting into the quilt at any moment.

"We embraced each other and shed tears of joy and of sadness at the thought that we had once been young and now were both gray-headed and near the grave. He dressed, and led me out to show me the estate.

" 'Well, how are you getting on here?' I asked.

" 'Oh, all right, thank God; I am getting on very well.'

"He was no more a poor timid clerk, but a real landowner, a gentleman. He was already accustomed to it, had grown used to it, and liked it. He ate a great deal, went to the bathhouse, was growing stout, was already at law with the village commune and both factories, and was very much offended when the peasants did not call him 'your Honor.' And he concerned himself with the salvation of his soul in a substantial, gentlemanly manner, and performed deeds of charity, not simply, but with an air of consequence. And what deeds of charity! He treated the peasants for every sort of disease with soda and castor oil, and on his name day had a thanksgiving service in the middle of the village, and then treated the peasants to a gallon of vodka—he thought that was the thing to do. Oh, those horrible gallons of vodka! One day the fat landowner hauls the peasants up before the district captain for trespass, and next day, in honor of a holiday, treats them to a gallon of vodka, and they drink and shout 'Hurrah!' and when they are drunk bow down to his feet. A change of life for the better and being well fed and idle develop in a Russian the most insolent self-conceit. Nikolay Ivanovich, who at one time in the government office was afraid to have any views of his own, now could say nothing that was not gospel truth, and uttered such truths in the tone of a prime minister. 'Education is essential, but for the peasants it is premature.' 'Corporal punishment is harmful as a rule, but in some cases it is necessary and there is nothing to take its place.'

" 'I know the peasants and understand how to treat them,' he would say. 'The peasants like me. I need only to hold up my little finger and the peasants will do anything I like.'

"And all this, observe, was uttered with a wise, benevolent smile. He repeated twenty times over 'We noblemen,' 'I as a noble'; obviously he did not remember that our grandfather was a peasant, and our father a soldier. Even our surname Chimsha-Himalaisky, in reality so incongruous, seemed to him now melodious, distinguished, and very agreeable.

"But the point just now is not he, but myself. I want to tell you about the change that took place in me during the brief hours I spent at his country place. In the evening, when we were drinking tea, the cook put on the table a plateful of gooseberries. They were not bought, but his own gooseberries, gathered for the first time since the bushes were planted. Nikolay Ivanovich laughed and looked for a minute in silence at the gooseberries, with tears in his eyes; he could not speak for excitement. Then he put one gooseberry in his mouth, looked at me with the triumph of a child who has at last received his favorite toy, and said:

" 'How delicious!'

"And he ate them greedily, continually repeating, 'Ah, how delicious! Do taste them!'

"They were sour and unripe, but, as Pushkin says:

> *Dearer to us the falsehood that exalts*
> *Than hosts of baser truths.*

"I saw a happy man whose cherished dream was so obviously fulfilled, who had attained his object in life, who had gained what he wanted, who was satisfied with his fate and himself. There is always, for some reason, an element of sadness mingled with my thoughts of human happiness, and, on this occasion, at the sight of a happy man I was overcome by an oppressive feeling that was close upon despair. It was particularly oppressive at night. A bed was made up for me in the room next to my brother's bedroom, and I could hear that he was awake, and that he kept getting up and going to the plate of gooseberries and taking one. I reflected how many satisfied, happy people there really are! What an overwhelming force it is! You look at life: the insolence and idleness of the strong, the ignorance and brutishness of the weak, incredible poverty all about us, overcrowding, degeneration, drunkenness, hypocrisy, lying. . . . Yet all is calm and stillness in the houses and in the streets; of the fifty thousand living in a town, there is not one who would cry out, who would give vent to his indignation aloud. We see the people going to market for provisions, eating by day, sleeping by night, talking their silly nonsense, getting married, growing old, serenely escorting their dead to the cemetery; but we do not see and we do not hear those who suffer, and what is terrible in life goes on somewhere behind the scenes. . . . Everything is quiet and peaceful, and nothing protests but mute statistics: so many people gone out of their minds, so many gallons of vodka drunk, so many children dead from malnutrition. . . . And this order of things is evidently necessary; evidently the happy man only feels at ease because the unhappy bear their burden in silence, and without that silence happiness would be impossible. It's a case of general hypnotism. There ought to be behind the door of every happy, contented man someone standing with a hammer continually reminding him with a tap that there are unhappy people; that however happy he may be, life will show him her jaws sooner or later, trouble will come for him—disease, poverty, losses, and no one will see or hear, just as now he neither sees nor hears others. But there is no man with a hammer; the happy man lives at his ease, the trivial daily cares faintly agitate him like the wind in the aspen tree—and all goes well.

"That night I realized that I, too, was happy and contented," Ivan Ivanovich went on, getting up. "I, too, at dinner and at the hunt liked to lay down the law on life and religion, and the way to manage the peasantry. I, too, used to say that science was light, that culture was essential, but for the simple people reading and writing was enough for the time. Freedom is a blessing, I used to say; we can no more do without it than without air, but we must wait a little. Yes, I used to talk like that, and now I ask, 'For what reason are we to wait?'" asked Ivan Ivanovich, looking angrily at Burkin. "Why wait, I ask you? What grounds have we for waiting? I shall be told, it can't be done all at once; every idea takes shape in life gradually, in its due time. But who is it says that? Where is the proof that it's right? You will fall back upon the natural order of things, the uniformity of phenomena; but is there order and uniformity in the fact that I, a living, thinking man, stand over a chasm and wait for it to close of itself, or to fill up with mud at the very time when perhaps I might leap over it or build a bridge across it? And again, wait for the sake of what? Wait till there's no strength to live? And meanwhile one must live, and one wants to live!

"I went away from my brother's early in the morning, and ever since then it has been unbearable for me to be among people. I am oppressed by peace and quiet; I am afraid to look at the windows, for there is no spectacle more painful to me now than the sight of a happy family sitting round the table drinking tea. I am old and am not fit for the struggle; I am not even capable of hatred; I can only grieve inwardly, feel irritated and vexed; but at night my head is hot from the rush of ideas, and I cannot sleep. . . . Ah, if I were young!"

Ivan Ivanovich walked backwards and forwards in excitement, and repeated: "If I were young!"

He suddenly went up to Alehin and began pressing first one of his hands and then the other.

"Pavel Konstantinovich," he said in an imploring voice, "don't be calm and contented, don't let yourself be put to sleep! While you are young, strong, confident, be not weary in well-doing! There is no happiness, and there ought not to be; but if there is a meaning and an object in life, that meaning and object is not our happiness, but something greater and more rational. Do good!"

And all this Ivan Ivanovich said with a pitiful, imploring smile, as though he were asking him a personal favor.

Then all three sat in armchairs at different ends of the drawing room and were silent. Ivan Ivanovich's story had not satisfied either Burkin or Alehin. When the generals and ladies gazed down from their gilt frames, looking in the dusk as though they were alive, it was dreary to listen to the story of the poor clerk who ate gooseberries. They felt inclined for some reason to talk about elegant people, about women. And their sitting in the drawing room where everything—the chandeliers in their covers, the armchairs, and the carpet under their feet—reminded them that those very people who were now looking down from their frames had once moved about, sat, drunk tea in this room, and the fact that lovely Pelageya was moving noiselessly about was better than any story.

Alehin was fearfully sleepy; he had got up early, before three o'clock in the morning, to look after his work, and now his eyes were closing; but he was afraid his visitors might tell some interesting story after he had gone, and he lingered on. He did not go into the question whether what Ivan Ivanovich had just said was right and true. His visitors did not talk of groats, nor of hay, nor of tar, but of something that had no direct bearing on his life, and he was glad and wanted them to go on.

"It's bedtime, though," said Burkin, getting up. "Allow me to wish you good night."

Alehin said good night and went downstairs to his own domain, while the visitors remained upstairs. They were both taken for the night to a big room where there stood two old wooden beds decorated with carvings, and in the corner was an ivory crucifix. The big cool beds, which had been made by the lovely Pelageya, smelt agreeably of clean linen.

Ivan Ivanovich undressed in silence and got into bed.

"Lord forgive us sinners!" he said, and put his head under the quilt.

His pipe lying on the table smelt strongly of stale tobacco, and Burkin could not sleep for a long while, and kept wondering where the oppressive smell came from.

The rain was pattering on the windowpanes all night.

A Simple Heart

G U S T A V E   F L A U B E R T

[1821–1880]

I

For half a century the women of Pont l'Evêque envied Mme Aubain her maidservant Félicité.

In return for a hundred francs a year she did all the cooking and the housework, the sewing, the washing, and the ironing. She could bridle a horse, fatten poultry, and churn butter, and she remained faithful to her mistress, who was by no means an easy person to get on with.

Mme Aubain had married a young fellow who was good-looking but badly off, and who died at the beginning of 1809, leaving her with two small children and a pile of debts. She then sold all her property except for the farms of Toucques and Geffosses, which together brought in five thousand francs a year at the most, and left her house at Saint Melaine for one behind the covered market which was cheaper to run and had belonged to her family.

This house had a slate roof and stood between an alleyway and a lane leading down to the river. Inside there were differences in level which were the cause of many a stumble. A narrow entrance hall separated the kitchen from the parlor, where Mme Aubain sat all day long in a wicker easy chair by the window. Eight mahogany chairs were lined up against the white-painted wainscoting, and under the barometer stood an old piano loaded with a pyramid of boxes and cartons. On either side of the chimney piece, which was carved out of yellow marble in the Louis Quinze style, there was a tapestry-covered armchair, and in the middle was a clock designed to look like a temple of Vesta. The whole room smelt a little musty, as the floor was on a lower level than the garden.

On the first floor was "Madame's" bedroom—very spacious, with a patterned wallpaper of pale flowers and a portrait of "Monsieur" dressed in what had once been the height of fashion. It opened into a smaller room in which there were two cots, without mattresses. Then came the drawing room, which was always shut up and full of furniture covered with dust sheets. Next there was a passage leading to the study, where books and papers filled the shelves of a bookcase in three sections built round a big writing table of dark wood. The two end panels were hidden under pen-and-ink drawings, landscapes in gouache, and etchings by Audran, souvenirs of better days and bygone luxury. On the second floor a dormer window gave light to Félicité's room, which looked out over the fields.

Every day Félicité got up at dawn, so as not to miss Mass, and worked until evening without stopping. Then, once dinner was over, the plates and dishes put away, and the door bolted, she piled ashes on the log fire and went to sleep in front of the hearth, with her rosary in her hands. Nobody could be more stubborn when it came to haggling over prices, and as for cleanliness, the shine on her saucepans was the despair of all the other servants. Being of a thrifty nature, she ate slowly, picking up from the table the crumbs from her loaf of bread—a twelve-pound loaf which was baked specially for her and lasted her twenty days.

All the year round she wore a kerchief of printed calico fastened behind with a pin, a bonnet which covered her hair, gray stockings, a red skirt, and over her jacket a bibbed apron such as hospital nurses wear.

Her face was thin and her voice was sharp. At twenty-five she was often taken for forty; once she reached fifty, she stopped looking any age in particular. Always silent and upright and deliberate in her movements, she looked like a wooden doll driven by clockwork.

II

Like everyone else, she had had her love story.

Her father, a mason, had been killed when he fell off some scaffolding. Then her mother died, and when her sisters went their separate ways, a farmer took her in, sending her, small as she was, to look after the cows out in the fields. She went about in rags, shivering with cold, used to lie flat on the ground to drink water out of the ponds, would be beaten for no reason at all, and was finally turned out of the house for stealing thirty sous, a theft of which she was innocent. She found work at another farm, looking after the poultry, and as she was liked by her employers the other servants were jealous of her.

One August evening—she was eighteen at the time—they took her off to the fete at Colleville. From the start she was dazed and bewildered by the noise of the fiddles, the lamps in the trees, the medley of gaily colored dresses, the gold crosses and lace, and the throng of people jigging up and down. She was standing shyly on one side when a smart young fellow, who had been leaning on the shaft of a cart, smoking his pipe, came up and asked her to dance. He treated her to cider, coffee, griddle-cake, and a silk neckerchief, and imagining that she knew what he was after, offered to see her home. At the edge of a field of oats, he pushed her roughly to the ground. Thoroughly frightened, she started screaming for help. He took to his heels.

Another night, on the road to Beaumont, she tried to get past a big, slow-moving wagon loaded with hay, and as she was squeezing by she recognized Théodore.

He greeted her quite calmly, saying that she must forgive him for the way he had behaved to her, as "it was the drink that did it."

She did not know what to say in reply and felt like running off.

Straight away he began talking about the crops and the notabilities of the commune, saying that his father had left Colleville for the farm at Les Écots, so that they were now neighbors.

"Ah!" she said.

He added that his family wanted to see him settled but that he was in no hurry and was waiting to find a wife to suit his fancy. She lowered her head. Then he asked her if she was thinking of getting married. She answered with a smile that it was mean of him to make fun of her.

"But I'm not making fun of you!" he said. "I swear I'm not!"

He put his left arm round her waist, and she walked on supported by his embrace. Soon they slowed down. There was a gentle breeze blowing, the stars were shining, the huge load of hay was swaying about in front of them, and the four horses were raising clouds of dust as they shambled along. Then, without being told, they turned off to the right. He kissed her once more, and she disappeared into the darkness.

The following week Théodore got her to grant him several rendezvous.

They would meet at the bottom of a farmyard, behind a wall, under a solitary tree. She was not ignorant of life as young ladies are, for the animals had taught her a great deal; but her reason and an instinctive sense of honor prevented her from giving way. The resistance she put up inflamed Théodore's passion to such an extent that in order to satisfy it (or perhaps out of sheer naiveté) he proposed to her. At first she refused to believe him, but he swore that he was serious.

Soon afterward he had a disturbing piece of news to tell her: the year before, his parents had paid a man to do his military service for him, but now he might be called up again any day, and the idea of going into the army frightened him. In Félicité's eyes this cowardice of his appeared to be a proof of his affection, and she loved him all the more for it. Every night she would steal out to meet him, and every night Théodore would plague her with his worries and entreaties.

In the end he said that he was going to the Prefecture himself to make inquiries, and that he would come and tell her how matters stood the following Sunday, between eleven and midnight.

At the appointed hour she hurried to meet her sweetheart, but found one of his friends waiting for her instead.

He told her that she would not see Théodore again. To make sure of avoiding conscription, he had married a very rich old woman, Mme Lehoussais of Toucques.

Her reaction was an outburst of frenzied grief. She threw herself on the ground, screaming and calling on God, and lay moaning all alone in the open until sunrise. Then she went back to the farm and announced her intention of leaving. At the end of the month, when she had received her wages, she wrapped her small belongings up in a kerchief and made her way to Pont l'Évêque.

In front of the inn there, she sought information from a woman in a widow's bonnet, who, as it happened, was looking for a cook. The girl did not know much about cooking, but she seemed so willing and expected so little that finally Mme Aubain ended up by saying: "Very well, I will take you on."

A quarter of an hour later Félicité was installed in her house.

At first she lived there in a kind of fearful awe caused by "the style of the house" and by the memory of "Monsieur" brooding over everything. Paul and Virginie, the boy aged seven and the girl barely four, seemed to her to be made of some precious substance. She used to carry them about pickaback and when Mme Aubain told her not to keep on kissing them she was cut to the quick. All the same, she was happy now, for her pleasant surroundings had dispelled her grief.

On Thursdays, a few regular visitors came in to play Boston, and Félicité got the cards and the footwarmers ready beforehand. They always arrived punctually at eight and left before the clock struck eleven.

Every Monday morning the second-hand dealer who lived down the alley put all his junk out on the pavement. Then the hum of voices began to fill the town, mingled with the neighing of horses, the bleating of lambs, the grunting of pigs, and the rattle of carts in the streets.

About midday, when the market was in full swing, a tall old peasant with a hooked nose and his cap on the back of his head would appear at the door. This was Robelin, the farmer from Geffosses. A little later, and Liébard, the farmer from Toucques, would arrive—a short, fat, red-faced fellow in a gray jacket and leather gaiters fitted with spurs.

Both men had hens or cheeses they wanted to sell to "Madame." But Félicité was up to all their tricks and invariably outwitted them, so that they went away full of respect for her.

From time to time Mme Aubain had a visit from an uncle of hers, the Marquis de Grémanville, who had been ruined by loose living and was now living at Falaise on his last remaining scrap of property. He always turned up at lunch time, accompanied by a hideous poodle which dirtied all the furniture with its paws. However hard he tried to behave like a gentleman, even going so far as to raise his hat every time he mentioned "my late father," the force of habit was usually too much for him, for he would start pouring himself one glass after another and telling bawdy stories. Félicité used to push him gently out of the house, saying politely: "You've had quite enough, Monsieur de Grémanville. See you another time!" and shutting the door on him.

She used to open it with pleasure to M. Bourais, who was a retired solicitor. His white tie and his bald head, his frilled shirt front and his ample brown frock coat, the way he had of rounding his arm to take a pinch of snuff, and indeed everything about him made an overwhelming impression on her such as we feel when we meet some outstanding personality.

As he looked after "Madame's" property, he used to shut himself up with her for hours in "Monsieur's" study. He lived in dread of compromising his reputation, had a tremendous respect for the Bench, and laid claim to some knowledge of Latin.

To give the children a little painless instruction, he made them a present of a geography book with illustrations. These represented scenes in different parts of the world, such as cannibals wearing feather headdresses, a monkey carrying off a young lady, Bedouins in the desert, a whale being harpooned, and so on.

Paul explained these pictures to Félicité, and that indeed was all the education she ever had. As for the children, they were taught by Guyot, a poor devil employed at the Town Hall, who was famous for his beautiful handwriting, and who had a habit of sharpening his penknife on his boots.

When the weather was fine the whole household used to set off early for a day at the Geffosses farm.

The farmyard there was on a slope, with the house in the middle; and the sea, in the distance, looked like a streak of gray. Félicité would take some slices of cold meat out of her basket, and they would have their lunch in a room adjoining the dairy. It was all that remained of a country house which had fallen into ruin, and the wallpaper hung in shreds, fluttering in the draft. Mme Aubain used to sit with bowed head, absorbed in her memories, so that the children were afraid to talk. "Why don't you run along and play?" she would say, and away they went.

Paul climbed up into the barn, caught birds, played ducks and drakes on the pond, or banged with a stick on the great casks, which sounded just like drums.

Virginie fed the rabbits or scampered off to pick cornflowers, showing her little embroidered knickers as she ran.

One autumn evening they came home through the fields. The moon, which was in its first quarter, lit up part of the sky, and there was some mist floating like a scarf over the winding Toucques. The cattle, lying out in the middle of the pasture, looked peacefully at the four people walking by. In the third field a few got up and made a half circle in front of them.

"Don't be frightened!" said Félicité, and crooning softly, she stroked the back of the nearest animal. It turned about and the others did the same. But while they were crossing the next field they suddenly heard a dreadful bellowing. It came from a bull which had been hidden by the mist, and which now came toward the two women.

Mme Aubain started to run.

"No! No!" said Félicité. "Not so fast!"

All the same they quickened their pace, hearing behind them a sound of heavy breathing which came nearer and nearer. The bull's hooves thudded like hammers on the turf, and they realized that it had broken into a gallop. Turning round, Félicité tore up some clods of earth and flung them at its eyes. It lowered its muzzle and thrust its horns forward, trembling with rage and bellowing horribly.

By now Mme Aubain had got to the end of the field with her two children and was frantically looking for a way over the high bank. Félicité was still backing away from the bull, hurling clods of turf which blinded it, and shouting: "Hurry! Hurry!"

Mme Aubain got down into the ditch, pushed first Virginie and then Paul up the other side, fell once or twice trying to climb the bank, and finally managed it with a valiant effort.

The bull had driven Félicité back against a gate, and its slaver was spurting into her face. In another second it would have gored her, but she just had time to slip between two of the bars, and the great beast halted in amazement.

This adventure was talked about at Pont l'Évêque for a good many years, but Félicité never prided herself in the least on what she had done, as it never occurred to her that she had done anything heroic.

Virginie claimed all her attention, for the fright had affected the little girl's nerves, and M. Poupart, the doctor, recommended sea-bathing at Trouville.

In those days the resort had few visitors. Mme Aubain made inquiries, consulted Bourais, and got everything ready as though for a long journey.

Her luggage went off in Liébard's cart the day before she left. The next morning he brought along two horses, one of which had a woman's saddle with a velvet back, while the other carried a cloak rolled up to make a kind of seat on its crupper. Mme Aubain sat on this, with Liébard in front. Félicité looked after Virginie on the other horse, and Paul mounted M. Lechaptois's donkey, which he had lent them on condition they took great care of it.

The road was so bad that it took two hours to travel the five miles to Toucques. The horses sank into the mud up to their pasterns and had to jerk their hindquarters to get out; often they stumbled in the ruts, or else they had to jump. In some places, Liébard's mare came to a sudden stop, and while he waited patiently for her to move off again, he talked about the people whose properties bordered the road, adding moral reflections to each story. For instance, in the middle of Toucques, as they were passing underneath some windows set in a mass of nasturtiums, he shrugged his shoulders and said:

"There's a Madame Lehoussais lives here. Now instead of taking a young man, she . . ."

Félicité did not hear the rest, for the horses had broken into a trot and the donkey was galloping along. All three turned down a bridle path, a gate swung open, a couple of boys appeared, and everyone dismounted in front of a manure heap right outside the farmhouse door.

Old Mother Liébard welcomed her mistress with every appearance of pleasure. She served up a sirloin of beef for lunch, with tripe and black pudding, a fricassee of chicken, sparkling cider, a fruit tart and brandy plums, garnishing the whole meal with compliments to Madame, who seemed to be enjoying better health, to Mademoiselle, who had turned into a "proper little beauty," and to Monsieur Paul, who had "filled out a lot." Nor did she forget their deceased grandparents, whom the Liébards had known personally, having been in the family's service for several generations.

Like its occupants, the farm had an air of antiquity. The ceiling beams were worm-eaten, the walls black with smoke, and the windowpanes gray with dust. There was an oak dresser laden with all sorts of odds and ends—jugs, plates, pewter bowls, wolf traps, sheep shears, and an enormous syringe which amused the children. In the three yards outside there was not a single tree without either mushrooms at its base or mistletoe in its branches. Several had been blown down and had taken root again at the middle; all of them were bent under the weight of their apples. The thatched roofs, which looked like brown velvet and varied in thickness, weathered the fiercest winds, but the cart shed was tumbling down. Mme Aubain said that she would have it seen to, and ordered the animals to be reharnessed.

It took them another half-hour to reach Trouville. The little caravan dismounted to make their way along the Écores, a cliff jutting right out over the boats moored below; and three minutes later they got to the end of the quay and entered the courtyard of the Golden Lamb, the inn kept by Mère David.

After the first few days Virginie felt stronger, as a result of the change of air and the sea-bathing. Not having a costume, she went into the water in her chemise and her maid dressed her afterward in a customs officer's hut which was used by the bathers.

In the afternoons they took the donkey and went off beyond the Roches-Noires, in the direction of Hennequeville. To begin with, the path went uphill between gentle slopes like the lawns in a park, and then came out on a plateau where pastureland and ploughed fields alternated. On either side there were holly bushes standing out from the tangle of brambles, and here and there a big dead tree spread its zigzag branches against the blue sky.

They almost always rested in the same field, with Deauville on their left, Le Havre on their right, and the open sea in front. The water glittered in the sunshine, smooth as a mirror, and so still that the murmur it made was scarcely audible; unseen sparrows could be heard twittering, and the sky covered the whole scene with its huge canopy. Mme Aubain sat doing her needlework, Virginie plaited rushes beside her, Félicité gathered lavender, and Paul, feeling profoundly bored, longed to get up and go.

Sometimes they crossed the Toucques in a boat and hunted for shells. When the tide went out, sea urchins, ormers,[1] and jellyfish were left behind; and the children scampered around, snatching at the foam flakes carried on the wind. The sleepy waves, breaking on the sand, spread themselves out along the shore. The beach stretched as far as the eye could see, bounded on the land side by the dunes which separated it from the Marais, a broad meadow in the shape of an arena. When they came back that way, Trouville, on the distant hillside, grew bigger at every step, and with its medley of oddly assorted houses seemed to blossom out in gay disorder.

On exceptionally hot days they stayed in their room. The sun shone in dazzling bars of light between the slats of the blind. There was not a sound to be heard in the village, and not a soul to be seen down in the street. Everything seemed more peaceful in the prevailing silence. In the distance caulkers

1 ormers: shells that are ear-shaped.

were hammering away at the boats, and the smell of tar was wafted along by a sluggish breeze.

The principal amusement consisted in watching the fishing boats come in. As soon as they had passed the buoys, they started tacking. With their canvas partly lowered and their foresails blown out like balloons they glided through the splashing waves as far as the middle of the harbor, where they suddenly dropped anchor. Then each boat came alongside the quay, and the crew threw ashore their catch of quivering fish. A line of carts stood waiting, and women in cotton bonnets rushed forward to take the baskets and kiss their men.

One day one of these women spoke to Félicité, who came back to the inn soon after in a state of great excitement. She explained that she had found one of her sisters—and Nastasie Barette, now Leroux, made her appearance, with a baby at her breast, another child holding her right hand, and on her left a little sailor boy, his arms akimbo and his cap over one ear.

Mme Aubain sent her off after a quarter of an hour. From then on they were forever hanging round the kitchen or loitering about when the family went for a walk, though the husband kept out of sight.

Félicité became quite attached to them. She bought them a blanket, several shirts, and a stove; and it was clear that they were bent on getting all they could out of her.

This weakness of hers annoyed Mme Aubain, who in any event disliked the familiar way in which the nephew spoke to Paul. And so, as Virginie had started coughing and the good weather was over, she decided to go back to Pont l'Évêque.

M. Bourais advised her on the choice of a school; Caen was considered the best, so it was there that Paul was sent. He said good-bye bravely, feeling really rather pleased to be going to a place where he would have friends of his own.

Mme Aubain resigned herself to the loss of her son, knowing that it was unavoidable. Virginie soon got used to it. Félicité missed the din he used to make, but she was given something new to do which served as a distraction: from Christmas onward she had to take the little girl to catechism every day.

III

After genuflecting at the door, she walked up the center isle under the nave, opened the door of Mme Aubain's pew, sat down, and started looking about her.

The choir stalls were all occupied, with the boys on the right and the girls on the left, while the curé stood by the lectern. In one of the stained-glass windows in the apse the Holy Ghost looked down on the Virgin; another window showed her kneeling before the Infant Jesus; and behind the tabernacle there was a wood-carving of St Michael slaying the dragon.

The priest began with a brief outline of sacred history. Listening to him,

Félicité saw in imagination the Garden of Eden, the Flood, the Tower of Babel, cities burning, peoples dying, and idols being overthrown; and this dazzling vision left her with a great respect for the Almighty and profound fear of His wrath.

Then she wept as she listened to the story of the Passion. Why had they crucified Him, when He loved children, fed the multitudes, healed the blind, and had chosen out of humility to be born among the poor, on the litter of a stable? The sowing of the seed, the reaping of the harvest, the pressing of the grapes—all those familiar things of which the Gospels speak had their place in her life. God had sanctified them in passing, so that she loved the lambs more tenderly for love of the Lamb of God, and the doves for the sake of the Holy Ghost.

She found it difficult, however, to imagine what the Holy Ghost looked like, for it was not just a bird but a fire as well, and sometimes a breath. She wondered whether that was its light she had seen flitting about the edge of the marshes at night, whether that was its breath she had felt driving the clouds across the sky, whether that was its voice she had heard in the sweet music of the bells. And she sat in silent adoration, delighting in the coolness of the walls and the quiet of the church.

Of dogma she neither understood nor even tried to understand anything. The curé discoursed, the children repeated their lesson, and she finally dropped off to sleep, waking up suddenly at the sound of their sabots clattering across the flagstones as they left the church.

It was in this manner, simply by hearing it expounded, that she learnt her catechism, for her religious education had been neglected in her youth. From then on she copied all Virginie's observances, fasting when she did and going to confession with her. On the feast of Corpus Christi the two of them made an altar of repose together.

The preparations for Virginie's first communion caused her great anxiety. She worried over her shoes, her rosary, her missal, and her gloves. And how she trembled as she helped Mme Aubain to dress the child!

All through the Mass her heart was in her mouth. One side of the choir was hidden from her by M. Bourais, but directly opposite her she could see the flock of maidens, looking like a field of snow with their white crowns perched on top of their veils; and she recognized her little darling from a distance by her dainty neck and her rapt attitude. The bell tinkled. Every head bowed low, and there was a silence. Then, to the thunderous accompaniment of the organ, choir and congregation joined in singing the *Agnus Dei*. Next the boys' procession began, and after that the girls got up from their seats. Slowly, their hands joined in prayer, they went toward the brightly lit altar, knelt on the first step, received the Host one by one, and went back to their places in the same order. When it was Virginie's turn, Félicité leant forward to see her, and in one of those imaginative flights born of real affection, it seemed to her that she herself was in the child's place. Virginie's face became her own,

Virginie's dress clothed her, Virginie's heart was beating in her breast; and as she closed her eyes and opened her mouth, she almost fainted away.

Early next morning she went to the sacristy and asked M. le Curé to give her communion. She received the sacrament with all due reverence, but did not feel the same rapture as she had the day before.

Mme Aubain wanted her daughter to possess every accomplishment, and since Guyot could not teach her English or music, she decided to send her as a boarder to the Ursuline Convent at Honfleur.

Virginie raised no objection, but Félicité went about sighing at Madame's lack of feeling. Then she thought that perhaps her mistress was right: such matters, after all, lay outside her province.

Finally the day arrived when an old wagonette stopped at their door, and a nun got down from it who had come to fetch Mademoiselle. Félicité hoisted the luggage up on top, gave the driver some parting instructions, and put six pots of jam, a dozen pears, and a bunch of violets in the boot.

At the last moment Virginie burst into a fit of sobbing. She threw her arms round her mother, who kissed her on the forehead, saying: "Come now, be brave, be brave." The step was pulled up and the carriage drove away.

Then Mme Aubain broke down, and that evening all her friends, M. and Mme Lormeau, Mme Lechaptois, the Rochefeuille sisters, M. de Houppeville, and Bourais, came in to console her.

To begin with she missed her daughter badly. But she had a letter from her three times a week, wrote back on the other days, walked round her garden, did a little reading, and thus contrived to fill the empty hours.

As for Félicité, she went into Virginie's room every morning from sheer force of habit and looked round it. It upset her not having to brush the child's hair any more, tie her bootlaces, or tuck her up in bed; and she missed seeing her sweet face all the time and holding her hand when they went out together. For want of something to do, she tried making lace, but her fingers were too clumsy and broke the threads. She could not settle to anything, lost her sleep, and, to use her own words, was "eaten up inside."

To "occupy her mind," she asked if her nephew Victor might come and see her, and permission was granted.

He used to arrive after Mass on Sunday, his cheeks flushed, his chest bare, and smelling of the countryside through which he had come. She laid a place for him straight away, opposite hers, and they had lunch together. Eating as little as possible herself, in order to save the expense, she stuffed him so full of food that he fell asleep after the meal. When the first bell for vespers rang, she woke him up, brushed his trousers, tied his tie, and set off for church, leaning on his arm with all a mother's pride.

His parents always told him to get something out of her—a packet of brown sugar perhaps, some soap, or a little brandy, sometimes even money. He brought her his clothes to be mended, and she did the work gladly, thankful for anything that would force him to come again.

In August his father took him on a coasting trip. The children's holidays were just beginning, and it cheered her up to have them home again. But Paul was turning capricious and Virginie was getting too old to be addressed familiarly—a state of affairs which put a barrier of constraint between them.

Victor went to Morlaix, Dunkirk, and Brighton in turn, and brought her a present after each trip. The first time it was a box covered with shells, the second a coffee cup, the third a big gingerbread man. He was growing quite handsome, with his trim figure, his little mustache, his frank open eyes, and the little leather cap that he wore on the back of his head like a pilot. He kept her amused by telling her stories full of nautical jargon.

One Monday—it was the fourteenth of July, 1819, a date she never forgot—Victor told her that he had signed on for an ocean voyage, and that on the Wednesday night he would be taking the Honfleur packet to join his schooner, which was due to sail shortly from Le Havre. He might be away, he said, for two years.

The prospect of such a long absence made Félicité extremely unhappy, and she felt she must bid him godspeed once more. So on the Wednesday evening, when Madame's dinner was over, she put on her clogs and swiftly covered the ten miles between Pont l'Évêque and Honfleur.

When she arrived at the Calvary she turned right instead of left, got lost in the shipyards, and had to retrace her steps. Some people she spoke to advised her to hurry. She went right round the harbor, which was full of boats, constantly tripping over moorings. Then the ground fell away, rays of light crisscrossed in front of her, and for a moment she thought she was going mad, for she could see horses up in the sky.

On the quayside more horses were neighing, frightened by the sea. A derrick was hoisting them into the air and dropping them into one of the boats, which was already crowded with passengers elbowing their way between barrels of cider, baskets of cheese, and sacks of grain. Hens were cackling and the captain swearing, while a cabin boy stood leaning on the cats-head, completely indifferent to it all. Félicité, who had not recognized him, shouted: "Victor!" and he raised his head. She rushed forward, but at that very moment the gangway was pulled ashore.

The packet moved out of the harbor with women singing as they hauled it along, its ribs creaking and heavy waves lashing its bows. The sail swung round, hiding everyone on board from view, and against the silvery, moonlit sea the boat appeared as a dark shape that grew ever fainter, until at last it vanished in the distance.

As Félicité was passing the Calvary, she felt a longing to commend to God's mercy all that she held most dear; and she stood there praying for a long time, her face bathed in tears, her eyes fixed upon the clouds. The town was asleep, except for the customs officers walking up and down. Water was pouring ceaselessly through the holes in the sluice-gate, making as much noise as a torrent. The clocks struck two.

The convent parlor would not be open before daybreak, and Madame would be annoyed if she were late; so, although she would have liked to give a kiss to the other child, she set off for home. The maids at the inn were just waking up as she got to Pont l'Évêque.

So the poor lad was going to be tossed by the waves for months on end! His previous voyages had caused her no alarm. People came back from England and Brittany; but America, the Colonies, the Islands, were all so far away, somewhere at the other end of the world.

From then on Félicité thought of nothing but her nephew. On sunny days she hoped he was not too thirsty, and when there was a storm she was afraid he would be struck by lightning. Listening to the wind howling in the chimney or blowing slates off the roof, she saw him being buffeted by the very same storm, perched on the top of a broken mast, with his whole body bent backwards under a sheet of foam; or again—and these were reminiscences of the illustrated geography book—he was being eaten by savages, captured by monkeys in a forest, or dying on a desert shore. But she never spoke of her worries.

Mme Aubain had worries of her own about her daughter. The good nuns said that she was an affectionate child, but very delicate. The slightest emotion upset her, and she had to give up playing the piano.

Her mother insisted on regular letters from the convent. One morning when the postman had not called, she lost patience and walked up and down the room, between her chair and the window. It was really extraordinary! Four days without any news!

Thinking her own example would comfort her, Félicité said:

"I've been six months, Madame, without news."

"News of whom?"

The servant answered gently:

"Why—of my nephew."

"Oh, your nephew!" And Mme Aubain started pacing up and down again, with a shrug of her shoulders that seemed to say: "I wasn't thinking of him—and indeed, why should I? Who cares about a young, good-for-nothing cabin boy? Whereas my daughter—why, just think!"

Although she had been brought up the hard way, Félicité was indignant with Madame, but she soon forgot. It struck her as perfectly natural to lose one's head where the little girl was concerned. For her, the two children were of equal importance; they were linked together in her heart by a single bond, and their destinies should be the same.

The chemist told her that Victor's ship had arrived at Havana: he had seen this piece of information in a newspaper.

Because of its association with cigars, she imagined Havana as a place where nobody did anything but smoke, and pictured Victor walking about among crowds of Negroes in a cloud of tobacco smoke. Was it possible, she wondered, "in case of need" to come back by land? And how far was it from Pont l'Évêque? To find out she asked M. Bourais.

He reached for his atlas, and launched forth into an explanation of latitudes and longitudes, smiling like the pedant he was at Félicité's bewilderment. Finally he pointed with his pencil at a minute black dot inside a ragged oval patch, saying:

"There it is."

She bent over the map, but the network of colored lines meant nothing to her and only tired her eyes. So when Bourais asked her to tell him what was puzzling her, she begged him to show her the house where Victor was living. He threw up his hands, sneezed, and roared with laughter, delighted to come across such simplicity. And Félicité—whose intelligence was so limited that she probably expected to see an actual portrait of her nephew—could not make out why he was laughing.

It was a fortnight later that Liébard came into the kitchen at market time, as he usually did, and handed her a letter from her brother-in-law. As neither of them could read, she turned to her mistress for help.

Mme Aubain, who was counting the stitches in her knitting, put it down and unsealed the letter. She gave a start, and, looking hard at Félicité, said quietly:

"They have some bad news for you . . . Your nephew . . ."

He was dead. That was all the letter had to say.

Félicité dropped on to a chair, leaning her head against the wall and closing her eyelids, which suddenly turned pink. Then, with her head bowed, her hands dangling, and her eyes set, she kept repeating:

"Poor little lad! Poor little lad!"

Liébard looked at her and sighed. Mme Aubain was trembling slightly. She suggested that she should go and see her sister at Trouville, but Félicité shook her head to indicate that there was no need for that.

There was a silence. Old Liébard thought it advisable to go.

Then Félicité said:

"It doesn't matter a bit, not to them it doesn't."

Her head fell forward again, and from time to time she unconsciously picked up the knitting needles lying on the worktable.

Some women went past carrying a tray full of dripping linen.

Catching sight of them through the window, she remembered her own washing; she had passed the lye through it the day before and today it needed rinsing. So she left the room.

Her board and tub were on the bank of the Toucques. She threw a pile of chemises down by the water's edge, rolled up her sleeves, and picked up her battledore. The lusty blows she gave with it could be heard in all the neighboring gardens.

The fields were empty, the river rippling in the wind; at the bottom long weeds were waving to and fro, like the hair of corpses floating in the water. She held back her grief, and was very brave until the evening; but in her room she gave way to it completely, lying on her mattress with her face buried in the pillow and her fists pressed against her temples.

Long afterward she learned the circumstances of Victor's death from the captain of his ship. He had gone down with yellow fever, and they had bled him too much at the hospital. Four doctors had held him at once. He had died straight away, and the chief doctor had said:

"Good! There goes another!"

His parents had always treated him cruelly. She preferred not to see them again, and they made no advances, either because they had forgotten about her or out of the callousness of the poor.

Meanwhile Virginie was growing weaker. Difficulty in breathing, fits of coughing, protracted bouts of fever, and mottled patches on the cheekbones all indicated some deep-seated complaint. M. Poupart had advised a stay in Provence. Mme Aubain decided to follow this suggestion, and, if it had not been for the weather at Pont l'Évêque, she would have brought her daughter home at once.

She arranged with a jobmaster to drive her out to the convent every Tuesday. There was a terrace in the garden, overlooking the Seine, and there Virginie, leaning on her mother's arm, walked up and down over the fallen vine leaves. Sometimes, while she was looking at the sails in the distance, or at the long stretch of horizon from the Château de Tancarville to the lighthouses of Le Havre, the sun would break through the clouds and make her blink. Afterward they would rest in the arbor. Her mother had secured a little cask of excellent Malaga, and, laughing at the idea of getting tipsy, Virginie used to drink a thimbleful, but no more.

Her strength revived. Autumn slipped by, and Félicité assured Mme Aubain that there was nothing to fear. But one evening, coming back from some errand in the neighborhood, she found M. Poupart's gig standing at the door. He was in the hall, and Mme Aubain was tying on her bonnet.

"Give me my foot warmer, purse, gloves. Quickly now!"

Virginie had pneumonia and was perhaps past recovery.

"Not yet!" said the doctor; and the two of them got into the carriage with snowflakes swirling around them. Night was falling and it was very cold.

Félicité rushed into the church to light a candle, and then ran after the gig. She caught up with it an hour later, jumped lightly up behind, and hung on to the fringe. But then a thought struck her: the courtyard had not been locked up, and burglars might get in. So she jumped down again.

At dawn the next day she went to the doctor's. He had come home and gone out again on his rounds. Then she waited at the inn, thinking that somebody who was a stranger to the district might call there with a letter. Finally, when it was twilight, she got into the coach for Lisieux.

The convent was at the bottom of a steep lane. When she was halfway down the hill, she heard a strange sound which she recognized as a death-bell tolling.

"It's for somebody else," she thought, as she banged the door-knocker hard.

After a few minutes she heard the sound of shuffling feet, the door opened a little way, and a nun appeared.

The good sister said with an air of compunction that "she had just passed away." At that moment the bell of Saint Léonard was tolled more vigorously than ever.

Félicité went up to the second floor. From the doorway of the room she could see Virginie lying on her back, her hands clasped together, her mouth open, her head tilted back under a black crucifix that leant over her, her face whiter than the curtains that hung motionless on either side. Mme Aubain was clinging to the foot of the bed and sobbing desperately. The Mother Superior stood on the right. Three candlesticks on the chest of drawers added touches of red to the scene, and fog was whitening the windows. Some nuns led Mme Aubain away.

For two nights Félicité never left the dead girl. She said the same prayers over and over again, sprinkled holy water on the sheets, then sat down again to watch. At the end of her first vigil, she noticed that the child's face had gone yellow, the lips were turning blue, the nose looked sharper, and the eyes were sunken. She kissed them several times, and would not have been particularly surprised if Virginie had opened them again: to minds like hers the supernatural is a simple matter. She laid her out, wrapped her in a shroud, put her in her coffin, placed a wreath on her, and spread out her hair. It was fair and amazingly long for her age. Félicité cut off a big lock, half of which she slipped into her bosom, resolving never to part with it.

The body was brought back to Pont l'Évêque at the request of Mme Aubain, who followed the hearse in a closed carriage.

After the Requiem Mass, it took another three quarters of an hour to reach the cemetery. Paul walked in front, sobbing. Then came M. Bourais, and after him the principal inhabitants of the town, the women all wearing long black veils, and Félicité. She was thinking about her nephew; and since she had been unable to pay him these last honors, she felt an added grief, just as if they were burying him with Virginie.

Mme Aubain's despair passed all bounds. First of all she rebelled against God, considering it unfair of Him to have taken her daughter from her—for she had never done any harm, and her conscience was quite clear. But was it? She ought to have taken Virginie to the south; other doctors would have saved her life. She blamed herself, wished she could have joined her daughter, and cried out in anguish in her dreams. One dream in particular obsessed her. Her husband, dressed like a sailor, came back from a long voyage, and told her amid tears that he had been ordered to take Virginie away—whereupon they put their heads together to discover somewhere to hide her.

One day she came in from the garden utterly distraught. A few minutes earlier—and she pointed to the spot—father and daughter had appeared to her, doing nothing, but simply looking at her.

For several months she stayed in her room in a kind of stupor. Félicité scolded her gently, telling her that she must take care of herself for her son's sake, and also in remembrance of "her."

"Her?" repeated Mme Aubain, as if she were waking from a sleep. "Oh, yes, of course! You don't forget her, do you!" This was an allusion to the cemetery, where she herself was strictly forbidden to go.

Félicité went there every day. She would set out on the stroke of four, going past the houses, up the hill, and through the gate, until she came to Virginie's grave. There was a little column of pink marble with a tablet at its base, and a tiny garden enclosed by chains. The beds were hidden under a carpet of flowers. She watered their leaves and changed the sand, going down on her knees to fork the ground thoroughly. The result was that when Mme Aubain was able to come here, she experienced a feeling of relief, a kind of consolation.

Then the years slipped by, each one like the last, with nothing to vary the rhythm of the great festivals: Easter, the Assumption, All Saints' Day. Domestic events marked dates that later served as points of reference. Thus in 1825 a couple of glaziers whitewashed the hall; in 1827 a piece of the roof fell into the courtyard and nearly killed a man; and in the summer of 1828 it was Madame's turn to provide the bread for consecration. About this time Bourais went away in a mysterious fashion; and one by one the old acquaintances disappeared: Guyot, Liébard, Mme Lechaptois, Robelin, and Uncle Grémanville, who had been paralysed for a long time.

One night the driver of the mail coach brought Pont l'Évêque news of the July Revolution. A few days later a new subprefect was appointed. This was the Baron de Larsonnière, who had been a consul in America, and who brought with him, besides his wife, his sister-in-law and three young ladies who were almost grown-up. They were to be seen on their lawn, dressed in loose-fitting smocks; and they had a Negro servant and a parrot. They paid a call on Mme Aubain, who made a point of returning it. As soon as Félicité saw them coming, she would run and tell her mistress. But only one thing could really awaken her interest, and that was her son's letters.

He seemed to be incapable of following any career and spent all his time in taverns. She paid his debts, but he contracted new ones, and the sighs Mme Aubain heaved as she knitted by the window reached Félicité at her spinning wheel in the kitchen.

The two women used to walk up and down together beside the espalier, forever talking of Virginie and debating whether such and such a thing would have appealed to her, or what she would have said on such and such an occasion.

All her little belongings were in a cupboard in the children's bedroom. Mme Aubain went through them as seldom as possible. One summer day she resigned herself to doing so, and the moths were sent fluttering out of the cupboard.

Virginie's frocks hung in a row underneath a shelf containing three dolls, a few hoops, a set of toy furniture, and the wash basin she had used. Besides the frocks, they took out her petticoats, her stockings, and her handkerchiefs, and spread them out on the two beds before folding them up again. The sunlight streamed in on these pathetic objects, bringing out the stains and showing up the creases made by the child's movements. The air was warm, the sky was blue, a blackbird was singing, and everything seemed to be utterly at peace.

They found a little chestnut-colored hat, made of plush with a long nap; but the moths had ruined it. Félicité asked if she might have it. The two women looked at each other, and their eyes filled with tears. Then the mistress opened her arms, the maid threw herself into them, and they clasped each other in a warm embrace, satisfying their grief in a kiss which made them equal.

It was the first time that such a thing had happened, for Mme Aubain was not of a demonstrative nature. Félicité was as grateful as if she had received a great favor, and henceforth loved her mistress with doglike devotion and religious veneration.

Her heart grew softer as time went by.

When she heard the drums of a regiment coming down the street she stood at the door with a jug of cider and offered the soldiers a drink. She looked after the people who went down with cholera. She watched over the Polish refugees, and one of them actually expressed a desire to marry her. But they fell out, for when she came back from the Angelus one morning, she found that he had got into her kitchen and was calmly eating an oil-and-vinegar salad.

After the Poles it was Père Colmiche, an old man who was said to have committed fearful atrocities in '93. He lived by the river in a ruined pigsty. The boys of the town used to peer at him through the cracks in the walls, and threw pebbles at him which landed on the litter where he lay, constantly shaken by fits of coughing. His hair was extremely long, his eyelids inflamed, and on one arm there was a swelling bigger than his head. Félicité brought him some linen, tried to clean out his filthy hovel, and even wondered if she could install him in the wash-house without annoying Madame. When the tumor had burst, she changed his dressings every day, brought him some cake now and then, and put him out in the sun on a truss of hay. The poor old fellow would thank her in a faint whisper, slavering and trembling all the while, fearful of losing her and stretching his hands out as soon as he saw her moving away.

He died, and she had a Mass said for the repose of his soul.

That same day a great piece of good fortune came her way. Just as she was serving dinner, Mme de Larsonnière's Negro appeared carrying the parrot in its cage, complete with perch, chain, and padlock. The Baroness had written a note informing Mme Aubain that her husband had been promoted to a Prefecture and they were leaving that evening; she begged her to accept the parrot as a keepsake and a token of her regard.

This bird had engrossed Félicité's thoughts for a long time, for it came from America, and that word reminded her of Victor. So she had asked the Negro all about it, and once she had even gone so far as to say:

"How pleased Madame would be if it were hers!"

The Negro had repeated this remark to his mistress, who, unable to take the parrot with her, was glad to get rid of it in this way.

IV

His name was Loulou. His body was green, the tips of his wings were pink, his poll blue, and his breast golden.

Unfortunately he had a tiresome mania for biting his perch and also used to pull his feathers out, scatter his droppings everywhere, and upset his bath water. He annoyed Mme Aubain, and so she gave him to Félicité for good.

Félicité started training him, and soon he could say: "Nice boy! Your servant, sir! Hail, Mary!" He was put near the door, and several people who spoke to him said how strange it was that he did not answer to the name of Jacquot, as all parrots were called Jacquot. They likened him to a turkey or a block of wood, and every sneer cut Félicité to the quick. How odd, she thought, that Loulou should be so stubborn, refusing to talk whenever anyone looked at him!

For all that, he liked having people around him, because on Sundays, while the Rochefeuille sisters, M. Houppeville and some new friends—the apothecary Onfroy, M. Varin, and Captain Mathieu—were having their game of cards, he would beat on the windowpanes with his wings and make such a din that it was impossible to hear oneself speak.

Bourais's face obviously struck him as terribly funny, for as soon as he saw it he was seized with uncontrollable laughter. His shrieks rang round the courtyard, the echo repeated them, and the neighbors came to their windows and started laughing too. To avoid being seen by the bird, M. Bourais used to creep along by the wall, hiding his face behind his hat, until he got to the river, and then come into the house from the garden. The looks he gave the parrot were far from tender.

Loulou had once been cuffed by the butcher's boy for poking his head into his basket; and since then he was always trying to give him a nip through his shirt. Fabu threatened to wring his neck, although he was not a cruel fellow, in spite of his tattooed arms and bushy whiskers. On the contrary, he rather liked the parrot, so much so indeed that in a spirit of jovial camaraderie he tried to teach him a few swear words. Félicité, alarmed at this development, put the bird in the kitchen. His little chain was removed, and he was allowed to wander all over the house.

Coming downstairs, he used to rest the curved part of his beak on each step and then raise first his right foot, then his left; and Félicité was afraid that this sort of gymnastic performance would make him giddy. He fell ill and could neither talk nor eat for there was a swelling under his tongue such as hens sometimes have. She cured him by pulling this pellicule out with her fingernails. One day M. Paul was silly enough to blow the smoke of his cigar at him; another time Mme Lormeau started teasing him with the end of her parasol, and he caught hold of the ferrule with his beak. Finally he got lost.

Félicité had put him down on the grass in the fresh air, and left him there for a minute. When she came back, the parrot had gone. First of all she looked for him in the bushes, by the river, and on the rooftops, paying no attention to her mistress's shouts of: "Be careful, now! You must be mad!" Next she went over all the gardens in Pont l'Évêque, stopping passers-by and asking them: "You don't happen to have seen my parrot by any chance?" Those who did not know him already were given a description of the bird. Suddenly she thought she could make out something green flying about behind the mills at the foot of the hill. But up on the hill there was nothing to be seen. A peddler told her that he had come upon the parrot a short time before in Mère Simon's shop at Saint Melaine. She ran all the way there, but no one knew what she was talking about. Finally she came back home, worn out, her shoes falling to pieces, and death in her heart. She was sitting beside Madame on the garden seat and telling her what she had been doing, when she felt something light drop on her shoulder. It was Loulou! What he had been up to, no one could discover: perhaps he had just gone for a little walk round the town.

Félicité was slow to recover from this fright, and indeed never really got over it.

As the result of a chill she had an attack of quinsy, and soon after that her ears were affected. Three years later she was deaf, and she spoke at the top of her voice, even in church. Although her sins could have been proclaimed over the length and breadth of the diocese without dishonor to her or offense to others, M. le Curé thought it advisable to hear her confession in the sacristy.

Imaginary buzzings in the head added to her troubles. Often her mistress would say: "Heavens, how stupid you are!" and she would reply: "Yes, Madame," at the same time looking all around her for something.

The little circle of her ideas grew narrower and narrower, and the pealing of bells and the lowing of cattle went out of her life. Every living thing moved about in a ghostly silence. Only one sound reached her ears now, and that was the voice of the parrot.

As if to amuse her, he would reproduce the click-clack of the turn-spit, the shrill call of a man selling fish, and the noise of the saw at the joiner's across the way; and when the bell rang he would imitate Mme Aubain's "Félicité! The door, the door!"

They held conversations with each other, he repeating *ad nauseam* the three phrases in his repertory, she replying with words which were just as disconnected but which came from the heart. In her isolation, Loulou was almost a son or a lover to her. He used to climb up her fingers, peck at her lips, and hang on to her shawl; and as she bent over him, wagging her head from side to side as nurses do, the great wings of her bonnet and the wings of the bird quivered in unison.

When clouds banked up in the sky and there was a rumbling of thunder, he would utter piercing cries, no doubt remembering the sudden downpours in his native forests. The sound of the rain falling roused him to frenzy. He would flap excitedly around, shoot up to the ceiling, knocking everything over, and fly out of the window to splash about in the garden. But he would soon come back to perch on one of the firedogs, hopping about to dry his feathers and showing tail and beak in turn.

One morning in the terrible winter of 1837, when she had put him in front of the fire because of the cold she found him dead in the middle of his cage, hanging head down with his claws caught in the bars. He had probably died of a stroke, but she thought he had been poisoned with parsley, and despite the absence of any proof, her suspicions fell on Fabu.

She wept so much that her mistress said to her: "Why don't you have him stuffed?"

Félicité asked the chemist's advice, remembering that he had always been kind to the parrot. He wrote to Le Havre, and a man called Fellacher agreed to do the job. As parcels sometimes went astray on the mail coach, she decided to take the parrot as far as Honfleur herself.

On either side of the road stretched an endless succession of apple trees, all stripped of their leaves, and there was ice in the ditches. Dogs were barking around the farms; and Félicité, with her hands tucked under her mantlet, her little black sabots and her basket, walked briskly along the middle of the road.

She crossed the forest, passed Le Haut-Chêne, and got as far as Saint Gatien.

Behind her, in a cloud of dust, and gathering speed as the horses galloped downhill, a mail coach swept along like a whirlwind. When he saw this woman making no attempt to get out of the way, the driver poked his head out above the hood, and he and the postilion shouted at her. His four horses could not be held in and galloped faster, the two leaders touching her as they went by. With a jerk of the reins the driver threw them to one side, and then, in a fury, he raised his long whip and gave her such a lash, from head to waist, that she fell flat on her back.

The first thing she did on regaining consciousness was to open her basket. Fortunately nothing had happened to Loulou. She felt her right cheek burning, and when she touched it her hand turned red; it was bleeding.

She sat down on a heap of stones and dabbed her face with her handkerchief. Then she ate a crust of bread which she had taken the precaution of putting in her basket, and tried to forget her wound by looking at the bird.

As she reached the top of the hill at Ecquemauville, she saw the lights of Honfleur twinkling in the darkness like a host of stars, and the shadowy expanse of the sea beyond. Then a sudden feeling of faintness made her stop; and the misery of her childhood, the disappointment of her first love, the departure of her nephew, and the death of Virginie all came back to her at once like the waves of a rising tide, and, welling up in her throat, choked her.

When she got to the boat she insisted on speaking to the captain, and without telling him what was in her parcel, asked him to take good care of it.

Fellacher kept the parrot a long time. Every week he promised it for the next; after six months he announced that a box had been sent off, and nothing more was heard of it. It looked as though Loulou would never come back, and Félicité told herself: "They've stolen him for sure!"

At last he arrived—looking quite magnificent, perched on a branch screwed into a mahogany base, one foot in the air, his head cocked to one side, and biting a nut which the taxidermist, out of a love of the grandiose, had gilded.

Félicité shut him up in her room.

This place, to which few people were ever admitted, contained such a quantity of religious bric-à-brac and miscellaneous oddments that it looked like a cross between a chapel and a bazaar.

A big wardrobe prevented the door from opening properly. Opposite the window that overlooked the garden was a little round one looking on to the courtyard. There was a table beside the bed, with a water jug, a couple of combs, and a block of blue soap in a chipped plate. On the walls there were rosaries, medals, several pictures of the Virgin, and a holy-water stoup made out of a coconut. On the chest of drawers, which was draped with a cloth just like an altar, was the shell box Victor had given her, and also a watering can and a ball, some copybooks, the illustrated geography book, and a pair of ankle boots. And on the nail supporting the looking glass, fastened by its ribbons, hung the little plush hat.

Félicité carried this form of veneration to such lengths that she even kept one of Monsieur's frock coats. All the old rubbish Mme Aubain had no more use for, she carried off to her room. That was how there came to be artificial flowers along the edge of the chest of drawers and a portrait of the Comte d'Artois in the window recess.

With the aid of a wall bracket, Loulou was installed on a chimney-breast that jutted out into the room. Every morning when she awoke, she saw him in the light of the dawn, and then she remembered the old days, and the smallest details of insignificant actions, not in sorrow but in absolute tranquillity.

Having no intercourse with anyone, she lived in the torpid state of a sleep-walker. The Corpus Christi processions roused her from this condition, for she would go round the neighbors collecting candlesticks and mats to decorate the altar of repose which they used to set up in the street.

In church she was forever gazing at the Holy Ghost, and one day she noticed that it had something of the parrot about it. This resemblance struck her as even more obvious in a color print depicting the baptism of Our Lord. With its red wings and its emerald-green body, it was the very image of Loulou.

She bought the print and hung it in the place of the Comte d'Artois, so that she could include them both in a single glance. They were linked together in her mind, the parrot being sanctified by this connection with the Holy Ghost, which itself acquired new life and meaning in her eyes. God the Father could not have chosen a dove as a means of expressing Himself, since doves cannot talk, but rather one of Loulou's ancestors. And although Félicité used to say her prayers with her eyes on the picture, from time to time she would turn slightly toward the bird.

She wanted to join the Children of Mary, but Mme Aubain dissuaded her from doing so.

An important event now loomed up—Paul's wedding.

After starting as a lawyer's clerk, he had been in business, in the Customs, and in Inland Revenue, and had even begun trying to get into the Department of Woods and Forests, when, at the age of thirty-six, by some heaven-sent inspiration, he suddenly discovered his real vocation—in the Wills and Probate Department. There he proved so capable that one of the auditors had offered him his daughter in marriage and promised to use his influence on his behalf.

Paul, grown serious-minded, brought her to see his mother. She criticized the way things were done at Pont l'Évêque, put on airs, and hurt Félicité's feelings. Mme Aubain was relieved to see her go.

The following week came news of M. Bourais's death in an inn in Lower Brittany. Rumors that he had committed suicide were confirmed, and doubts arose as to his honesty. Mme Aubain went over her accounts and was soon conversant with the full catalogue of his misdeeds—embezzlement of interest, secret sales of timber, forged receipts, etc. Besides all this, he was the father of an illegitimate child, and had had "relations with a person at Dozulé."

These infamies upset Mme Aubain greatly. In March, 1853, she was afflicted with a pain in the chest; her tongue seemed to be covered with a film; leeches failed to make her breathing any easier; and on the ninth evening of her illness she died. She had just reached the age of seventy-two.

She was thought to be younger because of her brown hair, worn in bandeaux round her pale, pock-marked face. There were few friends to mourn her, for she had a haughty manner which put people off. Yet Félicité wept for her as servants rarely weep for their masters. That Madame should die before her upset her ideas, seemed to be contrary to the order of things, monstrous and unthinkable.

Ten days later—the time it took to travel hot-foot from Besançon—the heirs arrived. The daughter-in-law ransacked every drawer, picked out some pieces of furniture and sold the rest; and then back they went to the Wills and Probate Department.

Madame's armchair, her pedestal table, her foot warmer, and the eight chairs had all gone. Yellow squares in the center of the wall panels showed where the pictures had hung. They had carried off the two cots with their mattresses, and no trace remained in the cupboard of all Virginie's things. Félicité climbed the stairs to her room, numbed with sadness.

The next day there was a notice on the door, and the apothecary shouted in her ear that the house was up for sale.

She swayed on her feet, and was obliged to sit down.

What distressed her most of all was the idea of leaving her room, which was so suitable for poor Loulou. Fixing an anguished look on him as she appealed to the Holy Ghost, she contracted the idolatrous habit of kneeling in front of the parrot to say her prayers. Sometimes the sun, as it came through the little window, caught his glass eye, so that it shot out a great luminous ray which sent her into ecstasies.

She had a pension of three hundred and eighty francs a year which her mistress had left her. The garden kept her in vegetables. As for clothes, she had enough to last her till the end of her days, and she saved on lighting by going to bed as soon as darkness fell.

She went out as little as possible, to avoid the second-hand dealer's shop, where some of the old furniture was on display. Ever since her fit of giddiness, she had been dragging one leg; and as her strength was failing, Mère Simon, whose grocery business had come to grief, came in every morning to chop wood and pump water for her.

Her eyes grew weaker. The shutters were not opened any more. Years went by, and nobody rented the house and nobody bought it.

For fear of being evicted, Félicité never asked for any repairs to be done. The laths in the roof rotted, and all through one winter her bolster was wet. After Easter she began spitting blood.

When this happened, Mère Simon called in a doctor. Félicité wanted to know what was the matter with her, but she was so deaf that only one word reached her: "Pneumonia." It was a word she knew, and she answered gently: "Ah! like Madame," thinking it natural that she should follow in her mistress's footsteps.

The time to set up the altars of repose was drawing near.

The first altar was always at the foot of the hill, the second in front of the post office, the third about halfway up the street. There was some argument as to the siting of this one, and finally the women of the parish picked on Mme Aubain's courtyard.

The fever and the tightness of the chest grew worse. Félicité fretted over not doing anything for the altar. If only she could have put something on it!

Then she thought of the parrot. The neighbors protested that it would not be seemly, but the curé gave his permission, and this made her so happy that she begged him to accept Loulou, the only thing of value she possessed, when she died.

From Tuesday to Saturday, the eve of Corpus Christi, she coughed more and more frequently. In the evening her face looked pinched and drawn, her lips stuck to her gums, and she started vomiting. At dawn the next day, feeling very low, she sent for a priest.

Three good women stood by her while she was given extreme unction. Then she said that she had to speak to Fabu.

He arrived in his Sunday best, very ill at ease in this funereal atmosphere.

"Forgive me," she said, making an effort to stretch out her arm. "I thought it was you who had killed him."

What could she mean by such nonsense? To think that she had suspected a man like him of murder! He got very indignant and was obviously going to make a scene.

"Can't you see," they said, "that she isn't in her right mind any more?"

From time to time Félicité would start talking to shadows. The women went away. Mère Simon had her lunch.

A little later she picked Loulou up and held him out to Félicité, saying: "Come now, say good-bye to him."

Although the parrot was not a corpse, the worms were eating him up. One of his wings was broken, and the stuffing was coming out of his stomach. But she was blind by now, and she kissed him on the forehead and pressed him against her cheek. Mère Simon took him away from her to put him on the altar.

V

The scents of summer came up from the meadows; there was a buzzing of flies; the sun was glittering in the river and warming the slates of the roof. Mère Simon had come back into the room and was gently nodding off to sleep.

The noise of church bells woke her up; the congregation was coming out from vespers. Félicité's delirium abated. Thinking of the procession, she could see it as clearly as if she had been following it.

All the school children, the choristers, and the firemen were walking along the pavements, while advancing up the middle of the street came the church officer armed with his halberd, the beadle carrying a great cross, the schoolmaster keeping an eye on the boys, and the nun fussing over her little girls—three of the prettiest, looking like curly-headed angels, were throwing rose petals into the air. Then came the deacon, with both arms outstretched, conducting the band, and a couple of censer-bearers who turned round at every step to face the Holy Sacrament, which the curé, wearing his splendid chasuble, was carrying under a canopy of poppy-red velvet held aloft by four churchwardens. A crowd of people surged along behind, between the white cloths covering the walls of the houses, and eventually they got to the bottom of the hill.

A cold sweat moistened Félicité's temples. Mère Simon sponged it up with a cloth, telling herself that one day she would have to go the same way.

The hum of the crowd increased in volume, was very loud for a moment, then faded away.

A fusillade shook the windowpanes. It was the postilions saluting the monstrance. Félicité rolled her eyes and said as loud as she could: "Is he all right?"—worrying about the parrot.

She entered into her death agony. Her breath, coming ever faster, with a rattling sound, made her sides heave. Bubbles of froth appeared at the corners of her mouth, and her whole body trembled.

Soon the booming of the ophicleides, the clear voices of the children, and the deep voices of the men could be heard near at hand. Now and then everything was quiet, and the tramping of feet, deadened by a carpet of flowers, sounded like a flock moving across pasture land.

The clergy appeared in the courtyard. Mère Simon climbed on to a chair to reach the little round window, from which she had a full view of the altar below.

It was hung with green garlands and adorned with a flounce in English needlepoint lace. In the middle was a little frame containing some relics, there were two orange trees at the corners, and all the way along stood silver candlesticks and china vases holding sunflowers, lilies, peonies, foxgloves, and bunches of hydrangea. This pyramid of bright colors stretched from the first floor right down to the carpet which was spread out over the pavement. Some rare objects caught the eye: a silver-gilt sugar basin wreathed in violets, some pendants of Alençon gems gleaming on a bed of moss, and two Chinese screens with landscape decorations. Loulou, hidden under roses, showed nothing but his blue poll, which looked like a plaque of lapis lazuli.

The churchwardens, the choristers, and the children lined up along the three sides of the courtyard. The priest went slowly up the steps and placed his great shining gold sun on the lace altar cloth. Everyone knelt down. There was a deep silence. And the censers, swinging at full tilt, slid up and down their chains.

A blue cloud of incense was wafted up into Félicité's room. She opened her nostrils wide and breathed it in with a mystical, sensuous fervor. Then she closed her eyes. Her lips smiled. Her heartbeats grew slower and slower, each a little fainter and gentler, like a fountain running dry, an echo fading away. And as she breathed her last, she thought she could see, in the opening heavens, a gigantic parrot hovering above her head.

A Good Man Is Hard to Find

FLANNERY O'CONNOR

[1925–1964]

The grandmother didn't want to go to Florida. She wanted to visit some of her connections in east Tennessee and she was seizing at every chance to change Bailey's mind. Bailey was the son she lived with, her only boy. He was sitting on the edge of his chair at the table, bent over the orange sports section of the *Journal*. "Now look here, Bailey," she said, "see here, read this," and she stood with one hand on her thin hip and the other rattling the newspaper at his bald head. "Here this fellow that calls himself The Misfit is aloose from the Federal Pen and headed toward Florida and you read what it says he did to these people. Just you read it. I wouldn't take my children in any direction with a criminal like that aloose in it. I couldn't answer to my conscience if I did."

Bailey didn't look up from his reading so she wheeled around then and faced the children's mother, a young woman in slacks, whose face was as broad and innocent as a cabbage and was tied around with a green headkerchief that had two points on the top like rabbit's ears. She was sitting on the sofa, feeding the baby his apricots out of a jar. "The children have been to Florida before," the old lady said. "You all ought to take them somewhere else for a change so they would see different parts of the world and be broad. They never have been to east Tennessee."

The children's mother didn't seem to hear her but the eight-year-old boy, John Wesley, a stocky child with glasses, said, "If you don't want to go to Florida, why dontcha stay at home?" He and the little girl, June Star, were reading the funny papers on the floor.

"She wouldn't stay at home to be queen for a day," June Star said without raising her yellow head.

"Yes, and what would you do if this fellow, The Misfit, caught you?" the grandmother asked.

"I'd smack his face," John Wesley said.

"She wouldn't stay at home for a million bucks," June Star said. "Afraid she'd miss something. She has to go everywhere we go."

"All right, Miss," the grandmother said. "Just remember that the next time you want me to curl your hair."

June Star said her hair was naturally curly.

The next morning the grandmother was the first one in the car, ready to go. She had her big black valise that looked like the head of a hippopotamus in one corner, and underneath it she was hiding a basket with Pitty Sing, the cat, in it. She didn't intend for the cat to be left alone in the house for three days because he would miss her too much and she was afraid he might brush against one of the gas burners and accidentally asphyxiate himself. Her son Bailey didn't like to arrive at a motel with a cat.

She sat in the middle of the back seat with John Wesley and June Star on either side of her. Bailey and the children's mother and the baby sat in front, and they left Atlanta at eight forty-five with the mileage on the car at 55890. The grandmother wrote this down because she thought it would be interesting to say how many miles they had been when they got back. It took them twenty minutes to reach the outskirts of the city.

The old lady settled herself comfortably, removing her white cotton gloves and putting them up with her purse on the shelf in front of the back window. The children's mother still had on slacks and still had her head tied up in a green kerchief, but the grandmother had on a navy blue straw sailor hat with a bunch of white violets on the brim and a navy blue dress with a small white dot in the print. Her collars and cuffs were white organdy trimmed with lace and at her neckline she had pinned a purple spray of cloth violets containing a sachet. In case of an accident, anyone seeing her dead on the highway would know at once that she was a lady.

She said she thought it was going to be a good day for driving, neither too hot nor too cold, and she cautioned Bailey that the speed limit was fifty-five miles an hour and that the patrolmen hid themselves behind billboards and small clumps of trees and sped out after you before you had a chance to slow down. She pointed out interesting details of the scenery: Stone Mountain; the blue granite that in some places came up to both sides of the highway; the brilliant red clay banks slightly streaked with purple; and the various crops that made rows of green lace-work on the ground. The trees were full of silver-white sunlight and the meanest of them sparkled. The children were reading comic magazines and their mother had gone back to sleep.

"Let's go through Georgia fast so we won't have to look at it much," John Wesley said.

"If I were a little boy," said the grandmother, "I wouldn't talk about my native state that way. Tennessee has the mountains and Georgia has the hills."

"Tennessee is just a hillbilly dumping ground," John Wesley said, "and Georgia is a lousy state too."

"You said it," June Star said.

"In my time," said the grandmother, folding her thin, veined fingers, "children were more respectful of their native states and their parents and everything else. People did right then. Oh, look at the cute little colored boy!" she said and pointed to a Negro child standing in the door of a shack. "Wouldn't that make a picture, now?" she asked, and they all turned and looked at the little Negro out of the back window. He waved.

"He didn't have any britches on," June Star said.

"He probably didn't have any," the grandmother explained. "Little colored children in the country don't have things like we do. If I could paint, I'd paint that picture," she said.

The children exchanged comic books.

The grandmother offered to hold the baby and the children's mother passed him over the front seat to her. She set him on her knee and bounced him and told him about the things they were passing. She rolled her eyes and screwed up her mouth and stuck her leathery thin face into his smooth bland one. Occasionally he gave her a faraway smile. They passed a large cotton field with five or six graves fenced in the middle of it, like a small island. "Look at the graveyard!" the grandmother said, pointing it out. "That was the old family burying ground. That belonged to the plantation."

"Where's the plantation?" John Wesley asked.

"Gone with the Wind," said the grandmother. "Ha. Ha."

When the children finished all the comic books they had brought, they opened the lunch and ate it. The grandmother ate a peanut butter sandwich and an olive and would not let the children throw the box and the paper napkins out the window. When there was nothing else to do, they played a game by choosing a cloud and making the other two guess what shape it suggested. John Wesley took one the shape of a cow and June Star guessed a cow and John Wesley said, no, an automobile, and June Star said he didn't play fair, and they began to slap each other over the grandmother.

The grandmother said she would tell them a story if they would keep quiet. When she told a story, she rolled her eyes and waved her head and was very dramatic. She said once when she was a maiden lady she had been courted by a Mr. Edgar Atkins Teagarden from Jasper, Georgia. She said he was a very good-looking man and a gentleman and that he brought her a watermelon every Saturday afternoon with his initials cut in it, E. A. T. Well, one Saturday, she said, Mr. Teagarden brought the watermelon and there was nobody at home and he left it on the front porch and returned in his buggy to Jasper, but she never got the watermelon, she said, because a boy ate it when he saw the initials, E. A. T.! This story tickled John Wesley's funny bone and he giggled and giggled but June Star didn't think it was any good. She said she wouldn't marry a man that just brought her a watermelon on Saturday. The grandmother said she would have done well to marry Mr. Teagarden because he was a gentleman and had bought Coca-Cola stock when it first came out and that he had died only a few years ago, a very wealthy man.

They stopped at The Tower for barbecued sandwiches. The Tower was a part stucco and part wood filling station and dance hall set in a clearing outside of Timothy. A fat man named Red Sammy Butts ran it and there were signs stuck here and there on the building and for miles up and down the highway saying, TRY RED SAMMY'S FAMOUS BARBECUE. NONE LIKE FAMOUS RED SAMMY'S! RED SAM! THE FAT BOY WITH THE HAPPY LAUGH. A VETERAN! SAMMY'S YOUR MAN!

Red Sammy was lying on the bare ground outside The Tower with his head under a truck while a gray monkey about a foot high, chained to a small chinaberry tree, chattered nearby. The monkey sprang back into the tree and got on the highest limb as soon as he saw the children jump out of the car and run toward him.

Inside, The Tower was a long dark room with a counter at one end and tables at the other and dancing space in the middle. They all sat down at a board table next to the nickelodeon and Red Sam's wife, a tall burnt-brown woman with hair and eyes lighter than her skin, came and took their order. The children's mother put a dime in the machine and played "The Tennessee Waltz," and the grandmother said that tune always made her want to dance. She asked Bailey if he would like to dance but he only glared at her. He didn't have a naturally sunny disposition like she did and trips made him nervous. The grandmother's brown eyes were very bright. She swayed her head from side to side and pretended she was dancing in her chair. June Star said play something she could tap to so the children's mother put in another dime and played a fast number and June Star stepped out onto the dance floor and did her tap routine.

"Ain't she cute?" Red Sam's wife said, leaning over the counter. "Would you like to come be my little girl?"

"No, I certainly wouldn't," June Star said. "I wouldn't live in a broken-down place like this for a million bucks!" and she ran back to the table.

"Ain't she cute?" the woman repeated, stretching her mouth politely.

"Aren't you ashamed?" hissed the grandmother.

Red Sam came in and told his wife to quit lounging on the counter and hurry up with these people's order. His khaki trousers reached just to his hip bones and his stomach hung over them like a sack of meal swaying under his shirt. He came over and sat down at a table nearby and let out a combination sigh and yodel. "You can't win," he said. "You can't win," and he wiped his sweating red face off with a gray handkerchief. "These days you don't know who to trust," he said. "Ain't that the truth?"

"People are certainly not nice like they used to be," said the grandmother.

"Two fellers come in here last week," Red Sammy said, "driving a Chrysler. It was a old beat-up car but it was a good one and these boys looked all right to me. Said they worked at the mill and you know I let them fellers charge the gas they bought? Now why did I do that?"

"Because you're a good man!" the grandmother said at once.

"Yes'm, I suppose so," Red Sam said as if he were struck with this answer.

His wife brought the orders, carrying the five plates all at once without a tray, two in each hand and one balanced on her arm. "It isn't a soul in this green world of God's that you can trust," she said. "And I don't count nobody out of that, not nobody," she repeated, looking at Red Sammy.

"Did you read about that criminal, The Misfit, that's escaped?" asked the grandmother.

"I wouldn't be a bit surprised if he didn't attack this place right here," said the woman. "If he hears about it being here, I wouldn't be none surprised to see him. If he hears it's two cents in the cash register, I wouldn't be at all surprised if he . . ."

"That'll do," Red Sam said. "Go bring these people their Co'-Colas," and the woman went off to get the rest of the order.

"A good man is hard to find," Red Sammy said. "Everything is getting terrible. I remember the day you could go off and leave your screen door unlatched. Not no more."

He and the grandmother discussed better times. The old lady said that in her opinion Europe was entirely to blame for the way things were now. She said the way Europe acted you would think we were made of money and Red Sam said it was no use talking about it, she was exactly right. The children ran outside into the white sunlight and looked at the monkey in the lacy chinaberry tree. He was busy catching fleas on himself and biting each one carefully between his teeth as if it were a delicacy.

They drove off again into the hot afternoon. The grandmother took cat naps and woke up every few minutes with her own snoring. Outside of Toombsboro she woke up and recalled an old plantation that she had visited in this neighborhood once when she was a young lady. She said the house had six white columns across the front and that there was an avenue of oaks leading up to it and two little wooden trellis arbors on either side in front where you sat down with your suitor after a stroll in the garden. She recalled exactly which road to turn off to get to it. She knew that Bailey would not be willing to lose any time looking at an old house, but the more she talked about it, the more she wanted to see it once again and find out if the little twin arbors were still standing. "There was a secret panel in this house," she said craftily, not telling the truth but wishing that she were, "and the story went that all the family silver was hidden in it when Sherman came through but it was never found . . ."

"Hey!" John Wesley said. "Let's go see it! We'll find it! We'll poke all the woodwork and find it! Who lives there? Where do you turn off at? Hey Pop, can't we turn off there?"

"We never have seen a house with a secret panel!" June Star shrieked. "Let's go to the house with the secret panel! Hey Pop, can't we go see the house with the secret panel!"

"It's not far from here, I know," the grandmother said. "It wouldn't take over twenty minutes."

Bailey was looking straight ahead. His jaw was as rigid as a horseshoe. "No," he said.

The children began to yell and scream that they wanted to see the house with the secret panel. John Wesley kicked the back of the front seat and June Star hung over her mother's shoulder and whined desperately into her ear that they never had any fun even on their vacation, that they could never do what

THEY wanted to do. The baby began to scream and John Wesley kicked the back of the seat so hard that his father could feel the blows in his kidney.

"All right!" he shouted and drew the car to a stop at the side of the road. "Will you all shut up? Will you all just shut up for one second? If you don't shut up, we won't go anywhere."

"It would be very educational for them," the grandmother murmured.

"All right," Bailey said, "but get this: this is the only time we're going to stop for anything like this. This is the one and only time."

"The dirt road that you have to turn down is about a mile back," the grandmother directed. "I marked it when we passed."

"A dirt road," Bailey groaned.

After they had turned around and were headed toward the dirt road, the grandmother recalled other points about the house, the beautiful glass over the front doorway and the candle-lamp in the hall. John Wesley said that the secret panel was probably in the fireplace.

"You can't go inside this house," Bailey said. "You don't know who lives there."

"While you all talk to the people in front, I'll run around behind and get in a window," John Wesley suggested.

"We'll all stay in the car," his mother said.

They turned onto the dirt road and the car raced roughly along in a swirl of pink dust. The grandmother recalled the times when there were no paved roads and thirty miles was a day's journey. The dirt road was hilly and there were sudden washes in it and sharp curves on dangerous embankments. All at once they would be on a hill, looking down over the blue tops of trees for miles around, then the next minute they would be in a red depression with the dust-coated trees looking down on them.

"This place had better turn up in a minute," Bailey said, "or I'm going to turn around."

The road looked as if no one had traveled on it in months.

"It's not much farther," the grandmother said and just as she said it, a horrible thought came to her. The thought was so embarrassing that she turned red in the face and her eyes dilated and her feet jumped up, upsetting her valise in the corner. The instant the valise moved, the newspaper top she had over the basket under it rose with a snarl and Pitty Sing, the cat, sprang onto Bailey's shoulder.

The children were thrown to the floor and their mother, clutching the baby, was thrown out the door onto the ground; the old lady was thrown into the front seat. The car turned over once and landed right-side-up in a gulch off the side of the road. Bailey remained in the driver's seat with the cat—gray-striped with a broad white face and an orange nose—clinging to his neck like a caterpillar.

As soon as the children saw they could move their arms and legs, they scrambled out of the car, shouting, "We've had an ACCIDENT!" The grandmother was curled up under the dashboard, hoping she was injured so that Bailey's wrath would not come down on her all at once. The horrible thought she had had before the accident was that the house she had remembered so vividly was not in Georgia but in Tennessee.

Bailey removed the cat from his neck with both hands and flung it out the window against the side of a pine tree. Then he got out of the car and started looking for the children's mother. She was sitting against the side of the red, gutted ditch, holding the screaming baby, but she only had a cut down her face and a broken shoulder. "We've had an ACCIDENT!" the children screamed in a frenzy of delight.

"But nobody's killed," June Star said with disappointment as the grandmother limped out of the car, her hat still pinned to her head but the broken front brim standing up at a jaunty angle and the violet spray hanging off the side. They all sat down in the ditch, except the children, to recover from the shock. They were all shaking.

"Maybe a car will come along," said the children's mother hoarsely.

"I believe I have an injured organ," said the grandmother, pressing her side, but no one answered her. Bailey's teeth were clattering. He had on a yellow sport shirt with bright blue parrots designed on it and his face was as yellow as the shirt. The grandmother decided that she would not mention that the house was in Tennessee.

The road was about ten feet above and they could see only the tops of the trees on the other side of it. Behind the ditch they were sitting in, there were more woods, tall and dark and deep. In a few minutes they saw a car some distance away on top of a hill, coming slowly as if the occupants were watching them. The grandmother stood up and waved both arms dramatically to attract their attention. The car continued to come on slowly, disappeared around a bend and appeared again, moving even slower, on top of the hill they had gone over. It was a big black battered hearse-like automobile. There were three men in it.

It came to a stop just over them and for some minutes, the driver looked down with a steady expressionless gaze to where they were sitting, and didn't speak. Then he turned his head and muttered something to the other two and they got out. One was a fat boy in black trousers and a red sweat shirt with a silver stallion embossed on the front of it. He moved around on the right side of them and stood staring, his mouth partly open in a kind of loose grin. The other had on khaki pants and a blue striped coat and a gray hat pulled down very low, hiding most of his face. He came around slowly on the left side. Neither spoke.

The driver got out of the car and stood by the side of it, looking down at them. He was an older man than the other two. His hair was just beginning to gray and he wore silver-rimmed spectacles that give him a scholarly look. He had a long creased face and didn't have on any shirt or undershirt. He had on blue jeans that were too tight for him and was holding a black hat and a gun. The two boys also had guns.

"We've had an ACCIDENT!" the children screamed.

The grandmother had the peculiar feeling that the bespectacled man was someone she knew. His face was as familiar to her as if she had known him all her life but she could not recall who he was. He moved away from the car and began to come down the embankment, placing his feet carefully so that he wouldn't slip. He had on tan and white shoes and no socks, and his ankles were red and thin. "Good afternoon," he said. "I see you all had you a little spill."

"We turned over twice!" said the grandmother.

"Oncet," he corrected. "We seen it happen. Try their car and see will it run, Hiram," he said quietly to the boy with the gray hat.

"What you got that gun for?" John Wesley asked. "Whatcha gonna do with that gun?"

"Lady," the man said to the children's mother, "would you mind calling them children to sit down by you? Children make me nervous. I want all you to sit down right together there where you're at."

"What are you telling US what to do for?" June Star asked.

Behind them the line of woods gaped like a dark open mouth. "Come here," said their mother.

"Look here now," Bailey began suddenly, "we're in a predicament! We're in . . ."

The grandmother shrieked. She scrambled to her feet and stood staring. "You're The Misfit!" she said. "I recognized you at once!"

"Yes'm," the man said, smiling slightly as if he were pleased in spite of himself to be known, "but it would have been better for all of you, lady, if you hadn't of reckernized me."

Bailey turned his head sharply and said something to his mother that shocked even the children. The old lady began to cry and The Misfit reddened.

"Lady," he said, "don't you get upset. Sometimes a man says things he don't mean. I don't reckon he meant to talk to you thataway."

"You wouldn't shoot a lady, would you?" the grandmother said and removed the clean handkerchief from her cuff and began to slap at her eyes with it.

The Misfit pointed the toe of his shoe into the ground and made a little hole and then covered it up again. "I would hate to have to," he said.

"Listen," the grandmother almost screamed, "I know you're a good man. You don't look a bit like you have common blood. I know you must come from nice people!"

"Yes, ma'am," he said, "finest people in the world." When he smiled he showed a row of strong white teeth. "God never made a finer woman than my mother and my daddy's heart was pure gold," he said. The boy with the red sweat shirt had come around behind them and was standing with his gun at his hip. The Misfit squatted down on the ground. "Watch them children, Bobby Lee," he said. "You know they make me nervous." He looked at the six of them huddled together in front of him and he seemed to be embarrassed as if he couldn't think of anything to say. "Ain't a cloud in the sky," he remarked, looking up at it. "Don't see no sun but don't see no cloud neither."

"Yes, it's a beautiful day," said the grandmother. "Listen," she said, "you shouldn't call yourself The Misfit because I know you're a good man at heart. I can just look at you and tell."

"Hush!" Bailey yelled. "Hush! Everybody shut up and let me handle this!" He was squatting in the position of a runner about to sprint forward but he didn't move.

"I pre-chate that, lady," The Misfit said and drew a little circle in the ground with the butt of his gun.

"It'll take a half a hour to fix this here car," Hiram called, looking over the raised hood of it.

"Well, first you and Bobby Lee get him and that little boy to step over yonder with you," The Misfit said, pointing to Bailey and John Wesley. "The boys want to ask you something," he said to Bailey. "Would you mind stepping back in them woods there with them?"

"Listen," Bailey began, "we're in a terrible predicament! Nobody realizes what this is," and his voiced cracked. His eyes were as blue and intense as the parrots on his shirt and he remained perfectly still.

The grandmother reached up to adjust her hat brim as if she were going to the woods with him but it came off in her hand. She stood staring at it and after a second she let it fall on the ground. Hiram pulled Bailey up by the arm as if he were assisting an old man. John Wesley caught hold of his father's hand and Bobby Lee followed. They went off toward the woods and just as they reached the dark edge, Bailey turned and supported himself against a gray naked pine trunk. He shouted, "I'll be back in a minute, Mamma, wait on me!"

"Come back this instant!" his mother shrilled but they all disappeared into the woods.

"Bailey Boy!" the grandmother called in a tragic voice but she found she was looking at The Misfit squatting on the ground in front of her. "I just know you're a good man," she said desperately. "You're not a bit common!"

"Nome, I ain't a good man," The Misfit said after a second as if he had considered her statement carefully, "but I ain't the worst in the world neither. My daddy said I was a different breed of dog from my brothers and sisters. 'You know,' Daddy said, 'It's some that can live their whole life out without asking about it and it's others has to know why it is, and this boy is one of the latters. He's going to be into everything.' " He put on his black hat and looked up suddenly and then away deep into the woods as if he were embarrassed again. "I'm sorry I don't have on a shirt before you ladies," he said, hunching his shoulders slightly. "We buried our clothes that we had on when we escaped and we're just making do until we can get better. We borrowed these from some folks we met," he explained.

"That's perfectly all right," the grandmother said. "Maybe Bailey has an extra shirt in his suitcase."

"I'll look and see terrectly," The Misfit said.

"Where are they taking him?" the children's mother screamed.

"Daddy was a card himself," The Misfit said. "You couldn't put anything over on him. He never got in trouble with the Authorities though. Just had the knack of handling them."

"You could be honest too if you'd only try," said the grandmother. "Think how wonderful it would be to settle down and live a comfortable life and not have to think about somebody chasing you all the time."

The Misfit kept scratching in the ground with the butt of his gun as if he were thinking about it. "Yes'm, somebody is always after you," he murmured.

The grandmother noticed how thin his shoulder blades were just behind his hat because she was standing up looking down on him. "Do you ever pray?" she asked.

He shook his head. All she saw was the black hat wiggle between his shoulder blades. "Nome," he said.

There was a pistol shot from the woods, followed closely by another. Then silence. The old lady's head jerked around. She could hear the wind move through the tree tops like a long satisfied insuck of breath. "Bailey Boy!" she called.

"I was a gospel singer for a while," The Misfit said. "I been most everything. Been in the arm service, both land and sea, at home and abroad, been twic't married, been an undertaker, been with the railroads, plowed Mother Earth, been in a tornado, seen a man burnt alive oncet," and he looked up at the children's mother and the little girl who were sitting close together, their faces white and their eyes glassy; "I even seen a woman flogged," he said.

"Pray, pray," the grandmother began, "pray, pray . . ."

"I never was a bad boy that I remember of," The Misfit said in an almost dreamy voice, "but somewheres along the line I done something wrong and got sent to the penitentiary. I was buried alive," and he looked up and held her attention to him by a steady stare.

"That's when you should have started to pray," she said. "What did you do to get sent to the penitentiary that first time?"

"Turn to the right, it was a wall," The Misfit said, looking up again at the cloudless sky. "Turn to the left, it was a wall. Look up it was a ceiling, look down it was a floor. I forget what I done, lady. I set there, and set there, trying to remember what it was I done and I ain't recalled it to this day. Oncet in a while, I would think it was coming to me, but it never come."

"Maybe they put you in by mistake," the old lady said vaguely.

"Nome," he said. "It wasn't no mistake. They had the papers on me."

"You must have stolen something," she said.

The Misfit sneered slightly. "Nobody had nothing I wanted," he said. "It was a head-doctor at the penitentiary said what I had done was kill my daddy but I known that for a lie. My daddy died in nineteen ought nineteen of the epidemic flu and I never had a thing to do with it. He was buried in the Mount Hopewell Baptist churchyard and you can go there and see for yourself."

"If you would pray," the old lady said, "Jesus would help you."

"That's right," The Misfit said.

"Well then, why don't you pray?" she asked, trembling with delight suddenly.

"I don't want no hep," he said. "I'm doing all right by myself."

Bobby Lee and Hiram came ambling back from the woods. Bobby Lee was dragging a yellow shirt with bright blue parrots in it.

"Throw me that shirt, Bobby Lee," The Misfit said. The shirt came flying at him and landed on his shoulder and he put it on. The grandmother couldn't name what the shirt reminded her of. "No, lady," The Misfit said while he was buttoning it up, "I found out the crime don't matter. You can do one thing or you can do another, kill a man or take a tire off his car, because sooner or later you're going to forget what it was you done and just be punished for it."

The children's mother had begun to make heaving noises as if she couldn't get her breath. "Lady," he asked, "would you and that little girl like to step off yonder with Bobby Lee and Hiram and join your husband?"

"Yes, thank you," the mother said faintly. Her left arm dangled helplessly and she was holding the baby, who had gone to sleep, in the other. "Hep that lady up, Hiram," The Misfit said as she struggled to climb out of the ditch, "and Bobby Lee, you hold onto that little girl's hand."

"I don't want to hold hands with him," June Star said. "He reminds me of a pig."

The fat boy blushed and laughed and caught her by the arm and pulled her off into the woods after Hiram and her mother.

Alone with The Misfit, the grandmother found that she had lost her voice. There was not a cloud in the sky nor any sun. There was nothing around her but woods. She wanted to tell him that he must pray. She opened and closed her mouth several times before anything came out. Finally she found herself saying, "Jesus, Jesus," meaning, Jesus will help you, but the way she was saying it, it sounded as if she might be cursing.

"Yes'm," The Misfit said as if he agreed. "Jesus thrown everything off balance. It was the same case with Him as with me except He hadn't committed any crime and they could prove I had committed one because they had the papers on me. Of course," he said, "they never shown me my papers. That's why I sign myself now. I said long ago, you get you a signature and sign everything you do and keep a copy of it. Then you'll know what you done and you can hold up the crime to the punishment and see do they match and in the end you'll have something to prove you ain't been treated right. I call myself The Misfit," he said, "because I can't make what all I done wrong fit what all I gone through in punishment."

There was a piercing scream from the woods, followed closely by a pistol report. "Does it seem right to you, lady, that one is punished a heap and another ain't punished at all?"

"Jesus!" the old lady cried. "You've got good blood! I know you wouldn't shoot a lady! I know you come from nice people! Pray! Jesus, you ought not to shoot a lady. I'll give you all the money I've got!"

"Lady," The Misfit said, looking beyond her far into the woods, "there never was a body that give the undertaker a tip."

There were two more pistol reports and the grandmother raised her head like a parched old turkey hen crying for water and called, "Bailey Boy, Bailey Boy!" as if her heart would break.

"Jesus was the only One that ever raised the dead," The Misfit continued, "and He shouldn't have done it. He thrown everything off balance. If He did what He said, then it's nothing for you to do but throw away everything and follow Him, and if He didn't, then it's nothing for you to do but enjoy the few minutes you got left the best way you can—by killing somebody or burning down his house or doing some other meanness to him. No pleasure but meanness," he said and his voice had become almost a snarl.

"Maybe He didn't raise the dead," the old lady mumbled, not knowing what she was saying and feeling so dizzy that she sank down in the ditch with her legs twisted under her.

"I wasn't there so I can't say He didn't," The Misfit said. "I wisht I had of been there," he said, hitting the ground with his fist. "It ain't right I wasn't there because if I had of been there I would of known. Listen lady," he said in a high voice, "if I had of been there I would of known and I wouldn't be like I am now." His voice seemed about to crack and the grandmother's head cleared for an instant. She saw the man's face twisted close to her own as if he were going to cry and she murmured, "Why you're one of my babies. You're one of my own children!" She reached out and touched him on the shoulder. The Misfit sprang back as if a snake had bitten him and shot her three times through the chest. Then he put his gun down on the ground and took off his glasses and began to clean them.

Hiram and Bobby Lee returned from the woods and stood over the ditch, looking down at the grandmother who half sat and half lay in a puddle of blood with her legs crossed under her like a child's and her face smiling up at the cloudless sky.

Without his glasses, The Misfit's eyes were red-rimmed and pale and defenseless-looking. "Take her off and throw her where you thrown the others," he said, picking up the cat that was rubbing itself against his leg.

"She was a talker, wasn't she?" Bobby Lee said, sliding down the ditch with a yodel.

"She would of been a good woman," The Misfit said, "if it had been somebody there to shoot her every minute of her life."

"Some fun!" Bobby Lee said.

"Shut up, Bobby Lee," The Misfit said. "It's no real pleasure in life."

most famous line

Bartleby the Scrivener

A STORY OF WALL STREET

HERMAN MELVILLE

[1819–1891]

I am a rather elderly man. The nature of my avocations, for the last thirty years, has brought me into more than ordinary contact with what would seem an interesting and somewhat singular set of men, of whom, as yet, nothing, that I know of, has ever been written—I mean, the law copyists, or scriveners. I have known very many of them, professionally and privately, and, if I pleased, could relate divers histories, at which good-natured gentlemen might smile, and sentimental souls might weep. But I waive the biographies of all other scriveners, for a few passages in the life of Bartleby, who was a scrivener, the strangest I ever saw, or heard of. While, of other law copyists, I might write the complete life, of Bartleby nothing of that sort can be done. I believe that no materials exist for a full and satisfactory biography of this man. It is an irreparable loss to literature. Bartleby was one of those beings of whom nothing is ascertainable, except from the original sources, and, in his case, those are very small. What my own astonished eyes saw of Bartleby, *that* is all I know of him, except, indeed, one vague report, which will appear in the sequel.

Ere introducing the scrivener, as he first appeared to me, it is fit I make some mention of myself, my *employés,* my business, my chambers, and general surroundings; because some such description is indispensable to an adequate understanding of the chief character about to be presented. *Imprimis* [1] I am a man who, from his youth upwards, has been filled with a profound conviction that the easiest way of life is the best. Hence, though I belong to a profession proverbially energetic and nervous, even to turbulence, at times, yet nothing of that sort have I ever suffered to invade my peace. I am one of those unambitious lawyers who never addresses a jury, or in any way draws down public applause; but, in the cool tranquillity of a snug retreat, do a snug business among rich men's bonds, and mortgages, and title deeds. All who know me consider me an eminently *safe* man. The late John Jacob Astor, a personage little given to poetic enthusiasm, had no hesitation in pronouncing my first grand point to be prudence; my next, method. I do not speak it in vanity, but simply record the fact, that I was not unemployed in my profession by the late John Jacob Astor; a name which, I admit, I love to repeat; for it hath a rounded and orbicular sound to it, and rings like unto bullion. I will freely add, that I was not insensible to the late John Jacob Astor's good opinion.

[1] *Imprimis:* in the first place.

Some time prior to the period at which this little history begins, my avocations had been largely increased. The good old office, now extinct in the State of New York, of a Master in Chancery, had been conferred upon me. It was not a very arduous office, but very pleasantly remunerative. I seldom lose my temper; much more seldom indulge in dangerous indignation at wrongs and outrages; but, I must be permitted to be rash here, and declare, that I consider the sudden and violent abrogation of the office of Master in Chancery, by the new Constitution, as a—premature act; inasmuch as I had counted upon a life-lease of the profits, whereas I only received those of a few short years. But this is by the way.

My chambers were upstairs, at No. — Wall Street. At one end, they looked upon the white wall of the interior of a spacious skylight shaft, penetrating the building from top to bottom.

This view might have been considered rather tame than otherwise, deficient in what landscape painters call "life." But, if so, the view from the other end of my chambers offered, at least, a contrast, if nothing more. In that direction, my windows commanded an unobstructed view of a lofty brick wall, black by age and everlasting shade; which wall required no spyglass to bring out its lurking beauties, but, for the benefit of all nearsighted spectators, was pushed up to within ten feet of my window panes. Owing to the great height of the surrounding buildings, and my chambers being on the second floor, the interval between this wall and mine not a little resembled a huge square cistern.

At the period just preceding the advent of Bartleby, I had two persons as copyists in my employment, and a promising lad as an office boy. First, Turkey; second, Nippers; third, Ginger Nut. These may seem names, the like of which are not usually found in the Directory. In truth, they were nicknames, mutually conferred upon each other by my three clerks, and were deemed expressive of their respective persons or characters. Turkey was a short, pursy Englishman, of about my own age—that is, somewhere not far from sixty. In the morning, one might say, his face was of a fine florid hue, but after twelve o'clock meridian—his dinner hour—it blazed like a grate full of Christmas coals; and continued blazing—but, as it were, with a gradual wane—till 6:00 P.M., or thereabouts; after which, I saw no more of the proprietor of the face, which, gaining its meridian with the sun, seemed to set with it, to rise, culminate, and decline the following day, with the like regularity and undiminished glory. There are many singular coincidences I have known in the course of my life, not the least among which was the fact, that, exactly when Turkey displayed his fullest beams from his red and radiant countenance, just then, too, at that critical moment, began the daily period when I considered his business capacities as seriously disturbed for the remainder of the twenty-four hours. Not that he was absolutely idle, or averse to business, then; far from it. The difficulty was, he was apt to be altogether too energetic. There was a strange, inflamed, flurried, flighty recklessness of activity about him. He would be incautious in dipping his pen into his inkstand. All his blots upon my documents were dropped there after twelve o'clock meridian. Indeed, not only would he be reckless, and sadly given to making blots in the afternoon, but, some days, he went further, and was rather noisy. At such times, too, his face flamed with augmented blazonry, as if cannel coal had been heaped on anthracite. He made an unpleasant racket with his chair; spilled his sand-box; in mending his pens, impatiently split them all to pieces, and threw them on the floor in a sudden passion; stood up, and leaned over his table, boxing his papers about in a most indecorous manner, very sad to behold in an elderly man like him. Nevertheless, as he was in many ways a most valuable person to me, and all the time before twelve o'clock meridian, was the quickest, steadiest creature, too, accomplishing a great deal of work in a style not easily to be matched—for these reasons, I was willing to overlook his eccentricities, though, indeed, occasionally, I remonstrated with him. I did this very gently, however, because, though the civilest, nay, the blandest and most reverential of men in the morning, yet, in the afternoon, he was disposed, upon provocation, to be slightly rash with his tongue—in fact, insolent. Now, valuing his morning services as I did, and resolved not to lose them—yet, at the same time, made uncomfortable by his inflamed ways after twelve o'clock—and being a man of peace, unwilling by my admonitions to call forth unseemly retorts from him, I took upon me, one Saturday noon (he was always worse on Saturdays) to hint to him, very kindly, that, perhaps, now that he was growing old, it might be well to abridge his labors; in short, he need not come to my chambers after twelve o'clock, but, dinner over, had best go home to his lodgings, and rest himself till teatime. But no; he insisted upon his afternoon devotions. His countenance became intolerably fervid, as he oratorically assured me— gesticulating with a long ruler at the other end of the room—that if his services in the morning were useful, how indispensable, then, in the afternoon?

"With submission, sir," said Turkey, on this occasion, "I consider myself your right-hand man. In the morning I but marshal and deploy my columns; but in the afternoon I put myself at their head, and gallantly charge the foe, thus"—and he made a violent thrust with the ruler.

"But the blots, Turkey," intimated I.

"True; but, with submission, sir, behold these hairs! I am getting old. Surely, sir, a blot or two of a warm afternoon is not to be severely urged against gray hairs. Old age—even if it blot the page—is honorable. With submission, sir, we *both* are getting old."

This appeal to my fellow feeling was hardly to be resisted. At all events, I saw that go he would not. So, I made up my mind to let him stay, resolving, nevertheless, to see to it that, during the afternoon, he had to do with my less important papers.

Nippers, the second on my list, was a whiskered, sallow, and, upon the whole, rather piratical-looking young man, of about five and twenty. I always deemed him the victim of two evil powers—ambition and indigestion. The ambition was evinced by a certain impatience of the duties of a mere copyist, an unwarrantable usurpation of strictly professional affairs, such as the original drawing up of legal documents. The indigestion seemed betokened in an occasional nervous testiness and grinning irritability, causing the teeth to audibly grind together over mistakes committed in copying; unnecessary maledictions, hissed, rather than spoken, in the heat of business; and especially by a continual discontent with the height of the table where he worked. Though of a very ingenious, mechanical turn, Nippers could never get this table to suit him. He put chips under it, blocks of various sorts, bits of pasteboard, and at last went so far as to attempt an exquisite adjustment, by final pieces of folded blotting paper. But no invention would answer. If, for the sake of easing his back, he brought the table lid at a sharp angle well up toward his chin, and wrote there like a man using the steep roof of a Dutch house for his desk, then he declared that it stopped the circulation in his arms. If now he lowered the table to his waistbands, and stooped over it in writing, then there was a sore aching in his back. In short, the truth of the matter was, Nippers knew not what he wanted. Or, if he wanted anything, it was to be rid of a scrivener's table altogether. Among the manifestations of his diseased ambition was a fondness he had for receiving visits from certain ambiguous-looking fellows in seedy coats, whom he called his clients. Indeed, I was aware that not only was he, at times, considerable of a ward politician, but he occasionally did a little business at the Justices' courts, and was not unknown on the steps of the Tombs. I have good reason to believe, however, that one individual who called upon him at my chambers, and who, with a grand air, he insisted was his client, was no other than a dun, and the alleged title deed, a bill. But, with all his failings, and the annoyances he caused me, Nippers, like his compatriot Turkey, was a very useful man to me; wrote a neat, swift hand; and, when he chose, was not deficient in a gentlemanly sort of deportment. Added to this, he always dressed in a gentlemanly sort of way; and so, incidentally, reflected credit upon my chambers. Whereas, with respect to Turkey, I had much ado to keep him from being a reproach to me. His clothes were apt to look oily, and smell of eating houses. He wore his pantaloons very loose and baggy in summer. His coats were execrable; his hat not to be handled. But while the hat was a thing of indifference to me, inasmuch as his natural civility and deference, as a dependent Englishman, always led him to doff it the moment he entered the room, yet his coat was another matter. Concerning his coats, I reasoned with him; but with no effect. The truth was, I suppose, that a man with so small an income could not afford to sport such a lustrous face and a lustrous coat at one and the same time. As Nippers once observed, Turkey's money went chiefly for red ink. One winter day, I presented Turkey with a highly respectable-looking coat of my own—a padded gray coat, of a most comfortable warmth, and which buttoned straight up from the knee to the neck. I thought Turkey would appreciate the favor, and abate his rashness and obstreperousness of afternoons. But no; I verily believe that buttoning himself up in so downy and blanketlike a coat had a pernicious effect upon him—upon the same principle that too much oats are bad for horses. In fact, precisely as a rash, restive horse is said to feel his oats, so Turkey felt his coat. It made him insolent. He was a man whom prosperity harmed.

Though, concerning the self-indulgent habits of Turkey, I had my own private surmises, yet, touching Nippers, I was well persuaded that, whatever might be his faults in other respects, he was, at least, a temperate young man. But, indeed, nature herself seemed to have been his vintner, and, at his birth, charged him so thoroughly with an irritable, brandylike disposition, that all subsequent potations were needless. When I consider how, amid the stillness of my chambers, Nippers would sometimes impatiently rise from his seat, and stooping over his table, spread his arms wide apart, seize the whole desk, and move it, and jerk it, with a grim, grinding motion on the floor, as if the table were a perverse voluntary agent and vexing him, I plainly perceive that, for Nippers, brandy-and-water were altogether superfluous.

It was fortunate for me that, owing to its peculiar cause—indigestion—the irritability and consequent nervousness of Nippers were mainly observable in the morning, while in the afternoon he was comparatively mild. So that, Turkey's paroxysms only coming on about twelve o'clock, I never had to do with their eccentricities at one time. Their fits relieved each other, like guards. When Nippers's was on, Turkey's was off; and *vice versa*. This was a good natural arrangement, under the circumstances.

Ginger Nut, the third on my list, was a lad some twelve years old. His father was a car-man, ambitious of seeing his son on the bench instead of a cart, before he died. So he sent him to my office, as student at law, errand boy, cleaner and sweeper, at the rate of one dollar a week. He had a little desk to himself; but he did not use it much. Upon inspection, the drawer exhibited a great array of the shells of various sorts of nuts. Indeed, to this quick-witted youth, the whole noble science of the law was contained in a nutshell. Not the least among the employments of Ginger Nut, as well as one which he discharged with the most alacrity, was his duty as cake and apple purveyor for Turkey and Nippers. Copying law papers being proverbially a dry, husky sort of business, my two scriveners were fain to moisten their mouths very often with Spitzenbergs, to be had at the numerous stalls nigh the Custom House and post office. Also, they sent Ginger Nut very frequently for that peculiar cake—small, flat, round, and very spicy—after which he had been named by them. Of a cold morning, when business was but dull, Turkey would gobble up scores of these cakes, as if they were mere wafers—indeed, they sell them at the rate of six or eight for a penny—the scrape of his pen blending with the crunching of the crisp particles in his mouth. Rashest of all the fiery afternoon blunders and flurried rashnesses of Turkey was his once moistening a ginger cake between his lips and clapping it on to a mortgage for a seal. I came within an ace of dismissing him then. But he mollified me by making an oriental bow, and saying—

"With submission, sir, it was generous of me to find you in stationery on my own account."

Now my original business—that of a conveyancer and title hunter, and drawer-up of recondite documents of all sorts—was considerably increased by receiving the master's office. There was now great work for scriveners. Not only must I push the clerks already with me, but I must have additional help.

In answer to my advertisement, a motionless young man one morning stood upon my office threshold, the door being open, for it was summer. I can see that figure now—pallidly neat, pitiably respectable, incurably forlorn! It was Bartleby.

After a few words touching his qualifications, I engaged him, glad to have among my corps of copyists a man of so singularly sedate an aspect, which I thought might operate beneficially upon the flighty temper of Turkey, and the fiery one of Nippers.

I should have stated before that ground glass folding doors divided my premises into two parts, one of which was occupied by my scriveners, the other by myself. According to my humor, I threw open these doors, or closed them. I resolved to assign Bartleby a corner by the folding doors, but on my side of them, so as to have this quiet man within easy call, in case any trifling thing was to be done. I placed his desk close up to a small side window in that part of the room, a window which originally had afforded a lateral view of certain grimy back yards and bricks, but which, owing to subsequent erections, commanded at present no view at all, though it gave some light. Within three feet of the panes was a wall, and the light came down from far above, between two lofty buildings, as from a very small opening in a dome. Still further to a satisfactory arrangement, I procured a high green folding screen, which might entirely isolate Bartleby from my sight, though not remove him from my voice. And thus, in a manner, privacy and society were conjoined.

At first, Bartleby did an extraordinary quantity of writing. As if long famishing for something to copy, he seemed to gorge himself on my documents. There was no pause for digestion. He ran a day and night line, copying by sunlight and by candlelight. I should have been quite delighted with his application, had he been cheerfully industrious. But he wrote on silently, palely, mechanically.

It is, of course, an indispensable part of a scrivener's business to verify the accuracy of his copy, word by word. Where there are two or more scriveners in an office, they assist each other in this examination, one reading from the copy, the other holding the original. It is a very dull, wearisome, and lethargic affair. I can readily imagine that, to some sanguine temperaments, it would be altogether intolerable. For example, I cannot credit that the mettlesome poet,

Byron, would have contentedly sat down with Bartleby to examine a law document of, say five hundred pages, closely written in a crimpy hand.

Now and then, in the haste of business it had been my habit to assist in comparing some brief document myself, calling Turkey or Nippers for this purpose. One object I had, in placing Bartleby so handy to me behind the screen, was to avail myself of his services on such trivial occasions. It was on the third day, I think, of his being with me, and before any necessity had arisen for having his own writing examined, that, being much hurried to complete a small affair I had in hand, I abruptly called to Bartleby. In my haste and natural expectancy of instant compliance, I sat with my head bent over the original on my desk, and my right hand sideways, and somewhat nervously extended with the copy, so that, immediately upon emerging from his retreat, Bartleby might snatch it and proceed to business without the least delay.

In this very attitude did I sit when I called to him, rapidly stating what it was I wanted him to do—namely, to examine a small paper with me. Imagine my surprise, nay, my consternation, when, without moving from his privacy, Bartleby, in a singularly mild, firm voice, replied, "I would prefer not to."

I sat awhile in perfect silence, rallying my stunned faculties. Immediately it occurred to me that my ears had deceived me, or Bartleby had entirely misunderstood my meaning. I repeated my request in the clearest tone I could assume; but in quite as clear a one came the previous reply, "I would prefer not to."

"Prefer not to," echoed I, rising in high excitement, and crossing the room with a stride. "What do you mean? Are you moon-struck? I want you to help me compare this sheet here—take it," and I thrust it toward him.

"I would prefer not to," said he.

I looked at him steadfastly. His face was leanly composed; his gray eye dimly calm. Not a wrinkle of agitation rippled him. Had there been the least uneasiness, anger, impatience, or impertinence in his manner; in other words, had there been anything ordinarily human about him, doubtless I should have violently dismissed him from the premises. But as it was, I should have as soon thought of turning my pale plaster-of-paris bust of Cicero out of doors. I stood gazing at him awhile, as he went on with his own writing, and then reseated myself at my desk. This is very strange, thought I. What had one best do? But my business hurried me. I concluded to forget the matter for the present, reserving it for my future leisure. So calling Nippers from the other room, the paper was speedily examined.

A few days after this, Bartleby concluded four lengthy documents, being quadruplicates of a week's testimony taken before me in my High Court of Chancery. It became necessary to examine them. It was an important suit, and great accuracy was imperative. Having all things arranged, I called Turkey, Nippers, and Ginger Nut from the next room, meaning to place the four copies in the hands of my four clerks, while I should read from the original. Accordingly, Turkey, Nippers, and Ginger Nut had taken their seats in a row, each with his document in his hand, when I called to Bartleby to join this interesting group.

"Bartleby! quick, I am waiting."

I heard a slow scrape of his chair legs on the uncarpeted floor, and soon he appeared standing at the entrance of his hermitage.

"What is wanted?" said he, mildly.

"The copies, the copies," said I, hurriedly. "We are going to examine them. There—" and I held toward him the fourth quadruplicate.

"I would prefer not to," he said, and gently disappeared behind the screen.

For a few moments I was turned into a pillar of salt, standing at the head of my seated column of clerks. Recovering myself, I advanced toward the screen, and demanded the reason for such extraordinary conduct.

"Why do you refuse?"

"I would prefer not to."

With any other man I should have flown outright into a dreadful passion, scorned all further words, and thrust him ignominiously from my presence. But there was something about Bartleby that not only strangely disarmed me, but in a wonderful manner, touched and disconcerted me. I began to reason with him.

"These are your own copies we are about to examine. It is labor-saving to you, because one examination will answer for your four papers. It is common usage. Every copyist is bound to help examine his copy. Is it not so? Will you not speak? Answer!"

"I prefer not to," he replied in a flutelike tone. It seemed to me that, while I had been addressing him, he carefully revolved every statement that I made; fully comprehended the meaning; could not gainsay the irresistible conclusion; but, at the same time, some paramount consideration prevailed with him to reply as he did.

"You are decided, then, not to comply with my request—a request made according to common usage and common sense?"

He briefly gave me to understand, that on that point my judgment was sound. Yes: his decision was irreversible.

It is not seldom the case that, when a man is browbeaten in some unprecedented and violently unreasonable way, he begins to stagger in his own plainest faith. He begins, as it were, vaguely to surmise that, wonderful as it may be, all the justice and all the reason is on the other side. Accordingly, if any disinterested persons are present, he turns to them for some reinforcement of his own faltering mind.

"Turkey," said I, "what do you think of this? Am I not right?"

"With submission, sir," said Turkey, in his blandest tone, "I think that you are."

"Nippers," said I, "what do *you* think of it?"

"I think I should kick him out of the office."

(The reader, of nice perceptions, will here perceive that, it being morning, Turkey's answer is couched in polite and tranquil terms, but Nippers replies in ill-tempered ones. Or, to repeat a previous sentence, Nippers's ugly mood was on duty, and Turkey's off.)

"Ginger Nut," said I, willing to enlist the smallest suffrage in my behalf, "what do *you* think of it?"

"I think, sir, he's a little *luny*," replied Ginger Nut, with a grin.

"You hear what they say," said I, turning toward the screen, "come forth and do your duty."

But he vouchsafed no reply. I pondered a moment in sore perplexity. But once more business hurried me. I determined again to postpone the consideration of this dilemma to my future leisure. With a little trouble we made out to examine the papers without Bartleby, though at every page or two Turkey deferentially dropped his opinion, that this proceeding was quite out of the common; while Nippers, twitching in his chair with a dyspeptic nervousness, ground out, between his set teeth, occasional hissing maledictions against the stubborn oaf behind the screen. And for his (Nippers's) part, this was the first and the last time he would do another man's business without pay.

Meanwhile Bartleby sat in his hermitage, oblivious to everything but his own peculiar business there.

Some days passed, the scrivener being employed upon another lengthy work. His late remarkable conduct led me to regard his ways narrowly. I observed that he never went to dinner; indeed, that he never went anywhere. As yet I had never, of my personal knowledge, known him to be outside of my office. He was a perpetual sentry in the corner. At about eleven o'clock though, in the morning, I noticed that Ginger Nut would advance toward the opening in Bartleby's screen, as if silently beckoned thither by a gesture invisible to me where I sat. The boy would then leave the office, jingling a few pence, and reappear with a handful of ginger nuts, which he delivered in the hermitage, receiving two of the cakes for his trouble.

He lives, then, on ginger nuts, thought I; never eats a dinner, properly speaking; he must be a vegetarian, then; but no; he never eats even vegetables; he eats nothing but ginger nuts. My mind then ran on in reveries concerning the probable effects upon the human constitution of living entirely on ginger nuts. Ginger nuts are so called, because they contain ginger as one of their peculiar constituents, and the final flavoring one. Now, what was ginger? A hot, spicy thing. Was Bartleby hot and spicy? Not at all. Ginger, then, had no effect upon Bartleby. Probably he preferred it should have none.

Nothing so aggravates an earnest person as a passive resistance. If the individual so resisted be of a not inhumane temper, and the resisting one perfectly harmless in his passivity, then, in the better moods of the former, he will endeavor charitably to construe to his imagination what proves impossible to be solved by his judgment. Even so, for the most part, I regarded

Bartleby and his ways. Poor fellow! thought I, he means no mischief; it is plain he intends no insolence; his aspect sufficiently evinces that his eccentricities are involuntary. He is useful to me. I can get along with him. If I turn him away, the chances are he will fall in with some less indulgent employer, and then he will be rudely treated, and perhaps driven forth miserably to starve. Yes. Here I can cheaply purchase a delicious self-approval. To befriend Bartleby; to humor him in his strange willfulness, will cost me little or nothing, while I lay up in my soul what will eventually prove a sweet morsel for my conscience. But this mood was not invariable with me. The passiveness of Bartleby sometimes irritated me. I felt strangely goaded on to encounter him in new opposition—to elicit some angry spark from him answerable to my own. But, indeed, I might as well have essayed to strike fire with my knuckles against a bit of Windsor soap. But one afternoon the evil impulse in me mastered me, and the following little scene ensued:

"Bartleby," said I, "when those papers are all copied, I will compare them with you."

"I would prefer not to."

"How? Surely you do not mean to persist in that mulish vagary?"

No answer.

I threw open the folding doors nearby, and, turning upon Turkey and Nippers, exclaimed:

"Bartleby a second time says he won't examine his papers. What do you think of it, Turkey?"

It was afternoon, be it remembered. Turkey sat glowing like a brass boiler; his bald head steaming; his hands reeling among his blotted papers.

"Think of it?" roared Turkey; "I think I'll just step behind his screen, and black his eyes for him!"

So saying, Turkey rose to his feet and threw his arms into a pugilistic position. He was hurrying away to make good his promise, when I detained him, alarmed at the effect of incautiously rousing Turkey's combativeness after dinner.

"Sit down, Turkey," said I, "and hear what Nippers has to say. What do you think of it, Nippers? Would I not be justified in immediately dismissing Bartleby?"

"Excuse me, that is for you to decide, sir. I think his conduct quite unusual, and, indeed, unjust, as regards Turkey and myself. But it may only be a passing whim."

"Ah," exclaimed I, "you have strangely changed your mind, then—you speak very gently of him now."

"All beer," cried Turkey; "gentleness is effects of beer—Nippers and I dined together today. You see how gentle *I* am, sir. Shall I go and black his eyes?"

"You refer to Bartleby, I suppose. No, not today, Turkey," I replied; "pray, put up your fists."

I closed the doors, and again advanced toward Bartleby. I felt additional incentives tempting me to my fate. I burned to be rebelled against again. I remembered that Bartleby never left the office.

"Bartleby," said I, "Ginger Nut is away; just step around to the post office, won't you? (it was but a three minutes' walk), and see if there is anything for me."

"I would prefer not to."

"You *will* not?"

"I *prefer* not."

I staggered to my desk, and sat there in a deep study. My blind inveteracy returned. Was there any other thing in which I could procure myself to be ignominiously repulsed by this lean, penniless wight?—my hired clerk? What added thing is 'here, perfectly reasonable, that he will be sure to refuse to do?

"Bartleby!"

No answer.

"Bartleby," in a louder tone.

No answer.

"Bartleby," I roared.

Like a very ghost, agreeably to the laws of magical invocation, at the third summons, he appeared at the entrance of his hermitage.

"Go to the next room, and tell Nippers to come to me."

"I prefer not to," he respectfully and slowly said, and mildly disappeared.

"Very good, Bartleby," said I, in a quiet sort of serenely severe, self-possessed tone, intimating the unalterable purpose of some terrible retribution very close at hand. At the moment I half intended something of the kind. But upon the whole, as it was drawing toward my dinner hour, I thought it best to put on my hat and walk home for the day, suffering much from perplexity and distress of mind.

Shall I acknowledge it? The conclusion of this whole business was, that it soon became a fixed fact of my chambers, that a pale young scrivener, by the name of Bartleby, had a desk there; that he copied for me at the usual rate of four cents a folio (one hundred words); but he was permanently exempt from examining the work done by him, that duty being transferred to Turkey and Nippers, out of compliment, doubtless, to their superior acuteness; moreover, said Bartleby was never, on any account, to be dispatched on the most trivial errand of any sort; and that even if entreated to take upon him such a matter, it was generally understood that he would "prefer not to"—in other words, that he would refuse point-blank.

As days passed on, I became considerably reconciled to Bartleby. His steadiness, his freedom from all dissipation, his incessant industry (except when he chose to throw himself into a standing revery behind his screen), his great stillness, his unalterableness of demeanor under all circumstances, made him a valuable acquisition. One prime thing was this—*he was always there*—

first in the morning, continually through the day, and the last at night. I had a singular confidence in his honesty. I felt my most precious papers perfectly safe in his hands. Sometimes, to be sure, I could not, for the very soul of me, avoid falling into sudden spasmodic passions with him. For it was exceeding difficult to bear in mind all the time those strange peculiarities, privileges, and unheard-of exemptions, forming the tacit stipulations on Bartleby's part under which he remained in my office. Now and then, in the eagerness of dispatching pressing business, I would inadvertently summon Bartleby, in a short, rapid tone, to put his finger, say, on the incipient tie of a bit of red tape with which I was about compressing some papers. Of course, from behind the screen the usual answer, "I prefer not to," was sure to come; and then, how could a human creature, with the common infirmities of our nature, refrain from bitterly exclaiming upon such perverseness—such unreasonableness. However, every added repulse of this sort which I received only tended to lessen the probability of my repeating the inadvertence.

Here it must be said that according to the custom of most legal gentlemen occupying chambers in densely populated law buildings, there were several keys to my door. One was kept by a woman residing in the attic, which person weekly scrubbed and daily swept and dusted my apartments. Another was kept by Turkey for convenience' sake. The third I sometimes carried in my own pocket. The fourth I knew not who had.

Now, one Sunday morning I happened to go to Trinity Church, to hear a celebrated preacher, and finding myself rather early on the ground I thought I would walk around to my chambers for a while. Luckily I had my key with me; but upon applying it to the lock, I found it resisted by something inserted from the inside. Quite surprised, I called out; when to my consternation a key was turned from within; and thrusting his lean visage at me, and holding the door ajar, the apparition of Bartleby appeared, in his shirt sleeves, and other-wise in a strangely tattered *déshabillé,* saying quietly that he was sorry, but he was deeply engaged just then, and—preferred not admitting me at present. In a brief word or two, he moreover added, that perhaps I had better walk around the block two or three times, and by that time he would probably have concluded his affairs.

Now, the utterly unsurmised appearance of Bartleby, tenanting my law chambers of a Sunday morning, with his cadaverously gentlemanly noncha-lance, yet withal firm and self-possessed, had such a strange effect upon me, that incontinently I slunk away from my own door, and did as desired. But not without sundry twinges of impotent rebellion against the mild effrontery of this unaccountable scrivener. Indeed, it was his wonderful mildness chiefly, which not only disarmed me, but unmanned me, as it were. For I consider that one, for the time, is somehow unmanned when he tranquilly permits his hired clerk to dictate to him, and order him away from his own premises. Furthermore, I was full of uneasiness as to what Bartleby could possibly be doing in my office in his shirt sleeves, and in an otherwise dismantled condition of a Sunday morning. Was anything amiss going on? Nay, that was out of the question. It was not to be thought of for a moment that Bartleby was an immoral person. But what could he be doing there?—copying? Nay again, whatever might be his eccentricities, Bartleby was an eminently decorous person. He would be the last man to sit down to his desk in any state approaching to nudity. Besides, it was Sunday; and there was something about Bartleby that forbade the supposition that he would by any secular occupation violate the proprieties of the day.

Nevertheless, my mind was not pacified; and full of a restless curiosity, at last I returned to the door. Without hindrance I inserted my key, opened it, and entered. Bartleby was not to be seen. I looked round anxiously, peeped behind his screen; but it was very plain that he was gone. Upon more closely examining the place, I surmised that for an indefinite period Bartleby must have eaten, dressed, and slept in my office, and that, too, without plate, mirror, or bed. The cushioned seat of a rickety old sofa in one corner bore the faint impress of a lean, reclining form. Rolled away under his desk, I found a blanket; under the empty grate, a blacking box and brush; on a chair, a tin basin, with soap and a ragged towel; in a newspaper a few crumbs of ginger nuts and a morsel of cheese. Yes, thought I, it is evident enough that Bartleby has been making his home here, keeping bachelor's hall all by himself. Immediately then the thought came sweeping across me, what miserable friendlessness and loneliness are here revealed! His poverty is great; but his solitude, how horrible! Think of it. Of a Sunday, Wall Street is deserted as Petra; and every night of every day it is an emptiness. This building, too, which of weekdays hums with industry and life, at nightfall echoes with sheer vacancy, and all through Sunday is forlorn. And here Bartleby makes his home; sole spectator of a solitude which he has seen all populous—a sort of innocent and transformed Marius brooding among the ruins of Carthage!

For the first time in my life a feeling of overpowering stinging melancholy seized me. Before, I had never experienced aught but a not unpleasing sadness. The bond of a common humanity now drew me irresistibly to gloom. A fraternal melancholy! For both I and Bartleby were sons of Adam. I remembered the bright silks and sparkling faces I had seen that day, in gala trim, swanlike, sailing down the Mississippi of Broadway; and I contrasted them with the pallid copyist, and thought to myself, Ah, happiness courts the light, so we deem the world is gay; but misery hides aloof, so we deem that misery there is none. These sad fancyings—chimeras, doubtless, of a sick and silly brain—led on to other and more special thoughts, concerning the eccentricities of Bartleby. Presentiments of strange discoveries hovered round me. The scrivener's pale form appeared to me laid out, among uncaring strangers, in its shivering winding sheet.

Suddenly I was attracted by Bartleby's closed desk, the key in open sight left in the lock.

I mean no mischief, seek the gratification of no heartless curiosity, thought

I; besides, the desk is mine, and its contents, too, so I will make bold to look within. Everything was methodically arranged, the papers smoothly placed. The pigeon holes were deep, and removing the files of documents, I groped into their recesses. Presently I felt something there, and dragged it out. It was an old bandanna handkerchief, heavy and knotted. I opened it, and saw it was a savings bank.

I now recalled all the quiet mysteries which I had noted in the man. I remembered that he never spoke but to answer; that, though at intervals he had considerable time to himself, yet I had never seen him reading—no, not even a newspaper; that for long periods he would stand looking out, at his pale window behind the screen, upon the dead brick wall; I was quite sure he never visited any refectory or eating house; while his pale face clearly indicated that he never drank beer like Turkey, or tea and coffee even, like other men; that he never went anywhere in particular that I could learn; never went out for a walk, unless, indeed, that was the case at present; that he had declined telling who he was, or whence he came, or whether he had any relatives in the world; that though so thin and pale, he never complained of ill health. And more than all, I remembered a certain unconscious air of pallid— how shall I call it?—of pallid haughtiness, say, or rather an austere reserve about him, which had positively awed me into my tame compliance with his eccentricities, when I had feared to ask him to do the slightest incidental thing for me, even though I might know, from his long-continued motionlessness, that behind his screen he must be standing in one of those dead-wall reveries of his.

Revolving all these things, and coupling them with the recently discovered fact that he made my office his constant abiding place and home, and not forgetful of his morbid moodiness; revolving all these things, a prudential feeling began to steal over me. My first emotions had been those of pure melancholy and sincerest pity; but just in proportion as the forlornness of Bartleby grew and grew to my imagination, did that same melancholy merge into fear, that pity into repulsion. So true it is, and so terrible, too, that up to a certain point the thought or sight of misery enlists our best affections; but, in certain special cases, beyond that point it does not. They err who would assert that invariably this is owing to the inherent selfishness of the human heart. It rather proceeds from a certain hopelessness of remedying excessive and organic ill. To a sensitive being, pity is not seldom pain. And when at last it is perceived that such pity cannot lead to effectual succor, common sense bids the soul be rid of it. What I saw that morning persuaded me that the scrivener was the victim of innate and incurable disorder. I might give alms to his body; but his body did not pain him; it was his soul that suffered, and his soul I could not reach.

I did not accomplish the purpose of going to Trinity Church that morning. Somehow, the things I had seen disqualified me for the time from church-going. I walked homeward, thinking what I would do with Bartleby. Finally, I resolved upon this—I would put certain calm questions to him the next morning, touching his history, etc., and if he declined to answer them openly and unreservedly (and I supposed he would prefer not), then to give him a twenty dollar bill over and above whatever I might owe him, and tell him his services were no longer required; but that if in any other way I could assist him, I would be happy to do so, especially if he desired to return to his native place, wherever that might be, I would willingly help to defray the expenses. Moreover, if, after reaching home, he found himself at any time in want of aid, a letter from him would be sure of a reply.

The next morning came.

"Bartleby," said I, gently calling to him behind his screen.

No reply.

"Bartleby," said I, in a still gentler tone, "come here; I am not going to ask you to do anything you would prefer not to do—I simply wish to speak to you."

Upon this he noiselessly slid into view.

"Will you tell me, Bartleby, where you were born?"

"I would prefer not to."

"Will you tell me *anything* about yourself?"

"I would prefer not to."

"But what reasonable objection can you have to speak to me? I feel friendly toward you."

He did not look at me while I spoke, but kept his glance fixed upon my bust of Cicero, which, as I then sat, was directly behind me, some six inches above my head.

"What is your answer, Bartleby," said I, after waiting a considerable time for a reply, during which his countenance remained immovable, only there was the faintest conceivable tremor of the white attenuated mouth.

"At present I prefer to give no answer," he said, and retired into his hermitage.

It was rather weak in me I confess, but his manner, on this occasion, nettled me. Not only did there seem to lurk in it a certain calm disdain, but his perverseness seemed ungrateful, considering the undeniable good usage and indulgence he had received from me.

Again I sat ruminating what I should do. Mortified as I was at his behavior, and resolved as I had been to dismiss him when I entered my office, nevertheless I strangely felt something superstitious knocking at my heart, and forbidding me to carry out my purpose, and denouncing me for a villain if I dared to breathe one bitter word against this forlornest of mankind. At last, familiarly drawing my chair behind his screen, I sat down and said: "Bartleby, never mind, then, about revealing your history; but let me entreat you, as a friend, to comply as far as may be with the usages of this office. Say now, you will help to examine papers tomorrow or next day: in short, say now, that in a day or two you will begin to be a little reasonable:—say so, Bartleby."

"At present I would prefer not to be a little reasonable," was his mildly cadaverous reply.

Just then the folding doors opened, and Nippers approached. He seemed suffering from an unusually bad night's rest, induced by severer indigestion than common. He overheard those final words of Bartleby.

"*Prefer not,* eh?" gritted Nippers—"I'd *prefer* him, if I were you, sir," addressing me—"I'd *prefer* him; I'd give him preferences, the stubborn mule! What is it, sir, pray, that he *prefers* not to do now?"

Bartleby moved not a limb.

"Mr. Nippers," said I, "I'd prefer that you would withdraw for the present."

Somehow, of late, I had got into the way of involuntarily using this word *prefer* upon all sorts of not exactly suitable occasions. And I trembled to think that my contact with the scrivener had already and seriously affected me in a mental way. And what further and deeper aberration might it not yet produce? This apprehension had not been without efficacy in determining me to summary measures.

As Nippers, looking very sour and sulky, was departing, Turkey blandly and deferentially approached.

"With submission, sir," said he, "yesterday I was thinking about Bartleby here, and I think that if he would but prefer to take a quart of good ale every day, it would do much toward mending him, and enabling him to assist in examining his papers."

"So you have got the word, too," said I, slightly excited.

"With submission, what word, sir?" asked Turkey, respectfully crowding himself into the contracted space behind the screen, and by so doing, making me jostle the scrivener. "What word, sir?"

"I would prefer to be left alone here," said Bartleby, as if offended at being mobbed in his privacy.

"*That's* the word, Turkey," said I—"*that's* it."

"Oh, *prefer?* oh yes—queer word. I never use it myself. But, sir, as I was saying, if he would but prefer—"

"Turkey," interrupted I, "you will please withdraw."

"Oh certainly, sir, if you prefer that I should."

As he opened the folding door to retire, Nippers at his desk caught a glimpse of me, and asked whether I would prefer to have a certain paper copied on blue paper or white. He did not in the least roguishly accent the word *prefer*. It was plain that it involuntarily rolled from his tongue. I thought to myself, surely I must get rid of a demented man, who already has in some degree turned the tongues, if not the heads of myself and clerks. But I thought it prudent not to break the dismission at once.

The next day I noticed that Bartleby did nothing but stand at his window in his dead-wall revery. Upon asking him why he did not write, he said that he had decided upon doing no more writing.

"Why, how now? What next?" exclaimed I. "Do no more writing?"

"No more."

"And what is the reason?"

"Do you not see the reason for yourself?" he indifferently replied.

I looked steadfastly at him, and perceived that his eyes looked dull and glazed. Instantly it occurred to me that his unexampled diligence in copying by his dim window for the first few weeks of his stay with me might have temporarily impaired his vision.

I was touched. I said something in condolence with him. I hinted that of course he did wisely in abstaining from writing for a while; and urged him to embrace that opportunity of taking wholesome exercise in the open air. This, however, he did not do. A few days after this, my other clerks being absent, and being in a great hurry to dispatch certain letters by the mail, I thought that, having nothing else earthly to do, Bartleby would surely be less inflexible than usual, and carry these letters to the post office. But he blankly declined. So, much to my inconvenience, I went myself.

Still added days went by. Whether Bartleby's eyes improved or not, I could not say. To all appearance I thought they did. But when I asked him if they did, he vouchsafed no answer. At all events, he would do no copying. At last, in reply to my urgings, he informed me that he had permanently given up copying.

"What!" exclaimed I. "Suppose your eyes should get entirely well—better than ever before—would you not copy then?"

"I have given up copying," he answered, and slid aside.

He remained as ever, a fixture in my chamber. Nay—if that were possible —he became still more of a fixture than before. What was to be done? He would do nothing in the office; why should he stay there? In plain fact, he had now become a millstone to me, not only useless as a necklace, but afflictive to bear. Yet I was sorry for him. I speak less than truth when I say that, on his own account, he occasioned me uneasiness. If he would but have named a single relative or friend, I would instantly have written, and urged their taking the poor fellow away to some convenient retreat. But he seemed alone, absolutely alone in the universe. A bit of wreck in the mid-Atlantic. At length, necessities connected with my business tyrannized over all other considerations. Decently as I could, I told Bartleby that in six days' time he must unconditionally leave the office. I warned him to take measures, in the interval, for procuring some other abode. I offered to assist him in his endeavor, if he himself would but take the first step towards a removal. "And when you finally quit me, Bartleby," added I, "I shall see that you go not away entirely unprovided. Six days from this hour, remember."

At the expiration of that period, I peeped behind the screen, and lo! Bartleby was there.

I buttoned up my coat, balanced myself; advanced slowly toward him, touched his shoulder, and said, "The time has come; you must quit this place; I am sorry for you; here is money; but you must go."

"I would prefer not," he replied, with his back still toward me.

"You *must*."

He remained silent.

Now I had an unbounded confidence in this man's common honesty. He had frequently restored to me sixpences and shillings carelessly dropped upon the floor, for I am apt to be very reckless in such shirt-button affairs. The proceeding, then, which followed will not be deemed extraordinary.

"Bartleby," said I, "I owe you twelve dollars on account; here are thirty-two; the odd twenty are yours— Will you take it?" and I handed the bills toward him.

But he made no motion.

"I will leave them here, then," putting them under a weight on the table. Then taking my hat and cane and going to the door, I tranquilly turned and added—"After you have removed your things from these offices, Bartleby, you will of course lock the door—since everyone is now gone for the day but you—and if you please, slip your key underneath the mat, so that I may have it in the morning. I shall not see you again; so good-bye to you. If, hereafter, in your new place of abode, I can be of any service to you, do not fail to advise me by letter. Good-bye, Bartleby, and fare you well."

But he answered not a word; like the last column of some ruined temple, he remained standing mute and solitary in the middle of the otherwise deserted room.

As I walked home in a pensive mood, my vanity got the better of my pity. I could not but highly plume myself on my masterly management in getting rid of Bartleby. Masterly I call it, and such it must appear to any dispassionate thinker. The beauty of my procedure seemed to consist in its perfect quietness. There was no vulgar bullying, no bravado of any sort, no choleric hectoring, and striding to and fro across the apartment, jerking out vehement commands for Bartleby to bundle himself off with his beggarly traps. Nothing of the kind. Without loudly bidding Bartleby depart—as an inferior genius might have done—I *assumed* the ground that depart he must; and upon that assumption built all I had to say. The more I thought over my procedure, the more I was charmed with it. Nevertheless, next morning, upon awakening, I had my doubts—I had somehow slept off the fumes of vanity. One of the coolest and wisest hours a man has, is just after he awakes in the morning. My procedure seemed as sagacious as ever—but only in theory. How it would prove in practice—there was the rub. It was truly a beautiful thought to have assumed Bartleby's departure; but, after all, that assumption was simply my own, and none of Bartleby's. The great point was, not whether I had assumed that he would quit me, but whether he would prefer so to do. He was more a man of preferences than assumptions.

After breakfast, I walked downtown, arguing the probabilities *pro* and *con*. One moment I thought it would prove a miserable failure, and Bartleby would be found all alive at my office as usual; the next moment it seemed certain that I should find his chair empty. And so I kept veering about. At the corner of Broadway and Canal Street, I saw quite an excited group of people standing in earnest conversation.

"I'll take odds he doesn't," said a voice as I passed.

"Doesn't go?—done!" said I; "put up your money."

I was instinctively putting my hand in my pocket to produce my own, when I remembered that this was an election day. The words I had overheard bore no reference to Bartleby, but to the success or nonsuccess of some candidate for the mayoralty. In my intent frame of mind, I had, as it were, imagined that all Broadway shared in my excitement, and were debating the same question with me. I passed on, very thankful that the uproar of the street screened my momentary absent-mindedness.

As I had intended, I was earlier than usual at my office door. I stood listening for a moment. All was still. He must be gone. I tried the knob. The door was locked. Yes, my procedure had worked to a charm; he indeed must be vanished. Yet a certain melancholy mixed with this: I was almost sorry for my brilliant success. I was fumbling under the door mat for the key, which Bartleby was to have left there for me, when accidentally my knee knocked against a panel, producing a summoning sound, and in response a voice came to me from within—"Not yet; I am occupied."

It was Bartleby.

I was thunderstruck. For an instant I stood like the man who, pipe in mouth, was killed one cloudless afternoon long ago in Virginia, by summer lightning; at his own warm open window he was killed, and remained leaning out there upon the dreamy afternoon, till some one touched him, when he fell.

"Not gone!" I murmured at last. But again obeying that wondrous ascendancy which the inscrutable scrivener had over me, and from which ascendancy, for all my chafing, I could not completely escape, I slowly went downstairs and out into the street, and while walking round the block, considered what I should next do in this unheard-of perplexity. Turn the man out by an actual thrusting I could not; to drive him away by calling him hard names would not do; calling in the police was an unpleasant idea; and yet, permit him to enjoy his cadaverous triumph over me—this, too, I could not think of. What was to be done? or, if nothing could be done, was there anything further that I could *assume* in the matter? Yes, as before I had prospectively assumed that Bartleby would depart, so now I might retrospectively assume that departed he was. In the legitimate carrying out of this assumption, I might enter my office in a great hurry, and pretending not to see Bartleby at all, walk straight against him as if he were air. Such a proceeding would in a singular degree have the appearance of a home thrust. It was hardly possible that Bartleby could withstand such an application of the doctrine of assumptions. But upon second thoughts the success of the plan seemed rather dubious. I resolved to argue the matter over with him again.

"Bartleby," said I, entering the office, with a quietly severe expression, "I am seriously displeased. I am pained, Bartleby. I had thought better of you. I had imagined you of such a gentlemanly organization, that in any delicate dilemma a slight hint would suffice—in short, an assumption. But it appears I am deceived. Why," I added, unaffectedly starting, "you have not even touched that money yet," pointing to it, just where I had left it the evening previous.

He answered nothing.

"Will you, or will you not, quit me?" I now demanded in a sudden passion, advancing close to him.

"I would prefer *not* to quit you," he replied, gently emphasizing the *not*.

"What earthly right have you to stay here? Do you pay any rent? Do you pay my taxes? Or is this property yours?"

He answered nothing.

"Are you ready to go on and write now? Are your eyes recovered? Could you copy a small paper for me this morning? or help examine a few lines? or step round to the post office? In a word, will you do anything at all, to give a coloring to your refusal to depart the premises?"

He silently retired into his hermitage.

I was now in such a state of nervous resentment that I thought it but prudent to check myself at present from further demonstrations. Bartleby and I were alone. I remembered the tragedy of the unfortunate Adams and the still more unfortunate Colt in the solitary office of the latter; and how poor Colt, being dreadfully incensed by Adams, and imprudently permitting himself to get wildly excited, was at unawares hurried into his fatal act—an act which certainly no man could possibly deplore more than the actor himself. Often it had occurred to me in my ponderings upon the subject, that had that altercation taken place in the public street, or at a private residence, it would not have terminated as it did. It was the circumstance of being alone in a solitary office, upstairs, of a building entirely unhallowed by humanizing domestic associations—an uncarpeted office, doubtless, of a dusty, haggard sort of appearance—this it must have been, which greatly helped to enhance the irritable desperation of the hapless Colt.

But when this old Adam of resentment rose in me and tempted me concerning Bartleby, I grappled him and threw him. How? Why, simply by recalling the divine injunction: "A new commandment give I unto you, that ye love one another." Yes, this it was that saved me. Aside from higher considerations, charity often operates as a vastly wise and prudent principle—a great safeguard to its possessor. Men have committed murder for jealousy's sake, and anger's sake, and hatred's sake, and selfishness' sake, and spiritual pride's sake; but no man, that ever I heard of, ever committed a diabolical murder for sweet charity's sake. Mere self-interest, then, if no better motive can be enlisted, should, especially with high-tempered men, prompt all beings to charity and philanthropy. At any rate, upon the occasion in question, I strove to drown my exasperated feelings toward the scrivener by benevolently construing his conduct. Poor fellow, poor fellow! thought I, he don't mean anything; and besides, he has seen hard times, and ought to be indulged.

I endeavored, also, immediately to occupy myself, and at the same time to comfort my despondency. I tried to fancy, that in the course of the morning, at such time as might prove agreeable to him, Bartleby, of his own free accord, would emerge from his hermitage and take up some decided line of march in the direction of the door. But no. Half past twelve o'clock came; Turkey began to glow in the face, overturn his inkstand, and become generally obstreperous; Nippers abated down into quietude and courtesy; Ginger Nut munched his noon apple; and Bartleby remained standing at his window in one of his profoundest dead-wall reveries. Will it be credited? Ought I to acknowledge it? That afternoon I left the office without saying one further word to him.

Some days now passed, during which, at leisure intervals I looked a little into "Edwards on the Will" and "Priestley on Necessity." Under the circumstances, those books induced a salutary feeling. Gradually I slid into the persuasion that these troubles of mine, touching the scrivener, had been all predestinated from eternity, and Bartleby was billeted upon me for some mysterious purpose of an all-wise Providence, which it was not for a mere mortal like me to fathom. Yes, Bartleby, stay there behind your screen, thought I; I shall persecute you no more; you are harmless and noiseless as any of these old chairs; in short, I never feel so private as when I know you are here. At last I see it, I feel it; I penetrate to the predestinated purpose of my life. I am content. Others may have loftier parts to enact; but my mission in this world, Bartleby, is to furnish you with office room for such period as you may see fit to remain.

I believe that this wise and blessed frame of mind would have continued with me, had it not been for the unsolicited and uncharitable remarks obtruded upon me by my professional friends who visited the rooms. But thus it often is, that the constant friction of illiberal minds wears out at last the best resolves of the more generous. Though to be sure, when I reflected upon it, it was not strange that people entering my office should be struck by the peculiar aspect of the unaccountable Bartleby, and so be tempted to throw out some sinister observations concerning him. Sometimes an attorney, having business with me, and calling at my office, and finding no one but the scrivener there, would undertake to obtain some sort of precise information from him touching my whereabouts; but without heeding his idle talk, Bartleby would remain standing immovable in the middle of the room. So after contemplating him in that position for a time, the attorney would depart, no wiser than he came.

Also, when a reference was going on, and the room full of lawyers and witnesses, and business driving fast, some deeply occupied legal gentleman present, seeing Bartleby wholly unemployed, would request him to run round to his (the legal gentleman's) office and fetch some papers for him. Thereupon, Bartleby would tranquilly decline, and yet remain idle as before. Then the lawyer would give a great stare, and turn to me. And what could I say? At last I was made aware that all through the circle of my professional acquaintance, a whisper of wonder was running round, having reference to the strange creature I kept at my office. This worried me very much. And as the idea came upon me of his possibly turning out a long-lived man, and keep occupying my chambers, and denying my authority; and perplexing my visitors; and scandalizing my professional reputation; and casting a general gloom over the premises; keeping soul and body together to the last upon his savings (for doubtless he spent but half a dime a day), and in the end perhaps outlive me, and claim possession of my office by right of his perpetual occupancy: as all these dark anticipations crowded upon me more and more, and my friends continually intruded their relentless remarks upon the apparition in my room, a great change was wrought in me. I resolved to gather all my faculties together, and forever rid me of this intolerable incubus.

Ere revolving any complicated project, however, adapted to this end, I first simply suggested to Bartleby the propriety of his permanent departure. In a calm and serious tone, I commended the idea to his careful and mature consideration. But, having taken three days to meditate upon it, he apprised me, that his original determination remained the same; in short, that he still preferred to abide with me.

What shall I do? I now said to myself, buttoning up my coat to the last button. What shall I do? What ought I to do? What does conscience say I *should* do with this man, or, rather, ghost? Rid myself of him, I must; go, he shall. But how? You will not thrust him, the poor, pale, passive mortal—you will not thrust such a helpless creature out of your door? You will not dishonor yourself by such cruelty? No, I will not, I cannot do that. Rather would I let him live and die here, and then mason up his remains in the wall. What, then, will you do? For all your coaxing, he will not budge. Bribes he leaves under your own paperweight on your table; in short, it is quite plain that he prefers to cling to you.

Then something severe, something unusual must be done. What! surely you will not have him collared by a constable, and commit his innocent pallor to the common jail? And upon what ground could you procure such a thing to be done?—a vagrant, is he? What! he a vagrant, a wanderer, who refuses to budge? It is because he will *not* be a vagrant, then, that you seek to count him *as* a vagrant. That it is too absurd. No visible means of support: there I have him. Wrong again: for indubitably he *does* support himself, and that is the only unanswerable proof that any man can show of his possessing the means so to do. No more, then. Since he will not quit me, I must quit him. I will change my offices; I will move elsewhere, and give him fair notice, that if I find him on my new premises I will then proceed against him as a common trespasser.

Acting accordingly, next day I thus addressed him: "I find these chambers too far from the City Hall; the air is unwholesome. In a word, I propose to remove my offices next week, and shall no longer require your services. I tell you this now, in order that you may seek another place."

He made no reply; and nothing more was said.

On the appointed day I engaged carts and men, proceeded to my chambers, and, having but little furniture, everything was removed in a few hours. Throughout, the scrivener remained standing behind the screen, which I directed to be removed the last thing. It was withdrawn; and, being folded up like a huge folio, left him the motionless occupant of a naked room. I stood in the entry watching him a moment, while something from within me upbraided me.

I reentered, with my hand in my pocket—and—and my heart in my mouth.

"Good-bye, Bartleby; I am going—good-bye, and God some way bless you; and take that," slipping something in his hand. But it dropped upon the floor, and then—strange to say—I tore myself from him whom I had so longed to be rid of.

Established in my new quarters, for a day or two I kept the door locked, and started at every footfall in the passages. When I returned to my rooms, after any little absence, I would pause at the threshold for an instant, and attentively listen, ere applying my key. But these fears were needless. Bartleby never came nigh me.

I thought all was going well, when a perturbed-looking stranger visited me, inquiring whether I was the person who had recently occupied rooms at No. — Wall Street.

Full of forebodings, I replied that I was.

"Then, sir," said the stranger, who proved a lawyer, "you are responsible for the man you left there. He refuses to do any copying; he refuses to do anything; he says he prefers not to; and he refuses to quit the premises."

"I am very sorry, sir," said I, with assumed tranquillity, but an inward tremor, "but, really, the man you allude to is nothing to me—he is no relation or apprentice of mine, that you should hold me responsible for him."

"In mercy's name, who is he?"

"I certainly cannot inform you. I know nothing about him. Formerly I employed him as a copyist; but he has done nothing for me now for some time past."

"I shall settle him, then—good morning, sir."

Several days passed, and I heard nothing more; and, though I often felt a charitable prompting to call at the place and see poor Bartleby, yet a certain squeamishness, of I know not what, withheld me.

All is over with him, by this time, thought I, at last, when, through another week, no further intelligence reached me. But, coming to my room the day after, I found several persons waiting at my door in a high state of nervous excitement.

"That's the man—here he comes," cried the foremost one, whom I recognized as the lawyer who had previously called upon me alone.

"You must take him away, sir, at once," cried a portly person among them, advancing upon me, and whom I knew to be the landlord of No. — Wall Street. "These gentlemen, my tenants, cannot stand it any longer; Mr. B—," pointing to the lawyer, "has turned him out of his room, and he now persists in haunting the building generally, sitting upon the banisters of the stairs by day, and sleeping in the entry by night. Everybody is concerned; clients are leaving the offices; some fears are entertained of a mob; something you must do, and that without delay."

Aghast at this torrent, I fell back before it, and would fain have locked myself in my new quarters. In vain I persisted that Bartleby was nothing to me—no more than to anyone else. In vain—I was the last person known to have anything to do with him, and they held me to the terrible account. Fearful, then, of being exposed in the papers (as one person present obscurely threatened), I considered the matter, and, at length, said, that if the lawyer would give me a confidential interview with the scrivener, in his (the lawyer's) own room, I would, that afternoon, strive my best to rid them of the nuisance they complained of.

Going upstairs to my old haunt, there was Bartleby silently sitting upon the banister at the landing.

"What are you doing here, Bartleby?" said I.

"Sitting upon the banister," he mildly replied.

I motioned him into the lawyer's room, who then left us.

"Bartleby," said I, "are you aware that you are the cause of great tribulation to me, by persisting in occupying the entry after being dismissed from the office?"

No answer.

"Now one of two things must take place. Either you must do something, or something must be done to you. Now what sort of business would you like to engage in? Would you like to reengage in copying for some one?"

"No; I would prefer not to make any change."

"Would you like a clerkship in a dry-goods store?"

"There is too much confinement about that. No, I would not like a clerkship; but I am not particular."

"Too much confinement," I cried, "why you keep yourself confined all the time!"

"I would prefer not to take a clerkship," he rejoined, as if to settle that little item at once.

"How would a bartender's business suit you? There is no trying of the eyesight in that."

"I would not like it at all; though, as I said before, I am not particular."

His unwonted wordiness inspirited me. I returned to the charge.

"Well, then, would you like to travel through the country collecting bills for the merchants? That would improve your health."

"No, I would prefer to be doing something else."

"How, then, would going as a companion to Europe, to entertain some young gentleman with your conversation—how would that suit you?"

"Not at all. It does not strike me that there is anything definite about that. I like to be stationary. But I am not particular."

"Stationary you shall be, then," I cried, now losing all patience, and, for the first time in all my exasperating connection with him, fairly flying into a passion. "If you do not go away from these premises before night, I shall feel bound—indeed, I *am* bound—to—to—to quit the premises myself!" I rather absurdly concluded, knowing not with what possible threat to try to frighten his immobility into compliance. Despairing of all further efforts, I was precipitately leaving him, when a final thought occurred to me—one which had not been wholly unindulged before.

"Bartleby," said I, in the kindest tone I could assume under such exciting circumstances, "will you go home with me now—not to my office, but my dwelling—and remain there till we can conclude upon some convenient arrangement for you at our leisure? Come, let us start now, right away."

"No: at present I would prefer not to make any change at all."

I answered nothing; but, effectually dodging everyone by the suddenness and rapidity of my flight, rushed from the building, ran up Wall Street toward Broadway, and, jumping into the first omnibus, was soon removed from pursuit. As soon as tranquility returned, I distinctly perceived that I had now done all that I possibly could, both in respect to the demands of the landlord and his tenants, and with regard to my own desire and sense of duty, to benefit Bartleby, and shield him from rude persecution. I now strove to be entirely carefree and quiescent; and my conscience justified me in the attempt; though, indeed, it was not so successful as I could have wished. So fearful was I of being again hunted out by the incensed landlord and his exasperated tenants, that, surrendering my business to Nippers for a few days, I drove about the upper part of the town and through the suburbs, in my rockaway; crossed over to Jersey City and Hoboken, and paid fugitive visits to Manhattanville and Astoria. In fact, I almost lived in my rockaway for the time.

When again I entered my office, lo, a note from the landlord lay upon the desk. I opened it with trembling hands. It informed me that the writer had sent to the police, and had Bartleby removed to the Tombs as a vagrant. Moreover, since I knew more about him than anyone else, he wished me to appear at that place, and make a suitable statement of the facts. These tidings had a conflicting effect upon me. At first I was indignant; but, at last, almost approved. The landlord's energetic, summary disposition had led him to adopt a procedure which I do not think I would have decided upon myself; and yet, as a last resort, under such peculiar circumstances, it seemed the only plan.

As I afterward learned, the poor scrivener, when told that he must be conducted to the Tombs, offered not the slightest obstacle, but, in his pale, unmoving way, silently acquiesced.

Some of the compassionate and curious bystanders joined the party; and headed by one of the constables arm-in-arm with Bartleby, the silent procession filed its way through all the noise, and heat, and joy of the roaring thoroughfares at noon.

The same day I received the note, I went to the Tombs, or, to speak more properly, the Halls of Justice. Seeking the right officer, I stated the purpose of my call, and was informed that the individual I described was, indeed, within. I then assured the functionary that Bartleby was a perfectly honest man, and greatly to be compassionated, however unaccountably eccentric. I narrated all I knew, and closed by suggesting the idea of letting him remain in as indulgent confinement as possible, till something less harsh might be done—though, indeed, I hardly knew what. At all events, if nothing else could be decided upon, the almshouse must receive him. I then begged to have an interview.

Being under no disgraceful charge, and quite serene and harmless in all his ways, they had permitted him freely to wander about the prison, and, especially, in the enclosed grass-platted yards thereof. And so I found him there, standing all alone in the quietest of the yards, his face toward a high wall, while all around, from the narrow slits of the jail windows, I thought I saw peering out upon him the eyes of murderers and thieves.

"Bartleby!"

"I know you," he said, without looking round—"and I want nothing to say to you."

"It was not I that brought you here, Bartleby," said I, keenly pained at his implied suspicion. "And to you, this should not be so vile a place. Nothing reproachful attaches to you by being here. And see, it is not so sad a place as one might think. Look, there is the sky, and here is the grass."

"I know where I am," he replied, but would say nothing more, and so I left him.

As I entered the corridor again, a broad meatlike man, in an apron, accosted me, and, jerking his thumb over his shoulder, said—"Is that your friend?"

"Yes."

"Does he want to starve? If he does, let him live on the prison fare, that's all."

"Who are you?" asked I, not knowing what to make of such an unofficially speaking person in such a place.

"I am the grub man. Such gentlemen as have friends here, hire me to provide them with something good to eat."

"Is this so?" said I, turning to the turnkey.

He said it was.

"Well, then," said I, slipping some silver into the grub man's hands (for so they called him), "I want you to give particular attention to my friend there; let him have the best dinner you can get. And you must be as polite to him as possible."

"Introduce me, will you?" said the grub man, looking at me with an expression which seemed to say he was all impatience for an opportunity to give a specimen of his breeding.

Thinking it would prove of benefit to the scrivener, I acquiesced; and, asking the grub man his name, went up with him to Bartleby.

"Bartleby, this is a friend; you will find him very useful to you."

"Your sarvant, sir, your sarvant," said the grub man, making a low salutation behind his apron. "Hope you find it pleasant here, sir; nice grounds—cool apartments—hope you'll stay with us sometime—try to make it agreeable. What will you have for dinner today?"

"I prefer not to dine today," said Bartleby, turning away. "It would disagree with me; I am unused to dinners." So saying, he slowly moved to the other side of the enclosure, and took up a position fronting the dead wall.

"How's this?" said the grub man, addressing me with a stare of astonishment. "He's odd, ain't he?"

"I think he is a little deranged," said I, sadly.

"Deranged? Deranged, is it? Well, now, upon my word, I thought that friend of yourn was a gentleman forger; they are always pale and genteel-like, them forgers. I can't help pity 'em—can't help it, sir. Did you know Monroe Edwards?" he added, touchingly, and paused. Then, laying his hand piteously on my shoulder, sighed, "he died of consumption at Sing Sing. So you weren't acquainted with Monroe?"

"No, I was never socially acquainted with any forgers. But I cannot stop longer. Look to my friend yonder. You will not lose by it. I will see you again."

Some few days after this, I again obtained admission to the Tombs, and went through the corridors in quest of Bartleby; but without finding him.

"I saw him coming from his cell not long ago," said a turnkey, "maybe he's gone to loiter in the yards."

So I went in that direction.

"Are you looking for the silent man?" said another turnkey, passing me. "Yonder he lies—sleeping in the yard there. 'Tis not twenty minutes since I saw him lie down."

The yard was entirely quiet. It was not accessible to the common prisoners. The surrounding walls, of amazing thickness, kept off all sounds behind them. The Egyptian character of the masonry weighed upon me with its gloom. But a soft imprisoned turf grew underfoot. The heart of the eternal pyramids, it seemed, wherein, by some strange magic, through the clefts, grass seed, dropped by birds, had sprung.

Strangely huddled at the base of the wall, his knees drawn up, and lying on his side, his head touching the cold stones, I saw the wasted Bartleby. But nothing stirred. I paused; then went close up to him; stooped over, and saw that his dim eyes were open; otherwise he seemed profoundly sleeping. Something prompted me to touch him. I felt his hand, when a tingling shiver ran up my arm and down my spine to my feet.

The round face of the grub man peered upon me now. "His dinner is ready. Won't he dine today, either? Or does he live without dining?"

"Lives without dining," said I, and closed the eyes.

"Eh!—He's asleep, ain't he?"

"With kings and counselors," [1] murmured I.

There would seem little need for proceeding further in this history. Imagination will readily supply the meager recital of poor Bartleby's interment. But, ere parting with the reader, let me say, that if this little narrative has sufficiently interested him, to awaken curiosity as to who Bartleby was, and what manner of life he led prior to the present narrator's making his acquaintance, I can only reply, that in such curiosity I fully share, but am wholly unable to gratify it. Yet here I hardly know whether I should divulge one little item of rumor, which came to my ear a few months after the scrivener's decease. Upon what basis it rested, I could never ascertain; and hence, how true it is I cannot now tell. But, inasmuch as this vague report has not been without a certain suggestive interest to me, however sad, it may prove the same with some others; and so I will briefly mention it. The report was this: that Bartleby had been a subordinate clerk in the Dead Letter Office at Washington, from which he had been suddenly removed by a change in the administration. When I think over this rumor, hardly can I express the emotions which seize me. Dead letters! Does it not sound like dead men? Conceive a man by nature and misfortune prone to a pallid hopelessness, can any business seem more fitted to heighten it than that of continually handling these dead letters, and assorting them for the flames? For by the cartload they are annually burned. Sometimes from out the folded paper the pale clerk takes a ring—the finger it was meant for, perhaps, molders in the grave; a bank note sent in swiftest charity—he whom it would relieve, nor eats nor hungers any more; pardon for those who died despairing; hope for those who died unhoping; good tidings for those who died, stifled by unrelieved calamities. On errands of life, these letters speed to death.

Ah, Bartleby! Ah, humanity!

---

[1] The allusion is to Job 3:13–14.

The Pupil

HENRY JAMES

[1843–1916]

I

The poor young man hesitated and procrastinated: it cost him such an effort to broach the subject of terms, to speak of money to a person who spoke only of feelings and, as it were, of the aristocracy. Yet he was unwilling to take leave, treating his engagement as settled, without some more conventional glance in that direction than he could find an opening for in the manner of the large affable lady who sat there drawing a pair of soiled *gants de Suède* through a fat jewelled hand and, at once pressing and gliding, repeated over and over everything but the thing he would have liked to hear. He would have liked to hear the figure of his salary; but just as he was nervously about to sound that note the little boy came back—the little boy Mrs. Moreen had sent out of the room to fetch her fan. He came back without the fan, only with the casual observation that he couldn't find it. As he dropped this cynical confession he looked straight and hard at the candidate for the honor of taking his education in hand. This personage reflected somewhat grimly that the first thing he should have to teach his little charge would be to appear to address himself to his mother when he spoke to her—especially not to make her such an improper answer as that.

When Mrs. Moreen bethought herself of this pretext for getting rid of their companion, Pemberton supposed it was precisely to approach the delicate subject of his remuneration. But it had been only to say some things about her son that it was better a boy of eleven shouldn't catch. They were extravagantly to his advantage save when she lowered her voice to sigh, tapping her left side familiarly, "And all overclouded by *this,* you know; all at the mercy of a weakness—!" Pemberton gathered that the weakness was in the region of the heart. He had known the poor child was not robust: this was the basis on which he had been invited to treat, through an English lady, an Oxford acquaintance, then at Nice, who happened to know both his needs and those of the amiable American family looking out for something really superior in the way of a resident tutor.

The young man's impression of his prospective pupil, who had come into the room as if to see for himself the moment Pemberton was admitted, was not quite the soft solicitation the visitor had taken for granted. Morgan Moreen was somehow sickly without being "delicate," and that he looked intelligent—it is true Pemberton wouldn't have enjoyed his being stupid—only added to the suggestion that, as with his big mouth and big ears he really couldn't be called pretty, he might too utterly fail to please. Pemberton was modest, was even timid; and the chance that his small scholar would prove cleverer than himself had quite figured, to his anxiety, among the dangers of an untried experiment. He reflected, however, that these were risks one had to run when one accepted a position, as it was called, in a private family; when as yet one's university honors had, pecuniarily speaking, remained barren. At any rate when Mrs. Moreen got up as to intimate that, since it was understood he would enter upon his duties within the week she would let him off now, he succeeded, in spite of the presence of the child, in squeezing out a phrase about the rate of payment. It was not the fault of the conscious smile which seemed a reference to the lady's expensive identity, it was not the fault of this demonstration, which had, in a sort, both vagueness and point, if the allusion didn't sound rather vulgar. This was exactly because she became still more gracious to reply: "Oh I can assure you that all that will be quite regular."

Pemberton only wondered, while he took up his hat, what "all that" was to amount to—people had such different ideas. Mrs. Moreen's words, however, seemed to commit the family to a pledge definite enough to elicit from the child a strange little comment in the shape of the mocking foreign ejaculation "Oh la-la!"

Pemberton, in some confusion, glanced at him as he walked slowly to the window with his back turned, his hands in his pockets and the air in his elderly shoulders of a boy who didn't play. The young man wondered if he should be able to teach him to play, though his mother had said it would never do and that this was why school was impossible. Mrs. Moreen exhibited no discomfiture; she only continued blandly: "Mr. Moreen will be delighted to meet your wishes. As I told you, he has been called to London for a week. As soon as he comes back you shall have it out with him."

This was so frank and friendly that the young man could only reply, laughing as his hostess laughed: "Oh I don't imagine we shall have much of a battle."

"They'll give you anything you like," the boy remarked unexpectedly, returning from the window. "We don't mind what anything costs—we live awfully well."

"My darling, you're too quaint!" his mother exclaimed, putting out to caress him a practiced but ineffectual hand. He slipped out of it, but looked with intelligent innocent eyes at Pemberton, who had already had time to notice that from one moment to the other his small satiric face seemed to change its time of life. At this moment it was infantine, yet it appeared also to be under the influence of curious intuitions and knowledges. Pemberton rather disliked precocity and was disappointed to find gleams of it in a disciple not yet in his teens. Nevertheless he divined on the spot that Morgan wouldn't prove a bore. He would prove on the contrary a source of agitation. This idea held the young man, in spite of a certain repulsion.

"You pompous little person! We're not extravagant!" Mrs. Moreen gaily protested, making another unsuccesful attempt to draw the boy to her side. "You must know what to expect," she went on to Pemberton.

"The less you expect the better!" her companion interposed. "But we *are* people of fashion."

"Only so far as *you* make us so!" Mrs. Moreen tenderly mocked. "Well then, on Friday—don't tell me you're superstitious—and mind you don't fail us. Then you'll see us all. I'm so sorry the girls are out. I guess you'll like the girls. And, you know, I've another son, quite different from this one."

"He tries to imitate me," Morgan said to their friend.

"He tries? Why he's twenty years old!" cried Mrs. Moreen.

"You're very witty," Pemberton remarked to the child—a proposition his mother echoed with enthusiasm, declaring Morgan's sallies to be the delight of the house.

The boy paid no heed to this; he only inquired abruptly of the visitor, who was surprised afterwards that he hadn't struck him as offensively forward: "Do you *want* very much to come?"

"Can you doubt it after such a description of what I shall hear?" Pemberton replied. Yet he didn't want to come at all; he was coming because he had to go somewhere, thanks to the collapse of his fortune at the end of a year abroad spent on the system of putting his scant patrimony into a single full wave of experience. He had had his full wave but couldn't pay the score at his inn. Moreover he had caught in the boy's eyes the glimpse of a far-off appeal.

"Well, I'll do the best I can for you," said Morgan; with which he turned away again. He passed out of one of the long windows; Pemberton saw him go and lean on the parapet of the terrace. He remained there while the young man took leave of his mother, who, on Pemberton's looking as if he expected a farewell from him, interposed with: "Leave him, leave him; he's so strange!" Pemberton supposed her to fear something he might say. "He's a genius—you'll love him," she added. "He's much the most interesting person in the family." And before he could invent some civility to oppose to this she wound up with: "But we're all good, you know!"

"He's a genius—you'll love him!" were words that recurred to our aspirant before the Friday, suggesting among many things that geniuses were not invariably lovable. However, it was all the better if there was an element that would make tutorship absorbing: he had perhaps taken too much for granted it would only disgust him. As he left the villa after his interview he looked up at the balcony and saw the child leaning over it. "We shall have great larks!" he called up.

Morgan hung fire a moment and then gaily returned: "By the time you come back I shall have thought of something witty!"

This made Pemberton say to himself, "After all he's rather nice."

II

On the Friday he saw them all, as Mrs. Moreen had promised, for her husband had come back and the girls and the other son were at home. Mr.

Moreen had a white mustache, a confiding manner and, in his buttonhole, the ribbon of a foreign order—bestowed, as Pemberton eventually learned, for services. For what services he never clearly ascertained: this was a point—one of a larger number—that Mr. Moreen's manner never confided. What it emphatically did confide was that he was even more a man of the world than you might first make out. Ulick, the first-born, was in visible training for the same profession—under the disadvantage as yet, however, of a buttonhole but feebly floral and a mustache with no pretensions to type. The girls had hair and figures and manners and small fat feet, but had never been out alone. As for Mrs. Moreen, Pemberton saw on a nearer view that her elegance was intermittent and her parts didn't always match. Her husband, as she had promised, met with enthusiasm Pemberton's ideas in regard to a salary. The young man had endeavored to keep these stammerings modest, and Mr. Moreen made it no secret that *he* found them wanting in "style." He further mentioned that he aspired to be intimate with his children, to be their best friend, and that he was always looking out for them. That was what he went off for, to London and other places—to look out; and this vigilance was the theory of life, as well as the real occupation, of the whole family. They all looked out, for they were very frank on the subject of its being necessary. They desired it to be understood that they were earnest people, and also that their fortune, though quite adequate for earnest people, required the most careful administration. Mr. Moreen, as the parent bird, sought sustenance for the nest. Ulick invoked support mainly at the club, where Pemberton guessed that it was usually served on green cloth. The girls used to do up their hair and their frocks themselves, and our young man felt appealed to to be glad, in regard to Morgan's education, that, though it must naturally be of the best, it didn't cost too much. After a little he *was* glad, forgetting at times his own needs in the interest inspired by the child's character and culture and the pleasure of making easy terms for him.

During the first weeks of their acquaintance Morgan had been as puzzling as a page in an unknown language—altogether different from the obvious little Anglo-Saxons who had misrepresented childhood to Pemberton. Indeed the whole mystic volume in which the boy had been amateurishly bound demanded some practice in translation. Today, after a considerable interval, there is something phantasmagoric, like a prismatic reflection or a serial novel, in Pemberton's memory of the queerness of the Moreens. If it were not for a few tangible tokens—a lock of Morgan's hair cut by his own hand, and the half dozen letters received from him when they were disjoined—the whole episode and the figures peopling it would seem too inconsequent for anything but dreamland. Their supreme quaintness was their success—as it appeared to him for a while at the time; since he had never seen a family so brilliantly equipped for failure. Wasn't it success to have kept him so hatefully long? Wasn't it success to have drawn him in that first morning at *déjeuner,* the Friday he came—it was enough to *make* one superstitious—so that he utterly committed himself, and this not by calculation or on a signal, but from a happy instinct which made them, like a band of gypsies, work so neatly together? They amused him as much as if they had really been a band of gypsies. He was still young and had not seen much of the world—his English years had been properly arid; therefore the reversed conventions of the Moreens—for they had *their* desperate properties—struck him as topsy-turvy. He had encountered nothing like them at Oxford; still less had any such note been struck to his younger American ear during the four years at Yale in which he had richly supposed himself to be reacting against a Puritan strain. The reaction of the Moreens, at any rate, went ever so much further. He had thought himself very sharp that first day in hitting them all off in his mind with the "cosmopolite" label. Later it seemed feeble and colorless—confessedly, helplessly provisional.

He yet, when he first applied it, felt a glow of joy—for an instructor he was still empirical—rise from the apprehension that living with them would really be to see life. Their sociable strangeness was an imitation of that—their chatter of tongues, their gaiety and good humor, their infinite dawdling (they were always getting themselves up, but it took forever, and Pemberton had once found Mr. Moreen shaving in the drawing room), their French, their Italian, and, cropping up in the foreign fluencies, their cold tough slices of American. They lived on macaroni and coffee—they had these articles prepared in perfection—but they knew recipes for a hundred other dishes. They overflowed with music and song, were always humming and catching each other up, and had a sort of professional acquaintance with continental cities. They talked of "good places" as if they had been pickpockets or strolling players. They had at Nice a villa, a carriage, a piano, and a banjo, and they went to official parties. They were a perfect calendar of the "days" of their friends, which Pemberton knew them, when they were indisposed, to get out of bed to go to, and which made the week larger than life when Mrs. Moreen talked of them with Paula and Amy. Their initiations gave their new inmate at first an almost dazzling sense of culture. Mrs. Moreen had translated something at some former period—an author whom it made Pemberton feel *borné* [1] never to have heard of. They could imitate Venetian and sing Neapolitan, and when they wanted to say something very particular communicated with each other in an ingenious dialect of their own, an elastic spoken cipher which Pemberton at first took for some *patois* of one of their countries, but which he "caught on to" as he would not have grasped provincial development of Spanish or German.

"It's the family language—Ultramoreen," Morgan explained to him drolly enough; but the boy rarely condescended to use it himself, though he dealt in colloquial Latin as if he had been a little prelate.

Among all the "days" with which Mrs. Moreen's memory was taxed she managed to squeeze in one of her own, which her friends sometimes forgot.

[1] *borné:* limited.

But the house drew a frequented air from the number of fine people who were freely named there and from several mysterious men with foreign titles and English clothes whom Morgan called the Princes and who, on sofas with the girls, talked French very loud—though sometimes with some oddity of accent —as if to show they were saying nothing improper. Pemberton wondered how the Princes could ever propose in that tone and so publicly: he took for granted cynically that this was what was desired of them. Then he recognized that even for the chance of such an advantage Mrs. Moreen would never allow Paula and Amy to receive alone. These young ladies were not at all timid, but it was just the safeguards that made them so candidly free. It was a houseful of Bohemians who wanted tremendously to be Philistines.

In one respect, however, certainly, they achieved no rigor—they were wonderfully amiable and ecstatic about Morgan. It was a genuine tenderness, an artless admiration, equally strong in each. They even praised his beauty, which was small, and were as afraid of him as if they felt him of finer clay. They spoke of him as a little angel and a prodigy—they touched on his want of health with long, vague faces. Pemberton feared at first an extravagance that might make him hate the boy, but before this happened he had become extravagant himself. Later, when he had grown rather to hate the others, it was a bribe to patience for him that they were at any rate nice about Morgan, going on tiptoe if they fancied he was showing symptoms, and even giving up somebody's "day" to procure him a pleasure. Mixed with this too was the oddest wish to make him independent, as if they had felt themselves not good enough for him. They passed him over to the new members of their circle very much as if wishing to force some charity of adoption on so free an agent and get rid of their own charge. They were delighted when they saw Morgan take so to his kind playfellow, and could think of no higher praise for the young man. It was strange how they contrived to reconcile the appearance, and indeed the essential fact, of adoring the child with their eagerness to wash their hands of him. Did they want to get rid of him before he should find them out? Pemberton was finding them out month by month. The boy's fond family, however this might be, turned their backs with exaggerated delicacy, as if to avoid the reproach of interfering. Seeing in time how little he had in common with them—it was by *them* he first observed it; they proclaimed it with complete humility—his companion was moved to speculate on the mysteries of transmission, the far jumps of heredity. Where his detachment from most of the things they represented had come from was more than an observer could say—it certainly had burrowed under two or three generations.

As for Pemberton's own estimate of his pupil, it was a good while before he got the point of view, so little had he been prepared for it by the smug young barbarians to whom the tradition of tutorship, as hitherto revealed to him, had been adjusted. Morgan was scrappy and surprising, deficient in many properties supposed common to the *genus* and abounding in others that were the portion only of the supernaturally clever. One day his friend made a great stride: it cleared up the question to perceive that Morgan *was* supernaturally clever and that, though the formula was temporarily meager, this would be the only assumption on which one could successfully deal with him. He had the general quality of a child for whom life had not been simplified by school, a kind of homebred sensibility which might have been bad for himself but was charming for others, and a whole range of refinement and perception—little musical vibrations as taking as picked-up airs—begotten by wandering about Europe at the tail of his migratory tribe. This might not have been an education to recommend in advance, but its results with so special a subject were as appreciable as the marks on a piece of fine porcelain. There was at the same time in him a small strain of stoicism, doubtless the fruit of having had to begin early to bear pain, which counted for pluck and made it of less consequence that he might have been thought at school rather a polyglot little beast. Pemberton indeed quickly found himself rejoicing that school was out of the question: in any million of boys it was probably good for all but one, and Morgan was that millionth. It would have made him comparative and superior—it might have made him really require kicking. Pemberton would try to be school himself—a bigger seminary than five hundred grazing donkeys, so that, winning no prizes, the boy would remain unconscious and irresponsible and amusing—amusing, because, though life was already intense in his childish nature, freshness still made there a strong draught for jokes. It turned out that even in the still air of Morgan's various disabilities jokes flourished greatly. He was a pale lean acute undeveloped little cosmopolite, who liked intellectual gymnastics and who also, as regards the behavior of mankind, had noticed more things than you might suppose, but who nevertheless had his proper playroom of superstitions, where he smashed a dozen toys a day.

III

At Nice once, toward evening, as the pair rested in the open air after a walk, and looked over the sea at the pink western lights, he said suddenly to his comrade: "Do you like it, you know—being with us all in this intimate way?"

"My dear fellow, why should I stay if I didn't?"

"How do I know you'll stay? I'm almost sure you won't, very long."

"I hope you don't mean to dismiss me," said Pemberton.

Morgan debated, looking at the sunset. "I think if I did right I ought to."

"Well, I know I'm supposed to instruct you in virtue; but in that case don't do right."

"You're very young—fortunately," Morgan went on, turning to him again.

"Oh yes, compared with you!"

"Therefore it won't matter so much if you do lose a lot of time."

"That's the way to look at it," said Pemberton accommodatingly.

They were silent a minute; after which the boy asked: "Do you like my father and my mother very much?"

"Dear me, yes. Charming people."

Morgan received this with another silence; then unexpectedly, familiarly, but at the same time affectionately, he remarked: "You're a jolly old humbug!"

For a particular reason the words made our young man change color. The boy noticed in an instant that he had turned red, whereupon he turned red himself and pupil and master exchanged a longish glance in which there was a consciousness of many more things than are usually touched upon, even tacitly, in such a relation. It produced for Pemberton an embarrassment; it raised in a shadowy form a question—this was the first glimpse of it—destined to play a singular and, as he imagined, owing to the altogether peculiar conditions, an unprecedented part in his intercourse with his little companion. Later, when he found himself talking with the youngster in a way in which few youngsters could ever have been talked with, he thought of that clumsy moment on the bench at Nice as the dawn of an understanding that had broadened. What had added to the clumsiness then was that he thought it his duty to declare to Morgan that he might abuse him, Pemberton, as much as he liked, but must never abuse his parents. To this Morgan had the easy retort that he hadn't dreamed of abusing them; which appeared to be true: it put Pemberton in the wrong.

"Then why am I a humbug for saying *I* think them charming?" the young man asked, conscious of a certain rashness.

"Well—they're not your parents."

"They love you better than anything in the world—never forget that," said Pemberton.

"Is that why you like them so much?"

"They're very kind to me," Pemberton replied evasively.

"You *are* a humbug!" laughed Morgan, passing an arm into his tutor's. He leaned against him looking off at the sea again and swinging his long thin legs.

"Don't kick my shins," said Pemberton while he reflected. "Hang it, I can't complain of them to the child!"

"There's another reason too," Morgan went on, keeping his legs still.

"Another reason for what?"

"Besides their not being your parents."

"I don't understand you," said Pemberton.

"Well, you will before long. All right!"

He did understand fully before long, but he made a fight even with himself before he confessed it. He thought it the oddest thing to have a struggle with the child about. He wondered he didn't hate the hope of the Moreens for bringing the struggle on. But by the time it began, any such sentiment for that scion was closed to him. Morgan was a special case, and to know him was to accept him on his own odd terms. Pemberton had spent his aversion to special cases before arriving at knowledge. When at last he did arrive, his quandary was great. Against every interest he had attached himself. They would have to meet things together. Before they went home that evening at Nice the boy had said, clinging to his arm:

"Well, at any rate you'll hang on to the last."

"To the last?"

"Till you're fairly beaten."

"*You* ought to be fairly beaten!" cried the young man, drawing him closer.

IV

A year after he had come to live with them, Mr. and Mrs. Moreen suddenly gave up the villa at Nice. Pemberton had got used to suddenness, having seen it practiced on a considerable scale during two jerky little tours—one in Switzerland the first summer, and the other late in the winter, when they all ran down to Florence and then, at the end of ten days, liking it much less than they had intended, straggled back in mysterious depression. They had returned to Nice "forever," as they said; but this didn't prevent their squeezing, one rainy muggy May night, into a second-class railway carriage—you could never tell by which class they would travel—where Pemberton helped them to stow away a wonderful collection of bundles and bags. The explanation of the maneuver was that they had determined to spend the summer "in some bracing place"; but in Paris they dropped into a small furnished apartment— a fourth floor in a third-rate avenue, where there was a smell on the staircase and the *portier* was hateful—and passed the next four months in blank indigence.

The better part of this baffled sojourn was for the preceptor and his pupil, who, visiting the Invalides and Notre Dame, the Conciergerie and all the museums, took a hundred remunerative rambles. They learned to know their Paris, which was useful, for they came back another year for a longer stay, the general character of which in Pemberton's memory today mixes pitiably and confusedly with that of the first. He sees Morgan's shabby knickerbockers —the everlasting pair that didn't match his blouse and that as he grew longer could only grow faded. He remembers the particular holes in his three or four pair of colored stockings.

Morgan was dear to his mother, but he never was better dressed than was absolutely necessary—partly, no doubt, by his own fault, for he was as indifferent to his appearance as a German philosopher. "My dear fellow, you *are* coming to pieces," Pemberton would say to him in skeptical remonstrance; to which the child would reply, looking at him serenely up and down: "My dear fellow, so are you! I don't want to cast you in the shade." Pemberton could have no rejoinder for this—the assertion so closely represented the fact. If however the deficiencies of his own wardrobe were a chapter by themselves he didn't like his little charge to look too poor. Later he used to say "Well, if we're poor, why, after all, shouldn't we look it?" and he consoled himself with thinking there was something rather elderly and gentlemanly in Morgan's disrepair—it differed from the untidiness of the urchin who plays and spoils his things. He could trace perfectly the degrees by which, in proportion as her little son confined himself to his tutor for society, Mrs. Moreen shrewdly forbore to renew his garments. She did nothing that didn't show, neglected him because he escaped notice, and then, as he illustrated this clever policy, discouraged at home his public appearances. Her position was logical enough—those members of her family who did show had to be showy.

During this period and several others Pemberton was quite aware of how he and his comrade might strike people; wandering languidly through the Jardin des Plantes as if they had nowhere to go, sitting on the winter days in the galleries of the Louvre, so splendidly ironical to the homeless, as if for the advantage of the *calorifère*.[1] They joked about it sometimes: it was the sort of joke that was perfectly within the boy's compass. They figured themselves as part of the vast vague hand-to-mouth multitude of the enormous city and pretended they were proud of their position in it—it showed them "such a lot of life" and made them conscious of a democratic brotherhood. If Pemberton couldn't feel a sympathy in destitution with his small companion—for after all Morgan's fond parents would never have let him really suffer—the boy would at least feel it with him, so it came to the same thing. He used sometimes to wonder what people would think they were—to fancy they were looked askance at, as if it might be a suspected case of kidnapping. Morgan wouldn't be taken for a young patrician with a preceptor—he wasn't smart enough; though he might pass for his companion's sickly little brother. Now and then he had a five-franc piece, and except once, when they bought a couple of lovely neckties, one of which he made Pemberton accept, they laid it out scientifically in old books. This was sure to be a great day, always spent on the quays, in a rummage of the dusty boxes that garnish the parapets. Such occasions helped them to live, for their books ran low very soon after the beginning of their acquaintance. Pemberton had a good many in England, but he was obliged to write to a friend and ask him kindly to get some fellow to give him something for them.

If they had to relinquish that summer the advantage of the bracing climate, the young man couldn't but suspect this failure of the cup when at their very lips to have been the effect of a rude jostle of his own. This had represented his first blowout, as he called it, with his patrons; his first successful attempt —though there was little other success about it—to bring them to a consideration of his impossible position. As the ostensible eve of a costly journey the moment had struck him as favorable to an earnest protest, the presentation of an ultimatum. Ridiculous as it sounded, he had never yet been able to com-

[1] *calorifère:* stove.

pass an uninterrupted private interview with the elder pair or with either of them singly. They were always flanked by their elder children, and poor Pemberton usually had his own little charge at his side. He was conscious of its being a house in which the surface of one's delicacy got rather smudged; nevertheless he had preserved the bloom of his scruple against announcing to Mr. and Mrs. Moreen with publicity that he shouldn't be able to go on longer without a little money. He was still simple enough to suppose Ulick and Paula and Amy might not know that since his arrival he had only had a hundred and forty francs; and he was magnanimous enough to wish not to compromise their parents in their eyes. Mr. Moreen now listened to him, as he listened to everyone and to everything, like a man of the world, and seemed to appeal to him—though not of course too grossly—to try and be a little more of one himself. Pemberton recognized in fact the importance of the character—from the advantage it gave Mr. Moreen. He was not even confused or embarrassed, whereas the young man in his service was more so than there was any reason for. Neither was he surprised—at least any more than a gentleman had to be who freely confessed himself a little shocked—though not perhaps strictly at Pemberton.

"We must go into this, mustn't we, dear?" he said to his wife. He assured his young friend that the matter should have his very best attention; and he melted into space as elusively as if, at the door, he were taking an inevitable but deprecatory precedence. When, the next moment, Pemberton found himself alone with Mrs. Moreen it was to hear her say "I see, I see"—stroking the roundness of her chin and looking as if she were only hesitating between a dozen easy remedies. If they didn't make their push Mr. Moreen could at least disappear for several days. During his absence his wife took up the subject again spontaneously, but her contribution to it was merely that she had thought all the while they were getting on so beautifully. Pemberton's reply to this revelation was that unless they immediately put down something on account he would leave them on the spot and forever. He knew she would wonder how he would get away, and for a moment expected her to inquire. She didn't for which he was almost grateful to her, so little was he in a position to tell.

"You won't, you _know_ you won't—you're too interested," she said. "You _are_ interested, you know you are, you dear kind man!" She laughed with almost condemnatory archness, as if it were a reproach—though she wouldn't insist; and flirted a soiled pocket handkerchief at him.

Pemberton's mind was fully made up to take his step the following week. This would give him time to get an answer to a letter he had dispatched to England. If he did in the event nothing of the sort—that is if he stayed another year and then went away only for three months—it was not merely because, before the answer to his letter came (most unsatisfactory when it did arrive), Mr. Moreen generously counted out to him, and again with the sacrifice to "form" of a marked man of the world, three hundred francs in elegant ringing gold. He was irritated to find that Mrs. Moreen was right, that he couldn't at the pinch bear to leave the child. This stood out clearer for the very reason that, the night of his desperate appeal to his patrons, he had seen fully for the first time where he was. Wasn't it another proof of the success with which those patrons practiced their arts that they had managed to avert for so long the illuminating flash? It descended on our friend with a breadth of effect which perhaps would have struck a spectator as comical, after he had returned to his little servile room, which looked into a close court where a bare dirty opposite wall took, with the sound of shrill clatter, the reflection of lighted back windows. He had simply given himself away to a band of adventurers. The idea, the word itself, wore a romantic horror for him—he had always lived on such safe lines. Later it assumed a more interesting, almost a soothing, sense: it pointed a moral, and Pemberton could enjoy a moral. The Moreens were adventurers not merely because they didn't pay their debts, because they lived on society, but because their whole view of life, dim and confused and instinctive, like that of clever color-blind animals, was speculative and rapacious and mean. Oh they were "respectable," and that only made them more *immondes!* [1] The young man's analysis, while he brooded, put it at last very simply—they were adventurers because they were toadies and snobs. That was the completest account of them—it was the law of their being. Even when this truth became vivid to their ingenious inmate he remained unconscious of how much his mind had been prepared for it by the extraordinary little boy who had now become such a complication in his life. Much less could he then calculate on the information he was still to owe the extraordinary little boy.

V

But it was during the ensuing time that the real problem came up—the problem of how far it was excusable to discuss the turpitude of parents with a child of twelve, of thirteen, of fourteen. Absolutely inexcusable and quite impossible it of course at first appeared; and indeed the question didn't press for some time after Pemberton had received his three hundred francs. They produced a temporary lull, a relief from the sharpest pressure. The young man frugally amended his wardrobe and even had a few francs in his pocket. He thought the Moreens looked at him as if he were almost too smart, as if they ought to take care not to spoil him. If Mr. Moreen hadn't been such a man of the world he would perhaps have spoken of the freedom of such neckties on the part of a subordinate. But Mr. Moreen was always enough a man of the world to let things pass—he had certainly shown that. It was singular how Pemberton guessed that Morgan, though saying nothing about it, knew something had happened. But three hundred francs, especially when one owed money, couldn't last forever; and when the treasure was gone—the boy knew

[1] *immondes:* unclean.

when it had failed—Morgan did break ground. The party had returned to Nice at the beginning of the winter, but not to the charming villa. They went to a hotel, where they stayed three months, and then moved to another establishment, explaining that they had left the first because, after waiting and waiting, they couldn't get the rooms they wanted. These apartments, the rooms they wanted, were generally very splendid; but fortunately they never *could* get them—fortunately, I mean, for Pemberton, who reflected always that if they had got them there would have been a still scanter educational fund. What Morgan said at last was said suddenly, irrelevantly, when the moment came, in the middle of a lesson, and consisted of the apparently unfeeling words: "You ought to *filer,* you know—you really ought."

Pemberton stared. He had learnt enough French slang from Morgan to know that to *filer* meant to cut sticks. "Ah my dear fellow, don't turn me off!"

Morgan pulled a Greek lexicon toward him—he used a Greek-German—to look out a word, instead of asking it of Pemberton. "You can't go on like this, you know."

"Like what, my boy?"

"You know they don't pay you up," said Morgan, blushing and turning his leaves.

"Don't pay me?" Pemberton stared again and feigned amazement. "What on earth put that into your head?"

"It has been there a long time," the boy replied rummaging his book.

Pemberton was silent, then he went on: "I say, what are you hunting for? They pay me beautifully."

"I'm hunting for the Greek for awful whopper," Morgan dropped.

"Find that rather for gross impertinence and disabuse your mind. What do I want of money?"

"Oh that's another question!"

Pemberton wavered—he was drawn in different ways. The severely correct thing would have been to tell the boy that such a matter was none of his business and bid him go on with his lines. But they were really too intimate for that; it was not the way he was in the habit of treating him; there had been no reason it should be. On the other hand Morgan had quite lighted on the truth—he really shouldn't be able to keep it up much longer; therefore why not let him know one's real motive for forsaking him? At the same time it wasn't decent to abuse to one's pupil the family of one's pupil; it was better to misrepresent than to do that. So in reply to his comrade's last exclamation he just declared, to dismiss the subject, that he had received several payments.

"I say—I say!" the boy ejaculated, laughing.

"That's all right," Pemberton insisted. "Give me your written rendering."

Morgan pushed a copybook across the table, and he began to read the page, but with something running in his head that made it no sense. Looking up after a minute or two he found the child's eyes fixed on him and felt in them something strange. Then Morgan said: "I'm not afraid of the stern reality."

"I haven't yet seen the thing you *are* afraid of—I'll do you that justice!"

This came out with a jump—it was perfectly true—and evidently gave Morgan pleasure. "I've thought of it a long time," he presently resumed.

"Well, don't think of it any more."

The boy appeared to comply, and they had a comfortable and even an amusing hour. They had a theory that they were very thorough, and yet they seemed always to be in the amusing part of lessons, the intervals between the dull dark tunnels, where there were waysides and jolly views. Yet the morning was brought to a violent end by Morgan's suddenly leaning his arms on the table, burying his head in them and bursting into tears: at which Pemberton was the more startled that, as it then came over him, it was the first time he had ever seen the boy cry and that the impression was consequently quite awful.

The next day, after much thought, he took a decision and, believing it to be just, immediately acted on it. He cornered Mr. and Mrs. Moreen again and let them know that if on the spot they didn't pay him all they owed him he wouldn't only leave their house but would tell Morgan exactly what had brought him to it.

"Oh you *haven't* told him?" cried Mrs. Moreen with a pacifying hand on her well-dressed bosom.

"Without warning you? For what do you take me?" the young man returned.

Mr. and Mrs. Moreen looked at each other; he could see that they appreciated, as tending to their security, his superstition of delicacy, and yet that there was a certain alarm in their relief. "My dear fellow," Mr. Moreen demanded, "what use *can* you have, leading the quiet life we all do, for such a lot of money?"—a question to which Pemberton made no answer, occupied as he was in noting that what passed in the mind of his patrons was something like: "Oh then, if we've felt that the child, dear little angel, has judged us and how he regards us, and we haven't been betrayed, he must have guessed—and in short it's *general!*" an inference that rather stirred up Mr. and Mrs. Moreen, as Pemberton had desired it should. At the same time, if he had supposed his threat would do something toward bringing them round, he was disappointed to find them taking for granted—how vulgar their perception *had* been!—that he had already given them away. There was a mystic uneasiness in their parental breasts, and that had been the inferior sense of it. None the less, however, his threat did touch them; for if they had escaped it was only to meet a new danger. Mr. Moreen appealed to him, on every precedent, as a man of the world; but his wife had recourse, for the first time since his domestication with them, to a fine *hauteur,* reminding him that a devoted mother, with her child, had arts that protected her against gross misrepresentation.

"I should misrepresent you grossly if I accused you of common honesty!" our friend replied; but as he closed the door behind him sharply, thinking he had not done himself much good, while Mr. Moreen lighted another cigarette, he heard his hostess shout after him more touchingly:

"Oh you do, you *do,* put the knife to one's throat!"

The next morning, very early, she came to his room. He recognised her knock, but had no hope she brought him money; as to which he was wrong, for she had fifty francs in her hand. She squeezed forward in her dressing gown, and he received her in his own, between his bathtub and his bed. He had been tolerably schooled by this time to the "foreign ways" of his hosts. Mrs. Moreen was ardent, and when she was ardent she didn't care what she did; so she now sat down on his bed, his clothes being on the chairs, and, in her preoccupation, forgot, as she glanced round, to be ashamed of giving him such a horrid room. What Mrs. Moreen's ardor now bore upon was the design of persuading him that in the first place she was very good-natured to bring him fifty francs, and that in the second, if he would only see it, he was really too absurd to expect to be *paid.* Wasn't he paid enough without perpetual money—wasn't he paid by the comfortable luxurious home he enjoyed with them all, without a care, an anxiety, a solitary want? Wasn't he sure of his position, and wasn't that everything to a young man like him, quite unknown, with singularly little to show, the ground of whose exorbitant pretensions it had never been easy to discover? Wasn't he paid above all by the sweet relation he had established with Morgan—quite ideal as from master to pupil —and by the simple privilege of knowing and living with so amazingly gifted a child; than whom really (and she meant literally what she said) there was no better company in Europe? Mrs. Moreen herself took to appealing to him as a man of the world; she said *"Voyons, mon cher,"* [1] and "My dear man, look here now"; and urged him to be reasonable, putting it before him that it was truly a chance for him. She spoke as if, according as he *should* be reasonable, he would prove himself worthy to be her son's tutor and of the extraordinary confidence they had placed in him.

After all, Pemberton reflected, it was only a difference of theory and the theory didn't matter much. They had hitherto gone on that of remunerated, as now they would go on that of gratuitous, service; but why should they have so many words about it? Mrs. Moreen at all events continued to be convincing; sitting there with her fifty francs she talked and reiterated as women reiterate, and bored and irritated him, while he leaned against the wall with his hands in the pockets of his wrapper, drawing it together round his legs and looking over the head of his visitor at the gray negations of his window. She wound up with saying: "You see I bring you a definite proposal."

"A definite proposal?"

"To make our relations regular, as it were—to put them on a comfortable footing."

[1] *Voyons, mon cher.* Come, my dear.

"I see—it's a system," said Pemberton. "A kind of organized blackmail."

Mrs. Moreen bounded up, which was exactly what he wanted. "What do you mean by that?"

"You practice on one's fears—one's fears about the child if one should go away."

"And pray what would happen to him in that event?" she demanded with majesty.

"Why he'd be alone with *you*."

"And pray with whom *should* a child be but with those whom he loves most?"

"If you think that, why don't you dismiss me?"

"Do you pretend he loves you more than he loves *us*?" cried Mrs. Moreen.

"I think he ought to. I make sacrifices for him. Though I've heard of those *you* make I don't see them."

Mrs. Moreen stared a moment; then with emotion she grasped her inmate's hand. *"Will* you make it—the sacrifice?"

He burst out laughing. "I'll see. I'll do what I can. I'll stay a little longer. Your calculation's just—I *do* hate intensely to give him up; I'm fond of him and he thoroughly interests me, in spite of the inconvenience I suffer. You know my situation perfectly. I haven't a penny in the world and, occupied as you see me with Morgan, am unable to earn money."

Mrs. Moreen tapped her undressed arm with her folded bank note. "Can't you write articles? Can't you translate as *I* do?"

"I don't know about translating; it's wretchedly paid."

"I'm glad to earn what I can," said Mrs. Moreen with prodigious virtue.

"You ought to tell me who you do it for." Pemberton paused a moment, and she said nothing; so he added: "I've tried to turn off some little sketches, but the magazines won't have them—they're declined with thanks."

"You see then you're not such a phoenix," his visitor pointedly smiled— "to pretend to abilities you're sacrificing for our sake."

"I haven't time to do things properly," he ruefully went on. Then as it came over him that he was almost abjectly good-natured to give these explanations he added: "If I stay on longer it must be on one condition—that Morgan shall know distinctly on what footing I am."

Mrs. Moreen demurred. "Surely you don't want to show off to a child?"

"To show *you* off, do you mean?"

Again she cast about, but this time it was to produce a still finer flower. "And *you* talk of blackmail!"

"You can easily prevent it," said Pemberton.

"And *you* talk of practicing on fears!" she bravely pushed on.

"Yes, there's no doubt I'm a great scoundrel."

His patroness met his eyes—it was clear she was in straits. Then she thrust out her money at him. "Mr. Moreen desired me to give you this on account."

"I'm much obliged to Mr. Moreen, but we *have* no account."

"You won't take it?"

"That leaves me more free," said Pemberton.

"To poison my darling's mind?" groaned Mrs. Moreen.

"Oh your darling's mind—!" the young man laughed.

She fixed him a moment, and he thought she was going to break out tormentedly, pleadingly: "For God's sake, tell me what *is* in it!" But she checked this impulse—another was stronger. She pocketed the money—the crudity of the alternative was comical—and swept out of the room with the desperate concession: "You may tell him any horror you like!"

VI

A couple of days after this, during which he had failed to profit by so free a permission, he had been for a quarter of an hour walking with his charge in silence when the boy became sociable again with the remark: "I'll tell you how I know it; I know it through Zénobie."

"Zénobie? Who in the world is *she?*"

"A nurse I used to have—ever so many years ago. A charming woman. I liked her awfully, and she liked me."

"There's no accounting for tastes. What is it you know through her?"

"Why what their idea is. She went away because they didn't fork out. She did like me awfully, and she stayed two years. She told me all about it—that at last she could never get her wages. As soon as they saw how much she liked me they stopped giving her anything. They thought she'd stay for nothing—just *because,* don't you know?" And Morgan had a queer little conscious lucid look. "She did stay ever so long—as long as she could. She was only a poor girl. She used to send money to her mother. At last she couldn't afford it any longer, and went away in a fearful rage one night—I mean of course in a rage against *them.* She cried over me tremendously, she hugged me nearly to death. She told me all about it," the boy repeated. "She told me it was their idea. So I guessed, ever so long ago, that they have had the same idea with you."

"Zénobie was very sharp," said Pemberton. "And she made you so."

"Oh that wasn't Zénobie; that was nature. And experience!" Morgan laughed.

"Well, Zénobie was a part of your experience."

"Certainly I was a part of hers, poor dear!" the boy wisely sighed. "And I'm part of yours."

"A very important part. But I don't see how you know I've been treated like Zénobie."

"Do you take me for the biggest dunce you've known?" Morgan asked. "Haven't I been conscious of what we've been through together?"

"What we've been through?"

"Our privations—our dark days."

"Oh our days have been bright enough."

Morgan went on in silence for a moment. Then he said: "My dear chap, you're a hero!"

"Well, you're another!" Pemberton retorted.

"No I'm not, but I ain't a baby. I won't stand it any longer. You must get some occupation that pays. I'm ashamed, I'm ashamed!" quavered the boy with a ring of passion, like some high silver note from a small cathedral chorister, that deeply touched his friend.

"We ought to go off and live somewhere together," the young man said.

"I'll go like a shot if you'll take me."

"I'd get some work that would keep us both afloat," Pemberton continued.

"So would I. Why shouldn't *I* work? I ain't such a beastly little muff as *that* comes to."

"The difficulty is that your parents wouldn't hear of it. They'd never part with you; they worship the ground you tread on. Don't you see the proof of it?" Pemberton developed. "They don't dislike me; they wish me no harm; they're very amiable people; but they're perfectly ready to expose me to any awkwardness in life for your sake."

The silence in which Morgan received his fond sophistry struck Pemberton somehow as expressive. After a moment the child repeated: "You *are* a hero!" Then he added: "They leave me with you altogether. You've all the responsibility. They put me off on you from morning till night. Why then should they object to my taking up with you completely? I'd help you."

"They're not particularly keen about my being helped, and they delight in thinking of you as *theirs*. They're tremendously proud of you."

"I'm not proud of *them*. But you know that," Morgan returned.

"Except for the little matter we speak of they're charming people," said Pemberton, not taking up the point made for his intelligence, but wondering greatly at the boy's own, and especially at this fresh reminder of something he had been conscious of from the first—the strangest thing in his friend's large little composition, a temper, a sensibility, even a private ideal, which made him as privately disown the stuff his people were made of. Morgan had in secret a small loftiness which made him acute about betrayed meanness; as well as a critical sense for the manners immediately surrounding him that was quite without precedent in a juvenile nature, especially when one noted that it had not made this nature "old-fashioned," as the word is of children—quaint or wizened or offensive. It was as if he had been a little gentleman and had paid the penalty by discovering that he was the only such person in his family. This comparison didn't make him vain, but it could make him melancholy and a trifle austere. While Pemberton guessed at these dim young things, shadows of shadows, he was partly drawn on and partly checked, as for a scruple, by the charm of attempting to sound the little cool shallows that were so quickly growing deeper. When he tried to figure to himself the morning twilight of childhood, so as to deal with it safely, he saw it was never fixed, never arrested, that ignorance, at the instant he touched it, was already flushing faintly into knowledge, that there was nothing that at a given moment you could say an intelligent child didn't know. It seemed to him that he himself knew too much to imagine Morgan's simplicity and too little to disembroil his tangle.

The boy paid no heed to his last remark; he only went on: "I'd have spoken to them about their idea, as I call it, long ago, if I hadn't been sure what they'd say."

"And what would they say?"

"Just what they said about what poor Zénobie told me—that it was a horrid dreadful story, that they had paid her every penny they owed her."

"Well, perhaps they had," said Pemberton.

"Perhaps they've paid you!"

"Let us pretend they have, and *n'en parlons plus.*" [1]

"They accused her of lying and cheating"—Morgan stuck to historic truth. "That's why I don't want to speak to them."

"Lest they should accuse me too?" To this Morgan made no answer, and his companion, looking down at him—the boy turned away his eyes, which had filled—saw that he couldn't have trusted himself to utter. "You're right. Don't worry them," Pemberton pursued. "Except for that, they *are* charming people."

"Except for *their* lying and *their* cheating?"

"I say—I say!" cried Pemberton, imitating a little tone of the lad's which was itself an imitation.

"We must be frank, at the last; we *must* come to an understanding," said Morgan with the importance of the small boy who lets himself think he is arranging great affairs—almost playing at shipwreck or at Indians. "I know all about everything."

"I dare say your father has his reasons," Pemberton replied, but too vaguely, as he was aware.

"For lying and cheating?"

"For saving and managing and turning his means to the best account. He has plenty to do with his money. You're an expensive family."

"Yes, I'm very expensive," Morgan concurred in a manner that made his preceptor burst out laughing.

"He's saving for *you*," said Pemberton. "They think of you in everything they do."

"He might, while he's about it, save a little—" The boy paused, and his friend waited to hear what. Then Morgan brought out oddly: "A little reputation."

"Oh there's plenty of that. That's all right!"

"Enough of it for the people they know, no doubt. The people they know are awful."

"Do you mean the Princes? We mustn't abuse the Princes."

[1] *n'en parlons plus:* let's speak no more of it.

"Why not? They haven't married Paula—they haven't married Amy. They only clean out Ulick."

"You *do* know everything!" Pemberton declared.

"No I don't after all. I don't know what they live on, or how they live, or *why* they live! What have they got and how did they get it? Are they rich, are they poor, or have they a *modeste aisance?* Why are they always chiveying me about—living one year like ambassadors and the next like paupers? Who are they, anyway, and what are they? I've thought of all that—I've thought of a lot of things. They're so beastly worldly. That's what I hate most—oh I've *seen* it! All they care about is to make an appearance and to pass for something or other. What the dickens do they want to pass for? What *do* they, Mr. Pemberton?"

"You pause for a reply," said Pemberton, treating the question as a joke, yet wondering too and greatly struck with his mate's intense if imperfect vision. "I haven't the least idea."

"And what good does it do? Haven't I seen the way people treat them—the 'nice' people, the ones they want to know? They'll take anything from them—they'll lie down and be trampled on. The nice ones hate that—they just sicken them. You're the only really nice person we know."

"Are you sure? They don't lie down for me!"

"Well, you shan't lie down for them. You've got to go—that's what you've got to do," said Morgan.

"And what will become of you?"

"Oh I'm growing up. I shall get off before long. I'll see you later."

"You had better let me finish you," Pemberton urged, lending himself to the child's strange superiority.

Morgan stopped in their walk, looking up at him. He had to look up much less than a couple of years before—he had grown, in his loose leanness, so long and high. "Finish me?" he echoed.

"There are such a lot of jolly things we can do together yet. I want to turn you out—I want you to do me credit."

Morgan continued to look at him. "To give you credit—do you mean?"

"My dear fellow, you're too clever to live."

"That's just what I'm afraid you think. No, no; it isn't fair—I can't endure it. We'll separate next week. The sooner it's over the sooner to sleep."

"If I hear of anything—any other chance—I promise to go," Pemberton said.

Morgan consented to consider this. "But you'll be honest," he demanded; "you won't pretend you haven't heard?"

"I'm much more likely to pretend I have."

"But what can you hear of, this way, stuck in a hole with us? You ought to be on the spot, to go to England—you ought to go to America."

"One would think you were *my* tutor!" said Pemberton.

Morgan walked on and after a little had begun again: "Well, now that you know I know and that we look at the facts and keep nothing back—it's much more comfortable, isn't it?"

"My dear boy, it's so amusing, so interesting, that it will surely be quite impossible for me to forego such hours as these."

This made Morgan stop once more. "You *do* keep something back. Oh you're not straight—*I* am!"

"How am I not straight?"

"Oh you've got your idea!"

"My idea?"

"Why that I probably shan't make old—make older—bones, and that you can stick it out till I'm removed."

"You *are* too clever to live!" Pemberton repeated.

"I call it a mean idea," Morgan pursued. "But I shall punish you by the way I hang on."

"Look out or I'll poison you!" Pemberton laughed.

"I'm stronger and better every year. Haven't you noticed that there hasn't been a doctor near me since you came?"

"*I'm* your doctor," said the young man, taking his arm and drawing him tenderly on again.

Morgan proceeded and after a few steps gave a sigh of mingled weariness and relief. "Ah now that we look at the facts it's all right!"

VII

They looked at the facts a good deal after this; and one of the first consequences of their doing so was that Pemberton stuck it out, in his friend's parlance, for the purpose. Morgan made the facts so vivid and so droll, and at the same time so bald and so ugly, that there was fascination in talking them over with him, just as there would have been heartlessness in leaving him alone with them. Now that the pair had such perceptions in common, it was useless for them to pretend they didn't judge such people; but the very judgement and the exchange of perceptions created another tie. Morgan had never been so interesting as now that he himself was made plainer by the sidelight of these confidences. What came out in it most was the small fine passion of his pride. He had plenty of that, Pemberton felt—so much that one might perhaps wisely wish for it some early bruises. He would have liked his people to have a spirit and had waked up to the sense of their perpetually eating humble pie. His mother would consume any amount, and his father would consume even more than his mother. He had a theory that Ulick had wriggled out of an "affair" at Nice: there had once been a flurry at home, a regular panic, after which they all went to bed and took medicine, not to be accounted for on any other supposition. Morgan had a romantic imagination, fed by poetry and history, and he would have liked those who "bore his name"—as he used to say to Pemberton with the humor that made his queer delicacies manly—to carry themselves with an air. But their one idea was to get in with people who didn't want them and to take snubs as if they were honorable scars. Why people didn't want them more he didn't know—that was people's own affair; after all they weren't superficially repulsive, they were a hundred times cleverer than most of the dreary grandees, the "poor swells" they rushed about Europe to catch up with. "After all they *are* amusing—they are!" he used to pronounce with the wisdom of the ages. To which Pemberton always replied: "Amusing—the great Moreen troupe? Why they're altogether delightful; and if it weren't for the hitch that you and I (feeble performers!) make in the *ensemble* they'd carry everything before them."

What the boy couldn't get over was the fact that this particular blight seemed, in a tradition of self-respect, so undeserved and so arbitrary. No doubt people had a right to take the line they liked; but why should *his* people have liked the line of pushing and toadying and lying and cheating? What had their forefathers—all decent folk, so far as he knew—done to them, or what had *he* done to them? Who had poisoned their blood with the fifth-rate social ideal, the fixed idea of making smart acquaintances and getting into the *monde chic,*[1] especially when it was foredoomed to failure and exposure? They showed so what they were after; that was what made the people they wanted not want *them*. And never a wince for dignity, never a throb of shame at looking each other in the face, never any independence or resentment or disgust. If his father or his brother would only knock some one down once or twice a year! Clever as they were they never guessed the impression they made. They were good-natured, yes—as good-natured as Jews at the doors of clothing shops! But was that the model one wanted one's family to follow? Morgan had dim memories of an old grandfather, the maternal, in New York, whom he had been taken across the ocean at the age of five to see: a gentleman with a high neckcloth and a good deal of pronunciation, who wore a dress coat in the morning, which made one wonder what he wore in the evening, and had, or was supposed to have, "property," and something to do with the Bible Society. It couldn't have been but that *he* was a good type. Pemberton himself remembered Mrs. Clancy, a widowed sister of Mr. Moreen's, who was as irritating as a moral tale and had paid a fortnight's visit to the family at Nice shortly after he came to live with them. She was "pure and refined," as Amy said over the banjo, and had the air of not knowing what they meant when they talked, and of keeping something rather important back. Pemberton judged that what she kept back was an approval of many of their ways; therefore it was to be supposed that she too was of a good type, and that Mr. and Mrs. Moreen and Ulick and Paula and Amy might easily have been of a better one if they would.

But that they wouldn't was more and more perceptible from day to day. They continued to "chivey," as Morgan called it, and in due time became aware of a variety of reasons for proceeding to Venice. They mentioned a

[1] *monde chic:* stylish world.

great many of them—they were always strikingly frank and had the brightest friendly chatter, at the late foreign breakfast in especial, before the ladies had made up their faces, when they leaned their arms on the table, had something to follow the *demi-tasse,* and, in the heat of familiar discussion as to what they "really ought" to do, fell inevitably into the languages in which they could *tutoyer.*[1] Even Pemberton liked them then; he could endure even Ulick when he heard him give his little flat voice for the "sweet sea-city." That was what made him have a sneaking kindness for them—that they were so out of the workaday world and kept him so out of it. The summer had waned when, with cries of ecstasy, they all passed out on the balcony that overhung the Grand Canal. The sunsets then were splendid and the Dorringtons had arrived. The Dorringtons were the only reason they hadn't talked of at breakfast; but the reasons they didn't talk of at breakfast always came out in the end. The Dorringtons on the other hand came out very little; or else when they did they stayed—as was natural—for hours, during which periods Mrs. Moreen and the girls sometimes called at their hotel (to see if they had returned) as many as three times running. The gondola was for the ladies, as in Venice too there were "days," which Mrs. Moreen knew in their order an hour after she arrived. She immediately took one herself, to which the Dorringtons never came, though on a certain occasion when Pemberton and his pupil were together at Saint Mark's—where, taking the best walks they had ever had and haunting a hundred churches, they spent a great deal of time—they saw the old lord turn up with Mr. Moreen and Ulick, who showed him the dim basilica as if it belonged to them. Pemberton noted how much less, among its curiosities, Lord Dorrington carried himself as a man of the world; wondering too whether, for such services, his companions took a fee from him. The autumn at any rate waned, the Dorringtons departed, and Lord Verschoyle, the eldest son, had proposed neither for Amy nor for Paula.

One sad November day, while the wind roared round the old palace and the rain lashed the lagoon, Pemberton, for exercise and even somewhat for warmth—the Moreens were horribly frugal about fires; it was a cause of suffering to their inmate—walked up and down the big bare *sala* with his pupil. The scagliola floor was cold, the high, battered casements shook in the storm, and the stately decay of the place was unrelieved by a particle of furniture. Pemberton's spirits were low, and it came over him that the fortune of the Moreens was now even lower. A blast of desolation, a portent of disgrace and disaster, seemed to draw through the comfortless hall. Mr. Moreen and Ulick were in the Piazza, looking out for something, strolling drearily, in mackintoshes, under the arcades; but still, in spite of mackintoshes, unmistakable men of the world. Paula and Amy were in bed—it might have been thought they were staying there to keep warm. Pemberton looked askance at the boy at his side, to see to what extent he was conscious of these

[1] *tutoyer:* address one another in an informal, familiar manner.

dark omens. But Morgan, luckily for him, was now mainly conscious of growing taller and stronger and indeed of being in his fifteenth year. This fact was intensely interesting to him and the basis of a private theory—which, however, he had imparted to his tutor—that in a little while he should stand on his own feet. He considered that the situation would change—that in short he should be "finished," grown up, producible in the world of affairs and ready to prove himself of sterling ability. Sharply as he was capable at times of analyzing, as he called it, his life, there were happy hours when he remained, as he also called it—and as the name, really, of their right ideal— "jolly" superficial; the proof of which was his fundamental assumption that he should presently go to Oxford, to Pemberton's college, and aided and abetted by Pemberton, do the most wonderful things. It depressed the young man to see how little in such a project he took account of ways and means: in other connections he mostly kept to the measure. Pemberton tried to imagine the Moreens at Oxford and fortunately failed; yet unless they were to adopt it as a residence there would be no *modus vivendi* [1] for Morgan. How could he live without an allowance, and where was the allowance to come from? He, Pemberton, might live on Morgan; but how could Morgan live on *him?* What was to become of him anyhow? Somehow the fact that he was a big boy now, with better prospects of health, made the question of his future more difficult. So long as he was markedly frail, the great consideration he inspired seemed enough of an answer to it. But at the bottom of Pemberton's heart was the recognition of his probably being strong enough to live and not yet strong enough to struggle or to thrive. Morgan himself at any rate was in the first flush of the rosiest consciousness of adolescence, so that the beating of the tempest seemed to him after all but the voice of life and the challenge of fate. He had on his shabby little overcoat, with the collar up, but was enjoying his walk.

It was interrupted at last by the appearance of his mother at the end of the *sala.* She beckoned him to come to her, and while Pemberton saw him, complaisant, pass down the long vista and over the damp false marble, he wondered what was in the air. Mrs. Moreen said a word to the boy and made him go into the room she had quitted. Then, having closed the door after him, she directed her steps swiftly to Pemberton. There *was* something in the air, but his wildest flight of fancy wouldn't have suggested what it proved to be. She signified that she had made a pretext to get Morgan out of the way, and then she inquired—without hesitation—if the young man could favor her with the loan of three louis. While, before bursting into a laugh, he stared at her with surprise, she declared that she was awfully pressed for the money; she was desperate for it—it would save her life.

"Dear lady, *c'est trop fort!*" [2] Pemberton laughed in the manner and with

[1] *modus vivendi:* way of living.
[2] *c'est trop fort:* that is too much.

the borrowed grace of idiom that marked the best colloquial, the best anecdotic, moments of his friends themselves. "Where in the world do you suppose I should get three louis, *du train dont vous allez?*" [1]

"I thought you worked—wrote things. Don't they pay you?"

"Not a penny."

"Are you such a fool as to work for nothing?"

"You ought surely to know that."

Mrs. Moreen stared, then she colored a little. Pemberton saw she had quite forgotten the terms—if "terms" they could be called—that he had ended by accepting from herself; they had burdened her memory as little as her conscience. "Oh yes, I see what you mean—you've been very nice about that; but why drag it in so often?" She had been perfectly urbane with him ever since the rough scene of explanation in his room the morning he made her accept *his* "terms"—the necessity of his making his case known to Morgan. She had felt no resentment after seeing there was no danger Morgan would take the matter up with her. Indeed, attributing this immunity to the good taste of his influence with the boy, she had once said to Pemberton "My dear fellow, it's an immense comfort you're a gentleman." She repeated this in substance now. "Of course you're a gentleman—that's a bother the less!" Pemberton reminded her that he had not "dragged in" anything that wasn't already in as much as his foot was in his shoe; and she also repeated her prayer that, somewhere and somehow, he would find her sixty francs. He took the liberty of hinting that if he could find them it wouldn't be to lend them to *her*—as to which he consciously did himself injustice, knowing that if he had them he would certainly put them at her disposal. He accused himself, at bottom and not unveraciously, of a fantastic, a demoralized sympathy with her. If misery made strange bedfellows it also made strange sympathies. It was moreover a part of the abasement of living with such people that one had to make vulgar retorts, quite out of one's own tradition of good manners. "Morgan, Morgan, to what pass have I come for you?" he groaned while Mrs. Moreen floated voluminously down the *sala* again to liberate the boy, wailing as she went that everything was too odious.

Before their young friend was liberated there came a thump at the door communicating with the staircase, followed by the apparition of a dripping youth who poked in his head. Pemberton recognized him as the bearer of a telegram and recognized the telegram as addressed to himself. Morgan came back as, after glancing at the signature—that of a relative in London—he was reading the words: "Found jolly job for you, engagement to coach opulent youth on own terms. Come at once." The answer happily was paid and the messenger waited. Morgan, who had drawn near, waited too and looked hard at Pemberton; and Pemberton, after a moment, having met his look, handed him the telegram. It was really by wise looks—they knew each other so well now—that, while the telegraph boy, in his waterproof cape, made a great

---

[1] *du train dont vous allez:* from the type of place where you go.

puddle on the floor, the thing was settled between them. Pemberton wrote the answer with a pencil against the frescoed wall, and the messenger departed. When he had gone the young man explained himself.

"I'll make a tremendous charge; I'll earn a lot of money in a short time, and we'll live on it."

"Well, I hope the opulent youth will be a dismal dunce—he probably will," Morgan parenthesized—"and keep you a long time a-hammering of it in."

"Of course the longer he keeps me the more we shall have for our old age."

"But suppose *they* don't pay you!" Morgan awfully suggested.

"Oh there are not two such—!" But Pemberton pulled up; he had been on the point of using too invidious a term. Instead of this he said "Two such fatalities."

Morgan flushed—the tears came to his eyes. *"Dites toujours* [1] two such rascally crews!" Then in a different tone he added: "Happy opulent youth!"

"Not if he's a dismal dunce."

"Oh they're happier then. But you can't have everything, can you?" the boy smiled.

Pemberton held him fast, hands on his shoulders—he had never loved him so. "What will become of *you,* what will you do?" He thought of Mrs. Moreen, desperate for sixty francs.

"I shall become an *homme fait.*" And then as if he recognized all the bearings of Pemberton's allusion: "I shall get on with them better when you're not here."

"Ah don't say that—it sounds as if I set you against them!"

"You do—the sight of you. It's all right; you know what I mean. I shall be beautiful. I'll take their affairs in hand; I'll marry my sisters."

"You'll marry yourself!" joked Pemberton; as high, rather tense pleasantry would evidently be the right, or the safest, tone for their separation.

It was, however, not purely in this strain that Morgan suddenly asked: "But I say—how will you get to your jolly job? You'll have to telegraph to the opulent youth for money to come on."

Pemberton bethought himself. "They won't like that, will they?"

"Oh look out for them!"

Then Pemberton brought out his remedy. "I'll go to the American Consul; I'll borrow some money of him—just for the few days, on the strength of the telegram."

Morgan was hilarious. "Show him the telegram—then collar the money and stay!"

Pemberton entered into the joke sufficiently to reply that for Morgan he was really capable of that; but the boy, growing more serious, and to prove he hadn't meant what he said, not only hurried him off to the Consulate—since he was to start that evening, as he had wired to his friend—but made sure of

[1] *Dites toujours:* say always.

their affair by going with him. They splashed through the tortuous perfora-
tions and over the humpbacked bridges, and they passed through the Piazza,
where they saw Mr. Moreen and Ulick go into a jeweller's shop. The Consul
proved accommodating—Pemberton said it wasn't the letter, but Morgan's
grand air—and on their way back they went into Saint Mark's for a hushed
ten minutes. Later they took up and kept up the fun of it to the very end; and
it seemed to Pemberton a part of that fun that Mrs. Moreen, who was very
angry when he had announced her his intention, should charge him, grotesquely and vulgarly and in reference to the loan she had vainly endeavored
to effect, with bolting lest they should "get something out" of him. On the
other hand he had to do Mr. Moreen and Ulick the justice to recognize that
when on coming in *they* heard the cruel news they took it like perfect men of
the world.

VIII

When he got at work with the opulent youth, who was to be taken in hand
for Balliol, he found himself unable to say if this aspirant had really such poor
parts or if the appearance were only begotten of his own long association with
an intensely living little mind. From Morgan he heard half a dozen times: the
boy wrote charming young letters, a patchwork of tongues, with indulgent
postscripts in the family Volapuk [1] and, in little squares and rounds and
crannies of the text, the drollest illustrations—letters that he was divided
between the impulse to show his present charge as a vain, a wasted incentive,
and the sense of something in them that publicity would profane. The opulent
youth went up in due course and failed to pass; but it seemed to add to the
presumption that brilliancy was not expected of him all at once that his
parents, condoning the lapse, which they good-naturedly treated as little as
possible as if it were Pemberton's, should have sounded the rally again,
begged the young coach to renew the siege.

The young coach was now in a position to lend Mrs. Moreen three louis,
and he sent her a post-office order even for a larger amount. In return for his
favor he received a frantic scribbled line from her: "Implore you to come
back instantly—Morgan dreadfully ill." They were on the rebound, once
more in Paris—often as Pemberton had seen them depressed he had never
seen them crushed—and communication was therefore rapid. He wrote to the
boy to ascertain the state of his health, but awaited the answer in vain. He
accordingly, after three days, took an abrupt leave of the opulent youth and,
crossing the Channel, alighted at the small hotel, in the quarter of the Champs
Élysées, of which Mrs. Moreen had given him the address. A deep if dumb
dissatisfaction with this lady and her companions bore him company: they
couldn't be vulgarly honest, but they could live at hotels, in velvety *entresols,*
amid a smell of burnt pastilles, surrounded by the most expensive city in

[1] *Volapuk:* world speech or language (comparable to Esperanto).

Europe. When he had left them in Venice it was with an irrepressible suspicion that something was going to happen; but the only thing that could have taken place was again their masterly retreat. "How is he? Where is he?" he asked of Mrs. Moreen; but before she could speak, these questions were answered by the pressure round his neck of a pair of arms, in shrunken sleeves, which still were perfectly capable of an effusive young foreign squeeze.

"Dreadfully ill—I don't see it!" the young man cried. And then to Morgan: "Why on earth didn't you relieve me? Why didn't you answer my letter?"

Mrs. Moreen declared that when she wrote he was very bad, and Pemberton learned at the same time from the boy that he had answered every letter he had received. This led to the clear inference that Pemberton's note had been kept from him so that the game to be practiced should not be interfered with. Mrs. Moreen was prepared to see the fact exposed, as Pemberton saw the moment he faced her that she was prepared for a good many other things. She was prepared above all to maintain that she had acted from a sense of duty, that she was enchanted she had got him over, whatever they might say, and that it was useless of him to pretend he didn't know in all his bones that his place at such a time was with Morgan. He had taken the boy away from them and now had no right to abandon him. He had created for himself the gravest responsibilities and must at least abide by what he had done.

"Taken him away from you?" Pemberton exclaimed indignantly.

"Do it—do it for pity's sake; that's just what I want. I can't stand this— and such scenes. They're awful frauds—poor dears!" These words broke from Morgan, who had intermitted his embrace, in a key which made Pemberton turn quickly to him and see that he had suddenly seated himself, was breathing in great pain and was very pale.

"*Now* do you say he's not in a state, my precious pet?" shouted his mother, dropping on her knees before him with clasped hands, but touching him no more than if he had been a gilded idol. "It will pass—it's only for an instant; but don't say such dreadful things!"

"I'm all right—all right," Morgan panted to Pemberton, whom he sat looking up at with a strange smile, his hands resting on either side on the sofa.

"Now do you pretend I've been dishonest, that I've deceived?" Mrs. Moreen flashed at Pemberton as she got up.

"It isn't *he* says it, it's I!" the boy returned, apparently easier but sinking back against the wall; while his restored friend, who had sat down beside him, took his hand and bent over him.

"Darling child, one does what one can; there are so many things to consider," urged Mrs. Moreen. "It's his *place*—his only place. You see *you* think it is now."

"Take me away—take me away," Morgan went on, smiling to Pemberton with his white face.

"Where shall I take you, and how—oh *how,* my boy?" the young man stammered, thinking of the rude way in which his friends in London held that, for his convenience, with no assurance of prompt return, he had thrown them over; of the just resentment with which they would already have called in a successor, and of the scant help to finding fresh employment that resided for him in the grossness of his having failed to pass his pupil.

"Oh we'll settle that. You used to talk about it," said Morgan. "If we can only go all the rest's a detail."

"Talk about it as much as you like, but don't think you can attempt it. Mr. Moreen would never consent—it would be so *very* hand-to-mouth," Pemberton's hostess beautifully explained to him. Then to Morgan she made it clearer: "It would destroy our peace, it would break our hearts. Now that he's back it will be all the same again. You'll have your life, your work, and your freedom, and we'll all be happy as we used to be. You'll bloom and grow perfectly well, and we won't have any more silly experiments, will we? They're too absurd. It's Mr. Pemberton's place—everyone in his place. You in yours, your papa in his, me in mine—*n'est-ce pas, chéri?* We'll all forget how foolish we've been and have lovely times."

She continued to talk and to surge vaguely about the little draped stuffy salon while Pemberton sat with the boy, whose color gradually came back; and she mixed up her reasons, hinting that there were going to be changes, that the other children might scatter (who knew?—Paula had her ideas) and that then it might be fancied how much the poor old parent birds would want the little nestling. Morgan looked at Pemberton, who wouldn't let him move; and Pemberton knew exactly how he felt at hearing himself called a little nestling. He admitted that he had had one or two bad days, but he protested afresh against the wrong of his mother's having made them the ground of an appeal to poor Pemberton. Poor Pemberton could laugh now, apart from the comicality of Mrs. Moreen's mustering so much philosophy for her defense— she seemed to shake it out of her agitated petticoats, which knocked over the light gilt chairs—so little did their young companion, *marked,* unmistakably marked at the best, strike him as qualified to repudiate any advantage.

He himself was in for it at any rate. He should have Morgan on his hands again indefinitely; though indeed he saw the lad had a private theory to produce which would be intended to smooth this down. He was obliged to him for it in advance; but the suggested amendment didn't keep his heart rather from sinking, any more than it prevented him from accepting the prospect on the spot, with some confidence moreover that he should do even better if he could have a little supper. Mrs. Moreen threw out more hints about the changes that were to be looked for, but she was such a mixture of smiles and shudders—she confessed she was very nervous—that he couldn't tell if she were in high feather or only in hysterics. If the family was really at last going to pieces why shouldn't she recognize the necessity of pitching Morgan into some sort of lifeboat? This presumption was fostered by the fact that they were established in luxurious quarters in the capital of pleasure; that was exactly where they naturally *would* be established in view of going to pieces. Moreover didn't she mention that Mr. Moreen and the others were enjoying themselves at the opera with Mr. Granger, and wasn't *that* also precisely where one would look for them on the eve of a smash? Pemberton gathered that Mr. Granger was a rich vacant American—a big bill with a flourishy heading and no items; so that one of Paula's "ideas" was probably that this time she hadn't missed fire—by which straight shot indeed she would have shattered the general cohesion. And if the cohesion was to crumble what would become of poor Pemberton? He felt quite enough bound up with them to figure to his alarm as a dislodged block in the edifice.

It was Morgan who eventually asked if no supper had been ordered for him; sitting with him below, later, at the dim delayed meal, in the presence of a great deal of corded green plush, a plate of ornamental biscuit and an aloofness marked on the part of the waiter. Mrs. Moreen had explained that they had been obliged to secure a room for the visitor out of the house; and Morgan's consolation—he offered it while Pemberton reflected on the nastiness of luke-warm sauces—proved to be, largely, that this circumstance would facilitate their escape. He talked of their escape—recurring to it often afterwards—as if they were making up a "boy's book" together. But he likewise expressed his sense that there was something in the air, that the Moreens couldn't keep it up much longer. In point of fact, as Pemberton was to see, they kept it up for five or six months. All the while, however, Morgan's contention was designed to cheer him. Mr. Moreen and Ulick, whom he had met the day after his return, accepted that return like perfect men of the world. If Paula and Amy treated it even with less formality an allowance was to be made for them, inasmuch as Mr. Granger hadn't come to the opera after all. He had only placed his box at their service, with a bouquet for each of the party; there was even one apiece, embittering the thought of his profusion, for Mr. Moreen and Ulick. "They're all like that," was Morgan's comment; "at the very last, just when we think we've landed them, they're back in the deep sea!"

Morgan's comments in these days were more and more free; they even included a large recognition of the extraordinary tenderness with which he had been treated while Pemberton was away. Oh yes, they couldn't do enough to be nice to him, to show him they had him on their mind and make up for his loss. That was just what made the whole thing so sad and caused him to rejoice after all in Pemberton's return—he had to keep thinking of their affection less, had less sense of obligation. Pemberton laughed out at this last reason, and Morgan blushed and said "Well, dash it, you know what I mean." Pemberton knew perfectly what he meant; but there were a good many things that—dash it too!—it didn't make any clearer. This episode of his second sojourn in Paris stretched itself out wearily, with their resumed readings and wanderings and maunderings, their potterings on the quays, their hauntings of the museums, their occasional lingerings in the Palais Royal when the first sharp weather came on, and there was a comfort in warm emanations, before Chevet's wonderful succulent window. Morgan wanted to hear all about the opulent youth—he took an immense interest in him. Some of the details of his opulence—Pemberton could spare him none of them—evidently fed the boy's appreciation of all his friend had given up to come back to him; but in addition to the greater reciprocity established by that heroism he had always his little brooding theory, in which there was a frivolous gaiety too, that their long probation was drawing to a close. Morgan's conviction that the Moreens couldn't go on much longer kept pace with the unexpended impetus with which, from month to month, they did go on. Three weeks after Pemberton had rejoined them they went on to another hotel, a dingier one than the first; but Morgan rejoiced that his tutor had at least still not sacrificed the advantage of a room outside. He clung to the romantic utility of this when the day, or rather the night, should arrive for their escape.

For the first time, in this complicated connection, our friend felt his collar gall him. It was, as he had said to Mrs. Moreen in Venice, *trop fort*—everything was *trop fort*. He could neither really throw off his blighting burden nor find in it the benefit of a pacified conscience or of a rewarded affection. He had spent all the money accruing to him in England, and he saw his youth going and that he was getting nothing back for it. It was all very well of Morgan to count it for reparation that he should now settle on him permanently—there was an irritating flash in such a view. He saw what the boy had in his mind; the conception that as his friend had had the generosity to come back he must show his gratitude by giving him his life. But the poor friend didn't desire the gift—what could he do with Morgan's dreadful little life? Of course at the same time that Pemberton was irritated he remembered the reason, which was very honorable to Morgan and which dwelt simply in his making one so forget that he was no more than a patched urchin. If one dealt with him on a different basis one's misadventures were one's own fault. So Pemberton waited in a queer confusion of yearning and alarm for the catastrophe which was held to hang over the house of Moreen, of which he certainly at moments felt the symptoms brush his cheek and as to which he wondered much in what form it would find its liveliest effect.

Perhaps it would take the form of sudden dispersal—a frightened *sauve qui peut*,[1] a scuttling into selfish corners. Certainly they were less elastic than of yore; they were evidently looking for something they didn't find. The Dorringtons hadn't reappeared, the Princes had scattered; wasn't that the beginning of the end? Mrs. Moreen had lost her reckoning of the famous "days"; her social calendar was blurred—it had turned its face to the wall. Pemberton suspected that the great, the cruel discomfiture had been the unspeakable behavior of Mr. Granger, who seemed not to know what he wanted, or, what was much worse, wha*t they* wanted. He kept sending flowers, as if to bestrew

---

[1] *sauve qui peut:* each to save himself as he is able.

the path of his retreat, which was never the path of a return. Flowers were all very well, but—Pemberton could complete the proposition. It was now positively conspicuous that in the long run the Moreens were a social failure; so that the young man was almost grateful the run had not been short. Mr. Moreen indeed was still occasionally able to get away on business and, what was more surprising, was likewise able to get back. Ulick had no club, but you couldn't have discovered it from his appearance, which was as much as ever that of a person looking at life from the window of such an institution; therefore Pemberton was doubly surprised at an answer he once heard him make his mother in the desperate tone of a man familiar with the worst privations. Her question Pemberton had not quite caught; it appeared to be an appeal for a suggestion as to whom they might get to take Amy. "Let the Devil take her!" Ulick snapped; so that Pemberton could see that they had not only lost their amiability but had ceased to believe in themselves. He could also see that if Mrs. Moreen was trying to get people to take her children she might be regarded as closing the hatches for the storm. But Morgan would be the last she would part with.

One winter afternoon—it was a Sunday—he and the boy walked far together in the Bois de Boulogne. The evening was so splendid, the cold lemon-colored sunset so clear, the stream of carriages and pedestrians so amusing and the fascination of Paris so great, that they stayed out later than usual and became aware that they should have to hurry home to arrive in time for dinner. They hurried accordingly, arm-in-arm, good-humored and hungry, agreeing that there was nothing like Paris after all and that after everything too that had come and gone they were not yet sated with innocent pleasures. When they reached the hotel they found that, though scandalously late, they were in time for all the dinner they were likely to sit down to. Confusion reigned in the apartments of the Moreens—very shabby ones this time, but the best in the house—and before the interrupted service of the table, with objects displaced almost as if there had been a scuffle and a great wine stain from an overturned bottle, Pemberton couldn't blink the fact that there had been a scene of the last proprietary firmness. The storm had come—they were all seeking refuge. The hatches were down, Paula and Amy were invisible—they had never tried the most casual art upon Pemberton, but he felt they had enough of an eye to him not to wish to meet him as young ladies whose frocks had been confiscated—and Ulick appeared to have jumped overboard. The host and his staff, in a word, had ceased to "go on" at the pace of their guests, and the air of embarrassed detention, thanks to a pile of gaping trunks in the passage, was strangely commingled with the air of indignant withdrawal.

When Morgan took all this in—and he took it in very quickly—he colored to the roots of his hair. He had walked from his infancy among difficulties and dangers, but he had never seen a public exposure. Pemberton noticed in a second glance at him that the tears had rushed into his eyes and that they were tears of a new and untasted bitterness. He wondered an instant, for the boy's sake, whether he might successfully pretend not to understand. Not successfully, he felt, as Mr. and Mrs. Moreen, dinnerless by their extinguished hearth, rose before him in their little dishonored salon, casting about with glassy eyes for the nearest port in such a storm. They were not prostrate but were horribly white, and Mrs. Moreen had evidently been crying. Pemberton quickly learned however that her grief was not for the loss of her dinner, much as she usually enjoyed it, but the fruit of a blow that struck even deeper, as she made all haste to explain. He would see for himself, so far as that went, how the great change had come, the dreadful bolt had fallen, and how they would now all have to turn themselves about. Therefore cruel as it was to them to part with their darling she must look to him to carry a little further the influence he had so fortunately acquired with the boy—to induce his young charge to follow him into some modest retreat. They depended on him—that was the fact—to take their delightful child temporarily under his protection: it would leave Mr. Moreen and herself so much more free to give the proper attention (too little, alas! had been given) to the readjustment of their affairs.

"We trust you—we feel we *can,*" said Mrs. Moreen, slowly rubbing her plump white hands and looking with compunction hard at Morgan, whose chin, not to take liberties, her husband stroked with a tentative paternal forefinger.

"Oh yes—we feel that we *can.* We trust Mr. Pemberton fully, Morgan," Mr. Moreen pursued.

Pemberton wondered again if he might pretend not to understand; but everything good gave way to the intensity of Morgan's understanding. "Do you mean he may take me to live with him for ever and ever? cried the boy. "May take me away, away, anywhere he likes?"

"Forever and ever? *Comme vous-y-allez!*" [1] Mr. Moreen laughed indulgently. "For as long as Mr. Pemberton may be so good."

"We've struggled, we've suffered," his wife went on; "but you've made him so your own that we've already been through the worst of the sacrifice."

Morgan had turned away from his father—he stood looking at Pemberton with a light in his face. His sense of shame for their common humiliated state had dropped; the case had another side—the thing was to clutch at *that.* He had a moment of boyish joy, scarcely mitigated by the reflection that with this unexpected consecration of his hope—too sudden and too violent; the turn taken was away from a *good* boy's book—the "escape" was left on their hands. The boyish joy was there an instant, and Pemberton was almost scared at the rush of gratitude and affection that broke through his first abasement. When he stammered "My dear fellow, what do you say to *that?*" how could one not say something enthusiastic? But there was more need for courage at something else that immediately followed and that made the lad sit down quickly on the nearest chair. He had turned quite livid and had raised his

[1] *Comme vous-y-allez:* as long as you like.

hand to his left side. They were all three looking at him, but Mrs. Moreen suddenly bounded forward. "Ah his darling little heart!" she broke out; and this time, on her knees before him and without respect for the idol, she caught him ardently in her arms. "You walked him too far, you hurried him too fast!" she hurled over her shoulder at Pemberton. Her son made no protest, and the next instant, still holding him, she sprang up with her face convulsed and with the terrified cry "Help, help! he's going, he's gone!" Pemberton saw with equal horror, by Morgan's own stricken face, that he was beyond their wildest recall. He pulled him half out of his mother's hands, and for a moment, while they held him together, they looked all their dismay into each other's eyes. "He couldn't stand it with his weak organ," said Pemberton— "the shock, the whole scene, the violent emotion."

"But I thought he *wanted* to go to you!" wailed Mrs. Moreen.

"I *told* you he didn't, my dear," her husband made answer. Mr. Moreen was trembling all over and was in his way as deeply affected as his wife. But after the very first he took his bereavement as a man of the world.

FICTION: FOR STUDY AND DISCUSSION

For the preceding six stories, you should attempt to specify the particular problem of goodness each is exploring. Be careful not to oversimplify; that is, do not assume in any given story that one character is entirely good, whereas another character is entirely bad. In this connection, read again my comments on "The Leader of the People" (page 243). Notice, also, how these comments apply to "Bartleby the Scrivener." Is Bartleby entirely good and his employer, the narrator, entirely bad? Of course not—and to think so would be to miss a major point of the story: namely, the impersonality of modern business and financial society, and how this impersonality affects various human lives. As a related point, remember, too, that you should be alert for different *kinds* of goodness. Again, "The Leader of the People" is a reminder. That the grandfather's superior qualities were valuable in opening up the West does not mean that the less dramatic qualities of his son-in-law's generation are not equally "good" for a nation at a later stage in its development.

To point up what I have been suggesting, let me propose some relevant questions:

1. In "Gooseberries," what is Ivan's attitude toward goodness? his brother's? his host's?
2. What is Flaubert saying about goodness in "The Simple Heart"?
3. In what ways does "A Good Man Is Hard to Find" deal with issues about goodness which are pertinent to our modern world?
4. To what extent can you distinguish the degrees of "goodness" and "badness" of the characters in "Bartleby the Scrivener"?
5. Henry James often chose situations where superior people become naïvely involved with persons less sensitive to goodness. Do you see the extent to which this type of situation is true of "The Pupil"?

I have not yet mentioned the term "point of view" in fictional technique. You may already know that point of view refers to whether the story is told in the first person or in the third person (sometimes called the omniscient point of view). Incidentally, be on guard against "a story within the story" (as in the case of "Gooseberries," where Ivan tells a story in the first person but where the overall point of view is clearly third person). Moreover, do not limit your investigation to stories in this section: go back to earlier ones for additional examples.

Another interesting characteristic of any short story is its "structure," which simply means how it is "put together" (just as the structure of one of your compositions might consist of an opening paragraph, followed by three paragraphs, ending in a concluding paragraph). Sometimes, the main structural units of a short story are identified by the author (for example, in "A Simple Heart" or in "The Pupil") and then these units become easily recognized— much as are the chapters of a novel or the acts of a play. Whether or not structural units are so physically evident, a structure exists, and you should be able to detect its fundamental pattern.

With respect to both "point of view" and "structure," always remember that I have chosen selections for this book in terms of the interesting insights they offer on the values of Truth, Beauty, and Goodness. Therefore, I am primarily concerned, here, that in each story you see how the chosen "point of view" and the chosen "structure" reinforce an individual attitude toward goodness which the story exemplifies.

For example, "Bartleby the Scrivener" is told in the first person, presumably because Melville wished us to feel intimately related to the narrator's personality, especially to his changing attitudes toward goodness. Comparably, the story is structured to suggest by episodes and scenes the development of the narrator from a man who is uncritically certain about goodness to one who becomes sensitive to a different type and dimension of goodness.

Ulysses

ALFRED, LORD TENNYSON
[1809–1892]

"Ulysses" represents a very considerable achievement by Tennyson. It is always difficult to write about famous men—whether they are real men or mythological. The author usually ends up by either perpetuating the accepted image of, say, a George Washington or by so desperately overpersonalizing such men that their significant symbolic value becomes blurred in a too great preoccupation with their private lives. In this poem Tennyson has avoided both of these dangers, and it is valuable to see how he has done so.

Tennyson chooses to use the Roman name Ulysses for the Greek Odysseus of Homer's epic. Ulysses has had ten years of a wandering, adventuresome life since his mighty exploits in the Trojan War. Now, at last, he is back in his own kingdom, the island of Ithaca. He has surely earned the pleasures, the honors, and the serenities of old age.

But it is on Ulysses' rejection of a comfortable future that Tennyson builds his interpretation of the hero's character, an interpretation which is established at the very beginning of the poem. Reread a few of the opening lines to see for yourself how effectively they lead you to the Ulysses whom Tennyson has portrayed. Reread them, also, to see the skill with which Tennyson has met his problem: portraying Ulysses as a man of stature but also as an individual human being whose personal endowments include a driving restlessness which makes prolonged leisure an impossible goal.

It little profits that an idle king,
By this still hearth, among these barren crags,
Matched with an aged wife, I mete and dole
Unequal laws unto a savage race,
That hoard, and sleep, and feed, and know not me.   5
I cannot rest from travel; I will drink
Life to the lees. All times I have enjoyed
Greatly, have suffered greatly, both with those
That loved me, and alone; on shore, and when
Through scudding drifts the rainy Hyades   10
Vexed the dim sea. I am become a name;
For always roaming with a hungry heart
Much have I seen and known—cities of men
And manners, climates, councils, governments,
Myself not least, but honored of them all—   15
And drunk delight of battle with my peers,

Far on the ringing plains of windy Troy.
I am a part of all that I have met;
Yet all experience is an arch where through
Gleams that untraveled world, whose margin fades   20
Forever and forever when I move.
How dull it is to pause, to make an end,
To rust unburnished, not to shine in use!
As though to breathe were life! Life piled on life
Were all too little, and of one to me   25
Little remains; but every hour is saved
From that eternal silence, something more,
A bringer of new things; and vile it were
For some three suns to store and hoard myself,
And this gray spirit yearning in desire   30
To follow knowledge like a sinking star,
Beyond the utmost bound of human thought.

    This is my son, mine own Telemachus,
To whom I leave the scepter and the isle—
Well-loved of me, discerning to fulfill   35
This labor, by slow prudence to make mild
A rugged people, and through soft degrees
Subdue them to the useful and the good.
Most blameless is he, centered in the sphere
Of common duties, decent not to fail   40
In offices of tenderness, and pay
Meet adoration to my household gods,
When I am gone. He works his work, I mine.

    There lies the port; the vessel puffs her sail;
There gloom the dark, broad seas. My mariners,   45
Souls that have toiled, and wrought, and thought with me—
That ever with a frolic welcome took
The thunder and the sunshine, and opposed
Free hearts, free foreheads—you and I are old;
Old age hath yet his honor and his toil.   50
Death closes all; but something ere the end,
Some work of noble note, may yet be done,
Not unbecoming men that strove with Gods.
The lights begin to twinkle from the rocks;
The long day wanes; the slow moon climbs; the deep   55
Moans round with many voices. Come, my friends.
'Tis not too late to seek a newer world.
Push off, and sitting well in order smite

The sounding furrows; for my purpose holds
To sail beyond the sunset, and the baths   60
Of all the western stars, until I die.
It may be that the gulfs will wash us down;
It may be we shall touch the Happy Isles,
And see the great Achilles, whom we knew.
Though much is taken, much abides; and though   65
We are not now that strength which in old days
Moved earth and heaven, that which we are, we are—
One equal temper of heroic hearts,
Made weak by time and fate, but strong in will
To strive, to seek, to find, and not to yield.   70

FOR STUDY AND DISCUSSION

1. This is the first poem offered under the heading of Goodness. What is Ulysses' conception of "the good life"?
2. Ulysses has decided to leave his kingdom to his son, Telemachus. In Ulysses' opinion, what is "the good life" for Telemachus and the people he will henceforth rule?
3. Assuming a considerable age difference in the two men, what is the irony implied by their different conceptions of "the good life"?

Try Tropic

(for a sick generation)

GENEVIEVE TAGGARD

[1894–1948]

Try tropic for your balm,
Try storm,
And after storm, calm.
Try snow of heaven, heavy, soft, and slow,
Brilliant and warm.   5
Nothing will help, and nothing do much harm.

Drink iron from rare springs; follow the sun;
Go far
To get the beam of some medicinal star;

Or in your anguish run　　　　　　　　　　10
The gauntlet of all zones to an ultimate one.
Fever and chill
Punish you still,
Earth has no zone to work against your ill.

Burn in the jeweled desert with the toad.　　15
Catch lace
Of evening mist across your haunted face;
Or walk in upper air, the slanted road.
It will not lift that load;
Nor will large seas undo your subtle ill.　　20

Nothing can cure and nothing kill
What ails your eyes, what cuts your pulse in two,
And not kill you.

The Last Word

MATTHEW ARNOLD
[1822–1888]

Creep into thy narrow bed,
Creep, and let no more be said!
Vain thy onset! all stands fast;
Thou thyself must break at last.

Let the long contention cease!　　　　　5
Geese are swans, and swans are geese.
Let them have it how they will!
Thou art tired; best be still!

They out-talked thee, hissed thee, tore thee.
Better men fared thus before thee;　　　10
Fired their ringing shot and passed,
Hotly charged—and sank at last.

Charge once more, then, and be dumb!
Let the victors, when they come,
When the forts of folly fall,　　　　　15
Find thy body by the wall.

Brahma

RALPH WALDO EMERSON
[1803–1882]

If the red slayer think he slays,
   Or if the slain think he is slain,
They know not well the subtle ways
   I keep, and pass, and turn again.

Far or forgot to me is near;   5
   Shadow and sunlight are the same;
The vanished gods to me appear;
   And one to me are shame and fame.

They reckon ill who leave me out;
   When me they fly, I am the wings;   10
I am the doubter and the doubt,
   And I the hymn the Brahmin sings.

The strong gods pine for my abode,
   And pine in vain the sacred Seven;
But thou, meek lover of the good!   15
   Find me, and turn thy back on heaven.[1]

[1] "Brahma" may seem very simple to you, for its structure presents no problem and the writing is fluent. Yet these "simplicities" represent a considerable achievement, since in this poem Emerson has given poetic expression to the very core of Hinduism's religion and philosophy. Briefly, the poem reflects the conviction that Brahma transcends space and time, thereby absorbing—or negating—all earthly opposites (for example, "Shadow and sunlight are the same"). At one time Emerson considered calling this poem "Song of the Soul," no doubt having in mind its affinity to his own views. He has expressed these views in an essay called "Over-Soul," in which he says: "We see the world piece by piece, as the sun, the moon, the animal, the tree; but the whole . . . is the soul." He adds: "The soul knows only the soul; the web of events is the flowing robe in which she is clothed."

Sonnet 116

WILLIAM SHAKESPEARE
[1564–1616]

Let me not to the marriage of true minds
Admit impediments. Love is not love
Which alters when it alteration finds,
Or bends with the remover to remove—
O, no! it is an ever-fixèd mark   5
That looks on tempests and is never shaken;
It is the star to every wandering bark,
Whose worth's unknown, although his height be taken.
Love's not Time's fool, though rosy lips and cheeks
Within his bending sickle's compass come;   10
Love alters not with his brief hours and weeks,
But bears it out even to the edge of doom—
If this be error, and upon me proved,
I never writ, nor no man ever loved.

The Heavy Bear Who Goes with Me

DELMORE SCHWARTZ
[1913–1966]

"the withness of the body"—WHITEHEAD

The heavy bear who goes with me,
A manifold honey to smear his face,
Clumsy and lumbering here and there,
The central ton of every place,
The hungry beating brutish one   5
In love with candy, anger, and sleep,
Crazy factotum, dishevelling all,
Climbs the building, kicks the football,
Boxes his brother in the hate-ridden city.

Breathing at my side, that heavy animal,   10
That heavy bear who sleeps with me,
Howls in his sleep for a world of sugar,
A sweetness intimate as the water's clasp,

Howls in his sleep because the tight-rope *weird line*
Trembles and shows the darkness beneath.   15
—The strutting show-off is terrified,
Dressed in his dress-suit, bulging his pants,
Trembles to think that his quivering meat
Must finally wince to nothing at all.

That inescapable animal walks with me,   20
Has followed me since the black womb held,
Moves where I move, distorting my gesture,
A caricature, a swollen shadow,
A stupid clown of the spirit's motive,
Perplexes and affronts with his own darkness,   25
The secret life of belly and bone,
Opaque, too near, my private, yet unknown,
Stretches to embrace the very dear
With whom I would walk without him near,
Touches her grossly, although a word   30
Would bare my heart and make me clear,
Stumbles, flounders, and strives to be fed
Dragging me with him in his mouthing care.
Amid the hundred million of his kind,
The scrimmage of appetite everywhere.   35

My Father Moved Through Dooms of Love

E. E. C U M M I N G S
[1894–1962]

my father moved through dooms of love
through sames of am through haves of give,
singing each morning out of each night
my father moved through depths of height

this motionless forgetful where   5
turned at his glance to shining here;
that if(so timid air is firm)
under his eyes would stir and squirm

newly as from unburied which
floats the first who,his april touch   10
drove sleeping selves to swarm their fates
woke dreamers to their ghostly roots

and should some why completely weep
my father's fingers brought her sleep:
vainly no smallest voice might cry   15
for he could feel the mountains grow.

Lifting the valleys of the sea
my father moved through griefs of joy;
praising a forehead called the moon
singing desire into begin   20

joy was his song and joy so pure
a heart of star by him could steer
and pure so now and now so yes
the wrists of twilight would rejoice

keen as midsummer's keen beyond   25
conceiving mind of sun will stand,
so strictly(over utmost him
so hugely)stood my father's dream

his flesh was flesh his blood was blood:
no hungry man but wished him food;   30
no cripple wouldn't creep one mile
uphill to only see him smile.

Scorning the pomp of must and shall
my father moved through dooms of feel;
his anger was as right as rain   35
his pity was as green as grain

septembering arms of year extend
less humbly wealth to foe and friend
than he to foolish and to wise
offered immeasurable is   40

proudly and(by octobering flame
beckoned)as earth will downward climb,
so naked for immortal work
his shoulders marched against the dark

his sorrow was as true as bread: 45
no liar looked him in the head;
if every friend became his foe
he'd laugh and build a world with snow.

My father moved through theys of we,
singing each new leaf out of each tree   50
(and every child was sure that spring
danced when she heard my father sing)

then let men kill which cannot share,
let blood and flesh be mud and mire,
scheming imagine,passion willed,   55
freedom a drug that's bought and sold

giving to steal and cruel kind,
a heart to fear, to doubt a mind,
to differ a disease of same,
conform the pinnacle of am   60

though dull were all we taste as bright,
bitter all utterly things sweet,
maggoty minus and dumb death
all we inherit,all bequeath

and nothing quite so least as truth   65
—i say though hate were why men breathe—
because my father lived his soul
love is the whole and more than all [1]

---

[1] The unconventionality of Cummings's verse commonly disturbs those who read his poems for the first time. In his experiments, I feel that Cummings sometimes fails because he too severely breaks the line of communication between himself and the inquiring reader. I have no such reservations about this poem. Its language, its rhythms, and its structural development subtly reinforce one another to evoke the insight and warmth with which Cummings recalls his father. You should attempt to specify these particular contributions to the poem's effectiveness. You might find an analogy helpful: for example, in what ways does a skillfully executed candid photograph of a loved one often "catch" the individuality of that person in a manner which a posed photograph does not?

Channel Firing

THOMAS HARDY
[1840–1928]

That night your great guns, unawares,
Shook all our coffins as we lay,
And broke the chancel window-squares,
We thought it was the Judgment Day

And sat upright. While drearisome   5
Arose the howl of wakened hounds:
The mouse let fall the altar crumb,
The worms drew back into the mounds,

The glebe ¹ cow drooled. Till God called, "No;
It's gunnery practice out at sea   10
Just as before you went below;
The world is as it used to be:

"All nations striving strong to make
Red war yet redder. Mad as hatters
They do no more for Christes sake   15
Than you who are helpless in such matters.

"That this is not the judgment hour
For some of them's a blessed thing,
For if it were they'd have to scour
Hell's floor for so much threatening . . .   20

"Ha, ha. It will be warmer when
I blow the trumpet (if indeed
I ever do; for you are men,
And rest eternal sorely need)."

So down we lay again. "I wonder,   25
Will the world ever saner be,"
Said one, "than when He sent us under
In our indifferent century!"

And many a skeleton shook his head.
"Instead of preaching forty year,"   30
My neighbor Parson Thirdly said,
"I wish I had stuck to pipes and beer."

¹ *glebe:* church.

Again the guns disturbed the hour,
Roaring their readiness to avenge,
As far inland as Stourton Tower,   35
And Camelot, and starlit Stonehenge.[1]

Two Look at Two

ROBERT FROST

[1875–1963]

Love and forgetting might have carried them
A little further up the mountain side
With night so near, but not much further up.
They must have halted soon in any case
With thoughts of the path back, how rough it was   5
With rock and washout, and unsafe in darkness;
When they were halted by a tumbled wall
With barbed-wire binding. They stood facing this,
Spending what onward impulse they still had
In one last look the way they must not go,   10
On up the failing path, where, if a stone
Or earthslide moved at night, it moved itself;
No footstep moved it. "This is all," they sighed,
"Good-night to woods." But not so; there was more.
A doe from round a spruce stood looking at them   15
Across the wall, as near the wall as they.
She saw them in their field, they her in hers.
The difficulty of seeing what stood still,
Like some up-ended boulder split in two,

---

[1] "Channel Firing" is a demanding poem. Hardy wrote some lovely lyrics, but in this poem he does not attempt to be mellifluous. Training for war has long since lost its romantic appeal. The guns roar again; the skeletons in the graveyard are pictured as awakened from their "rest eternal" by man's suicidal preparations for yet another war. I have indicated the *situation* of the poem, and I have implied Hardy's attitude toward this situation. To unravel the complexities of "Channel Firing" further, I ask you the following questions:

1. Who "speaks" the poem? Why is this point significant?
2. What is the relevance of Parson Thirdly's reflection about his life as a clergyman?
3. In *Areopagitica*, Milton wrote that "Good and evil . . . grow up together almost inseparably. . . ." How is this observation pertinent to "Channel Firing," especially to God's colloquially phrased comments?

Was in her clouded eyes: they saw no fear there.   20
She seemed to think that two thus they were safe.
Then, as if they were something that, though strange,
She could not trouble her mind with too long,
She sighed and passed unscared along the wall.
"This, then, is all. What more is there to ask?"   25
But no, not yet. A snort to bid them wait.
A buck from round the spruce stood looking at them
Across the wall, as near the wall as they.
This was an antlered buck of lusty nostril,
Not the same doe come back into her place.   30
He viewed them quizzically with jerks of head,
As if to ask, "Why don't you make some motion?
Or give some sign of life? Because you can't.
I doubt if you're as living as you look."
Thus till he had them almost feeling dared   35
To stretch a proffering hand—and a spell-breaking.
Then he too passed unscared along the wall.
Two had seen two, whichever side you spoke from.
"This *must* be all." It was all. Still they stood,
A great wave from it going over them,   40
As if the earth in one unlooked-for favor
Had made them certain earth returned their love.

Rest from Loving and Be Living

C. DAY LEWIS

[BORN 1904]

Rest from loving and be living.
Fallen is fallen past retrieving
The unique flyer dawn's dove
Arrowing down feathered with fire.

Cease denying, begin knowing.   5
Comes peace this way, here comes renewing
With dower of bird and bud, knocks
Loud on winter wall on death's door.

Here's no meaning but of morning.
Naught soon of night but stars remaining,   10
Sink lower, fade, as dark womb
Recedes creation will step clear.[1]

Blindman's Buff

PETER VIERECK

[BORN 1916]

Night watchmen think of dawn and things auroral.
Clerks wistful for Bermudas think of coral.
The poet in New York still thinks of laurel.
(But lovers think of death and touch each other
As if to prove that love is still alive.)   5

The Martian space crew, in an Earthward dive,
Think of their sweet unearthly earth Up There,
Where darling monsters romp in airless air.
(Two lovers think of death and touch each other,
Fearing that day when only one's alive.)   10

[1] You should appreciate Lewis's great technical virtuosity—for example, his variation on "true" rhyming, his unconventional sentence structures, his arbitrary punctuation—but these details should not distract you from the contemporary relevance of Lewis's advice: "Rest from loving and be living." By the way, I find that as an unconscious tribute to Lewis's verbal skill students commonly slide over the apparent paradox in the first line. Is not *loving* also *living?* Then why does Lewis say rest from loving when the whole insistence of his poem is on "activist" living? What kinds of love might be described negatively as being restful?

We think of cash, but cash does not arrive.
We think of fun, but fate will not connive.
We never mention death. Do we survive?
(The lovers think of death and touch each other
To live their love while love is yet alive.)   15

Prize winners are so avid when they strive;
They race so far; they pile their toys so high.
Only a cad would trip them. Yet they die.
(The lovers think of death and touch each other;
Of all who live, these are the most alive.)   20

When all the lemming-realists contrive
To swim—where to?—in life's enticing tide,
Only a fool would stop and wait outside.
(The lovers stop and wait and touch each other
Who twinly think of death are twice alive.)   25

Plump creatures smack their lips and think they thrive;
The hibernating bear, but half alive,
Dreams of free honey in a stingless hive.
He thinks of life at every lifeless breath.
(The lovers think of death.) [1]   30

---

[1] Sometimes titles of poems have very little significance, but at other times they are highly indicative. If the allusion in Viereck's title is unfamiliar to you, look up the phrase in any good dictionary. A knowledge of its meaning is expected by Viereck in his sophisticated application of the phrase to adult situations.

Karma [1]

EDWIN ARLINGTON ROBINSON
[1869–1935]

Christmas was in the air and all was well
With him, but for a few confusing flaws
In divers of God's images. Because
A friend of his would neither buy nor sell,
Was he to answer for the ax that fell?   5
He pondered; and the reason for it was,
Partly, a slowly freezing Santa Claus
Upon the corner, with his beard and bell.

Acknowledging an improvident surprise,
He magnified a fancy that he wished   10
The friend whom he had wrecked were here again.
Not sure of that, he found a compromise;
And from the fullness of his heart he fished
A dime for Jesus who had died for man.

The Wisdom of the World

SIEGFRIED SASSOON
[1886–1967]

The wisdom of the world is this: to say, *"There is*
No other wisdom but to gulp what time can give" . . .
To guard no inward vision winged with mysteries;
To hear no voices haunt the hurrying hours we live;
To keep no faith with ghostly friends; never to know
Vigils of sorrow crowned when loveless passions fade . . .
From wisdom such as this to find my gloom I go,
Companioned by those powers who keep me unafraid.

---

[1] *Karma:* basically associated with Buddhistic and Hinduistic religious convictions, the word has become a loose synonym for *fate.*

As a Plane Tree by the Water

ROBERT LOWELL

[BORN 1917]

Darkness has called to darkness, and disgrace
Elbows about our windows in this planned
Babel of Boston where our money talks
And multiplies the darkness of a land
Of preparation where the Virgin walks   5
And roses spiral her enameled face
Or fall to splinters on unwatered streets.
Our Lady of Babylon, go by, go by,
I was once the apple of your eye;
Flies, flies are on the plane tree, on the streets.   10

The flies, the flies, the flies of Babylon
Buzz in my eardrums while the devil's long
Dirge of the people detonates the hour
For floating cities where his golden tongue
Enchants the masons of the Babel Tower   15
To raise tomorrow's city to the sun
That never sets upon these hell-fire streets
Of Boston, where the sunlight is a sword
Striking at the withholder of the Lord:
Flies, flies are on the plane tree, on the streets.   20

Flies strike the miraculous waters of the iced
Atlantic and the eyes of Bernadette
Who saw Our Lady standing in the cave
At Massabielle, saw her so squarely that
Her vision put out reason's eyes. The grave   25
Is open-mouthed and swallowed up in Christ.
O walls of Jericho! And all the streets
To our Atlantic wall are singing: "Sing,
Sing for the resurrection of the King."
Flies, flies are on the plane tree, on the streets.[1]   30

---

[1] Lowell's poem might well remind you of Benét's short story "By the Waters of Babylon" (p. 25). For Benét, New York City is the modern Babylon; for Lowell, it is Boston. In neither case is the specific city of primary significance, for each writer is concerned with the ways in which *any* modern city represents the false values symbolized by ancient Babylon. In Lowell's poem the emphasis is clearly on the extent to which we have commercialized (and hence vulgarized) the most sensitive insights of our religious heritage. You should observe how he employs imagery and allusion to underscore his profound distaste for this contemporary tendency.

Good and Bad

JAMES STEPHENS
[1882–1950]

Good and bad and right and wrong,
Wave the silly words away:
This is wisdom to be strong,
This is virtue to be gay:
Let us sing and dance until
We shall know the final art,
How to banish good and ill
With the laughter of the heart.

The Ballad of Father Gilligan

WILLIAM BUTLER YEATS
[1865–1939]

The old priest Peter Gilligan
Was weary night and day;
For half his flock were in their beds,
Or under green sods lay.

Once, while he nodded on a chair,   5
At the moth-hour of eve,
Another poor man sent for him,
And he began to grieve.

"I have no rest, nor joy, nor peace,
For people die and die";   10
And after cried he, "God forgive!
My body spake, not I!"

He knelt, and leaning on the chair
He prayed and fell asleep;
And the moth-hour went from the fields,   15
And stars began to peep.

They slowly into millions grew,
And leaves shook in the wind;
And God covered the world with shade,
And whispered to mankind.   20

Upon the time of sparrow chirp
When the moths came once more,
The old priest Peter Gilligan
Stood upright on the floor.

"Mavrone, mavrone! the man has died,   25
While I slept on the chair";
He roused his horse out of its sleep
And rode with little care.

He rode now as he never rode,
By rocky lane and fen;   30
The sick man's wife opened the door:
"Father! You come again!"

"And is the poor man dead?" he cried.
"He died an hour ago."
The old priest Peter Gilligan   35
In grief swayed to and fro.

"When you were gone, he turned and died
As merry as a bird."
The old priest Peter Gilligan
He knelt him at that word.   40

"He who hath made the night of stars
For souls, who tire and bleed,
Sent one of His great angels down
To help me in my need.

"He who is wrapped in purple robes,   45
With planets in His care,
Had pity on the least of things
Asleep upon a chair." [1]

---

[1] You are no doubt acquainted with many folk ballads such as the Scottish "Sir Patrick Spence" or "Lord Randall" and with such American ones as "Jesse James" or "Frankie and Johnny." Literary ballads—that is, ballads composed by professional poets —often follow folk ballad traditions in both form and content, but their greater subtlety of treatment is quickly apparent. Thus Yeats in this ballad outwardly follows a metrical pattern commonly found in folk ballads (in each stanza the first and third lines have four stresses while the second and fourth—the rhyming lines—have only three), but a sensitive reading of the poem suggests no monotony of metrical repetition. In a like manner the imagery in a literary ballad reveals a sophistication of insight and expression. (See, for example, the fifth stanza of Yeats's poem.)

Arms and the Boy

WILFRED OWEN
[1893–1918]

Let the boy try along this bayonet blade
How cold steel is, and keen with hunger of blood;
Blue with all malice, like a madman's flash;
And thinly drawn with famishing for flesh.

Lend him to stroke these blind, blunt bullet leads   5
Which long to nuzzle in the hearts of lads,
Or give him cartridges of fine zinc teeth,
Sharp with the sharpness of grief and death.

For his teeth seem for laughing round an apple.
There lurk no claws behind his fingers supple;   10
And God will grow no talons at his heels,
Nor antlers through the thickness of his curls.

An Elementary School Classroom in a Slum ✳

STEPHEN SPENDER
[BORN 1909]

Far far from gusty waves these children's faces.
Like rootless weeds, the hair torn round their pallor.
The tall girl with her weighed-down head. The paper-
seeming boy, with rat's eyes. The stunted, unlucky heir
Of twisted bones, reciting a father's gnarled disease,   5
His lesson from his desk. At back of the dim class
One unnoted, sweet and young. His eyes live in a dream   *one eye's hope*
Of squirrel's game, in tree room, other than this.

On sour cream walls, donations. Shakespeare's head,
Cloudless at dawn, civilized dome riding all cities.   10
Belled, flowery, Tyrolese valley. Open-handed map
Awarding the world its world. And yet, for these
Children, these windows, not this world, are world,

Where all their future's painted with a fog,
A narrow street sealed in with a lead sky,   15
Far far from rivers, capes, and stars of words.

Surely, Shakespeare is wicked, the map a bad example
With ships and sun and love tempting them to steal—
For lives that slyly turn in their cramped holes
From fog to endless night? On their slag heap, these children   20
Wear skins peeped through by bones and spectacles of steel
With mended glass, like bottle bits on stones.
All of their time and space are foggy slum.
So blot their maps with slums as big as doom.

Unless, governor, teacher, inspector, visitor,   25
This map becomes their window and these windows
That shut upon their lives like catacombs,
Break O break open till they break the town
And show the children to green fields, and make their world
Run azure on gold sands, and let their tongues   30
Run naked into books, the white and green leaves open
History theirs whose language is the sun.[1]

weirdest line

[1] Spender's poem was written a generation ago, but its eloquent anger at the educational conditions for many underprivileged children remains persuasive. Much of this persuasiveness rests on our recognition that such conditions still exist. Any formal report on slum classrooms could provide a factual but less effective reminder of this situation. Investigate the special means by which Spender shocks us to attention. For example, what is the relevance to his theme of the use of nature? of his description of the classroom? In what sense can it be said that "Shakespeare is wicked"? that "Tyrol is wicked"? How does he use the words *map* and *window* as symbols of the conditions against which he is protesting? In answering these questions you will be answering, most emphatically, the rhetorical question of a much earlier poet, William Blake [1757–1827]:

> Is this a holy thing to see
> In a rich and fruitful land . . . ?

Shine, Perishing Republic ✳

ROBINSON JEFFERS
[1887–1962]

While this America settles in the mold of its vulgarity, heavily
    thickening to empire,
And protest, only a bubble in the molten mass, pops and sighs out,
    and the mass hardens,

Beautiful thing: disapears but will come back — Platonic cuz moth is still there

I sadly smiling remember that the flower fades to make fruit, the   5
    fruit rots to make earth.
Out of the mother; and through the spring exultances, ripeness and
    decadence; and home to the mother.

You making haste, haste on decay: not blameworthy; life is good,
    be it stubbornly long or suddenly   10
A mortal splendor: meteors are not needed less than mountains:
    shine, perishing republic.

America will fall at some point

But for my children, I would have them keep their distance from
    the thickening center; corruption
Never has been compulsory, when the cities lie at the monster's   15
    feet there are left the mountains.

And boys, be in nothing so moderate as in love of man, a clever
    servant, insufferable master.
There is the trap that catches noblest spirits, that caught—they say
    —God, when he walked on earth.   20

People in gen. you should be careful of

The Habit of Perfection

GERARD MANLEY HOPKINS
[1844–1889]

Elected Silence, sing to me
And beat upon my whorlèd ear,
Pipe me to pastures still and be
The music that I care to hear.

Shape nothing, lips; be lovely-dumb: 5
It is the shut, the curfew sent
From there where all surrenders come
Which only makes you eloquent.

Be shellèd, eyes, with double dark
And find the uncreated light: 10
This ruck and reel which you remark
Coils, keeps, and teases simple sight.

Palate, the hutch of tasty lust,
Desire not to be rinsed with wine:
The can must be so sweet, the crust   15
So fresh that come in fasts divine!

Nostrils, your careless breath that spend
Upon the stir and keep of pride,
What relish shall the censers send
Along the sanctuary side!   20

O feel-of-primrose hands, O feet
That want the yield of plushy sward,
But you shall walk the golden street
And you unhouse and house the Lord.

And, Poverty, be thou the bride   25
And now the marriage feast begun,
And lily-colored clothes provide
Your spouse not labored-at nor spun.

POETRY: FOR STUDY AND DISCUSSION

The late French novelist and essayist Albert Camus remains a glowing spokesman for the many who assert that philosophical ideals only achieve relevance when they are "acted out": whether in personal action or, vicariously, in the arts. The poems in this section, therefore, might well be examined in terms of the concept of "the good life" to which each attempts to give dramatic presentation.

Some of these poems deal with goodness in religious terms (for example, Yeats's "The Ballad of Father Gilligan"); some in sociological terms (for example, Spender's "An Elementary School Classroom in a Slum"); some in psychological terms (for example, Taggard's "Try Tropic"). I suggest that you look again at the other poems in this section and try to specify how each makes concrete its own philosophical attitude about "the good life."

In this regard, please always remember to divorce (so far as possible) your personal standards of "the good life" from those represented in the different poems. Judge each poem as an effective expression of what *it* suggests "the good life" to be. Here, I emphasize the word *it* because it is a common mistake for students to generalize about a poet's philosophy on the basis of a single example or too few examples. From such an assumption, one might improperly conclude that Shakespeare disapproved of ambition (*Macbeth*), interracial marriage (*Othello*), and intellectualism (*Hamlet*).

I would like to remind you of two supplementary points. The first is that the poet may not necessarily realize all that his poem is saying. Poets vary in this respect, but the fact remains that often the poem "takes over," as it were, and achieves its own identity. Certainly, once it is published, the poem becomes exposed to interpretation and its author loses some of his paternal rights. An interesting example of a poem which has "gone beyond" its author is Robert Frost's familiar "Stopping by Woods on a Snowy Evening":

> Whose woods these are I think I know.
> His house is in the village though;
> He will not see me stopping here
> To watch his woods fill up with snow.
>
> My little horse must think it queer   5
> To stop without a farmhouse near
> Between the woods and frozen lake
> The darkest evening of the year.
>
> He gives his harness bells a shake
> To ask if there is some mistake.   10
> The only other sound's the sweep
> Of easy wind and downy flake.
>
> The woods are lovely, dark and deep,
> But I have promises to keep,
> And miles to go before I sleep,   15
> And miles to go before I sleep.

To be sure, this poem can be enjoyed as a picture of a New England experience that was common in past generations. Frost, himself, denied further proposed significance. Yet numerous qualified readers have found the poem to be a striking metaphor of our arduous passage toward death. Very often this type of "extension of meaning" can give increased dimension to a poem—regardless, as I have suggested, of what the poet may have consciously intended. However (and this is the second point), you must always be most careful to be certain that any such extension of meaning is clearly consistent with the poem's own aesthetic logic: its images, its rhythm, and the like. The argument that a poem once read becomes one's own is enticing but superficial: not until one has thought through a poem with the utmost diligence can the reader confidently say, "This poem is mine."

COMMITMENT

Introduction

Commitment is one of the most recurring values of Western civilization, as you will better realize when you have read Antigone. In the past, the word dedication was more commonly used to suggest the same absorption of one's self in a cause or principle. Here, a reminder to you of the distinction between the quantitative and qualitative aspects of values in general is relevant to an investigation of the particular value of commitment. One is "committed" to pay a financial debt; one is "committed" to meet a particular social obligation; one is "committed" to fulfill all manner of precise promises of this or that sort. These types of commitment are usually limited to fairly clearly defined legal or social conventionalities.

What, then, comes closer to the kinds of qualitative commitments which make commitment itself worth examination as a significant value? A list of names taken from this century alone suggests an answer: Gandhi, Schweitzer, Lenin, Madame Curie, Picasso, Martin Luther King. Such people (and, of course, many others) evidence a superior capacity to identify themselves with a purpose fully believed in—to, in Emerson's familiar phrase, "hitch their wagons to a star." That the chosen star may in itself be sometimes of debatable worth is not the issue here; it is enough that such people have made larger commitments than are possible for most of us but which serve as symbols of our own comparable capacities to find ourselves (for better or worse) through dedication.

What I have been saying strongly implies one major presupposition: the possibility of genuine choice. Whether man has, in a fundamental sense, freedom of choice is a philosophical problem beyond the scope of this volume. George Russell ("A.E.") once wrote,

> In the lost childhood of Judas
> Christ was betrayed . . .

You are already acquainted with T. S. Eliot's early negativism in "Preludes" (p. 113). Indeed, it may well be true that our actions are basically determined by factors beyond our control, but it is equally true that we act—and make judgments on acts—as if we were free to choose among available possibilities.[1] This observation would be accepted by Sartre, an atheist; by Stace, an agnostic; by Niebuhr, a theist. It is applicable to Kurtz in Heart of Darkness and to the symbolic Mr. Antrobus in The Skin of Our Teeth. Long ago Saint Joan of Arc heard the voice of Saint Catherine (or so she believed) and it led her, disdainful of adversity, to a commitment

---

[1] The phrase as if is the recognized translation of als-ob, a key concept from Hans Vaihinger, a German philosopher (1852–1933), for whom freedom of the will was a necessary moral "fiction."

of great magnitude. Fully committed people commonly "hear voices," and as Sartre has said, ". . . if I hear voices, what proof is there that they come from heaven and not from hell, or from the subconscious, or a pathological condition . . . ? I'll never find any proof or sign to convince me. . . . If a voice addresses me, it is always for me to decide that this is the angel's voice; if I consider that such an act is a good one, it is I who will choose to say that it is good rather than bad."

The selections which follow have not been chosen to persuade you to adopt any particular commitment. They have been chosen because they represent a variety of stimulating positions relevant to man's deepest and most persistent concerns in a "value world" which both changes—and does not.

Jean-Paul Sartre

[B O R N 1905]

Sartre represents to modern generations the most dramatic (and dramatized) spokesman of existentialism. In point of fact, he would be among the first to acknowledge that existentialism has considerable historical background and a variety of philosophical expressions. In short, existentialism is a mansion of many rooms: it includes Friedrich Nietzsche (prophet of the "God is dead" movement), the Catholic philosopher Gabriel Marcel, the Protestant philosopher Paul Tillich, and the Jewish philosopher Martin Buber. It also includes the atheism of Jean-Paul Sartre. Indeed, given the adaptability of its basic point of view, the only persons who cannot find comfort in the hospitality of existentialism are the agnostics[1] and the rationalists: the former because of their aversion toward all philosophies demanding commitment, the latter because they disagree with the cardinal principles of existentialism.

For a philosophical position as broad as this, it is proper to ask what core it contains to justify widespread acceptance by men whose specific philosophical and religious views vary so widely. Probably the most agreed-upon core is found in Sartre's phrase that "existence precedes essence." In this phrase is embodied the revolt of all existentialists against the more conventional formula (for example, Plato's) that some Plan (here, the essence of Man) precedes his existence. Existentialists believe that each man becomes Man (that is, achieves his essence) either by his own efforts (as Sartre, an atheist, would say) or through the search for a meaningful God (as a religious existentialist would profess). In each instance (I repeat), for the existentialists a man is significantly and responsibly free to fulfill the degree of Manhood of which he is capable.

You will see how Sartre emphasizes this conviction from his own atheistic point of view. Thus, after his introductory remarks, he makes his assertion that existence precedes essence and proceeds to give an excellent example of what he has in mind. He then links this basic doctrine to the subjectivity which he feels is inherent in existentialism. Note carefully that he rejects subjectivity of a narrow (or egoistic) sort: ". . . when we say that a man is responsible for himself, we do not only mean that he is responsible for his own individuality, but that he is responsible for all men." Next, Sartre examines the "anguish" which is the inevitable accompaniment of a freedom combined with such responsibility: ". . . man, with no support and no aid, is condemned every moment to invent man." Finally, he concludes by

[1] Students are often confused between the terms agnosticism and skepticism. In philosophy, the distinction normally holds that whereas the agnostic merely questions the possibility of verifiable knowledge (for or against) of ultimate beliefs of a moral or religious nature, the skeptic questions the possibility of verifiable knowledge of any ultimate beliefs (including, for example, scientific beliefs).

returning to his "existence precedes essence" thesis and by summarizing the major implication of that phrase: "What we mean is that a man is nothing else than a series of undertakings, that he is the sum, the organization, the ensemble of the relationships which make up these undertakings."

Existentialism

. . . What is meant by the term *existentialism?*

Most people who use the word would be rather embarrassed if they had to explain it, since, now that the word is all the rage, even the work of a musician or painter is being called existentialist. A gossip columnist in *Clartés* signs himself *The Existentialist,* so that by this time the word has been·so stretched and has taken on so broad a meaning, that it no longer means anything at all. It seems that for want of an avant-garde doctrine analogous to surrealism, the kind of people who are eager for scandal and flurry turn to this philosophy which in other respects does
10 not at all serve their purposes in this sphere.

Actually, it is the least scandalous, the most austere of doctrines. It is intended strictly for specialists and philosophers. Yet it can be defined easily. What complicates matters is that there are two kinds of existentialist; first, those who are Christian, among whom I would include Jaspers and Gabriel Marcel, both Catholic; and on the other hand the atheistic existentialists, among whom I class Heidegger, and then the French existentialists and myself. What they have in common is that they think that existence precedes essence, or, if you prefer, that subjectivity must be the starting point.

20 Just what does that mean? Let us consider some object that is manufactured, for example, a book or a paper cutter; here is an object which has been made by an artisan whose inspiration came from a concept. He referred to the concept of what a paper cutter is and likewise to a known method of production, which is part of the concept, something which is, by and large, a routine. Thus, the paper cutter is at once an object produced in a certain way and, on the other hand, one having a specific use; and one cannot postulate a man who produces a paper cutter but does not know what it is used for. Therefore, let us say that, for the paper cutter, essence—that is, the ensemble of both the production routines and the properties which enable it to be both produced and
30 defined—precedes existence. Thus, the presence of the paper cutter or book in front of me is determined. Therefore, we have here a technical view of the world whereby it can be said that production precedes existence. . . .

Man is nothing else but what he makes of himself. Such is the first

Excerpt from *Existentialism* by Jean-Paul Sartre, translated by Bernhard Frechtman.

principle of existentialism. It is also what is called subjectivity, the name we are labeled with when charges are brought against us. But what do we mean by this, if not that man has a greater dignity than a stone or a table? For we mean that man first exists, that is, that man first of all is the being who hurls himself toward a future and who is conscious of imagining himself as being in the future. Man is at the start a plan which is aware of itself, rather than a patch of moss, a piece of garbage, or a cauliflower; nothing exists prior to this plan; there is nothing in heaven; man will be what he will have planned to be. Not what he will want to be. Because by the word *will* we generally mean a conscious decision, which is subsequent to what we have already made of ourselves. I may want to belong to a political party, write a book, get married; but all that is only a manifestation of an earlier, more spontaneous choice that is called *will*. But if existence really does precede essence, man is responsible for what he is. Thus, existentialism's first move is to make every man aware of what he is and to make the full responsibility of his existence rest on him. And when we say that a man is responsible for himself, we do not only mean that he is responsible for his own individuality, but that he is responsible for all men. . . .

Now, I'm not being singled out as an Abraham, and yet at every moment I'm obliged to perform exemplary acts. For every man, everything happens as if all mankind had its eyes fixed on him and were guiding itself by what he does. And every man ought to say to himself, "Am I really the kind of man who has the right to act in such a way that humanity might guide itself by my actions?" And if he does not say that to himself, he is masking his anguish.

There is no question here of the kind of anguish which would lead to quietism, to inaction. It is a matter of a simple sort of anguish that anybody who has had responsibilities is familiar with. For example, when a military officer takes the responsibility for an attack and sends a certain number of men to death, he chooses to do so, and in the main he alone makes the choice. Doubtless, orders come from above, but they are too broad; he interprets them, and on this interpretation depend the lives of ten or fourteen or twenty men. In making a decision he cannot help having a certain anguish. All leaders know this anguish. That doesn't keep them from acting; on the contrary, it is the very condition of their action. For it implies that they envisage a number of possibilities, and when they choose one, they realize that it has value only because it is chosen. We shall see that this kind of anguish, which is the kind that existentialism describes, is explained, in addition, by a direct responsibility to the other men whom it involves. It is not a curtain separating us from action, but is part of action itself. . . .

That is the idea I shall try to convey when I say that man is condemned to be free. Condemned, because he did not create himself, yet,

80 in other respects is free; because, once thrown into the world, he is responsible for everything he does. The existentialist does not believe in the power of passion. He will never agree that a sweeping passion is a ravaging torrent which fatally leads a man to certain acts and is therefore an excuse. He thinks that man is responsible for his passion.

The existentialist does not think that man is going to help himself by finding in the world some omen by which to orient himself. Because he thinks that man will interpret the omen to suit himself. Therefore, he thinks that man, with no support and no aid, is condemned every moment to invent man. Ponge, in a very fine article, has said, "Man is the 90 future of man." That's exactly it. But if it is taken to mean that this future is recorded in heaven, that God sees it, then it is false, because it would really no longer be a future. If it is taken to mean that, whatever a man may be, there is a future to be forged, a virgin future before him, then this remark is sound. But then we are forlorn. . . .

Actually, things will be as man will have decided they are to be. Does that mean that I should abandon myself to quietism? No. First, I should involve myself; then act on the old saw, "Nothing ventured, nothing gained." Nor does it mean that I shouldn't belong to a party, but rather that I shall have no illusions and shall do what I can. For example, 100 suppose that I ask myself, "Will socialization, as such, ever come about?" I know nothing about it. All I know is that I'm going to do everything in my power to bring it about. Beyond that, I can't count on anything. Quietism is the attitude of people who say, "Let others do what I can't do." The doctrine I am presenting is the very opposite of quietism, since it declares, "There is no reality except in action." Moreover, it goes further, since it adds, "Man is nothing else than his plan; he exists only to the extent that he fufills himself; he is therefore nothing else than the ensemble of his acts, nothing else than his life. . . .

A man is involved in life, leaves his impress on it, and outside of that 110 there is nothing. To be sure, this may seem a harsh thought to someone whose life hasn't been a success. But, on the other hand, it prompts people to understand that reality alone is what counts, that dreams, expectations, and hopes warrant no more than to define a man as a disappointed dream, as miscarried hopes, as vain expectations. In other words, to define him negatively and not positively. However, when we say, "You are nothing else than your life," that does not imply that the artist will be judged solely on the basis of his works of art; a thousand other things will contribute toward summing him up. What we mean is that a man is nothing else than a series of undertakings, that he is the 120 sum, the organization, the ensemble of the relationships which make up these undertakings.

FOR STUDY AND DISCUSSION

1. As I have said in my introduction, very early in the selection Sartre lays down the basic premise of the different kinds of existentialism: that existence precedes essence. He then gives the example of a paper cutter. How does this example clarify the distinction between a man-made object and man himself?

2. "Man is nothing else but what he makes of himself. Such is the first principle of existentialism. It is also what is called subjectivity. . . ." Why do you think the last sentence of this paragraph (lines 52–54) is an important one?

3. How is this same sentence (lines 52–54) related in meaning to Sartre's discussion of "anguish"?

4. What does Sartre have in mind when he remarks that ". . . man is condemned to be free"?

5. In the last two paragraphs, Sartre is insisting that existentialism is a philosophy of activism. Point to phrases and examples which he uses to underline this emphasis. Can you show how the emphasis on activity is consistent with the earlier material of the selection?

W. T. Stace

[1886–1967]

I would suppose W. T. Stace to be an agnostic: that is, one who, in contrast to both atheists and theists, takes the position of "I cannot know" when asked for his answer to such philosophical problems (for example) as the freedom of the will or the existence of God. As you recall, William James (p. 14) takes the stand that such a posture is unnecessary, even improper, in moral and religious situations, and you will remember his doctrine that "forced options" are indispensable in these areas. On page 16, James has summed up his objection to agnosticism explicitly:

> I, therefore, for one, cannot see my way to accepting the agnostic rules for truth-seeking [never to believe any hypothesis when there is no evidence or insufficient evidence] or to willfully agree to keep my willing nature out of the game. I cannot do so for this plain reason: that a rule of thinking which would absolutely prevent me from acknowledging certain kinds of truth, if those kinds of truths were really there, would be an irrational rule.

This is a criticism with which many philosophers would agree: Jean-Paul Sartre, who is an atheist, would concur as much as would Reinhold Niebuhr, a theist. Yet agnostics reject James's position. T. H. Huxley speaks for most agnostics in the following assertion:

> My only consolation lies in the reflection that, however bad our posterity may become, so far as they hold by the plain rule of not pretending to believe what they have no reason to believe, because it may be to their advantage so to pretend, they will not have reached the lowest depth of immorality.

Stace's position is essentially a development and contemporary refinement of this statement by Huxley. As you will see, Stace begins by pointing out how Renaissance and post-Renaissance science changed "the old comfortable picture of a friendly universe governed by spiritual values." He proceeds to show that this new orientation has made impossible continued belief in a "final cause" (such as a God) through which the universe might have a meaning and a purpose. The result, he continues, is to force men to develop "a new imaginative picture of the world": a picture of a world without any purpose whatsoever. As Stace expresses it, "To ask any question about why things are thus, or what purpose their being so serves, is to ask a senseless question, because they serve no purpose at all." He concludes that we must face the truth of such a meaningless universe if we are to outgrow a childish dependence on dreams and to emerge as men who—on their own— create ideals and persist in striving for "great ends and noble achievements."

You may wonder why, given the inherent character of agnosticism, I have included an exponent of this conviction under the general heading of Commitment. My answer is hinted at by my use of the word conviction. I believe that agnosticism can be usefully examined and discussed as a type of "anticommitment commitment."

Man Against Darkness

It was Galileo and Newton—notwithstanding that Newton himself was a deeply religious man—who destroyed the old comfortable picture of a friendly universe governed by spiritual values. And this was effected, not by Newton's discovery of the law of gravitation nor by any of Galileo's brilliant investigations, but by the general picture of the world which these men and others of their time made the basis of science, not only of their own day, but of all succeeding generations down to the present. That is why the century immediately following Newton, the eighteenth century, was notoriously an age of religious
10 skepticism. Skepticism did not have to wait for the discoveries of Darwin and the geologists in the nineteenth century. It flooded the world immediately after the age of the rise of science.

Neither the Copernican hypothesis nor any of Newton's or Galileo's particular discoveries were the real causes. Religious faith might well have accommodated itself to the new astronomy. The real turning point between the medieval age of faith and the modern age of unfaith came when the scientists of the seventeenth century turned their backs upon what used to be called "final causes." The final cause of a thing meant the purpose which it was supposed to serve in the universe, its cosmic
20 purpose. What lay back of this was the presupposition that there is a cosmic order or plan and that everything which exists could in the last analysis be explained in terms of its place in this cosmic plan, that is, in terms of its purpose.

Plato and Aristotle believed this, and so did the whole medieval Christian world. For instance, if it were true that the sun and the moon were created and exist for the purpose of giving light to man, then this fact would explain why the sun and the moon exist. We might not be able to discover the purpose of everything, but everything must have a purpose. Belief in final causes thus amounted to a belief that the world is
30 governed by purposes, presumably the purposes of some overruling mind. This belief was not the invention of Christianity. It was basic to the whole of Western civilization, whether in the ancient pagan world or in Christendom, from the time of Socrates to the rise of science in the seventeenth century.

[It came about] that for the past three hundred years there has been

Excerpt from an article in the *Atlantic Monthly* magazine, September 1948.

growing up in men's minds, dominated as they are by science, a new imaginative picture of the world. The world, according to this new picture, is purposeless, senseless, meaningless. Nature is nothing but matter in motion. The motions of matter are governed, not by any purpose, but
40 by blind forces and laws. Nature on this view, says Whitehead—to whose writings I am indebted in this part of my paper—is "merely the hurrying of material, endlessly, meaninglessly." You can draw a sharp line across the history of Europe dividing it into two epochs of very unequal length. The line passes through the lifetime of Galileo. European man before Galileo—whether ancient pagan or more recent Christian—thought of the world as controlled by plan and purpose. After Galileo, European man thinks of it as utterly purposeless.

The picture of a meaningless world and a meaningless human life is, I think, the basic theme of much modern art and literature. Certainly it
50 is the basic theme of modern philosophy. According to the most characteristic philosophies of the modern period from Hume in the eighteenth century to the so-called positivists [1] of today, the world is just what it is, and that is the end of all inquiry. There is no reason for its being what it is. Everything might just as well have been quite different, and there would have been no reason for that either. When you have stated what things are, what things the world contains, there is nothing more which could be said, even by an omniscient being. To ask any question about *why* things are thus, or what purpose their being so serves, is to ask a senseless question, because they serve no purpose at all.

60 The widespread belief in "ethical relativity" among philosophers, psychologists, ethnologists, and sociologists is the theoretical counterpart of the repudiation of principle which we see all around us, especially in international affairs, the field in which morals have always had the weakest foothold. No one any longer effectively believes in moral principles except as the private prejudices either of individual men or of nations or cultures. This is the inevitable consequence of believing in a purposeless world.

No civilization can live without ideals, or to put it in another way, without a firm faith in moral ideas. Our ideals and moral ideas have in
70 the past been rooted in religion. But the religious basis of our ideals has been undermined, and the superstructure of ideals is plainly tottering. None of the commonly suggested remedies on examination seems likely to succeed. It would therefore look as if the early death of our civilization were inevitable.

I am sure that the first thing we have to do is to face the truth, however bleak it may be, and then next we have to learn to live with it. Let me say a word about each of these two points. What I am urging as

[1] *positivists:* loosely, those philosophers who believe that only natural (that is, scientific) phenomena are knowable.

regards the first is complete honesty. Those who wish to resurrect Christian dogmas are not, of course, consciously dishonest. But they have
80 that kind of unconscious dishonesty which consists in lulling oneself with opiates and dreams. Those who talk of a new religion are merely hoping for a new opiate. Both alike refuse to face the truth that there is, in the universe outside man, no spirituality, no regard for values, no friend in the sky, no help or comfort for man of any sort. To be perfectly honest in the admission of this fact, not to seek shelter in new or old illusions, not to indulge in wishful dreams about this matter, this is the first thing we shall have to do.

Man has not yet grown up. He is not adult. Like a child he cries for the moon and lives in a world of fantasies. And the race as a whole has
90 perhaps reached the great crisis of its life. Can it grow up as a race in the same sense as individual men grow up? Can man put away childish things and adolescent dreams? Can he grasp the real world as it actually is, stark and bleak, without its romantic or religious halo, and still retain his ideals, striving for great ends and noble achievements? If he can, all may yet be well. If he cannot, he will probably sink back into the savagery and brutality from which he came, taking a humble place once more among the lower animals.

FOR STUDY AND DISCUSSION

1. What does Stace mean by his statement in lines 10–13: "Skepticism did not have to wait for the discoveries of Darwin and the geologists in the nineteenth century. It flooded the world immediately after the age of the rise of science"?
2. Why does Stace go on to say, "To ask any question about *why* things are thus, or what purpose they so serve, is to ask a senseless question, because they serve no purpose at all"?
3. What does he mean by the phrase "ethical relativity," and how is its prevalence today related to our sense of a world without essential meaning or purpose?
4. Stace agrees that "no civilization can live without ideals," but he adds that "the religious basis of our ideals has been undermined." Do you agree (or disagree) with the contention that ideals must have a religious basis? Whatever your opinion, do you agree (or disagree) that our traditional religious basis has been "undermined"?
5. Stace concludes that (a) we must face the truth and that (b) we must learn to live with it and build our ideals upon it. He explains his first point in the next-to-last paragraph, and he explains his second point in his concluding paragraph. How are both points intimately related to the general development of his argument throughout the selection?

Reinhold Niebuhr

[BORN 1892]

Niebuhr is one of the most searching and influential thinkers of our time. As a theologian, he is primarily concerned with religion and the philosophy of religion. Whether you agree or disagree with his particular expression of Christian "truths," his views deserve your thoughtful attention, since they have been a major source for the contemporary reexamination of the validity and relevance of religious commitment.

It is Niebuhr's contention that many of Christianity's traditional convictions should be accepted for their symbolic truth rather than for their literal truth. You will recall Plato's Allegory of the Den (p. 5). Clearly, Plato did not believe that we are literally prisoners in a den, but he composed his "story" to convey imaginatively the extent to which we are enslaved by dependence on our senses. In a like manner, Niebuhr is asserting that Christianity's fundamental insights are embodied in "myths" which have no unquestionable historical validity but which are profoundly true as symbolic representations of man's basic spiritual concerns. It is to reinforce the authority of this view that Niebuhr emphasizes the observation of Saint Paul: "We are deceivers, yet true."

For Niebuhr, then, the religious commitment is one to a type of truth which transcends historical-scientific truth and which captures a significant dimension of reality that escapes more conventional observation or analysis. In this respect, Niebuhr's position is very similar to that of William James (p. 14) and Martin Buber (p. 238).

The Christian Commitment

[What] is true in the Christian religion can be expressed only in symbols which contain a certain degree of provisional and superficial deception. Every apologist of the Christian faith might well, therefore, make the Pauline phrase his own.[1] We do teach the truth by deception. We are deceivers, yet true.

The necessity for the deception is given in the primary characteristic of the Christian world view. Christianity does not believe that the natural, temporal, and historical world is self-derived or self-explanatory. . . .

Before analyzing the deceptive symbols which the Christian faith uses to express this dimension of eternity in time, it might be clarifying to recall that artists are forced to use deceptive symbols when they seek to

Excerpts from *Beyond Tragedy* and *An Interpretation of Christian Ethics*.
[1] See II Corinthians 6:8.

402

portray two dimensions of space upon the single dimension of a flat canvas. Every picture which suggests depth and perspective draws angles not as they are but as they appear to the eye when it looks into depth. Parallel lines are not drawn as parallel lines but are made to appear as if they converged on the horizon; for so they appear to the eye when it envisages a total perspective. Only the most primitive art and the drawings made by very small children reveal the mistake of portraying things in their true proportions rather than as they are seen. The neces-
20 sity of picturing things as they seem rather than as they are, in order to record on one dimension what they are in two dimensions, is a striking analogy, in the field of space, of the problem of religion in the sphere of time. . . .

Great art faces the problem of the two dimensions of time as well as the two dimensions of space. The portrait artist, for instance, is confronted with the necessity of picturing a character. Human personality is more than a succession of moods. The moods of a moment are held together in a unity of thought and feeling, which gives them, however seemingly capricious, a considerable degree of consistency. The problem
30 of the artist is to portray the inner consistency of a character which is never fully expressed in any one particular mood or facial expression. This can be done only by falsifying physiognomic details. Portraiture is an art which can never be sharply distinguished from caricature. A moment of time in a personality can be made to express what transcends the moment of time only if the moment is not recorded accurately. It must be made into a symbol of something beyond itself.

This technique of art explains why art is more closely related to religion than science. Art describes the world not in terms of its exact relationships. It constantly falsifies these relationships, as analyzed by
40 science, in order to express their total meaning. . . .

[Thus] the idea of the fall is subject to the error of regarding the primitive myth of the garden, the apple, and the serpent, as historically true. But even if this error is not committed, Christian thought is still tempted to regard the fall as an historical occurrence. The fall is not historical. It does not take place in any concrete human act. It is the presupposition of such acts. It deals with an area of human freedom which, when once expressed in terms of an act, is always historically related to a previous act or predisposition. External descriptions of human behavior are therefore always deterministic. That is the decep-
50 tion into which those are betrayed who seek to avoid the errors of introspection by purely external descriptions of human behavior. What Christianity means by the idea of the fall can only be known in introspection. The consciousness of sin and the consciousness of God are inextricably involved with each other. Only as the full dimension of human existence is measured, which includes not only the dimension of

historical breadth but the dimension of trans-historical freedom, does the idea of the fall of man achieve significance and relevance.

. . . We are deceivers, yet true, in clinging to the idea of the fall as a symbol of the origin and the nature of evil in human life.

60   Only a vital Christian faith, renewing its youth in its prophetic origin, is capable of dealing adequately with the moral and social problems of our age; only such a faith can affirm the significance of temporal and mundane existence without capitulating unduly to the relativities of the temporal process. Such a faith alone can point to a source of meaning which transcends all the little universes of value and meaning which "have their day and cease to be" and yet not seek refuge in an eternal world where all history ceases to be significant. Only such a faith can outlast the death of old cultures and the birth of new civilizations, and yet deal in terms of moral responsibility with the world in which cultures 70 and civilizations engage in struggles for death and life.

FOR STUDY AND DISCUSSION

1. What does Niebuhr mean by his observation that in Christianity "we are deceivers, yet true"?
2. To illustrate this point, Niebuhr discusses the extent to which art "distorts" reality, and he comments that "this technique of art explains why art is more closely related to religion than science." What common characteristics of art and religion does he have in mind? What characteristics would you say science and history share?
3. In referring to the Christian belief in the fall of man, Niebuhr remarks that "we are deceivers, yet true in clinging to the idea of the fall as a symbol of the origin and the nature of evil in human life." What does he mean by this statement? Can you think of other Christian convictions which Niebuhr would probably interpret in a like manner?
4. Is Niebuhr's view of the role which "symbols" and "myths" play in Christianity (and, by extension, in all religions) new to you? Do you find that it enriches religion for you, or do you prefer the more literal and traditional interpretations? Why?
5. Reread Niebuhr's concluding paragraph. What commitment is he expressing there which neither Sartre nor Stace would support?

FICTION

Heart of Darkness

JOSEPH CONRAD

[1857–1924]

Conrad once made a trip up the Congo, and we have diary evidence of an itinerary close to that of Marlow's, the central character of Conrad's brooding story Heart of Darkness. Remember, however, that a work of art is never simply the reproduction of an author's own experience; rather, that experience has provided suggestions which stimulate his creative capacities to articulate significances of theme and personality. Thomas Mann once remarked that "all subject matter is boring if no ideas shine through it." Thomas Wolfe also expressed very well the relationship of the author to his material when he said, ". . . it is impossible for a man who has the stuff of creation in him to make a literal transcription of his own experience. Everything in a work of art is changed and transfigured by the personality of the artist."

Heart of Darkness is, then, far more than a remembered account by Conrad told in the person of Marlow. That the "darkness" of the title implies significantly more than the geographical darkness of "darkest Africa" is foreshadowed very early in the tale. Similarly, although the Congo is at first the physical "heart" of this darkness to Marlow, it increasingly takes on symbolic force. In this connection, try to imaginatively identify yourself with Marlow as you read. The early Marlow is a restless, somewhat cynical young man, searching for adventure as the young have always done. But as the story proceeds, he becomes more and more puzzled by the situations and personalities he encounters, then more and more involved in the types of values and forms of commitment which they represent. When he returns home to London, he has had considerable "initiation" into the intricacies of human character and its potentialities for truth and falsity, good and evil, beauty and ugliness. These insights are shared with us in Heart of Darkness.

I

The *Nellie,* a cruising yawl, swung to her anchor without a flutter of the sails, and was at rest. The flood had made, the wind was nearly calm, and being bound down the river, the only thing for it was to come to and wait for the turn of the tide.

The sea-reach of the Thames stretched before us like the beginning of an interminable waterway. In the offing the sea and the sky were welded together without a joint, and in the luminous space the tanned sails of the barges drifting up with the tide seemed to stand still in red clusters of canvas sharply peaked, with gleams of varnished sprits. A haze rested on the low shores that ran out to sea in vanishing flatness. The air was dark above Gravesend, and farther back still seemed condensed into a mournful gloom, brooding motionless over the biggest, and the greatest, town on earth.

The Director of Companies was our captain and our host. We four affectionately watched his back as he stood in the bows looking to seaward. On the whole river there was nothing that looked half so nautical. He resembled a pilot, which to a seaman is trustworthiness personified. It was difficult to realize his work was not out there in the luminous estuary, but behind him, within the brooding gloom.

Between us there was, as I have already said somewhere, the bond of the sea. Besides holding our hearts together through long periods of separation, it had the effect of making us tolerant of each other's yarns—and even convictions. The lawyer—the best of old fellows—had, because of his many years and many virtues, the only cushion on deck, and was lying on the only rug. The Accountant had brought out already a box of dominoes, and was toying architecturally with the bones. Marlow sat cross-legged right aft, leaning against the mizzenmast. He had sunken cheeks, a yellow complexion, a straight back, an ascetic aspect, and, with his arms dropped, the palms of hands outwards, resembled an idol. The Director, satisfied the anchor had good hold, made his way aft and sat down among us. We exchanged a few words lazily. Afterward there was silence on board the yacht. For some reason or other we did not begin that game of dominoes. We felt meditative, and fit for nothing but placid staring. The day was ending in a serenity of still and exquisite brilliance. The water shone pacifically; the sky, without a speck, was a benign immensity of unstained light; the very mist on the Essex marshes was like a gauzy and radiant fabric, hung from the wooded rises inland, and draping the low shores in diaphanous folds. Only the gloom to the west, brooding over the upper reaches, became more somber every minute, as if angered by the approach of the sun.

And at last, in its curved and imperceptible fall, the sun sank low, and from glowing white changed to a dull red without rays and without heat, as if about to go out suddenly, stricken to death by the touch of that gloom brooding over a crowd of men.

Forthwith a change came over the waters, and the serenity became less brilliant but more profound. The old river in its broad reach rested unruffled at the decline of day, after ages of good service done to the race that peopled its banks, spread out in the tranquil dignity of a waterway leading to the uttermost ends of the earth. We looked at the venerable stream not in the vivid flush of a short day that comes and departs for ever, but in the august light of abiding memories. And indeed nothing is easier for a man who has, as the phrase goes, "followed the sea" with reverence and affection, than to evoke the great spirit of the past upon the lower reaches of the Thames. The tidal current runs to and fro in its unceasing service, crowded with memories of men and ships it has borne to the rest of home or to the battles of the sea.

It had known and served all the men of whom the nation is proud, from Sir Francis Drake to Sir John Franklin, knights all, titled and untitled—the great knights-errant of the sea. It had borne all the ships whose names are like jewels flashing in the night of time, from the *Golden Hind* returning with her round flanks full of treasure, to be visited by the Queen's Highness and thus pass out of the gigantic tale, to the *Erebus* and *Terror,* bound on other conquests—and that never returned. It had known the ships and the men. They had sailed from Deptford, from Greenwich, from Erith—the adventurers and the settlers; kings' ships and the ships of men on 'Change; captains, admirals, the dark "interlopers" of the Eastern trade, and the commissioned "generals" of East India fleets. Hunters for gold or pursuers of fame, they all had gone out on that stream, bearing the sword, and often the torch, messengers of the might within the land, bearers of a spark from the sacred fire. What greatness had not floated on the ebb of that river into the mystery of an unknown earth! . . . The dreams of men, the seed of commonwealths, the germs of empires.

The sun set; the dusk fell on the stream, and lights began to appear along the shore. The Chapman lighthouse, a three-legged thing erect on a mud-flat, shone strongly. Lights of ships moved in the fairway—a great stir of lights going up and going down. And farther west on the upper reaches the place of the monstrous town was still marked ominously on the sky, a brooding gloom in sunshine, a lurid glare under the stars.

"And this also," said Marlow suddenly, "has been one of the dark places of the earth."

He was the only man of us who still "followed the sea." The worst that could be said of him was that he did not represent his class. He was a seaman, but he was a wanderer too, while most seamen lead, if one may so express it, a sedentary life. Their minds are of the stay-at-home order, and their home is always with them—the ship; and so is their country—the sea. One ship is very much like another, and the sea is always the same. In the immutability of their surroundings the foreign shores, the foreign faces, the changing immensity of life, glide past, veiled not by a sense of mystery but by a slightly disdainful ignorance; for there is nothing mysterious to a seaman unless it be the sea itself, which is the mistress of his existence and as inscrutable as Destiny. For the rest, after his hours of work, a casual stroll or a casual spree on shore suffices to unfold for him the secret of a whole continent, and generally he finds the secret not worth knowing. The yarns of seamen have a direct simplicity, the whole meaning of which lies within the shell of a cracked nut. But Marlow was not typical (if his propensity to spin yarns be excepted), and to him the meaning of an episode was not inside like a kernel but outside, enveloping the tale which brought it out only as a glow brings out a haze, in the likeness of one of these misty halos that sometimes are made visible by the spectral illumination of moonshine.

His remark did not seem at all surprising. It was just like Marlow. It was accepted in silence. No one took the trouble to grunt even; and presently he said, very slow:

"I was thinking of very old times, when the Romans first came here, nineteen hundred years ago—the other day. . . . Light came out of this river since—you say Knights? Yes; but it is like a running blaze on a plain, like a flash of lightning in the clouds. We live in the flicker—may it last as long as the old earth keeps rolling! But darkness was here yesterday. Imagine the feelings of a commander of a fine—what d'ye call 'em?—trireme in the Mediterranean, ordered suddenly to the north; run overland across the Gauls in a hurry; put in charge of one of these craft the legionaries—a wonderful lot of handy men they must have been too—used to build, apparently by the hundred, in a month or two, if we may believe what we read. Imagine him here—the very end of the world, a sea the color of lead, a sky the color of smoke, a kind of ship about as rigid as a concertina—and going up this river with stores, or orders, or what you like. Sandbanks, marshes, forests, savages —precious little to eat fit for a civilized man, nothing but Thames water to drink. No Falernian wine here, no going ashore. Here and there a military camp lost in a wilderness, like a needle in a bundle of hay—cold, fog, tempests, disease, exile, and death—death skulking in the air, in the water, in the bush. They must have been dying like flies here. Oh yes—he did it. Did it very well, too, no doubt, and without thinking much about it either, except afterward to brag of what he had gone through in his time, perhaps. They were men enough to face the darkness. And perhaps he was cheered by keeping his eye on a chance of promotion to the fleet at Ravenna by and by, if he had good friends in Rome and survived the awful climate. Or think of a decent young citizen in a toga—perhaps too much dice, you know—coming out here in the train of some prefect, or tax gatherer, or trader, even to mend his fortunes. Land in a swamp, march through the woods, and in some inland post feel the savagery, the utter savagery, had closed round him—all that mysterious life of the wilderness that stirs in the forest, in the jungles, in the hearts of wild men. There's no initiation either into such mysteries. He has to live in the midst of the incomprehensible, which is also detestable. And it has a fascination, too, that goes to work upon him. The fascination of the abomination—you know. Imagine the growing regrets, the longing to escape, the powerless disgust, the surrender, the hate."

He paused.

"Mind," he began again, lifting one arm from the elbow, the palm of the hand outwards, so that, with his legs folded before him, he had the pose of a Buddha preaching in European clothes and without a lotus flower—"Mind, none of us would feel exactly like this. What saves us is efficiency—the devotion to efficiency. But these chaps were not much account, really. They were no colonists; their administration was merely a squeeze, and nothing more, I suspect. They were conquerors, and for that you want only brute force—nothing to boast of, when you have it, since your strength is just an accident arising from the weakness of others. They grabbed what they could get for the sake of what was to be got. It was just robbery with violence, aggravated murder on a great scale, and men going at it blind—as is very proper for those who tackle a darkness. The conquest of the earth, which mostly means the taking it away from those who have a different complexion or slightly flatter noses than ourselves, is not a pretty thing when you look into it too much. What redeems it is the idea only. An idea at the back of it; not a sentimental pretense but an idea; and an unselfish belief in the idea—something you can set up, and bow down before, and offer a sacrifice to. . . ."

He broke off. Flames glided in the river, small green flames, red flames, white flames, pursuing, overtaking, joining, crossing each other—then separating slowly or hastily. The traffic of the great city went on in the deepening night upon the sleepless river. We looked on, waiting patiently—there was nothing else to do till the end of the flood; but it was only after a long silence, when he said, in a hesitating voice, "I suppose you fellows remember I did once turn freshwater sailor for a bit," that we knew we were fated, before the ebb began to run, to hear about one of Marlow's inconclusive experiences.

"I don't want to bother you much with what happened to me personally," he began, showing in this remark the weakness of many tellers of tales who seem so often unaware of what their audience would best like to hear; "yet to understand the effect of it on me you ought to know how I got out there, what I saw, how I went up that river to the place where I first met the poor chap. It was the farthest point of navigation and the culminating point of my experience. It seemed somehow to throw a kind of light on everything about me—and into my thoughts. It was somber enough too—and pitiful—not extraordinary in any way—not very clear either. No, not very clear. And yet it seemed to throw a kind of light.

"I had then, as you remember, just returned to London after a lot of Indian Ocean, Pacific, China Seas—a regular dose of the East—six years or so, and I was loafing about, hindering you fellows in your work and invading your homes, just as though I had got a heavenly mission to civilize you. It was very fine for a time but after a bit I did get tired of resting. Then I began to look for a ship—I should think the hardest work on earth. But the ships wouldn't even look at me. And I got tired of that game too.

"Now when I was a little chap I had a passion for maps. I would look for hours at South America, or Africa, or Australia, and lose myself in all the glories of exploration. At that time there were many blank spaces on the earth, and when I saw one that looked particularly inviting on a map (but they all look that) I would put my finger on it and say, When I grow up I will go there. The North Pole was one of these places, I remember. Well, I haven't been there yet, and shall not try now. The glamor's off. Other places were scattered about the Equator, and in every sort of latitude all over the two hemispheres. I have been in some of them, and . . . well, we won't talk about that. But there was one yet—the biggest, the most blank, so to speak—that I had a hankering after.

"True, by this time it was not a blank space any more. It had got filled since my boyhood with rivers and lakes and names. It had ceased to be a blank space of delightful mystery—a white patch for a boy to dream gloriously over. It had become a place of darkness. But there was in it one river especially, a mighty big river, that you could see on the map, resembling an immense snake uncoiled, with its head in the sea, its body at rest curving afar over a vast country, and its tail lost in the depths of the land. And as I looked at the map of it in a shop window, it fascinated me as a snake would a bird—a silly little bird. Then I remembered there was a big concern, a Company for trade on that river. Dash it all! I thought to myself, they can't trade without using some kind of craft on that lot of fresh water—steamboats! Why shouldn't I try to get charge of one? I went on along Fleet Street, but could not shake off the idea. The snake had charmed me.

"You understand it was a Continental concern, that Trading Society; but I have a lot of relations living on the Continent, because it's cheap and not so nasty as it looks, they say.

"I am sorry to own I began to worry them. This was already a fresh departure for me. I was not used to get things that way, you know. I always went my own road and on my own legs where I had a mind to go. I wouldn't have believed it of myself; but, then—you see—I felt somehow I must get there by hook or by crook. So I worried them. The men said, 'My dear fellow,' and did nothing. Then—would you believe it?—I tried the women. I, Charlie Marlow, set the women to work—to get a job. Heavens! Well, you see, the notion drove me. I had an aunt, a dear enthusiastic soul. She wrote: 'It will be delightful. I am ready to do anything, anything for you. It is a glorious idea. I know the wife of a very high personage in the Administration, and also a man who has lots of influence with,' etc. etc. She was determined to make no end of fuss to get me appointed skipper of a river steamboat, if such was my fancy.

"I got my appointment—of course; and I got it very quick. It appears the Company had received news that one of their captains had been killed in a scuffle with the natives. This was my chance, and it made me the more anxious to go. It was only months and months afterward, when I made the attempt to recover what was left of the body, that I heard the original quarrel arose from a misunderstanding about some hens. Yes, two black hens. Fresleven—that was the fellow's name, a Dane—thought himself wronged somehow in the bargain, so he went ashore and started to hammer the chief of the village with a stick. Oh, it didn't surprise me in the least to hear this, and at the same time to be told that Fresleven was the gentlest, quietest creature that ever walked on two legs. No doubt he was; but he had been a couple of years already out there engaged in the noble cause, you know, and he probably felt the need at last of asserting his self-respect in some way. Therefore he whacked the old black man mercilessly, while a big crowd of his people watched him, thunderstruck, till some man—I was told the chief's son—in desperation at hearing the old chap yell, made a tentative jab with a spear at the white man—and of course it went quite easy between the shoulder blades. Then the whole population cleared into the forest, expecting all kinds of calamities to happen, while, on the other hand, the steamer Fresleven commanded left also in a bad panic, in charge of the engineer, I believe. Afterward nobody seemed to trouble much about Fresleven's remains, till I got out and stepped into his shoes. I couldn't let it rest, though; but when an opportunity offered at last to meet my predecessor, the grass growing through his ribs was tall enough to hide his bones. They were all there. The supernatural being had not been touched after he fell. And the village was deserted, the huts gaped black, rotting, all askew within the fallen enclosures. A calamity had come to it, sure enough. The people had vanished. Mad terror had scattered them, men, women, and children, through the bush, and they had never returned. What became of the hens I don't know either. I should think the cause of progress got them, anyhow. However, through this glorious affair I got my appointment, before I had fairly begun to hope for it.

"I flew around like mad to get ready, and before forty-eight hours I was crossing the Channel to show myself to my employers, and sign the contract. In a very few hours I arrived in a city that always makes me think of a whited sepulcher. Prejudice no doubt. I had no difficulty in finding the Company's offices. It was the biggest thing in the town, and everybody I met was full of it. They were going to run an oversea empire, and make no end of coin by trade.

"A narrow and deserted street in deep shadow, high houses, innumerable windows with venetian blinds, a dead silence, grass sprouting between the stones, imposing carriage archways right and left, immense double doors standing ponderously ajar. I slipped through one of these cracks, went up a swept and ungarnished staircase, as arid as a desert, and opened the first door I came to. Two women, one fat and the other slim, sat on straw-bottomed chairs, knitting black wool. The slim one got up and walked straight at me—still knitting with downcast eyes—and only just as I began to think of getting out of her way, as you would for a somnambulist, stood still, and looked up. Her dress was as plain as an umbrella cover, and she turned round without a word and preceded me into a waiting room. I gave my name, and looked about. Deal table in the middle, plain chairs all round the walls, on one end a large shining map, marked with all the colors of a rainbow. There was a vast amount of red—good to see at any time, because one knows that some real work is done in there, a deuce of a lot of blue, a little green, smears of orange, and, on the East Coast, a purple patch, to show where the jolly pioneers of progress drink the jolly lager beer. However, I wasn't going into any of these. I was going into the yellow. Dead in the center. And the river was there—fascinating—deadly—like a snake. Ough! A door opened, a white-haired secretarial head, but wearing a compassionate expression, appeared, and a skinny forefinger beckoned me into the sanctuary. Its light was dim, and a heavy writing desk squatted in the middle. From behind that structure came out an impression of pale plumpness in a frock coat. The great man himself. He was five feet six, I should judge, and had his grip on the handle-end of ever so many millions. He shook hands, I fancy, murmured vaguely, was satisfied with my French. *Bon voyage.*

"In about forty-five seconds I found myself again in the waiting room with the compassionate secretary, who, full of desolation and sympathy, made me sign some document. I believe I undertook amongst other things not to disclose any trade secrets. Well, I am not going to.

"I began to feel slightly uneasy. You know I am not used to such ceremonies, and there was something ominous in the atmosphere. It was just as though I had been let into some conspiracy—I don't know—something not quite right; and I was glad to get out. In the outer room the two women knitted black wool feverishly. People were arriving, and the younger one was walking back and forth introducing them. The old one sat on her chair. Her flat cloth slippers were propped up on a foot warmer, and a cat reposed on her lap. She wore a starched white affair on her head, had a wart on one cheek, and silver-rimmed spectacles hung on the tip of her nose. She glanced at me above the glasses. The swift and indifferent placidity of that look troubled me. Two youths with foolish and cheery countenances were being piloted over, and she threw at them the same quick glance of unconcerned wisdom. She seemed to know all about them and about me too. An eerie feeling came over me. She seemed uncanny and fateful. Often far away there I thought of these two, guarding the door of Darkness, knitting black wool as for a warm pall, one introducing, introducing continuously to the unknown, the other scrutinizing the cheery and foolish faces with unconcerned old eyes. *Ave!* Old knitter of black wool. *Morituri te salutant.*[1] Not many of those she looked at ever saw her again—not half, by a long way.

"There was yet a visit to the doctor. 'A simple formality,' assured me the secretary, with an air of taking an immense part in all my sorrows. Accordingly a young chap wearing his hat over the left eyebrow, some clerk I suppose—there must have been clerks in the business, though the house was as still as a house in a city of the dead—came from somewhere upstairs, and led me forth. He was shabby and careless, with inkstains on the sleeves of his jacket, and his cravat was large and billowy, under a chin shaped like the toe of an old boot. It was a little too early for the doctor, so I proposed a drink, and thereupon he developed a vein of joviality. As we sat over our vermouths he glorified the Company's business, and by and by I expressed casually my surprise at him not going out there. He became very cool and collected all at

---

[1] *Morituri te salutant:* "They who are about to die salute you," the greeting Roman gladiators gave to Caesar before they fought in the amphitheater.

once. 'I am not such a fool as I look, quoth Plato to his disciples,' he said sententiously, emptied his glass with great resolution, and we rose.

"The old doctor felt my pulse, evidently thinking of something else the while. 'Good, good for there,' he mumbled, and then with a certain eagerness asked me whether I would let him measure my head. Rather surprised, I said Yes, when he produced a thing like callipers and got the dimensions back and front and every way, taking notes carefully. He was an unshaven little man in a threadbare coat like a gaberdine, with his feet in slippers, and I thought him a harmless fool. 'I always ask leave, in the interests of science, to measure the crania of those going out there,' he said. 'And when they come back too?' I asked. 'Oh, I never see them,' he remarked; 'and, moreover, the changes take place inside, you know.' He smiled, as if at some quiet joke. 'So you are going out there. Famous. Interesting too.' He gave me a searching glance, and made another note. 'Ever any madness in your family?' he asked, in a matter-of-fact tone. I felt very annoyed. 'Is that question in the interests of science too?' 'It would be,' he said, without taking notice of my irritation, 'interesting for science to watch the mental changes of individuals, on the spot, but . . .' 'Are you an alienist?' [1] I interrupted. 'Every doctor should be—a little,' answered that original imperturbably. 'I have a little theory which you Messieurs who go out there must help me to prove. This is my share in the advantages my country shall reap from the possession of such a magnificent dependency. The mere wealth I leave to others. Pardon my questions, but you are the first Englishman coming under my observation . . .' I hastened to assure him I was not in the least typical. 'If I were,' said I, 'I wouldn't be talking like this with you.' 'What you say is rather profound, and probably erroneous,' he said, with a laugh. 'Avoid irritation more than exposure to the sun. *Adieu*. How do you English say, eh? Good-bye. Ah! Good-bye. *Adieu*. In the tropics one must before everything keep calm.' . . . He lifted a warning forefinger. . . . '*Du calme, du calme. Adieu.*'

"One thing more remained to do—say good-bye to my excellent aunt. I found her triumphant. I had a cup of tea—the last decent cup of tea for many days—and in a room that most soothingly looked just as you would expect a lady's drawing room to look, we had a long quiet chat by the fireside. In the course of these confidences it became quite plain to me I had been represented to the wife of the high dignitary, and goodness knows to how many more people besides, as an exceptional and gifted creature—a piece of good fortune for the Company—a man you don't get hold of every day. Good heavens! and I was going to take charge of a two-penny-halfpenny river steamboat with a penny whistle attached! It appeared, however, I was also one of the Workers, with a capital—you know. Something like an emissary of light, something like a lower sort of apostle. There had been a lot of such rot let loose in print and talk just about that time, and the excellent woman, living right in the rush of all that humbug, got carried off her feet. She talked about 'weaning those

[1] *alienist:* psychiatrist.

ignorant millions from their horrid ways,' till, upon my word, she made me quite uncomfortable. I ventured to hint that the Company was run for profit.

" 'You forget, dear Charlie, that the laborer is worthy of his hire,' she said brightly. It's queer how out of touch with truth women are. They live in a world of their own, and there had never been anything like it, and never can be. It is too beautiful altogether, and if they were to set it up it would go to pieces before the first sunset. Some confounded fact we men have been living contentedly with ever since the day of creation would start up and knock the whole thing over.

"After this I got embraced, told to wear flannel, be sure to write often, and so on—and I left. In the street—I don't know why—a queer feeling came to me that I was an impostor. Odd thing that I, who used to clear out for any part of the world at twenty-four hours' notice, with less thought than most men give to the crossing of a street, had a moment—I won't say of hesitation, but of startled pause, before this commonplace affair. The best way I can explain it to you is by saying that, for a second or two, I felt as though, instead of going to the center of a continent, I were about to set off for the center of the earth.

"I left in a French steamer, and she called in every blamed port they have out there, for, as far as I could see, the sole purpose of landing soldiers and customhouse officers. I watched the coast. Watching a coast as it slips by the ship is like thinking about an enigma. There it is before you—smiling, frowning, inviting, grand, mean, insipid, or savage, and always mute with an air of whispering, Come and find out. This one was almost featureless, as if still in the making, with an aspect of monotonous grimness. The edge of a colossal jungle, so dark green as to be almost black, fringed with white surf, ran straight, like a ruled line, far, far away along a blue sea whose glitter was blurred by a creeping mist. The sun was fierce, the land seemed to glisten and drip with steam. Here and there grayish-whitish specks showed up clustered inside the white surf, with a flag flying above them perhaps—settlements some centuries old, and still no bigger than pin heads on the untouched expanse of their background. We pounded along, stopped, landed soldiers; went on, landed customhouse clerks to levy toll in what looked like a god forsaken wilderness, with a tin shed and a flagpole lost in it; landed more soldiers—to take care of the customhouse clerks presumably. Some, I heard, got drowned in the surf; but whether they did or not, nobody seemed particularly to care. They were just flung out there, and on we went. Every day the coast looked the same, as though we had not moved; but we passed various places— trading places—with names like Gran' Bassam, Little Popo; names that seemed to belong to some sordid farce acted in front of a sinister back cloth. The idleness of a passenger, my isolation amongst all these men with whom I had no point of contact, the oily and languid sea, the uniform somberness of the coast, seemed to keep me away from the truth of things, within the toil of a mournful and senseless delusion. The voice of the surf heard now and then was a positive pleasure, like the speech of a brother. It was something natural, that had its reason, that had a meaning. Now and then a boat from the shore gave one a momentary contact with reality. It was paddled by black fellows. You could see from afar the white of their eyeballs glistening. They shouted, sang; their bodies streamed with perspiration; they had faces like grotesque masks—these chaps; but they had bone, muscle, a wild vitality, an intense energy of movement, that was as natural and true as the surf along their coast. They wanted no excuse for being there. They were a great comfort to look at. For a time I would feel I belonged still to a world of straightforward facts; but the feeling would not last long. Something would turn up to scare it away. Once, I remember, we came upon a man-of-war anchored off the coast. There wasn't even a shed there, and she was shelling the bush. It appears the French had one of their wars going on thereabouts. Her ensign dropped limp like a rag; the muzzles of the long six-inch guns stuck out all over the low hull; the greasy, slimy swell swung her up lazily and let her down, swaying her thin masts. In the empty immensity of earth, sky, and water, there she was, incomprehensible, firing into a continent. Pop, would go one of the six-inch guns; a small flame would dart and vanish, a little white smoke would disappear, a tiny projectile would give a feeble screech—and nothing happened. Nothing could happen. There was a touch of insanity in the proceeding, a sense of lugubrious drollery in the sight; and it was not dissipated by somebody on board assuring me earnestly there was a camp of natives—he called them enemies!—hidden out of sight somewhere.

"We gave her her letters (I heard the men in that lonely ship were dying of fever at the rate of three a day) and went on. We called at some more places with farcical names, where the merry dance of death and trade goes on in a still and earthy atmosphere as of an overheated catacomb; all along the formless coast bordered by dangerous surf, as if Nature herself had tried to ward off intruders; in and out of rivers, streams of death in life, whose banks were rotting into mud, whose waters, thickened into slime, invaded the contorted mangroves, that seemed to writhe at us in the extremity of an impotent despair. Nowhere did we stop long enough to get a particularized impression, but the general sense of vague and oppressive wonder grew upon me. It was like a weary pilgrimage among hints for nightmares.

"It was upward of thirty days before I saw the mouth of the big river. We anchored off the seat of the government. But my work would not begin till some two hundred miles farther on. So as soon as I could I made a start for a place thirty miles higher up.

"I had passage on a little seagoing steamer. Her captain was a Swede, and knowing me for a seaman, invited me on the bridge. He was a young man, lean, fair, and morose, with lanky hair and a shuffling gait. As we left the miserable little wharf, he tossed his head contemptuously at the shore. 'Been living there?' he asked. I said, 'Yes.' 'Fine lot these government chaps —are they not?' he went on, speaking English with great precision and considerable bitterness. 'It is funny what some people will do for a few francs a month. I wonder what becomes of that kind when it goes up country?' I said to him I expected to see that soon. 'So-o-o!' he exclaimed. He shuffled athwart, keeping one eye ahead vigilantly. 'Don't be too sure,' he continued. 'The other day I took up a man who hanged himself on the road. He was a Swede, too.' 'Hanged himself! Why, in God's name?' I cried. He kept on looking out watchfully. 'Who knows? The sun too much for him, or the country perhaps.'

"At last we opened a reach. A rocky cliff appeared, mounds of turned-up earth by the shore, houses on a hill, others with iron roofs, amongst a waste of excavations, or hanging to the declivity. A continuous noise of the rapids above hovered over this scene of inhabited devastation. A lot of people, mostly black and naked, moved about like ants. A jetty projected into the river. A blinding sunlight drowned all this at times in a sudden recrudescence of glare. 'There's your Company's station,' said the Swede, pointing to three wooden barracklike structures on the rocky slope. 'I will send your things up. Four boxes did you say? So. Farewell.'

"I came upon a boiler wallowing in the grass, then found a path leading up the hill. It turned aside for the boulders, and also for an undersized railway truck lying there on its back with its wheels in the air. One was off. The thing looked as dead as the carcass of some animal. I came upon more pieces of decaying machinery, a stack of rusty nails. To the left a clump of trees made a shady spot, where dark things seemed to stir feebly. I blinked, the path was steep. A horn tooted to the right, and I saw the black people run. A heavy and dull detonation shook the ground, a puff of smoke came out of the cliff, and that was all. No change appeared on the face of the rock. They were building a railway. The cliff was not in the way or anything; but this objectless blasting was all the work going on.

"A slight clinking behind me made me turn my head. Six black men advanced in a file, toiling up the path. They walked erect and slow, balancing small baskets full of earth on their heads, and the clink kept time with their footsteps. Black rags were wound round their loins, and the short ends behind waggled to and fro like tails. I could see every rib, the joints of their limbs were like knots in a rope; each had an iron collar on his neck, and all were connected together with a chain whose bights swung between them, rhythmically clinking. Another report from the cliff made me think suddenly of that ship of war I had seen firing into a continent. It was the same kind of ominous voice; but these men could by no stretch of imagination be called enemies. They were called criminals, and the outraged law, like the bursting shells, had come to them, an insoluble mystery from the sea. All their meager breasts panted together, the violently dilated nostrils quivered, the eyes stared stonily uphill. They passed me within six inches, without a glance, with that complete, deathlike indifference of unhappy savages. Behind this raw matter one of the reclaimed, the product of the new forces at work, strolled despondently, carrying a rifle by its middle. He had a uniform jacket with one button off, and seeing a white man on the path, hoisted his weapon to his shoulder with alacrity. This was simple prudence, white men being so much alike at a distance that he could not tell who I might be. He was speedily reassured, and with a large, white, rascally grin, and a glance at his charge, seemed to take me into partnership in his exalted trust. After all, I also was a part of the great cause of these high and just proceedings.

"Instead of going up, I turned and descended to the left. My idea was to let that chain gang get out of sight before I climbed the hill. You know I am not particularly tender; I've had to strike and to fend off. I've had to resist and to attack sometimes—that's only one way of resisting—without counting the exact cost, according to the demands of such sort of life as I had blundered into. I've seen the devil of violence, and the devil of greed, and the devil of hot desire; but, by all the stars! these were strong, lusty, red-eyed devils, that swayed and drove men—men, I tell you. But as I stood on this hillside, I foresaw that in the blinding sunshine of that land I would become acquainted with a flabby, pretending, weak-eyed devil of a rapacious and pitiless folly. How insidious he could be, too, I was only to find out several months later and a thousand miles farther. For a moment I stood appalled, as though by a warning. Finally I descended the hill, obliquely, towards the trees I had seen.

"I avoided a vast artificial hole somebody had been digging on the slope, the purpose of which I found it impossible to divine. It wasn't a quarry or a sandpit, anyhow. It was just a hole. It might have been connected with the philanthropic desire of giving the criminals something to do. I don't know. Then I nearly fell into a very narrow ravine, almost no more than a scar in the hillside. I discovered that a lot of imported drainage pipes for the settlement had been tumbled in there. There wasn't one that was not broken. It was a wanton smash-up. At last I got under the trees. My purpose was to stroll into the shade for a moment; but no sooner within than it seemed to me I had stepped into the gloomy circle of some Inferno. The rapids were near, and an uninterrupted, uniform, headlong, rushing noise filled the mournful stillness of the grove, where not a breath stirred, not a leaf moved, with a mysterious sound—as though the tearing pace of the launched earth had suddenly become audible.

"Black shapes crouched, lay, sat between the trees, leaning against the trunks, clinging to the earth, half coming out, half effaced within the dim light, in all the attitudes of pain, abandonment, and despair. Another mine on the cliff went off, followed by a slight shudder of the soil under my feet. The work was going on. The work! And this was the place where some of the helpers had withdrawn to die.

"They were dying slowly—it was very clear. They were not enemies, they were not criminals, they were nothing earthly now—nothing but black shadows of disease and starvation, lying confusedly in the greenish gloom.

Brought from all the recesses of the coast in all the legality of time contracts, lost in uncongenial surroundings, fed on unfamiliar food, they sickened, became inefficient, and were then allowed to crawl away and rest. These moribund shapes were free as air—and nearly as thin. I began to distinguish the gleam of eyes under the trees. Then, glancing down, I saw a face near my hand. The black bones reclined at full length with one shoulder against the tree, and slowly the eyelids rose and the sunken eyes looked up at me, enormous and vacant, a kind of blind, white flicker in the depths of the orbs, which died out slowly. The man seemed young—almost a boy—but you know with them it's hard to tell. I found nothing else to do but to offer him one of my good Swede's ship's biscuits I had in my pocket. The fingers closed slowly on it and held—there was no other movement and no other glance. He had tied a bit of white worsted round his neck—Why? Where did he get it? Was it a badge—an ornament—a charm—a propitiatory act? Was there any idea at all connected with it? It looked startling round his black neck, this bit of white thread from beyond the seas.

"Near the same tree two more bundles of acute angles sat with their legs drawn up. One, with his chin propped on his knees, stared at nothing, in an intolerable and appalling manner: his brother phantom rested its forehead, as if overcome with a great weariness; and all about others were scattered in every pose of contorted collapse, as in some picture of a massacre or a pestilence. While I stood horror-struck, one of these creatures rose to his hands and knees, and went off on all fours towards the river to drink. He lapped out of his hand, then sat up in the sunlight, crossing his shins in front of him, and after a time let his woolly head fall on his breastbone.

"I didn't want any more loitering in the shade, and I made haste towards the station. When near the buildings I met a white man, in such an unexpected elegance of getup that in the first moment I took him for a sort of vision. I saw a high starched collar, white cuffs, a light alpaca jacket, snowy trousers, a clear necktie, and varnished boots. No hat. Hair parted, brushed, oiled, under a green-lined parasol held in a big white hand. He was amazing, and had a penholder behind his ear.

"I shook hands with this miracle, and I learned he was the Company's chief accountant, and that all the bookkeeping was done at this station. He had come out for a moment, he said, 'to get a breath of fresh air.' The expression sounded wonderfully odd, with its suggestion of sedentary desk life. I wouldn't have mentioned the fellow to you at all, only it was from his lips that I first heard the name of the man who is so indissolubly connected with the memories of that time. Moreover, I respected the fellow. Yes; I respected his collars, his vast cuffs, his brushed hair. His appearance was certainly that of a hairdresser's dummy; but in the great demoralization of the land he kept up his appearance. That's backbone. His starched collars and got-up shirt fronts were achievements of character. He had been out nearly three years; and, later, I could not help asking him how he managed to sport such linen. He had just the faintest blush, and said modestly, 'I've been teaching one of the native women about the station. It was difficult. She had a distaste for the work.' Thus this man had verily accomplished something. And he was devoted to his books, which were in apple-pie order.

"Everything else in the station was in a muddle—heads, things, buildings. Strings of dusty natives with splay feet arrived and departed; a stream of manufactured goods, rubbishy cottons, beads, and brass wire set into the depths of darkness, and in return came a precious trickle of ivory.

"I had to wait in the station for ten days—an eternity. I lived in a hut in the yard, but to be out of the chaos I would sometimes get into the accountant's office. It was built of horizontal planks, and so badly put together that, as he bent over his high desk, he was barred from neck to heels with narrow strips of sunlight. There was no need to open the big shutter to see. It was hot there too; big flies buzzed fiendishly, and did not sting, but stabbed. I sat generally on the floor, while, of faultless appearance (and even slightly scented), perching on a high stool, he wrote, he wrote. Sometimes he stood up for exercise. When a truckle bed with a sick man (some invalided agent from upcountry) was put in there, he exhibited a gentle annoyance. 'The groans of this sick person,' he said, 'distract my attention. And without that it is extremely difficult to guard against clerical errors in this climate.'

"One day he remarked, without lifting his head, 'In the interior you will no doubt meet Mr. Kurtz.' On my asking who Mr. Kurtz was, he said he was a first-class agent; and seeing my disappointment at this information, he added slowly, laying down his pen, 'He is a very remarkable person.' Further questions elicited from him that Mr. Kurtz was at present in charge of a trading post, a very important one, in the true ivory country, at 'the very bottom of there. Sends in as much ivory as all the others put together. . . .' He began to write again. The sick man was too ill to groan. The flies buzzed in a great peace.

"Suddenly there was a growing murmur of voices and a great tramping of feet. A caravan had come in. A violent babble of uncouth sounds burst out on the other side of the planks. All the carriers were speaking together, and in the midst of the uproar the lamentable voice of the chief agent was heard 'giving it up' tearfully for the twentieth time that day. . . . He rose slowly. 'What a frightful row,' he said. He crossed the room gently to look at the sick man, and returning, said to me, 'He does not hear.' 'What! Dead?' I asked, startled. 'No, not yet,' he answered, with great composure. Then, alluding with a toss of the head to the tumult in the station yard, 'When one has got to make correct entries, one comes to hate those savages—hate them to the death.' He remained thoughtful for a moment. 'When you see Mr. Kurtz,' he went on, 'tell him from me that everything here'—he glanced at the desk—'is very satisfactory. I don't like to write to him—with those messengers of ours you never know who may get hold of your letter—at that Central Station.' He stared at me for a moment with his mild, bulging eyes. 'Oh, he will go far, very far,' he began again. 'He will be a somebody in the Administration before long. They, above—the Council in Europe, you know—mean him to be.'

"He turned to his work. The noise outside had ceased, and presently in going out I stopped at the door. In the steady buzz of flies the homeward-bound agent was lying flushed and insensible; the other, bent over his books, was making correct entries of perfectly correct transactions; and fifty feet below the doorstep I could see the still treetops of the grove of death.

"Next day I left that station at last, with a caravan of sixty men, for a two-hundred-mile tramp.

"No use telling you much about that. Paths, paths, everywhere; a stamped-in network of paths spreading over the empty land, through long grass, through burnt grass, through thickets, down and up chilly ravines, up and down stony hills ablaze with heat; and a solitude, a solitude, nobody, not a hut. The population had cleared out a long time ago. Well, if a lot of mysterious Negroes armed with all kinds of fearful weapons suddenly took to travelling on the road between Deal and Gravesend, catching the yokels right and left to carry heavy loads for them, I fancy every farm and cottage thereabouts would get empty very soon. Only here the dwellings were gone too. Still, I passed through several abandoned villages. There's something pathetically childish in the ruins of grass walls. Day after day, with the stamp and shuffle of sixty pair of bare feet behind me, each pair under a sixty-pound load. Camp, cook, sleep, strike camp, march. Now and then a carrier dead in harness, at rest in the long grass near the path, with an empty water gourd and his long staff lying by his side. A great silence around and above. Perhaps on some quiet night the tremor of far-off drums, sinking, swelling, a tremor vast, faint; a sound weird, appealing, suggestive, and wild—and perhaps with as profound a meaning as the sound of bells in a Christian country. Once a white man in an unbuttoned uniform, camping on the path with an armed escort of lank Zanzibaris, very hospitable and festive—not to say drunk. Was looking after the upkeep of the road, he declared. Can't say I saw any road or any upkeep, unless the body of a middle-aged Negro, with a bullet-hole in the forehead, upon which I absolutely stumbled three miles farther on, may be considered as a permanent improvement. I had a white companion too, not a bad chap, but rather too fleshy and with the exasperating habit of fainting on the hot hillsides, miles away from the least bit of shade and water. Annoying, you know, to hold your own coat like a parasol over a man's head while he is coming to. I couldn't help asking him once what he meant by coming there at all. 'To make money, of course. What do you think?' he said scornfully. Then he got fever, and had to be carried in a hammock slung under a pole. As he weighed sixteen stone I had no end of rows with the carriers. They jibbed, ran away, sneaked off with their loads in the night—quite a mutiny. So, one evening, I made a speech in English with gestures, not one of which was lost to the sixty pairs of eyes before me, and the next morning I started the hammock off in front all right. An hour afterward I came upon the whole concern wrecked in a bush—man, hammock, groans, blankets, horrors. The heavy pole had skinned his poor nose. He was very anxious for me to kill somebody, but there wasn't the shadow of a carrier near. I remembered the old doctor—'It would be interesting for science to watch the mental changes of individuals, on the spot.' I felt I was becoming scientifically interesting. However, all that is to no purpose. On the fifteenth day I came in sight of the big river again, and hobbled into the Central Station. It was on a backwater surrounded by scrub and forest, with a pretty border of smelly mud on one side, and on the three others enclosed by a crazy fence of rushes. A neglected gap was all the gate it had, and the first glance at the place was enough to let you see the flabby devil was running that show. White men with long staves in their hands appeared languidly from among the buildings, strolling up to take a look at me, and then retired out of sight somewhere. One of them, a stout, excitable chap with black mustaches, informed me with great volubility and many digressions, as soon as I told him who I was, that my steamer was at the bottom of the river. I was thunderstruck. What, how, why? Oh, it was 'all right.' The 'manager himself' was there. All quite correct. 'Everybody had behaved splendidly! splendidly!'—'You must,' he said in agitation, 'go and see the general manager at once. He is waiting!'

"I did not see the real significance of that wreck at once. I fancy I see it now, but I am not sure—not at all. Certainly the affair was too stupid—when I think of it—to be altogether natural. Still. . . . But at the moment it presented itself simply as a confounded nuisance. The steamer was sunk. They had started two days before in a sudden hurry up the river with the manager on board, in charge of some volunteer skipper, and before they had been out three hours they tore the bottom out of her on stones, and she sank near the south bank. I asked myself what I was to do there, now my boat was lost. As a matter of fact, I had plenty to do in fishing my command out of the river. I had to set about it the very next day. That, and the repairs when I brought the pieces to the station, took some months.

"My first interview with the manager was curious. He did not ask me to sit down after my twenty-mile walk that morning. He was commonplace in complexion, in feature, in manners, and in voice. He was of middle size and of ordinary build. His eyes, of the usual blue, were perhaps remarkably cold, and he certainly could make his glance fall on one as trenchant and heavy as an ax. But even at these times the rest of his person seemed to disclaim the intention. Otherwise there was only an indefinable, faint expression of his lips, something stealthy—a smile—not a smile—I remember it, but I can't explain. It was unconscious, this smile was, though just after he had said something it got intensified for an instant. It came at the end of his speeches like a seal applied on the words to make the meaning of the commonest phrase appear absolutely inscrutable. He was a common trader, from his youth up employed in these parts—nothing more. He was obeyed, yet he inspired neither love nor fear, nor even respect. He inspired uneasiness. That was it! Uneasiness. Not a definite mistrust—just uneasiness—nothing more. You have no idea how effective such a . . . a . . . faculty can be. He had no genius for organizing, for initiative, or for order even. That was evident in such things as the deplorable state of the station. He had no learning, and no intelligence. His position had come to him—why? Perhaps because he was never ill. . . . He had served three terms of three years out there. . . . Because triumphant health in the general rout of constitutions is a kind of power in itself. When he went home on leave he rioted on a large scale—pompously. Jack ashore—with a difference—in externals only. This one could gather from his casual talk. He originated nothing, he could keep the routine going—that's all. But he was great. He was great by this little thing that it was impossible to tell what could control such a man. He never gave that secret away. Perhaps there was nothing within him. Such a suspicion made one pause—for out there there were no external checks. Once when various tropical diseases had laid low almost every 'agent' in the station, he was heard to say, 'Men who come out here should have no entrails.' He sealed the utterance with that smile of his, as though it had been a door opening into a darkness he had in his keeping. You fancied you had seen things—but the seal was on. When annoyed at mealtimes by the constant quarrels of the white men about precedence, he ordered an immense round table to be made, for which a special house had to be built. This was the station's mess room. Where he sat was the first place—the rest were nowhere. One felt this to be his unalterable conviction. He was neither civil nor uncivil. He was quiet. He allowed his 'boy'—an overfed young Negro from the coast—to treat the white men, under his very eyes, with provoking insolence.

"He began to speak as soon as he saw me. I had been very long on the road. He could not wait. Had to start without me. The upriver stations had to be relieved. There had been so many delays already that he did not know who was dead and who was alive, and how they got on—and so on, and so on. He paid no attention to my explanations, and, playing with a stick of sealing wax, repeated several times that the situation was 'very grave, very grave.' There were rumors that a very important station was in jeopardy, and its chief, Mr. Kurtz, was ill. Hoped it was not true. Mr. Kurtz was. . . . I felt weary and irritable. Hang Kurtz, I thought. I interrupted him by saying I had heard of Mr. Kurtz on the coast. 'Ah! So they talk of him down there,' he murmured to himself. Then he began again, assuring me Mr. Kurtz was the best agent he had, an exceptional man, of the greatest importance to the Company; therefore I could understand his anxiety. He was, he said, 'very, very uneasy.' Certainly he fidgeted on his chair a good deal, exclaimed, 'Ah, Mr. Kurtz!' broke the stick of sealing wax and seemed dumbfounded by the accident. Next thing he wanted to know 'how long it would take to' . . . I interrupted him again. Being hungry, you know, and kept on my feet too, I was getting savage. 'How can I tell?' I said. 'I haven't even seen the wreck yet—some months, no doubt.' All this talk seemed to me so futile. 'Some months,' he said. 'Well, let us say three months before we can make a start. Yes. That ought to do the affair.' I flung out of his hut (he lived all alone in a clay hut with a sort of verandah) muttering to myself my opinion of him. He was a chattering idiot. Afterward I took it back when it was borne in upon me startlingly with what extreme nicety he had estimated the time requisite for the 'affair.'

"I went to work the next day, turning, so to speak, my back on that station. In that way only it seemed to me I could keep my hold on the redeeming facts of life. Still, one must look about sometimes; and then I saw this station, these men strolling aimlessly about in the sunshine of the yard. I asked myself sometimes what it all meant. They wandered here and there with their absurd long staves in their hands, like a lot of faithless pilgrims bewitched inside a rotten fence. The word *ivory* rang in the air, was whispered, was sighed. You would think they were praying to it. A taint of imbecile rapacity blew through it all, like a whiff from some corpse. By Jove! I've never seen anything so unreal in my life. And outside, the silent wilderness surrounding this cleared speck on the earth struck me as something great and invincible, like evil or truth, waiting patiently for the passing away of this fantastic invasion.

"Oh, these months! Well, never mind. Various things happened. One evening a grass shed full of calico, cotton prints, beads, and I don't know what else, burst into a blaze so suddenly that you would have thought the earth had opened to let an avenging fire consume all that trash. I was smoking my pipe quietly by my dismantled steamer, and saw them all cutting capers in the light, with their arms lifted high, when the stout man with mustaches came tearing down to the river, a tin pail in his hand, assured me that everybody was 'behaving splendidly, splendidly,' dipped about a quart of water and tore back again. I noticed there was a hole in the bottom of his pail.

"I strolled up. There was no hurry. You see the thing had gone off like a box of matches. It had been hopeless from the very first. The flame had leaped high, driven everybody back, lighted up everything—and collapsed. The shed was already a heap of embers glowing fiercely. A Negro was being beaten near by. They said he had caused the fire in some way; be that as it may, he was screeching most horribly. I saw him, later, for several days, sitting in a bit of shade looking very sick and trying to recover himself: afterward he arose and went out—and the wilderness without a sound took him into its bosom again. As I approached the glow from the dark I found myself at the back of two men, talking. I heard the name of Kurtz pronounced, then the words, 'take advantage of this unfortunate accident.' One of the men was the manager. I wished him a good evening. 'Did you ever see anything like it—eh? it is incredible,' he said, and walked off. The other man remained. He was a first-class agent, young, gentlemanly, a bit reserved, with a forked little beard and a hooked nose. He was standoffish with the other agents, and they on their side said he was the manager's spy upon them. As to me, I had hardly ever spoken to him before. We got into talk, and by and by we strolled away from the hissing ruins. Then he asked me to his room, which was in the main building of the station. He struck a match, and I perceived that this young aristocrat had not only a silver-mounted dressing case but also a whole candle all to himself. Just at that time the manager was the only man supposed to have any right to candles. Native mats covered the clay walls; a collection of spears, assagais, shields, knives, was hung up in trophies. The business entrusted to this fellow was the making of bricks—so I had been informed; but there wasn't a fragment of a brick anywhere in the station, and he had been there more than a year—waiting. It seems he could not make bricks without something. I don't know what—straw maybe. Anyway, it could not be found there, and as it was not likely to be sent from Europe, it did not appear clear to me what he was waiting for. An act of special creation perhaps. However, they were all waiting—all the sixteen or twenty pilgrims of them—for something; and upon my word it did not seem an uncongenial occupation, from the way they took it, though the only thing that ever came to them was disease—as far as I could see. They beguiled the time by backbiting and intriguing against each other in a foolish kind of way. There was an air of plotting about that station, but nothing came of it, of course. It was as unreal as everything else—as the philanthropic pretense of the whole concern, as their talk, as their government, as their show of work. The only real feeling was a desire to get appointed to a trading post where ivory was to be had, so that they could earn percentages. They intrigued and slandered and hated each other only on that account—but as to effectually lifting a little finger— oh no. By heavens! there is something after all in the world allowing one man to steal a horse while another must not look at a halter. Steal a horse straight out. Very well. He has done it. Perhaps he can ride. But there is a way of looking at a halter that would provoke the most charitable of saints into a kick.

"I had no idea why he wanted to be sociable, but as we chatted in there it suddenly occurred to me the fellow was trying to get at something—in fact, pumping me. He alluded constantly to Europe, to the people I was supposed to know there—putting leading questions as to my acquaintances in the sepulchral city, and so on. His little eyes glittered like mica discs—with curiosity— though he tried to keep up a bit of superciliousness. At first I was astonished, but very soon I became awfully curious to see what he would find out from me. I couldn't possibly imagine what I had in me to make it worth his while. It was very pretty to see how he baffled himself, for in truth my body was full only of chills, and my head had nothing in it but that wretched steamboat business. It was evident he took me for a perfectly shameless prevaricator. At last he got angry, and, to conceal a movement of furious annoyance, he yawned. I rose. Then I noticed a small sketch in oils, on a panel, representing a woman, draped and blindfolded, carrying a lighted torch. The background was somber—almost black. The movement of the woman was stately, and the effect of the torchlight on the face was sinister.

"It arrested me, and he stood by civilly, holding an empty half pint champagne bottle (medical comforts) with the candle stuck in it. To my question he said Mr. Kurtz had painted this—in this very station more than a year ago—while waiting for means to go to his trading post. 'Tell me, pray,' said I, 'who is this Mr. Kurtz?'

" 'The chief of the Inner Station,' he answered in a short tone, looking away. 'Much obliged,' I said, laughing. 'And you are the brickmaker of the Central Station. Everyone knows that.' He was silent for a while. 'He is a prodigy,' he said at last. 'He is an emissary of pity, and science, and progress, and devil knows what else. We want,' he began to declaim suddenly, 'for the guidance of the cause entrusted to us by Europe, so to speak, higher intelligence, wide sympathies, a singleness of purpose.' 'Who says that?' I asked. 'Lots of them,' he replied. 'Some even write that; and so *he* comes here, a special being, as you ought to know.' 'Why ought I to know?' I interrupted, really surprised. He paid no attention. 'Yes. Today he is chief of the best station, next year he will be assistant manager, two years more and . . . but I daresay you know what he will be in two years' time. You are of the new gang—the gang of virtue. The same people who sent him specially also recommended you. Oh, don't say no. I've my own eyes to trust.' Light dawned upon me. My dear aunt's influential acquaintances were producing an unexpected effect upon that young man. I nearly burst into a laugh. 'Do you read the Company's confidential correspondence?' I asked. He hadn't a word to say. It was great fun. 'When Mr. Kurtz,' I continued severely, 'is General Manager, you won't have the opportunity.'

"He blew the candle out suddenly, and we went outside. The moon had risen. Black figures strolled about listlessly, pouring water on the glow, whence proceeded a sound of hissing; steam ascended in the moonlight; the beaten native groaned somewhere. 'What a row the brute makes!' said the indefatigable man with the mustaches, appearing near us. 'Serve him right. Transgression—punishment—bang! Pitiless, pitiless. That's the only way. This will prevent all conflagrations for the future. I was just telling the manager. . . .' He noticed my companion, and became crestfallen all at once. 'Not in bed yet,' he said, with a kind of servile heartiness; 'it's so natural. Ha! Danger—agitation.' He vanished. I went on to the riverside, and the other followed me. I heard a scathing murmur at my ear, 'Heap of muffs—go to.' The pilgrims could be seen in knots gesticulating, discussing. Several had still their staves in their hands. I verily believe they took these sticks to bed with them. Beyond the fence the forest stood up spectrally in the moonlight, and through the dim stir, through the faint sounds of that lamentable courtyard, the silence of the land went home to one's very heart—its mystery, its greatness, the amazing reality of its concealed life. The hurt native moaned feebly somewhere near by, and then fetched a deep sigh that made me mend my pace away from there. I felt a hand introducing itself under my arm. 'My dear sir,' said the fellow, 'I don't want to be misunderstood, and especially by you, who will see Mr. Kurtz long before I can have that pleasure. I wouldn't like him to get a false idea of my disposition. . . . '

"I let him run on, this papier-mâché Mephistopheles, and it seemed to me that if I tried I could poke my forefinger through him, and would find nothing inside but a little loose dirt, maybe. He, don't you see, had been planning to be assistant manager by and by under the present man, and I could see that the coming of that Kurtz had upset them both not a little. He talked precipitately, and I did not try to stop him. I had my shoulders against the wreck of my steamer, hauled up on the slope like a carcass of some big river animal. The smell of mud, of primeval mud, by Jove! was in my nostrils, the high stillness of primeval forest was before my eyes; there were shiny patches on the black creek. The moon had spread over everything a thin layer of silver— over the rank grass, over the mud, upon the wall of matted vegetation standing higher than the wall of a temple, over the great river I could see through a somber gap glittering, glittering, as it flowed broadly by without a murmur. All this was great, expectant, mute, while the man jabbered about himself. I wondered whether the stillness on the face of the immensity looking at us two were meant as an appeal or as a menace. What were we who had strayed in here? Could we handle that dumb thing, or would it handle us? I felt how big, how confoundedly big, was that thing that couldn't talk and perhaps was deaf as well. What was in there? I could see a little ivory coming out from there, and I had heard Mr. Kurtz was in there. I had heard enough about it too— God knows! Yet somehow it didn't bring any image with it—no more than if I had been told an angel or a fiend was in there. I believed it in the same way one of you might believe there are inhabitants in the planet Mars. I knew once a Scotch sailmaker who was certain, dead sure, there were people in Mars. If you asked him for some idea how they looked and behaved, he would get shy and mutter something about 'walking on all fours.' If you as much as smiled, he would—though a man of sixty—offer to fight you. I would not have gone so far as to fight for Kurtz, but I went for him near enough to a lie. You know I hate, detest, and can't bear a lie, not because I am straighter than the rest of us, but simply because it appalls me. There is a taint of death, a flavor of mortality in lies—which is exactly what I hate and detest in the world—what I want to forget. It makes me miserable and sick, like biting something rotten would do. Temperament, I suppose. Well, I went near enough to it by letting the young fool there believe anything he liked to imagine as to my influence in Europe. I became in an instant as much of a pretense as the rest of the bewitched pilgrims. This simply because I had a notion it somehow would be of help to that Kurtz whom at the time I did not see—you understand. He was just a word for me. I did not see the man in the name any more than you do. Do you see him? Do you see the story? Do you see anything? It seems to me I am trying to tell you a dream—making a vain attempt, because no relation of a dream can convey the dream sensation, that commingling of absurdity, surprise, and bewilderment in a tremor of struggling revolt, that notion of being captured by the incredible which is of the very essence of dreams. . . ."

He was silent for a while.

". . . No, it is impossible; it is impossible to convey the life sensation of any given epoch of one's existence—that which makes its truth, its meaning—its subtle and penetrating essence. It is impossible. We live, as we dream—alone. . . ."

He paused again as if reflecting, then added:

"Of course in this you fellows see more than I could then. You see me, whom you know. . . ."

It had become so pitch dark that we listeners could hardly see one another. For a long time already he, sitting apart, had been no more to us than a voice. There was not a word from anybody. The others might have been asleep, but I was awake. I listened, I listened on the watch for the sentence, for the word, that would give me the clue to the faint uneasiness inspired by this narrative that seemed to shape itself without human lips in the heavy night air of the river.

". . . Yes—I let him run on," Marlow began again, "and think what he pleased about the powers that were behind me. I did! And there was nothing behind me! There was nothing but that wretched, old, mangled steamboat I was leaning against, while he talked fluently about 'the necessity for every man to get on.' 'And when one comes out here, you conceive, it is not to gaze at the moon.' Mr. Kurtz was a 'universal genius,' but even a genius would find it easier to work with 'adequate tools—intelligent men.' He did not make bricks—why, there was a physical impossibility in the way—as I was well aware; and if he did secretarial work for the manager, it was because 'no sensible man rejects wantonly the confidence of his superiors.' Did I see it? I saw it. What more did I want? What I really wanted was rivets, by heaven! Rivets. To get on with the work—to stop the hole. Rivets I wanted. There were cases of them down at the coast—cases—piled up—burst—split! You kicked a loose rivet at every second step in that station yard on the hillside. Rivets had rolled into the grove of death. You could fill your pockets with rivets for the trouble of stooping down—and there wasn't one rivet to be found where it was wanted. We had plates that would do, but nothing to fasten them with. And every week the messenger, a lone Negro, letter bag on shoulder and staff in hand, left our station for the coast. And several times a week a coast caravan came in with trade goods—ghastly glazed calico that made you shudder only to look at it, glass beads value about a penny a quart, confounded spotted cotton handkerchiefs. And no rivets. Three carriers could have brought all that was wanted to set that steamboat afloat.

"He was becoming confidential now, but I fancy my unresponsive attitude must have exasperated him at last, for he judged it necessary to inform me he feared neither God nor devil, let alone any mere man. I said I could see that very well, but what I wanted was a certain quantity of rivets—and rivets were what really Mr. Kurtz wanted, if he had only known it. Now letters went to the coast every week. . . . 'My dear sir,' he cried, 'I write from dictation.' I demanded rivets. There was a way—for an intelligent man. He changed his manner; became very cold, and suddenly began to talk about a hippopotamus; wondered whether sleeping on board the steamer (I stuck to my salvage night and day) I wasn't disturbed. There was an old hippo that had the bad habit of getting out on the bank and roaming at night over the station grounds. The pilgrims used to turn out in a body and empty every rifle they could lay hands on at him. Some even had sat up o' nights for him. All this energy was wasted, though. 'That animal has a charmed life,' he said; 'but you can say this only of brutes in this country. No man—you apprehend me?—no man here bears a charmed life.' He stood there for a moment in the moonlight with his delicate hooked nose set a little askew, and his mica eyes glittering without a wink, then, with a curt 'Good-night,' he strode off. I could see he was disturbed and considerably puzzled, which made me feel more hopeful than I had been for days. It was a great comfort to turn from that chap to my influential friend, the battered, twisted, ruined, tin-pot steamboat. I clambered on board. She rang under my feet like an empty Huntley & Palmer biscuit tin kicked along a gutter; she was nothing so solid in make, and rather less pretty in shape, but I had expended enough hard work on her to make me love her. No influential friend would have served me better. She had given me a chance to come out a bit—to find out what I could do. No, I don't like work. I had rather laze about and think of all the fine things that can be done. I don't like work—no man does—but I like what is in the work—the chance to find yourself. Your own reality—for yourself, not for others—what no other man can ever know. They can only see the mere show, and never can tell what it really means.

"I was not surprised to see somebody sitting aft, on the deck, with his legs dangling over the mud. You see I rather chummed with the few mechanics there were in that station, whom the other pilgrims naturally despised—on account of their imperfect manners, I suppose. This was the foreman—a boiler maker by trade—a good worker. He was a lank, bony, yellow-faced man, with big intense eyes. His aspect was worried, and his head was as bald as the palm of my hand; but his hair in falling seemed to have stuck to his chin, and had prospered in the new locality, for his beard hung down to his waist. He was a widower with six young children (he had left them in charge of a sister of his to come out there), and the passion of his life was pigeon-flying. He was an enthusiast and a connoisseur. He would rave about pigeons. After work hours he used sometimes to come over from his hut for a talk about his children and his pigeons; at work, when he had to crawl in the mud under the bottom of the steamboat, he would tie up that beard of his in a kind of white serviette he brought for the purpose. It had loops to go over his ears. In the evening he could be seen squatted on the bank rinsing that wrapper in the creek with great care, then spreading it solemnly on a bush to dry.

"I slapped him on the back and shouted 'We shall have rivets!' He scrambled to his feet exclaiming 'No! Rivets!' as though he couldn't believe his ears. Then in a low voice, 'You . . . eh?' I don't know why we behaved like lunatics. I put my finger to the side of my nose and nodded mysteriously. 'Good for you!' he cried, snapped his fingers above his head, lifting one foot. I tried a jig. We capered on the iron deck. A frightful clatter came out of that hulk, and the virgin forest on the other bank of the creek sent it back in a thundering roll upon the sleeping station. It must have made some of the pilgrims sit up in their hovels. A dark figure obscured the lighted doorway of the manager's hut, vanished, then, a second or so after, the doorway itself vanished too. We stopped, and the silence driven away by the stamping of our feet flowed back again from the recesses of the land. The great wall of vegetation, an exuberant and entangled mass of trunks, branches, leaves, boughs, festoons, motionless in the moonlight, was like a rioting invasion of soundless life, a rolling wave of plants, piled up, crested, ready to topple over the creek, to sweep every little man of us out of his little existence. And it moved not. A deadened burst of mighty splashes and snorts reached us from afar, as though an ichthyosaurus had been taking a bath of glitter in the great river. 'After all,' said the boiler maker in a reasonable tone, 'why shouldn't we get the rivets?' Why not, indeed! I did not know of any reason why we shouldn't. 'They'll come in three weeks,' I said confidently.

"But they didn't. Instead of rivets there came an invasion, an infliction, a visitation. It came in sections during the next three weeks, each section headed by a donkey carrying a white man in new clothes and tan shoes, bowing from that elevation right and left to the impressed pilgrims. A quarrelsome band of footsore sulky natives trod on the heels of the donkey; a lot of tents, campstools, tin boxes, white cases, brown bales would be shot down in the courtyard, and the air of mystery would deepen a little over the muddle of the station. Five such installments came, with their absurd air of disorderly flight with the loot of innumerable outfit shops and provision stores, that, one would think, they were lugging, after a raid, into the wilderness for equitable division. It was an inextricable mess of things decent in themselves but that human folly made look like the spoils of thieving.

"This devoted band called itself the Eldorado Exploring Expedition, and l believe they were sworn to secrecy. Their talk, however, was the talk of sordid buccaneers: it was reckless without hardihood, greedy without audacity, and cruel without courage; there was not an atom of foresight or of serious intention in the whole batch of them, and they did not seem aware these things are wanted for the work of the world. To tear treasure out of the bowels of the land was their desire, with no more moral purpose at the back of it than there is in burglars breaking into a safe. Who paid the expenses of the noble enterprise I don't know; but the uncle of our manager was leader of that lot.

"In exterior he resembled a butcher in a poor neighborhood, and his eyes had a look of sleepy cunning. He carried his fat paunch with ostentation on his short legs, and during the time his gang infested the station spoke to no one but his nephew. You could see these two roaming about all day long with their heads close together in an everlasting confab.

"I had given up worrying myself about the rivets. One's capacity for that kind of folly is more limited than you would suppose. I said Hang!—and let things slide. I had plenty of time for meditation, and now and then I would give some thought to Kurtz. I wasn't very interested in him. No. Still, I was curious to see whether this man, who had come out equipped with moral ideas of some sort, would climb to the top after all, and how he would set about his work when there."

II

"One evening as I was lying flat on the deck of my steamboat, I heard voices approaching—and there were the nephew and the uncle strolling along the bank. I laid my head on my arm again, and had nearly lost myself in a doze, when somebody said in my ear, as it were: 'I am as harmless as a little child, but I don't like to be dictated to. Am I the manager—or am I not? I was ordered·to send him there. It's incredible.' . . . I became aware that the two were standing on the shore alongside the forepart of the steamboat, just below my head. I did not move; it did not occur to me to move: I was sleepy. 'It *is* unpleasant,' grunted the uncle. 'He has asked the Administration to be sent there,' said the other, 'with the idea of showing what he could do; and I was instructed accordingly. Look at the influence that man must have. Is it not frightful?' They both agreed it was frightful, then made several bizarre remarks: 'Make rain and fine weather—one man—the Council—by the nose' —bits of absurd sentences that got the better of my drowsiness, so that I had pretty near the whole of my wits about me when the uncle said, 'The climate may do away with this difficulty for you. Is he alone there?' 'Yes,' answered the manager; 'he sent his assistant down the river with a note to me in these terms: "Clear this poor devil out of the country, and don't bother sending more of that sort. I had rather be alone than have the kind of men you can dispose of with me." It was more than a year ago. Can you imagine such impudence?' 'Anything since then?' asked the other hoarsely. 'Ivory,' jerked the nephew; 'lots of it—prime sort—lots—most annoying, from him.' 'And with that?' questioned the heavy rumble. 'Invoice,' was the reply fired out, so to speak. Then silence. They had been talking about Kurtz.

"I was broad awake by this time, but, lying perfectly at ease, remained still, having no inducement to change my position. 'How did that ivory come all this way?' growled the elder man, who seemed very vexed. The other explained that it had come with a fleet of canoes in charge of an English half-caste clerk Kurtz had with him; that Kurtz had apparently intended to return himself, the station being by that time bare of goods and stores, but after coming three hundred miles, had suddenly decided to go back, which he started to do alone in a small dugout with four paddlers, leaving the half-caste to continue down the river with the ivory. The two fellows there seemed astounded at anybody attempting such a thing. They were at a loss for an adequate motive. As for me, I seemed to see Kurtz for the first time. It was a distinct glimpse: the dugout, four paddling savages, and the lone white man turning his back suddenly on the headquarters, on relief, on thoughts of home—perhaps; setting his face toward the depths of the wilderness, toward his empty and desolate station. I did not know the motive. Perhaps he was just simply a fine fellow who stuck to his work for its own sake. His name, you understand, had not been pronounced once. He was 'that man.' The half-caste, who, as far as I could see, had conducted a difficult trip with great prudence and pluck, was invariably alluded to as 'that scoundrel.' The 'scoundrel' had reported that the 'man' had been very ill—had recovered imperfectly. . . . The two below me moved away then a few paces, and strolled back and forth at some little distance. I heard: 'Military post—doctor—two hundred miles—quite alone now—unavoidable delays—nine months no news—strange rumors.' They approached again, just as the manager was saying, 'No one, as far as I know, unless a species of wandering trader—a pestilential fellow, snapping ivory from the natives.' Who was it they were talking about now? I gathered in snatches that this was some man supposed to be in Kurtz's district, and of whom the manager did not approve. 'We will not be free from unfair competition till one of these fellows is hanged for an example,' he said. 'Certainly,' grunted the other; 'get him hanged! Why not? Anything—anything can be done in this country. That's what I say; nobody here, you understand, *here,* can endanger your position. And why? You stand the climate—you outlast them all. The danger is in Europe; but there before I left I took care to—' They moved off and whispered, then their voices rose again. 'The extraordinary series of delays is not my fault. I did my best.' The fat man sighed, 'Very sad.' 'And the pestiferous absurdity of his talk,' continued the other; 'he bothered me enough when he was here. "Each station should be like a beacon on the road toward better things, a center for trade of course, but also for humanizing, improving, instructing." Conceive you—that ass! And he wants to be manager! No, it's—' Here he got choked by excessive indignation, and I lifted my head the least bit. I was surprised to see how near they were—right under me. I could have spat upon their hats. They were looking on the ground, absorbed in thought. The manager was switching his leg with a slender twig: his sagacious relative lifted his head. 'You have been well since you came out this time?' he asked. The other gave a start. 'Who? I? Oh! Like a charm—like a charm. But the rest—oh, my goodness! All sick. They die so quick, too, that I haven't the time to send them out of the country—it's incredible!' 'H'm. Just so,' grunted the uncle. 'Ah! my boy, trust to this—I say, trust to this.' I saw him extend his short flipper of an arm for a gesture that took in the forest, the creek, the mud, the river—seemed to beckon with a dishonoring flourish before the sunlit face of the land a treacherous appeal to the lurking death, to the hidden evil, to the profound darkness of its heart. It was so startling that I leaped to my feet and looked back at the edge of the forest, as though I had expected an answer of some sort to that black display of confidence. You know the foolish notions that come to one sometimes. The high stillness confronted these two figures with its ominous patience, waiting for the passing away of a fantastic invasion.

"They swore aloud together—out of sheer fright, I believe—then, pretending not to know anything of my existence, turned back to the station. The sun was low; and leaning forward side by side, they seemed to be tugging painfully uphill their two ridiculous shadows of unequal length, that trailed behind them slowly over the tall grass without bending a single blade.

"In a few days the Eldorado Expedition went into the patient wilderness, that closed upon it as the sea closes over a diver. Long afterward the news came that all the donkeys were dead. I know nothing as to the fate of the less valuable animals. They, no doubt, like the rest of us, found what they deserved. I did not inquire. I was then rather excited at the prospect of meeting Kurtz very soon. When I say very soon I mean it comparatively. It was just two months from the day we left the creek when we came to the bank below Kurtz's station.

"Going up that river was like traveling back to the earliest beginnings of the world, when vegetation rioted on the earth and the big trees were kings. An empty stream, a great silence, an impenetrable forest. The air was warm, thick, heavy, sluggish. There was no joy in the brilliance of sunshine. The long stretches of the waterway ran on, deserted, into the gloom of overshadowed distances. On silvery sandbanks hippos and alligators sunned themselves side by side. The broadening waters flowed through a mob of wooded islands; you lost your way on that river as you would in a desert, and butted all day long against shoals, trying to find the channel, till you thought yourself bewitched and cut off forever from everything you had known once—somewhere—far away—in another existence perhaps. There were moments when one's past came back to one, as it will sometimes when you have not a moment to spare to yourself; but it came in the shape of an unrestful and noisy dream, remembered with wonder among the overwhelming realities of this strange world of plants, and water, and silence. And this stillness of life did not in the least resemble a peace. It was the stillness of an implacable force brooding over an inscrutable intention. It looked at you with a vengeful aspect. I got used to it afterward; I did not see it anymore; I had no time. I had to keep guessing at the channel; I had to discern, mostly by inspiration, the signs of hidden banks; I watched for sunken stones; I was learning to clap my teeth smartly before my heart flew out, when I shaved by a fluke some infernal sly old snag that would have ripped the life out of the tin-pot steamboat and drowned all the pilgrims; I had to keep a lookout for the signs of dead wood we could cut up in the night for next day's steaming. When you have to attend to things of that sort, to the mere incidents of the surface, the reality—the reality, I tell you—fades. The inner truth is hidden—luckily, luckily. But I felt it all the same; I felt often its mysterious stillness watching me at my monkey tricks, just as it watches you fellows performing on your respective tightropes for— what is it? half a crown a tumble—"

"Try to be civil, Marlow," growled a voice, and I knew there was at least one listener awake besides myself.

"I beg your pardon. I forgot the heartache which makes up the rest of the price. And indeed what does the price matter, if the trick be well done? You do your tricks very well. And I didn't do badly either, since I managed not to sink that steamboat on my first trip. It's a wonder to me yet. Imagine a blindfolded man set to drive a van over a bad road. I sweated and shivered over that business considerably, I can tell you. After all, for a seaman, to scrape the bottom of the thing that's supposed to float all the time under his care is the unpardonable sin. No one may know of it, but you never forget the thump—eh? A blow on the very heart. You remember it, you dream of it, you wake up at night and think of it—years after—and go hot and cold all over. I don't pretend to say that steamboat floated all the time. More than once she had to wade for a bit, with twenty cannibals splashing around and pushing. We had enlisted some of these chaps on the way for a crew. Fine fellows— cannibals—in their place. They were men one could work with, and I am grateful to them. And, after all, they did not eat each other before my face: they had brought along a provision of hippo meat which went rotten, and made the mystery of the wilderness stink in my nostrils. Phoo! I can sniff it now. I had the manager on board and three or four pilgrims with their staves—all complete. Sometimes we came upon a station close by the bank, clinging to the skirts of the unknown, and the white men rushing out of a tumble-down hovel, with great gestures of joy and surprise and welcome, seemed very strange—had the appearance of being held there captive by a spell. The word *ivory* would ring in the air for a while—and on we went again into the silence, along empty reaches, round the still bends, between the high walls of our winding way, reverberating in hollow claps the ponderous beat of the stern-wheel. Trees, trees, millions of trees, massive, immense, running up high; and at their foot, hugging the bank against the stream, crept the little begrimed steamboat, like a sluggish beetle crawling on the floor of a lofty portico. It made you feel very small, very lost, and yet it was not altogether depressing, that feeling. After all, if you were small, the grimy beetle crawled on—which was just what you wanted it to do. Where the pilgrims imagined it crawled to I don't know. To some place where they expected to get something, I bet! For me it crawled toward Kurtz—exclusively; but when the steampipes started leaking we crawled very slow. The reaches opened before us and closed behind, as if the forest had stepped leisurely across the water to bar the way for our return. We penetrated deeper and deeper into the heart of darkness. It was very quiet there. At night sometimes the roll of drums behind the curtain of trees would run up the river and remain sustained faintly, as if hovering in the air high over our heads, till the first break of day. Whether it meant war, peace, or prayer we could not tell. The dawns were heralded by the descent of a chill stillness; the woodcutters slept, their fires burned low; the snapping of a twig would make you start. We were wanderers on a prehistoric earth, on an earth that wore the aspect of an unknown planet. We could have fancied ourselves the first of men taking possession of an accursed inheritance, to be subdued at the cost of profound anguish and of excessive toil. But suddenly, as we struggled round a bend, there would be a glimpse of rush walls, of peaked grass roofs, a burst of yells, a whirl of black limbs, a mass of hands clapping, of feet stamping, of bodies swaying, of eyes rolling, under the droop of heavy and motionless foliage. The steamer toiled along slowly on the edge of a black and incomprehensible frenzy. The prehistoric man was cursing us, praying to us, welcoming us—who could tell? We were cut off from the comprehension of our surroundings; we glided past like phantoms, wondering and secretly appalled, as sane men would be before an enthusiastic outbreak in a madhouse. We could not understand because we were too far and could not remember, because we were travelling in the night of first ages, of those ages that are gone, leaving hardly a sign—and no memories.

"The earth seemed unearthly. We are accustomed to look upon the shackled form of a conquered monster, but there—there you could look at a thing monstrous and free. It was unearthly, and the men were—No, they were not inhuman. Well, you know, that was the worst of it—this suspicion of their not being inhuman. It would come slowly to one. They howled and leaped, and spun, and made horrid faces; but what thrilled you was just the thought of their humanity—like yours—the thought of your remote kinship with this wild and passionate uproar. Ugly. Yes, it was ugly enough; but if you were man enough you would admit to yourself that there was in you just the faintest trace of a response to the terrible frankness of that noise, a dim suspicion of there being a meaning in it which you—you so remote from the night of first ages—could comprehend. And why not? The mind of man is capable of anything—because everything is in it, all the past as well as all the future. What was there after all? Joy, fear, sorrow, devotion, valor, rage—who can tell?—but truth—truth stripped of its cloak of time. Let the fool gape and shudder—the man knows, and can look on without a wink. But he must at least be as much of a man as these on the shore. He must meet that truth with his own true stuff—with his own inborn strength. Principles? Principles won't do. Acquisitions, clothes, pretty rags—rags that would fly off at the first good shake. No; you want a deliberate belief. An appeal to me in this fiendish row—is there? Very well; I hear; I admit, but I have a voice too, and for good or evil mine is the speech that cannot be silenced. Of course, a fool, what with sheer fright and fine sentiments, is always safe. Who's that grunting? You wonder I didn't go ashore for a howl and a dance? Well, no—I didn't. Fine sentiments, you say? Fine sentiments be hanged! I had no time. I had to mess about with white lead and strips of woolen blanket helping to put bandages on those leaky steampipes—I tell you. I had to watch the steering, and circumvent those snags, and get the tin-pot along by hook or by crook. There was surface truth enough in these things to save a wiser man. And between whiles I had to look after the savage who was fireman. He was an improved specimen; he could fire up a vertical boiler. He was there below me, and, upon my word, to look at him was as edifying as seeing a dog in a parody of breeches and a feather hat, walking on his hind legs. A few months of training had done for that really fine chap. He squinted at the steam gauge and at the water gauge with an evident effort of intrepidity—and he had filed teeth too, the poor devil, and the wool of his pate shaved into queer patterns, and three ornamental scars on each of his cheeks. He ought to have been clapping his hands and stamping his feet on the bank, instead of which he was hard at work, a thrall to strange witchcraft, full of improving knowledge. He was useful because he had been instructed; and what he knew was this—that should the water in that transparent thing disappear, the evil spirit inside the boiler would get angry through the greatness of his thirst, and take a terrible vengeance. So he sweated and fired up and watched the glass fearfully (with an impromptu charm, made of rags, tied to his arm, and a piece of polished bone, as big as a watch, stuck flatways through his lower lip), while the wooded banks slipped past us slowly, the short noise was left behind, the interminable miles of silence—and we crept on, toward Kurtz. But the snags were thick, the water was treacherous and shallow, the boiler seemed indeed to have a sulky devil in it, and thus neither that fireman nor I had any time to peer into our creepy thoughts.

"Some fifty miles below the Inner Station we came upon a hut of reeds, an inclined and melancholy pole, with the unrecognizable tatters of what had been a flag of some sort flying from it, and a neatly stacked woodpile. This was unexpected. We came to the bank, and on the stack of firewood found a flat piece of board with some faded pencil writing on it. When deciphered it said: 'Wood for you. Hurry up. Approach cautiously.' There was a signature, but it was illegible—not Kurtz—a much longer word. Hurry up. Where? Up the river? 'Approach cautiously.' We had not done so. But the warning could not have been meant for the place where it could be only found after approach. Something was wrong above. But what—and how much? That was the question. We commented adversely upon the imbecility of that telegraphic style. The bush around said nothing, and would not let us look very far, either. A torn curtain of red twill hung in the doorway of the hut, and flapped sadly in our faces. The dwelling was dismantled; but we could see a white man had lived there not very long ago. There remained a rude table—a plank on two posts; a heap of rubbish reposed in a dark corner, and by the door I picked up a book. It had lost its covers, and the pages had been thumbed into a state of extremely dirty softness; but the back had been lovingly stitched afresh with white cotton thread, which looked clean yet. It was an extraordinary find. Its title was, *An Inquiry into some Points of Seamanship,* by a man Towser, Towson—some such name—Master in His Majesty's Navy. The matter looked dreary reading enough, with illustrative diagrams and repulsive tables of figures, and the copy was sixty years old. I handled this amazing antiquity with the greatest possible tenderness, lest it should dissolve in my hands. Within, Towson or Towser was inquiring earnestly into the breaking strain of ships' chains and tackle, and other such matters. Not a very enthralling book; but at the first glance you could see there a singleness of intention, an honest concern for the right way of going to work, which made these humble pages, thought out so many years ago, luminous with another than a professional light. The simple old sailor, with his talk of chains and purchases, made me forget the jungle and the pilgrims in a delicious sensation of having come upon something unmistakably real. Such a book being there was wonderful enough; but still more astounding were the notes penciled in the margin, and plainly referring to the text. I couldn't believe my eyes! They were in cipher! Yes, it looked like cipher. Fancy a man lugging with him a book of that description into this nowhere and studying it—and making notes —in cipher at that! It was an extravagant mystery.

"I had been dimly aware for some time of a worrying noise, and when I lifted my eyes I saw the woodpile was gone, and the manager, aided by all the pilgrims, was shouting at me from the riverside. I slipped the book into my pocket. I assure you to leave off reading was like tearing myself away from the shelter of an old and solid friendship.

"I started the lame engine ahead. 'It must be this miserable trader—this intruder,' exclaimed the manager, looking back malevolently at the place we had left. 'He must be English,' I said. 'It will not save him from getting into trouble if he is not careful,' muttered the manager darkly. I observed with assumed innocence that no man was safe from trouble in this world.

"The current was more rapid now, the steamer seemed at her last gasp, the stern-wheel flopped languidly, and I caught myself listening on tiptoe for the next beat of the float, for in sober truth I expected the wretched thing to give up every moment. It was like watching the last flickers of a life. But still we crawled. Sometimes I would pick out a tree a little way ahead to measure our progress toward Kurtz by, but I lost it invariably before we got abreast. To keep the eyes so long on one thing was too much for human patience. The manager displayed a beautiful resignation. I fretted and fumed and took to arguing with myself whether or no I would talk openly with Kurtz; but before I could come to any conclusion it occurred to me that my speech or my silence, indeed any action of mine, would be a mere futility. What did it matter what anyone knew or ignored? What did it matter who was manager? One gets sometimes such a flash of insight. The essentials of this affair lay deep under the surface, beyond my reach, and beyond my power of meddling.

"Toward the evening of the second day we judged ourselves about eight miles from Kurtz's station. I wanted to push on; but the manager looked grave, and told me the navigation up there was so dangerous that it would be advisable, the sun being very low already, to wait where we were till next morning. Moreover, he pointed out that if the warning to approach cautiously were to be followed, we must approach in daylight—not at dusk, or in the dark. This was sensible enough. Eight miles meant nearly three hours' steaming for us, and I could also see suspicious ripples at the upper end of the reach. Nevertheless, I was annoyed beyond expression at the delay, and most unreasonably too, since one night more could not matter much after so many months. As we had plenty of wood, and caution was the word, I brought up in the middle of the stream. The reach was narrow, straight, with high sides like a railway cutting. The dusk came gliding into it long before the sun had set. The current ran smooth and swift, but a dumb immobility sat on the banks. The living trees, lashed together by the creepers and every living bush of the undergrowth, might have been changed into stone, even to the slenderest twig, to the lightest leaf. It was not sleep—it seemed unnatural, like a state of trance. Not the faintest sound of any kind could be heard. You looked on amazed, and began to suspect yourself of being deaf—then the night came suddenly, and struck you blind as well. About three in the morning some large fish leaped, and the loud splash made me jump as though a gun had been fired. When the sun rose there was a white fog, very warm and clammy, and more blinding than the night. It did not shift or drive; it was just there, standing all round you like something solid. At eight or nine, perhaps, it lifted as a shutter lifts. We had a glimpse of the towering multitude of trees, of the immense matted jungle, with the blazing little ball of the sun hanging over it—all perfectly still—and then the white shutter came down again, smoothly, as if sliding in greased grooves. I ordered the chain, which we had begun to heave in, to be paid out again. Before it stopped running with a muffled rattle, a cry, a very loud cry, as of infinite desolation, soared slowly in the opaque air. It ceased. A complaining clamor, modulated in savage discords, filled our ears. The sheer unexpectedness of it made my hair stir under my cap. I don't know how it struck the others: to me it seemed as though the mist itself had screamed, so suddenly, and apparently from all sides at once, did this tumultuous and mournful uproar arise. It culminated in a hurried outbreak of almost intolerably excessive shrieking, which stopped short, leaving us stiffened in a variety of silly attitudes, and obstinately listening to the nearly as appalling and excessive silence. 'Good God! What is the meaning—?' stammered at my elbow one of the pilgrims—a little fat man, with sandy hair and red whiskers, who wore side-spring boots, and pink pajamas tucked into his socks. Two others remained open-mouthed a whole minute, then dashed into the little cabin, to rush out incontinently and stand darting scared glances, with Winchesters at 'ready' in their hands. What we could see was just the steamer we were on, her outlines blurred as though she had been on the point of dissolving, and a misty strip of water, perhaps two feet broad, around her—and that was all. The rest of the world was nowhere, as far as our eyes and ears were concerned. Just nowhere. Gone, disappeared; swept off without leaving a whisper or a shadow behind.

"I went forward, and ordered the chain to be hauled in short, so as to be ready to trip the anchor and move the steamboat at once if necessary. 'Will they attack?' whispered an awed voice. 'We will all be butchered in this fog,' murmured another. The faces twitched with the strain, the hands trembled slightly, the eyes forgot to wink. It was very curious to see the contrast of expressions of the white men and of the black fellows of our crew, who were as much strangers to that part of the river as we, though their homes were only eight hundred miles away. The whites, of course greatly discomposed, had besides a curious look of being painfully shocked by such an outrageous row. The others had an alert, naturally interested expression; but their faces were essentially quiet, even those of the one or two who grinned as they hauled at the chain. Several exchanged short, grunting phrases, which seemed to settle the matter to their satisfaction. Their headman, a young, broad-chested black, severely draped in dark blue fringed cloths, with fierce nostrils and his hair all done up artfully in oily ringlets, stood near me. 'Ah!' I said, just for good fellowship's sake. 'Catch 'im,' he snapped, with a bloodshot widening of his eyes and a flash of sharp teeth—'catch 'im. Give 'im to us.' 'To you, eh?' I asked; 'what would you do with them?' 'Eat 'im!' he said curtly, and, leaning his elbow on the rail, looked out into the fog in a dignified and profoundly pensive attitude. I would no doubt have been properly horrified, had it not occurred to me that he and his chaps must be very hungry: that they must have been growing increasingly hungry for at least this month past. They had been engaged for six months (I don't think a single one of them had any clear idea of time, as we at the end of countless ages have. They still belonged to the beginnings of time—had no inherited experience to teach them, as it were), and of course, as long as there was a piece of paper written over in accordance with some farcical law or other made down the river, it didn't enter anybody's head to trouble how they would live. Certainly they had brought with them some rotten hippo meat, which couldn't have lasted very long, anyway, even if the pligrims hadn't, in the midst of a shocking hullabaloo, thrown a considerable quantity of it overboard. It looked like a high-handed proceeding; but it was really a case of legitimate self-defense. You can't breathe dead hippo waking, sleeping, and eating, and at the same time keep your precarious grip on existence. Besides that, they had given them every week three pieces of brass wire, each about nine inches long; and the theory was they were to buy their provisions with that currency in riverside villages. You can see how *that* worked. There were either no villages, or the people were hostile, or the director, who like the rest of us fed out of tins, with an occasional old he-goat thrown in, didn't want to stop the steamer for some more or less recondite reasons. So, unless they swallowed the wire itself, or made loops of it to snare the fishes with, I don't see what good their extravagant salary could be to them. I must say it was paid with a regularity worthy of a large and honorable trading company. For the rest, the only thing to eat—though it didn't look eatable in the least—I saw in their possession was a few lumps of some stuff like half-cooked dough, of a dirty lavender color, they kept wrapped in leaves, and now and then swallowed a piece of, but so small that it seemed done more for the look of the thing than for any serious purpose of sustenance. Why in the name of all the gnawing devils of hunger they didn't go for us—they were thirty to five—and have a good tuck-in for once, amazes me now when I think of it. They were big powerful men, with not much capacity to weigh the consequences, with courage, with strength, even yet, though their skins were no longer glossy and their muscles no longer hard. And I saw that something restraining, one of those human secrets that baffle probability, had come into play there. I looked at them with a swift quickening of interest—not because it occurred to me I might be eaten by them before very long, though I own to you that just then I perceived—in a new light, as it were—how unwholesome the pilgrims looked, and I hoped, yes, I positively hoped, that my aspect was not so—what shall I say?—so—unappetizing: a touch of fantastic vanity which fitted well with the dream-sensation that pervaded all my days at that time. Perhaps I had a little fever too. One can't live with one's finger everlastingly on one's pulse. I had often 'a little fever,' or a little touch of other things—the playful paw strokes of the wilderness, the preliminary trifling before the more serious onslaught which came in due course. Yes; I looked at them as you would on any human being, with a curiosity of their impulses, motives, capacities, weaknesses, when brought to the test of an inexorable physical necessity. Restraint! What possible restraint? Was it superstition, disgust, patience, fear—or some kind of primitive honor? No fear can stand up to hunger, no patience can wear it out, disgust simply does not exist where hunger is; and as to superstition, beliefs, and what you may call principles, they are less than chaff in a breeze. Don't you know the deviltry of lingering starvation, its exasperating torment, its black thoughts, its somber and brooding ferocity? Well, I do. It takes a man all his inborn strength to fight hunger properly. It's really easier to face bereavement, dishonor, and the perdition of one's soul—than this kind of prolonged hunger. Sad, but true. And these chaps too had no earthly reason for any kind of scruple. Restraint! I would just as soon have expected restraint from a hyena prowling among the corpses of a battlefield. But there was the fact facing me—the fact dazzling, to be seen, like the foam on the depths of the sea, like a ripple on an unfathomable enigma, a mystery greater—when I thought of it—than the curious, inexplicable note of desperate grief in this savage clamor that had swept by us on the riverbank, behind the blind whiteness of the fog.

"Two pilgrims were quarreling in hurried whispers as to which bank. 'Left.' 'No, no; how can you? Right, right, of course.' 'It is very serious,' said the manager's voice behind me; 'I would be desolated if anything should happen to Mr. Kurtz before we came up.' I looked at him, and had not the slightest doubt he was sincere. He was just the kind of man who would wish to preserve appearances. That was his restraint. But when he muttered something about going on at once, I did not even take the trouble to answer him. I knew, and he knew, that it was impossible. Were we to let go our hold of the bottom, we would be absolutely in the air—in space. We wouldn't be able to tell where we were going to—whether up or down stream, or across—till we fetched against one bank or the other—and then we wouldn't know at first which it was. Of course I made no move. I had no mind for a smash-up. You couldn't imagine a more deadly place for a shipwreck. Whether drowned at once or not, we were sure to perish speedily in one way or another. 'I authorize you to take all the risks,' he said, after a short silence. 'I refuse to take any,' I said shortly; which was just the answer he expected, though its tone might have surprised him. 'Well, I must defer to your judgment. You are captain,' he said, with marked civility. I turned my shoulder to him in sign of my appreciation, and looked into the fog. How long would it last? It was the most hopeless lookout. The approach to this Kurtz grubbing for ivory in the wretched bush was beset by as many dangers as though he had been an enchanted princess sleeping in a fabulous castle. 'Will they attack, do you think?' asked the manager, in a confidential tone.

"I did not think they would attack, for several obvious reasons. The thick fog was one. If they left the bank in their canoes they would get lost in it, as we would be if we attempted to move. Still, I had also judged the jungle of both banks quite impenetrable—and yet eyes were in it, eyes that had seen us. The riverside bushes were certainly very thick; but the undergrowth behind was evidently penetrable. However, during the short lift I had seen no canoes anywhere in the reach—certainly not abreast of the steamer. But what made the idea of attack inconceivable to me was the nature of the noise—of the cries we had heard. They had not the fierce character boding of immediate hostile intention. Unexpected, wild, and violent as they had been, they had given me an irresistible impression of sorrow. The glimpse of the steamboat had for some reason filled those savages with unrestrained grief. The danger, if any, I expounded, was from our proximity to a great human passion let loose. Even extreme grief may ultimately vent itself in violence—but more generally takes the form of apathy. . . .

"You should have seen the pilgrims stare! They had no heart to grin, or even to revile me; but I believe they thought me gone mad—with fright, maybe. I delivered a regular lecture. My dear boys, it was no good bothering. Keep a lookout? Well, you may guess I watched the fog for the signs of lifting as a cat watches a mouse; but for anything else our eyes were of no more use to us than if we had been buried miles deep in a heap of cotton wool. It felt like it too—choking, warm, stifling. Besides, all I said, though it sounded extravagant, was absolutely true to fact. What we afterward alluded to as an attack was really an attempt at repulse. The action was very far from being aggressive—it was not even defensive, in the usual sense: it was undertaken under the stress of desperation, and in its essence was purely protective.

"It developed itself, I should say, two hours after the fog lifted, and its commencement was at a spot, roughly speaking, about a mile and a half below Kurtz's station. We had just floundered and flopped round a bend, when I saw an islet, a mere grassy hummock of bright green, in the middle of the stream. It was the only thing of the kind; but as we opened the reach more, I perceived it was the head of a long sandbank, or rather of a chain of shallow patches stretching down the middle of the river. They were discolored, just awash, and the whole lot was seen just under the water, exactly as a man's backbone is seen running down the middle of his back under the skin. Now, as far as I did see, I could go to the right or to the left of this. I didn't know either channel, of course. The banks looked pretty well alike, the depth appeared the same; but as I had been informed the station was on the west side, I naturally headed for the western passage.

"No sooner had we fairly entered it than I became aware it was much narrower than I had supposed. To the left of us there was the long uninterrupted shoal, and to the right a high steep bank heavily overgrown with bushes. Above the bush the trees stood in serried ranks. The twigs overhung the current thickly, and from distance to distance a large limb of some tree projected rigidly over the stream. It was then well on in the afternoon, the face of the forest was gloomy, and a broad strip of shadow had already fallen on the water. In this shadow we steamed up—very slowly, as you may imagine. I sheered her well inshore—the water being deepest near the bank, as the sounding pole informed me.

"One of my hungry and forbearing friends was sounding in the bows just below me. This steamboat was exactly like a decked scow. On the deck there were two little teakwood houses, with doors and windows. The boiler was in the fore-end, and the machinery right astern. Over the whole there was a light roof, supported on stanchions. The funnel projected through that roof, and in front of the funnel a small cabin built of light planks served for a pilothouse. It contained a couch, two campstools, a loaded Martini-Henry leaning in one corner, a tiny table, and the steering wheel. It had a wide door in front and a broad shutter at each side. All these were always thrown open, of course. I spent my days perched up there on the extreme fore-end of that roof, before the door. At night I slept, or tried to, on the couch. An athletic black belonging to some coast tribe, and educated by my poor predecessor, was the helmsman. He sported a pair of brass earrings, wore a blue cloth wrapper from the waist to the ankles, and thought all the world of himself. He was the most unstable kind of fool I had ever seen. He steered with no end of a swagger while you were by; but if he lost sight of you, he became instantly the prey of an abject funk, and would let that cripple of a steamboat get the upper hand of him in a minute.

"I was looking down at the sounding pole, and feeling much annoyed to see at each try a little more of it stick out of that river, when I saw my poleman give up the business suddenly, and stretch himself flat on the deck, without even taking the trouble to haul his pole in. He kept hold on it though, and it trailed in the water. At the same time the fireman, whom I could also see below me, sat down abruptly before his furnace and ducked his head. I was amazed. Then I had to look at the river mighty quick, because there was a snag in the fairway. Sticks, little sticks, were flying about—thick: they were whizzing before my nose, dropping below me, striking behind me against my pilothouse. All this time the river, the shore, the woods, were very quiet— perfectly quiet. I could only hear the heavy splashing thump of the stern-wheel and the patter of these things. We cleared the snag clumsily. Arrows, by Jove! We were being shot at! I stepped in quickly to close the shutter on the land side. That fool helmsman, his hands on the spokes, was lifting his knees high, stamping his feet, champing his mouth, like a reined-in horse. Confound him! And we were staggering within ten feet of the bank. I had to lean right out to swing the heavy shutter, and I saw a face among the leaves on the level with my own, looking at me very fierce and steady; and then suddenly, as though a veil had been removed from my eyes, I made out, deep in the tangled gloom, naked breasts, arms, legs, glaring eyes—the bush was swarming with human limbs in movement, glistening, of bronze color. The twigs shook, swayed, and rustled, the arrows flew out of them, and then the shutter came to. 'Steer her straight,' I said to the helmsman. He held his head rigid, face forward; but his eyes rolled, he kept on lifting and setting down his feet gently, his mouth foamed a little. 'Keep quiet!' I said in a fury. I might just as well have ordered a tree not to sway in the wind. I darted out. Below me there was a great scuffle of feet on the iron deck; confused exclamations; a voice screamed, 'Can you turn back?' I caught sight of a V-shaped ripple on the water ahead. What? Another snag! A fusillade burst out under my feet. The pilgrims had opened with their Winchesters, and were simply squirting lead into that bush. A deuce of a lot of smoke came up and drove slowly forward. I swore at it. Now I couldn't see the ripple or the snag either. I stood in the doorway, peering, and the arrows came in swarms. They might have been poisoned, but they looked as though they wouldn't kill a cat. The bush began to howl. Our woodcutters raised a warlike whoop; the report of a rifle just at my back deafened me. I glanced over my shoulder, and the pilothouse was yet full of noise and smoke when I made a dash at the wheel. The fool had dropped everything, to throw the shutter open and let off that Martini-Henry. He stood before the wide opening, glaring, and I yelled at him to come back, while I straightened the sudden twist out of that steamboat. There was no room to turn even if I had wanted to, the snag was somewhere very near ahead in that confounded smoke, there was no time to lose, so I just crowded her into the bank—right into the bank, where I knew the water was deep.

"We tore slowly along the overhanging bushes in a whirl of broken twigs and flying leaves. The fusillade below stopped short, as I had foreseen it would when the squirts got empty. I threw my head back to a glinting whizz that traversed the pilothouse, in at one shutter hole and out at the other. Looking past that mad helmsman, who was shaking the empty rifle and yelling at the shore, I saw vague forms of men running bent double, leaping, gliding, distinct, incomplete, evanescent. Something big appeared in the air before the shutter, the rifle went overboard, and the man stepped back swiftly, looked at me over his shoulder in an extraordinary, profound, familiar manner, and fell upon my feet. The side of his head hit the wheel twice, and the end of what appeared a long cane clattered round and knocked over a little campstool. It looked as though after wrenching that thing from somebody ashore he had lost his balance in the effort. The thin smoke had blown away, we were clear of the snag, and looking ahead I could see that in another hundred yards or so I would be free to sheer off, away from the bank; but my feet felt so very warm and wet that I had to look down. The man had rolled on his back and stared straight up at me; both his hands clutched that cane. It was the shaft of a spear that, either thrown or lunged through the opening, had caught him in the side just below the ribs; the blade had gone in out of sight, after making a frightful gash; my shoes were full; a pool of blood lay very still, gleaming dark red under the wheel; his eyes shone with an amazing luster. The fusillade burst out again. He looked at me anxiously, gripping the spear like something precious, with an air of being afraid I would try to take it away from him. I had to make an effort to free my eyes from his gaze and attend to the steering. With one hand I felt above my head for the line of the steam whistle, and jerked out screech after screech hurriedly. The tumult of angry and warlike yells was checked instantly, and then from the depths of the woods went out such a tremulous and prolonged wail of mournful fear and utter despair as may be imagined to follow the flight of the last hope from the earth. There was a great commotion in the bush; the shower of arrows stopped, a few dropping shots rang out sharply—then silence, in which the languid beat of the stern-wheel came plainly to my ears. I put the helm hard a-starboard at the moment when the pilgrim in pink pajamas, very hot and agitated, appeared in the doorway. 'The manager sends me—' he began in an official tone, and stopped short. 'Good God!' he said, glaring at the wounded man.

"We two whites stood over him, and his lustrous and inquiring glance enveloped us both. I declare it looked as though he would presently put to us some question in an understandable language; but he died without uttering a sound, without moving a limb, without twitching a muscle. Only in the very last moment, as though in response to some sign we could not see, to some whisper we could not hear, he frowned heavily, and that frown gave to his black death mask an inconceivably somber, brooding, and menacing expression. The luster of inquiring glance faded swiftly into vacant glassiness. 'Can you steer?' I asked the agent eagerly. He looked very dubious; but I made a grab at his arm, and he understood at once I meant him to steer whether or no. To tell you the truth, I was morbidly anxious to change my shoes and socks. 'He is dead,' murmured the fellow, immensely impressed. 'No doubt about it,' said I, tugging like mad at the shoelaces. 'And by the way, I suppose Mr. Kurtz is dead as well by this time.'

"For the moment that was the dominant thought. There was a sense of extreme disappointment, as though I had found out I had been striving after something altogether without a substance. I couldn't have been more disgusted if I had traveled all this way for the sole purpose of talking with Mr. Kurtz. Talking with . . . I flung one shoe overboard, and became aware that that was exactly what I had been looking forward to—a talk with Kurtz. I made the strange discovery that I had never imagined him as doing, you know, but as discoursing. I didn't say to myself, 'Now I will never see him,' or 'Now I will never shake him by the hand,' but, 'Now I will never hear him.' The man presented himself as a voice. Not of course that I did not connect him with some sort of action. Hadn't I been told in all the tones of jealousy and admiration that he had collected, bartered, swindled, or stolen more ivory than all the other agents together? That was not the point. The point was in his being a gifted creature, and that of all his gifts the one that stood out preeminently, that carried with it a sense of real presence, was his ability to talk, his words—the gift of expression, the bewildering, the illuminating, the most exalted and the most contemptible, the pulsating stream of light, or the deceitful flow from the heart of an impenetrable darkness.

"The other shoe went flying unto the devil-god of that river. I thought, By Jove! it's all over. We are too late; he has vanished—the gift has vanished, by means of some spear, arrow, or club. I will never hear that chap speak after all—and my sorrow had a startling extravagance of emotion, even such as I had noticed in the howling sorrow of these savages in the bush. I couldn't have felt more of lonely desolation somehow, had I been robbed of a belief or had missed my destiny in life. . . . Why do you sigh in this beastly way, somebody? Absurd? Well, absurd. Good Lord! mustn't a man ever— Here, give me some tobacco." . . .

There was a pause of profound stillness, then a match flared, and Marlow's lean face appeared, worn, hollow, with downward folds and dropped eyelids, with an aspect of concentrated attention; and as he took vigorous draws at his pipe, it seemed to retreat and advance out of the night in the regular flicker of the tiny flame. The match went out.

"Absurd!" he cried. "This is the worst of trying to tell. . . . Here you all are, each moored with two good addresses, like a hulk with two anchors, a butcher round one corner, a policeman round another, excellent appetites, and temperature normal—you hear—normal from year's end to year's end. And you say, Absurd! Absurd be—exploded! Absurd! My dear boys, what can you expect from a man who out of sheer nervousness had just flung overboard a pair of new shoes? Now I think of it, it is amazing I did not shed tears. I am, upon the whole, proud of my fortitude. I was cut to the quick at the idea of having lost the inestimable privilege of listening to the gifted Kurtz. Of course I was wrong. The privilege was waiting for me. Oh yes, I heard more than enough. And I was right, too. A voice. He was very little more than a voice. And I heard—him—it—this voice—other voices—all of them were so little more than voices—and the memory of that time itself lingers around me, impalpable, like a dying vibration of one immense jabber, silly, atrocious, sordid, savage, or simply mean, without any kind of sense. Voices, voices—even the girl herself—now—"

He was silent for a long time.

"I laid the ghost of his gifts at last with a lie," he began suddenly. "Girl! What? Did I mention a girl? Oh, she is out of it—completely. They—the women I mean—are out of it—should be out of it. We must help them to stay in that beautiful world of their own, lest ours gets worse. Oh, she had to be out of it. You should have heard the disinterred body of Mr. Kurtz saying, 'My Intended.' You would have perceived directly then how completely she was out of it. And the lofty frontal bone of Mr. Kurtz! They say the hair goes on growing sometimes, but this—ah—specimen was impressively bald. The wilderness had patted him on the head, and, behold, it was like a ball—an ivory ball; it had caressed him, and—lo!—he had withered; it had taken him, loved him, embraced him, got into his veins, consumed his flesh, and sealed his soul to its own by the inconceivable ceremonies of some devilish initiation. He was its spoiled and pampered favorite. Ivory? I should think so. Heaps of it, stacks of it. The old mud shanty was bursting with it. You would think there was not a single tusk left either above or below the ground in the whole country. 'Mostly fossil,' the manager had remarked disparagingly. It was no more fossil than I am; but they call it fossil when it is dug up. It appears these natives do bury the tusks sometimes—but evidently they couldn't bury this parcel deep enough to save the gifted Mr. Kurtz from his fate. We filled the steamboat with it, and had to pile a lot on the deck. Thus he could see and enjoy as long as he could see, because the appreciation of this favor had remained with him to the last. You should have heard him say, 'My ivory.' Oh yes, I heard him. 'My Intended, my ivory, my station, my river, my—' everything belonged to him. It made me hold my breath in expectation of hearing the wilderness burst into a prodigious peal of laughter that would shake the fixed stars in their places. Everything belonged to him—but that was a trifle. The thing was to know what he belonged to, how many powers of darkness claimed him for their own. That was the reflection that made you creepy all over. It was impossible—it was not good for one either—trying to imagine. He had taken a high seat among the devils of the land—I mean literally.

You can't understand. How could you?—with solid pavement under your feet, surrounded by kind neighbors ready to cheer you or to fall on you, stepping delicately between the butcher and the policeman, in the holy terror of scandal and gallows and lunatic asylums—how can you imagine what particular region of the first ages a man's untrammeled feet may take him into by the way of solitude—utter solitude without a policeman—by the way of silence—utter silence, where no warning voice of a kind neighbor can be heard whispering of public opinion? These little things make all the great difference. When they are gone you must fall back upon your own innate strength, upon your own capacity for faithfulness. Of course you may be too much of a fool to go wrong—too dull even to know you are being assaulted by the powers of darkness. I take it, no fool ever made a bargain for his soul with the devil: the fool is too much of a fool, or the devil too much of a devil—I don't know which. Or you may be such a thunderingly exalted creature as to be altogether deaf and blind to anything but heavenly sights and sounds. Then the earth for you is only a standing place—and whether to be like this is your loss or your gain I won't pretend to say. But most of us are neither one nor the other. The earth for us is a place to live in, where we must put up with sights, with sounds, with smells, too, by Jove!—breathe dead hippo, so to speak, and not be contaminated. And there, don't you see? your strength comes in, the faith in your ability for the digging of unostentatious holes to bury the stuff in—your power of devotion, not to yourself, but to an obscure, back-breaking business. And that's difficult enough. Mind, I am not trying to excuse or even explain—I am trying to account to myself for—for—Mr. Kurtz—for the shade of Mr. Kurtz. This initiated wraith from the back of Nowhere honored me with its amazing confidence before it vanished altogether. This was because it could speak English to me. The original Kurtz had been educated partly in England, and—as he was good enough to say himself —his sympathies were in the right place. His mother was half-English, his father was half-French. All Europe contributed to the making of Kurtz; and by and by I learned that, most appropriately, the International Society for the Suppression of Savage Customs had entrusted him with the making of a report, for its future guidance. And he had written it too. I've seen it. I've read it. It was eloquent, vibrating with eloquence, but too high-strung, I think. Seventeen pages of close writing he had found time for! But this must have been before his—let us say—nerves went wrong, and caused him to preside at certain midnight dances ending with unspeakable rites, which—as far as I reluctantly gathered from what I heard at various times—were offered up to him—do you understand?—to Mr. Kurtz himself. But it was a beautiful piece of writing. The opening paragraph, however, in the light of later information, strikes me now as ominous. He began with the argument that we whites, from the point of development we had arrived at, 'must necessarily appear to them [savages] in the nature of supernatural beings—we approach them with the might as of a deity,' and so on, and so on. 'By the simple exercise of our will we can exert a power for good practically unbounded,' etc. etc. From that point he soared and took me with him. The peroration was magnificent, though difficult to remember, you know. It gave me the notion of an exotic Immensity ruled by an august Benevolence. It made me tingle with enthusiasm. This was the unbounded power of eloquence—of words—of burning noble words. There were no practical hints to interrupt the magic current of phrases, unless a kind of note at the foot of the last page, scrawled evidently much later, in an unsteady hand, may be regarded as the exposition of a method. It was very simple, and at the end of that moving appeal to every altruistic sentiment it blazed at you, luminous and terrifying, like a flash of lightning in a serene sky: 'Exterminate all the brutes!' The curious part was that he had apparently forgotten all about that valuable postscriptum, because, later on, when he in a sense came to himself, he repeatedly entreated me to take good care of 'my pamphlet' (he called it), as it was sure to have in the future a good influence upon his career. I had full information about all these things, and, besides, as it turned out, I was to have the care of his memory. I've done enough for it to give me the indisputable right to lay it, if I choose, for an everlasting rest in the dustbin of progress, among all the sweepings and, figuratively speaking, all the dead cats of civilization. But then, you see, I can't choose. He won't be forgotten. Whatever he was, he was not common. He had the power to charm or frighten rudimentary souls into an aggravated witch dance in his honor; he could also fill the small souls of the pilgrims with bitter misgivings: he had one devoted friend at least, and he had conquered one soul in the world that was neither rudimentary nor tainted with self-seeking. No; I can't forget him, though I am not prepared to affirm the fellow was exactly worth the life we lost in getting to him. I missed my late helmsman awfully—I missed him even while his body was still lying in the pilothouse. Perhaps you will think it passing strange this regret for a savage who was no more account than a grain of sand in a black Sahara. Well, don't you see, he had done something, he had steered; for months I had him at my back—a help—an instrument. It was a kind of partnership. He steered for me—I had to look after him, I worried about his deficiencies, and thus a subtle bond had been created, of which I only became aware when it was suddenly broken. And the intimate profundity of that look he gave me when he received his hurt remains to this day in my memory—like a claim of distant kinship affirmed in a supreme moment.

"Poor fool! If he had only left that shutter alone. He had no restraint, no restraint—just like Kurtz—a tree swayed by the wind. As soon as I had put on a dry pair of slippers, I dragged him out, after first jerking the spear out of his side, which operation I confess I performed with my eyes shut tight. His heels leaped together over the little doorstep; his shoulders were pressed to my breast; I hugged him from behind desperately. Oh! he was heavy, heavy; heavier than any man on earth, I should imagine. Then without more ado I tipped him overboard. The current snatched him as though he had been a wisp of grass, and I saw the body roll over twice before I lost sight of it for ever. All the pilgrims and the manager were then congregated on the awning deck about the pilothouse, chattering at each other like a flock of excited magpies, and there was a scandalized murmur at my heartless promptitude. What they wanted to keep that body hanging about for I can't guess. Embalm it, maybe. But I had also heard another, and a very ominous, murmur on the deck below. My friends the woodcutters were likewise scandalized, and with a better show of reason—though I admit that the reason itself was quite inadmissible. Oh, quite! I had made up my mind that if my late helmsman was to be eaten, the fishes alone should have him. He had been a very second-rate helmsman while alive, but now he was dead he might have become a first-class temptation, and possibly cause some startling trouble. Besides, I was anxious to take the wheel, the man in pink pajamas showing himself a hopeless duffer at the business.

"This I did directly the simple funeral was over. We were going half-speed, keeping right in the middle of the stream, and I listened to the talk about me. They had given up Kurtz, they had given up the station; Kurtz was dead, and the station had been burnt—and so on—and so on. The red-haired pilgrim was beside himself with the thought that at least this poor Kurtz had been properly revenged. 'Say! We must have made a glorious slaughter of them in the bush. Eh? What do you think? Say?' He positively danced, the bloodthirsty little gingery beggar. And he had nearly fainted when he saw the wounded man! I could not help saying, 'You made a glorious lot of smoke, anyhow.' I had seen, from the way the tops of the bushes rustled and flew, that almost all the shots had gone too high. You can't hit anything unless you take aim and fire from the shoulder; but these chaps fired from the hip with their eyes shut. The retreat, I maintained—and I was right—was caused by the screeching of the steam whistle. Upon this they forgot Kurtz, and began to howl at me with indignant protests.

"The manager stood by the wheel murmuring confidentially about the necessity of getting well away down the river before dark at all events, when I saw in the distance a clearing on the riverside and the outlines of some sort of building. 'What's this?' I asked. He clapped his hands in wonder. 'The station!' he cried. I edged in at once, still going half-speed.

"Through my glasses I saw the slope of a hill interspersed with rare trees and perfectly free from undergrowth. A long decaying building on the summit was half buried in the high grass; the large holes in the peaked roof gaped black from afar; the jungle and the woods made a background. There was no enclosure or fence of any kind; but there had been one apparently, for near the house half a dozen slim posts remained in a row, roughly trimmed, and with their upper ends ornamented with round carved balls. The rails, or whatever there had been between, had disappeared. Of course the forest surrounded all that. The riverbank was clear, and on the water side I saw a white man under a hat like a cartwheel beckoning persistently with his whole arm.

Examining the edge of the forest above and below, I was almost certain I could see movements—human forms gliding here and there. I steamed past prudently, then stopped the engines and let her drift down. The man on the shore began to shout, urging us to land. 'We have been attacked,' screamed the manager. 'I know—I know. It's all right,' yelled back the other, as cheerful as you please. 'Come along. It's all right. I am glad.'

"His aspect reminded me of something I had seen—something funny I had seen somewhere. As I maneuvered to get alongside, I was asking myself, 'What does this fellow look like?' Suddenly I got it. He looked like a harlequin. His clothes had been made of some stuff that was brown holland probably, but it was covered with patches all over, with bright patches, blue, red, and yellow —patches on the back, patches on the front, patches on elbows, on knees; colored binding round his jacket, scarlet edging at the bottom of his trousers; and the sunshine made him look extremely gay and wonderfully neat withal, because you could see how beautifully all this patching had been done. A beardless, boyish face, very fair, no features to speak of, nose peeling, little blue eyes, smiles and frowns chasing each other over that open countenance like sunshine and shadow on a wind-swept plain. 'Look out, captain!' he cried; 'there's a snag lodged in here last night.' What! Another snag? I confess I swore shamefully. I had nearly holed my cripple, to finish off that charming trip. The harlequin on the bank turned his little pug nose up to me. 'You English?' he asked, all smiles. 'Are you?' I shouted from the wheel. The smiles vanished, and he shook his head as if sorry for my disappointment. Then he brightened up. 'Never mind!' he cried encouragingly. 'Are we in time?' I asked. 'He is up there,' he replied, with a toss of the head up the hill, and becoming gloomy all of a sudden. His face was like the autumn sky, overcast one moment and bright the next.

"When the manager, escorted by the pilgrims, all of them armed to the teeth, had gone to the house, this chap came on board. 'I say, I don't like this. These natives are in the bush,' I said. He assured me earnestly it was all right. 'They are simple people,' he added; 'well, I am glad you came. It took me all my time to keep them off.' 'But you said it was all right,' I cried. 'Oh, they meant no harm,' he said; and as I stared he corrected himself, 'Not exactly.' Then vivaciously, 'My faith, your pilothouse wants a clean up!' In the next breath he advised me to keep enough steam on the boiler to blow the whistle in case of any trouble. 'One good screech will do more for you than all your rifles. They are simple people,' he repeated. He rattled away at such a rate he quite overwhelmed me. He seemed to be trying to make up for lots of silence, and actually hinted, laughing, that such was the case. 'Don't you talk with Mr. Kurtz?' I said. 'You don't talk with that man—you listen to him,' he exclaimed with severe exaltation. 'But now—' He waved his arm, and in the twinkling of an eye was in the uttermost depths of despondency. In a moment he came up again with a jump, possessed himself of both my hands, shook them continuously, while he gabbled: 'Brother sailor . . . honor . . .

pleasure . . . delight . . . introduce myself . . . Russian . . . son of an arch-priest . . . Government of Tambov . . . What? Tobacco! English tobacco; the excellent English tobacco! Now, that's brotherly. Smoke? Where's a sailor that does not smoke?'

"The pipe soothed him, and gradually I made out he had run away from school, had gone to sea in a Russian ship; ran away again; served some time in English ships; was not reconciled with the arch-priest. He made a point of that. 'But when one is young, one must see things, gather experience, ideas; enlarge the mind.' 'Here!' I interrupted. 'You can never tell! Here I met Mr. Kurtz,' he said, youthfully solemn and reproachful. I held my tongue after that. It appears he had persuaded a Dutch trading house on the coast to fit him out with stores and goods, and had started for the interior with a light heart, and no more idea of what would happen to him than a baby. He had been wandering about that river for nearly two years alone, cut off from everybody and everything. 'I am not so young as I look. I am twenty-five,' he said. 'At first old Van Shuyten would tell me to go to the devil,' he narrated with keen enjoyment; 'but I stuck to him, and talked and talked, till at last he got afraid I would talk the hind leg off his favorite dog, so he gave me some cheap things and a few guns, and told me he hoped he would never see my face again. Good old Dutchman, Van Shuyten. I sent him one small lot of ivory a year ago, so that he can't call me a little thief when I get back. I hope he got it. And for the rest I don't care. I had some wood stacked for you. That was my old house. Did you see?'

"I gave him Towson's book. He made as though he would kiss me, but restrained himself. 'The only book I had left, and I thought I had lost it,' he said, looking at it ecstatically. 'So many accidents happen to a man going about alone, you know. Canoes get upset sometimes—and sometimes you've got to clear out so quick when the people get angry.' He thumbed the pages. 'You made notes in Russian?' I asked. He nodded. 'I thought they were written in cipher,' I said. He laughed, then became serious. 'I had lots of trouble to keep these people off,' he said. 'Did they want to kill you?' I asked. 'Oh no!' he cried, and checked himself. 'Why did they attack us?' I pursued. He hesitated, then said shamefacedly, 'They don't want him to go.' 'Don't they?' I said curiously. He nodded a nod full of mystery and wisdom. 'I tell you,' he cried, 'this man has enlarged my mind.' He opened his arms wide, staring at me with his little blue eyes that were perfectly round."

III

"I looked at him, lost in astonishment. There he was before me, in motley, as though he had absconded from a troupe of mimes, enthusiastic, fabulous. His very existence was improbable, inexplicable, and altogether bewildering. He was an insoluble problem. It was inconceivable how he had existed, how he had succeeded in getting so far, how he had managed to remain—why he did not instantly disappear. 'I went a little farther,' he said, 'then still a little farther—till I had gone so far that I don't know how I'll ever get back. Never mind. Plenty time. I can manage. You take Kurtz away quick—quick—I tell you.' The glamor of youth enveloped his particolored rags, his destitution, his loneliness, the essential desolation of his futile wanderings. For months—for years—his life hadn't been worth a day's purchase; and there he was gallantly, thoughtlessly alive, to all appearance indestructible solely by the virtue of his few years and of his unreflecting audacity. I was seduced into something like admiration—like envy. Glamor urged him on, glamor kept him unscathed. He surely wanted nothing from the wilderness but space to breathe in and to push on through. His need was to exist, and to move onwards at the greatest possible risk, and with a maximum of privation. If the absolutely pure, uncalculating, unpractical spirit of adventure had ever ruled a human being, it ruled this bepatched youth. I almost envied him the possession of this modest and clear flame. It seemed to have consumed all thought of self so completely, that, even while he was talking to you, you forgot that it was he—the man before your eyes—who had gone through these things. I did not envy him his devotion to Kurtz, though. He had not meditated over it. It came to him, and he accepted it with a sort of eager fatalism. I must say that to me it appeared about the most dangerous thing in every way he had come upon so far.

"They had come together unavoidably, like two ships becalmed near each other, and lay rubbing sides at last. I suppose Kurtz wanted an audience, because on a certain occasion, when encamped in the forest, they had talked all night, or more probably Kurtz had talked. 'We talked of everything,' he said, quite transported at the recollection. 'I forgot there was such a thing as sleep. The night did not seem to last an hour. Everything! Everything! . . . Of love too.' 'Ah, he talked to you of love!' I said, much amused. 'It isn't what you think,' he cried, almost passionately. 'It was in general. He made me see things—things.'

"He threw his arms up. We were on deck at the time, and the head man of my woodcutters, lounging nearby, turning upon him his heavy and glittering eyes. I looked around, and I don't know why, but I assure you that never, never before, did this land, this river, this jungle, the very arch of this glazing sky, appear to me so hopeless and so dark, so impenetrable to human thought, so pitiless to human weakness. 'And, ever since, you have been with him, of course?' I said.

"On the contrary. It appears their intercourse had been very much broken by various causes. He had, as he informed me proudly, managed to nurse Kurtz through two illnesses (he alluded to it as you would to some risky feat), but as a rule Kurtz wandered alone, far in the depths of the forest. 'Very often coming to this station, I had to wait days and days before he would turn up,' he said. 'Ah, it was worth waiting for!—sometimes.' 'What was he doing? exploring or what?' I asked. 'Oh, yes, of course'; he had discovered lots of villages, a lake too—he did not know exactly in what direction; it was dangerous to inquire too much—but mostly his expeditions had been for ivory. 'But he had no goods to trade with by that time,' I objected. 'There's a good lot of cartridges left even yet,' he answered, looking away. 'To speak plainly, he raided the country,' I said. He nodded. 'Not alone, surely!' He muttered something about the villages round that lake. 'Kurtz got the tribe to follow him, did he?' I suggested. He fidgeted a little. 'They adored him,' he said. The tone of these words was so extraordinary that I looked at him searchingly. It was curious to see his mingled eagerness and reluctance to speak of Kurtz. The man filled his life, occupied his thoughts, swayed his emotions. 'What can you expect?' he burst out; 'he came to them with thunder and lightning, you know—and they had never seen anything like it—and very terrible. He could be very terrible. You can't judge Mr. Kurtz as you would an ordinary man. No, no, no! Now—just to give you an idea—I don't mind telling you, he wanted to shoot me too one day—but I don't judge him.' 'Shoot you!' I cried. 'What for?' 'Well, I had a small lot of ivory the chief of that village near my house gave me. You see I used to shoot game for them. Well, he wanted it, and wouldn't hear reason. He declared he would shoot me unless I gave him the ivory and then cleared out of the country, because he could do so, and had a fancy for it, and there was nothing on earth to prevent him killing whom he jolly well pleased. And it was true too. I gave him the ivory. What did I care! But I didn't clear out. No, no. I couldn't leave him. I had to be careful, of course, till we got friendly again for a time. He had his second illness then. Afterward I had to keep out of the way; but I didn't mind. He was living for the most part in those villages on the lake. When he came down to the river, sometimes he would take to me, and sometimes it was better for me to be careful. This man suffered too much. He hated all this, and somehow he couldn't get away. When I had a chance I begged him to try and leave while there was time; I offered to go back with him. And he would say yes, and then he would remain; go off on another ivory hunt; disappear for weeks; forget himself among these people—forget himself—you know.' 'Why! he's mad,' I said. He protested indignantly. Mr. Kurtz couldn't be mad. If I had heard him talk, only two days ago, I wouldn't dare hint at such a thing. . . . I had taken up my binoculars while we talked, and was looking at the shore, sweeping the limit of the forest at each side and at the back of the house. The consciousness of there being people in that bush, so silent, so quiet—as silent and quiet as the ruined house on the hill—made me uneasy. There was no sign on the face of nature of this amazing tale that was not so much told as suggested to me in desolate exclamations, completed by shrugs, in interrupted phrases, in hints ending in deep sighs. The woods were unmoved, like a mask—heavy, like the closed door of a prison—they looked with their air of hidden knowledge, of patient expectation, of unapproachable silence. The Russian was explaining to me that it was only lately that Mr. Kurtz had come down to the river, bringing along with him all the fighting men of that lake tribe. He had been absent for several months—getting himself adored, I suppose—and had come down unexpectedly, with the intention to all appearances of making a raid either across the river or downstream. Evidently the appetite for more ivory had got the better of the—what shall I say?—less material aspirations. However, he had got much worse suddenly. 'I heard he was lying helpless, and so I came up—took my chance,' said the Russian. 'Oh, he is bad, very bad.' I directed my glass to the house. There were no signs of life, but there was the ruined roof, the long mud wall peeping above the grass, with three little square window holes, no two of the same size; all this brought within reach of my hand, as it were. And then I made a brusque movement, and one of the remaining posts of that vanished fence leaped up in the field of my glass. You remember I told you I had been struck at the distance by certain attempts at ornamentation, rather remarkable in the ruinous aspect of the place. Now I had suddenly a nearer view, and its first result was to make me throw my head back as if before a blow. Then I went carefully from post to post with my glass, and I saw my mistake. These round knobs were not ornamental but symbolic; they were expressive and puzzling, striking and disturbing—food for thought and also for the vultures if there had been any looking down from the sky; but at all events for such ants as were industrious enough to ascend the pole They would have been even more impressive, those heads on the stakes, if their faces had not been turned to the house. Only one, the first I had made out, was facing my way. I was not so shocked as you may think. The start back I had given was really nothing but a movement of surprise. I had expected to see a knob of wood there, you know. I returned deliberately to the first I had seen—and there it was, black, dried, sunken, with closed eyelids—a head that seemed to sleep at the top of that pole, and, with the shrunken dry lips showing a narrow white line of the teeth, was smiling too, smiling continuously at some endless and jocose dream of that eternal slumber.

"I am not disclosing any trade secrets. In fact the manager said afterward that Mr. Kurtz's methods had ruined the district. I have no opinion on that point, but I want you clearly to understand that there was nothing exactly profitable in these heads being there. They only showed that Mr. Kurtz lacked restraint in the gratification of his various lusts, that there was something wanting in him—some small matter which, when the pressing need arose, could not be found under his magnificent eloquence. Whether he knew of this deficiency himself I can't say. I think the knowledge came to him at last— only at the very last. But the wilderness had found him out early, and had taken on him a terrible vengeance for the fantastic invasion. I think it had whispered to him things about himself which he did not know, things of which he had no conception till he took counsel with this great solitude—and the whisper had proved irresistibly fascinating. It echoed loudly within him because he was hollow at the core. . . . I put down the glass, and the head that had appeared near enough to be spoken to seemed at once to have leaped away from me into inaccessible distance.

"The admirer of Mr. Kurtz was a bit crestfallen. In a hurried, indistinct voice he began to assure me he had not dared to take these—say, symbols—down. He was not afraid of the natives; they would not stir till Mr. Kurtz gave the word. His ascendancy was extraordinary. The camps of these people surrounded the place, and the chiefs came every day to see him. They would crawl. . . . 'I don't want to know anything of the ceremonies used when approaching Mr. Kurtz,' I shouted. Curious, this feeling that came over me that such details would be more intolerable than those heads drying on the stakes under Mr. Kurtz's windows. After all, that was only a savage sight, while I seemed at one bound to have been transported into some lightless region of subtle horrors, where pure, uncomplicated savagery was a positive relief, being something that had a right to exist—obviously—in the sunshine. The young man looked at me with surprise. I suppose it did not occur to him that Mr. Kurtz was no idol of mine. He forgot I hadn't heard any of these splendid monologues on, what was it? on love, justice, conduct of life—or what not. If it had come to crawling before Mr. Kurtz, he crawled as much as the veriest savage of them all. I had no idea of the conditions, he said: these heads were the heads of rebels. I shocked him excessively by laughing. Rebels! What would be the next definition I was to hear? There had been enemies, criminals, workers—and these were rebels. Those rebellious heads looked very subdued to me on their sticks. 'You don't know how such a life tries a man like Kurtz,' cried Kurtz's last disciple. 'Well, and you?' I said. 'I! I! I am a simple man. I have no great thoughts. I want nothing from anybody. How can you compare me to . . . ?' His feelings were too much for speech, and suddenly he broke down. 'I don't understand,' he groaned. 'I've been doing my best to keep him alive, and that's enough. I had no hand in all this. I have no abilities. There hasn't been a drop of medicine or a mouthful of invalid food for months here. He was shamefully abandoned. A man like this, with such ideas. Shamefully! Shamefully! I—I—haven't slept for the last ten nights. . . .'

"His voice lost itself in the calm of the evening. The long shadows of the forest had slipped downhill while we talked, had gone far beyond the ruined hovel, beyond the symbolic row of stakes. All this was in the gloom, while we down there were yet in the sunshine, and the stretch of the river abreast of the clearing glittered in a still and dazzling splendor, with a murky and over-shadowed bend above and below. Not a living soul was seen on the shore. The bushes did not rustle.

"Suddenly round the corner of the house a group of men appeared, as though they had come up from the ground. They waded waist-deep in the grass, in a compact body, bearing an improvised stretcher in their midst. Instantly, in the emptiness of the landscape, a cry arose whose shrillness pierced the still air like a sharp arrow flying straight to the very heart of the land; and, as if by enchantment, streams of human beings—of naked human beings—with spears in their hands, with bows, with shields, with wild glances and savage movements, were poured into the clearing by the dark-faced and pensive forest. The bushes shook, the grass swayed for a time, and then everything stood still in attentive immobility.

" 'Now, if he does not say the right thing to them we are all done for,' said the Russian at my elbow. The knot of men with the stretcher had stopped too, halfway to the steamer, as if petrified. I saw the man on the stretcher sit up, lank and with an uplifted arm, above the shoulders of the bearers. 'Let us hope that the man who can talk so well of love in general will find some particular reason to spare us this time,' I said. I resented bitterly the absurd danger of our situation, as if to be at the mercy of that atrocious phantom had been a dishonoring necessity. I could not hear a sound, but through my glasses I saw the thin arm extended commandingly, the lower jaw moving, the eyes of that apparition shining darkly far in its bony head that nodded with grotesque jerks. Kurtz—Kurtz—that means 'short' in German—don't it? Well, the name was as true as everything else in his life—and death. He looked at least seven feet long. His covering had fallen off, and his body emerged from it pitiful and appalling as from a winding sheet. I could see the cage of his ribs all astir, the bones of his arm waving. It was as though an animated image of death carved out of old ivory had been shaking its hand with menaces at a motionless crowd of men made of dark and glittering bronze. I saw him open his mouth wide—it gave him a weirdly voracious aspect, as though he had wanted to swallow all the air, all the earth, all the men before him. A deep voice reached me faintly. He must have been shouting. He fell back suddenly. The stretcher shook as the bearers staggered forward again, and almost at the same time I noticed that the crowd of savages was vanishing without any perceptible movement of retreat, as if the forest that had ejected these beings so suddenly had drawn them in again as the breath is drawn in a long aspiration.

"Some of the pilgrims behind the stretcher carried his arms—two shotguns, a heavy rifle, and a light revolver-carbine—the thunderbolts of that pitiful Jupiter. The manager bent over him murmuring as he walked beside his head. They laid him down in one of the little cabins—just a room for a bedplace and a campstool or two, you know. We had brought his belated correspondence, and a lot of torn envelopes and open letters littered his bed. His hand roamed feebly among these papers. I was struck by the fire of his eyes and the composed languor of his expression. It was not so much the exhaustion of disease. He did not seem in pain. This shadow looked satiated and calm, as though for the moment it had had its fill of all the emotions.

"He rustled one of the letters, and looking straight in my face said, 'I am glad.' Somebody had been writing to him about me. These special recommendations were turning up again. The volume of tone he emitted without effort, almost without the trouble of moving his lips, amazed me. A voice! a voice! It was grave, profound, vibrating, while the man did not seem capable of a whisper. However, he had enough strength in him—factitious no doubt—to very nearly make an end of us, as you shall hear directly.

"The manager appeared silently in the doorway; I stepped out at once and he drew the curtain after me. The Russian, eyed curiously by the pilgrims, was staring at the shore. I followed the direction of his glance.

"Dark human shapes could be made out in the distance, flitting indistinctly against the gloomy border of the forest, and near the river two bronze figures, leaning on tall spears, stood in the sunlight under fantastic headdresses of spotted skins, warlike and still in statuesque repose. And from right to left along the lighted shore moved a wild and gorgeous apparition of a woman.

"She walked with measured steps, draped in striped and fringed cloths, treading the earth proudly, with a slight jingle and flash of barbarous ornaments. She carried her head high; her hair was done in the shape of a helmet; she had brass leggings to the knee, brass wire gauntlets to the elbow, a crimson spot on her tawny cheek, innumerable necklaces of glass beads on her neck; bizarre things, charms, gifts of witchmen, that hung about her, glittered and trembled at every step. She must have had the value of several elephant tusks upon her. She was savage and superb, wild-eyed and magnificent; there was something ominous and stately in her deliberate progress. And in the hush that had fallen suddenly upon the whole sorrowful land, the immense wilderness, the colossal body of the fecund and mysterious life seemed to look at her, pensive, as though it had been looking at the image of its own tenebrous and passionate soul.

"She came abreast of the steamer, stood still, and faced us. Her long shadow fell to the water's edge. Her face had a tragic and fierce aspect of wild sorrow and of dumb pain mingled with the fear of some struggling, half-shaped resolve. She stood looking at us without a stir, and like the wilderness itself, with an air of brooding over an inscrutable purpose. A whole minute passed, and then she made a step forward. There was a low jingle, a glint of yellow metal, a sway of fringed draperies, and she stopped as if her heart had failed her. The young fellow by my side growled. The pilgrims murmured at my back. She looked at us all as if her life had depended upon the unswerving steadiness of her glance. Suddenly she opened her bared arms and threw them up rigid above her head, as though in an uncontrollable desire to touch the sky, and at the same time the swift shadows darted out on the earth, swept around on the river, gathering the steamer into a shadowy embrace. A formidable silence hung over the scene.

"She turned away slowly, walked on, following the bank, and passed into the bushes to the left. Once only her eyes gleamed back at us in the dusk of the thickets before she disappeared.

" 'If she had offered to come aboard I really think I would have tried to shoot her,' said the man of patches nervously. 'I had been risking my life every day for the last fortnight to keep her out of the house. She got in one day and kicked up a row about those miserable rags I picked up in the storeroom to mend my clothes with. I wasn't decent. At least it must have been that, for she talked like a fury to Kurtz for an hour, pointing at me now and then. I don't understand the dialect of this tribe. Luckily for me, I fancy Kurtz felt too ill that day to care, or there would have been mischief. I don't understand. . . . No—it's too much for me. Ah, well, it's all over now.'

"At this moment I heard Kurtz's deep voice behind the curtain: 'Save me!—save the ivory, you mean. Don't tell me. Save *me!* Why, I've had to save you. You are interrupting my plans now. Sick! Sick! Not so sick as you would like to believe. Never mind. I'll carry my ideas out yet—I will return. I'll show you what can be done. You with your little peddling notions—you are interfering with me. I will return. I. . . .'

"The manager came out. He did me the honor to take me under the arm and lead me aside. 'He is very low, very low,' he said. He considered it necessary to sigh, but neglected to be consistently sorrowful. 'We have done all we could for him—haven't we? But there is no disguising the fact, Mr. Kurtz has done more harm than good to the Company. He did not see the time was not ripe for vigorous action. Cautiously, cautiously—that's my principle. We must be cautious yet. The district is closed to us for a time. Deplorable! Upon the whole, the trade will suffer. I don't deny there is a remarkable quantity of ivory—mostly fossil. We must save it, at all events—but look how precarious the position is—and why? Because the method is unsound.' 'Do you,' said I, looking at the shore, 'call it "unsound method"?' 'Without doubt,' he exclaimed hotly. 'Don't you?' . . . 'No method at all,' I murmured after a while. 'Exactly,' he exulted. 'I anticipated this. Shows a complete want of judgment. It is my duty to point it out in the proper quarter.' 'Oh,' said I, 'that fellow—what's his name?—the brickmaker, will make a readable report for you.' He appeared confounded for a moment. It seemed to me I had never breathed an atmosphere so vile, and I turned mentally to Kurtz for relief—positively for relief. 'Nevertheless, I think Mr. Kurtz is a remarkable man,' I said with emphasis. He started, dropped on me a cold heavy glance, said very quietly, 'He *was,*' and turned his back on me. My hour of favor was over; I found myself lumped along with Kurtz as a partisan of methods for which the time was not ripe: I was unsound! Ah! but it was something to have at least a choice of nightmares.

"I had turned to the wilderness really, not to Mr. Kurtz, who, I was ready to admit, was as good as buried. And for a moment it seemed to me as if I also were buried in a vast grave full of unspeakable secrets. I felt an intolerable weight oppressing my breast, the smell of the damp earth, the unseen presence of victorious corruption, the darkness of an impenetrable night. . . . The Russian tapped me on the shoulder. I heard him mumbling and stammering something about 'brother seaman—couldn't conceal—knowledge of matters that would affect Mr. Kurtz's reputation.' I waited. For him evidently Mr. Kurtz was not in his grave; I suspect that for him Mr. Kurtz was one of the immortals. 'Well!' said I at last, 'speak out. As it happens, I am Mr. Kurtz's friend—in a way.'

"He stated with a good deal of formality that had we not been 'of the same profession,' he would have kept the matter to himself without regard to consequences. He suspected 'there was an active ill will toward him on the part of these white men that—' 'You are right,' I said, remembering a certain conversation I had overheard. 'The manager thinks you ought to be hanged.' He showed a concern at this intelligence which amused me at first. 'I had better get out of the way quietly,' he said earnestly. 'I can do no more for Kurtz now, and they would soon find some excuse. What's to stop them? There's a military post three hundred miles from here.' 'Well, upon my word,' said I, 'perhaps you had better go if you have any friends among the savages nearby.' 'Plenty,' he said. 'They are simple people—and I want nothing, you know.' He stood biting his lip, then: 'I don't want any harm to happen to these whites here, but of course I was thinking of Mr. Kurtz's reputation—but you are a brother seaman and—' 'All right,' said I, after a time. 'Mr. Kurtz's reputation is safe with me.' I did not know how truly I spoke.

"He informed me, lowering his voice, that it was Kurtz who had ordered the attack to be made on the steamer. 'He hated sometimes the idea of being taken away—and then again. . . . But I don't understand these matters. I am a simple man. He thought it would scare you away—that you would give it up, thinking him dead. I could not stop him. Oh, I had an awful time of it this last month.' 'Very well,' I said. 'He is all right now.' 'Ye-e-es,' he muttered, not very convinced apparently. 'Thanks,' said I; 'I shall keep my eyes open.' 'But quiet—eh?' he urged anxiously. 'It would be awful for his reputation if anybody here—' I promised a complete discretion with great gravity. 'I have a canoe and three black fellows waiting not very far. I am off. Could you give me a few Martini-Henry cartridges?' I could, and did, with proper secrecy. He helped himself, with a wink at me, to a handful of my tobacco. 'Between sailors—you know—good English tobacco.' At the door of the pilothouse he turned round—'I say, haven't you a pair of shoes you could spare?' He raised one leg. 'Look.' The soles were tied with knotted strings sandalwise under his bare feet. I rooted out an old pair, at which he looked with admiration before tucking it under his left arm. One of his pockets (bright red) was bulging with cartridges, from the other (dark blue) peeped 'Towson's Inquiry,' etc. etc. He seemed to think himself excellently well equipped for a renewed encounter with the wilderness. 'Ah! I'll never, never meet such a man again. You ought to have heard him recite poetry—his own too it was, he told me. Poetry!' He rolled his eyes at the recollection of these delights. 'Oh, he enlarged my mind!' 'Good-bye,' said I. He shook hands and vanished in the night. Sometimes I ask myself whether I had ever really seen him—whether it was possible to meet such a phenomenon! . . .

"When I woke up shortly after midnight his warning came to my mind with its hint of danger that seemed, in the starred darkness, real enough to make me get up for the purpose of having a look round. On the hill a big fire burned, illuminating fitfully a crooked corner of the station house. One of the agents with a picket of a few of our blacks, armed for the purpose, was keeping guard over the ivory; but deep within the forest, red gleams that wavered, that seemed to sink and rise from the ground among confused columnar shapes of intense blackness, showed the exact position of the camp where Mr. Kurtz's adorers were keeping their uneasy vigil. The monotonous beating of a big drum filled the air with muffled shocks and a lingering vibration. A steady droning sound of many men chanting each to himself some weird incantation came out from the black, flat wall of the woods as the humming of bees comes out of a hive, and had a strange narcotic effect upon my half-awake senses. I believe I dozed off leaning over the rail, till an abrupt burst of yells, an overwhelming outbreak of a pent-up and mysterious frenzy, woke me up in a bewildered wonder. It was cut short all at once, and the low droning went on with an effect of audible and soothing silence. I glanced casually into the little cabin. A light was burning within, but Mr. Kurtz was not there.

"I think I would have raised an outcry if I had believed my eyes. But I didn't believe them at first—the thing seemed so impossible. The fact is I was completely unnerved by a sheer blank fright, pure abstract terror, unconnected with any distinct shape of physical danger. What made this emotion so overpowering was—how shall I define it?—the moral shock I received, as if something altogether monstrous, intolerable to thought and odious to the soul, had been thrust upon me unexpectedly. This lasted of course the merest fraction of a second, and then the usual sense of commonplace, deadly danger, the possibility of a sudden onslaught and massacre, or something of the kind, which I saw impending, was positively welcome and composing. It pacified me, in fact, so much, that I did not raise an alarm.

"There was an agent buttoned up inside an ulster and sleeping on a chair on deck within three feet of me. The yells had not awakened him; he snored very slightly; I left him to his slumbers and leaped ashore. I did not betray Mr. Kurtz—it was ordered I should never betray him—it was written I should be loyal to the nightmare of my choice. I was anxious to deal with this shadow by myself alone—and to this day I don't know why I was so jealous of sharing with anyone the peculiar blackness of that experience.

"As soon as I got on the bank I saw a trail—a broad trail through the grass. I remember the exultation with which I said to myself, 'He can't walk —he is crawling on all fours—I've got him.' The grass was wet with dew. I strode rapidly with clenched fists. I fancy I had some vague notion of falling upon him and giving him a drubbing. I don't know. I had some imbecile thoughts. The knitting old woman with the cat obtruded herself upon my memory as a most improper person to be sitting at the other end of such an affair. I saw a row of pilgrims squirting lead in the air out of Winchesters held to the hip. I thought I would never get back to the steamer, and imagined myself living alone and unarmed in the woods to an advanced age. Such silly things—you know. And I remember I confounded the beat of the drum with the beating of my heart, and was pleased at its calm regularity.

"I kept to the track though—then stopped to listen. The night was very clear; a dark blue space, sparkling with dew and starlight, in which black things stood very still. I thought I could see a kind of motion ahead of me. I was strangely cocksure of everything that night. I actually left the track and ran in a wide semicircle (I verily believe chuckling to myself) so as to get in front of that stir, of that motion I had seen—if indeed I had seen anything. I was circumventing Kurtz as though it had been a boyish game.

"I came upon him, and, if he had not heard me coming, I would have fallen over him too, but he got up in time. He rose, unsteady, long, pale, indistinct, like a vapor exhaled by the earth, and swayed slightly, misty and silent before me; while at my back the fires loomed between the trees, and the murmur of many voices issued from the forest. I had cut him off cleverly; but when actually confronting him I seemed to come to my senses, I saw the danger in its right proportion. It was by no means over yet. Suppose he began to shout? Though he could hardly stand, there was still plenty of vigor in his voice. 'Go away—hide yourself,' he said, in that profound tone. It was very awful. I glanced back. We were within thirty yards of the nearest fire. A black figure stood up, strode on long black legs, waving long black arms, across the glow. It had horns—antelope horns, I think—on its head. Some sorcerer, some witchman no doubt: it looked fiendlike enough. 'Do you know what you are doing?' I whispered. 'Perfectly,' he answered, raising his voice for that single word: it sounded to me far off and yet loud, like a hail through a speaking-trumpet. If he makes a row we are lost, I thought to myself. This clearly was not a case for fisticuffs, even apart from the very natural aversion I had to beat that Shadow—this wandering and tormented thing. 'You will be lost,' I said—'utterly lost.' One gets sometimes such a flash of inspiration, you know. I did say the right thing, though indeed he could not have been more irretrievably lost than he was at this very moment, when the foundations of our intimacy were being laid—to endure—to endure—even to the end—even beyond.

" 'I had immense plans,' he muttered irresolutely. 'Yes,' said I; 'but if you try to shout I'll smash your head with—' There was not a stick or a stone near. 'I will throttle you for good,' I corrected myself. 'I was on the threshold of great things,' he pleaded, in a voice of longing, with a wistfulness of tone that made my blood run cold. 'And now for this stupid scoundrel—' 'Your success in Europe is assured in any case,' I affirmed steadily. I did not want to have the throttling of him, you understand—and indeed it would have been very little use for any practical purpose. I tried to break the spell—the heavy, mute spell of the wilderness—that seemed to draw him to its pitiless breast by the awakening of forgotten and brutal instincts, by the memory of gratified and monstrous passions. This alone, I was convinced, had driven him out to the edge of the forest, to the bush, toward the gleam of fires, the throb of drums, the drone of weird incantations; this alone had beguiled his unlawful soul beyond the bounds of permitted aspirations. And, don't you see, the terror of the position was not in being knocked on the head—though I had a very lively sense of that danger too—but in this, that I had to deal with a being to whom I could not appeal in the name of anything high or low. I had, even like the natives, to invoke him—himself—his own exalted and incredible degradation. There was nothing either above or below him, and I knew it. He had kicked himself loose of the earth. Confound the man! he had kicked the very earth to pieces. He was alone, and I before him did not know whether I stood on the ground or floated in the air. I've been telling you what we said—repeating the phrases we pronounced—but what's the good? They were common everyday words—the familiar, vague sounds exchanged on every waking day of life. But what of that? They had behind them, to my mind, the terrific suggestiveness of words heard in dreams, of phrases spoken in nightmares. Soul! If anybody had ever struggled with a soul, I am the man. And I wasn't arguing with a lunatic either. Believe me or not, his intelligence was perfectly clear—concentrated, it is true, upon himself with horrible intensity, yet clear; and therein was my only chance—barring, of course, the killing him there and then, which wasn't so good, on account of unavoidable noise. But his soul was mad. Being alone in the wilderness, it had looked within itself, and, by heavens! I tell you, it had gone mad. I had—for my sins, I suppose, to go through the ordeal of looking into it myself. No eloquence could have been so withering to one's belief in mankind as his final burst of sincerity. He struggled with himself too. I saw it—I heard it. I saw the inconceivable mystery of a soul that knew no restraint, no faith, and no fear, yet struggling blindly with itself. I kept my head pretty well; but when I had him at last stretched on the couch, I wiped my forehead, while my legs shook under me as though I had carried half a ton on my back down that hill. And yet I had only supported him, his bony arm clasped round my neck—and he was not much heavier than a child.

"When next day we left at noon, the crowd, of whose presence behind the curtain of trees I had been acutely conscious all the time, flowed out of the woods again, filled the clearing, covered the slope with a mass of naked, breathing, quivering, bronze bodies. I steamed up a bit, then swung downstream, and two thousand eyes followed the evolutions of the splashing, thumping, fierce river demon beating the water with its terrible tail and breathing black smoke into the air. In front of the first rank, along the river, three men, plastered with bright red earth from head to foot, strutted to and fro restlessly. When we came abreast again, they faced the river, stamped their feet, nodded their horned heads, swayed their scarlet bodies; they shook towards the fierce river demon a bunch of black feathers, a mangy skin with a pendent tail—something that looked like a dried gourd; they shouted periodically together strings of amazing words that resembled no sounds of human language; and the deep murmurs of the crowd, interrupted suddenly, were like the responses of some satanic litany.

"We had carried Kurtz into the pilothouse: there was more air there. Lying on the couch, he stared through the open shutter. There was an eddy in the mass of human bodies, and the woman with helmeted head and tawny cheeks rushed out to the very brink of the stream. She put out her hands, shouted something, and all that wild mob took up the shout in a roaring chorus of articulated, rapid, breathless utterance.

" 'Do you understand this?' I asked.

"He kept on looking out past me with fiery, longing eyes, with a mingled expression of wistfulness and hate. He made no answer, but I saw a smile, a smile of indefinable meaning, appear on his colorless lips that a moment after twitched convulsively. 'Do I not?' he said slowly, gasping, as if the words had been torn out of him by a supernatural power.

"I pulled the string of the whistle, and I did this because I saw the pilgrims on deck getting out their rifles with an air of anticipating a jolly lark. At the sudden screech there was a movement of abject terror through that wedged mass of bodies. 'Don't! don't you frighten them away,' cried someone on deck disconsolately. I pulled the string time after time. They broke and ran, they leaped, they crouched, they swerved, they dodged the flying terror of the sound. The three red chaps had fallen flat, face down on the shore, as though they had been shot dead. Only the barbarous and superb woman did not so much as flinch, and stretched tragically her bare arms after us over the somber and glittering river.

"And then that imbecile crowd down on the deck started their little fun, and I could see nothing more for smoke.

"The brown current ran swiftly out of the heart of darkness, bearing us down toward the sea with twice the speed of our upward progress; and Kurtz's life was running swiftly too, ebbing, ebbing out of his heart into the sea of inexorable time. The manager was very placid, he had no vital anxieties now, he took us both in with a comprehensive and satisfied glance: the 'affair' had come off as well as could be wished. I saw the time approaching when I would be left alone of the party of 'unsound method.' The pilgrims looked upon me with disfavor. I was, so to speak, numbered with the dead. It is strange how I accepted this unforeseen partnership, this choice of nightmares forced upon me in the tenebrous land invaded by these mean and greedy phantoms.

"Kurtz discoursed. A voice! a voice! It rang deep to the very last. It survived his strength to hide in the magnificent folds of eloquence the barren darkness of his heart. Oh, he struggled! he struggled! The wastes of his weary brain were haunted by shadowy images now—images of wealth and fame revolving obsequiously round his unextinguishable gift of noble and lofty expression. My Intended, my station, my career, my ideas—these were the subjects for the occasional utterances of elevated sentiments. The shade of the original Kurtz frequented the bedside of the hollow sham, whose fate it was to be buried presently in the mould of primeval earth. But both the diabolic love and the unearthly hate of the mysteries it had penetrated fought for the possession of that soul satiated with primitive emotions, avid of lying fame, of sham distinction, of all the appearances of success and power.

"Sometimes he was contemptibly childish. He desired to have kings meet him at railway stations on his return from some ghastly Nowhere, where he intended to accomplish great things. 'You show them you have in you something that is really profitable, and then there will be no limits to the recognition of your ability,' he would say. 'Of course you must take care of the motives—right motives—always.' The long reaches that were like one and the same reach, monotonous bends that were exactly alike, slipped past the steamer with their multitude of secular trees looking patiently after this grimy fragment of another world, the forerunner of change, of conquest, of trade, of massacres, of blessings. I looked ahead—piloting. 'Close the shutter,' said Kurtz suddenly one day; 'I can't bear to look at this.' I did so. There was a silence. 'Oh, but I will wring your heart yet!' he cried at the invisible wilderness.

"We broke down—as I had expected—and had to lie up for repairs at the head of an island. This delay was the first thing that shook Kurtz's confidence. One morning he gave me a packet of papers and a photograph—the lot tied together with a shoestring. 'Keep this for me,' he said. 'This noxious fool' (meaning the manager) 'is capable of prying into my boxes when I am not looking.' In the afternoon I saw him. He was lying on his back with closed eyes, and I withdrew quietly, but I heard him mutter, 'Live rightly, die, die. . . .' I listened. There was nothing more. Was he rehearsing some speech in his sleep, or was it a fragment of a phrase from some newspaper article? He had been writing for the papers and meant to do so again, 'for the furthering of my ideas. It's a duty.'

"His was an impenetrable darkness. I looked at him as you peer down at a man who is lying at the bottom of a precipice where the sun never shines. But I had not much time to give him, because I was helping the engine driver to take to pieces the leaky cylinders, to straighten a bent connecting rod, and in other such matters. I lived in an infernal mess of rust, filings, nuts, bolts, spanners, hammers, ratchet drills—things I abominate, because I don't get on with them. I tended the little forge we fortunately had aboard; I toiled wearily in a wretched scrap heap—unless I had the shakes too bad to stand.

"One evening coming in with a candle I was startled to hear him say a little tremulously, 'I am lying here in the dark waiting for death.' The light was within a foot of his eyes. I forced myself to murmur, 'Oh, nonsense!' and stood over him as if transfixed.

"Anything approaching the change that came over his features I have never seen before, and hope never to see again. Oh, I wasn't touched. I was fascinated. It was as though a veil had been rent. I saw on that ivory face the expression of somber pride, of ruthless power, of craven terror—of an intense and hopeless despair. Did he live his life again in every detail of desire, temptation, and surrender during that supreme moment of complete knowledge? He cried in a whisper at some image, at some vision—he cried out twice, a cry that was no more than a breath:

" 'The horror! The horror!'

"I blew the candle out and left the cabin. The pilgrims were dining in the mess room and I took my place opposite the manager, who lifted his eyes to give me a questioning glance, which I successfully ignored. He leaned back, serene, with that peculiar smile of his sealing the unexpressed depths of his meanness. A continuous shower of small flies streamed upon the lamp, upon the cloth, upon our hands and faces. Suddenly the manager's boy put his insolent black head in the doorway, and said in a tone of scathing contempt:

" 'Mistah Kurtz—he dead.'

"All the pilgrims rushed out to see. I remained, and went on with my dinner. I believe I was considered brutally callous. However, I did not eat much. There was a lamp in there—light, don't you know—and outside it was so beastly, beastly dark. I went no more near the remarkable man who had pronounced a judgment upon the adventures of his soul on this earth. The voice was gone. What else had been there? But I am of course aware the next day the pilgrims buried something in a muddy hole.

"And then they very nearly buried me.

"However, as you see, I did not go to join Kurtz there and then. I did not. I remained to dream the nightmare out to the end, and to show my loyalty to Kurtz once more. Destiny. My destiny! Droll thing life is—that mysterious arrangement of merciless logic for a futile purpose. The most you can hope from it is some knowledge of yourself—that comes too late—a crop of unextinguishable regrets. I have wrestled with death. It is the most unexciting contest you can imagine. It takes place in an impalpable grayness, with nothing underfoot, with nothing around, without spectators, without clamor, without glory, without the great desire of victory, without the great fear of defeat, in a sickly atmosphere of tepid skepticism, without much belief in your own right, and still less in that of your adversary. If such is the form of ultimate wisdom, then life is a greater riddle than some of us think it to be. I was within a hairbreadth of the last opportunity for pronouncement, and I found with humiliation that probably I would have nothing to say. This is the reason why I affirm that Kurtz was a remarkable man. He had something to say. He said it. Since I had peeped over the edge myself, I understand better the meaning of his stare, that could not see the flame of the candle, but was wide enough to embrace the whole universe, piercing enough to penetrate all the hearts that beat in the darkness. He had summed up—he had judged. 'The horror!' He was a remarkable man. After all, this was the expression of some sort of belief; it had candor, it had conviction, it had a vibrating note of revolt in its whisper, it had the appalling face of a glimpsed truth—the strange commingling of desire and hate. And it is not my own extremity I remember best—a vision of grayness without form filled with physical pain, and a careless contempt for the evanescence of all things—even of this pain itself. No! It is his extremity that I seem to have lived through. True, he had made that last stride, he had stepped over the edge, while I had been permitted to draw back my hesitating foot. And perhaps in this is the whole difference; perhaps all the wisdom, and all truth, and all sincerity, are just compressed into that inappreciable moment of time in which we step over the threshold of the invisible. Perhaps! I like to think my summing-up would not have been a word of careless contempt. Better his cry—much better. It was an affirmation, a moral victory paid for by innumerable defeats, by abominable terrors, by abominable satisfactions. But it was a victory! That is why I have remained loyal to Kurtz to the last, and even beyond, when a long time after I heard once more, not his own voice, but the echo of his magnificent eloquence thrown to me from a soul as translucently pure as a cliff of crystal.

"No, they did not bury me, though there is a period of time which I remember mistily, with a shuddering wonder, like a passage through some inconceivable world that had no hope in it and no desire. I found myself back in the sepulchral city resenting the sight of people hurrying through the streets to filch a little money from each other, to devour their infamous cookery, to gulp their unwholesome beer, to dream their insignificant and silly dreams. They trespassed upon my thoughts. They were intruders whose knowledge of life was to me an irritating pretense, because I felt so sure they could not possibly know the things I knew. Their bearing, which was simply the bearing of commonplace individuals going about their business in the assurance of perfect safety, was offensive to me like the outrageous flauntings of folly in the face of a danger it is unable to comprehend. I had no particular desire to enlighten them, but I had some difficulty in restraining myself from laughing in their faces, so full of stupid importance. I daresay I was not very well at that time. I tottered about the streets—there were various affairs to settle—grinning bitterly at perfectly respectable persons. I admit my behavior was inexcusable, but then my temperature was seldom normal in these days. My dear aunt's endeavors to 'nurse up my strength' seemed altogether beside the mark. It was not my strength that wanted nursing, it was my imagination that wanted soothing. I kept the bundle of papers given me by Kurtz, not knowing exactly what to do with it. His mother had died lately, watched over, as I was told, by his Intended. A clean-shaved man, with an official manner and wearing gold-rimmed spectacles, called on me one day and made inquiries, at first circuitous, afterward suavely pressing, about what he was pleased to denominate certain 'documents.' I was not surprised, because I had had two rows with the manager on the subject out there. I had refused to give up the smallest scrap out of that package, and I took the same attitude with the spectacled man. He became darkly menacing at last, and with much heat argued that the Company had the right to every bit of information about its 'territories.' And, said he, 'Mr. Kurtz's knowledge of unexplored regions must have been necessarily extensive and peculiar—owing to his great abilities and to the deplorable circumstances in which he had been placed: therefore—' I assured him Mr. Kurtz's knowledge, however extensive, did not bear upon the problems of commerce or administration. He invoked then the name of science. 'It would be an incalculable loss, if,' etc. etc. I offered him the report on the 'Suppression of Savage Customs,' with the postscriptum torn off. He took it up eagerly, but ended by sniffing at it with an air of contempt. 'This is not what we had a right to expect,' he remarked. 'Expect nothing else,' I said. 'There are only private letters.' He withdrew upon some threat of legal proceedings, and I saw him no more; but another fellow, calling himself Kurtz's cousin, appeared two days later, and was anxious to hear all the details about his dear relative's last moments. Incidentally he gave me to understand that Kurtz had been essentially a great musician. 'There was the making of an immense success,' said the man, who was an organist, I believe, with lank gray hair flowing over a greasy coat collar. I had no reason to doubt his statement; and to this day I am unable to say what was Kurtz's profession, whether he ever had any—which was the greatest of his talents. I had taken him for a painter who wrote for the papers, or else for a journalist who could paint—but even the cousin (who took snuff during the interview) could not tell me what he had been—exactly. He was a universal genius—on that point I agreed with the old chap, who thereupon blew his nose noisily into a large cotton handkerchief and withdrew in senile agitation, bearing off some family letters and memoranda without importance. Ultimately a journalist anxious to know something of the fate of his 'dear colleague' turned up. This visitor informed me Kurtz's proper sphere ought to have been politics 'on the popular side.' He had furry straight eyebrows, bristly hair cropped short, an eyeglass on a broad ribbon, and, becoming expansive, confessed his opinion that Kurtz really couldn't write a bit —'but heavens! how that man could talk! He electrified large meetings. He had faith—don't you see?—he had the faith. He could get himself to believe anything—anything. He would have been a splendid leader of an extreme party.' 'What party?' I asked. 'Any party,' answered the other. 'He was an—an —extremist.' Did I not think so? I assented. Did I know, he asked, with a sudden flash of curiosity, 'what it was that had induced him to go out there?' 'Yes,' said I, and forthwith handed him the famous Report for publication, if he thought fit. He glanced through it hurriedly, mumbling all the time, judged 'it would do,' and took himself off with this plunder.

"Thus I was left at last with a slim packet of letters and the girl's portrait. She struck me as beautiful—I mean she had a beautiful expression. I know that the sunlight can be made to lie too, yet one felt that no manipulation of light and pose could have conveyed the delicate shade of truthfulness upon those features. She seemed ready to listen without mental reservation, without suspicion, without a thought for herself. I concluded I would go and give her back her portrait and those letters myself. Curiosity? Yes; and also some other feeling perhaps. All that had been Kurtz's had passed out of my hands: his soul, his body, his station, his plans, his ivory, his career. There remained only his memory and his Intended—and I wanted to give that up too to the past, in a way—to surrender personally all that remained of him with me to that oblivion which is the last word of our common fate. I don't defend myself. I had no clear perception of what it was I really wanted. Perhaps it was an impulse of unconscious loyalty, or the fulfilment of one of those ironic necessities that lurk in the fact of human existence. I don't know. I can't tell. But I went.

"I thought his memory was like the other memories of the dead that accumulate in every man's life—a vague impress on the brain of shadows that had fallen on it in their swift and final passage; but before the high and ponderous door, between the tall houses of a street as still and decorous as a well-kept alley in a cemetery, I had a vision of him on the stretcher, opening his mouth voraciously, as if to devour all the earth with all its mankind. He lived then before me; he lived as much as he had ever lived—a shadow insatiable of splendid appearances, of frightful realities; a shadow darker than the shadow of the night, and draped nobly in the folds of a gorgeous eloquence. The vision seemed to enter the house with me—the stretcher, the phantom bearers, the wild crowd of obedient worshipers, the gloom of the forests, the glitter of the reach between the murky bends, the beat of the drum, regular and muffled like the beating of a heart—the heart of a conquering darkness. It was a moment of triumph for the wilderness, an invading and vengeful rush which, it seemed to me, I would have to keep back alone for the salvation of another soul. And the memory of what I had heard him say afar there, with the horned shapes stirring at my back, in the glow of fires, within the patient woods, those broken phrases came back to me, were heard again in their ominous and terrifying simplicity. I remembered his abject pleading, his abject threats, the colossal scale of his vile desires, the meanness, the torment, the tempestuous anguish of his soul. And later on I seemed to see his collected languid manner, when he said one day, 'this lot of ivory now is really mine. The Company did not pay for it. I collected it myself at a very great personal risk. I am afraid they will try to claim it as theirs though. H'm. It is a difficult case. What do you think I ought to do—resist? Eh? I want no more than justice.' . . . He wanted no more than justice—no more than justice. I rang the bell before a mahogany door on the first floor, and while I waited he seemed to stare at me out of the glassy panel—stare with that wide and immense stare, embracing, condemning, loathing all the universe. I seemed to hear the whispered cry, 'The horror! The horror!'

"The dusk was falling. I had to wait in a lofty drawing room with three long windows from floor to ceiling that were like three luminous and bedraped columns. The bent gilt legs and backs of the furniture shone in distinct curves. The tall marble fireplace had a cold and monumental whiteness. A grand piano stood massively in a corner, with dark gleams on the flat surfaces like a somber and polished sarcophagus. A high door opened—closed. I rose.

"She came forward, all in black, with a pale head, floating towards me in the dusk. She was in mourning. It was more than a year since his death, more than a year since the news came; she seemed as though she would remember and mourn forever. She took both my hands in hers and murmured, 'I had heard you were coming.' I noticed she was not very young—I mean not girlish. She had a mature capacity for fidelity, for belief, for suffering. The room seemed to have grown darker, as if all the sad light of the cloudy evening had taken refuge on her forehead. This fair hair, this pale visage, this pure brow, seemed surrounded by an ashy halo from which the dark eyes looked out at me. Their glance was guileless, profound, confident, and trustful. She carried her sorrowful head as though she were proud of that sorrow, as though she would say, I—I alone know how to mourn for him as he deserves. But while we were still shaking hands, such a look of awful desolation came upon her face that I perceived she was one of those creatures that are not the playthings of Time. For her he had died only yesterday. And, by Jove! the impression was so powerful that for me too he seemed to have died only yesterday—nay, this very minute. I saw her and him in the same instant of time—his death and her sorrow—I saw her sorrow in the very moment of his death. Do you understand? I saw them together—I heard them together. She had said, with a deep catch of the breath, 'I have survived'; while my strained ears seemed to hear distinctly, mingled with her tone of despairing regret, the summing-up whisper of his eternal condemnation. I asked myself what I was doing there, with a sensation of panic in my heart as though I had blundered into a place of cruel and absurd mysteries not fit for a human being to behold. She motioned me to a chair. We sat down. I laid the packet gently on the little table, and she put her hand over it. . . . 'You knew him well,' she murmured, after a moment of mourning silence.

" 'Intimacy grows quickly out there,' I said. 'I knew him as well as it is possible for one man to know another.'

" 'And you admired him,' she said. 'It was impossible to know him and not to admire him. Was it?'

" 'He was a remarkable man,' I said unsteadily. Then before the appealing fixity of her gaze, that seemed to watch for more words on my lips, I went on, 'It was impossible not to—'

" 'Love him,' she finished eagerly, silencing me into an appalled dumbness. 'How true! how true! But when you think that no one knew him so well as I! I had all his noble confidence. I knew him best.'

" 'You knew him best,' I repeated. And perhaps she did. But with every word spoken the room was growing darker, and only her forehead, smooth and white, remained illumined by the unextinguishable light of belief and love.

" 'You were his friend,' she went on. 'His friend,' she repeated, a little louder. 'You must have been, if he had given you this, and sent you to me. I feel I can speak to you—and oh! I must speak. I want you—you who have heard his last words—to know I have been worthy of him. . . . It is not pride. . . . Yes! I am proud to know I understood him better than anyone on earth—he told me so himself. And since his mother died I have had no one—no one—to—to—'

"I listened. The darkness deepened. I was not even sure whether he had given me the right bundle. I rather suspect he wanted me to take care of another batch of his papers which, after his death, I saw the manager examining under the lamp. And the girl talked, easing her pain in the certitude of my sympathy; she talked as thirsty men drink. I had heard that her engagement with Kurtz had been disapproved by her people. He wasn't rich enough or something. And indeed I don't know whether he had not been a pauper all his life. He had given me some reason to infer that it was his impatience of comparative poverty that drove him out there.

" '. . . Who was not his friend who had heard him speak once?' she was saying. 'He drew men toward him by what was best in them.' She looked at me with intensity. 'It is the gift of the great,' she went on, and the sound of her low voice seemed to have the accompaniment of all the other sounds, full of mystery, desolation, and sorrow, I had ever heard—the ripple of the river, the soughing of the trees swayed by the wind, the murmurs of the crowds, the faint ring of incomprehensible words cried from afar, the whisper of a voice speaking from beyond the threshold of an eternal darkness. 'But you have heard him! You know!' she cried.

" 'Yes, I know,' I said with something like despair in my heart, but bowing my head before the faith that was in her, before that great and saving illusion that shone with an unearthly glow in the darkness, in the triumphant darkness from which I could not have defended her—from which I could not even defend myself.

" 'What a loss to me—to us!'—she corrected herself with beautiful generosity; then added in a murmur, 'to the world.' By the last gleams of twilight I could see the glitter of her eyes, full of tears—of tears that would not fall.

" 'I have been very happy—very fortunate—very proud,' she went on. 'Too fortunate. Too happy for a little while. And now I am unhappy for—for life.'

"She stood up; her fair hair seemed to catch all the remaining light in a glimmer of gold. I rose too.

" 'And of all this,' she went on mournfully, 'of all his promise, and of all his greatness, of his generous mind, of his noble heart, nothing remains—nothing but a memory. You and I—'

" 'We shall always remember him,' I said hastily.

" 'No!' she cried. 'It is impossible that all this should be lost—that such a life should be sacrificed to leave nothing—but sorrow. You know what vast plans he had. I knew of them too—I could not perhaps understand—but others knew of them. Something must remain. His words, at least, have not died.'

" 'His words will remain,' I said.

" 'And his example,' she whispered to herself. 'Men looked up to him—his goodness shone in every act. His example—'

" 'True,' I said; 'his example too. Yes, his example. I forgot that.'

" 'But I do not. I cannot—I cannot believe—not yet. I cannot believe that I shall never see him again, that nobody will see him again, never, never, never.'

"She put out her arms as if after a retreating figure, stretching them black and with clasped pale hands across the fading and narrow sheen of the window. Never see him! I saw him clearly enough then. I shall see this eloquent phantom as long as I live, and I shall see her too, a tragic and familiar Shade, resembling in this gesture another one, tragic also, and bedecked with powerless charms, stretching bare brown arms over the glitter of the infernal stream, the stream of darkness. She said suddenly very low, 'He died as he lived.'

" 'His end,' said I, with dull anger stirring in me, 'was in every way worthy of his life.'

" 'And I was not with him,' she murmured. My anger subsided before a feeling of infinite pity.

" 'Everything that could be done—' I mumbled.

" 'Ah, but I believed in him more than anyone on earth—more than his own mother, more than—himself. He needed me! Me! I would have treasured every sigh, every word, every sign, every glance.'

"I felt like a chill grip on my chest. 'Don't,' I said in a muffled voice.

" 'Forgive me. I—I—have mourned so long in silence—in silence. . . . You were with him—to the last? I think of his loneliness. Nobody near to understand him as I would have understood. Perhaps no one to hear. . . .'

" 'To the very end,' I said shakily. 'I heard his very last words. . . .' I stopped in a fright.

" 'Repeat them,' she murmured in a heartbroken tone. 'I want—I want—something—something—to—to live with.'

"I was on the point of crying at her, 'Don't you hear them?' The dusk was repeating them in a persistent whisper all around us, in a whisper that seemed to swell menacingly like the first whisper of a rising wind. 'The horror! The horror!'

" 'His last word—to live with,' she insisted. 'Don't you understand I loved him—I loved him—I loved him!'

"I pulled myself together and spoke slowly.

" 'The last word he pronounced was—your name.'

"I heard a light sigh and then my heart stood still, stopped dead short by an exulting and terrible cry, by the cry of inconceivable triumph and of unspeakable pain. 'I knew it—I was sure!' . . . She knew. She was sure. I heard her weeping; she had hidden her face in her hands. It seemed to me that the house would collapse before I could escape, that the heavens would fall upon my head. But nothing happened. The heavens do not fall for such a trifle. Would they have fallen, I wonder, if I had rendered Kurtz that justice which was his due? Hadn't he said he wanted only justice? But I couldn't. I could not tell her. It would have been too dark—too dark altogether. . . ."

Marlow ceased, and sat apart, indistinct and silent, in the pose of a meditating Buddha. Nobody moved for a time. "We have lost the first of the ebb," said the Director suddenly. I raised my head. The offing was barred by a black bank of clouds, and the tranquil waterway leading to the uttermost ends of the earth flowed somber under an overcast sky—seemed to lead into the heart of an immense darkness.

FOR STUDY AND DISCUSSION

1. Now that you have finished *Heart of Darkness* you will better appreciate the effectiveness of Conrad's introductory pages. Observe how often he uses the word *gloom*. This deliberate repetition is clearly valuable toward establishing the atmosphere of the tale, but it is also a foreshadowing of that more symbolic gloom which Marlow is to experience. Ask yourself, too, why Conrad does not give names to Marlow's listeners. Why does he have Marlow reflect at length on the Roman occupation of Britain? How does Marlow's phrase "the fascination of the abomination" (p. 408) prepare the reader both for the causes of Kurtz's spiritual degeneration and for Marlow's complex reaction to that degeneration?

2. To what extent is Marlow a committed man? to whom? to what? How and why do his degrees of commitment vary during different stages of the experience he recounts?

   Ask yourself the same questions (to the extent that they are relevant) about the following characters:

   the manager of the Central Station (and those whom he represents)
   Kurtz
   the Intended
   the audience on the *Nellie* whom Marlow is addressing

3. Marlow occasionally interrupts his narrative to speak quite fiercely to his audience. What is the purpose of these interruptions? Here, I would like you to read a poem by Ralph Waldo Emerson.

Grace

How much, preventing God! how much I owe
To the defenses thou hast round me set:
Example, custom, fear, occasion slow,—
These scorned bondmen were my parapet.
I dare not peep over this parapet
To gauge with glance the roaring gulf below,
The depths of sin to which I had descended,
Had not these me against myself defended.

How is the point of this poem very close to the reason for Marlow's interruptions? To what extent do both raise the enduring question of whether moral behavior is enforced by external restraints or by self-discipline? Here, you might well consider Marlow's reaction to the neatly groomed accountant at the Outer Station, to the cannibals on his boat, and to Kurtz's degradation.

4. By temperament Marlow is a highly introspective and reflective man. Conrad remarks, ". . . Marlow was not typical (if his propensity to spin yarns be excepted), and to him the meaning of an episode was not inside like a kernel but outside, enveloping the tale which brought it out only as a glow brings out a haze, in the likeness of one of these misty halos that sometimes are made visible by the spectral illumination of moonshine." This tendency develops (one might say matures) as Marlow's experiences take on greater meaning for him. For example, contrast his early reaction to the knitting women and the doctor in Belgium with the significances he later sees in them. In the same vein, observe how the actual rivets which he needs for his boat become symbolic of the need to remain "riveted" to reality. Thus, he exclaims at one point, ". . . and rivets were what really Mr. Kurtz wanted if he had only known it."

5. Marlow, at last, is forced to an agonizing decision: between loyalty to a depraved Kurtz or loyalty to conventional values of the company which has employed him. He, himself, refers to his selection of loyalty to Kurtz as ". . . the nightmare of my choice." I would like you to examine his problem and to realize that it is one which most of us have to face in our own (less dramatic) situations.

6. This last point—Marlow's decisive commitment to Kurtz—leads very quickly to the concluding events of the story: Kurtz's death and its effect on Marlow; Marlow's return to "the sepulchral city" and his sense of alienation there; finally, his visit to Kurtz's Intended and the lie he tells her. You should attempt to relate these points to Marlow's developing character and to the thematic thrust of the story.

7. Lastly, I would wish you to read again Conrad's final paragraph. Observe how, structurally, it brings the reader back from the Congo to the Thames. Observe, also, that this return is, for Marlow, no lasting escape from our common "heart of darkness."

DRAMA

Antigone

SOPHOCLES

[496?–406 B.C.]

Antigone dramatizes what philosophers sometimes call "the problem of conflicting claims." A simplified illustration of this problem would be to imagine a situation in which a man with a wife and one child awoke, late at night, to find his house in flames and to find himself in a position to be able to save only one of his two loved ones: which one should he choose to save? You may answer that the decision might well be forced upon him so that he had to choose the person whose room was closest to his own, but your answer would miss the ethical problem involved: assuming that a genuine choice were possible, which person should he choose to save?

Antigone dramatizes this "should" element in the problem of conflicting claims within a far more complex situation than the one I have suggested for illustrative purposes. Antigone herself is aware of the claim made upon her by her state: that she should not disobey the authority of that state. She is caught between this claim and the one she chooses: that she must not disobey the "higher law" of religion and conscience. Seen in this fashion, you may better sense the lasting appeal of the play. To be sure, on the plot level the conflict is between a girl named Antigone and a man named Creon, both mythical Greeks from a remote past. Yet on the theme level, the play deals with issues which perplex us today in those areas where individuals find that the position taken by the state is against their own consciences.

I would urge you to remember that one is dealing with a most subtle problem in *Antigone*. After all, there would be no such thing in philosophy as "the problem of conflicting claims" if there were no complex issues involved. Thus, it is natural to side with Antigone in the play and to cast Creon in the role of villain, but is not Antigone somewhat arrogant, somewhat presumptuous, in her confidence that she knows the "higher law" of the gods? And is it not proper to appreciate Creon's position (as head of the state) that Antigone's action, if tolerated, could lead to social and political anarchy? Try, in short, as you read the play to sense the problems it is exploring and to withhold your final judgments of the relative "guilt" or "innocence" of its characters until you have had time for reflection.[1]

---

[1] Two very good books available in paperback editions (Mentor) which might interest you are Edith Hamilton's Mythology and G. Lowes Dickinson's The Greek View of Life. The first will acquaint you with many Greek legends and will give you background information for an increased understanding of Antigone. The second is a more general account of Greek opinions on such subjects as religion, the state, the individual, and art.

Antigone

An English Version by Dudley Fitts and Robert Fitzgerald

PROLOGUE		[Antigone, Ismene]
PARODOS		[Chorus]
SCENE	I	[Creon, Sentry, Chorus]
ODE	I	[Chorus]
SCENE	II	[Sentry, Creon, Antigone, Ismene, Chorus]
ODE	II	[Chorus]
SCENE	III	[Haimon, Creon, Chorus]
ODE	III	[Chorus]
SCENE	IV	[Antigone, Creon, Chorus]
ODE	IV	[Chorus]
SCENE	V	[Teiresias, Creon, Chorus]
PAEAN		[Chorus]
EXODOS		[Messenger, Creon, Eurydice, Chorus]

PERSONS REPRESENTED

ANTIGONE (an·tig′ō·nē)   HAIMON (hā′mon)
ISMENE (is·mā′nē)   TEIRESIAS (ter·ē′sē·us)
EURYDICE (ū·rid′i·sē)   A SENTRY
CREON (krē′on)   A MESSENGER
CHORUS

SCENE: *Before the palace of* CREON, *King of Thebes. A central double door, and two lateral doors. A platform extends the length of the façade, and from this platform three steps lead down into the "orchestra," or chorus ground.*

TIME: *Dawn of the day after the repulse of the Argive army from the assault on Thebes.*

Prologue [1]

[ANTIGONE *and* ISMENE *enter from the central door of the palace.*]

ANTIGONE.   Ismene, dear sister,
   You would think that we had already suffered enough
   For the curse on Oedipus: [2]
   I cannot imagine any grief

---

[1] *Prologue:* an account of events that precede the action of the play.

[2] *curse on Oedipus:* Oedipus unknowingly married his own mother (as told in Sophocles' *Oedipus Rex*), a crime for which he and his children were punished.

That you and I have not gone through. And now—
Have they told you of the new decree of our King Creon?

ISMENE. I have heard nothing: I know
That two sisters lost two brothers, a double death
In a single hour; and I know that the Argive army
Fled in the night; but beyond this, nothing.

ANTIGONE. I thought so. And that is why I wanted you
To come out here with me. There is something we must do.

ISMENE. Why do you speak so strangely?

ANTIGONE. Listen, Ismene:
Creon buried our brother Eteocles
With military honors, gave him a soldier's funeral,
And it was right that he should; but Polyneices,
Who fought as bravely and died as miserably—
They say that Creon has sworn
No one shall bury him, no one mourn for him,
But his body must lie in the fields, a sweet treasure
For carrion birds to find as they search for food.
That is what they say, and our good Creon is coming here
To announce it publicly; and the penalty—
Stoning to death in the public square!

                    There it is,
And now you can prove what you are:
A true sister, or a traitor to your family.

ISMENE. Antigone, you are mad! What could I possibly do?

ANTIGONE. You must decide whether you will help me or not.

ISMENE. I do not understand you. Help you in what?

ANTIGONE. Ismene, I am going to bury him. Will you come?

ISMENE. Bury him! You have just said the new law forbids it.

ANTIGONE. He is my brother. And he is your brother, too.

ISMENE. But think of the danger! Think what Creon will do!

ANTIGONE. Creon is not strong enough to stand in my way.

ISMENE. Ah sister!
Oedipus died, everyone hating him
For what his own search brought to light, his eyes
Ripped out by his own hand; and Iocaste died,
His mother and wife at once: she twisted the cords
That strangled her life; and our two brothers died,
Each killed by the other's sword. And we are left:
But oh, Antigone,
Think how much more terrible than these
Our own death would be if we should go against Creon
And do what he has forbidden! We are only women,
We cannot fight with men, Antigone!
The law is strong, we must give in to the law

In this thing, and in worse. I beg the Dead
To forgive me, but I am helpless: I must yield
To those in authority. And I think it is dangerous business
To be always meddling.
ANTIGONE.   If that is what you think,
I should not want you, even if you asked to come.
You have made your choice, you can be what you want to be.
But I will bury him; and if I must die,
I say that this crime is holy: I shall lie down
With him in death, and I shall be as dear
To him as he to me.
                        It is the dead,
Not the living, who make the longest demands:
We die forever . . .
                        You may do as you like,
Since apparently the laws of the gods mean nothing to you.
ISMENE.   They mean a great deal to me; but I have no strength
To break laws that were made for the public good.
ANTIGONE.   That must be your excuse, I suppose. But as for me,
I will bury the brother I love.
ISMENE.   Antigone,
I am so afraid for you!
ANTIGONE.   You need not be:
You have yourself to consider, after all.
ISMENE.   But no one must hear of this, you must tell no one!
I will keep it a secret, I promise!
ANTIGONE.   Oh tell it! Tell everyone!
Think how they'll hate you when it all comes out
If they learn that you knew about it all the time!
ISMENE.   So fiery! You should be cold with fear.
ANTIGONE.   Perhaps. But I am doing only what I must.
ISMENE.   But can you do it? I say that you cannot.
ANTIGONE.   Very well: when my strength gives out, I shall do no more.
ISMENE.   Impossible things should not be tried at all.
ANTIGONE.   Go away, Ismene:
I shall be hating you soon, and the dead will too,
For your words are hateful. Leave me my foolish plan:
I am not afraid of the danger; if it means death,
It will not be the worst of deaths—death without honor.
ISMENE.   Go then, if you feel that you must.
You are unwise,
But a loyal friend indeed to those who love you.
                        [*Exit into the palace.* ANTIGONE *goes off, L.*[1] *Enter the* CHORUS.]

[1] *L.:* stage left.

Parodos [1]

CHORUS.   [STROPHE 1

    Now the long blade of the sun, lying
    Level east to west, touches with glory
    Thebes of the Seven Gates. Open, unlidded
    Eye of golden day! O marching light
    Across the eddy and rush of Dirce's [2] stream,
    Striking the white shields of the enemy
    Thrown headlong backward from the blaze of morning!

CHORAGOS.[3]

    Polyneices their commander
    Roused them with windy phrases,
    He the wild eagle screaming
    Insults above our land,
    His wings their shields of snow,
    His crest their marshalled helms.

CHORUS.   [ANTISTROPHE 1

    Against our seven gates in a yawning ring
    The famished spears came onward in the night;
    But before his jaws were sated with our blood,
    Or pinefire took the garland of our towers,
    He was thrown back; and as he turned, great Thebes—
    No tender victim for his noisy power—
    Rose like a dragon behind him, shouting war.

CHORAGOS.

    For God hates utterly
    The bray of bragging tongues;
    And when he beheld their smiling,
    Their swagger of golden helms,
    The frown of his thunder blasted
    Their first man from our walls.

CHORUS.   [STROPHE 2

    We heard his shout of triumph high in the air
    Turn to a scream; far out in a flaming arc
    He fell with his windy torch, and the earth struck him.
    And others storming in fury no less than his
    Found shock of death in the dusty joy of battle.

---

  [1] *Parodos:* the "parade" or entrance of the Chorus. *Strophe* and *antistrophe* are alternating stanzas of choral song. When singing the strophe, the Chorus turned in one direction. Then, as the antistrophe was sung, the Chorus turned in the opposite direction.
  [2] *Dirce:* a mythological character who was thrown into a spring near Thebes.
  [3] *Choragos:* the leader of the Chorus.

CHORAGOS.

> Seven captains at seven gates
> Yielded their clanging arms to the god
> That bends the battle-line and breaks it.
> These two only, brothers in blood,
> Face to face in matchless rage,
> Mirroring each the other's death,
> Clashed in long combat.

CHORUS. [ANTISTROPHE 2

> But now in the beautiful morning of victory
> Let Thebes of the many chariots sing for joy!
> With hearts for dancing we'll take leave of war:
> Our temples shall be sweet with hymns of praise,
> And the long night shall echo with our chorus.

Scene I

CHORAGOS. But now at last our new King is coming:
> Creon of Thebes, Menoikeus' son.
> In this auspicious dawn of his reign
> What are the new complexities
> That shifting Fate has woven for him?
> What is his counsel? Why has he summoned
> The old men to hear him?

[*Enter* CREON *from the palace, C.*[1] *He addresses the* CHORUS *from the top step.*]

CREON. Gentlemen: I have the honor to inform you that our Ship of State, which recent storms have threatened to destroy, has come safely to harbor at last, guided by the merciful wisdom of Heaven. I have summoned you here this morning because I know that I can depend upon you: your devotion to King Laios was absolute; you never hesitated in your duty to our late ruler Oedipus; and when Oedipus died, your loyalty was transferred to his children. Unfortunately, as you know, his two sons, the princes Eteocles and Polyneices, have killed each other in battle; and I, as the next in blood, have succeeded to the full power of the throne.

I am aware, of course, that no Ruler can expect complete loyalty from his subjects until he has been tested in office. Nevertheless, I say to you at the very outset that I have nothing but contempt for the kind of Governor who is afraid, for whatever reason, to follow the course

[1] *C:* center. This stage direction indicates that Creon enters from the center doors of the palace.

that he knows is best for the State; and as for the man who sets private friendship above the public welfare, I have no use for him, either. I call God to witness that if I saw my country headed for ruin, I should not be afraid to speak out plainly; and I need hardly remind you that I would never have any dealings with an enemy of the people. No one values friendship more highly than I; but we must remember that friends made at the risk of wrecking our Ship are not real friends at all.

These are my principles, at any rate, and that is why I have made the following decision concerning the sons of Oedipus: Eteocles, who died as a man should die, fighting for his country, is to be buried with full military honors, with all the ceremony that is usual when the greatest heroes die; but his brother Polyneices, who broke his exile to come back with fire and sword against his native city and the shrines of his father's gods, whose one idea was to spill the blood of his blood and sell his own people into slavery—Polyneices, I say, is to have no burial: no man is to touch him or say the least prayer for him; he shall lie on the plain, unburied; and the birds and the scavenging dogs can do with him whatever they like.

This is my command, and you can see the wisdom behind it. As long as I am King, no traitor is going to be honored with the loyal man. But whoever shows by word and deed that he is on the side of the State—he shall have my respect while he is living, and my reverence when he is dead.

CHORAGOS. If that is your will, Creon son of Menoikeus,
You have the right to enforce it: we are yours.
CREON. That is my will. Take care that you do your part.
CHORAGOS. We are old men: let the younger ones carry it out.
CREON. I do not mean that: the sentries have been appointed.
CHORAGOS. Then what is it that you would have us do?
CREON. You will give no support to whoever breaks this law.
CHORAGOS. Only a crazy man is in love with death!
CREON. And death it is; yet money talks, and the wisest
Have sometimes been known to count a few coins too many.

[*Enter* SENTRY *from L.*]

SENTRY. I'll not say that I'm out of breath from running, King, because every time I stopped to think about what I have to tell you, I felt like going back. And all the time a voice kept saying, "You fool, don't you know you're walking straight into trouble?"; and then another voice, "Yes, but if you let somebody else get the news to Creon first, it will be even worse than that for you!" But good sense won out, at least I hope it was good sense, and here I am with a story that makes no sense at all; but I'll tell it anyhow, because, as they say, what's going to happen's going to happen, and—

CREON.   Come to the point. What have you to say?

SENTRY.   I did not do it. I did not see who did it. You must not punish me
for what someone else has done.

CREON.   A comprehensive defense! More effective, perhaps,
If I knew its purpose. Come: what is it?

SENTRY.   A dreadful thing . . . I don't know how to put it—

CREON.   Out with it!

SENTRY.   Well, then;
The dead man—

Polyneices—

[*Pause. The* SENTRY *is overcome, fumbles for words.* CREON *waits
impassively.*]

out there—

someone—

New dust on the slimy flesh!

[*Pause. No sign from* CREON]

Someone has given it burial that way, and
Gone . . .

[*Long pause.* CREON *finally speaks with deadly control.*]

CREON.   And the man who dared do this?

SENTRY.   I swear I
Do not know! You must believe me!

Listen:
The ground was dry, not a sign of digging, no,
Not a wheeltrack in the dust, no trace of anyone.
It was when they relieved us this morning: and one of them,
The corporal, pointed to it.

There it was,
The strangest—

Look:
The body, just mounded over with light dust: you see?
Not buried really, but as if they'd covered it
Just enough for the ghost's peace. And no sign
Of dogs or any wild animal that had been there.

And then what a scene there was! Every man of us
Accusing the other: we all proved the other man did it,
We all had proof that we could not have done it.
We were ready to take hot iron in our hands,
Walk through fire, swear by all the gods,
It was not I!

I do not know who it was, but it was not I!

[CREON'S *rage has been mounting steadily, but the* SENTRY *is too intent upon his story to notice it.*]

And then, when this came to nothing, someone said
A thing that silenced us and made us stare
Down at the ground: you had to be told the news,
And one of us had to do it! We threw the dice,
And the bad luck fell to me. So here I am,
No happier to be here than you are to have me:
Nobody likes the man who brings bad news.

CHORAGOS.   I have been wondering, King: can it be that the gods have done
this?
CREON.   [*Furiously*] Stop!
Must you doddering wrecks
Go out of your heads entirely? "The gods!"
Intolerable!
The gods favor this corpse? Why? How had he served them?
Tried to loot their temples, burn their images,
Yes, and the whole State, and its laws with it!
Is it your senile opinion that the gods love to honor bad men?
A pious thought!
                    No, from the very beginning
There have been those who have whispered together,
Stiff-necked anarchists, putting their heads together,
Scheming against me in alleys. These are the men,
And they have bribed my own guard to do this thing.

[*Sententiously*] Money!
There's nothing in the world so demoralizing as money.
Down go your cities,
Homes gone, men gone, honest hearts corrupted,
Crookedness of all kinds, and all for money!
                    [*To* SENTRY] But you!
I swear by God and by the throne of God,
The man who has done this thing shall pay for it!
Find that man, bring him here to me, or your death
Will be the least of your problems: I'll string you up
Alive, and there will be certain ways to make you
Discover your employer before you die;
And the process may teach you a lesson you seem to have missed:
The dearest profit is sometimes all too dear:
That depends on the source. Do you understand me?
A fortune won is often misfortune.

SENTRY.   King, may I speak?

CREON.   Your very voice distresses me.

SENTRY.   Are you sure that it is my voice, and not your conscience?

CREON.   By God, he wants to analyze me now!

SENTRY.   It is not what I say, but what has been done, that hurts you.

CREON.   You talk too much.

SENTRY.   Maybe; but I've done nothing.

CREON.   Sold your soul for some silver: that's all you've done.

SENTRY.   How dreadful it is when the right judge judges wrong!

CREON.   Your figures of speech
        May entertain you now; but unless you bring me the man,
        You will get little profit from them in the end.

                                   [*Exit* CREON *into the palace.*]

SENTRY.   "Bring me the man!"
        I'd like nothing better than bringing him the man!
        But bring him or not, you have seen the last of me here.
        At any rate, I am safe!

                                            [*Exit* SENTRY.]

Ode I [1]

CHORUS.   [STROPHE 1
        Numberless are the world's wonders, but none
        More wonderful than man; the storm-gray sea
        Yields to his prows, the huge crests bear him high;
        Earth, holy and inexhaustible, is graven
        With shining furrows where his plows have gone
        Year after year, the timeless labor of stallions.

        The light-boned birds and beasts that cling to cover, [ANTISTROPHE 1
        The lithe fish lighting their reaches of dim water,
        All are taken, tamed in the net of his mind;
        The lion on the hill, the wild horse windy-maned,
        Resign to him; and his blunt yoke has broken
        The sultry shoulders of the mountain bull.

        Words also, and thought as rapid as air,   [STROPHE 2
        He fashions to his good use; statecraft is his,
        And his the skill that deflects the arrows of snow,
        The spears of winter rain: from every wind
        He has made himself secure—from all but one:
        In the late wind of death he cannot stand.

[1] *Ode:* a dignified poem, sung or chanted by the Chorus.

O clear intelligence, force beyond all measure!   [ANTISTROPHE 2
O fate of man, working both good and evil!
When the laws are kept, how proudly his city stands!
When the laws are broken, what of his city then?
Never may the anarchic man find rest at my hearth,
Never be it said that my thoughts are his thoughts.

Scene II

[*Reenter* SENTRY *leading* ANTIGONE.]

CHORAGOS.   What does this mean? Surely this captive woman
   Is the Princess, Antigone. Why should she be taken?
SENTRY.   Here is the one who did it! We caught her
   In the very act of burying him. Where is Creon?
CHORAGOS.   Just coming from the house.

[*Enter* CREON, *C.*]

CREON.   What has happened?
   Why have you come back so soon?
SENTRY.   [*Expansively*] O King,
   A man should never be too sure of anything:
   I would have sworn
   That you'd not see me here again: your anger
   Frightened me so, and the things you threatened me with;
   But how could I tell then
   That I'd be able to solve the case so soon?

No dice-throwing this time: I was only too glad to come!

Here is this woman. She is the guilty one:
   We found her trying to bury him.
   Take her, then; question her; judge her as you will.
   I am through with the whole thing now, and glad of it.
CREON.   But this is Antigone! Why have you brought her here?
SENTRY.   She was burying him, I tell you!
CREON.   [*Severely*] Is this the truth?
SENTRY.   I saw her with my own eyes. Can I say more?
CREON.   The details: come, tell me quickly!
SENTRY.   It was like this:
   After those terrible threats of yours, King,
   We went back and brushed the dust away from the body.
   The flesh was soft by now, and stinking,

So we sat on a hill to windward and kept guard.
No napping this time! We kept each other awake.
But nothing happened until the white round sun
Whirled in the center of the round sky over us:
Then, suddenly,
A storm of dust roared up from the earth, and the sky
Went out, the plain vanished with all its trees
In the stinging dark. We closed our eyes and endured it.
The whirlwind lasted a long time, but it passed;
And then we looked, and there was Antigone!
I have seen
A mother bird come back to a stripped nest, heard
Her crying bitterly a broken note or two
For the young ones stolen. Just so, when this girl
Found the bare corpse, and all her love's work wasted,
She wept, and cried on heaven to damn the hands
That had done this thing.
                        And then she brought more dust
And sprinkled wine three times for her brother's ghost.

We ran and took her at once. She was not afraid,
Not even when we charged her with what she had done.
She denied nothing.
                     And this was a comfort to me,
And some uneasiness: for it is a good thing
To escape from death, but it is no great pleasure
To bring death to a friend.
                           Yet I always say
There is nothing so comfortable as your own safe skin!
CREON.   [*Slowly, dangerously*] And you, Antigone,
    You with your head hanging, do you confess this thing?
ANTIGONE.   I do. I deny nothing.
CREON.   [*To* SENTRY] You may go.

                                              [*Exit* SENTRY.]

    [*To* ANTIGONE] Tell me, tell me briefly:
    Had you heard my proclamation touching this matter?
ANTIGONE.   It was public. Could I help hearing it?
CREON.   And yet you dared defy the law.
ANTIGONE.   I dared.
    It was not God's proclamation. That final Justice
    That rules the world below makes no such laws.
    Your edict, King, was strong,
    But all your strength is weakness itself against

The immortal unrecorded laws of God.[1]
They are not merely now: they were, and shall be,
Operative forever, beyond man utterly.

I knew I must die, even without your decree:
I am only mortal. And if I must die
Now, before it is my time to die,
Surely this is no hardship: can anyone
Living, as I live, with evil all about me,
Think Death less than a friend? This death of mine
Is of no importance; but if I had left my brother
Lying in death unburied, I should have suffered.
Now I do not.

        You smile at me. Ah Creon,
Think me a fool, if you like; but it may well be
That a fool convicts me of folly.

CHORAGOS.   Like father, like daughter: both headstrong, deaf to reason!
    She has never learned to yield.

CREON.   She has much to learn.
    The inflexible heart breaks first, the toughest iron
    Cracks first, and the wildest horses bend their necks
    At the pull of the smallest curb.
                   Pride? In a slave?
    This girl is guilty of a double insolence,
    Breaking the given laws and boasting of it.
    Who is the man here,
    She or I, if this crime goes unpunished?
    Sister's child, or more than sister's child,
    Or closer yet in blood—she and her sister
    Win bitter death for this!

        [*To* SERVANTS] Go, some of you,
    Arrest Ismene. I accuse her equally.
    Bring her: you will find her sniffling in the house there.

    Her mind's a traitor: crimes kept in the dark
    Cry for light, and the guardian brain shudders;
    But how much worse than this
    Is brazen boasting of barefaced anarchy!

ANTIGONE.   Creon, what more do you want than my death?

CREON.   Nothing.
    That gives me everything.

---

[1] The ancient Greeks had no written, authoritative work prescribing their religious or moral code.

ANTIGONE.   Then I beg you: kill me.
This talking is a great weariness: your words
Are distasteful to me, and I am sure that mine
Seem so to you. And yet they should not seem so:
I should have praise and honor for what I have done.
All these men here would praise me
Were their lips not frozen shut with fear of you.

[*Bitterly*] Ah the good fortune of kings,
Licensed to say and do whatever they please!
CREON.   You are alone here in that opinion.
ANTIGONE.   No, they are with me. But they keep their tongues in leash.
CREON.   Maybe. But you are guilty, and they are not.
ANTIGONE.   There is no guilt in reverence for the dead.
CREON.   But Eteocles—was he not your brother too?
ANTIGONE.   My brother too.
CREON.   And you insult his memory?
ANTIGONE.   [*Softly*] The dead man would not say that I insult it.
CREON.   He would: for you honor a traitor as much as him.
ANTIGONE.   His own brother, traitor or not, and equal in blood.
CREON.   He made war on his country. Eteocles defended it.
ANTIGONE.   Nevertheless, there are honors due all the dead.
CREON.   But not the same for the wicked as for the just.
ANTIGONE.   Ah Creon, Creon,
Which of us can say what the gods hold wicked?
CREON.   An enemy is an enemy, even dead.
ANTIGONE.   It is my nature to join in love, not hate.
CREON.   [*Finally, losing patience*] Go join them, then; if you must have
    your love,
Find it in hell!
CHORAGOS.   But see, Ismene comes:

[*Enter* ISMENE, *guarded.*]

Those tears are sisterly, the cloud
That shadows her eyes rains down gentle sorrow.
CREON.   You, too, Ismene,
Snake in my ordered house, sucking my blood
Stealthily—and all the time I never knew
That these two sisters were aiming at my throne!
                                        Ismene,
Do you confess your share in this crime, or deny it?
Answer me.
ISMENE.   Yes, if she will let me say so. I am guilty.

ANTIGONE. [*Coldly*] No, Ismene. You have no right to say so.
You would not help me, and I will not have you help me.
ISMENE. But now I know what you meant; and I am here
To join you, to take my share of punishment.
ANTIGONE. The dead man and the gods who rule the dead
Know whose act this was. Words are not friends.
ISMENE. Do you refuse me, Antigone? I want to die with you:
I too have a duty that I must discharge to the dead.
ANTIGONE. You shall not lessen my death by sharing it.
ISMENE. What do I care for life when you are dead?
ANTIGONE. Ask Creon. You're always hanging on his opinions.
ISMENE. You are laughing at me. Why, Antigone?
ANTIGONE. It's a joyless laughter, Ismene.
ISMENE.   But can I do nothing?
ANTIGONE. Yes. Save yourself. I shall not envy you.
There are those who will praise you; I shall have honor, too.
ISMENE. But we are equally guilty!
ANTIGONE.   No more, Ismene.
You are alive, but I belong to Death.
CREON. [*To the* CHORUS] Gentlemen, I beg you to observe these girls:
One has just now lost her mind; the other,
It seems, has never had a mind at all.
ISMENE. Grief teaches the steadiest minds to waver, King.
CREON. Yours certainly did, when you assumed guilt with the guilty!
ISMENE. But how could I go on living without her?
CREON.   You are.
She is already dead.
ISMENE.   But your own son's bride!
CREON. There are places enough for him to push his plow.
I want no wicked women for my sons!
ISMENE. O dearest Haimon, how your father wrongs you!
CREON. I've had enough of your childish talk of marriage!
CHORAGOS. Do you really intend to steal this girl from your son?
CREON. No; Death will do that for me.
CHORAGOS.   Then she must die?
CREON. [*Ironically*] You dazzle me.
                         —But enough of this talk!
[*To* GUARDS] You, there, take them away and guard them well:
For they are but women, and even brave men run
When they see Death coming.
                         [*Exeunt* ISMENE, ANTIGONE, *and* GUARDS.]

Ode II

CHORUS. [STROPHE 1

Fortunate is the man who has never tasted God's vengeance!
Where once the anger of heaven has struck, that house is shaken
Forever: damnation rises behind each child
Like a wave cresting out of the black northeast,
When the long darkness under sea roars up
And bursts drumming death upon the wind-whipped sand.

I have seen this gathering sorrow from time long past [ANTISTROPHE 1
Loom upon Oedipus' children: generation from generation
Takes the compulsive rage of the enemy god.
So lately this last flower of Oedipus' line
Drank the sunlight! but now a passionate word
And a handful of dust have closed up all its beauty.

What mortal arrogance [STROPHE 2
Transcends the wrath of Zeus?
Sleep cannot lull him, nor the effortless long months
Of the timeless gods: but he is young for ever,
And his house is the shining day of high Olympos.
All that is and shall be,
And all the past, is his.
No pride on earth is free of the curse of heaven.

The straying dreams of men [ANTISTROPHE 2
May bring them ghosts of joy:
But as they drowse, the waking embers burn them;
Or they walk with fixed eyes, as blind men walk.
But the ancient wisdom speaks for our own time:
Fate works most for woe
With Folly's fairest show.
Man's little pleasure is the spring of sorrow.

Scene III

CHORAGOS.   But here is Haimon, King, the last of all your sons.
Is it grief for Antigone that brings him here,
And bitterness at being robbed of his bride?

[*Enter* HAIMON.]

CREON.   We shall soon see, and no need of diviners.
Son,

You have heard my final judgment on that girl:
Have you come here hating me, or have you come
With deference and with love, whatever I do?
HAIMON.   I am your son, Father. You are my guide.
You make things clear for me, and I obey you.
No marriage means more to me than your continuing wisdom.
CREON.   Good. That is the way to behave: subordinate
Everything else, my son, to your father's will.
This is what a man prays for, that he may get
Sons attentive and dutiful in his house,
Each one hating his father's enemies,
Honoring his father's friends. But if his sons
Fail him, if they turn out unprofitably,
What has he fathered but trouble for himself
And amusement for the malicious?
                                So you are right
Not to lose your head over this woman.
Your pleasure with her would soon grow cold, Haimon.
Let her find her husband in hell!
Of all the people in this city, only she
Has had contempt for my law and broken it.

Do you want me to show myself weak before the people?
Or to break my sworn word? No, and I will not.
The woman dies.
I suppose she'll plead "family ties." Well, let her.
If I permit my own family to rebel,
How shall I earn the world's obedience?
Show me the man who keeps his house in hand,
He's fit for public authority.
                                I'll have no dealings
With lawbreakers, critics of the government:
Whoever is chosen to govern should be obeyed—
Must be obeyed, in all things, great and small,
Just and unjust! O Haimon,
The man who knows how to obey, and that man only,
Knows how to give commands when the time comes.
You can depend on him, no matter how fast
The spears come: he's a good soldier, he'll stick it out.

Anarchy, anarchy! Show me a greater evil!
This is why cities tumble and the great houses rain down,
This is what scatters armies!

No, no: good lives are made so by discipline.
We keep the laws then, and the lawmakers,
And no woman shall seduce us. If we must lose,
Let's lose to a man, at least! Is a woman stronger than we?
CHORAGOS.   Unless time has rusted my wits,
What you say, King, is said with point and dignity.
HAIMON.   [*Boyishly earnest*] Father:
Reason is God's crowning gift to man, and you are right
To warn me against losing mine. I cannot say—
I hope that I shall never want to say!—that you
Have reasoned badly. Yet there are other men
Who can reason, too; and their opinions might be helpful.
You are not in a position to know everything
That people say or do, or what they feel:
Your temper terrifies them—everyone
Will tell you only what you like to hear.
But I, at any rate, can listen; and I have heard them
Muttering and whispering in the dark about this girl.
They say no woman has ever, so unreasonably,
Died so shameful a death for a generous act:
"She covered her brother's body. Is this indecent?
She kept him from dogs and vultures. Is this a crime?
Death?—She should have all the honor that we can give her!"

This is the way they talk out there in the city.

You must believe me:
Nothing is closer to me than your happiness.
What could be closer? Must not any son
Value his father's fortune as his father does his?
I beg you, do not be unchangeable:
Do not believe that you alone can be right.
The man who thinks that,
The man who maintains that only he has the power
To reason correctly, the gift to speak, the soul—
A man like that, when you know him, turns out empty.

It is not reason never to yield to reason!

In floodtime you can see how some trees bend,
And because they bend, even their twigs are safe,
While stubborn trees are torn up, roots and all.
And the same thing happens in sailing:
Make your sheet fast, never slacken—and over you go,

Head over heels and under: and there's your voyage.
Forget you are angry! Let yourself be moved!
I know I am young; but please let me say this:
The ideal condition
Would be, I admit, that men should be right by instinct;
But since we are all too likely to go astray,
The reasonable thing is to learn from those who can teach.

CHORAGOS.   You will do well to listen to him, King,
 If what he says is sensible. And you, Haimon,
 Must listen to your father. Both speak well.

CREON.   You consider it right for a man of my years and experience
 To go to school to a boy?

HAIMON.   It is not right
 If I am wrong. But if I am young, and right,
 What does my age matter?

CREON.   You think it right to stand up for an anarchist?

HAIMON.   Not at all. I pay no respect to criminals.

CREON.   Then she is not a criminal?

HAIMON.   The City would deny it, to a man.

CREON.   And the City proposes to teach me how to rule?

HAIMON.   Ah. Who is it that's talking like a boy now?

CREON.   My voice is the one voice giving orders in this City!

HAIMON.   It is no City if it takes orders from one voice.

CREON.   The State is the King!

HAIMON.   Yes, if the State is a desert. [*Pause*]

CREON.   This boy, it seems, has sold out to a woman.

HAIMON.   If you are a woman: my concern is only for you.

CREON.   So? Your "concern"! In a public brawl with your father!

HAIMON.   How about you, in a public brawl with justice?

CREON.   With justice, when all that I do is within my rights?

HAIMON.   You have no right to trample on God's right.

CREON.   [*Completely out of control*] Fool, adolescent fool! Taken in by a
 woman!

HAIMON.   You'll never see me taken in by anything vile.

CREON.   Every word you say is for her!

HAIMON.   [*Quietly, darkly*] And for you.
 And for me. And for the gods under the earth.

CREON.   You'll never marry her while she lives.

HAIMON.   Then she must die. But her death will cause another.

CREON.   Another?
 Have you lost your senses? Is this an open threat?

HAIMON.   There is no threat in speaking to emptiness.

CREON.   I swear you'll regret this superior tone of yours!
 You are the empty one!

HAIMON. If you were not my father,
   I'd say you were perverse.
CREON. You girl-struck fool, don't play at words with me!
HAIMON. I am sorry. You prefer silence.
CREON. Now, by God!
   I swear, by all the gods in heaven above us,
   You'll watch it, I swear you shall!
             [*To the* SERVANTS] Bring her out!
   Bring the woman out! Let her die before his eyes!
   Here, this instant, with her bridegroom beside her!
HAIMON. Not here, no; she will not die here, King.
   And you will never see my face again.
   Go on raving as long as you've a friend to endure you.

                                   [*Exit* HAIMON.]

CHORAGOS. Gone, gone.
   Creon, a young man in a rage is dangerous!
CREON. Let him do, or dream to do, more than a man can.
   He shall not save these girls from death.
CHORAGOS. These girls?
   You have sentenced them both?
CREON. No, you are right.
   I will not kill the one whose hands are clean.
CHORAGOS. But Antigone?
CREON. [*Somberly*] I will carry her far away
   Out there in the wilderness, and lock her
   Living in a vault of stone. She shall have food,
   As the custom is, to absolve the State of her death.
   And there let her pray to the gods of hell:
   They are her only gods:
   Perhaps they will show her an escape from death,
   Or she may learn,
            though late,
   That piety shown the dead is pity in vain.

                                   [*Exit* CREON.]

Ode III

CHORUS.   [STROPHE
   Love, unconquerable
   Waster of rich men, keeper
   Of warm lights and all-night vigil
   In the soft face of a girl:
   Sea-wanderer, forest-visitor!

Even the pure Immortals cannot escape you,
And mortal man, in his one day's dusk,
Trembles before your glory.

Surely you swerve upon ruin   [ANTISTROPHE
The just man's consenting heart,
As here you have made bright anger
Strike between father and son—
And none has conquered but Love!
A girl's glance working the will of heaven:
Pleasure to her alone who mocks us,
Merciless Aphrodite.[1]

Scene IV

CHORAGOS.   [As ANTIGONE enters guarded]
     But I can no longer stand in awe of this,
     Nor, seeing what I see, keep back my tears.
     Here is Antigone, passing to that chamber
     Where all find sleep at last.
ANTIGONE.   [STROPHE 1
     Look upon me, friends, and pity me
     Turning back at the night's edge to say
     Good-by to the sun that shines for me no longer;
     Now sleepy Death
     Summons me down to Acheron,[2] that cold shore:
     There is no bridesong there, nor any music.
CHORUS.
     Yet not unpraised, not without a kind of honor,
     You walk at last into the underworld;
     Untouched by sickness, broken by no sword.
     What woman has ever found your way to death?
ANTIGONE.   [ANTISTROPHE 1
     How often I have heard the story of Niobe,[3]
     Tantalos's wretched daughter, how the stone
     Clung fast about her, ivy-close: and they say
     The rain falls endlessly
     And sifting soft snow; her tears are never done.
     I feel the loneliness of her death in mine.

---

[1] *Aphrodite* (af·rō·dī′tē): Greek goddess of love and beauty.
[2] *Acheron* (aᴸ′e·ron): the river of woe, one of the rivers surrounding Hades.
[3] *Niobe* (nī′o·bē): mother whose fourteen children were killed by the gods because she boasted of them. Niobe wept for them and was transformed into a stone from which her tears continued to flow.

CHORUS.

But she was born of heaven, and you
Are woman, woman-born. If her death is yours,
A mortal woman's, is this not for you
Glory in our world and in the world beyond?

ANTIGONE.   [STROPHE 2

You laugh at me. Ah, friends, friends,
Can you not wait until I am dead? O Thebes,
O men many-charioted, in love with Fortune,
Dear springs of Dirce, sacred Theban grove,
Be witnesses for me, denied all pity,
Unjustly judged! and think a word of love
For her whose path turns
Under dark earth, where there are no more tears.

CHORUS.

You have passed beyond human daring and come at last
Into a place of stone where Justice sits.
I cannot tell
What shape of your father's guilt appears in this.

ANTIGONE.   [ANTISTROPHE 2

You have touched it at last: that bridal bed
Unspeakable, horror of son and mother mingling:
Their crime, infection of all our family!
O Oedipus, father and brother!
Your marriage strikes from the grave to murder mine.
I have been a stranger here in my own land:
All my life
The blasphemy of my birth has followed me.

CHORUS.

Reverence is a virtue, but strength
Lives in established law: that must prevail.
You have made your choice,
Your death is the doing of your conscious hand.

ANTIGONE.   [EPODE ¹

Then let me go, since all your words are bitter,
And the very light of the sun is cold to me.
Lead me to my vigil, where I must have
Neither love nor lamentation; no song, but silence.

[CREON *interrupts impatiently.*]

CREON.   If dirges and planned lamentations could put off death,
Men would be singing forever.
[*To the* SERVANTS] Take her, go!

¹ *Epode:* the part of a choral ode which follows the strophe and the antistrophe.

You know your orders: take her to the vault
And leave her alone there. And if she lives or dies,
That's her affair, not ours: our hands are clean.
ANTIGONE.   O tomb, vaulted bride-bed in eternal rock,
Soon I shall be with my own again
Where Persephone [1] welcomes the thin ghosts underground:
And I shall see my father again, and you, mother,
And dearest Polyneices—
                                    dearest indeed
To me, since it was my hand
That washed him clean and poured the ritual wine:
And my reward is death before my time!

And yet, as men's hearts know, I have done no wrong,
I have not sinned before God. Or if I have,
I shall know the truth in death. But if the guilt
Lies upon Creon who judged me, then, I pray,
May his punishment equal my own.
CHORAGOS.   O passionate heart,
Unyielding, tormented still by the same winds!
CREON.   Her guards shall have good cause to regret their delaying.
ANTIGONE.   Ah! That voice is like the voice of death!
CREON.   I can give you no reason to think you are mistaken.
ANTIGONE.   Thebes, and you my fathers' gods,
And rulers of Thebes, you see me now, the last
Unhappy daughter of a line of kings,
Your kings, led away to death. You will remember
What things I suffer, and at what men's hands,
Because I would not transgress the laws of heaven.
[*To the* GUARDS, *simply*] Come: let us wait no longer.

[*Exit* ANTIGONE, *L., guarded.*]

Ode IV [2]

CHORUS.   [STROPHE 1
All Danae's [3] beauty locked away

---

[1] *Persephone* (per·sef'ō·nē): the daughter of Zeus and Demeter. She was carried away from earth by Pluto to Hades to become Queen of the Lower World but was allowed to return to the earth for a part of each year.

[2] Ode IV gives three examples of the punishment of the gods. These examples are legendary parallels to Antigone's fate.

[3] *Danae* (dan'ā·ē): a princess of Argos, who was imprisoned by her father in a bronze house sunk underground. Zeus visited her as a shower of golden rain, and she bore his son, Perseus.

In a brazen cell where the sunlight could not come:
A small room, still as any grave, enclosed her.
Yet she was a princess too,
And Zeus in a rain of gold poured love upon her.
O child, child,
No power in wealth or war
Or tough sea-blackened ships
Can prevail against untiring Destiny!

And Dryas' son [1] also, that furious king,   [ANTISTROPHE 1
Bore the god's prisoning anger for his pride:
Sealed up by Dionysus in deaf stone,
His madness died among echoes.
So at the last he learned what dreadful power
His tongue had mocked:
For he had profaned the revels,
And fired the wrath of the nine
Implacable Sisters [2] that love the sound of the flute.

And old men tell a half-remembered tale [3]   [STROPHE 2
Of horror done where a dark ledge splits the sea
And a double surf beats on the gray shores:
How a king's new woman, sick
With hatred for the queen he had imprisoned,
Ripped out his two sons' eyes with her bloody hands
While grinning Ares [4] watched the shuttle plunge
Four times: four blind wounds crying for revenge,

Crying, tears and blood mingled. Piteously born,   [ANTISTROPHE 2
Those sons whose mother was of heavenly birth!
Her father was the god of the North Wind
And she was cradled by gales,
She raced with young colts on the glittering hills
And walked untrammeled in the open light:
But in her marriage deathless Fate found means
To build a tomb like yours for all her joy.

---

[1] *Dryas' son:* Lycurgus (lī·kur′gus), a Thracian king who insulted the god Dionysus. As punishment Lycurgus was imprisoned in a cave where he became mad.

[2] *nine Implacable Sisters:* nine daughters of Zeus; the nine Muses.

[3] This section refers to Cleopatra, daughter of Boreas (the North Wind).

[4] *Ares* (ar′ēz): god of war.

Scene V

[*Enter blind* TEIRESIAS, *led by a boy. The opening speeches of*
TEIRESIAS *should be in singsong contrast to the realistic lines*
of CREON.]

TEIRESIAS.   This is the way the blind man comes, Princes, Princes,
Lock-step, two heads lit by the eyes of one.
CREON.   What new thing have you to tell us, old Teiresias?
TEIRESIAS.   I have much to tell you: listen to the prophet, Creon.
CREON.   I am not aware that I have ever failed to listen.
TEIRESIAS.   Then you have done wisely, King, and ruled well.
CREON.   I admit my debt to you. But what have you to say?
TEIRESIAS.   This, Creon: you stand once more on the edge of fate.
CREON.   What do you mean? Your words are a kind of dread.
TEIRESIAS.   Listen, Creon:
I was sitting in my chair of augury, at the place
Where the birds gather about me. They were all achatter,
As is their habit, when suddenly I heard
A strange note in their jangling, a scream, a
Whirring fury; I knew that they were fighting,
Tearing each other, dying
In a whirlwind of wings clashing. And I was afraid.
I began the rites of burnt offering at the altar,
But Hephaistos [1] failed me: instead of bright flame,
There was only the sputtering slime of the fat thigh-flesh
Melting: the entrails dissolved in gray smoke,
The bare bone burst from the welter. And no blaze!

This was a sign from heaven. My boy described it,
Seeing for me as I see for others.

I tell you, Creon, you yourself have brought
This new calamity upon us. Our hearths and altars
Are stained with the corruption of dogs and carrion birds
That glut themselves on the corpse of Oedipus' son.
The gods are deaf when we pray to them, their fire
Recoils from our offering, their birds of omen
Have no cry of comfort, for they are gorged
With the thick blood of the dead.
                    O my son,

---

[1] *Hephaistos* (also spelled *Hephaestus*): god of fire and maker of thunderbolts.

These are no trifles! Think: all men make mistakes,
But a good man yields when he knows his course is wrong,
And repairs the evil. The only crime is pride.

Give in to the dead man, then: do not fight with a corpse—
What glory is it to kill a man who is dead?
Think, I beg you:
It is for your own good that I speak as I do.
You should be able to yield for your own good.

CREON. It seems that prophets have made me their especial province.
All my life long
I have been a kind of butt for the dull arrows
Of doddering fortune-tellers!
     No, Teiresias:
If your birds—if the great eagles of God himself
Should carry him stinking bit by bit to heaven,
I would not yield. I am not afraid of pollution:
No man can defile the gods.
     Do what you will,
Go into business, make money, speculate
In India gold or that synthetic gold from Sardis,
Get rich otherwise than by my consent to bury him.
Teiresias, it is a sorry thing when a wise man
Sells his wisdom, lets out his words for hire!

TEIRESIAS. Ah Creon! Is there no man left in the world—

CREON. To do what? Come, let's have the aphorism!

TEIRESIAS. No man who knows that wisdom outweighs any wealth?

CREON. As surely as bribes are baser than any baseness.

TEIRESIAS. You are sick, Creon! You are deathly sick!

CREON. As you say: it is not my place to challenge a prophet.

TEIRESIAS. Yet you have said my prophecy is for sale.

CREON. The generation of prophets has always loved gold.

TEIRESIAS. The generation of kings has always loved brass.

CREON. You forget yourself! You are speaking to your King.

TEIRESIAS. I know it. You are a king because of me.

CREON. You have a certain skill; but you have sold out.

TEIRESIAS. King, you will drive me to words that—

CREON.   Say them, say them!
Only remember: I will not pay you for them.

TEIRESIAS. No, you will find them too costly.

CREON.   No doubt. Speak:
Whatever you say, you will not change my will.

TEIRESIAS. Then take this, and take it to heart!
The time is not far off when you shall pay back

Corpse for corpse, flesh of your own flesh.
You have thrust the child of this world into living night,
You have kept from the gods below the child that is theirs:
The one in a grave before her death, the other,
Dead, denied the grave. This is your crime:
And the Furies [1] and the dark gods of hell
Are swift with terrible punishment for you.

Do you want to buy me now, Creon?

                               Not many days,
And your house will be full of men and women weeping,
And curses will be hurled at you from far
Cities grieving for sons unburied, left to rot
Before the walls of Thebes.

These are my arrows, Creon: they are all for you.

[*To* BOY] But come, child: lead me home.
Let him waste his fine anger upon younger men.
Maybe he will learn at last
To control a wiser tongue in a better head.

                                      [*Exit* TEIRESIAS.]

CHORAGOS. The old man has gone, King, but his words
   Remain to plague us. I am old, too,
   But I cannot remember that he was ever false.
CREON. That is true. . . . It troubles me.
   Oh it is hard to give in! but it is worse
   To risk everything for stubborn pride.
CHORAGOS. Creon: take my advice.
CREON.   What shall I do?
CHORAGOS. Go quickly: free Antigone from her vault
   And build a tomb for the body of Polyneices.
CREON. You would have me do this?
CHORAGOS.   Creon, yes!
   And it must be done at once: God moves
   Swiftly to cancel the folly of stubborn men.
CREON. It is hard to deny the heart! But I
   Will do it: I will not fight with destiny.
CHORAGOS. You must go yourself, you cannot leave it to others.
CREON. I will go.
           Bring axes, servants:

[1] *Furies* (also called the *Erinyes*): three goddesses who punished evildoers. They especially avenged crimes involving the violation of ties of kinship.

Come with me to the tomb. I buried her, I
Will set her free.
                    Oh quickly!
My mind misgives—
The laws of the gods are mighty, and a man must serve them
To the last day of his life!

                                                    [*Exit* CREON.]

Paean [1]

CHORAGOS.   [STROPHE 1
    God of many names
CHORUS.   O Iacchus
                    son
    of Kadmeian Semele
                    O born of the Thunder!
    Guardian of the West
                    Regent
    of Eleusis' plain
                    O Prince of maenad Thebes
    and the Dragon Field by rippling Ismenos:
CHORAGOS.   [ANTISTROPHE 1
    God of many names
CHORUS.   the flame of torches
    flares on our hills
                    the nymphs of Iacchus
    dance at the spring of Castalia.[2]
    from the vine-close mountain
                    come ah come in ivy:
    Evohé evohé! [3] sings through the streets of Thebes
CHORAGOS.   [STROPHE 2
    God of many names
CHORUS.   Iacchus of Thebes
    heavenly Child
                    of Semele, bride of the Thunderer!
    The shadow of plague is upon us:
                                    come
    with clement feet

---

[1] *Paean:* a hymn of praise. This hymn to Dionysus (Iacchus), son of Zeus and the Theban princess Semele, asks the god to come to Thebes to restore peace and joy.

[2] *Castalia:* a nymph who threw herself into a spring on Mt. Parnassos when she was pursued by the god Apollo.

[3] *Evohé:* a shout of joy at Dionysian festivals, similar to "alleluia."

oh come from Parnassos [1]
down the long slopes
across the lamenting water

CHORAGOS. [ANTISTROPHE 2
Iô Fire! [2] Chorister of the throbbing stars!
O purest among the voices of the night!
Thou son of God, blaze for us!

CHORUS.
Come with choric rapture of circling Maenads [3]
Who cry *Iô Iacche!*
God of many names!

Exodos [4]

[*Enter* MESSENGER, L.]

MESSENGER.   Men of the line of Kadmos, you who live
Near Amphion's [5] citadel:
I cannot say
Of any condition of human life "This is fixed,
This is clearly good, or bad." Fate raises up,
And Fate casts down the happy and unhappy alike:
No man can foretell his Fate.
Take the case of Creon:
Creon was happy once, as I count happiness:
Victorious in battle, sole governor of the land,
Fortunate father of children nobly born.
And now it has all gone from him! Who can say
That a man is still alive when his life's joy fails?
He is a walking dead man. Grant him rich,
Let him live like a king in his great house:
If his pleasure is gone, I would not give
So much as the shadow of smoke for all he owns.

CHORAGOS.   Your words hint at sorrow: what is your news for us?

MESSENGER.   They are dead. The living are guilty of their death.

---

[1] *Parnassos:* a mountain north of Delphi with two summits, one of which was sacred to Dionysus.

[2] *Iô Fire!:* Hail, Fire! The "fire" refers to the circumstances of Dionysus' birth. Semele, his mother, asked to see Zeus as King of Heaven and Lord of the Thunderbolt. No mortal could see Zeus thus and survive. Semele was consumed by a Thunderbolt, but Zeus rescued Dionysus and cared for him until he was born.

[3] *Maenads* (mē'nadz): literally, "mad women"; nymphs who attended Dionysus.

[4] *Exodos:* the final, or exit, song of the chorus.

[5] *Amphion* (am·fī'on): a gentle musician, husband of Niobe. Amphion and his twin brother once undertook to build a wall around Thebes.

CHORAGOS.   Who is guilty? Who is dead? Speak!

MESSENGER.   Haimon.
Haimon is dead; and the hand that killed him
Is his own hand.

CHORAGOS.   His father's? or his own?

MESSENGER.   His own, driven mad by the murder his father had done.

CHORAGOS.   Teiresias, Teiresias, how clearly you saw it all!

MESSENGER.   This is my news: you must draw what conclusions you can
    from it.

CHORAGOS.   But look: Eurydice, our Queen:
Has she overheard us?

[*Enter* EURYDICE *from the palace, C.*]

EURYDICE.   I have heard something, friends:
As I was unlocking the gate of Pallas's ¹ shrine,
For I needed her help today, I heard a voice
Telling of some new sorrow. And I fainted
There at the temple with all my maidens about me.
But speak again: whatever it is, I can bear it:
Grief and I are no strangers.

MESSENGER.   Dearest Lady,
I will tell you plainly all that I have seen.
I shall not try to comfort you: what is the use,
Since comfort could lie only in what is not true?
The truth is always best.

                              I went with Creon
To the outer plain where Polyneices was lying,
No friend to pity him, his body shredded by dogs.
We made our prayers in that place to Hecate ²
And Pluto,³ that they would be merciful. And we bathed
The corpse with holy water, and we brought
Fresh-broken branches to burn what was left of it,
And upon the urn we heaped up a towering barrow
Of the earth of his own land.

                              When we were done, we ran
To the vault where Antigone lay on her couch of stone.
One of the servants had gone ahead,
And while he was yet far off he heard a voice
Grieving within the chamber, and he came back

---

¹ *Pallas:* the goddess Pallas Athena, daughter of Zeus. She sprang from Zeus' head, full-grown and in full armor. Athena is the personification of wisdom, reason, and purity.

² *Hecate:* Greek goddess associated with the underworld, also called Goddess of the Dark of the Moon.

³ *Pluto:* also called Hades, god of the underworld.

And told Creon. And as the King went closer,
The air was full of wailing, the words lost,
And he begged us to make all haste. "Am I a prophet?"
He said, weeping, "And must I walk this road,
The saddest of all that I have gone before?
My son's voice calls me on. Oh quickly, quickly!
Look through the crevice there, and tell me
If it is Haimon, or some deception of the gods!"

We obeyed; and in the cavern's farthest corner
We saw her lying:
She had made a noose of her fine linen veil
And hanged herself. Haimon lay beside her,
His arms about her waist, lamenting her,
His love lost under ground, crying out
That his father had stolen her away from him.

When Creon saw him the tears rushed to his eyes
And he called to him: "What have you done, child? Speak to me.
What are you thinking that makes your eyes so strange?
O my son, my son, I come to you on my knees!"
But Haimon spat in his face. He said not a word,
Staring—
        And suddenly drew his sword
And lunged. Creon shrank back, the blade missed; and the boy,
Desperate against himself, drove it half its length
Into his own side, and fell. And as he died
He gathered Antigone close in his arms again,
Choking, his blood bright red on her white cheek.
And now he lies dead with the dead, and she is his
At last, his bride in the houses of the dead.

                        [*Exit* EURYDICE *into the palace.*]

CHORAGOS.   She has left us without a word. What can this mean?
MESSENGER.   It troubles me, too; yet she knows what is best,
   Her grief is too great for public lamentation,
   And doubtless she has gone to her chamber to weep
   For her dead son, leading her maidens in his dirge.
CHORAGOS.   It may be so: but I fear this deep silence. [*Pause*]
MESSENGER.   I will see what she is doing. I will go in.

                        [*Exit* MESSENGER *into the palace.*]

   [*Enter* CREON *with attendants, bearing* HAIMON'S *body.*]

CHORAGOS.   But here is the King himself: oh look at him,
   Bearing his own damnation in his arms.

CREON. Nothing you say can touch me any more.
My own blind heart has brought me
From darkness to final darkness. Here you see
The father murdering, the murdered son—
And all my civic wisdom!

Haimon my son, so young, so young to die,
I was the fool, not you; and you died for me.
CHORAGOS. That is the truth; but you were late in learning it.
CREON. This truth is hard to bear. Surely a god
Has crushed me beneath the hugest weight of heaven,
And driven me headlong a barbaric way
To trample out the thing I held most dear.

The pains that men will take to come to pain!

[*Enter* MESSENGER *from the palace.*]

MESSENGER. The burden you carry in your hands is heavy,
But it is not all: you will find more in your house.
CREON. What burden worse than this shall I find there?
MESSENGER. The Queen is dead.
CREON. O port of death, deaf world,
Is there no pity for me? And you, Angel of evil,
I was dead, and your words are death again.
Is it true, boy? Can it be true?
Is my wife dead? Has death bred death?
MESSENGER. You can see for yourself.

[*The doors are opened, and the body of* EURYDICE *is disclosed within.*]

CREON. Oh pity!
All true, all true, and more than I can bear!
O my wife, my son!
MESSENGER. She stood before the altar, and her heart
Welcomed the knife her own hand guided,
And a great cry burst from her lips for Megareus [1] dead,
And for Haimon dead, her sons; and her last breath
Was a curse for their father, the murderer of her sons.
And she fell, and the dark flowed in through her closing eyes.
CREON. O God, I am sick with fear.
Are there no swords here? Has no one a blow for me?
MESSENGER. Her curse is upon you for the deaths of both.

---

[1] *Megareus* (me·gar'ē·us): son of Creon and Eurydice, killed in battle between Theban and Argive armies.

CREON. It is right that it should be. I alone am guilty.
I know it, and I say it. Lead me in,
Quickly, friends.
I have neither life nor substance. Lead me in.
CHORAGOS. You are right, if there can be right in so much wrong.
The briefest way is best in a world of sorrow.
CREON. Let it come,
Let death come quickly, and be kind to me.
I would not ever see the sun again.
CHORAGOS. All that will come when it will; but we, meanwhile,
Have much to do. Leave the future to itself.
CREON. All my heart was in that prayer!
CHORAGOS. Then do not pray any more: the sky is deaf.
CREON. Lead me away. I have been rash and foolish.
I have killed my son and my wife.
I look for comfort; my comfort lies here dead.
Whatever my hands have touched has come to nothing.
Fate has brought all my pride to a thought of dust.

[As CREON is being led into the house, the CHORAGOS *advances and
speaks directly to the audience.*]

CHORAGOS. There is no happiness where there is no wisdom;
No wisdom but in submission to the gods.
Big words are always punished,
And proud men in old age learn to be wise.

FOR STUDY AND DISCUSSION

1. In the light of this section's heading (Commitment), you should first analyze, most carefully, the respective commitments of Antigone and Creon. In each case you should be able to identify the object of the commitment and the reason for the commitment. You should also be able to refer to lines in the play which support your opinions.
2. You should also consider the few minor characters of the play in terms of their particular commitments. Be careful about this direction. It would be tempting, for example, to dismiss Ismene since she is clearly weaker in conviction and courage than her sister. Yet does she not faithfully represent the attitude which most of us might reluctantly take were we faced with the hard realities of comparable choices today? Examine the reactions of Eurydice, Haimon, and the Sentry in the same manner.
3. Consider the function of the Chorus and of the Choragos. That they contribute background information is clear enough, but to which of their lines could you point as evidence that they are also used to comment on the theme of the play? Do you think Sophocles is suggesting, through them, his own attitude toward the moral problems with which the play is dealing? Or do you think that he

uses them (neutrally, as it were) to represent the attitude of the city's elder statesmen? Or do they, perhaps, represent the attitude of "the common citizen" of the city, somewhat bewildered by the momentous events of which he is the condemned observer? Since no one knows with certainty the answers to these questions, each might well be the subject for a paper utilizing (a) the fluctuating attitudes of the Chorus as it is confronted with the unfolding events and (b) such underlying consistency of philosophy that the Chorus exhibits.

4. Consider Teiresias, the seer. Observe that his contribution to the play is much more important to the theme than to the plot. Why would one expect this to be true? Teiresias is not sharply defined as a character. Again, why might one expect this lack of characterization?

Mention of Teiresias is a reminder of the Greek view of "fate." The Greeks believed in a rational, orderly universe. They believed that the essence of this rational order (*logos*) is so unknowable that—both for reasons of morality and enduring happiness—one must submit to its inscrutable laws. To the Greeks their gods were responsible for the proper operations of *logos* and inflicted awesome punishment on those who defied the essential harmonies of life. In terms of theme, then, Greek tragedy customarily emphasizes the dire results to such individuals (or, by relationship, to whole families) as they are "fatefully" driven to their doom. As W. H. Auden has pointed out, "Greek tragedy is the tragedy of necessity: 'What a pity it had to be this way ' "

The general relevance of these observations to the theme of *Antigone* and to the conflict between its two principal characters is evident. Its particular relevance to Teiresias is that the Greek gods commonly revealed their will (and their warnings) through the medium of seers, of whom Teiresias is one. The passages dealing with Creon's reactions to Teiresias might well be reread in this perspective.

5. Lastly, I mention two words first associated with Greek tragedy which have become common currency in modern critical vocabulary. The first of these is *hubris,* which denotes an excess of the kind of pride, usually spiritual pride, that is the "fatal flaw" of principal characters in the tragedies and leads to their destruction. The concept of *hubris* is clearly related to certain points I have made in point 4 above. That Creon was guilty of *hubris* is obvious enough; I would like you to be able to show in what manner Antigone, too, suffered from this fatal flaw.

6. The second word with which I want to be sure you are familiar is *catharsis.* Originally from Aristotle's *Poetics,* Runes's *Dictionary of Philosophy* defines *catharsis* as "purification; purgation; specifically the purging of the emotions of pity and fear effected by tragedy." Aristotle seems to have meant that through our imaginative participation in the heroic problems and struggles of great tragic characters we find release ("purgation") from our own anxieties. (Incidentally, I suspect that an audience of ancient Greece might experience *catharsis* far more readily than a modern one because religious convictions and tragic drama were more closely identified in ancient Greece than they are in contemporary times.)

The Skin of Our Teeth

THORNTON WILDER

[BORN 1897]

The Skin of Our Teeth *is best approached as an allegory. I first mentioned the term allegory in my introduction to Plato's "Allegory of the Den" (p. 5). Since then, you have seen varying degrees of allegory in such short stories as "By the Waters of Babylon," "The Penal Colony," and "The Birthmark," to remind you of a few. Now you encounter this technique (or form) in drama, and it will help you to fathom the deliberately unrealistic characters and situations of the play if you do not permit the perplexities on the story level to distract you from the relative simplicities on the meaning level.*

I have referred to perplexities. From the opening pages one confronts them. The radio announcer quite matter-of-factly speaks of a wall of glacial ice moving southward from Canada; we are introduced to Mr. Antrobus, the inventor of the wheel; the scenery of the Antrobuses' home behaves most strangely; and additional bizarre events (and remarks) keep tumbling on. But from the very first there are hints that there is meaning in this apparent madness, and this becomes especially apparent if one rereads the early lines after having finished Act I. The following details emerge as significantly interrelated foreshadowings of the play's theme: the name of the town, Excelsior, in which the Antrobus family lives; the ring found in the theater (inscribed: To Eva from Adam. Genesis II: 18); the name of the hero, Antrobus (look up anthropo- in a dictionary); the reference to the fact that Mr. Antrobus had once been a gardener.

Such considerations also apply to the bewildering shifts of time, style, and tone within the play. With respect to time, the reader begins in the present, is often thrown back (by allusions) many centuries, then is again confronted with the world of today. The style, for the most part, is a satirical parody of "Americanese" (especially in the language of Sabina), yet Mr. Antrobus is sometimes allowed to speak with considerable dignity before returning to his usual role (and phraseology) of a contemporary husband and father. So, too, there are subtle shifts of tone, for although Wilder's tone in its most conspicuous appearances is satirical, there are primary undertones of seriousness which reinforce the play's comment on life.

This comment, or theme, is a profound one and a basically optimistic one: that Man is a somewhat comical figure who since his beginning has been buffeted by forces larger than himself but who achieves stature by his refusal to ever admit final defeat. The theme reminds one of some lines from a poem (significantly titled "Everyman") by the British poet Siegfried Sassoon:

> And then once more the impassioned pygmy fist
> Clenched cloudward and defiant;

In short, Man, like Mr. Antrobus, is half ape, half angel. He is ludicrously unequipped to deserve Hamlet's adulation ("What a piece of work is a man!"), but he commands our respect for his indomitable capacity for survival—if only by the skin of his teeth.

CHARACTERS *(in the order of their appearance)*

ANNOUNCER	MISS E. MUSE
SABINA	MISS T. MUSE
MR. FITZPATRICK	MISS M. MUSE
MRS. ANTROBUS	TWO USHERS
DINOSAUR	TWO DRUM MAJORETTES
MAMMOTH	FORTUNE TELLER
TELEGRAPH BOY	TWO CHAIR PUSHERS
GLADYS	SIX CONVEENERS
HENRY	BROADCAST OFFICIAL
MR. ANTROBUS	DEFEATED CANDIDATE
DOCTOR	MR. TREMAYNE
PROFESSOR	HESTER
JUDGE	IVY
HOMER	FRED BAILEY

ACT I.

Home, Excelsior, New Jersey.

ACT II.

Atlantic City Boardwalk.

ACT III.

Home, Excelsior, New Jersey.

Act I

A projection screen in the middle of the curtain. The first lantern slide: the name of the theater, and the words: NEWS EVENTS OF THE WORLD. *An* ANNOUNCER'S *voice is heard.*

ANNOUNCER. The management takes pleasure in bringing to you—The News Events of the World:

[*Slide of the sun appearing above the horizon*]

Freeport, Long Island.

The sun rose this morning at 6:32 A.M. This gratifying event was first reported by Mrs. Dorothy Stetson of Freeport, Long Island, who promptly telephoned the Mayor.

The Society for Affirming the End of the World at once went into a special session and postponed the arrival of that event for TWENTY-FOUR HOURS.

All honor to Mrs. Stetson for her public spirit.

New York City.

> [*Slide of the front doors of the theater in which this play is playing; three cleaning* WOMEN *with mops and pails*]

The X Theater. During the daily cleaning of this theater a number of lost objects were collected as usual by Mesdames Simpson, Pateslewski, and Moriarty.

Among these objects found today was a wedding ring, inscribed: To Eva from Adam. Genesis II:18.

The ring will be restored to the owner or owners, if their credentials are satisfactory.

Tippehatchee, Vermont.

> [*Slide representing a glacier*]

The unprecedented cold weather of this summer has produced a condition that has not yet been satisfactorily explained. There is a report that a wall of ice is moving southward across these counties. The disruption of communications by the cold wave now crossing the country has rendered exact information difficult, but little credence is given to the rumor that the ice had pushed the Cathedral of Montreal as far as St. Albans, Vermont.

For further information see your daily papers.

Excelsior, New Jersey.

> [*Slide of a modest suburban home*]

The home of Mr. George Antrobus, the inventor of the wheel. The discovery of the wheel, following so closely on the discovery of the lever, has centered the attention of the country on Mr. Antrobus of this attractive suburban residence district. This is his home, a commodious seven-room house, conveniently situated near a public school, a Methodist church, and a firehouse; it is right handy to an A. and P.

> [*Slide of* MR. ANTROBUS *on his front steps, smiling and lifting his straw hat. He holds a wheel.*]

Mr. Antrobus, himself. He comes of very old stock and has made his way up from next to nothing.

It is reported that he was once a gardener, but left that situation under circumstances that have been variously reported.

Mr. Antrobus is a veteran of foreign wars, and bears a number of scars, front and back.

[*Slide of* MRS. ANTROBUS, *holding some roses*]

This is Mrs. Antrobus, the charming and gracious president of the Excelsior Mothers' Club.

Mrs. Antrobus is an excellent needlewoman; it is she who invented the apron on which so many interesting changes have been rung since.

[*Slide of the* FAMILY *and* SABINA]

Here we see the Antrobuses with their two children, Henry and Gladys, and friend. The friend in the rear is Lily Sabina, the maid.

I know we all want to congratulate this typical American family on its enterprise. We all wish Mr. Antrobus a successful future. Now the management takes you to the interior of this home for a brief visit.

[*Curtain rises. Living room of a commuter's home.* SABINA— *straw-blonde, over-rouged—is standing by the window back center, a feather duster under her elbow.*]

SABINA. Oh, oh, oh! Six o'clock and the master not home yet.

Pray God nothing serious has happened to him crossing the Hudson River. If anything happened to him, we would certainly be inconsolable and have to move into a less desirable residence district.

The fact is I don't know what'll become of us. Here it is the middle of August and the coldest day of the year. It's simply freezing; the dogs are sticking to the sidewalks; can anybody explain that? No.

But I'm not surprised. The whole world's at sixes and sevens, and why the house hasn't fallen down about our ears long ago is a miracle to me.

[*A fragment of the right wall leans precariously over the stage.* SABINA *looks at it nervously and it slowly rights itself.*]

Every night this same anxiety as to whether the master will get home safely: whether he'll bring home anything to eat. In the midst of life we are in the midst of death, a truer word was never said.

[*The fragment of scenery flies up into the lofts.* SABINA *is struck dumb with surprise, shrugs her shoulders and starts dusting* MR. ANTROBUS'S *chair, including the under side.*]

Of course, Mr. Antrobus is a very fine man, an excellent husband and father, a pillar of the church, and has all the best interests of the community at heart. Of course, every muscle goes tight every time he passes a policeman; but what I think is that there are certain charges that ought not to be made, and I think I may add, ought not to be allowed to be made; we're all human; who isn't?

[*She dusts* MRS. ANTROBUS'S *rocking chair.*]

Mrs. Antrobus is as fine a woman as you could hope to see. She lives only for her children; and if it would be any benefit to her children she'd see the rest of us stretched out dead at her feet without turning a hair,—that's the truth. If you want to know anything more about Mrs. Antrobus, just go and look at a tigress, and look hard.

As to the children—

Well, Henry Antrobus is a real, clean-cut American boy. He'll graduate from high school one of these days, if they make the alphabet any easier.—Henry, when he has a stone in his hand, has a perfect aim; he can hit anything from a bird to an older brother—Oh! I didn't mean to say that!—but it certainly was an unfortunate accident, and it was very hard getting the police out of the house.

Mr. and Mrs. Antrobus's daughter is named Gladys. She'll make some good man a good wife some day, if he'll just come down off the movie screen and ask her.

So here we are!

We've managed to survive for some time now, catch as catch can, the fat and the lean, and if the dinosaurs don't trample us to death, and if the grass-hoppers don't eat up our garden, we'll all live to see better days, knock on wood.

Each new child that's born to the Antrobuses seems to them to be sufficient reason for the whole universe's being set in motion; and each new child that dies seems to them to have been spared a whole world of sorrow, and what the end of it will be is still very much an open question.

We've rattled along, hot and cold, for some time now—

[*A portion of the wall above the door, right, flies up into the air and disappears.*]

—and my advice to you is not to inquire into why or whither, but just enjoy your ice cream while it's on your plate,—that's my philosophy.

Don't forget that a few years ago we came through the depression by the skin of our teeth! One more tight squeeze like that and where will we be?

[*This is a cue line.* SABINA *looks angrily at the kitchen door and repeats:*]

. . . we came through the depression by the skin of our teeth; one more tight squeeze like that and where will we be?

[*Flustered, she looks through the opening in the right wall, then goes to the window and reopens the act.*]

Oh, oh, oh! Six o'clock and the master not home yet. Pray God nothing has happened to him crossing the Hudson. Here it is the middle of August and the coldest day of the year. It's simply freezing; the dogs are sticking. One more tight squeeze like that and where will we be?

VOICE. [*Off-stage*] Make up something! Invent something!

SABINA. Well . . . uh . . . this certainly is a fine American home . . . and—uh . . . everybody's very happy . . . and—uh . . .

[*Suddenly flings pretense to the winds and coming downstage says with indignation:*]

I can't invent any words for this play, and I'm glad I can't. I hate this play and every word in it.

As for me, I don't understand a single word of it, anyway,—all about the troubles the human race has gone through, there's a subject for you.

Besides, the author hasn't made up his silly mind as to whether we're all living back in caves or in New Jersey today, and that's the way it is all the way through.

Oh—why can't we have plays like we used to have—*Peg o' My Heart,* and *Smilin' Thru,* and *The Bat*—good entertainment with a message you can take home with you?

I took this hateful job because I had to. For two years I've sat up in my room living on a sandwich and a cup of tea a day, waiting for better times in the theater. And look at me now: I—I who've played *Rain* and *The Barretts of Wimpole Street* and *First Lady*—God in Heaven!

[*The* STAGE MANAGER *puts his head out from the hole in the scenery.*]

MR. FITZPATRICK. Miss Somerset!! Miss Somerset!

SABINA. Oh! Anyway!—nothing matters! It'll all be the same in a hundred years. [*Loudly*] We came through the depression by the skin of our teeth,— that's true!—one more tight squeeze like that and where will we be?

[*Enter* MRS. ANTROBUS, *a mother.*]

MRS. ANTROBUS. Sabina, you've let the fire go out.

SABINA. [*In a lather*] One-thing-and-another; don't-know-whether-my-wits-are-upside-or-down; might-as-well-be-dead-as-alive-in-a-house-all-sixes-and-sevens. . . .

MRS. ANTROBUS. You've let the fire go out. Here it is the coldest day of the year right in the middle of August, and you've let the fire go out.

SABINA. Mrs. Antrobus, I'd like to give my two weeks' notice, Mrs. Antrobus. A girl like I can get a situation in a home where they're rich enough to have a fire in every room, Mrs. Antrobus, and a girl don't have to carry the responsibility of the whole house on her two shoulders. And a home without children, Mrs. Antrobus, because children are a thing only a parent can stand,

and a truer word was never said; and a home, Mrs. Antrobus, where the master of the house don't pinch decent, self-respecting girls when he meets them in a dark corridor. I mention no names and make no charges. So you have my notice, Mrs. Antrobus. I hope that's perfectly clear.

MRS. ANTROBUS. You've let the fire go out!—Have you milked the mammoth?

SABINA. I don't understand a word of this play.—Yes, I've milked the mammoth.

MRS. ANTROBUS. Until Mr. Antrobus comes home we have no food and we have no fire. You'd better go over to the neighbors and borrow some fire.

SABINA. Mrs. Antrobus! I can't! I'd die on the way, you know I would. It's worse than January. The dogs are sticking to the sidewalks. I'd die.

MRS. ANTROBUS. Very well, I'll go.

SABINA. [*Even more distraught, coming forward and sinking on her knees*] You'd never come back alive; we'd all perish; if you weren't here, we'd just perish. How do we know Mr. Antrobus'll be back? We don't know. If you go out, I'll just kill myself.

MRS. ANTROBUS. Get up, Sabina.

SABINA. Every night it's the same thing. Will he come back safe, or won't he? Will we starve to death, or freeze to death, or boil to death or will we be killed by burglars? I don't know why we go on living. I don't know why we go on living at all. It's easier being dead.

[*She flings her arms on the table and buries her head in them. In each of the succeeding speeches she flings her head up—and sometimes her hands—then quickly buries her head again.*]

MRS. ANTROBUS. The same thing! Always throwing up the sponge, Sabina. Always announcing your own death. But give you a new hat—or a plate of ice cream—or a ticket to the movies, and you want to live forever.

SABINA. You don't care whether we live or die; all you care about is those children. If it would be any benefit to them you'd be glad to see us all stretched out dead.

MRS. ANTROBUS. Well, maybe I would.

SABINA. And what do they care about? Themselves—that's all they care about. [*Shrilly*] They make fun of you behind your back. Don't tell me: they're ashamed of you. Half the time, they pretend they're someone else's children. Little thanks you get from them.

MRS. ANTROBUS. I'm not asking for any thanks.

SABINA. And Mr. Antrobus—you don't understand *him*. All that work he does—trying to discover the alphabet and the multiplication table. Whenever he tries to learn anything you fight against it.

MRS. ANTROBUS. Oh, Sabina, I know you.

When Mr. Antrobus raped you home from your Sabine hills, he did it to insult me.

He did it for your pretty face, and to insult me.

You were the new wife, weren't you?

For a year or two you lay on your bed all day and polished the nails on your hands and feet:

You made puffballs of the combings of your hair and you blew them up to the ceiling.

And I washed your underclothes and I made you chicken broths.

I bore children and between my very groans I stirred the cream that you'd put on your face.

But I knew you wouldn't last.

You didn't last.

SABINA. But it was I who encouraged Mr. Antrobus to make the alphabet. I'm sorry to say it, Mrs. Antrobus, but you're not a beautiful woman, and you can never know what a man could do if he tried. It's girls like I who inspire the multiplication table.

I'm sorry to say it, but you're not a beautiful woman, Mrs. Antrobus, and that's the God's truth.

MRS. ANTROBUS. And you didn't last—you sank to the kitchen. And what do you do there? *You let the fire go out!*

No wonder to you it seems easier being dead.

Reading and writing and counting on your fingers is all very well in their way, —but I keep the home going.

—There's that dinosaur on the front lawn again. —Shoo! Go away. Go away.

[*The baby* DINOSAUR *puts his head in the window.*]

DINOSAUR. It's cold.

MRS. ANTROBUS. You go around to the back of the house where you belong.

DINOSAUR. It's cold.

[*The* DINOSAUR *disappears.* MRS. ANTROBUS *goes calmly out.* SABINA *slowly raises her head and speaks to the audience. The central portion of the center wall rises, pauses, and disappears into the loft.*]

SABINA. Now that you audience are listening to this, too, I understand it a little better.

I wish eleven o'clock were here; I don't want to be dragged through this whole play again.

[*The* TELEGRAPH BOY *is seen entering along the back wall of the stage from the right. She catches sight of him and calls:*]

Mrs. Antrobus! Mrs. Antrobus! Help! There's a strange man coming to the house. He's coming up the walk, help!

[*Enter* MRS. ANTROBUS *in alarm, but efficient.*]

MRS. ANTROBUS. Help me quick!

> [*They barricade the door by piling the furniture against it.*]

Who is it? What do you want?

TELEGRAPH BOY. A telegram for Mrs. Antrobus from Mr. Antrobus in the city.

SABINA. Are you sure, are you sure? Maybe it's just a trap!

MRS. ANTROBUS. I know his voice, Sabina. We can open the door.

> [*Enter the* TELEGRAPH BOY, *twelve years old, in uniform. The* DINOSAUR *and* MAMMOTH *slip by him into the room and settle down front right.*]

I'm sorry we kept you waiting. We have to be careful, you know.

> [*To the* ANIMALS]

Hm! . . . Will you be quiet?

> [*They nod.*]

Have you had your supper?

> [*They nod.*]

Are you *ready* to come in?

> [*They nod.*]

Young man, have you any fire with you? Then light the grate, will you?

> [*He nods, produces something like a briquet, and kneels by the imagined fireplace, footlights center. Pause.*]

What are people saying about this cold weather?

> [*He makes a doubtful shrug with his shoulders.*]

Sabina, take this stick and go and light the stove.

SABINA. Like I told you, Mrs. Antrobus; two weeks. That's the law. I hope that's perfectly clear. [*Exit*]

MRS. ANTROBUS. What about this cold weather?

TELEGRAPH BOY. [*Lowered eyes*] Of course, I don't know anything . . . but they say there's a wall of ice moving down from the North, that's what they say. We can't get Boston by telegraph, and they're burning pianos in Hartford.

. . . It moves everything in front of it, churches and post offices and city halls.

I live in Brooklyn myself.

MRS. ANTROBUS. What are people doing about it?

TELEGRAPH BOY. Well . . . uh . . . Talking, mostly.

Or just what you'd do a day in February.

There are some that are trying to go South and the roads are crowded; but you can't take old people and children very far in a cold like this.

MRS. ANTROBUS. —What's this telegram you have for me?

TELEGRAPH BOY. [*Fingertips to his forehead*] If you wait just a minute; I've got to remember it.

> [*The* ANIMALS *have left their corner and are nosing him. Presently they take places on either side of him, leaning against his hips, like heraldic beasts.*]

This telegram was flashed from Murray Hill to University Heights! And then by puffs of smoke from University Heights to Staten Island.

And then by lantern from Staten Island to Plainfield, New Jersey. What hath God wrought! [*He clears his throat.*]

"To Mrs. Antrobus, Excelsior, New Jersey:

My dear wife, will be an hour late. Busy day at the office. Don't worry the children about the cold just keep them warm burn everything except Shakespeare." [*Pause*]

MRS. ANTROBUS. Men! —He knows I'd burn ten Shakespeares to prevent a child of mine from having one cold in the head. What does it say next?

> [*Enter* SABINA.]

TELEGRAPH BOY. "Have made great discoveries today have separated em from en."

SABINA. I know what that is, that's the alphabet, yes it is. Mr. Antrobus is just the cleverest man. Why, when the alphabet's finished, we'll be able to tell the future and everything.

TELEGRAPH BOY. Then listen to this: "Ten tens make a hundred semi-colon consequences far-reaching." [*Watches for effect*]

MRS. ANTROBUS. The earth's turning to ice, and all he can do is to make up new numbers.

TELEGRAPH BOY. Well, Mrs. Antrobus, like the head man at our office said: a few more discoveries like that and we'll be worth freezing.

MRS. ANTROBUS. What does he say next?

TELEGRAPH BOY. l . . . l can't do this last part very well. [*He clears his throat and sings*] "Happy w'dding ann'vers'ry to you, Happy ann'vers'ry to you—"

> [*The* ANIMALS *begin to howl soulfully;* SABINA *screams with pleasure.*]

MRS. ANTROBUS. Dolly! Frederick! Be quiet.

TELEGRAPH BOY. [*Above the din*] "Happy w'dding ann'vers'ry, dear Eva; happy w'dding ann'vers'ry to you."

MRS. ANTROBUS. Is that in the telegram? Are they singing telegrams now?

[*He nods.*]

The earth's getting so silly no wonder the sun turns cold.

SABINA. Mrs. Antrobus, I want to take back the notice I gave you. Mrs. Antrobus, I don't want to leave a house that gets such interesting telegrams and I'm sorry for anything I said. I really am.

MRS. ANTROBUS. Young man, I'd like to give you something for all this trouble; Mr. Antrobus isn't home yet and I have no money and no food in the house—

TELEGRAPH BOY. Mrs. Antrobus . . . I don't like to . . . appear to . . . ask for anything, but . . .

MRS. ANTROBUS. What is it you'd like?

TELEGRAPH BOY. Do you happen to have an old needle you could spare? My wife just sits home all day thinking about needles.

SABINA. [*Shrilly*] We only got two in the house. Mrs. Antrobus, you know we only got two in the house.

MRS. ANTROBUS. [*After a look at* SABINA *taking a needle from her collar*] Why yes, I can spare this.

TELEGRAPH BOY. [*Lowered eyes*] Thank you, Mrs. Antrobus. Mrs. Antrobus, can I ask you something else? I have two sons of my own; if the cold gets worse, what should I do?

SABINA. I think we'll all perish, that's what I think. Cold like this in August is just the end of the whole world.

[*Silence*]

MRS. ANTROBUS. I don't know. After all, what does one do about anything? Just keep as warm as you can. And don't let your wife and children see that you're worried.

TELEGRAPH BOY. Yes. . . . Thank you, Mrs. Antrobus. Well, I'd better be going.—Oh, I forgot! There's one more sentence in the telegram. "Three cheers have invented the wheel."

MRS. ANTROBUS. A wheel? What's a wheel?

TELEGRAPH BOY. I don't know. That's what it said. The sign for it is like this. Well, good-by.

[*The* WOMEN *see him to the door, with good-bys and injunctions to keep warm.*]

SABINA. [*Apron to her eyes, wailing*] Mrs. Antrobus, it looks to me like all the nice men in the world are already married; I don't know why that is. [*Exit*]

MRS. ANTROBUS. [*Thoughtful, to the* ANIMALS] Do you ever remember hearing tell of any cold like this in August?

[*The* ANIMALS *shake their heads.*]

From your grandmothers or anyone?

> [*They shake their heads.*]

Have you any suggestions?

> [*They shake their heads. She pulls her shawl around, goes to the front door and opening it an inch calls:*]

HENRY. GLADYS. CHILDREN. Come right in and get warm. No, no, when mama says a thing she means it.
Henry! HENRY. Put down that stone. You know what happened last time. [*Shriek*]
HENRY! Put down that stone!
Gladys! Put down your dress!! Try and be a lady.

> [*The* CHILDREN *bound in and dash to the fire. They take off their winter things and leave them in heaps on the floor.*]

GLADYS. Mama, I'm hungry. Mama, why is it so cold?
HENRY. [*At the same time*] Mama, why doesn't it snow? Mama, when's supper ready? Maybe it'll snow and we can make snowballs.
GLADYS. Mama, it's so cold that in one more minute I just couldn't of stood it.
MRS. ANTROBUS. Settle down, both of you, I want to talk to you.

> [*She draws up a hassock and sits front center over the orchestra pit before the imaginary fire. The* CHILDREN *stretch out on the floor, leaning against her lap. Tableau by Raphael. The* ANIMALS *edge up and complete the triangle.*]

It's just a cold spell of some kind. Now listen to what I'm saying:
When your father comes home I want you to be extra quiet. He's had a hard day at the office and I don't know but what he may have one of his moods.
I just got a telegram from him very happy and excited, and you know what that means. Your father's temper's uneven; I guess you know that. [*Shriek*]
Henry! Henry!
Why—why can't you remember to keep your hair down over your forehead? You must keep that scar covered up. Don't you know that when your father sees it he loses all control over himself? He goes crazy. He wants to die.

> [*After a moment's despair she collects herself decisively, wets the hem of her apron in her mouth and starts polishing his forehead vigorously.*]

Lift your head up. Stop squirming. Blessed me, sometimes I think that it's going away—and then there it is: just as red as ever.
HENRY. Mama, today at school two teachers forgot and called me by my old name. They forgot, Mama. You'd better write another letter to the

principal, so that he'll tell them I've changed my name. Right out in class they called me: Cain.

MRS. ANTROBUS. [*Putting her hand on his mouth, too late; hoarsely*] Don't say it. [*Polishing feverishly*] If you're good they'll forget it. Henry, you didn't hit anyone . . . today, did you?

HENRY. Oh . . . no-o-o!

MRS. ANTROBUS. [*Still working, not looking at Gladys*] And, Gladys, I want you to be especially nice to your father tonight. You know what he calls you when you're good—his little angel, his little star. Keep your dress down like a little lady. And keep your voice nice and low. Gladys Antrobus!! What's that red stuff you have on your face? [*Slaps her*] You're a filthy detestable child! [*Rises in real, though temporary, repudiation and despair*] Get away from me, both of you! I wish I'd never seen sight or sound of you. Let the cold come! I can't stand it. I don't want to go on. [*She walks away.*]

GLADYS. [*Weeping*] All the girls at school do, Mama.

MRS. ANTROBUS. [*Shrieking*] I'm through with you, that's all!—Sabina! Sabina!—Don't you know your father'd go crazy if he saw that paint on your face? Don't you know your father thinks you're perfect? Don't you know he couldn't live if he didn't think you were perfect?—Sabina!

[*Enter* SABINA.]

SABINA. Yes, Mrs. Antrobus!

MRS. ANTROBUS. Take this girl out into the kitchen and wash her face with the scrubbing brush.

MR. ANTROBUS. [*Outside, roaring*] "I've been working on the railroad, all the livelong day . . . etc."

[*The* ANIMALS *start running around in circles, bellowing.* SABINA *rushes to the window.*]

MRS. ANTROBUS. Sabina, what's that noise outside?

SABINA. Oh, it's a drunken tramp. It's a giant, Mrs. Antrobus. We'll all be killed in our beds, I know it!

MRS. ANTROBUS. Help me quick. Quick. Everybody.

[*Again they stack all the furniture against the door.* MR. ANTROBUS *pounds and bellows.*]

Who is it? What do you want?—Sabina, have you any boiling water ready? —Who is it?

MR. ANTROBUS. Broken-down camel of a pig's snout, open this door.

MRS. ANTROBUS. God be praised! It's your father.—Just a minute, George! —Sabina, clear the door, quick. Gladys, come here while I clean your nasty face!

MR. ANTROBUS. She-bitch of a goat's gizzard, I'll break every bone in your body. Let me in or I'll tear the whole house down.

MRS. ANTROBUS. Just a minute, George, something's the matter with the lock.

MR. ANTROBUS. Open the door or I'll tear your livers out. I'll smash your brains on the ceiling, and Devil take the hindmost.

MRS. ANTROBUS. Now, you can open the door, Sabina. I'm ready.

[*The door is flung open. Silence.* MR. ANTROBUS—*face of a Keystone Comedy Cop—stands there in fur cap and blanket. His arms are full of parcels, including a large stone wheel with a center in it. One hand carries a railroad man's lantern. Suddenly he bursts into joyous roar.*]

MR. ANTROBUS. Well, how's the whole crooked family?

[*Relief. Laughter. Tears. Jumping up and down.* ANIMALS *cavorting.* ANTROBUS *throws the parcels on the ground. Hurls his cap and blanket after them. Heroic embraces. Melee of* HUMANS *and* ANIMALS, SABINA *included.*]

I'll be scalded and tarred if a man can't get a little welcome when he comes home. Well, Maggie, you old gunny-sack, how's the broken down old weather hen?—Sabina, old fishbait, old skunkpot.—And the children,—how've the little smellers been?

GLADYS. Papa, Papa, Papa, Papa, Papa.

MR. ANTROBUS. How've they been, Maggie?

MRS. ANTROBUS. Well, I must say, they've been as good as gold. I haven't had to raise my voice once. I don't know what's the matter with them.

ANTROBUS. [*Kneeling before* GLADYS] Papa's little weasel, eh?—Sabina, there's some food for you. Papa's little gopher?

GLADYS. [*Her arm around his neck*] Papa, you're always teasing me.

ANTROBUS. And Henry? Nothing rash today, I hope. Nothing rash?

HENRY. No, Papa.

ANTROBUS. [*Roaring*] Well that's good, that's good—I'll bet Sabina let the fire go out.

SABINA. Mr. Antrobus. I've given my notice. I'm leaving two weeks from today. I'm sorry, but I'm leaving.

ANTROBUS. [*Roar*] Well, if you leave now you'll freeze to death, so go and cook the dinner.

SABINA. Two weeks, that's the law. [*Exit*]

ANTROBUS. Did you get my telegram?

MRS. ANTROBUS. Yes.—What's a wheel?

[*He indicates the wheel with a glance.* HENRY *is rolling it around the floor. Rapid, hoarse interchange:* MRS. ANTROBUS: *What does this cold weather mean? It's below freezing.* ANTROBUS: *Not before the children!* MRS. ANTROBUS: *Shouldn't we do some-*

thing about it?—start off, move? ANTROBUS: *Not before the children!!! He gives* HENRY *a sharp slap.*]

HENRY. Papa, you hit me!

ANTROBUS. Well, remember it. That's to make you remember today. Today. The day the alphabet's finished; and the day that we *saw* the hundred—the hundred, the hundred, the hundred, the hundred, the hundred—there's no end to 'em.

I've had a day at the office!

Take a look at that wheel, Maggie—when I've got that to rights: you'll see a sight.

There's a reward there for all the walking you've done.

MRS. ANTROBUS. How do you mean?

ANTROBUS. [*On the hassock looking into the fire; with awe*] Maggie, we've reached the top of the wave. There's not much more to be done. We're there!

MRS. ANTROBUS. [*Cutting across his mood sharply*] And the ice?

ANTROBUS. The ice!

HENRY. [*Playing with the wheel*] Papa, you could put a chair on this.

ANTROBUS. [*Broodingly*] Ye-e-s, any booby can fool with it now,—but I thought of it first.

MRS. ANTROBUS. Children, go out in the kitchen. I want to talk to your father alone.

[*The* CHILDREN *go out.* ANTROBUS *has moved to his chair up left. He takes the goldfish bowl on his lap; pulls the canary cage down to the level of his face. Both the* ANIMALS *put their paws up on the arm of his chair.* MRS. ANTROBUS *faces him across the room, like a judge.*]

MRS. ANTROBUS. Well?

ANTROBUS. [*Shortly*] It's cold.—How things been, eh? Keck, keck, keck. —And you, Millicent?

MRS. ANTROBUS. I know it's cold.

ANTROBUS. [*To the canary*] No spilling of sunflower seed, eh? No singing after lights-out, y'know what I mean?

MRS. ANTROBUS. You can try and prevent us freezing to death, can't you? You can do something? We can start moving. Or we can go on the animals' backs?

ANTROBUS. The best thing about animals is that they don't talk much.

MAMMOTH. It's cold.

ANTROBUS. Eh, eh, eh! Watch that!—

—By midnight we'd turn to ice. The roads are full of people now who can scarcely lift a foot from the ground. The grass out in front is like iron,— which reminds me, I have another needle for you.—The people up north— where are they?

Frozen . . . crushed. . . .

MRS. ANTROBUS. Is that what's going to happen to us?—Will you answer me?

ANTROBUS. I don't know. I don't know anything. Some say that the ice is going slower. Some say that it's stopped. The sun's growing cold. What can I do about that? Nothing we can do but burn everything in the house, and the fenceposts and the barn. Keep the fire going. When we have no more fire, we die.

MRS. ANTROBUS. Well, why didn't you say so in the first place?

[MRS. ANTROBUS *is about to march off when she catches sight of two* REFUGEES, *men, who have appeared against the back wall of the theater and who are soon joined by others.*]

REFUGEES. Mr. Antrobus! Mr. Antrobus! Mr. An-nn-tro-bus!

MRS. ANTROBUS. Who's that? Who's that calling you?

ANTROBUS. [*Clearing his throat guiltily*] Hm—let me see.

[*Two* REFUGEES *come up to the window.*]

REFUGEE. Could we warm our hands for a moment, Mr. Antrobus. It's very cold, Mr. Antrobus.

ANOTHER REFUGEE. Mr. Antrobus, I wonder if you have a piece of bread or something that you could spare.

[*Silence. They wait humbly.* MRS. ANTROBUS *stands rooted to the spot. Suddenly a knock at the door, then another hand knocking in short rapid blows.*]

MRS. ANTROBUS. Who are these people? Why, they're all over the front yard. What have they come *here* for?

[*Enter* SABINA.]

SABINA. Mrs. Antrobus! There are some tramps knocking at the back door.

MRS. ANTROBUS. George, tell these people to go away. Tell them to move right along. I'll go and send them away from the back door. Sabina, come with me.

[*She goes out energetically.*]

ANTROBUS. Sabina! Stay here! I have something to say to you. [*He goes to the door and opens it a crack and talks through it.*] Ladies and gentlemen! I'll have to ask you to wait a few minutes longer. It'll be all right . . . while you're waiting you might each one pull up a stake of the fence. We'll need them all for the fireplace. There'll be coffee and sandwiches in a moment.

[SABINA *looks out door over his shoulder and suddenly extends her arm pointing, with a scream.*]

SABINA. Mr. Antrobus, what's that??—that big white thing? Mr. Antrobus, it's ICE. It's ICE!!

ANTROBUS. Sabina, I want you to go in the kitchen and make a lot of coffee. Make a whole pail full.

SABINA. Pail full!!

ANTROBUS. [*With gesture*] And sandwiches . . . piles of them . . . like this.

SABINA. Mr. An . . . !!

[*Suddenly she drops the play, and says in her own person as* MISS SOMERSET, *with surprise.*]

Oh, *I* see what this part of the play means now! This means refugees.

[*She starts to cross to the proscenium.*]

Oh, I don't like it. I don't like it.

[*She leans against the proscenium and bursts into tears.*]

ANTROBUS. Miss Somerset!

[*Voice of the* STAGE MANAGER]

Miss Somerset!

SABINA. [*Energetically, to the audience*] Ladies and gentlemen! Don't take this play serious. The world's not coming to an end. You know it's not. People exaggerate! Most people really have enough to eat and a roof over their heads. Nobody actually starves—you can always eat grass or something. That ice-business—why, it was a long, long time ago. Besides they were only savages. Savages don't love their families—not like we do.

ANTROBUS *and* STAGE MANAGER. Miss Somerset!!

[*There is renewed knocking at the door.*]

SABINA. All right. I'll say the lines, but I won't think about the play.

[*Enter* MRS. ANTROBUS.]

SABINA. [*Parting thrust at the audience*] And I advise *you* not to think about the play, either. [*Exit* SABINA.]

MRS. ANTROBUS. George, these tramps say that you asked them to come to the house. What does this mean?

[*Knocking at the door*]

ANTROBUS. Just . . . uh. . . . There are a few friends, Maggie, I met on the road. Real nice, real useful people. . . .

MRS. ANTROBUS. [*Back to the door*] Now, don't you ask them in!
George Antrobus, not another soul comes in here over my dead body.

ANTROBUS. Maggie, there's a doctor there. Never hurts to have a good doctor in the house. We've lost a peck of children, one way and another. You can never tell when a child's throat will get stopped up. What you and I have seen—!!!

[*He puts his fingers on his throat, and imitates diphtheria.*]

MRS. ANTROBUS. Well, just one person then, the Doctor. The others can go right along the road.

ANTROBUS. Maggie, there's an old man, particular friend of mine—

MRS. ANTROBUS. I won't listen to you—

ANTROBUS. It was he that really started off the ABC's.

MRS. ANTROBUS. I don't care if he perishes. We can do without reading or writing. We can't do without food.

ANTROBUS. Then let the ice come!! Drink your coffee!! I don't want any coffee if I can't drink it with some good people.

MRS. ANTROBUS. Stop shouting. Who else is there trying to push us off the cliff?

ANTROBUS. Well, there's the man . . . who makes all the laws. Judge Moses!

MRS. ANTROBUS. Judges can't help us now.

ANTROBUS. And if the ice melts? . . . and if we pull through? Have you and I been able to bring up Henry? What have we done?

MRS. ANTROBUS. Who are those old women?

ANTROBUS. [*Coughs*] Up in town there are nine sisters. There are three or four of them here. They're sort of music teachers . . . and one of them recites and one of them—

MRS. ANTROBUS. That's the end. A singing troupe! Well, take your choice, live or die. Starve your own children before your face.

ANTROBUS. [*Gently*] These people don't take much. They're used to starving.
They'll sleep on the floor.
Besides, Maggie, listen: no, listen:
Who've we got in the house, but Sabina? Sabina's always afraid the worst will happen. Whose spirits can she keep up? Maggie, these people never give up. They think they'll live and work forever.

MRS. ANTROBUS. [*Walks slowly to the middle of the room*] All right, let them in. Let them in. You're master here. [*Softly*]—But these animals must go. Enough's enough. They'll soon be big enough to push the walls down, anyway. Take them away.

ANTROBUS. [*Sadly*] All right. The dinosaur and mammoth—! Come on, baby, come on Frederick. Come for a walk. That's a good little fellow.

DINOSAUR. It's cold.

ANTROBUS. Yes, nice cold fresh air. Bracing.

[*He holds the door open and the ANIMALS go out. He beckons to his friends. The REFUGEES are typical elderly out-of-works*] *from the streets of New York today.* JUDGE MOSES *wears a skull cap.* HOMER *is a blind beggar with a guitar. The seedy crowd shuffles in and waits humbly and expectantly.* ANTROBUS *introduces them to his wife, who bows to each with a stately bend of her head.*]

Make yourself at home, Maggie, this the doctor . . . m . . . Coffee'll be here in a minute. . . . Professor, this is my wife. . . . And: . . . Judge . . . Maggie, you know the Judge.

[*An old blind man with a guitar*]

Maggie, you know . . . you know Homer?—Come right in, Judge.—Miss Muse—are some of your sisters here? Come right in. . . . Miss E. Muse; Miss T. Muse, Miss M. Muse.
MRS. ANTROBUS. Pleased to meet you.
Just . . . make yourself comfortable. Supper'll be ready in a minute. [*She goes out, abruptly.*]
ANTROBUS. Make yourself at home, friends. I'll be right back.

[*He goes out. The* REFUGEES *stare about them in awe. Presently several voices start whispering "Homer! Homer!" All take it up.* HOMER *strikes a chord or two on his guitar, then starts to speak:*]

HOMER.

Μῆνιν ἄειδε, θεὰ, Πηληϊάδεω 'Αχιλῆος,
οὐλομένην, ἣ μυρί' 'Αχαιοῖς ἄλγε' ἔθηκεν,
πολλὰς δ' ἰφθίμους ψυχὰς—

[HOMER'S *face shows he is lost in thought and memory and the words die away on his lips. The* REFUGEES *likewise nod in dreamy recollection. Soon the whisper "Moses, Moses!" goes around. An aged Jew parts his beard and recites dramatically:*]

MOSES.

בְּרֵאשִׁית בָּרָא אֱלֹהִים אֵת הַשָּׁמַיִם וְאֵת הָאָרֶץ: וְהָאָרֶץ הָיְתָה תֹהוּ

וָבֹהוּ וְחֹשֶׁךְ עַל־פְּנֵי תְהוֹם וְרוּחַ אֱלֹהִים מְרַחֶפֶת עַל־פְּנֵי הַמָּיִם:²

[*The same dying away of the words take place, and on the part of the* REFUGEES *the same retreat into recollection. Some of them murmur, "Yes, yes." The mood is broken by the abrupt entrance of* MR. *and* MRS. ANTROBUS *and* SABINA *bearing platters of sandwiches and a pail of coffee.* SABINA *stops and stares at the guests.*]

MR. ANTROBUS. Sabina, pass the sandwiches.
SABINA. I thought I was working in a respectable house that had respecta-

ble guests. I'm giving my notice, Mr. Antrobus: two weeks, that's the law.

MR. ANTROBUS. Sabina! Pass the sandwiches.

SABINA. Two weeks, that's the law.

MR. ANTROBUS. There's the law. That's Moses.

SABINA. [Stares] The Ten Commandments—FAUGH!!—[To Audience] That's the worst line I've ever had to say on any stage.

ANTROBUS. I think the best thing to do is just not to stand on ceremony, but pass the sandwiches around from left to right.—Judge, help yourself to one of these.

MRS. ANTROBUS. The roads are crowded, I hear?

THE GUESTS. [All talking at once] Oh, ma'am, you can't imagine. . . . You can hardly put one foot before you . . . people are trampling one another.

[Sudden silence]

MRS. ANTROBUS. Well, you know what I think it is,—I think it's sun-spots!

THE GUESTS. [Discreet hubbub] Oh, you're right, Mrs. Antrobus . . . that's what it is. . . . That's what I was saying the other day.

[Sudden silence]

ANTROBUS. Well, I don't believe the whole world's going to turn to ice.

[All eyes are fixed on him, waiting.]

I can't believe it. Judge! Have we worked for nothing? Professor! Have we just failed in the whole thing?

MRS. ANTROBUS. It is certainly very strange—well fortunately on both sides of the family we come of very hearty stock.—Doctor, I want you to meet my children. They're eating their supper now. And of course I want them to meet you.

MISS M. MUSE. How many children have you, Mrs. Antrobus?

MRS. ANTROBUS. I have two,—a boy and a girl.

MOSES. [Softly] I understood you had two sons, Mrs. Antrobus.

[MRS. ANTROBUS in blind suffering; she walks toward the footlights.]

MRS. ANTROBUS. [In a low voice] Abel, Abel, my son, my son, Abel, my son, Abel, Abel, my son.

[The REFUGEES move with few steps toward her as though in comfort murmuring words in Greek, Hebrew, German, et cetera. A piercing shriek from the kitchen,—SABINA'S voice. All heads turn.]

ANTROBUS. What's that?

[SABINA enters, bursting with indignation, pulling on her gloves.]

SABINA. Mr. Antrobus—that son of yours, that boy Henry Antrobus—I don't stay in this house another moment!—He's not fit to live among respectable folks and that's a fact.

MRS. ANTROBUS. Don't say another word, Sabina. I'll be right back. [*Without waiting for an answer she goes past her into the kitchen.*]

SABINA. Mr. Antrobus, Henry has thrown a stone again and if he hasn't killed the boy that lives next door, I'm very much mistaken. He finished his supper and went out to play; and I heard such a fight; and then I saw it. I saw it with my own eyes. And it looked to me like stark murder.

[MRS. ANTROBUS *appears at the kitchen door, shielding* HENRY *who follows her. When she steps aside, we see on* HENRY'S *forehead a large ochre and scarlet scar in the shape of a C.* MR. ANTROBUS *starts toward him. A pause.* HENRY *is heard saying under his breath:*]

HENRY. He was going to take the wheel away from me. He started to throw a stone at me first.

MRS. ANTROBUS. George, it was just a boyish impulse. Remember how young he is. [*Louder, in an urgent wail*] George, he's only four thousand years old.

SABINA. And everything was going along so nicely! [*Silence.* ANTROBUS *goes back to the fireplace.*]

ANTROBUS. Put out the fire! Put out all the fires. [*Violently*] No wonder the sun grows cold. [*He starts stamping on the fireplace.*]

MRS. ANTROBUS. Doctor! Judge! Help me!—George, have you lost your mind?

ANTROBUS. There is no mind. We'll not try to live. [*To the guests*] Give it up. Give up trying.

[MRS. ANTROBUS *seizes him.*]

SABINA. Mr. Antrobus! I'm downright ashamed of you.

MRS. ANTROBUS. George, have some more coffee.—Gladys! Where's Gladys gone?

[GLADYS *steps in, frightened.*]

GLADYS. Here I am, mama.

MRS. ANTROBUS. Go upstairs and bring your father's slippers. How could you forget a thing like that, when you know how tired he is?

[ANTROBUS *sits in his chair. He covers his face with his hands.* MRS. ANTROBUS *turns to the* REFUGEES:]

Can't some of you sing? It's your business in life to sing, isn't it? Sabina!

[*Several of the women clear their throats tentatively, and with frightened faces gather around* HOMER'S *guitar. He establishes a few chords. Almost inaudibly they start singing, led by* SABINA: *"Jingle Bells."* MRS. ANTROBUS *continues to* ANTROBUS *in a low voice, while taking off his shoes:*]

George, remember all the other times. When the volcanoes came right up in the front yard.

And the time the grasshoppers ate every single leaf and blade of grass, and all the grain and spinach you'd grown with your own hands. And the summer there were earthquakes every night.

ANTROBUS. Henry! Henry! [*Puts his hand on his forehead*] Myself. All of us, we're covered with blood.

MRS. ANTROBUS. Then remember all the times you were pleased with him and when you were proud of yourself.—Henry! Henry! Come here and recite to your father the multiplication table that you do so nicely.

[HENRY *kneels on one knee beside his father and starts whispering the multiplication table.*]

HENRY. [*Finally*] Two times six is twelve; three times six is eighteen—I don't think I know the sixes.

[*Enter* GLADYS *with the slippers.* MRS. ANTROBUS *makes stern gestures to her: Go in there and do your best. The* GUESTS *are now singing "Tenting Tonight."*]

GLADYS. [*Putting slippers on his feet*] Papa . . . papa . . . I was very good in school today. Miss Conover said right out in class that if all the girls had as good manners as Gladys Antrobus, that the world would be a very different place to live in.

MRS. ANTROBUS. You recited a piece at assembly, didn't you? Recite it to your father.

GLADYS. Papa, do you want to hear what I recited in class?

[*Fierce directorial glance from her mother*]

"THE STAR" by Henry Wadsworth LONGFELLOW.

MRS. ANTROBUS. Wait!!! The fire's going out. There isn't enough wood! Henry, go upstairs and bring down the chairs and start breaking up the beds.

[*Exit* HENRY. *The singers return to "Jingle Bells," still very softly.*]

GLADYS. Look, Papa, here's my report card. Lookit. Conduct A! Look, Papa. Papa, do you want to hear the Star, by Henry Wadsworth Longfellow? Papa, you're not mad at me, are you?—I know it'll get warmer. Soon it'll be just like spring, and we can go to a picnic at the Hibernian Picnic Grounds like you always like to do, don't you remember? Papa, just look at me once.

[*Enter* HENRY *with some chairs.*]

ANTROBUS. You recited in assembly, did you? [*She nods eagerly.*] You didn't forget it?

GLADYS. No!!! I was perfect.

> [*Pause. Then* ANTROBUS *rises, goes to the front door and opens it. The* REFUGEES *draw back timidly; the song stops; he peers out of the door, then closes it.*]

ANTROBUS. [*With decision, suddenly*] Build up the fire. It's cold. Build up the fire. We'll do what we can. Sabina, get some more wood. Come around the fire, everybody. At least the young ones may pull through. Henry, have you eaten something?

HENRY. Yes, papa.

ANTROBUS. Gladys, have you had some supper?

GLADYS. I ate in the kitchen, papa.

ANTROBUS. If you do come through this—what'll you be able to do? What do you know? Henry, did you take a good look at that wheel?

HENRY. Yes, papa.

ANTROBUS. [*Sitting down in his chair*] Six times two are—

HENRY. —twelve; six times three are eighteen; six times four are—Papa, it's hot and cold. It makes my head all funny. It makes me sleepy.

ANTROBUS. [*Gives him a cuff*] Wake up. I don't care if your head is sleepy. Six times four are twenty-four. Six times five are—

HENRY. Thirty. Papa!

ANTROBUS. Maggie, put something into Gladys' head on the chance she can use it.

MRS. ANTROBUS. What do you mean, George?

ANTROBUS. Six times six are thirty-six.
Teach her the beginning of the Bible.

GLADYS. But, Mama, it's so cold and close.

> [HENRY *has all but drowsed off. His father slaps him sharply and the lesson goes on.*]

MRS. ANTROBUS. "In the beginning God created the heavens and the earth; and the earth was waste and void; and the darkness was upon the face of the deep—"

> [*The singing starts up again louder.* SABINA *has returned with wood.*]

SABINA. [*After placing wood on the fireplace comes down to the footlights and addresses the audience:*] Will you please start handing up your chairs?

We'll need everything for this fire. Save the human race.—Ushers, will you pass the chairs up here? Thank you.

HENRY. Six times nine are fifty-four; six times ten are sixty.

> [*In the back of the auditorium the sound of chairs being ripped up can be heard.* USHERS *rush down the aisles with chairs and hand them over.*]

GLADYS. "And God called the light Day and the darkness he called Night."

SABINA. Pass up your chairs, everybody. Save the human race.

Curtain

Act II

> [*Toward the end of the intermission, though with the houselights still up, lantern slide projections begin to appear on the curtain. Timetables for trains leaving Pennsylvania Station for Atlantic City. Advertisements of Atlantic City hotels, drugstores, churches, rug merchants, fortune tellers, Bingo parlors.*
>
> *When the house lights go down, the voice of an* ANNOUNCER *is heard.*]

ANNOUNCER. The Management now brings you the News Events of the World. Atlantic City, New Jersey:

> [*Projection of a chrome postcard of the waterfront, trimmed in mica with the legend:* FUN AT THE BEACH]

This great convention city is playing host this week to the anniversary convocation of that great fraternal order,—the Ancient and Honorable Order of Mammals, Subdivision Humans. This great fraternal, militant, and burial society is celebrating on the Boardwalk, ladies and gentlemen, its six hundred thousandth Annual Convention.

It has just elected its president for the ensuing term,—

> [*Projection of* MR. *and* MRS. ANTROBUS *posed as they will be shown a few moments later*]

Mr. George Antrobus of Excelsior, New Jersey. We show you President Antrobus and his gracious and charming wife, every inch a mammal. Mr. Antrobus has had a long and chequered career. Credit has been paid to him for many useful enterprises including the introduction of the lever, of the wheel, and the brewing of beer. Credit has been also extended to President

Antrobus's gracious and charming wife for many practical suggestions, including the hem, the gore, and the gusset; and the novelty of the year,—frying in oil. Before we show you Mr. Antrobus accepting the nomination, we have an important announcement to make. As many of you know, this great celebration of the Order of the Mammals has received delegations from the other rival Orders,—or shall we say: esteemed concurrent Orders: the WINGS, the FINS, the SHELLS, and so on. These Orders are holding their conventions also, in various parts of the world, and have sent representatives to our own, two of a kind.

Later in the day we will show you President Antrobus broadcasting his words of greeting and congratulation to the collected assemblies of the whole natural world.

Ladies and Gentlemen! We give you President Antrobus!

> [*The screen becomes a transparency.* MR. ANTROBUS *stands beside a pedestal;* MRS. ANTROBUS *is seated wearing a corsage of orchids.* ANTROBUS *wears an untidy Prince Albert; spats; from a red rosette in his buttonhole hangs a fine long purple ribbon of honor. He wears a gay lodge hat,—something between a fez and a legionnaire's cap.*]

ANTROBUS. Fellow-mammals, fellow-vertebrates, fellow-humans, I thank you. Little did my dear parents think,—when they told me to stand on my own two feet,—that I'd arrive at this place.

My friends, we have come a long way.

During this week of happy celebration it is perhaps not fitting that we dwell on some of the difficult times we have been through. The dinosaur is extinct— [*Applause*]—the ice has retreated; and the common cold is being pursued by every means within our power.

> [MRS. ANTROBUS *sneezes, laughs prettily, and murmurs: "I beg your pardon."*]

In our memorial service yesterday we did honor to all our friends and relatives who are no longer with us, by reason of cold, earthquakes, plagues, and . . . and . . . [*Coughs*] differences of opinion.

As our Bishop so ably said . . . uh . . . so ably said. . . .

MRS. ANTROBUS. [*Closed lips*] Gone, but not forgotten.

ANTROBUS. "They are gone, but not forgotten."

I think I can say, I think I can prophesy with complete . . . uh . . . with complete. . . .

MRS. ANTROBUS. Confidence.

ANTROBUS. Thank you, my dear,—With complete lack of confidence, that a new day of security is about to dawn.

The watchword of the closing year was: Work. I give you the watchword for the future: Enjoy Yourselves.

MRS. ANTROBUS. George, sit down!

ANTROBUS. Before I close, however, I wish to answer one of those unjust and malicious accusations that were brought against me during this last electoral campaign.

Ladies and gentlemen, the charge was made that at various points in my career I leaned toward joining some of the rival orders,—that's a lie.

As I told reporters of the *Atlantic City Herald,* I do not deny that a few months before my birth I hesitated between . . . uh . . . between pinfeathers and gill-breathing,—and so did many of us here,—but for the last million years I have been viviparous, hairy, and diaphragmatic.

> [*Applause. Cries of* "*Good old Antrobus,*" "*The Prince chap!*"
> "*Georgie,*" *etc.*]

ANNOUNCER. Thank you. Thank you very much, Mr. Antrobus.

Now I know that our visitors will wish to hear a word from that gracious and charming mammal, Mrs. Antrobus, wife and mother,—Mrs. Antrobus!

> [MRS. ANTROBUS *rises, lays her program on her chair, bows, and says:*]

MRS. ANTROBUS. Dear friends, I don't really think I should say anything. After all, it was my husband who was elected and not I.

Perhaps, as president of the Women's Auxiliary Bed and Board Society,— I had some notes here, oh, yes, here they are:—I should give a short report from some of our committees that have been meeting in this beautiful city.

Perhaps it may interest you to know that it has at last been decided that the tomato is edible. Can you all hear me? The tomato *is* edible.

A delegate from across the sea reports that the thread woven by the silkworm gives a cloth . . . I have a sample of it here . . . can you see it? smooth, elastic. I should say that it's rather attractive,—though personally I prefer less shiny surfaces. Should the windows of a sleeping apartment be open or shut? I know all mothers will follow our debates on this matter with close interest. I am sorry to say that the most expert authorities have not yet decided. It does seem to me that the night air would be bound to be unhealthy for our children, but there are many distinguished authorities on both sides. Well, I could go on talking forever,—as Shakespeare says: a woman's work is seldom done; but I think I'd better join my husband in saying thank you, and sit down. Thank you. [*She sits down.*]

ANNOUNCER. Oh, Mrs. Antrobus!

MRS. ANTROBUS. Yes?

ANNOUNCER. We understand that you are about to celebrate a wedding anniversary. I know our listeners would like to extend their felicitations and hear a few words from you on that subject.

MRS. ANTROBUS. I have been asked by this kind gentleman . . . yes, my friends, this spring Mr. Antrobus and I will be celebrating our five thousandth wedding anniversary.

I don't know if I speak for my husband, but I can say that, as for me, I regret every moment of it.

[*Laughter of confusion*]

I beg your pardon. What I *mean* to say is that I do not regret one moment of it. I hope none of you catch my cold. We have two children. We've always had two children, though it hasn't always been the same two. But as I say, we have two fine children, and we're very grateful for that. Yes, Mr. Antrobus and I have been married five thousand years. Each wedding anniversary reminds me of the times when there were no weddings. We had to crusade for marriage. Perhaps there are some women within the sound of my voice who remember that crusade and those struggles; we fought for it, didn't we? We chained ourselves to lampposts and we made disturbances in the Senate,—anyway, at last we women got the ring.

A few men helped us, but I must say that most men blocked our way at every step: they said we were unfeminine.

I only bring up these unpleasant memories, because I see some signs of backsliding from that great victory.

Oh, my fellow mammals, keep hold of that.

My husband says that the watchword for the year is Enjoy Yourselves. I think that's very open to misunderstanding.

My watchword for the year is: Save the Family. It's held together for over five thousand years: Save it! Thank you.

ANNOUNCER. Thank you, Mrs. Antrobus.

[*The transparency disappears.*]

We had hoped to show you the Beauty Contest that took place here today. President Antrobus, an experienced judge of pretty girls, gave the title of Miss Atlantic City 1942, to Miss Lily-Sabina Fairweather, charming hostess of our Boardwalk Bingo Parlor.

Unfortunately, however, our time is up, and I must take you to some views of the Convention City and conveeners,—enjoying themselves.

[*A burst of music; the curtain rises.*
The Boardwalk. The audience is sitting in the ocean. A handrail of scarlet cord stretches across the front of the stage. A ramp—also with scarlet handrail—descends to the right corner of the orchestra pit where a great scarlet beach umbrella or a cabana stands. Front and right stage left are benches facing the sea; attached to each bench is a street lamp.
The only scenery is two cardboard cutouts six feet high, rep-

resenting shops at the back of the stage. Reading from left to right they are: SALT WATER TAFFY; FORTUNE TELLER; *then the blank space;* BINGO PARLOR; TURKISH BATH. *They have practical doors, that of the Fortune Teller's being hung with bright gypsy curtains.*

By the left proscenium and rising from the orchestra pit is the weather signal; it is like the mast of a ship with crossbars. From time to time black disks are hung on it to indicate the storm and hurricane warnings. Three roller chairs, pushed by melancholy NEGROES *file by empty. Throughout the act they traverse the stage in both directions.*

From time to time, CONVEENERS, *dressed like* MR. ANTROBUS, *cross the stage. Some walk sedately by; others engage in inane horseplay. The old gypsy* FORTUNE TELLER *is seated at the door of her shop, smoking a corncob pipe.*

From the Bingo Parlor comes the voice of the CALLER.]

BINGO CALLER. A-nine; A-nine. C-twenty-six; C-twenty-six. A-four; A-four. B-twelve.

CHORUS. [*Backstage*] Bingo!!!

[*The front of the Bingo Parlor shudders, rises a few feet in the air and returns to the ground trembling.*]

FORTUNE TELLER. [*Mechanically, to the unconscious back of a passerby, pointing with her pipe*] Bright's disease! Your partner's deceiving you in that Kansas City deal. You'll have six grandchildren. Avoid high places. [*She rises and shouts after another:*] Cirrhosis of the liver!

[SABINA *appears at the door of the Bingo Parlor. She hugs about her a blue raincoat that almost conceals her red bathing suit. She tries to catch the* FORTUNE TELLER'S *attention.*]

SABINA. Sssssst! Esmeralda! Sssssst!

FORTUNE TELLER. Keck!

SABINA. Has President Antrobus come along yet?

FORTUNE TELLER. No, no, no. Get back there. Hide yourself.

SABINA. I'm afraid I'll miss him. Oh, Esmeralda, if I fail in this, I'll die; I know I'll die. President Antrobus!!! And I'll be his wife! If it's the last thing I'll do, I'll be Mrs. George Antrobus.—Esmeralda, tell me my future.

FORTUNE TELLER. Keck!

SABINA. All right, I'll tell *you* my future. [*Laughing dreamily and tracing it out with one finger on the palm of her hand*] I've won the Beauty Contest in Atlantic City,—well, I'll win the Beauty Contest of the whole world. I'll take President Antrobus away from that wife of his. Then I'll take every man away from his wife. I'll turn the whole earth upside down.

FORTUNE TELLER. Keck!

SABINA. When all those husbands just think about me they'll get dizzy. They'll faint in the streets. They'll have to lean against lampposts.—Esmeralda, who was Helen of Troy?

FORTUNE TELLER. [*Furiously*] Shut your foolish mouth. When Mr. Antrobus comes along you can see what you can do. Until then,—go away.

> [SABINA *laughs. As she returns to the door of her Bingo Parlor a group of* CONVEENERS *rush over and smother her with attentions:* "Oh, Miss Lily, you know me. You've known me for years."]

SABINA. Go away, boys, go away. I'm after bigger fry than you are. —Why, Mr. Simpson!! How *dare* you!! I expect that even you nobodies must have girls to amuse you; but where you find them and what you do with them, is of absolutely no interest to me.

> [*Exit. The* CONVEENERS *squeal with pleasure and stumble in after her. The* FORTUNE TELLER *rises, puts her pipe down on the stool, unfurls her voluminous skirts, gives a sharp wrench to her bodice and strolls toward the audience, swinging her hips like a young woman.*]

FORTUNE TELLER. I tell the future. Keck. Nothing easier. Everybody's future is in their face. Nothing easier.

But who can tell your past,—eh? Nobody!

Your youth,—where did it go? It slipped away while you weren't looking. While you were asleep. While you were drunk? Puh! You're like our friends, Mr. and Mrs. Antrobus; you lie awake nights trying to know your past. What did it mean? What was it trying to say to you?

Think! Think! Split your heads. I can't tell the past and neither can you. If anybody tries to tell you the past, take my word for it they're charlatans! Charlatans! But I can tell the future.

> [*She suddenly barks at a passing chair-pusher.*]

Apoplexy!

> [*She returns to the audience.*]

Nobody listens.—Keck! I see a face among you now—I won't embarrass him by pointing him out, but, listen, it may be you: Next year the watchsprings inside you will crumple up. Death by regret,—Type Y. It's in the corners of your mouth. You'll decide that you should have lived for pleasure, but that you missed it. Death by regret,—Type Y. . . . Avoid mirrors. You'll try to be angry,—but no!—no anger.

> [*Far forward, confidentially*]

And now what's the immediate future of our friends, the Antrobuses? Oh, you've seen it as well as I have, keck,—that dizziness of the head; that Great Man dizziness? The inventor of beer and gunpowder. The sudden fits of temper and then the long stretches of inertia? "I'm a sultan; let my slave girls fan me?"

You know as well as I what's coming. Rain. Rain. Rain in floods. The deluge. But first you'll see shameful things—shameful things. Some of you will be saying: "Let him drown. He's not worth saving. Give the whole thing up." I can see it in your faces. But you're wrong. Keep your doubts and despairs to yourselves.

Again there'll be the narrow escape. The survival of a handful. From destruction,—total destruction.

[*She points sweeping with her hand to the stage.*]

Even of the animals, a few will be saved: two of a kind, male and female, two of a kind.

[*The heads of* CONVEENERS *appear about the stage and in the orchestra pit, jeering at her.*]

CONVEENERS. Charlatan! Madam Kill-joy! Mrs. Jeremiah! Charlatan!

FORTUNE TELLER. And *you!* Mark my words before it's too late. Where'll *you* be?

CONVEENERS. The croaking raven. Old dust and ashes. Rags, bottles, sacks.

FORTUNE TELLER. Yes, stick out your tongues. You can't stick your tongues out far enough to lick the death-sweat from your foreheads. It's too late to work now—bail out the flood with your soup spoons. You've had your chance and you've lost.

CONVEENERS. Enjoy yourselves!!!

[*They disappear. The* FORTUNE TELLER *looks off left and puts her finger on her lip.*]

FORTUNE TELLER. They're coming—the Antrobuses. Keck. Your hope. Your despair. Your selves.

[*Enter from the left,* MR. *and* MRS. ANTROBUS *and* GLADYS.]

MRS. ANTROBUS. Gladys Antrobus, stick your stummick in.

GLADYS. But it's easier this way.

MRS. ANTROBUS. Well, it's too bad the new president has such a clumsy daughter, that's all I can say. Try and be a lady.

FORTUNE TELLER. Aijah! That's been said a hundred billion times.

MRS. ANTROBUS. Goodness! Where's Henry? He was here just a minute ago. Henry!

[*Sudden violent stir. A roller chair appears from the left. About it are dancing in great excitement* HENRY *and a* NEGRO CHAIR-PUSHER.]

HENRY. [*Slingshot in hand*] I'll put your eye out. I'll make you yell, like you never yelled before.

NEGRO. [*At the same time*] Now, I warns you. I warns you. If you make me mad, you'll get hurt.

ANTROBUS. Henry! What is this? Put down that slingshot.

MRS. ANTROBUS. [*At the same time*] Henry! HENRY! Behave yourself.

FORTUNE TELLER. That's right, young man. There are too many people in the world as it is. Everybody's in the way, except one's self.

HENRY. All I wanted to do was—have some fun.

NEGRO. Nobody can't touch my chair, nobody, without I allow 'em to. You get clean away from me and you get away fast.

[*He pushes his chair off, muttering.*]

ANTROBUS. What were you doing, Henry?

HENRY. Everybody's always getting mad. Everybody's always trying to push you around. I'll make him sorry for this; I'll make him sorry.

ANTROBUS. Give me that slingshot.

HENRY. I won't. I'm sorry I came to this place. I wish I weren't here. I wish I weren't anywhere.

MRS. ANTROBUS. Now, Henry, don't get so excited about nothing. I declare I don't know what we're going to do with you. Put your slingshot in your pocket, and don't try to take hold of things that don't belong to you.

ANTROBUS. After this you can stay home. I wash my hands of you.

MRS. ANTROBUS. Come now, let's forget all about it. Everybody take a good breath of that sea air and calm down.

[*A passing* CONVEENER *bows to* ANTROBUS *who nods to him.*]

Who was that you spoke to, George?

ANTROBUS. Nobody, Maggie. Just the candidate who ran against me in the election.

MRS. ANTROBUS. The man who ran against you in the election!!

[*She turns and waves her umbrella after the disappearing* CONVEENER.]

My husband didn't speak to you and he never will speak to you.

ANTROBUS. Now, Maggie.

MRS. ANTROBUS. After those lies you told about him in your speeches! Lies, that's what they were.

GLADYS AND HENRY. Mama, everybody's looking at you. Everybody's laughing at you.

MRS. ANTROBUS. If you must know, my husband's a SAINT, a downright SAINT, and you're not fit to speak to him on the street.

ANTROBUS. Now, Maggie, now, Maggie, that's enough of that.

MRS. ANTROBUS. George Antrobus, you're a perfect worm. If you won't stand up for yourself, I will.

GLADYS. Mama, you just act awful in public.

MRS. ANTROBUS. [*Laughing*] Well, I must say I enjoyed it. I feel better. Wish his wife had been there to hear it. Children, what do you want to do?

GLADYS. Papa, can we ride in one of those chairs? Mama, I want to ride in one of those chairs.

MRS. ANTROBUS. No, sir. If you're tired you just sit where you are. We have no money to spend on foolishness.

ANTROBUS. I guess we have money enough for a thing like that. It's one of the things you do at Atlantic City.

MRS. ANTROBUS. Oh, we have? I tell you it's a miracle my children have shoes to stand up in. I didn't think I'd ever live to see them pushed around in chairs.

ANTROBUS. We're on a vacation, aren't we? We have a right to some treats, I guess. Maggie, some day you're going to drive me crazy.

MRS. ANTROBUS. All right, go. I'll just sit here and laugh at you. And you can give me my dollar right in my hand. Mark my words, a rainy day is coming. There's a rainy day ahead of us. I feel it in my bones. Go on, throw your money around. I can starve. I've starved before. I know how.

> [*A* CONVEENER *puts his head through Turkish Bath window, and says with raised eyebrows:*]

CONVEENER. Hello, George. How are ya? I see where you brought the WHOLE family along.

MRS. ANTROBUS. And what do you mean by that?

> [CONVEENER *withdraws head and closes window.*]

ANTROBUS. Maggie, I tell you there's a limit to what I can stand. God's Heaven, haven't I worked *enough?* Don't I get *any* vacation? Can't I even give my children so much as a ride in a roller chair?

MRS. ANTROBUS. [*Putting out her hand for raindrops*] Anyway, it's going to rain very soon and you have your broadcast to make.

ANTROBUS. Now, Maggie, I warn you. A man can stand a family only just so long. I'm warning you.

> [*Enter* SABINA *from the Bingo Parlor. She wears a flounced red silk bathing suit, 1905. Red stockings, shoes, parasol. She bows demurely to* ANTROBUS *and starts down the ramp.* ANTROBUS *and the* CHILDREN *stare at her.* ANTROBUS *bows gallantly.*]

MRS. ANTROBUS. Why, George Antrobus, how can you say such a thing! You have the best family in the world.

ANTROBUS. Good morning, Miss Fairweather.

> [SABINA *finally disappears behind the beach umbrella or in a cabana in the orchestra pit.*]

MRS. ANTROBUS. Who on earth was that you spoke to, George?

ANTROBUS. [*Complacent, mock-modest*] Hm . . . m . . . just a . . . solambaka keray.

MRS. ANTROBUS. What? I can't understand you.

GLADYS. Mama, wasn't she beautiful?

HENRY. Papa, introduce her to me.

MRS. ANTROBUS. Children, will you be quiet while I ask your father a simple question?—Who did you say it was, George?

ANTROBUS. Why-uh . . . a friend of mine. Very nice refined girl.

MRS. ANTROBUS. I'm waiting.

ANTROBUS. Maggie, that's the girl I gave the prize to in the beauty contest, —that's Miss Atlantic City 1942.

MRS. ANTROBUS. Hm! She looked like Sabina to me.

HENRY. [*At the railing*] Mama, the lifeguard knows her, too. Mama, he knows her well.

ANTROBUS. Henry, come here.—She's a very nice girl in every way and the sole support of her aged mother.

MRS. ANTROBUS. So was Sabina, so was Sabina; and it took a wall of ice to open your eyes about Sabina.—Henry, come over and sit down on this bench.

ANTROBUS. She's a very different matter from Sabina. Miss Fairweather is a college graduate, Phi Beta Kappa.

MRS. ANTROBUS. Henry, you sit here by Mama. Gladys—

ANTROBUS. [*Sitting*] Reduced circumstances have required her taking a position as hostess in a Bingo Parlor; but there isn't a girl with higher principles in the country.

MRS. ANTROBUS. Well, let's not talk about it.—Henry, I haven't seen a whale yet.

ANTROBUS. She speaks seven languages and has more culture in her little finger than you've acquired in a lifetime.

MRS. ANTROBUS. [*Assumed amiability*] All right, all right, George. I'm glad to know there are such superior girls in the Bingo Parlors.—Henry, what's that?

[*Pointing at the storm signal, which has one black disk*]

HENRY. What is it, Papa?

ANTROBUS. What? Oh, that's the storm signal. One of those black disks means bad weather; two means storm; three means hurricane; and four means the end of the world.

[*As they watch it a second black disk rolls into place.*]

MRS. ANTROBUS. Goodness! I'm going this very minute to buy you all some raincoats.

GLADYS. [*Putting her cheek against her father's shoulder*] Mama, don't go yet. I like sitting this way. And the ocean coming in and coming in. Papa, don't you like it?

MRS. ANTROBUS. Well, there's only one thing I lack to make me a perfectly happy woman: I'd like to see a whale.

HENRY. Mama, we saw two. Right out there. They're delegates to the convention. I'll find you one.

GLADYS. Papa, ask me something. Ask me a question.

ANTROBUS. Well . . . how big's the ocean?

GLADYS. Papa, you're teasing me. It's—three-hundred and sixty million square-miles—and—it—covers—three-fourths—of—the—earth's—surface —and—its—deepest-place—is—five—and—a—half—miles—deep—and— its—average—depth—is—twelve-thousand—feet. No, Papa, ask me something hard, real hard.

MRS. ANTROBUS. [*Rising*] Now I'm going off to buy those raincoats. I think that bad weather's going to get worse and worse. I hope it doesn't come before your broadcast. I should think we have about an hour or so.

HENRY. I hope it comes and zzzzzz everything before it. I hope it—

MRS. ANTROBUS. Henry!—George, I think . . . maybe, it's one of those storms that are just as bad on land as on the sea. When you're just as safe and safer in a good stout boat.

HENRY. There's a boat out at the end of the pier.

MRS. ANTROBUS. Well, keep your eye on it. George, you shut your eyes and get a good rest before the broadcast.

ANTROBUS. Thundering Judas, do I have to be told when to open and shut my eyes? Go and buy your raincoats.

MRS. ANTROBUS. Now, children, you have ten minutes to walk around. Ten minutes. And, Henry: control yourself. Gladys, stick by your brother and don't get lost.

    [*They run off.*]

Will you be all right, George?

    [CONVEENERS *suddenly stick their heads out of the Bingo Parlor and Salt Water Taffy store, and voices rise from the orchestra pit.*]

CONVEENERS. George. Geo-r-r-rge! George! Leave the old hen-coop at home, George. Do-mes-ticated Georgie!

MRS. ANTROBUS. [*Shaking her umbrella*] Low common oafs! That's what they are. Guess a man has a right to bring his wife to a convention, if he wants to. [*She starts off.*] What's the matter with a family, I'd like to know. What else have they got to offer?

    [*Exit.* ANTROBUS *has closed his eyes. The* FORTUNE TELLER *comes out of her shop and goes over to the left proscenium. She leans against it watching* SABINA *quizzically.*]

FORTUNE TELLER. Heh! Here she comes!

SABINA. [*Loud whisper*] What's he doing?

FORTUNE TELLER. Oh, he's ready for you. Bite your lips, dear, take a long breath and come on up.

SABINA. I'm nervous. My whole future depends on this. I'm nervous.

FORTUNE TELLER. Don't be a fool. What more could you want? He's forty-five. His head's a little dizzy. He's just been elected president. He's never known any other woman than his wife. Whenever he looks at her he realizes that she knows every foolish thing he's ever done.

SABINA. [*Still whispering*] I don't know why it is, but every time I start one of these I'm nervous.

> [*The* FORTUNE TELLER *stands in the center of the stage watching the following.*]

FORTUNE TELLER. You make me tired.

SABINA. First tell me my fortune.

> [*The* FORTUNE TELLER *laughs dryly and makes the gesture of brushing away a nonsensical question.* SABINA *coughs and says:*]

Oh, Mr. Antrobus,—dare I speak to you for a moment?

ANTROBUS. What?—Oh, certainly, certainly, Miss Fairweather.

SABINA. Mr. Antrobus . . . I've been so unhappy. I've wanted . . . I've wanted to make sure that you don't think that I'm the kind of girl who goes out for beauty contests.

FORTUNE TELLER. That's the way!

ANTROBUS. Oh, I understand. I understand perfectly.

FORTUNE TELLER. Give it a little more. Lean on it.

SABINA. I knew you would. My mother said to me this morning: Lily, she said, that fine Mr. Antrobus gave you the prize because he saw at once that you weren't the kind of girl who'd go in for a thing like that. But, honestly, Mr. Antrobus, in this world, honestly, a good girl doesn't know where to turn.

FORTUNE TELLER. Now you've gone too far.

ANTROBUS. My dear Miss Fairweather!

SABINA. You wouldn't know how hard it is. With that lovely wife and daughter you have. Oh, I think Mrs. Antrobus is the finest woman I ever saw. I wish I were like her.

ANTROBUS. There, there. There's . . . uh . . . room for all kinds of people in the world, Miss Fairweather.

SABINA. How wonderful of you to say that. How generous!—Mr. Antrobus, have you a moment free? . . . I'm afraid I may be a little conspicuous here . . . could you come down, for just a moment, to my beach cabana . . . ?

ANTROBUS. Why-uh . . . yes, certainly . . . for a moment . . . just for a moment.

SABINA. There's a deck chair there. Because: you know you *do* look tired. Just this morning my mother said to me: Lily, she said, I hope Mr. Antrobus is getting a good rest. His fine strong face has deep deep lines in it. Now isn't it true, Mr. Antrobus: you work too hard?

FORTUNE TELLER. Bingo! [*She goes into her shop.*]

SABINA. Now you will just stretch out. No, I shan't say a word, not a word. I shall just sit there,—privileged. That's what I am.

ANTROBUS. [*Taking her hand*] Miss Fairweather . . . you'll . . . spoil me.

SABINA. Just a moment. I have something I wish to say to the audience.— Ladies and gentlemen. I'm not going to play this particular scene tonight. It's just a short scene and we're going to skip it. But I'll tell you what takes place and then we can continue the play from there on. Now in this scene—

ANTROBUS. [*Between his teeth*] But, Miss Somerset!

SABINA. I'm sorry. I'm sorry. But I have to skip it. In this scene, I talk to Mr. Antrobus, and at the end of it he decides to leave his wife, get a divorce at Reno and marry me. That's all.

ANTROBUS. Fitz!—Fitz!

SABINA. So that now I've told you we can jump to the end of it,—where you say:

[*Enter in fury* MR. FITZPATRICK, *the stage manager.*]

MR. FITZPATRICK. Miss Somerset, we insist on your playing this scene.

SABINA. I'm sorry, Mr. Fitzpatrick, but I can't and I won't. I've told the audience all they need to know and now we can go on.

[*Other* ACTORS *begin to appear on the stage, listening.*]

MR. FITZPATRICK. And *why* can't you play it?

SABINA. Because there are some lines in that scene that would hurt some people's feelings and I don't think the theater is a place where people's feelings ought to be hurt.

MR. FITZPATRICK. Miss Somerset, you can pack up your things and go home. I shall call the understudy and I shall report you to Equity.

SABINA. I sent the understudy up to the corner for a cup of coffee and if Equity tries to penalize me I'll drag the case right up to the Supreme Court. Now listen, everybody, there's no need to get excited.

MR. FITZPATRICK *and* ANTROBUS. Why can't you play it . . . what's the matter with the scene?

SABINA. Well, if you must know, I have a personal guest in the audience tonight. Her life hasn't been exactly a happy one. I wouldn't have my friend hear some of these lines for the whole world. I don't suppose it occurred to the author that some other women might have gone through the experience of losing their husbands like this. Wild horses wouldn't drag from me the details of my friend's life, but . . . well, they'd been married twenty years, and before he got rich, why, she'd done the washing and everything.

MR. FITZPATRICK. Miss Somerset, your friend will forgive you. We must play this scene.

SABINA. Nothing, nothing will make me say some of those lines . . . about "a man outgrows a wife every seven years" and . . . and that one about "the Mohammedans being the only people who looked the subject square in the face." Nothing.

MR. FITZPATRICK. Miss Somerset! Go to your dressing room. I'll *read* your lines.

SABINA. Now everybody's nerves are on edge.

ANTROBUS. Skip the scene.

[MR. FITZPATRICK *and the other* ACTORS *go off.*]

SABINA. Thank you. I knew you'd understand. We'll do just what I said. So Mr. Antrobus is going to divorce his wife and marry me. Mr. Antrobus, you say: "It won't be easy to lay all this before my wife."

[*The* ACTORS *withdraw.* ANTROBUS *walks about, his hand to his forehead, muttering:*]

ANTROBUS. Wait a minute. I can't get back into it as easily as all that. "My wife is a very obstinate woman." Hm . . . then you say . . . hm . . . Miss Fairweather, I mean Lily, it won't be easy to lay all this before my wife. It'll hurt her feelings a little.

SABINA. Listen, George: *other* people haven't got feelings. Not in the same way that we have,—we who are presidents like you and prize-winners like me. Listen, other people haven't got feelings; they just imagine they have. Within two weeks they go back to playing bridge and going to the movies. Listen, dear: everybody in the world except a few people like you and me are just people of straw. Most people have no insides at all. Now that you're president you'll see that. Listen, darling, there's a kind of secret society at the top of the world,—like you and me,—that know this. The world was made for us. What's life anyway? Except for two things, pleasure and power, what is life? Boredom! Foolishness. You know it is. Except for those two things, life's nau-se-at-ing. So,—come here!

[*She moves close. They kiss.*]

So.

Now when your wife comes, it's really very simple; just tell her.

ANTROBUS. Lily, Lily: you're a wonderful woman.

SABINA. Of course I am.

[*They enter the cabana and it hides them from view. Distant roll of thunder. A third black disk appears on the weather signal. Distant thunder is heard.* MRS. ANTROBUS *appears carrying parcels. She looks about, seats herself on the bench left, and fans herself with her handkerchief. Enter* GLADYS *right, followed by two* CONVEENERS. *She is wearing red stockings.*]

MRS. ANTROBUS. Gladys!

GLADYS. Mama, here I am.

MRS. ANTROBUS. Gladys Antrobus!!! Where did you get those dreadful things?

GLADYS. Wha-a-t? Papa liked the color.

MRS. ANTROBUS. You go back to the hotel this minute!

GLADYS. I won't. I won't. Papa liked the color.

MRS. ANTROBUS. All right. All right. You stay here. I've a good mind to let your father see you that way. You stay right here.

GLADYS. I . . . I don't want to stay if . . . if you don't think he'd like it.

MRS. ANTROBUS. Oh . . . it's all one to me. I don't care what happens. I don't care if the biggest storm in the whole world comes. Let it come. [*She folds her hands.*] Where's your brother?

GLADYS. [*In a small voice*] He'll be here.

MRS. ANTROBUS. Will he? Well, let him get into trouble. I don't care. I don't know where your father is, I'm sure.

[*Laughter from the cabana*]

GLADYS. [*Leaning over the rail*] I think he's . . . Mama, he's talking to the lady in the red dress.

MRS. ANTROBUS. Is that so? [*Pause*] We'll wait till he's through. Sit down here beside me and stop fidgeting . . . what are you crying about?

[*Distant thunder. She covers* GLADYS'S *stockings with a raincoat.*]

GLADYS. You don't like my stockings.

[*Two* CONVEENERS *rush in with a microphone on a standard and various paraphernalia. The* FORTUNE TELLER *appears at the door of her shop. Other characters gradually gather.*]

BROADCAST OFFICIAL. Mrs. Antrobus! Thank God we've found you at last. Where's Mr. Antrobus? We've been hunting everywhere for him. It's about time for the broadcast to the conventions of the world.

MRS. ANTROBUS. [*Calm*] I expect he'll be here in a minute.

BROADCAST OFFICIAL. Mrs. Antrobus, if he doesn't show up in time, I hope you will consent to broadcast in his place. It's the most important broadcast of the year.

[SABINA *enters from cabana followed by* ANTROBUS.]

MRS. ANTROBUS. No, I shan't. I haven't one single thing to say.

BROADCAST OFFICIAL. Then won't you help us find him, Mrs. Antrobus? A storm's coming up. A hurricane. A deluge!

SECOND CONVEENER. [*Who has sighted* ANTROBUS *over the rail*] Joe! Joe! Here he is.

BROADCAST OFFICIAL. In the name of God, Mr. Antrobus, you're on the air in five minutes. Will you kindly please come and test the instrument? That's all we ask. If you just please begin the alphabet slowly.

> [ANTROBUS, *with set face, comes ponderously up the ramp. He stops at the point where his waist is level with the stage and speaks authoritatively to the* OFFICIALS.]

ANTROBUS. I'll be ready when the time comes. Until then, move away. Go away. I have something I wish to say to my wife.

BROADCAST OFFICIAL. [*Whimpering*] Mr. Antrobus! This is the most important broadcast of the year.

> [*The* OFFICIALS *withdraw to the edge of the stage.* SABINA *glides up the ramp behind* ANTROBUS.]

SABINA. [*Whispering*] Don't let her argue. Remember arguments have nothing to do with it.

ANTROBUS. Maggie, I'm moving out of the hotel. In fact, I'm moving out of everything. For good. I'm going to marry Miss Fairweather. I shall provide generously for you and the children. In a few years you'll be able to see that it's all for the best. That's all I have to say.

BROADCAST OFFICIAL. Mr. Antrobus! I hope you'll be ready. This is the most important broadcast of the year.

GLADYS. What did Papa say, Mama? I didn't hear what Papa said.

BROADCAST OFFICIAL. Mr. Antrobus. All we want to do is test your voice with the alphabet.

BINGO ANNOUNCER. A—nine; A—nine. D—forty-two; D—forty-two. C—thirty; C—thirty.
B—seventeen; B—seventeen. C—forty; C—forty.

CHORUS. Bingo!!

ANTROBUS. Go away. Clear out.

MRS. ANTROBUS. [*Composedly with lowered eyes*] George, I can't talk to you until you wipe those silly red marks off your face.

ANTROBUS. I think there's nothing to talk about. I've said what I have to say.

SABINA. Splendid!!

ANTROBUS. You're a fine woman, Maggie, but . . . but a man has his own life to lead in the world.

MRS. ANTROBUS. Well, after living with you for five thousand years I guess I have a right to a word or two, haven't I?

ANTROBUS. [*To* SABINA] What can I answer to that?

SABINA. Tell her that conversation would only hurt her feelings. It's-kinder-in-the-long-run-to-do-it-short-and-quick.

ANTROBUS. I want to spare your feelings in every way I can, Maggie.

BROADCAST OFFICIAL. Mr. Antrobus, the hurricane signal's gone up. We could begin right now.

MRS. ANTROBUS. [*Calmly, almost dreamily*] I didn't marry you because you were perfect. I didn't even marry you because I loved you. I married you because you gave me a promise.

[*She takes off her ring and looks at it.*]

That promise made up for your faults. And the promise I gave you made up for mine. Two imperfect people got married and it was the promise that made the marriage.

ANTROBUS. Maggie, . . . I was only nineteen.

MRS. ANTROBUS. [*She puts her ring back on her finger.*] And when our children were growing up, it wasn't a house that protected them; and it wasn't our love, that protected them—it was that promise.
And when that promise is broken—this can happen!

[*With a sweep of the hand she removes the raincoat from* GLADYS'S *stockings.*]

ANTROBUS. [*Stretches out his arm, apoplectic*] Gladys!! Have you gone crazy? Has everyone gone crazy? [*Turning on* SABINA] You did this. You gave them to her.

SABINA. I never said a word to her.

ANTROBUS. [*To* GLADYS] You go back to the hotel and take those horrible things off.

GLADYS. [*Pert*] Before I go, I've got something to tell you,—it's about Henry.

MRS. ANTROBUS. [*Claps her hands peremptorily*] Stop your noise,—I'm taking her back to the hotel, George. Before I go I have a letter. . . . I have a message to throw into the ocean. [*Fumbling in her handbag*] Where is the plagued thing? Here it is.

[*She flings something—invisible to us—far over the heads of the audience to the back of the auditorium.*]

It's a bottle. And in the bottle's a letter. And in the letter is written all the things that a woman knows.
It's never been told to any man and it's never been told to any woman, and if it finds its destination, a new time will come. We're not what books and plays say we are. We're not what advertisements say we are. We're not in the movies and we're not on the radio.
We're not what you're all told and what you think we are: We're ourselves.

And if any man can find one of us he'll learn why the whole universe was set in motion. And if any man harm any one of us, his soul—the only soul he's got—had better be at the bottom of that ocean,—and that's the only way to put it. Gladys, come here. We're going back to the hotel.

[*She drags* GLADYS *firmly off by the hand, but* GLADYS *breaks away and comes down to speak to her father.*]

SABINA. Such goings-on. Don't give it a minute's thought.

GLADYS. Anyway, I think you ought to know that Henry hit a man with a stone. He hit one of those colored men that push the chairs and the man's very sick. Henry ran away and hid and some policemen are looking for him very hard. And I don't care a bit if you don't want to have anything to do with mama and me, because I'll never like you again and I hope nobody ever likes you again,—so there!

[*She runs off.* ANTROBUS *starts after her.*]

ANTROBUS. I . . . I have to go and see what I can do about this.

SABINA. You stay right here. Don't you go now while you're excited. Gracious sakes, all these things will be forgotten in a hundred years. Come, now, you're on the air. Just say anything,—it doesn't matter what. Just a lot of birds and fishes and things.

BROADCAST OFFICIAL. Thank you, Miss Fairweather. Thank you very much. Ready, Mr. Antrobus.

ANTROBUS. [*Touching the microphone*] What is it, what is it? Who am I talking to?

BROADCAST OFFICIAL. Why, Mr. Antrobus! To our order and to all the other orders.

ANTROBUS. [*Raising his head*] What are all those birds doing?

BROADCAST OFFICIAL. Those are just a few of the birds. Those are the delegates to our convention,—two of a kind.

ANTROBUS. [*Pointing into the audience*] Look at the water. Look at them all. Those fishes jumping. The children should see this!—There's Maggie's whales!! Here are your whales, Maggie!!

BROADCAST OFFICIAL. I hope you're ready, Mr. Antrobus.

ANTROBUS. And look on the beach! You didn't tell me these would be here!

SABINA. Yes, George. Those are the animals.

BROADCAST OFFICIAL. [*Busy with the apparatus*] Yes, Mr. Antrobus, those are the vertebrates. We hope the lion will have a word to say when you're through. Step right up, Mr. Antrobus, we're ready. We'll just have time before the storm. [*Pause. In a hoarse whisper*] They're wait-ing.

[*It has grown dark. Soon after he speaks a high whistling noise begins. Strange veering lights start whirling about the stage. The other characters disappear from the stage.*]

ANTROBUS. Friends. Cousins. Four score and ten billion years ago our forefather brought forth upon this planet the spark of life,—

[*He is drowned out by thunder. When the thunder stops the* FORTUNE TELLER *is seen standing beside him.*]

FORTUNE TELLER. Antrobus, there's not a minute to be lost. Don't you see the four disks on the weather signal? Take your family into that boat at the end of the pier.

ANTROBUS. My family? I have no family. Maggie! Maggie! They won't come.

FORTUNE TELLER. They'll come.—Antrobus! Take these animals into that boat with you. All of them,—two of each kind.

SABINA. George, what's the matter with you? This is just a storm like any other storm.

ANTROBUS. Maggie!

SABINA. Stay with me, we'll go . . . [*Losing conviction*] This is just another thunderstorm,—isn't it? Isn't it?

ANTROBUS. Maggie!!!

[MRS. ANTROBUS *appears beside him with* GLADYS.]

MRS. ANTROBUS. [*Matter-of-fact*] Here I am and here's Gladys.

ANTROBUS. Where've you been? Where have you been? Quick, we're going into that boat out there.

MRS. ANTROBUS. I know we are. But I haven't found Henry.

[*She wanders off into the darkness calling "Henry!"*]

SABINA. [*Low urgent babbling, only occasionally raising her voice*] I don't believe it. I don't believe it's anything at all. I've seen hundreds of storms like this.

FORTUNE TELLER. There's no time to lose. Go. Push the animals along before you. Start a new world. Begin again.

SABINA. Esmeralda! George! Tell me,—is it really serious?

ANTROBUS. [*Suddenly very busy*] Elephants first. Gently, gently.—Look where you're going.

GLADYS. [*Leaning over the ramp and striking an animal on the back*] Stop it or you'll be left behind!

ANTROBUS. Is the kangaroo there? *There* you are! Take those turtles in your pouch, will you? [*To some other animals, pointing to his shoulder*] Here! You jump up here. You'll be trampled on.

GLADYS. [*To her father, pointing below*] Papa, look,—the snakes!

MRS. ANTROBUS. I can't find Henry. Hen-ry!

ANTROBUS. Go along. Go along. Climb on their backs.—Wolves! Jackals, —whatever you are,—tend to your own business!

GLADYS. [*Pointing, tenderly*] Papa,—look.

SABINA. Mr. Antrobus—take me with you. Don't leave me here. I'll work. I'll help. I'll do anything.

[THREE CONVEENERS *cross the stage, marching with a banner.*]

CONVEENERS. George! What are you scared of?—George! Fellas, it looks like rain.—"Maggie, where's my umbrella?"—George, setting up for Barnum and Bailey.

ANTROBUS. [*Again catching his wife's hand*] Come on now, Maggie,—the pier's going to break any minute.

MRS. ANTROBUS. I'm not going a step without Henry. Henry!

GLADYS. [*On the ramp*] Mama! Papa! Hurry. The pier's cracking, Mama. It's going to break.

MRS. ANTROBUS. Henry! Cain! CAIN!

[HENRY *dashes onto the stage and joins his mother.*]

HENRY. Here I am, Mama.

MRS. ANTROBUS. Thank God!—now come quick.

HENRY. I didn't think you wanted me.

MRS. ANTROBUS. Quick! [*She pushes him down before her into the aisle.*]

SABINA. [*All the* ANTROBUSES *are now in the theater aisle.* SABINA *stands at the top of the ramp.*] Mrs. Antrobus, take me. Don't you remember me? I'll work. I'll help. Don't leave me here!

MRS. ANTROBUS. [*Impatiently, but as though it were of no importance*] Yes, yes. There's a lot of work to be done. Only hurry.

FORTUNE TELLER. [*Now dominating the stage. To* SABINA *with a grim smile*] Yes, go—back to the kitchen with you.

SABINA. [*Half down the ramp. To* FORTUNE TELLER] I don't know why my life's always being interrupted—just when everything's going fine!!

[*She dashes up the aisle. Now the* CONVEENERS *emerge doing a serpentine dance on the stage. They jeer at the* FORTUNE TELLER.]

CONVEENERS. Get a canoe—there's not a minute to be lost! Tell me my future, Mrs. Croaker.

FORTUNE TELLER. Paddle in the water, boys—enjoy yourselves.

VOICE from the BINGO PARLOR. A-nine; A-nine. C-twenty-four. C-twenty-four.

CONVEENERS. Rags, bottles, and sacks.

FORTUNE TELLER. Go back and climb on your roofs. Put rags in the cracks under your doors.—Nothing will keep out the flood. You've had your chance. You've had your day. You've failed. You've lost.

VOICE from the BINGO PARLOR. B-fifteen. B-fifteen.

FORTUNE TELLER. [*Shading her eyes and looking out to sea*] They're safe. George Antrobus! Think it over! A new world to make,—think it over!

Curtain

Act III

[*Just before the curtain rises, two sounds are heard from the stage: a cracked bugle call.*

The curtain rises on almost total darkness. Almost all the flats composing the walls of MR. ANTROBUS'S *house, as of Act I, are up, but they lean helter-skelter against one another, leaving irregular gaps. Among the flats missing are two in the back wall, leaving the frames of the window and door crazily out of line. Off stage, back right, some red Roman fire is burning. The bugle call is repeated. Enter* SABINA *through the tilted door. She is dressed as a Napoleonic camp follower, "la fille du regiment," in begrimed reds and blues.*]

SABINA. Mrs. Antrobus! Gladys! Where are you?
The war's over. The war's over. You can come out. The peace treaty's been signed.
Where are they?—Hmpf! Are they dead, too? Mrs. Annnntrobus! Glaaaadus! Mr. Antrobus'll be here this afternoon. I just saw him downtown. Huuuurry and put things in order. He says that now that the war's over we'll all have to settle down and be perfect.

[*Enter* MR. FITZPATRICK, *the stage manager, followed by the whole company, who stand waiting at the edges of the stage.* MR. FITZPATRICK *tries to interrupt* SABINA.]

MR. FITZPATRICK. Miss Somerset, we have to stop a moment.
SABINA. They may be hiding out in the back—
MR. FITZPATRICK. Miss Somerset! We have to stop a moment.
SABINA. What's the matter?
MR. FITZPATRICK. There's an explanation we have to make to the audience.—Lights, please. [*To the actor who plays* MR. ANTROBUS] Will you explain the matter to the audience?

[*The lights go up. We now see that a balcony or elevated runway has been erected at the back of the stage, back of the wall of the Antrobus house. From its extreme right and left ends ladderlike steps descend to the floor of the stage.*]

ANTROBUS. Ladies and gentlemen, an unfortunate accident has taken place backstage. Perhaps I should say *another* unfortunate accident.
SABINA. I'm sorry. I'm sorry.
ANTROBUS. The management feels, in fact, we all feel that you are due an

apology. And now we have to ask your indulgence for the most serious mishap of all. Seven of our actors have . . . have been taken ill. Apparently, it was something they ate. I'm not exactly clear what happened.

[*All the* ACTORS *start to talk at once.* ANTROBUS *raises his hand.*]

Now, now—not all at once. Fitz, do you know what it was?

MR. FITZPATRICK. Why, it's perfectly clear. These seven actors had dinner together, and they ate something that disagreed with them.

SABINA. Disagreed with them!!! They have ptomaine poisoning. They're in Bellevue Hospital this very minute in agony. They're having their stomachs pumped out this very minute, in perfect agony.

ANTROBUS. Fortunately, we've just heard they'll all recover.

SABINA. It'll be a miracle if they do, a downright miracle. It was the lemon meringue pie.

ACTORS. It was the fish . . . it was the canned tomatoes . . . it was the fish.

SABINA. It was the lemon meringue pie. I saw it with my own eyes; it had blue mold all over the bottom of it.

ANTROBUS. Whatever it was, they're in no condition to take part in this performance. Naturally, we haven't enough understudies to fill all those roles; but we do have a number of splendid volunteers who have kindly consented to help us out. These friends have watched our rehearsals, and they assure me that they know the lines and the business very well. Let me introduce them to you—my dresser, Mr. Tremayne,—himself a distinguished Shakespearean actor for many years; our wardrobe mistress, Hester; Miss Somerset's maid, Ivy; and Fred Bailey, captain of the ushers in this theater.

[*These persons bow modestly.* IVY *and* HESTER *are Negro women.*]

Now this scene takes place near the end of the act. And I'm sorry to say we'll need a short rehearsal, just a short run-through. And as some of it takes place in the auditorium, we'll have to keep the curtain up. Those of you who wish can go out in the lobby and smoke some more. The rest of you can listen to us, or . . . or just talk quietly among yourselves, as you choose. Thank you. Now will you take it over, Mr. Fitzpatrick?

MR. FITZPATRICK. Thank you.—Now for those of you who are listening perhaps I should explain that at the end of this act, the men have come back from the War and the family's settled down in the house. And the author wants to show the hours of the night passing by over their heads, and the planets crossing the sky . . . uh . . . over their heads. And he says—this is hard to explain—that each of the hours of the night is a philosopher, or a great thinker. Eleven o'clock, for instance, is Aristotle. And nine o'clock is Spinoza. Like that. I don't suppose it means anything. It's just a kind of poetic effect.

SABINA. Not mean anything! Why, it certainly does. Twelve o'clock goes by saying those wonderful things. I think it means that when people are asleep they have all those lovely thoughts, much better than when they're awake.

IVY. Excuse me, I think it means,—excuse me, Mr. Fitzpatrick—

SABINA. What were you going to say, Ivy?

IVY. Mr. Fitzpatrick, you let my father come to a rehearsal; and my father's a Baptist minister, and he said that the author meant that—just like the hours and stars go by over our heads at night, in the same way the ideas and thoughts of the great men are in the air around us all the time and they're working on us, even when we don't know it.

MR. FITZPATRICK. Well, well, maybe that's it. Thank you, Ivy. Anyway,— the hours of the night are philosophers. My friends, are you ready? Ivy, can you be eleven o'clock? "This good estate of the mind possessing its object in energy we call divine." Aristotle.

IVY. Yes, sir. I know that and I know twelve o'clock and I know nine o'clock.

MR. FITZPATRICK. Twelve o'clock? Mr. Tremayne, the Bible.

TREMAYNE. Yes.

MR. FITZPATRICK. Ten o'clock? Hester,—Plato?

[*She nods eagerly.*]

Nine o'clock, Spinoza,—Fred?

BAILEY. Yes, *sir.*

[FRED BAILEY *picks up a great gilded cardboard numeral IX and starts up the steps to the platform.* MR. FITZPATRICK *strikes his forehead.*]

MR. FITZPATRICK. The planets!! We forgot all about the planets.

SABINA. O my God! The planets! Are they sick too?

[ACTORS *nod.*]

MR. FITZPATRICK. Ladies and gentlemen, the planets are singers. Of course, we can't replace them, so you'll have to imagine them singing in this scene. Saturn sings from the orchestra pit down here. The Moon is way up there. And Mars with a red lantern in his hand, stands in the aisle over there— Tz-tz-tz. It's too bad; it all makes a very fine effect. However! Ready—nine o'clock: Spinoza.

BAILEY. [*Walking slowly across the balcony, left to right*] "After experience had taught me that the common occurrences of daily life are vain and futile—"

FITZPATRICK. Louder, Fred. "And I saw that all the objects of my desire and fear—"

BAILEY. "And I saw that all the objects of my desire and fear were in themselves nothing good nor bad save insofar as the mind was affected by them—"

FITZPATRICK. Do you know the rest? All right. Ten o'clock. Hester, Plato.

HESTER. "Then tell me, O Critias, how will a man choose the ruler that shall rule over him? Will he not—"

FITZPATRICK. Thank you. Skip to the end, Hester.

HESTER. ". . . can be multiplied a thousandfold in its effects among the citizens."

FITZPATRICK. Thank you.—Aristotle, Ivy?

IVY. "This good estate of the mind possessing its object in energy we call divine. This we mortals have occasionally and it is this energy which is pleasantest and best. But God has it always. It is wonderful in us; but in him how much more wonderful."

FITZPATRICK. Midnight. Midnight, Mr. Tremayne. That's right,—you've done it before.—All right, everybody. You know what you have to do.— Lower the curtain. House lights up. Act Three of *The Skin of Our Teeth*.

[*As the curtain descends he is heard saying:*]

You volunteers, just wear what you have on. Don't try to put on the costumes today.

[*House lights go down. The Act begins again. The bugle call. Curtain rises. Enter* SABINA.]

SABINA. Mrs. Antrobus! Gladys! Where are you?
The war's over.—You've heard all this—

[*She gabbles the main points.*]

Where—are—they? Are—they—dead, too, et cetera.
I—just—saw—Mr.—Antrobus—downtown, et cetera. [*Slowing up.*]
He says that now that the war's over we'll all have to settle down and be perfect. They may be hiding out in the back somewhere. Mrs. An-tro-bus.

[*She wanders off. It has grown lighter.*
A trap door is cautiously raised and MRS. ANTROBUS *emerges waist-high and listens. She is disheveled and worn; she wears a tattered dress and a shawl half covers her head. She talks down through the trap door.*]

MRS. ANTROBUS. It's getting light. There's still something burning over there—Newark, or Jersey City. What? Yes, I could swear I heard someone moving about up here. But I can't see anybody. I say: I can't see anybody.

[*She starts to move about the stage.* GLADYS's *head appears at the trap door. She is holding a* BABY.]

GLADYS. Oh, Mama. Be careful.

MRS. ANTROBUS. Now, Gladys, you stay out of sight.

GLADYS. Well, let me stay here just a minute. I want the baby to get some of this fresh air.

MRS. ANTROBUS. All right, but keep your eyes open. I'll see what I can find. I'll have a good hot plate of soup for you before you can say Jack Robinson. Gladys Antrobus! Do you know what I think I see? There's old Mr. Hawkins sweeping the sidewalk in front of his A. and P. store. Sweeping it with a broom. Why, he must have gone crazy, like the others! I see some other people moving about, too.

GLADYS. Mama, come back, come back.

[MRS. ANTROBUS *returns to the trap door and listens.*]

MRS. ANTROBUS. Gladys, there's something in the air. Everybody's movement's sort of different. I see some women walking right out in the middle of the street.

SABINA'S VOICE. Mrs. An-tro-bus!

MRS. ANTROBUS AND GLADYS. What's that?!!

SABINA'S VOICE. Glaaaadys! Mrs. An-tro-bus!

[*Enter* SABINA.]

MRS. ANTROBUS. Gladys, that's Sabina's voice as sure as I live.—Sabina! Sabina!—Are you *alive?!!*

SABINA. Of course, I'm alive. How've you girls been?—*Don't* try and kiss me. I never want to kiss another human being as long as I live. Sh-sh, there's nothing to get emotional about. Pull yourself together, the war's over. Take a deep breath,—the war's over.

MRS. ANTROBUS. The war's over!! I don't believe you. I don't believe you. I can't believe you.

GLADYS. Mama!

SABINA. Who's that?

MRS. ANTROBUS. That's Gladys and her baby. I don't believe you. Gladys, Sabina says the war's over. Oh, Sabina.

SABINA. [*Leaning over the* BABY] Goodness! Are there any babies left in the world! Can it *see?* And can it cry and everything?

GLADYS. Yes, he can. He notices everything very well.

SABINA. Where on earth did you get it? Oh, I won't ask.—Lord, I've lived all these seven years around camp and I've forgotten how to behave.—Now we've got to think about the men coming home.—Mrs. Antrobus, go and wash your face, I'm ashamed of you. Put your best clothes on. Mr. Antrobus'll be here this afternoon. I just saw him downtown.

MRS. ANTROBUS *and* GLADYS. He's alive!! He'll be here!! Sabina, you're not joking?

MRS. ANTROBUS. And Henry?

SABINA. [*Dryly*] Yes, Henry's alive, too, that's what they say. Now don't stop to talk. Get yourselves fixed up. Gladys, you look terrible. Have you any decent clothes?

[SABINA *has pushed them toward the trap door.*]

MRS. ANTROBUS. [*Half down*] Yes, I've something to wear just for this very day. But, Sabina,—who won the war?

SABINA. Don't stop now,—just wash your face.

> [*A whistle sounds in the distance.*]

Oh, my God, what's that silly little noise?

MRS. ANTROBUS. Why, it sounds like . . . it sounds like what used to be the noon whistle at the shoe-polish factory. [*Exit.*]

SABINA. That's what it is. Seems to me like peacetime's coming along pretty fast—shoe polish!

GLADYS. [*Half down*] Sabina, how soon after peacetime begins does the milkman start coming to the door?

SABINA. As soon as he catches a cow. Give him time to catch a cow, dear.

> [*Exit* GLADYS. SABINA *walks about a moment, thinking.*]

Shoe polish! My, I'd forgotten what peacetime was like.

> [*She shakes her head, then sits down by the trap door and starts talking down the hole.*]

Mrs. Antrobus, guess what I saw Mr. Antrobus doing this morning at dawn. He was tacking up a piece of paper on the door of the Town Hall. You'll die when you hear: it was a recipe for grass soup, for a grass soup that doesn't give you the diarrhea. Mr. Antrobus is still thinking up new things.—He told me to give you his love. He's got all sorts of ideas for peacetime, he says. No more laziness and idiocy, he says. And oh, yes! Where are his books? What? Well, pass them up. The first thing he wants to see are his books. He says if you've burnt those books, or if the rats have eaten them, he says it isn't worthwhile starting over again. Everybody's going to be beautiful, he says, and diligent, and very intelligent.

> [*A hand reaches up with two volumes.*]

What language is that? Pu-u-gh,—mold! And he's got such plans for you, Mrs. Antrobus. You're going to study history and algebra—and so are Gladys and I—and philosophy. You should hear him talk:

> [*Taking two more volumes*]

Well, these are in English, anyway.—To hear him talk, seems like he expects you to be a combination, Mrs. Antrobus, of a saint and a college professor, and a dancehall hostess, if you know what I mean.

> [*Two more volumes*]

Ugh. German!

> [*She is lying on the floor; one elbow bent, her cheek on her hand, meditatively.*]

Yes, peace will be here before we know it. In a week or two we'll be asking the Perkinses in for a quiet evening of bridge. We'll turn on the radio and hear how to be big successes with a new toothpaste. We'll trot down to the movies and see how girls with wax faces live—all *that* will begin again. Oh, Mrs. Antrobus, God forgive me but I enjoyed the war. Everybody's at their best in wartime. I'm sorry it's over. And, oh, I forgot! Mr. Antrobus sent you another message—can you hear me?—

> [*Enter* HENRY, *blackened and sullen. He is wearing torn overalls, but has one gaudy admiral's epaulette hanging by a thread from his right shoulder, and there are vestiges of gold and scarlet braid running down his left trouser leg. He stands listening.*]

Listen! Henry's never to put foot in this house again, he says. He'll kill Henry on sight, if he sees him.

You don't know about Henry??? Well, where have you been? What? Well, Henry rose right to the top. Top of *what?* Listen, I'm telling you. Henry rose from corporal to captain, to major, to general.—I don't know how to say it, but the enemy is *Henry;* Henry *is* the enemy. Everybody knows that.

HENRY. He'll kill me, will he?

SABINA. Who are *you?* I'm not afraid of you. The war's over.

HENRY. I'll kill him so fast. I've spent seven years trying to find him; the others I killed were just substitutes.

SABINA. Goodness! It's Henry!—

> [*He makes an angry gesture.*]

Oh, I'm not afraid of you. The war's over, Henry Antrobus, and you're not any more important than any other unemployed. You go away and hide yourself, until we calm your father down.

HENRY. The first thing to do is to burn up those old books; it's the ideas he gets out of those old books that . . . that makes the whole world so you can't live in it.

> [*He reels forward and starts kicking the books about, but suddenly falls down in a sitting position.*]

SABINA. You leave those books alone!! Mr. Antrobus is looking forward to them a-special.—Gracious sakes, Henry, you're so tired you can't stand up. Your mother and sister'll be here in a minute and we'll think what to do about you.

HENRY. What did they ever care about me?

SABINA. There's that old whine again. All you people think you're not loved enough, nobody loves you. Well, you start being lovable and we'll love you.

HENRY. [*Outraged*] I don't want anybody to love me.

SABINA. Then stop talking about it all the time.

HENRY. I *never* talk about it. The last thing I want is anybody to pay any attention to me.

SABINA. I can hear it behind every word you say.

HENRY. I want everybody to hate me.

SABINA. Yes, you've decided that's second best, but it's still the same thing. —Mrs. Antrobus! Henry's here. He's so tired he can't stand up.

[MRS. ANTROBUS *and* GLADYS, *with her* BABY, *emerge. They are dressed as in Act I.* MRS. ANTROBUS *carries some objects in her apron, and* GLADYS *has a blanket over her shoulder.*]

MRS. ANTROBUS *and* GLADYS. Henry! Henry! Henry!

HENRY. [*Glaring at them*] Have you anything to eat?

MRS. ANTROBUS. Yes, I have, Henry. I've been saving it for this very day, —two good baked potatoes. No! Henry! one of them's for your father. Henry!! Give me that other potato back this minute.

[SABINA *sidles up behind him and snatches the other potato away.*]

SABINA. He's so dog-tired he doesn't know what he's doing.

MRS. ANTROBUS. Now you just rest there, Henry, until I can get your room ready. Eat that potato good and slow, so you can get all the nourishment out of it.

HENRY. You all might as well know right now that I haven't come back here to live.

MRS. ANTROBUS. Sh. . . . I'll put this coat over you. Your room's hardly damaged at all. Your football trophies are a little tarnished, but Sabina and I will polish them up tomorrow.

HENRY. Did you hear me? I don't live here. I don't belong to anybody.

MRS. ANTROBUS. Why, how can you say a thing like that! You certainly do belong right here. Where else would you want to go? Your forehead's feverish, Henry, seems to me. You'd better give me that gun, Henry. You won't need that any more.

GLADYS. [*Whispering*] Look, he's fallen asleep already, with his potato half-chewed.

SABINA. Puh! The terror of the world.

MRS. ANTROBUS. Sabina, you mind your own business, and start putting the room to rights.

[HENRY *has turned his face to the back of the sofa.* MRS. ANTROBUS *gingerly puts the revolver in her apron pocket, then helps* SABINA. SABINA *has found a rope hanging from the ceiling. Grunting, she hangs all her weight on it, and as she pulls the walls begin to move into their right places.* MRS. ANTROBUS *brings the overturned tables, chairs and hassock into the positions of Act I.*]

SABINA. That's all we do—always beginning again! Over and over again. Always beginning again.

[*She pulls on the rope and a part of the wall moves into place. She stops. Meditatively*]

How do we know that it'll be any better than before? Why do we go on pretending? Some day the whole earth's going to have to turn cold anyway, and until that time all these other things'll be happening again: it will be more wars and more walls of ice and floods and earthquakes.

MRS. ANTROBUS. Sabina!! Stop arguing and go on with your work.

SABINA. All right. I'll go on just out of *habit,* but I won't believe in it.

MRS. ANTROBUS. [*Aroused*] Now, Sabina. I've let you talk long enough. I don't want to hear any more of it. Do I have to explain to you what everybody knows,—everybody who keeps a home going? Do I have to say to you what nobody should ever *have* to say, because they can read it in each other's eyes?

Now listen to me:

[MRS. ANTROBUS *takes hold of the rope.*]

I could live for seventy years in a cellar and make soup out of grass and bark, without ever doubting that this world has a work to do and will do it. Do you hear me?

SABINA. [*Frightened*] Yes, Mrs. Antrobus.

MRS. ANTROBUS. Sabina, do you see this house,—216 Cedar Street,—do you see it?

SABINA. Yes, Mrs. Antrobus.

MRS. ANTROBUS. Well, just to have known this house is to have seen the idea of what we can do some day if we keep our wits about us. Too many people have suffered and died for my children for us to start reneging now. So we'll start putting this house to rights. Now, Sabina, go and see what you can do in the kitchen.

SABINA. Kitchen! Why is it that however far I go away, I always find myself back in the kitchen? [*Exit.*]

MRS. ANTROBUS. [*Still thinking over her last speech, relaxes and says with a reminiscent smile*] Goodness gracious, wouldn't you know that my father was a parson? It was just like I heard his own voice speaking and he's been dead five thousand years. There! I've gone and almost waked Henry up.

HENRY. [*Talking in his sleep, indistinctly*] Fellows . . . what have they done for us? . . . Blocked our way at every step. Kept everything in their own hands. And you've stood it. When are you going to wake up?

MRS. ANTROBUS. Sh, Henry. Go to sleep. Go to sleep. Go to sleep.—Well, that looks better. Now let's go and help Sabina.

GLADYS. Mama, I'm going out into the backyard and hold the baby right up in the air. And show him that we don't have to be afraid any more.

[*Exit* GLADYS *to the kitchen.* MRS. ANTROBUS *glances at* HENRY, *exits into kitchen.* HENRY *thrashes about in his sleep. Enter* AN-TROBUS, *his arms full of bundles, chewing the end of a carrot. He has a slight limp. Over the suit of Act I he is wearing an overcoat too long for him, its skirts trailing on the ground. He lets his bundles fall and stands looking about. Presently his attention is fixed on* HENRY, *whose words grow clearer.*]

HENRY. All right! What have you got to lose? What have they done for us? That's right—nothing. Tear everything down. I don't care what you smash. We'll begin again and we'll show 'em.

[ANTROBUS *takes out his revolver and holds it pointing downward. With his back toward the audience he moves toward the footlights.* HENRY'S *voice grows louder and he wakes with a start. They stare at one another. Then* HENRY *sits up quickly. Throughout the following scene* HENRY *is played, not as a misunderstood or misguided young man, but as a representation of strong unreconciled evil.*]

All right! Do something. [*Pause*] Don't think I'm afraid of you, either. All right, do what you were going to do. Do it. [*Furiously*] Shoot me, I tell you. You don't have to think I'm any relation of yours. I haven't got any father or any mother, or brothers or sisters. And I don't want any. And what's more I haven't got anybody over me; and I never will have. I'm alone, and that's all I want to be: alone. So you can shoot me.

ANTROBUS. You're the last person I wanted to see. The sight of you dries up all my plans and hopes. I wish I were back at war still, because it's easier to fight you than to live with you. War's a pleasure—do you hear me?—War's a pleasure compared to what faces us now: trying to build up a peacetime with you in the middle of it. [ANTROBUS walks up to the window.]

HENRY. I'm not going to be a part of any peacetime of yours. I'm going a long way from here and make my own world that's fit for a man to live in. Where a man can be free, and have a chance, and do what he wants to do in his own way.

ANTROBUS. [*His attention arrested; thoughtfully. He throws the gun out of the window and turns with hope*] . . . Henry, let's try again.

HENRY. Try what? Living *here?*—Speaking polite downtown to all the old men like you? Standing like a sheep at the street corner until the red light turns to green? Being a good boy and a good sheep, like all the stinking ideas you get out of your books? Oh, no. I'll make a world, and I'll show you.

ANTROBUS. [*Hard*] How can you make a world for people to live in, unless you've first put order in yourself? Mark my words: I shall continue fighting you until my last breath as long as you mix up your idea of liberty with your idea of hogging everything for yourself. I shall have no pity on you. I shall pursue you to the far corners of the earth. You and I want the same thing; but until you think of it as something that everyone has a right to, you are my deadly enemy and I will destroy you.—I hear your mother's voice in the kitchen. Have you seen her?

HENRY. I have no mother. Get it into your head. I don't belong here. I have nothing to do here. I have no home.

ANTROBUS. Then why did you come here? With the whole world to choose from, why did you come to this one place: 216 Cedar Street, Excelsior, New Jersey. . . . Well?

HENRY. What if I did? What if I wanted to look at it once more, to see if—

ANTROBUS. Oh, you're related, all right—When your mother comes in you must behave yourself. Do you hear me?

HENRY. [*Wildly*] What is this?—*must behave* yourself. Don't you say *must* to me.

ANTROBUS. Quiet!

[*Enter* MRS. ANTROBUS *and* SABINA.]

HENRY. Nobody can say *must* to me. All my life everybody's been crossing me,—everybody, everything, all of you. I'm going to be free, even if I have to kill half the world for it. Right now, too. Let me get my hands on his throat. I'll show him.

[*He advances toward* ANTROBUS. *Suddenly,* SABINA *jumps between them and calls out in her own person:*]

SABINA. Stop! Stop! Don't play this scene. You know what happened last night. Stop the play.

[*The men fall back, panting.* HENRY *covers his face with his hands.*]

Last night you almost strangled him. You became a regular savage. Stop it!

HENRY. It's true. I'm sorry. I don't know what comes over me. I have nothing against him personally. I respect him very much . . . I . . . I admire him. But something comes over me. It's like I become fifteen years old again. I . . . I . . . listen: my own father used to whip me and lock me up every Saturday night. I never had enough to eat. He never let me have enough money to buy decent clothes. I was ashamed to go downtown. I never could go to the dances. My father and my uncle put rules in the way of everything I wanted to do. They tried to prevent my living at all.—I'm sorry. I'm sorry.

MRS. ANTROBUS. [*Quickly*] No, go on. Finish what you were saying. Say it all.

HENRY. In this scene it's as though I were back in high school again. It's like I had some big emptiness inside me,—the emptiness of being hated and blocked at every turn. And the emptiness fills up with the one thought that you have to strike and fight and kill. Listen, it's as though you have to kill somebody else so as not to end up killing yourself.

SABINA. That's not true. I knew your father and your uncle and your mother. You imagined all that. Why, they did everything they could for you. How can you say things like that? They didn't lock you up.

HENRY. They did. They did. They wished I hadn't been born.

SABINA. That's not true.

ANTROBUS. [*In his own person, with self-condemnation, but cold and proud*] Wait a minute. I have something to say, too. It's not wholly his fault that he wants to strangle me in this scene. It's my fault, too. He wouldn't feel that way unless there were something in me that reminded him of all that. He talks about an emptiness. Well, there's an emptiness in me, too. Yes,—work, work, work,—that's all I do. I've ceased to *live*. No wonder he feels that anger coming over him.

MRS. ANTROBUS. There! At least you've said it.

SABINA. We're all just as wicked as we can be, and that's the God's truth.

MRS. ANTROBUS. [*Nods a moment, then comes forward; quietly*] Come. Come and put your head under some cold water.

SABINA. [*In a whisper*] I'll go with him. I've known him a long while. You have to go on with the play. Come with me.

[HENRY *starts out with* SABINA, *but turns at the exit and says to* ANTROBUS:]

HENRY. Thanks. Thanks for what you said. I'll be all right tomorrow. I won't lose control in that place. I promise.

[*Exeunt* HENRY *and* SABINA. ANTROBUS *starts toward the front door, fastens it.* MRS. ANTROBUS *goes up stage and places the chair close to table.*]

MRS. ANTROBUS. George, do I see you limping?

ANTROBUS. Yes, a little. My old wound from the other war started smarting again. I can manage.

MRS. ANTROBUS. [*Looking out of the window*] Some lights are coming on, —the first in seven years. People are walking up and down looking at them. Over in Hawkins's open lot they've built a bonfire to celebrate the peace. They're dancing around it like scarecrows.

ANTROBUS. A bonfire! As though they hadn't seen enough things burning, —Maggie,—the dog died?

MRS. ANTROBUS. Oh, yes. Long ago. There are no dogs left in Excelsior.— You're back again! All these years. I gave up counting on letters. The few that arrived were anywhere from six months to a year late.

ANTROBUS. Yes, the ocean's full of letters, along with the other things.

MRS. ANTROBUS. George, sit down, you're tired.

ANTROBUS. No, you sit down. I'm tired but I'm restless. [*Suddenly, as she comes forward*] Maggie! I've lost it. I've lost it.

MRS. ANTROBUS. What, George? What have you lost?

ANTROBUS. The most important thing of all: The desire to begin again, to start building.

MRS. ANTROBUS. [*Sitting in the chair right of the table*] Well, it will come back.

ANTROBUS. [*At the window*] I've lost it. This minute I feel like all those people dancing around the bonfire—just relief. Just the desire to settle down; to slip into the old grooves and keep the neighbors from walking over my lawn.—Hm. But during the war,—in the middle of all that blood and dirt and hot and cold—every day and night, I'd have moments, Maggie, when I *saw* the things that we could do when it was over. When you're at war you think about a better life; when you're at peace you think about a more comfortable one. I've lost it. I feel sick and tired.

MRS. ANTROBUS. Listen! The baby's crying.
I hear Gladys talking. Probably she's quieting Henry again. George, while Gladys and I were living here—like moles, like rats, and when we were at our wits' end to save the baby's life—the only thought we clung to was that you were going to bring something good out of this suffering. In the night, in the dark, we'd whisper about it, starving and sick.—Oh, George, you'll have to get it back again. Think! What else kept us alive all these years? Even now, it's not comfort we want. We can suffer whatever's necessary; only give us back that promise.

[*Enter* SABINA *with a lighted lamp. She is dressed as in Act I.*]

SABINA. Mrs. Antrobus . . .

MRS. ANTROBUS. Yes, Sabina?

SABINA. Will you need me?

MRS. ANTROBUS. No. Sabina, you can go to bed.

SABINA. Mrs. Antrobus, if it's all right with you, I'd like to go to the bonfire and celebrate seeing the war's over. And, Mrs. Antrobus, they've opened the Gem Movie Theater and they're giving away a hand-painted soup tureen to every lady, and I thought one of us ought to go.

ANTROBUS. Well, Sabina, I haven't any money. I haven't seen any money for quite a while.

SABINA. Oh, you don't need money. They're taking anything you can give them. And I have some . . . some . . . Mrs. Antrobus, promise you won't tell anyone. It's a little against the law. But I'll give you some, too.

ANTROBUS. What is it?

SABINA. I'll give you some, too. Yesterday I picked up a lot of . . . of beef cubes!

[MRS. ANTROBUS *turns and says calmly:*]

MRS. ANTROBUS. But, Sabina, you know you ought to give that in to the Center downtown. They know who needs them most.

SABINA. [*Outburst*] Mrs. Antrobus, I didn't make this war. I didn't ask for it. And, in my opinion, after anybody's gone through what we've gone through, they have a right to grab what they can find. You're a very nice man, Mr. Antrobus, but you'd have got on better in the world if you'd realized that dog-eat-dog was the rule in the beginning and always will be. And most of all now. [*In tears*] Oh, the world's an awful place, and you know it is. I used to think something could be done about it; but I know better now. I hate it. I hate it.

[*She comes forward slowly and brings six cubes from the bag.*]

All right. All right. You can have them.

ANTROBUS. Thank you, Sabina.

SABINA. Can I have . . . can I have one to go to the movies?

[ANTROBUS *in silence gives her one.*]

Thank you.

ANTROBUS. Good night, Sabina.

SABINA. Mr. Antrobus, don't mind what I say. I'm just an ordinary girl, you know what I mean, I'm just an ordinary girl. But you're a bright man, you're a very bright man, and of course you invented the alphabet and the wheel, and, my God, a lot of things . . . and if you've got any other plans, my God, don't let me upset them. Only every now and then I've got to go to the movies. I mean my nerves can't stand it. But if you have any ideas about improving the crazy old world, I'm really with you. I really am. Because it's . . . it's . . . Good night.

[*She goes out.* ANTROBUS *starts laughing softly with exhilaration.*]

ANTROBUS. Now I remember what three things always went together when I was able to see things most clearly: three things. Three things: [*He points to where* SABINA *has gone out.*] The voice of the people in their confusion and their need. And the thought of you and the children and this house. And . . . Maggie! I didn't dare ask you: my books! They haven't been lost, have they?

MRS. ANTROBUS. No. There are some of them right here. Kind of tattered.

ANTROBUS. Yes.—Remember, Maggie, we almost lost them once before? And when we finally did collect a few torn copies out of old cellars they ran in everyone's head like a fever. They as good as rebuilt the world. [*Pauses, book in hand, and looks up*] Oh, I've never forgotten for long at a time that living is struggle. I know that every good and excellent thing in the world stands moment by moment on the razor-edge of danger and must be fought for—whether it's a field, or a home, or a country. All I ask is the chance to build new worlds and God has always given us that. And has given us [*Open-*

ing the book] voices to guide us; and the memory of our mistakes to warn us. Maggie, you and I will remember in peacetime all the resolves that were so clear to us in the days of war. We've come a long ways. We've learned. We're learning. And the steps of our journey are marked for us here.

[*He stands by the table turning the leaves of a book.*]

Sometimes out there in the war,—standing all night on a hill—I'd try and remember some of the words in these books. Parts of them and phrases would come back to me. And after a while I used to give names to the hours of the night.

[*He sits, hunting for a passage in the book.*]

Nine o'clock I used to call Spinoza. Where is it: "After experience had taught me—"

[*The back wall has disappeared, revealing the platform.* FRED BAILEY *carrying his numeral has started from left to right.* MRS. ANTROBUS *sits by the table sewing.*]

BAILEY. "After experience had taught me that the common occurrences of daily life are vain and futile; and I saw that all the objects of my desire and fear were in themselves nothing good nor bad save insofar as the mind was affected by them; I at length determined to search out whether there was something truly good and communicable to man."

[*Almost without break* HESTER, *carrying a large Roman numeral ten, starts crossing the platform.* GLADYS *appears at the kitchen door and moves toward her mother's chair.*]

HESTER. "Then tell me, O Critias, how will a man choose the ruler that shall rule over him? Will he not choose a man who has first established order in himself, knowing that any decision that has its spring from anger or pride or vanity can be multiplied a thousandfold in its effects upon the citizens?"

[HESTER *disappears and* IVY, *as eleven o'clock, starts speaking.*]

IVY. "This good estate of the mind possessing its object in energy we call divine. This we mortals have occasionally and it is this energy which is pleasantest and best. But God has it always. It is wonderful in us; but in him how much more wonderful."

[*As* MR. TREMAYNE *starts to speak,* HENRY *appears at the edge of the scene, brooding and unreconciled, but present.*]

TREMAYNE. "In the beginning, God created the Heavens and the Earth; And the Earth was waste and void; And the darkness was upon the face of the deep. And the Lord said let there be light and there was light."

[*Sudden blackout and silence, except for the last strokes of the midnight bell. Then just as suddenly the lights go up, and* SABINA *is standing at the window, as at the opening of the play.*]

SABINA. Oh, oh, oh. Six o'clock and the master not home yet. Pray God nothing serious has happened to him crossing the Hudson River. But I wouldn't be surprised. The whole world's at sixes and sevens, and why the house hasn't fallen down about our ears long ago is a miracle to me.

[*She comes down to the footlights.*]

This is where you came in. We have to go on for ages and ages yet.
You go home.
The end of this play isn't written yet.
Mr. and Mrs. Antrobus! Their heads are full of plans and they're as confident as the first day they began,—and they told me to tell you: good night.

Curtain

FOR STUDY AND DISCUSSION

1. A recurring judgment about man is that his technological advances have not been matched by comparable advances in his general morality. What material in *The Skin of Our Teeth* could be used to support such a judgment? In this context, what is the role of *woman* in the play? of Mrs. Antrobus, for example? of Sabina? of Gladys?

2. Why does Wilder sometimes suggest, usually through Sabina, that the production of the play is not proceeding very smoothly? Along this same line, notice that the play, at its end, returns to its beginning, even to the extent of Sabina's repeating exact lines from the opening scene. Why do you think Wilder has done this? What do you think he has in mind when he has Sabina say, "The end of this play isn't written yet"?

3. There are many examples of conflict in *The Skin of Our Teeth*—both on the story level and on the meaning level—and you should be able to identify them. One of the most interesting is the conflict between Henry and his father. Toward the end of Act II, as "the flood" approaches, Mrs. Antrobus says she will not leave without Henry. She calls out, "Henry! Cain! CAIN!" What is the point here? Later, in Act III, after "the war," Mr. Antrobus and Henry have a most serious confrontation. What points of view toward war, toward books, toward life itself do Mr. Antrobus and Henry represent in this scene?

4. The setting of *Antigone* is ancient Greece; *The Skin of Our Teeth* takes place in contemporary America. With the reminder that the term *setting* is not restricted to the physical environment alone but includes also the prevailing "climate of opinion," can you specify in the case of each play how the setting contributes to the comment on life which the particular play is making?

5. Nowadays, well-known plays are frequently adapted for movie or television

production. What do you think would be the special qualities of each of the two plays that might come through well on these media? Which qualities of each might be diminished or marred by the "cutting" that normally accompanies such adaptations?

6. A play is written to be staged, and certainly much is lost by merely reading it. (Incidentally, can you specify some of the effects likely to be lost if you are confined to reading a play rather than seeing it?) However, there are advantages to the reading approach. What advantages can you suggest? To what extent do the advantages vary for each of the two plays?

7. Following are quotations from three distinguished writers: a poet, a philosopher, and a novelist. All three remarks are especially relevant to the theme of *The Skin of Our Teeth,* but they are also relevant to the more general concern of this section: Commitment. I should like you to be able to express the relevance of each remark.

A. I have been treading on leaves all day until I am autumn-tired.

. . .

They spoke to the fugitive in my heart as if it were leaf to leaf;
They tapped at my eyelids and touched my lips with an invitation to grief.
But it was no reason I had to go because they had to go.
Now up my knee to keep on top of another year of snow.

—ROBERT FROST

B. It is better to be a human being dissatisfied than a pig satisfied; better to be a Socrates dissatisfied than a fool satisfied. And if the fool, or the pig, is of a different opinion, it is because they only know their own side of the question. The other party to the comparison knows both sides.

—JOHN STUART MILL

C. What's wrong with this world is, it's not finished yet. It is not completed to that point where man can put his final signature to the job and say "It is finished. We made it, and it works."

Because only man can complete it. Not God, but man. It is man's high destiny and proof of his immortality too, that his is the choice between ending the world, effacing it from the long annal of time and space, and completing it. This is not only his right, but his privilege too. Like the phoenix it rises from the ashes of its own failure with each generation, until it is your turn now in your flash and flick of time and space which we call today, in this and in all the stations in time and space today and yesterday and tomorrow, where a handful of aged people like me, who should know but no longer can, are facing young people like you who can do, if they only knew where and how to perform this duty, accept this privilege, bear this right.

—WILLIAM FAULKNER

Author Biographies

Conrad Aiken was born in Savannah, Georgia, in 1889. He went to live with a great-grandaunt in New Bedford, Massachusetts at the age of ten, after his father had killed the boy's mother and then committed suicide. Conrad Aiken was graduated with the Harvard class of 1911, together with T. S. Eliot, Walter Lippmann, and several others who became prominent writers. His first book of poetry, Earth Triumphant and Other Tales in Verse, appeared in 1914. His fourth book, Nocturnes of Remembered Spring (1917), was savagely attacked as derivative by one anonymous reviewer in a Chicago newspaper. The reviewer was Aiken himself. He also wrote short stories and novels. Many of the short stories have been deemed remarkable. Aiken's collected Short Stories appeared in 1950. In 1952 he published Ushant, an autobiography which neglected the usual chronological order, both bewildering and delighting its reviewers. His Collected Poems appeared in 1953. Conrad Aiken, one of America's most distinguished poets, has received many awards.

CONRAD AIKEN

Aristotle was born in 384 B.C. in southern Macedonia to a father who was a physician and personal friend of Macedonia's ruler. He went to Athens at the age of seventeen to enter Plato's Academy and remained there until Plato's death some twenty years later. Aristotle then left Athens, and in 343 B.C. he became the tutor of Alexander of Macedon, who eventually won a prodigious empire in a few short years. In 335 B.C. Aristotle returned to Athens, where he founded his own school. Here, as he had done earlier in his career, he not only taught but also carried out and fostered scientific research. After the death of Alexander in 323 B.C., Aristotle found it advisable to withdraw from Athens. He died the following year in Chalcis. Aristotle's surviving works reveal the enormous range of his interests, which included philosophy, logic, rhetoric, politics, social questions, and the physical sciences, especially biology. It is scarcely possible to overstate Aristotle's influence on both Arab and Christian thought during the Middle Ages. From the Renaissance on, the theory of tragedy he developed in his Poetics had a decisive impact upon the development of the drama in France and elsewhere in Europe.

ARISTOTLE

Matthew Arnold was born in Laleham, England, in 1822. He was the son of Dr. Thomas Arnold who, when the boy was six years old, was named headmaster of Rugby School in England. Under Dr. Arnold's firm guidance, what had been a den of disorder and bullying became the prototype of the British "public school." Matthew Arnold studied there for five years, and in 1841 entered Balliol College, Oxford. For most of his life Arnold was Her Majesty's Inspector of Schools, and in this capacity he traveled widely all over England. As a poet he made his mark early, for his winning of the poetry prize at Rugby and of the Newdigate Prize for poetry at Oxford was soon followed by genuine poetic achievement. Among Arnold's best-known poems are "The Scholar-Gypsy" and "Dover

MATTHEW ARNOLD

Beach." In his later years he published many volumes of prose. He wrote on religious matters, and on the social problems to which rapid industrialization had given rise. He also produced an impressive quantity of excellent literary criticism. Arnold earned himself a distinguished place as an "eminent Victorian." He died in 1888, two years after he retired as school inspector.

STEPHEN
VINCENT
BENÉT

Stephen Vincent, the younger brother of William Rose Benét, was born in Bethlehem, Pennsylvania, in 1898, to a family with a long military tradition and marked literary interests. As his father was transferred from one military post to another, the boy moved also, spending long periods of time in Benicia, California, and in Georgia. He was graduated from Yale University in 1919, and took his M.A. degree there the following year. At the age of seventeen, while still an undergraduate, Stephen Vincent Benét had already published his first volume, a series of dramatic monologues in verse. At no later time did he earn his livelihood in any way except as a writer. His greatest and perhaps his most enduring success came to him with the long narrative poem John Brown's Body (1928), which he wrote during a year spent in France. Shortly before his death he wrote another long narrative poem, Western Star (1943), which also was warmly received. The needs of a growing family had stimulated him to turn, however, to the writing of magazine fiction. He proved to have a genuine gift for this, and it is generally recognized that his stories have great literary merit. His best-known and often reprinted story is "The Devil and Daniel Webster" (1936). Like so much of his writing, it reflects his deep involvement in the nation's history. During World War II Benét served in the Office of War Information, writing radio scripts for propaganda purposes. So zealously did he labor at radio scripts and other materials required by the emergency that he seriously affected his health. He died in New York City in 1943.

WILLIAM
ROSE
BENÉT

William, who was twelve years older than his brother Stephen, was born in Fort Hamilton, in New York Harbor, in 1886. The family name, usually assumed to be French, actually comes from the province of Catalonia in northeastern Spain. The boy's great-great-grandfather, an officer in the Spanish navy, settled in St. Augustine, Florida. The grandfather was a Brigadier General in the United States Army, and the boy's father, at the time of his retirement, held the rank of Colonel. William did not adhere to the family's military tradition, however, and emerged with a degree from the Sheffield Scientific School of Yale University in 1907. He did editorial work for a number of magazines, including the Century Magazine and the Saturday Review of Literature which he helped found in 1924, and published a variety of books in prose. But poetry was at the center of his ambitions. In his earlier years as a writer, William Rose Benét published colorful, romantic volumes of verse entitled Merchants of Cathay (1913), The Falcon of God (1914), and Moons of Grandeur (1920). Much later he brought out a long autobiographical poem, The Dust Which Is God (1941), inspired by memories of his second wife, the poet Elinor Wylie, who had died in 1928. The poem was awarded a Pulitzer prize. Benét died in 1950.

Born in Willard, New York, in 1893, Morris Bishop attended high school MORRIS BISHOP in Yonkers, New York, and went on to Cornell University. He graduated in 1914 with an M.A. degree in Romance Languages. Work for a textbook publisher in Boston was brought to an end by military service during World War I. At war's end, the young officer was dispatched as a member of the American Relief Administration mission to Finland. Back in civilian life, Bishop spent a dreary year with a New York advertising agency. He was happy to return to academic life in 1921 as instructor in French and Spanish at Cornell. There he remained throughout his teaching career. Professor Bishop has published a number of biographies, including lives of Pascal, Ronsard, and La Rochefoucauld. On the nonacademic side, he published a mystery novel under a pseudonym and a great amount of light verse. Professor Bishop was named University Historian at Cornell.

Martin Buber was born in Vienna, Austria, in 1878. He studied at the MARTIN BUBER universities of Vienna, Berlin, Zürich, and Leipzig. He held a chair in Jewish philosophy and taught at the university at Frankfurt from 1924 until 1933, when Hitler's accession to power barred him, as a Jew, from further teaching. He left Germany in 1938 and went to Palestine, where he taught at the Hebrew University. Buber's reputation is based on his work in Jewish mysticism and biblical interpretation, and also on his personal philosophy. He became equally well known in Jewish and non-Jewish intellectual and religious circles. The most widely read, in English, of all his books is I and Thou (1937), which stresses the central position of dialogue, of the authentic personal confrontation of man and man. Between Man and Man (1947) clearly marks a rather diminished interest in mysticism and the adoption of an attitude that might be called existential. One great concern of his later years was the need for reconciliation between Arab and Jew. Buber died in 1965.

Chekhov was born in 1860 in the city of Taganrog on the Sea of Azov in ANTON P. CHEKHOV southwestern Russia. His origins were humble. Chekhov's grandfather had bought his freedom from serfdom; his father owned a grocery store. Nevertheless, the boy was enrolled in the local secondary school. His last three years of schooling were spent in considerable isolation, for his father, who had gone bankrupt, went off to Moscow with the other members of the family. Chekhov's first literary endeavors date from this period. In 1879 he too went to Moscow, in order to study medicine. The stories he began to publish in humorous magazines were the only source of income for him and for his mother, two younger brothers, and a sister. By 1885 Chekhov had become a doctor, a career he was never to abandon, and had also attained literary fame. Continuing his work as a writer, he wrote many more excellent short stories, failed as a novelist, and demonstrated his qualities as a dramatist in such remarkable plays as The Sea Gull (1896) and The Cherry Orchard (1904). The Moscow Art Theater founded in 1898, produced Chekhov's plays. If it had not been for this admirably trained company, audiences might not so readily have recognized the plays' strengths and subtleties. Chekhov suffered from tuberculosis and during his last years was obliged to leave the harsh climate of Moscow. He died in 1904 in the little German spa of Badenweiler.

JOSEPH
CONRAD

Teodor Jozef Konrad Nalecz Korzeniowski was born in 1857 in the Russian Ukraine to Polish parents. The parents were arrested in 1863 in connection with an abortive uprising to establish Polish independence, and were forced to live in Vologda, a town to the north of Moscow. The climate was frightful, and within a few years both mother and father were dead. Placed in the charge of a maternal uncle in Cracow, the boy soon grew restive. He was happy to be allowed to join the French navy in 1874. Four years later he signed up with a British merchant ship, and in the sixteen years that followed he spent most of his time on British ships. He passed the examinations for the master's certificate, learned the English language, and became a British citizen. Conrad's long years of travel and bouts of adventure in many corners of the earth provided much of the material for his novels. His first novel, Almayer's Folly, was published in 1895. Forced by ill health to abandon the sea, Conrad and his English wife settled in England. The next few years were a depressing combination of sickness and poverty. Nevertheless, he continued to write steadily and won the esteem of prominent writers and critics. He did not win a substantial following among the public until the eve of World War I. Since then, the great bulk of his work has been rescued from its comparative obscurity. It can be read today with a sense of intimate involvement, with the conviction that Conrad has transposed into literature essential and eternally valid reactions of hope and despair. The Nigger of the Narcissus (1897), Lord Jim (1900), and Youth (1902) are some of his earlier novels. The Secret Agent (1907) depicts the underworld of crime and anarchist conspiracy. At the time of his death in 1924, Conrad left an unfinished novel, Suspense (1925), about Napoleon during his period of exile on the island of Elba.

STEPHEN
CRANE

Stephen Crane, the youngest of fourteen children, was born in 1871 in Newark, New Jersey. His father was a Methodist minister. As a boy Crane led an active life and at the same time was strongly attracted to literature and the theater. Crane spent only a short time at Lafayette College and Syracuse University, where he found more time for baseball than for studying. He made his way to New York City and there, for five years, earned a living by free-lance writing and reporting. His first book, published under a pseudonym and at his own expense, was Maggie: A Girl of the Streets (1893). The subject was too shocking, at that time, to attract a publisher or win an audience. The Red Badge of Courage (1895), on the other hand, brought Crane immediate fame, both at home and abroad. The author of this study of a man's reactions under battle conditions had never known war at first-hand (he had relied, he said, on his own football squad experiences), and he now set out to remedy that lack. As a war correspondent, he reported on the Greco-Turkish War of 1897 and the Spanish-American War of 1898. He did not again live permanently in the United States: His association with Cora Talor gave rise to difficulties, for she had never been divorced from her second husband. Crane settled with her as his wife in Sussex, England where he entertained such friendships as Joseph Conrad and Henry James. But he was unable to shake off the dread disease of tuberculosis, and he died in 1900 in Badenweiler, Germany before he was thirty. Crane is often called one of the first realists in American literature. His prose style and his free verse poems have also been compared to the techniques of the Impressionist painters.

Edward Estlin Cummings was born in 1894 in Cambridge, Massachusetts. He went to school there and entered Harvard University in 1911. He soon involved himself in undergraduate literary activities and published the first of his poems in Eight Harvard Poets (1917). With the entrance of the United States into World War I, Cummings volunteered to serve with an ambulance unit in Europe. The experiences obtained in this way later formed the basis of his autobiographical prose work The Enormous Room (1922). His first individual collection of poetry, Tulips and Chimneys (1923), won him immediate acclaim. Throughout his life he continued to publish volumes of verse at relatively brief intervals. Cummings died in 1962, and his total output is to be found in Poems 1923–1954 (1954) and 95 Poems (1958). Cummings also exhibited his work as a painter and graphic artist. CIOPW (1931) contains reproductions of his works executed in charcoal, ink, pencil, oil, and water colors. The shock aroused by Cummings's innovations in the printed form of his poems has long since receded into the past, and his reputation as a genuine, moving, and sensuous lyric poet is firmly established.

E. E.
CUMMINGS

René Descartes was born in 1596 in the Touraine region of France. In 1604 he was sent to the highly regarded Jesuit school at La Flèche, where he was to remain for eight years. After two years spent in obtaining a law degree, he volunteered in 1618 to serve as an officer in the army of Prince Maurice of Nassau. As a result, he traveled widely in central Europe. Upon his return to Paris, he set out to formulate in writing the views that—as he assures us in his Discourse on Method (1637)—he had begun to reach during his school days at La Flèche. After 1628 he lived in Holland. The condemnation of Galileo by the Church in 1633 for having heretically maintained that the earth moved in orbit around the sun, was a warning to Descartes that too frank an expression of novel opinions could get him into trouble. He did all he could to establish his Catholic orthodoxy, and he clung to the comparative safety of residence among moneymaking Dutch Protestants. Only in 1649 did he give up residence in Holland in answer to a summons from Queen Christina of Sweden. The rigors of a Swedish winter and the eccentric Queen's insistence that he offer her tutoring in the early morning hours were too great a shock for Descartes, who had always coddled himself. In February of the following year, he was carried off by a chill. In addition to the Discourse, which recommends a stance of universal doubt as a means of arriving at absolute certainties, Descartes is renowned for his work in optics, meteorology, mathematics, and mechanics. In his voluminous correspondence Descartes evidenced an unshakable faith in the powers of the human mind in his proposed solutions for a wide range of problems. As a scientific thinker, Descartes was closer to being a pure rationalist and was less of an experimenter than his older contemporary Galileo. He has often been called the father of modern philosophy.

RENÉ
DESCARTES

John Dewey was born in 1859 near Burlington, Vermont. At the age of twenty he received his degree from the University of Vermont. For several years he taught school while continuing his studies. The Johns Hopkins University granted him the degree of Doctor of Philosophy. Dewey's long career as a university professor took him from the University of Michigan to the University of Chicago, where he remained from 1894

JOHN
DEWEY

to 1904, and from there to Columbia University, where he stayed until his retirement in 1929. One of Dewey's most significant activities during the Chicago years was his founding, together with his wife, of the highly original "laboratory school," which set standards for improvements in education. The basis of his practices are expounded in The School and Society (1899) and in many other works. Dewey is regarded as the great inspirer of "progressive education" within the school systems of the United States. He emphasized learning through experience and experimentation rather than by rote. As a philosopher, Dewey has propounded views that have been variously termed "radical empiricism" and "instrumentalism." The term pragmatism is also frequently applied to his thinking, as it is to that of William James. Dewey died in 1952.

EMILY
DICKINSON

Emily Dickinson was born in 1830 in Amherst, Massachusetts, and there she spent her whole life. She never married, and for the last ten years of her existence she never left home. Among the visitors to the house were many people of position and culture, but Emily's strictly literary contacts were very few. She did correspond with Thomas Wentworth Higginson, a literary critic, and asked him if her poems were "alive." Only seven of her poems were published while she lived—all of them anonymous. Her immediate family had no idea of the body of work that Emily was accumulating. After her death in 1886, close to 1,800 poems were discovered, some neatly copied out in the form of little books, but others left incomplete or in a fragmentary state. In the early editions of her work, which Higginson helped edit, punctuation was supplied and rhymes and words were changed to smooth out the poems. The definitive edition of Emily Dickinson's poems was prepared by Thomas H. Johnson and published in three volumes in 1955. The same scholar also edited three volumes of Emily's letters (1958). Her poems, popular in the 1890's when they first appeared, were rediscovered in the 1920's and highly acclaimed. The amazing thing about her work is how she, living in so circumscribed a fashion and with a constricted acquaintance with literature, could express such insights into basic human emotions.

HILDA
DOOLITTLE
(H. D.)

Hilda Doolittle was born in 1886 in Bethlehem, Pennsylvania, where her father was a professor at Lehigh University. He later accepted a position in the Philadelphia area, and there his daughter received her schooling. She went on to Bryn Mawr College, but was forced to leave because of ill health. While convalescing, she turned to the writing of stories and poems. A planned trip to Europe in 1911 turned into lifelong residence. She first spent some time in Italy and France, but a meeting with Ezra Pound in London drew her into the "Imagist" movement. (Later she would be called "the perfect Imagist.") The movement was a revolt against the immediate past in poetry, against the self-indulgent flabbiness and verbal imprecision of much Romantic and later nineteenth-century poetry. Imagists admired the economy and precision of ancient Greek lyric poetry and also found qualities worthy of imitation in the poetry of the Far East. Ezra Pound sent off some of Hilda Doolittle's poems for publication in 1913 in Harriet Monroe's Chicago-based magazine Poetry. The young woman signed her poems simply "H. D.," a practice she was never to abandon. Her first published collection of verse was Sea Garden (1916), and she followed it with a number of translations from the Greek. During the World War II years she found a means of uniting her life-

long interest in the old Greek world with a passionate concern for the present. A trilogy, made up of The Walls Do Not Fall (1944), Tribute to the Angels (1945), and Flowering of the Rod (1946), linked up Christian and Jewish symbolism and pagan myth with the ongoing crisis and with men's hope for a better future. She died in 1961.

Thomas Stearns Eliot was born in 1888 in St. Louis, Missouri. He entered Harvard University in 1906 and, after spending a year at the Sorbonne in Paris, returned to Harvard for advanced study in philosophy and linguistics. During a stay at Merton College, Oxford, he completed his doctoral dissertation. Eliot remained in England and for a while taught school. Then he worked in Lloyd's Bank for eight years, resigning in order to become a director of what is now the Faber and Faber publishing firm. By this time he had been writing poetry for many years and had made the acquaintance in England of Ezra Pound, whose advice he listened to and sometimes accepted. Eliot established for himself a dual reputation, as a poet and as a critic and theoretician of poetry. A number of verse plays, which were both admired and scenically successful, enhanced his prestige. Two of his plays are Murder in the Cathedral (1935) and The Cocktail Party (1949). Eliot came to be the most idolized literary personage on either side of the Atlantic. In 1927 he announced simultaneously his acquisition of British citizenship and conversion to the Church of England. Religious concerns continued to hold his attention for the rest of his life, a fact that is reflected in innumerable ways in his poetry, plays, and criticism. A volume entitled The Complete Poems and Plays was published in 1952. A revised edition of Eliot's Selected Essays appeared in 1950. Eliot died in 1965.

T. S. ELIOT

Ralph Waldo Emerson was born in 1803 in Boston, Massachusetts, the son of a Unitarian minister and descendant of a long line of ecclesiastical personages. It was assumed that he too would enter the Church, and after completion of undergraduate work at Harvard College, he went on to the Harvard Divinity School. For some years he served as pastor in the Second Church of Boston, but a difference of opinion on a theological issue led to his resignation. About this time his young wife died, and to conquer his despondency Emerson set off on a European trip. Upon his return he preached from various pulpits, and instead of seeking a living as a pastor, he transformed himself into a lecturer. Emerson became an outstandingly successful lecturer who could attract crowds even in towns far from New England. He was at the center of a group of friends who, inspired more or less vaguely by German idealist philosophy, gathered together for discussions and acquired the name of Transcendentalists. Somewhat later Emerson was swept up in the antislavery movement. On a second visit to Europe, in 1847 and 1848, he gave many lectures in England and Scotland and was handsomely received by the foremost literary men. In his English Traits (1856), Emerson published an excellent, sympathetic account of that nation's character and history. Emerson died in 1882, and his collected works were published in twelve volumes in 1903–04. Estimates of his stature as a writer have varied considerably. There is widespread agreement, however, that he had, and that some of his writings still retain, the capacity to stimulate younger readers with their message of self-reliance and trust in the inner vision.

RALPH WALDO EMERSON

WILLIAM
FAULKNER

William Faulkner, oldest of four brothers, was born in 1897 in a small town near Oxford, Mississippi. Except for a few years, Faulkner spent all of his life in Oxford. He left high school without graduating, and served for a short time in the Canadian Royal Air Force during World War I. After the war, he attended the University of Mississippi in Oxford for a year, where he did rather badly in English. Faulkner then held a series of odd jobs, including local postmaster, traveled to New Orleans, where he met Sherwood Anderson, and settled down in Oxford to become a writer. His early novels, Soldiers' Pay (1926) and Mosquitoes (1927), received little attention. It was not until Sanctuary, a rather more sensational book, was published that Faulkner was able to make a living as a writer. Faulkner wrote a series of novels about life in Yoknapatawpha County, a name he made up, and its county seat Jefferson, which was very much like Oxford, Mississippi. The Sound and the Fury (1929), As I Lay Dying (1930), Light in August (1932), Absalom, Absalom! (1936) and The Hamlet (1940) are a few titles in the Yoknapatawpha saga. Faulkner wrote about life in the Deep South as it once was and as he saw it in the present. Faulkner won the Nobel prize for literature in 1950. He died in Oxford in 1962.

GUSTAVE
FLAUBERT

Gustave Flaubert, the son of a doctor, was born in 1821 in Rouen, France, and lived there almost all his life until he died in 1880. Three years in Paris did not bring him the law degree he had little interest in obtaining, and a nervous complaint of an obscure nature reinforced in the young man a cautious attitude toward life. Much later he told a friend: "I have always been afraid of life, and life has taken its revenge." Apart from traveling, a taste which his private income made easy to satisfy, Flaubert concentrated single-mindedly on writing novels that would be without an aesthetic flaw. He was in no hurry to break into print and in his maturity congratulated himself on his restraint. He sometimes entertained his friends by reading to them from his unpublished, furiously romantic tales. Writing, as Flaubert practiced it, became an arduous, demanding task. All of his novels, whether contemporary in theme or remote in time, had to be thoroughly researched. To acquire a close familiarity with the period or milieu, he assembled masses of information, but he did not pour all of this into his novels. His aim was to utilize reality in order to create the beautiful. The task of writing was even more agonizing than the gathering of material. Flaubert's most celebrated novel is Madame Bovary (1857). After its publication, the author had to appear in court on a charge of obscenity, but he was acquitted. Subsequent novels include The Sentimental Education (1869) and The Temptation of Saint Anthony (1874). Some modern readers prefer the greater freedom and the careless variety Flaubert revealed in the Correspondence (1887–93), a judgment which would scarcely have pleased Flaubert.

ROBERT
FROST

Robert Lee Frost was born in 1874 in San Francisco. At the age of eleven, he was taken by his widowed mother to live in Lawrence, Massachusetts. He attended classes briefly at Dartmouth College, but left to eke out a living by means of casual employment. Later he entered Harvard University, but once again abandoned his studies to make ends meet. From 1900 on, he combined farming, near Derry, New Hampshire, with teaching. He sold his farm in 1912 and set off with his family for England. His first book of poems, A Boy's Will, was published there in 1913. Ezra Pound helped Frost, as he helped so many other poets, to acquire a reputation in his own country. Returning to the United States in 1915, Frost went back to teaching, but in a more informal way. At a whole series of colleges, in the course of his long life, he functioned as "poet in residence." He also gave frequent readings of his own poetry. As a consequence, he became the most widely known and most affectionately regarded of all American poets. The Complete Poems of Robert Frost were published in 1949; a later collection is In the Clearing (1962). Frost died in 1963.

Of mixed Irish and German ancestry, Robert Graves was born in London, England, in 1895. Military service in World War I interrupted his education, and he did not receive his degree from St. John's College, Oxford, until 1926. In that same year he went to Cairo, Egypt, to teach English literature at the university there. He established his reputation as a poet in the 1920's and has never ceased to write poetry. His name would be found on almost anyone's short list of the most impressive English poets writing in the twentieth century. But after taking up residence on the Spanish Mediterranean island of Majorca, Graves turned with increasing frequency to prose. The novels I, Claudius (1934) and Claudius the God (1935) reconstitute the personality of that Roman emperor, and The White Goddess (1948) is a highly original interpretation of myth. On many different subjects that require immense erudition, Robert Graves never feared to challenge and contradict the established specialists. His poetry has been gathered in Collected Poems (1959), followed by More Poems (1961) and New Poems (1963). A special place in his work is occupied by the autobiographical Goodbye to All That (1929).

ROBERT GRAVES

Thomas Hardy was born in 1840 in a village near Dorchester, England, a region that was later to serve as a setting for some of his fiction. Though his family had been known in those parts since the fifteenth century, they were no longer even modestly prosperous. The boy received a rather slipshod education, supplemented by his own reading, and was apprenticed to a local architect. His move to London in 1862, to work for another architect, offered the young man a fresh start. He continued to read widely and tried his hand at writing verse. Once again living in Dorchester, he turned to the writing of fiction, more out of necessity than from inclination. In 1871 he found acceptance for his second novel, Desperate Remedies, by financing part of the costs of publication. With the publication of Far from the Madding Crowd in 1874, the author, who had recently married, abandoned the profession of architecture. In his later years as a novelist, Hardy became a center of controversy because of the "daring" or "inconoclastic" nature of his work. Jude the Obscure (1896) was declared particularly obnoxious, and Hardy was so embittered at the criticism that he resolved to write no more novels. His Wessex Poems (1898) mark the beginning of a new era in his life. During the next thirty years he wrote more than one thousand poems, varied in theme and evoking different atmospheres. These poems were often knotted and quirky, in striking contrast to the mellifluous verses of other contemporary poets. A particularly ambitious work is The Dynasts (1904–08), an epic drama not intended for the stage. It provides a panorama of all Europe in the years

THOMAS HARDY

that led up to the climactic *Battle of Waterloo*. Hardy died in 1928. His many works were brought together in the twenty-four volumes of the *Wessex* edition (1912–31).

NATHANIEL
HAWTHORNE

Nathaniel Hawthorne (he added the "w" to the family name of Hathorne) was born in 1804 in Salem, Massachusetts. Hawthorne's father, a sea captain, died when the boy was only four years old, and Nathaniel led a sequestered life surrounded by women. He read a great deal and developed an abiding interest in local and colonial history. In 1825 he was graduated from Bowdoin College in Maine. Returning to Salem, he lived an isolated existence for twelve years. During these years he began to publish sketches and tales in newspapers and magazines. His first novel, *Fanshawe*, was published at his own expense in 1828. Later, he tried to obtain and destroy every copy of the novel. A position in the Boston Custom House, which he held from 1837 to 1841, brought him in contact with cultivated people in Boston and Cambridge. Hawthorne continued, however, to suffer from great shyness even in small gatherings. Among his acquaintances was Sophia Peabody, whom he married in 1842. For financial reasons, he went to work in the Salem Custom House. It was during this period of his life that he published his most celebrated novels, *The Scarlet Letter* (1850) and *The House of the Seven Gables* (1851), in which he made use of his unique knowledge of Salem lore. *The Blithedale Romance* (1852) reflects the life of the communal experiment at Brook Farm, in which Hawthorne had briefly participated. In 1852 Hawthorne set sail for Europe. President Franklin Pierce, Hawthorne's friend from college days, had made him the American consul in Liverpool, England. Hawthorne did not return to the United States until 1861. At his death in 1864, four novels in manuscript form were found among his papers. To the present day, the subtlety and passion of Hawthorne's writings and the secretiveness of his personality continue to exercise their fascination on readers and literary scholars.

ERNEST
HEMINGWAY

Born in 1899 in Oak Park, Illinois, Ernest Hemingway was educated in the local schools. His father, a doctor, took the family to the woods of northern Michigan for the summers, and there the boy acquired a lifelong affection for hunting and outdoor living. On leaving high school, Hemingway began to write for the Kansas City Star. An eye injury barred him from service with the armed forces in World War I, but he saw action as an ambulance driver with the Red Cross and was wounded while on the Italian front. After the war Hemingway came home for a short time but found his way back to Europe as a roving correspondent for the Toronto Star. In Paris he made the acquaintance of other expatriate Americans. He began to establish his reputation with the stories collected in *In Our Time* (1925) and especially with the short novel *The Sun Also Rises* (1926). The lean, laconic style that Hemingway achieved in his novels and his many fine short stories came to have an immense effect on fictional writing in English and in many other languages. In his later work, the outstanding novels are *For Whom the Bell Tolls* (1940), which depicts an American hero in Spain during the Spanish-Civil War of 1936–39, and the short novel *The Old Man and the Sea* (1952), at once acclaimed as a classic. Hemingway died in 1961 in his hunting lodge in Ketchum, Idaho, an apparent suicide.

Herrick was born in 1591 in Cheapside, London. His father was a gold-smith, and the boy was apprenticed to his uncle, a jeweler. In 1613 Herrick abandoned his apprenticeship for academic studies at Cambridge University, where he graduated four years later. Back in London, he was friendly with the dramatist Ben Jonson and other prominent literary men. After serving for a while as a military chaplain, in 1629 he became vicar of a parish in Devonshire. His strongly Royalist views led to his expulsion in 1647. Only after the death of Oliver Cromwell and the restoration of the monarchy was he able, in 1662, to return to his parish. Herrick's collected poems published in 1648, contained 1,130 nonreligious poems and only 272 religious ones. These figures may represent the comparative importance of the religious and nonreligious elements in Herrick's outlook. Herrick died in 1674, but his reputation as a lyric poet has survived intact to our own day.

ROBERT
HERRICK

Hopkins, the oldest of nine children, was born in 1844 at Stratford in the English county of Essex. In 1863 he entered Balliol College, Oxford, where he made the acquaintance of Robert Bridges, who later became poet laureate of England. While still an undergraduate, Hopkins, under the influence of John Henry (later Cardinal) Newman, was converted to the Catholic faith. Two years later he decided to become a Jesuit, and he burned all his youthful poems. He was ordained in 1877 and worked thereafter in several parishes. Then he was directed into teaching—first at the Catholic secondary school of Stonyhurst and, from 1884, at University College, Dublin, where he was Professor of Greek. He died in Dublin as a result of typhoid fever. After Hopkins's death in 1889, Bridges edited for publication in 1918 the first collection of Hopkins's poems. For the first time Hopkins's poetry became widely known and appreciated, not only because of its originality but also for its poetic and emotional depth. It was a technical aspect, however—the poet's conception of "sprung rhythm"—that gave rise to particularly intense debate. Hopkins coined the phrase "sprung rhythm" to describe rhythm in which the metrical feet have varying number of syllables but are of equal time length, with accents usually falling on the first syllable.

GERARD
MANLEY
HOPKINS

Aldous Huxley was born in 1894 at Godalming, Surrey, into a family whose members had already shown great intellectual distinction. He was the grandson of Thomas H. Huxley, the celebrated Victorian defender of the theory of organic evolution, and he was also related to the poet Matthew Arnold. Huxley's older brother Julian is a prominent biologist. Because of his poor eyesight, Aldous Huxley was barred from military service in World War I. For a few years he practiced literary journalism, but soon made bold to support himself by writing only what he chose to write. The author of many essays and novels, Huxley was a man of encyclopedic knowledge who also wrote nonfictional words on a wide range of topics. In The Perennial Philosophy (1945), for instance, he attempted, with the help of lavish quotations, to establish the identity of basic doctrine between mystics of many different faiths. Huxley's most famous novel is probably Brave New World (1932). Written during a period when fascism was on the rise, it presents a bleak picture of the human race's political future. Huxley settled in California in 1937, and never again took up residence in England. He died in 1963.

ALDOUS
HUXLEY

HENRY
JAMES

The younger brother of the psychologist William James, Henry James was born in New York City in 1843. His father, an adherent of the occult doctrines known as Swedenborgianism, traveled widely with his family. Henry, as a consequence, was educated mainly by private tutors in the United States, France, Switzerland, and Germany. For a while he attended Harvard Law School but had no interest in obtaining a degree or in practicing law. A back injury made it impossible for him to serve in the Civil War. In 1872 he found his way back to Europe, and from 1875 on he lived there. He soon discovered London to be more to his liking than Paris, and he lived in England for the rest of his life, becoming a British citizen in 1915. He died in 1916. Though not without private means, James was familiar with financial worries, and he supported himself by writing fiction. His inability to succeed as a dramatist was a sore disappointment to him. His later novels are marked by great complexity of style, a fact that some think was caused by his having begun to dictate his writing to a secretary. The English writer H. G. Wells, though a personal friend, unkindly declared that James's style reminded him of a hippopotamus trying to pick up a pea. James replied with typical dignity and restraint. Admiration for his work has increased, of recent years, and has been the subject of many scholarly studies.

WILLIAM
JAMES

William James (older brother of the novelist Henry James) was born in New York City in 1842 and educated in a large number of places both at home and abroad. His own reading, in English, French, and German, was quite extensive and more than made up for the inadequacies of his schooling. At Harvard he went on to take a medical degree. For a while he thought of turning to art, but abandoned the idea to accept a position at Harvard as instructor in physiology. He proceeded to study psychology and philosophy, and wrote on these subjects with a most refreshing verve and picturesqueness. The Principles of Psychology (1890) still finds readers, and his approach to philosophy, to which the label "Pragmatism" has been applied, has become a permanent strand in philosophical thinking. Another remarkable work is The Varieties of Religious Experience (1902). James never reconciled himself to the nineteenth-century conviction that human free will was an illusion and that the interaction of particles of matter determined everything. In his view the testimony of religious experience validated men's belief in the existence of "higher powers." William James remained remarkably open-minded, however, and later in life took the unusual step of declaring himself an adherent of the conclusions reached by a younger philosopher, the Frenchman Henri Bergson. He died in 1910.

ROBINSON
JEFFERS

Jeffers was born in 1887 in Pittsburgh, Pennsylvania. He early acquired an abiding interest in the classics, and in college he studied medicine and forestry. From 1913 on Jeffers lived in Carmel, California, ". . . where for the first time in my life I could see people living—amid magnificent unspoiled scenery—essentially as they did in the Idyls or the Sagas, or in Homer's Ithaca." Jeffers found in the countryside around him a sense of what was abiding and permanent in human life. In the introduction to The Selected Poetry of Robinson Jeffers, he wrote that ". . . poetry must deal with things that a reader two thousand years away could understand and be moved by." Jeffers's long narrative poems weld together his sense of the majesty of nature, local tales of Monterey people, and the literary influences from the ancient Greek writers of tragedy and from the Roman dramatist Seneca. Directly based on Classical tragedy are Jeffers's plays Medea (1946) and The Cretan Woman (1954). The Selected Poetry of Robinson Jeffers was published in 1938. Among later volumes of verse is Hungerfield and Other Poems (1954).

Franz Kafka was born in 1883 into a Jewish family of Prague, Czechoslo-vakia, which was then in Austria-Hungary. Kafka studied law and found employment in an office that handled accident insurance. His cultural background was German, not Czech, and only in his later years did he seek to increase his familiarity with the Jewish cultural tradition. He published little in his lifetime and left many of his stories unfinished. Two of the best known of his short stories are "The Judgment" (1913), which directly reflects his ambiguous feelings toward his own father, and "Meta-morphosis" (1915). This latter story tells of a hero who awakened one morning to find himself transformed into a cockroach. Kafka's two main novels are The Trial (1925) and The Castle (1926). All of his work seems to cry out for symbolical interpretation, and at the same time to rebut all attempts at interpretation. Nevertheless, even those critics who make this declaration may go on to propose their own solutions to the enigma. The author's own life was a series of frustrations. Only toward the end, while he was living in Berlin, did he appear to have achieved a degree of reconciliation to the necessities of existence. Kafka died of tuberculosis in 1924 in Vienna. The prestige of his writings has grown to extraordinary proportions, for many people feel that his portrait of the individual in conflict with higher powers, be they earthly or supernatural, is central for our own time.

FRANZ
KAFKA

Immanuel Kant was born in 1724 in Königsberg, East Prussia—the town is now known as Kaliningrad and is part of the Soviet Union—and there he spent his whole life. He studied at Königsberg University, but did not fulfill the family's expectations of becoming a Lutheran minister. Instead, for long years he eked out a bare existence first as a private tutor and then as a Privatdozent, a university lecturer whose only remuneration was in the form of fees paid him directly by his students. Finally, in 1770, he was named Professor of Logic and Metaphysics. Kant was small and frail, and he led an abstemious and closely regulated life. He retired from public life in 1797 and died in 1804. His work has come to occupy a central position in Western philosophical thinking. The main volumes in which his views find expression are the Critique of Pure Reason (1781), the Critique of Practical Reason (1788), and the Critique of Judgment (1789–90). Among nonspecialists Kant's ethical "Categorical Imperative" is mentioned rather often. The imperative states that one should always so act that the deed could serve as the base for a general ethical precept. One interesting short work by Kant is the essay entitled Perpetual Peace (1795), which sketches the base for a union of all democratic states.

IMMANUEL
KANT

John Keats was born in Finsbury, London, in 1795. After the death in 1804 of his father, who managed a livery stable, he went to live with his maternal grandmother. His school days appear to have been normal and happy. He began to read widely when in his teens. The Faerie Queene of

JOHN
KEATS

the sixteenth-century poet Edmund Spenser fired him with enthusiasm for poetry and the desire to be a poet. For a while the young man studied medicine, but in 1817 he gave up these studies and published his Poems. Though the volume attracted little attention, Keats persevered and published the long poem Endymion the following year. In 1819 his health began to fail, and from 1820 on, it was impossible for him to write. Accompanied by his devoted friend, the painter Joseph Severn, he left for Italy in September 1820. He died in Rome the following February. Keats is regarded as one of the greatest English romantic poets, and his brief life and his hopeless passion for Fanny Brawne have themselves been "romanticized."

C. DAY
LEWIS

Cecil Day Lewis was born in 1904 in Ballintogher, Ireland. His father, a pastor, moved to England while the boy was still very young. Day Lewis was educated at Sherbourne School and Wadham College, Oxford. He had begun writing verses at the age of six, and there was no doubt about his poetic vocation. But poetry rarely provides a livelihood, and the young poet turned to teaching school. He gave this up in 1935, and thereafter based his existence on writing and editorial work. Under the pseudonym Nicholas Blake, he became the author of first-class mystery stories. After World War II he lectured on poetry at Trinity College, Cambridge, and between 1951 and 1956 he held the university chair of poetry at Oxford University. A noteworthy aspect of Day Lewis's literary production is the number of books he has written about poetry. Among them are his Cambridge lectures, published as The Poetic Image (1947), The Poet's Task (1951), The Poet's Way (1959). In the 1930's he had associated with W. H. Auden and Stephen Spender, and had been known as a "revolutionary" poet. That reputation vanished along with that decade, and the poet is now a member in good standing of the British literary "establishment." He published his Collected Poems in 1954 and Selected Poems in 1967. He has also published translations of Virgil's Georgics, Eclogues, and Aeneid.

SINCLAIR
LEWIS

Harry Sinclair Lewis was born in 1885 in Sauk Center, Minnesota, where his father was a doctor. He went to the local high school, and was graduated from Yale University in 1908, one year behind his class. He had left the university in 1906 for a series of odd jobs and to try his hand at free-lance writing. After graduation he once more worked at a variety of undistinguished jobs and published fiction of no great value or promise. His first novel, Our Mr. Wrenn, was published in 1914. Success came to him with his sixth novel, Main Street (1920). The novels immediately following—Babbitt (1922), Arrowsmith (1925), Elmer Gantry (1927), and Dodsworth (1929)—maintained his reputation while infuriating many readers with their assaults on American provincialism, materialism, and hypocrisy. In 1930 Lewis was awarded the Nobel prize for literature. The later novels continued to sell, but few people could feel that they were a worthy continuation of the earlier work. Lewis's private life was erratic and unhappy. He saw few old friends and quarreled with the new. He died in 1951 in Rome of a heart attack.

ROBERT
LOWELL

Robert Lowell was born in 1917 in Boston, Massachusetts. His father was a naval officer who subsequently became a stockbroker. Previous generations of the family had contributed to American literature two poets, James Russell Lowell and Amy Lowell. Robert studied at St. Mark's School and at Harvard University, but transferred to Kenyon College, where he took a degree in classics in 1940. That same year Lowell became a Catholic, and America's entry into World War II found him a conscientious objector. As such, he served a jail sentence. Lord Weary's Castle (1946), his second book of poetry, brought him a Pulitzer prize and wide acclaim. In the eyes of many, he is today the foremost American poet. In addition to publishing his own poetry, Robert Lowell has translated and adapted the work of foreign poets from a number of different languages including Greek, Latin, and Russian. Among his books are The Mills of the Kavanaghs (1951), Life Studies (1959), For the Union Dead (1964), and Near the Ocean (1967). Many colleges and universities have utilized his services as visiting lecturer.

Masters was born in Garnett, Kansas, in 1869. He practiced law in Chicago for several years, but abandoned the law when it became amply evident that he could support himself as a writer. He published nearly fifty volumes of plays, novels, and poems, but his lasting fame rests on a single work, his Spoon River Anthology (1915). This book, with its representative portrait of American life, had considerable effect on the American literary revival that flowered in the years following World War I. Masters' autobiography is entitled Across Spoon River (1936). He died in 1950.

EDGAR LEE MASTERS

Melville was born in 1819 in New York City and lived there until 1830, when his father failed in business and moved with the family to Albany, New York. Two years later, after the father's death, Herman Melville began to earn his living. He worked in a bank, in a fur factory, and on his uncle's farm. He taught school for a few weeks and he studied surveying. In 1839 he went to sea, and in 1841 sailed on board a whaling ship from New Bedford harbor. Eighteen months' service under a brutal captain was enough for him. He deserted and for a month lived on one of the Marquesas Islands. Then he returned to whaling, though on other vessels, and wound up his nautical career as an enlisted man in the American Navy. He was discharged in 1843, returned home, and soon began to write. By 1850 he had published no fewer than five novels. Already a married man, he now settled in Pittsfield, Massachusetts and there wrote Moby Dick. Published in 1851, it proved less successful than the earlier works. Indeed, so great have been the praise and the volume of comment of recent years, that one tends to forget the general indifference to Melville's work that lasted until after World War I. Melville visited Europe and Palestine in the 1850's and made a last sea voyage in 1860 around the Cape to San Francisco. The rest of his life was unadventurous. In 1866 he became an inspector of customs in New York City, a post which he retained for nineteen years. Melville died in 1891. Typee (1846) and Omoo (1847), which draw on Melville's South Seas experiences, are among the early novels. Pierre (1852) appears to reflect its author's bitterness at lack of public response to Moby Dick, and shows a deepening interest in psychological problems. The unfinished Billy Budd (1924) has been praised as Melville's second greatest work.

HERMAN MELVILLE

EDNA ST.
VINCENT
MILLAY

Edna St. Vincent Millay was born in Rockland, Maine, in 1892. She studied at Vassar, where she remained until 1917, the year in which she published her first book of poems, Renascence. With it she at once established her reputation as a strongly subjective lyric poet with considerable popular appeal. Among her later works is Fatal Interview (1931), a series of sonnets. In Conversation at Midnight (1937) she tried to do justice to public issues, but few feel that she achieved much success in this new vein. She died in 1950. Currently available editions of her works are Collected Sonnets (1941) and Collected Lyrics (1959), both of which have also been brought out as paperbacks.

MARIANNE
MOORE

Marianne Moore was born in 1887 in St. Louis, Missouri, and was graduated from Bryn Mawr College in 1909. For some years she taught in Carlisle, Pennsylvania, and later spent four years as an assistant in the New York Public Library. Her first volume, Poems, appeared in 1921, and was followed at a steady pace by others. For her Collected Poems (1951) she received both the Pulitzer prize and the National Book Award. Her reputation far transcends such official recognitions, however, and it would be hard to find a reputable critic of poetry who does not place her work very high indeed—even though the quirks and oddities that mark her poems may lead a critic to write, for example, of her "bone-dry dottiness." Miss Moore is also famous for her devotion to baseball and to the borough of Brooklyn, where she lived for many years.

OGDEN NASH

Ogden Nash was born in 1902 in Rye, New York. He studied at St. George's School, Newport, Rhode Island, and at Harvard University. He spent several years at a variety of occupations, principally as an editor with book publishing firms. The immense success of his light verse, from the early Hard Lines (1931) to the recent Marriage Lines—Notes of a Student Husband (1964), soon freed him from regular office hours. Noteworthy features of his verse are the irregularly and sometimes disproportionately long lines and the preposterousness of the rhyme words. He has also written a considerable number of books especially for children. The successful musical of 1943, One Touch of Venus, had lyrics by Ogden Nash, a text by S. J. Perelman, and the music of Kurt Weil. Mr. Nash has traveled extensively in the United States, giving lectures and reading his poems to audiences on and off university campuses.

EDWARD
NEWHOUSE

Born in Budapest, Hungary, in 1911, Edward Newhouse arrived in the United States with his parents in 1923. He attended Townsend Harris High School in New York City, and until the age of eighteen scarcely ventured outside the city boundaries. Rejecting the offer of a college athletic scholarship, he began to write and to publish fiction, and spent nine months hopping on and off freight trains in both Mexico and the United States. Returning to New York, he became a regular contributor of short stories to the New Yorker Magazine. The Army Air Force provided Newhouse with a plethora of experiences during World War II. Rising from the ranks, he became a major, and continued after the war in the United States Air Force Reserves. He has written a few novels, and his numerous stories have been collected in several volumes, including The Iron Chain (1946) and Many Are Called (1951).

Born in 1892 in what he has called the "backwoods" of Wright City, Missouri, Reinhold Niebuhr (pronounced nē'bōōr) spent his boyhood years in St. Charles, Missouri and Lincoln, Illinois. After study at the Eden Theological Seminary, he went east for the first time to study at the Yale Divinity School, where he received his B.A. in 1914 and his M.A. degree the following year. For fourteen years he served as pastor at an Evangelical church in a poor district of Detroit, Michigan. As Detroit doubled in population, Niebuhr became increasingly concerned about the impact of social conditions on men's lives and about the current relevance or lack of relevance of the pastoral message. In 1928 Niebuhr accepted an offer from the Union Theological Seminary, remaining there until his retirement in 1960. The courses he taught there dealt with Christian ethics and the philosophy of religion. Over the years, Niebuhr's outlook evolved significantly. He ceased to be a religious liberal and declared his adherence to Christian orthodoxy. A pacifist in the 1930's, he advocated armed resistance to the Nazis during World War II. In politics, he might be described as an active adherent of the anti-Communist Left. His views are amply documented in the pages of Christianity and Crisis, a periodical which he edited from 1941 to 1946. Among his many impressive volumes are Moral Man and Immoral Society (1932) and The Nature and Destiny of Man (1941).

Born in Savannah, Georgia, in 1925, Flannery O'Connor went to school and college (the Georgia State College for Women) in the town of Milledgeville, Georgia. After graduation in 1945, she studied creative writing for two years with Paul Engle at the State University of Iowa. For many years she was seriously handicapped by lupus, a practically incurable disease, and often had to make use of crutches. She lived on a large farm outside Milledgeville, and for reasons of health seldom traveled far afield. As a consequence, the territory available for her inspection was much more restricted than that of most writers. But her insight, by way of compensation, may have gained in sharpness and perspicacity. Flannery O'Connor's first short story was published in Accent in 1946, and she continued to publish in magazines of high quality, including the Sewanee Review, Kenyon Review, and Harper's Bazaar. Her novel Wise Blood (1952) was favorably received, as were her collections of stories A Good Man Is Hard to Find (1955) and Everything That Rises Must Converge (1965). No reader can fail to be struck by the grotesque and often disturbing elements of character and event in Miss O'Connor's work. All this finds its place, however, in a coherent picture of the world that was shaped by her deep religious conviction and Roman Catholic faith. "To be able to recognize a freak," she once said, "you have to have some conception of the whole man." Miss O'Connor died in 1964.

Frank O'Connor was the pen name of Michael O'Donovan, who was born in 1903 and grew up in Cork, Ireland. The family was poor and the boy, who did not seem to live in quite the same world as his schoolmates, dreamed of literary glory. He taught himself German and, becoming enthused by the Irish literary and nationalist revival, learned the Irish language. He served, briefly and ineffectively, in the rebel forces during the Irish Civil War. A more suitable career as librarian opened up for him, and he worked hard to build his reputation as an outstanding short story writer. His first collection of stories, Guests of the Nation, was followed by many others. He also wrote plays and novels but did not achieve the same success as he had with his short stories. For a number of years he was a director of Dublin's Abbey Theatre, a position from which he was ousted. After World War II he lectured at colleges and universities in the United States, and he lived in the States for several years. His death occurred in Dublin, Ireland in 1966. The best account of Frank O'Connor's life is to be found in his autobiography, An Only Child (1961).

WILFRED
OWEN

Born in 1893 in Shropshire, England, Wilfred Owen began writing poetry while he was still a child. Ill health interrupted his university studies, and he spent some time in France. There he met a French poet of some note, Laurent Tailhade, and was in some measure affected by Tailhade's nonreligious pacifist views. Returning to England in 1915, Owen enlisted, received a commission, and returned wounded to England in 1917. While in the hospital he made the acquaintance of and was influenced by Siegfried Sassoon, whose antiwar poems were already in circulation. Owen returned to France, was awarded the Military Cross, and was killed in action on November 4, 1918. A volume of his poems was published in 1920, and a larger selection in 1931. His work achieves the difficult fusion of "protest poetry" and the evocation of horrible happenings within a firm, personal poetic structure.

PLATO

Plato was born around 429 B.C. into an Athenian family of considerable distinction. His own writings reveal how great an influence the life and death of Socrates had on his whole outlook. He withdrew from Athens after Socrates' death, traveling extensively and visiting Italy and Sicily. Some twelve years later he returned to Athens to found his famous Academy, a project which engaged his attention for the remaining forty years of his existence. He died in 347 B.C. All of Plato's works—and this is unusual for a writer so remote in time—have been preserved. In addition to the twenty-five dialogues, there are the Apology and a few letters that Plato may have written. The earliest dialogues present a remarkable picture of Socrates as an earthy, ugly, physically tough person who is possessed by an extraordinary passion to discover and practice what is morally right. This is accompanied by a sublime confidence that people can be taught to see and abide by the good. The chief dialogue of Plato's middle period is the Republic. From this time on, Plato develops his own views and speculations with extraordinary brilliance, and handles the dialogue form in a way that produces great literature as well as profound thinking. His conception of the ideal city, worked out in the Republic, is often mentioned. In a very late dialogue, the Laws, Plato presented a more balanced notion of the ideal city state. Plato's influence on Western thought, up to and including our own time, has been immense. Wherever, indeed, there is any mention of philosophical "idealism," Plato's shadow hovers in the background.

EZRA
POUND

Ezra Pound was born in 1885 in Hailey, Indiana, and received his college education at the University of Pennsylvania and Hamilton College. He taught briefly in Indiana, but soon abandoned the prospect of teaching the Romance languages for lifelong residence in Europe. He published his first volume of poems, A Lume Spento, in Venice in 1908, and in that same year settled in London. His first critical work, The Spirit of Romance, was published in 1910. His poetic doctrine called for sparseness of language and clear images. As the London representative of Harriet Monroe's Poetry Magazine, published in Chicago, and later of Margaret Anderson's Little Review, and as the direct adviser of other poets, Ezra Pound became a remarkable fosterer of literary talent in both prose and poetry. It is due to him that T. S. Eliot's famous Love Song of J. Alfred Prufrock was published, and the same is true for James Joyce's Portrait of the Artist as a Young Man and Ulysses. Without Pound's intervention, too, Eliot's Waste Land might have appeared in a form twice as long as the poem we know. As for Pound's own work, he poured by far the greatest share of his energies into a long poem, published over the years in successive batches. This poem, the Cantos, has bewildered many, with its historical allusions and discourses on economics and its quotations in the original Greek and Chinese. It has also had enthusiastic defenders. Pound's London period ended in 1920, when he moved to Paris. Four years later he went to live at Rapallo, on the Italian Riviera, and in Italy he remained, even after the United States declared war on Italy. During the war he broadcast remarks critical of American policy. In 1945 he was arrested by American troops and returned to the United States to face a charge of treason. However, he was declared mentally unfit to stand trial and was interned in St. Elizabeth's Hospital in Washington, D.C. from 1946 to 1958. The award to him, in 1949, of the Bollingen Prize for Poetry aroused a storm of controversy. After his release from hospital, Pound returned to Italy.

JOHN CROWE RANSOM

John Crowe Ransom was born in 1888 in Pulaski, Tennessee. He received a degree from Vanderbilt University in 1909 and, four years later, a degree from Oxford University, where he was a Rhodes Scholar. For many years he taught at Vanderbilt, with an intermission for service in the Field Artillery during World War I. In 1937 Ransom went to teach in Kenyon College, Kenyon, Ohio, where he edited the Kenyon Review. A member of the group of Southern Agrarians and a proponent of the New Criticism, through both precept and example, Ransom has had considerable influence on younger poets and critics. His own reputation as a poet has shone steadily for many years. A revised edition of his Selected Poems was published in 1945, and a collection of Poems and Essays has been made available in paperback.

EDWIN ARLINGTON ROBINSON

Born in 1869 in Head Tide, Maine, Robinson was taken at the age of six months to live in Gardiner. He went to Harvard University, but a decline in the family fortunes after his father's death forced him to leave college. After his mother's death in 1896, Robinson went to live in New York City. He saw little of the town of Gardiner after that, but it remains enshrined as Tillbury Town in many of his poems. Though without private means and for some years without any recognition as a poet, Robinson refused to use his pen for profit. He preferred any nonliterary odd job that would keep him alive. President Theodore Roosevelt opened the poet's way to a post in the New York Custom House, and there Robinson remained from 1905 to 1909. His life acquired a different cast when he took up residence in the MacDowell Colony in Peterborough, New Hampshire. Though he did not readily make new friends and had few old ones, his existence nevertheless became less hermitlike. He died in 1935. Robinson's Collected Poems are still in print, and there is a paperback edition of Selected Poems and Letters.

CARL
SANDBURG

Carl Sandburg was born in 1878 in Galesburg, Illinois, the son of a Swedish-born blacksmith. He left school at thirteen and held a wide variety of jobs as he traveled about the country. Sandburg volunteered to serve as a soldier in the Spanish-American War. In 1914 he was writing for the Chicago Daily News when his poem "Chicago" won a prize from Poetry Magazine. After that he published many volumes of poems: Chicago Poems (1916), Smoke and Steel (1920), Good Morning, America (1928), and The People, Yes (1936). Sandburg wrote his poetry in free verse, "in the American language," as he liked to say. Much of it celebrates the city and its people—laughing, brawling, real people. Sandburg's prose writings include a book of stories for children, Rootabaga Stories (1922), a novel, Remembrance Rock, and the autobiographical novel Always the Young Strangers. His many-volume biography of Abraham Lincoln won the Pulitzer prize in history in 1940.

GEORGE
SANTAYANA

George Santayana was born in 1863 in Madrid, Spain. In 1872 his family moved to Boston. There the boy attended the Boston Latin School. He went on to Harvard College, studied in Berlin for two years, and returned to Harvard to teach philosophy. He remained on the faculty from 1889 until 1912. In that year Santayana came into an inheritance and at once abandoned teaching. He lived in Europe thereafter, spending most of his time in Rome, where he died in 1952. Santayana's philosophy is best represented, in the view of some scholars, in The Life of Reason (1905), but others prefer his later work, for example the four volumes grouped together under the title Realms of Being. Santayana's philosophy is not currently in vogue, however. Indeed, to all those who, in one direction or another, have looked for some startling breakthrough in philosophy, Santayana's studies have always seemed too conservative and traditionalist— even "too well written." A unique place in the philosopher's work is occupied by his one novel, The Last Puritan (1935), described in the subtitle as "A Novel in the Form of a Memoir."

JEAN-PAUL
SARTRE

Born in 1905 in La Rochelle, on the French Atlantic coast, as the son of a French naval officer, Jean-Paul Sartre later lived in Paris. His father died when the boy was only two years old, whereupon the boy and his mother went to live under the roof of Madame Sartre's parents. Sartre was a brilliant university student and in 1929 took first place in a competitive examination that opened up for him a career of teaching in the better class of French secondary schools. He taught first in the provinces and later in Paris, with interruptions only for his period of military service and for service (in meteorology) in World War II. Imprisoned by the Germans after the French collapse, he obtained his freedom through the subterfuge of a forged medical release. Back in Paris, he was active in the underground literary opposition to the German occupation. Though an active pen-wielder from a very early age, Sartre had not attempted to publish much in the prewar years. He became instantaneously well known in 1943 with the staging of his play The Flies, which made use of the Orestes myth to preach resistance to illicit authority, and with Being and Nothingness, a philosophical work of immense length and not inconsiderable difficulty. It sold, however, "like hot cakes," and after the war's end served to spread Sartre's fame throughout the world as the prophet of philosophy's "latest thing": existentialism. Sartre's philosophical writings of recent years are studied in university courses and are much written about, his plays are frequently performed, and his novels continue to be discussed, though he has published no new fiction since the early 1950's. A left-winger in politics, Sartre has never been a member of the French Communist Party, and his relations with the Party, depending on the current political constellation, have run the gamut from expressions of support and sympathy to hostile and acrimonious exchanges.

SIEGFRIED
SASSOON

The Sassoons were a Sephardic Jewish family who had reached England from Spain via Persia and the city of Bombay. Siegfried, who was born in London in 1886, had all the "advantages" of a British upper-class education. He studied for a while at Clare College, Cambridge, but his devotion to tennis and hunting interfered with his studies. He left Cambridge without a degree. The horrors of service in the front lines during World War I turned this "fox-hunting man" and dilettante poet into an avowed pacifist. His conversion found an outlet in a series of savage antiwar poems and, some time later, in his refusal to return to the front. Influential friends took steps in his behalf, with the result that, instead of being court-martialed, as he desired, he was declared insane. He did, however, return to his regiment before the war had ended. Sassoon first attracted substantial public attention as a writer with his autobiographical Memoirs of a Fox-Hunting Man (1928), the first volume of a trilogy. The overall title is Meredith: A Biography (1948). While he continued his work as a poet, he chose to publish little. Sassoon's Collected Poems appeared in 1947. He died in 1967.

DELMORE
SCHWARTZ

Delmore Schwartz was born in 1914 in Brooklyn, New York. He took a B.A. in philosophy at New York University in 1935 and studied for two more years at Harvard University. From 1940 to 1947 he taught in the Harvard English Department. A brilliant intellect and at times a nonstop talker, Delmore Schwartz's ambitions centered upon the writing of great literature. A harsh self-critic, he was not always satisfied with his achievement, and he led an irregular, tortured existence that saw him move from one hotel room and one mental institution to another. For a year prior to his death, his friends had known nothing of his whereabouts. In 1966 they learned by reading the obituary notices that he had collapsed and died in New York City. Delmore Schwartz's first volume of poetry, In Dreams Begin Responsibilities (1939), made an immediate impact upon reviewers. While his subsequent work was not judged to be of uniformly high quality, time and again he astounded sensitive readers, for instance with the long introspective poem Genesis, Book I (1943) and with a collection of short stories with Jewish settings, The World's a Wedding (1948). He was awarded the Bollingen Prize for Poetry in 1959, the year that saw the publication of Summer Knowledge: New and Selected Poems, 1938–1958. He was sometimes compared to Arthur Rimbaud (1854–1891), the exceptionally precocious French poet who abandoned poetry forever at an age when most poets have scarcely begun

to write. Schwartz had published a translation of Rimbaud's A Season in
Hell in 1939.

WILLIAM
SHAKESPEARE

Shakespeare was born in 1564 at Stratford-on-Avon, in Warwickshire, the
child of well-situated middle-class parents. The Stratford Grammar School
had an excellent reputation, and it may be presumed that the boy learned
there his "little Latin" and his "less Greek." The young man married Ann
Hathaway in November 1582, becoming a father the following year. Twins
were born in 1585, one of whom was named Hamnet. Records for the succeeding seven years of Shakespeare's life are entirely lacking. In 1592 he
reemerges, in London, as an actor and playwright. One year later, with the
publication of a long poem entitled Venus and Adonis, he emerges as a
poet. The first official recording of a play by Shakespeare is found in 1594,
for the Comedy of Errors, and an entry of 1595 reveals him to be a distinguished associate of the Lord Chamberlain's Company of actors. In
1597 the flourishing actor and dramatist was able to purchase a large
house and garden in his native town. By 1612, and possibly earlier, Shakespeare had retired from the stage and was living in Stratford. A series
of investments in rents and real estate prove that Shakespeare had derived
substantial profits from his dual career. He had indeed been industrious.
A reference, printed in 1598, to his dramatic work lists no fewer than
twelve plays. Shakespeare died in 1616. A sign of his increasing popularity
is the increase in the number of his plays that found their way into print.
Sixteen were published in quarto form in Shakespeare's lifetime, and the
First Folio edition, which omits only Pericles, appeared in 1623. The
Sonnets had been published in 1609. Shakespeare's renown, at least since
the early nineteenth century, has been worldwide. The Germans, thanks
to the remarkable Tieck-Schlegel translation, have annexed him as a
German dramatist. All the early nineteenth-century Romantics saw themselves in Hamlet, and for the Russian Romantics "the Hamlet question"
had a precise meaning: whether to go on living or to commit suicide. Despite the inevitable reactions against "Shakespearolatry," no sign is dis-
cernible that men will cease to find a multiplicity of deeply relevant insights in Shakespeare's plays.

SOPHOCLES

Sophocles was born about 491 B.C. at Colonus, one mile north of Athens.
As a youth he was noted for his beauty and for his skill in music and
the dance. He had some success as an actor, but was handicapped by an
insufficiently powerful voice. His first victory as a writer of tragedy came
to him in 468 B.C. when he defeated the older dramatist Aeschylus in
the competition for best play. He is said to have won no fewer than
twenty-four times in the course of his long life and never to have been
placed lower than second. Sophocles himself listed three periods in his
work, which he saw as progressing from the "bombastic" through the
"artificial" to the style best fitted for conveying character. Of the 123
plays he is said to have written, seven survive. Perhaps the most frequently
read and commented upon today are Antigone, Oedipus Rex, and Oedipus
at Colonus. Everything that is recorded about Sophocles the man reveals
him as a harmonious personality, liked by all and content to remain
throughout his life a resident of Athens, where he played a prominent
role in public affairs. He died about 406 B.C.

Stephen Spender was born in London, England, in 1909. His father was a journalist and lecturer, his mother was of German-Jewish descent. Spender attended University College, Oxford, supporting himself by printing prescription labels and handling other small jobs on his hand press. He left Oxford in 1931 without having taken a degree. He spent several months every year in Germany before Hitler's rise to power in 1933, and for some time during the Civil War of 1936–39 he was in Spain. While still at Oxford he was a member, together with W. H. Auden, Louis MacNeice, and Cecil Day Lewis, of what came to be called the Oxford Group. A first volume of poetry, the Poems of 1933, brought him acclaim as "another Shelley." Stephen Spender continued to write poetry, though much less intensively after World War II. He published translations from German and Spanish poets and wrote prose works of many different kinds, including literary studies and travel books that are largely concerned with people's expression of their views. World Within World (1951) is a painfully frank autobiography. In it, as in his contribution to The God That Failed (1949), Spender discusses his membership, which extended over several weeks in the winter of 1936–37, in the British Communist Party. He was associated with the now extinct periodical Horizon and from 1953 to 1967 was coeditor of the magazine Encounter.

STEPHEN
SPENDER

Walter Terence Stace was born in 1886 in London, England. He was granted a B.A. degree by Trinity College, Dublin, and a little later settled down to a long career (1910–1932) in the British Civil Service in Ceylon. For one more year (1932–1933) he was mayor of Colombo, Ceylon, but then he embarked upon an entirely new career in fresh surroundings. He became lecturer in philosophy, then Professor of Philosophy at Princeton University, where he remained until his retirement in 1955. Professor Stace's previous work had been done in the field of Greek philosophy. However, after immigration to the United States he attracted wider attention with two books on more general topics. These were Religion and the Modern Mind (1960) and Mysticism and Philosophy (1960). Without attempting to hide his own predilections, Professor Stace endeavored, in these books, to do justice to as great a variety as possible of human experience and opinions.

W. T. STACE

Born in 1886 in Greensboro, North Carolina, Wilbur Daniel Steele received an education that ranged geographically from kindergarten in Berlin, Germany, to the University of Denver, Colorado, which granted him a B.A. degree in 1907, to the study of painting in Boston, Paris, and New York. While living in the artists' colony of Provincetown, Massachusetts, he tried his hand at writing. With the exception of a stint as naval correspondent off the coasts of Ireland, England, and France during World War I, the writing of fiction was to constitute Steele's whole career. His stories were published in such leading magazines as Harper's and the Atlantic Monthly, and he received a number of awards for them. He also wrote several novels, and two plays in collaboration. Among his later works are That Girl from Memphis (1945), Best Stories (1946), Diamond Wedding (1950), and Their Town (1952). Mr. Steele once confessed that words do not come to him easily. "They're always fighting me . . . I'm in a pure funk the whole time I'm writing."

WILBUR
DANIEL
STEELE

JOHN
STEINBECK

Born in 1902 to parents of German and Irish descent in Salinas, California, John Steinbeck read extensively from an early age and developed an interest in science. He attended Stanford University for several years, but left in 1926 without a degree. Then, as he had done previously at intervals, he worked at a wide variety of occupations. He worked on ranches and farms, he was a laboratory assistant, and as a construction worker he helped build the old Madison Square Garden in New York City. He published his first novel in 1929, and several others in the ensuing years, before writing the three works that established his reputation. These are In Dubious Battle (1936), Of Mice and Men (1937), and The Grapes of Wrath (1939). All three deal with the lives of migrant laborers. During World War II, Steinbeck worked for the United States Government and reported home from overseas. He was awarded the Nobel prize for literature in 1962. He died in New York City in 1968.

JAMES
STEPHENS

James Stephens was born in 1882. He grew up in the slums of Dublin, Ireland, without ever quite reaching the height of five feet. He impressed some of those who met him as being a real-life leprechaun. Though he had little formal schooling, he taught himself shorthand and so qualified for office work. He immersed himself in Irish myth and legend and wrote poems and stories that remained unpublished. But he was encouraged to persevere by the older Irish writer George Russell. Success came to Stephens in 1912 with the publication of his novel The Crock of Gold. Thereafter, he devoted all his time to writing. He lived for many years in Paris and moved to London because of the outbreak of war in 1939. He had visited the United States a number of times, lecturing and reciting poetry. His Collected Poems were published in 1926. He died in 1950.

GENEVIEVE
TAGGARD

Born in 1894 in Waitsburg, Washington, to a schoolteaching mother and father, Genevieve Taggard was of mixed Scottish-Irish, Scottish, and French Huguenot descent. At the age of two she was taken by her parents to Hawaii. The parents were devoutly religious, and the child acquired great familiarity with the Bible and with the church hymns. She began to write verse at the age of thirteen. In 1914 she entered the University of California at San Francisco and worked her way through college in five years. She then moved to New York City, worked briefly for a publisher, began to publish her poems, and married. She taught, first at Mount Holyoke College and later at Bennington College. Her travels took her to Spain and England, and she spent one summer in the Soviet Union on the Black Sea coast. At the time of her death in 1948, she was living in Jamaica, Vermont. Her Collected Poems: 1918–1938 were published in 1938. Her last book was Origin: Hawaii (1948).

ALLEN TATE

Born in 1899 in the Blue Grass country of Clarke County, Kentucky, Allen Tate received private instruction until he was nine years old. When he did enter school in Louisville, Kentucky, he astounded his teacher by reciting Oliver Wendell Holmes's "The Chambered Nautilus" and Edgar Allan Poe's "To Helen." His formal education was rounded off with a degree granted him by Vanderbilt University in 1922. Allen Tate then set out to become a writer—"because," he declared, "I could not put my mind on anything else." He came to be known both as one of the

Agrarian group of Southern writers and as a proponent of the New Criticism. He also established his reputation as an outstanding poet. His poems and his writings on literature have been gathered in Poems (1960) and Collected Essays (1960). Throughout his active career Allen Tate taught in a number of colleges and universities, and retired from his last position as Professor of English at the University of Minnesota in 1966.

Sara Teasdale was born in 1884 in St. Louis, Missouri, to parents well advanced in years. She received tuition at home and later attended a private school. Ample means made it possible for the young woman to travel in Europe and the Middle East. After her return to the United States she settled in Chicago, where she made the acquaintance of other young writers. Vachel Lindsay was strongly attracted to her, and she permitted him to court her for a number of years, alternately inspiring in him hope and despair. That situation came to an end in 1914, when she married a businessman, Ernest R. Filsinger. The marriage ended in divorce in 1929. Her last years were spent in New York City. With one exception, her entire literary production consisted of poetry. Among the collections of poems are Sonnets to Duse and Other Poems (1917), a collection of verse for children called Stars Tonight (1930), and the posthumous Collected Poems (1937). The nonpoetic exception is an unfinished and unpublished biography of the English poetess Christina Rossetti, whom she had idolized. Sara Teasdale, always a tortured personality, became increasingly unhappy. She was greatly upset by the suicide of Vachel Lindsay in 1931. Two years later she was found dead after she had taken an overdose of a sleeping medicine.

SARA
TEASDALE

The future Poet Laureate and future Lord Tennyson was born in 1809, the third of eleven children. His father was an English rural clergyman whose parish was in Lincolnshire. This father, who was unhappy in his profession and who, in his later years, became a "problem drinker," undertook the education of his son. Alfred Tennyson appears to have benefited thereby. He early revealed his creative involvement with literature and acquitted himself well at grammar school and at Trinity College, Cambridge. In 1829, while still an undergraduate, Tennyson published a first, slim volume of poems. A brief flirtation, during the summer of 1830, with revolutionary activities cured him for life of any interest in such causes. With his friend Arthur Hallam he had set out to bring money to Spaniards hoping to overthrow the reactionary Spanish monarchy. The death of his father in the following year made it necessary for Tennyson to leave Cambridge. His second volume of poems, published in 1832, contains poems still admired today. Yet the reviewers were harsh, and as a result Tennyson published nothing for several years. His reemergence, after this period of silence, brought him fame and a steadily increasing respect. In 1850 he published In Memoriam. This long poem, which tries to come to grips with the distress he felt upon the death of his friend Hallam, is central in his work. It was at this time that Tennyson married, and some time later he went to live on the Isle of Wight. He wrote a number of plays in verse, which today are largely forgotten. Yet at least one of them, Becket, had considerable success during his lifetime. The poet, in the last years of his life, and for reasons both literary and non-literary, was the object of a veneration that no writer, in our own less reverent era, could hope to arouse. He died in 1892.

ALFRED,
LORD
TENNYSON

DYLAN
THOMAS

Dylan Thomas was born in 1914 in Carmarthenshire, Wales, and attended the Swansea Grammar School. At no time did he show interest in any career except a literary one. His first volume, the 18 Poems of 1934, revealed him to be resolutely distinct from the "social consciousness" school of poetry that was then coming to the fore in the persons of W. H. Auden, Stephen Spender, and Louis MacNeice. Thomas's later work continued to be richly musical and loaded with imagery either splendidly rich or, as hostile critics saw it, at times confused. A talented reader of poetry (both his own and that of other poets whose work he liked), Thomas earned some money in this way and, for monetary reasons, gave many readings in the United States. The task of supporting a family, however, together with the poet's addiction to drink, imposed an impossible burden. In 1953 Thomas died, at the early age of thirty-nine, in New York City. In addition to his poetic work, he wrote the autobiographical Portrait of the Artist as a Young Dog (1940) and a remarkably evocative play, Under Milk Wood (1954).

FRANCIS
THOMPSON

Francis Thompson was born in 1859 in Preston, Lancashire, England to parents who had become converts to the Roman Catholic faith. He himself studied for the priesthood but was declared to be unfit, for temperamental reasons, to exercise that calling. An attempt to qualify for the medical profession ended in failure and the poet, who had acquired the habit of taking laudanum, lived for two years in London in the most appalling circumstances. Among other means of warding off starvation, he opened cab doors and sold matches on the street. A good Samaritan appeared in the form of a Catholic editor, Wilfrid Meynell. He and his wife Alice Meynell brought some order into Francis Thompson's life and made it possible for him to earn a living by writing articles. Thompson died in London of tuberculosis in 1907. During his lifetime he published several volumes of poetry. Today, his best-known poem is "The Hound of Heaven," which describes God's pursuit of the errant human soul.

LEO TOLSTOY

Leo Tolstoy was born in 1828 on his aristocratic family's estate at Yasnaya Polyana, in Tula province, Russia. Up to the age of sixteen he received all his education from tutors. His experience of university life in Kazan did not reconcile him to formal education, and he left without graduating. The following years were spent, idly enough, in Moscow and St. Petersburg. Disgusted with this existence, in 1851 Tolstoy went off to fight the Caucasian tribes then engaging the attention of the Russian Army. Three years later he saw service in the Crimean War. It was during these years of military activity that Tolstoy began to write, and he rapidly made a reputation for himself. But he refused to yield to the temptations offered by society, lived on his estate, traveled abroad, and returned to start a school on original lines for the children living on the estate. Marriage to a girl of eighteen transformed Count Tolstoy's life. In the succeeding period he wrote his two great novels, War and Peace (1863–69) and Anna Karenina (1873–76), and became the father of thirteen children. Religious and ethical concerns came to preoccupy him, and he endeavored to formulate the essence of Christianity as he saw it. He saw it as requiring not only certain views and beliefs, but also a radical transformation of everyday existence. He stopped drinking and smoking and became a vegetarian. His prestige was so great that others declared themselves his disciples, some of them establishing "colonies" where Tolstoyan Christianity could be more frictionlessly practiced. Tolstoy's relations with his wife had sadly deteriorated, however. While he struggled to live simply, she fought for the rights of her family. There was practically open warfare between them. In 1910, at the age of eighty-two, Tolstoy left home. He died of pneumonia a few days later, at the Astapovo railroad junction in Ryazan province.

Born in New York City in 1916, Peter Viereck went to school there and showed himself to be an outstanding student. He was graduated summa cum laude from Harvard University. A volume of verse, Terror and Decorum (1948), brought him a Pulitzer prize. He continued to write poetry but attracted even greater attention through his writings on politics and history. His Shame and Glory of the Intellectuals (1953) established him as a spokesman for the "New Conservatism," defined by him as a "revolt against revolt," whether the attack on society came from Left or Right. His Meta-politics, the Roots of the Nazi Mind (1961), was a reworking of an earlier book. Peter Viereck saw service in the United States Army in World War II as a sergeant and was involved in the African and Italian campaigns. A brother was killed in the war. Peter, the son of George Sylvester Viereck, who came under attack during both World War I and World War II for his pro-German views, long ago made it entirely plain that he did not share his father's views. He has been Professor of European and Russian History at Mount Holyoke College.

PETER
VIERECK

Walt Whitman was born near Huntington, Long Island, in 1819, the son of a carpenter. At the age of four he was taken to live in the small town, as then it was, of Brooklyn. After attending public school there, he became a printer's apprentice. By the age of fifteen he was standing firmly on his own feet, and took a keen interest in the literary and intellectual activities of New York City. In the following years he worked for a variety of newspapers in Manhattan and Brooklyn and was associated for a while with Tammany Hall. His first published literary (or semiliterary) work took the form of stories published in popular magazines. In 1848 he briefly edited the New Orleans Crescent, but returned to the North to publish a paper of his own, the Brooklyn Freeman, which ran for about one year. Whitman then tried his hand at various other activities, including building. In 1855 he published the first edition of Leaves of Grass at his own expense. It was set in part by Whitman himself. Few people cared for these unusual poems. But one of the few admirers was Ralph Waldo Emerson, who bestowed high praise on them. Whitman, for the rest of his life, continued to publish new, expanded editions of his one great work. During the Civil War he nursed the wounded, and after peace was restored he remained in Washington as a government employee. In 1873, stricken by paralysis, he went to live with his brother George in Camden, New Jersey. Later he was able to buy himself a small house there. He died in 1892. Whitman, during his lifetime, perhaps received more recognition abroad than he had at home. Today, however, his position as a great American poet seems beyond challenge.

WALT
WHITMAN

THORNTON
WILDER

Born in Madison, Wisconsin, in 1897, Thornton Wilder was to travel far before completing his primary and secondary schooling. His father served as American Consul-General in Hong Kong and Shanghai, and the boy studied in those towns and went to secondary school in Chefoo. His college career in the United States was interrupted by a year spent with the Coast Artillery Corps during World War I. After graduation from Yale University in 1920, Wilder spent two years at the American Academy in Rome. His first great literary success came to him with his novel The Bridge of San Luis Rey (1927). He continued his career as a novelist, taking Julius Caesar for his hero in The Ides of March (1948) and publishing most recently The Eighth Day (1967). Beginning in the 1930's he also established his reputation as a dramatist. Among his plays are the surprisingly simple and optimistic Our Town (1938), in which he himself acted, and The Skin of Our Teeth (1942), which ranges with immense freedom and sophistication over five thousand years of history. This play was undoubtedly influenced by James Joyce's last, mystifying work, Finnegans Wake. The eminent literary critic Edmund Wilson characterized The Skin of Our Teeth as "the marriage of Plato and Groucho Marx." Thornton Wilder, while a man of great erudition, nevertheless refrained from writing literary history or criticism, preferring to center his energies on literary creation. For him the theater is "the greatest of all art forms." He considers that the dramatist should strive to reach an audience made up of the widest possible spectrum of tastes and cultural levels. He announced, on one occasion, that he "would love to be the poet laureate of Coney Island."

WILLIAM
CARLOS
WILLIAMS

The future medical doctor and poet was born in 1883 in Rutherford, New Jersey. His parents were married in New York City, but they had met while living in the Virgin Islands. Williams received some of his schooling in Europe, studied medicine at the University of Pennsylvania, and went to Leipzig, Germany, for advanced medical studies. Throughout his life he remained a busy doctor, practicing in the town of his birth until his death in 1963. In spite of the heavy inroads his profession made on his time, Williams became a prolific writer. He published his first collection of poems in 1909. The bulk of his poetic work is available today in Collected Earlier Poems (1951) and the revised edition of Collected Later Poems (1962). His most ambitious poem consists of the five books of Paterson, which revolves around the life and the people of that New Jersey town. Williams also wrote fiction and essays, including the essays that make up In the American Grain (1925), a series of meditations on American history.

WILLIAM
WORDSWORTH

In 1770 William Wordsworth was born in Cockermouth, Cumberland, in the Lake District of England. He received an excellent schooling at Hawkshead, in Lancashire, and in 1787 went to St. John's College, Cambridge. Reading of his own choice claimed more of his attention than his studies, and the summers were spent walking in the Lake District and neighboring areas. He also went to France in 1790 and again in 1791. Wordsworth's enthusiasm for the French Revolution is echoed in a well-known passage ("Joy was it in that age to be alive") in his long autobiographical poem The Prelude. On returning to England, Wordsworth lived first of all in London and, after receiving a small legacy, in Dorsetshire with his sister Dorothy. The great years of his poetic achievement had begun. In 1798 he published, in collaboration with Samuel Taylor Coleridge, the famous Lyrical Ballads. In 1799 he went with Dorothy to live in the Lake District, and there he spent the rest of his life. In 1802 Wordsworth married. He had five children, two of whom died young. Dorothy continued to live under her brother's roof. With the end of the Napoleonic Wars, Wordsworth could again travel, and on a number of occasions he saw something of Switzerland, Italy, Belgium, Holland, Germany, and Ireland. By 1814 he had written by far the greater number of poems read widely today, but his poetic productivity continued for a considerable time to come. The "pantheism" we associate with Wordsworth disappeared entirely, and was replaced by a staunch adherence to the Church of England. He opposed Catholic Emancipation and wrote some sonnets in defense of slavery. In other ways, however, he revealed his continued sympathy with the poor and the afflicted. Wordsworth died in 1850.

ELINOR WYLIE

Elinor Hoyt was born in 1885 in Somerville, New Jersey, and attended private schools in Bryn Mawr, Pennsylvania and in Washington, D.C. The family was a distinguished one, and at the age of eighteen Elinor Hoyt made her debut in society in Paris and London. Two years later, she married. This marriage was terminated in 1910, when she eloped with Horace Wylie, a married man. They lived abroad until 1915, when both found themselves free to marry. They returned to the United States and lived in various places. Not surprisingly, in view of their unconventional behavior, they found residence in Washington impossible and New York much more congenial. In 1921 the marriage was dissolved. Two years later Elinor married the writer William Rose Benét. In 1928 she died of a stroke while sitting beside her husband. Her period of most intense activity as a poet covered the years from 1921 to 1928. Her poetic work can be read in the Collected Poems (1932). In 1933 there appeared the companion volume of Collected Prose, which reprints her four historical novels.

WILLIAM BUTLER YEATS

William Butler Yeats was born in 1865 in Dublin, Ireland. During his boyhood he spent a good deal of time in the house of his mother's father in County Sligo, in the west of the country. This region is frequently evoked in his later works. Much of his early schooling he received in England, for his father, the painter John Butler Yeats, had moved to London. The boy's last years of school extended from 1880 to 1883, in Dublin. Yeats had no desire to continue his formal education, attended art school for a time, and by 1886 or so knew that writing was his vocation. Though he became known primarily as a poet, Yeats also published plays, essays, and some fiction. He rounded out his experience of the literary life by translating and by editing volumes by other writers. Yeats was one of the founders, and for many years a director, of Dublin's Abbey Theater. He became one of the uncontested leaders of the Irish literary revival. After the founding of the Irish Free State, in 1922 Yeats was elected a senator, retiring in 1928. One aspect of Yeats's private life that had a strong impact on his poetry was his unrequited passion for Maude Gonne, later Maude Gonne McBride, a great beauty who devoted her life to the cause of Irish nationhood. Yeats first met her in 1889. In 1917, his notion of marrying her daughter having come to naught, Yeats married an English girl. His wife, acting as a medium, put him in touch with the spirit world, as is recounted in a book filled with occult speculation, A Vision (1925). The poetry of Yeats's last period developed in an unforseeable direction. Shaking off all "Celtic twilight" romanticism, the poet wrote poems noted for their harshness, their "unmusical" musicality, and their blunt avowal of passion felt in old age. Yeats died in 1939.

Index

OF AUTHORS AND TITLES

B 9
C 0
D 1
E 2
F 3
G 4
H 5
I 6
J 7
8

CPSIA information can be obtained at www.ICGtesting.com
Printed in the USA
BVOW04s1103160115

383486BV00001B/5/P